White Fire

Douglas Preston
and
Lincoln Child

W F HOWES LTD

This large print edition published in 2015 by
W F Howes Ltd
Unit 4, Rearsby Business Park, Gaddesby Lane,
Rearsby, Leicester LE7 4YH

1 3 5 7 9 10 8 6 4 2

First published in the United Kingdom in 2014
by Head of Zeus Ltd.

A CIP catalogue record for this book is available
from the British Library

ISBN 978 1 47129 448 8

Typeset by Palimpsest Book Production Limited,
Falkirk, Stirlingshire

Printed and bound in Great Britain
by TJ International, Padstow, Cornwall

Lincoln Child dedicates this book to his daughter,
VERONICA

Douglas Preston dedicates this book to
DAVID MORRELL

PROLOGUE

A TRUE STORY

August 30, 1889

The young doctor bid his wife good-bye on the Southsea platform, boarded the 4:15 express for London, and arrived three hours later at Victoria Station. Threading his way through the noise and bustle, he exited the station and flagged down a hansom cab.

'The Langham Hotel, if you please,' he told the driver as he stepped up into the compartment, flushed with a feeling of anticipation.

He sat back in the worn leather seat as the cabbie started down Grosvenor Place. It was a fine late-summer evening, the rarest kind in London, with a dying light falling through the carriage-choked streets and sooty buildings, enchanting everything with a golden radiance. At half past seven the lamps were only just starting to be lit.

The doctor did not often get the chance to come up to London, and he looked out the window of the hansom cab with interest. As the driver turned right onto Piccadilly, he took in St James's Palace and the Royal Academy, bathed in the afterglow

1

of sunset. The crowds, noise, and stench of the city, so different from his home countryside, filled him with energy. Countless horseshoes rang out against the cobbles, and the sidewalks thronged with people from all walks of life: clerks, barristers, and swells rubbed shoulders with chimneysweeps, costermongers, and cat's-meat dealers.

At Piccadilly Circus, the cab took a sharp left onto Regent Street, passing Carnaby and the Oxford Circus before pulling up beneath the porte cochère of the Langham. It had been the first grand hotel erected in London, and it remained by far the most stylish. As he paid off the cabbie, the doctor glanced up at the ornate sandstone façade, with its French windows and balconies of wrought iron, its high gables and balustrades. He had a small interest in architecture, and he guessed the façade was a mixture of Beaux-Arts and North German Renaissance Revival.

As he entered the great portal, the sound of music reached him: a string quartet, hidden behind a screen of hothouse lilies, playing Schubert. He paused to take in the magnificent lobby, crowded with men seated in tall-backed chairs, reading freshly ironed copies of *The Times* and drinking port or sherry. Expensive cigar smoke hung in the air, mingling with the scent of flowers and ladies' perfume.

At the entrance to the dining room, he was met by a small, rather portly man in a broadcloth frock coat and dun-colored trousers, who approached him with brisk steps. 'You must be Doyle,' he said, taking his hand. He had a bright smile and a broad American accent. 'I'm Joe Stoddart. So glad you could make it. Come in – the others just arrived.'

The doctor followed Stoddart as the man made his way among linen-covered tables to a far corner of the room. The restaurant was even more opulent than the lobby, with wainscoting of olive-stained oak, a cream-colored frieze, and an ornate ceiling of raised plasterwork. Stoddart stopped beside a sumptuous table at which two men were already seated.

'Mr William Gill, Mr Oscar Wilde,' Stoddart said. 'Allow me to introduce Dr A. Conan Doyle.'

Gill – whom Doyle recognized as a well-known Irish MP – stood and bowed with good-humored gravitas. A heavy gold Albert watch chain swayed across his ample waistcoat. Wilde, who was in the midst of taking a glass of wine, dabbed at his rather full lips with a damask napkin and motioned Conan Doyle toward the empty chair beside him.

'Mr Wilde was just entertaining us with the story of a tea party he attended this afternoon,' Stoddart said as they took their seats.

'At Lady Featherstone's,' Wilde said. 'She was recently widowed. Poor dear – her hair has gone quite gold from grief.'

'Oscar,' Gill said with a laugh, 'you really are wicked. Talking about a lady in such a manner.'

Wilde waved his hand dismissively. 'My lady would thank me. There is only one thing in the world worse than being talked about, and that is not being talked about.' He spoke rapidly, in a low, mannered voice.

Doyle examined Wilde with a covert look. The man was striking. Almost gigantic in stature, he had unfashionably long hair parted in the middle and carelessly thrown back, his facial features heavy. His choice of clothing was of an eccentricity bordering on madness. He wore a suit of black velvet that fitted tightly to his large frame, the sleeves embroidered in flowery designs and puffed at the shoulders. Around his neck he had donned a narrow, three-rowed frill of the same brocaded material as the sleeves. He had the sartorial audacity to sport knee breeches, equally tight fitting, with stockings of black silk and slippers with grosgrain bows. A *boutonnière* of an immense white orchid drooped pendulously from his fawn-colored vest, looking as if it might dribble nectar at any moment. Heavy gold rings glittered on the fingers of his indolent hands. Despite the idiosyncrasy of his clothing, the expression on his face was mild, balancing the keen quality of his eager brown eyes. And for all this the man displayed a remarkable delicacy of feeling and tact. He spoke in a curious precision of statement, with a unique trick of small gestures to illustrate his meaning.

'You're most kind to be treating us out like this,

4

Stoddart,' Wilde was saying. 'At the Langham, no less. I'd have been left to my own devices other- wise. It's not that I want for supper money, of course. It is only people who pay their bills who lack money, you see, and I never pay mine.'

'I fear you'll find my motives are completely mercenary,' Stoddart replied. 'You might as well know that I'm over here to establish a British edition of *Lippincott's Monthly.*'

'Philadelphia not large enough for you, then?' Gill asked.

Stoddart chuckled, then looked at Wilde and Doyle in turn. 'It is my intention, before this meal is complete, to secure a new novel from each of you.'

Hearing this, a current of excitement coursed through Doyle. In his telegram, Stoddart had been vague about the reasons for asking him to come to London for dinner, but the man was a well-known American publisher and this was exactly what Doyle had been hoping to hear. His medical practice had had a slower start than he would have liked. To fill the time, he'd taken to scribbling novels while waiting for patients. His last few had met with a small success. Stoddart was precisely the man he needed to further his progress. Doyle found him pleasant, even charming – for an American.

The dinner was proving delightful.

Gill was an amusing fellow, but Oscar Wilde was nothing short of remarkable. Doyle was captivated by the graceful wave of his hands; the languid expression that became quite animated when he delivered his peculiar anecdotes or amusing *bons mots*. It was almost magical, Doyle considered, that – thanks to modern technology – he'd been transported in a few short hours from a sleepy seacoast town to this elegant place, surrounded by an eminent editor, a member of Parliament, and the famous champion of aestheticism.

The dishes came thick and fast: potted shrimps, galantine of chicken, tripe fried in batter, *bisque de homard*. Red and yellow wine had appeared at the beginning of the evening, and the generous flow never ceased. It was astonishing how much money the Americans had; Stoddart was spending a fortune.

The timing was excellent. Doyle had just begun a new novel that Stoddart would surely like. His penultimate story, *Micah Clarke*, had been favorably reviewed, although his most recent novel, about a detective, based in part on his old university professor Joseph Bell, had been rather disappointingly received after appearing in *Beeton's Christmas Annual* . . . He forced himself back to the conversation at hand. Gill, the Irish MP, was questioning the veracity of the maxim that the good fortune of one's friends made one discontented.

Hearing this, a gleam appeared in Wilde's eyes. 'The devil,' he replied, 'was once crossing the desert, and he came upon a spot where a number of fiends were tormenting a holy hermit. The man easily shook off their evil suggestions. The devil watched their failure and then stepped forward to give them a lesson. "What you do is too crude," said he. "Permit me for one moment." With that he whispered to the holy man, "Your brother has just been made bishop of Alexandria." A scowl of malignant jealousy at once clouded the serene face of the hermit. "That," said the devil to his imps, "is the sort of thing which I should recommend."'

Stoddart and Gill laughed heartily, then began to fall into an argument about politics. Wilde turned to Doyle. 'You must tell me,' he said. 'Will you do a book for Stoddart?'

'I was rather thinking I would. The fact is, I've started work on a new novel already. I was thinking of calling it *A Tangled Skein*, or perhaps *The Sign of the Four*.'

Wilde pressed his hands together in delight. 'My dear fellow, that's wonderful news. I certainly hope it will be another Holmes story.'

Doyle looked at him in surprise. 'You mean to say you've read *A Study in Scarlet*?'

'I didn't read it, dear boy. I *devoured* it.' Reaching into his vest, Wilde pulled out a copy of the Ward Lock & Co. edition of the book, with its vaguely Oriental lettering so in vogue. 'I even looked through it again when I heard you would be dining with us this evening.'

'You're very kind,' Conan Doyle said, at a loss

for a better reply. He found himself surprised and gratified that the prince of English decadence would enjoy a humble detective novel.

'I feel you have the makings of a great character in Holmes. But . . .' And here Wilde stopped.

'Yes?' Doyle said.

'What I found most remarkable was the *credibility* of the thing. The details of the police work, Holmes's inquiries, were enlightening. I have much to learn from you in this way. You see, between me and life there is a mist of words always. I throw probability out of the window for the sake of a phrase, and the chance of an epigram makes me desert truth. You don't share that failing. And yet . . . and yet I believe you could do more with this Holmes of yours.'

'I would be much obliged if you'd explain,' Doyle said.

Wilde took a sip of wine. 'If he's to be a truly great detective, a great *persona*, he should be more eccentric. The world doesn't need another Sergeant Cuff or Inspector Dupin. No – make his humanity aspire to the greatness of his art.' He paused a moment, thinking, idly stroking the orchid that drooped from his buttonhole. 'In *Scarlet*, you call Watson "extremely lazy." In my opinion, you should allow the virtues of dissipation and idleness to be bestowed on your hero, not his errand boy. And make Holmes more reserved. Don't have *delight shining on his features*, or have him *barking with laughter*.'

Doyle colored, recognizing the infelicitous phraseology.

'You must confer on him a vice,' Wilde went on. 'Virtuous people are so banal; I simply cannot bear them.' He paused again. 'Not just a vice, Doyle – give him a *weakness*. Let me think – ah, yes! I recall.' He opened his copy of *A Study in Scarlet*, leafed quickly through the pages, found a passage, and began to quote Dr Watson: '"I might have suspected him of being addicted to the use of some narcotic, had not the temperance and cleanliness of his whole life forbidden such a notion."' He returned the book to his vest pocket. 'There – you had the perfect weakness in your hands, but you let it go. Pluck it up again! Deliver Holmes into the clutches of some addiction. Opium, say. But no: opium is so dreadfully common these days, it's become quite overrun by the lower classes.' Suddenly Wilde snapped his fingers. 'I have it! Cocaine hydrochloride. There's a novel and elegant vice for you.'

'Cocaine,' Doyle repeated a little uncertainly. As a doctor, he had sometimes prescribed a seven percent solution to patients suffering from exhaustion or depression, but the idea of making Holmes an addict was, on the face of it, quite absurd. Although Doyle had asked for Wilde's opinion, he found himself slightly put out at actually receiving criticism from the man. Across the table, the good-humored argument between Stoddart and Gill continued.

The aesthete took another sip of wine and tossed his hair back.

'And what about you?' Doyle asked. 'Will you do a book for Stoddart?'

'I shall. And it shall be under your influence – or rather, Holmes's influence – that I will proceed. Do you know, I've always believed there's no such thing as a moral or immoral book. Books are well written or badly written – that's all. But I find myself taken with the idea of writing a book about both art *and* morals. I'm planning to call it *The Picture of Dorian Gray*. And do you know, I believe it will be rather a ghastly story. Not a ghost story, exactly, but one in which the protagonist comes to a beastly end. The kind of story one wishes to read by daylight – not lamplight.'

'Such a story doesn't seem to be exactly in your line.'

Wilde looked at Doyle with something like amusement. 'Indeed? Did you think that – as one who would happily sacrifice himself on the pyre of aestheticism – I do not recognize the face of horror when I stare into it? Let me tell you: the shudder of fear is as sensual as the shudder of pleasure, if not more so.' He underscored this with another wave of his hand. 'Besides, I was once told a story so dreadful, so distressing in its particulars and in the extent of its evil, that now I truly believe nothing I hear could ever frighten me again.'

'How interesting,' Doyle replied a little absently, still mulling over the criticism of Holmes.

Wilde regarded him, a small smile forming on his large, pale features. 'Would you care to hear it? It is not for the faint of heart.'

The way Wilde phrased this, it sounded like a challenge. 'By all means.'

'It was told to me during my lecture tour of America a few years back. On my way to San Francisco, I stopped at a rather squalid yet picturesque mining camp known as Roaring Fork. I gave my lecture at the bottom of their mine, and it was frightfully well received by the good gentlemen of the camp. After my lecture, one of the miners approached me, an elderly chap somewhat the worse – or, perhaps, the better – for drink. He took me aside, said he'd enjoyed my story so much that he had one of his own to share with me.'

Wilde paused, wetting his thick, red lips with a delicate sip of wine. 'Here, lean in a little closer, that's a good fellow, and I'll tell it you exactly as it was told to me . . .'

Ten minutes later, a diner at the restaurant in the Langham Hotel would have been surprised to note – amid the susurrus of genteel conversation and the tinkle of cutlery – a young man in the dress of a country doctor abruptly rise from his table, very pale. Knocking over his chair in his agitation, one hand to his forehead, the man staggered from

11

the room, nearly upsetting a waiter's tray of delicacies. And as he vanished in the direction of the gentlemen's toilet area, his face displayed a perfect expression of revulsion and horror.

CHAPTER 1

PRESENT DAY

Corrie Swanson stepped into the ladies' room for the third time to check how she looked. A lot had changed with her since she'd transferred to the John Jay College of Criminal Justice at the beginning of her sophomore year. John Jay was a buttoned-down place. She had resisted it for a while, but finally realized she needed to grow up and play the game of life instead of acting the rebel forever. Gone were the purple hair, the piercings, the black leather jacket, the dark eye shadow and other Goth accoutrements. There was nothing she could do about the Möbius strip tattoo on the nape of her neck, beyond combing her hair back and wearing high collars. But someday, she realized, that would have to go as well.

If she was going to play the game, she was going to play it well.

Unfortunately, her personal transformation had taken place too late for her advisor, a former NYPD cop who had gone back to school and turned professor. She got the feeling his first impression of her had been that of a perp, and nothing she'd done in the year since she'd first met him had erased that. Clearly, he had it in for her. He had already rejected her first proposal for the Rosewell thesis, which involved a trip to Chile to do a perimortem analysis on skeletal remains discovered in a mass grave of Communist peasants murdered by the Pinochet regime back in the 1970s. Too far away, he said, too expensive for a research project, and besides it was old history. When Corrie replied that this was the point – these were old graves, requiring specialized forensic techniques – he said something about not involving herself in foreign political controversies, especially Communist ones.

Now she had another idea for her thesis, an even better one, and she was willing to do almost anything to see it happen.

Examining herself in the mirror, she rearranged a few strands of hair, touched up her conservative lipstick, adjusted her gray worsted suit jacket, and gave her nose a quick powdering. She hardly recognized herself; God, she might even be mistaken for a Young Republican. So much the better.

She exited the ladies' room and walked briskly down the hall, her conservative pumps clicking professionally against the hard linoleum. Her advisor's door was shut, as usual, and she gave it a brisk, self-confident rap. A voice inside said, 'Come in.'

She entered. The office was, as always, neat as a pin, the books and journals all lined up flush with the edges of the bookshelves, the comfortable, masculine leather furniture providing a cozy air. Professor Greg Carbone sat behind his large desk, its acreage of burnished mahogany unbroken by books, papers, family photographs, or knickknacks.

'Good morning, Corrie,' Carbone said, rising and buttoning his blue serge suit. 'Please sit down.'

'Thank you, Professor.' She knew he liked to be called that. Woe to the student who called him Mister or, worse, Greg.

He settled back down as she did. Carbone was a strikingly handsome man with salt-and-pepper hair, wonderful teeth, trim and fit, a good dresser, articulate, soft-spoken, intelligent, and successful. Everything he did, he did well, and as a result he was an accomplished asshole indeed.

'Well, Corrie,' Carbone began, 'you are looking well today.'

'Thank you, Dr Carbone.'

'I'm excited to hear about your new idea.'

'Thanks.' Corrie opened her briefcase (no backpacks at John Jay) and took out a manila file folder, placing it on her knee. 'I'm sure you've been reading about the archaeological investigation going on down in City Hall Park. Next to the location of the old prison known as the Tombs.'

'Tell me about it.'

'The parks department has been excavating a small cemetery of executed criminals to make way for a new subway entrance.'

'Ah yes, I did read about that,' said Carbone.

15

'The cemetery was operational from 1858 to 1865. After 1865, all execution burials were moved to Hart Island and remain unavailable.'

A slow nod from Carbone. He looked interested; she felt encouraged.

'I think this would make for a great opportunity to do an osteological study of those skeletons – to see if severe childhood malnourishment, which as you know leaves osteological markers, might correlate with later criminal behavior.'

Another nod from Carbone.

'I've got it all outlined here.' She laid a proposal on the table. 'Hypotheses, methodology, control group, observations, and analysis.'

Carbone laid a hand on the document, drew it toward himself, opened it, and began perusing.

'There are a number of reasons why this is a great opportunity,' she went on. 'First, the city has good records on most of these executed criminals – names, rap sheets, and trial records. Those who were orphans raised in the Five Points House of Industry – about half a dozen – also have some childhood records. They were all executed in the same way – hanging – so the cause of death is identical. And the cemetery was used for only seven years, so all the remains come from roughly the same time period.'

She paused. Carbone was slowly turning over the pages, one after another, apparently reading. There was no way to tell what he was thinking; his face was a blank.

'I made a few inquiries, and it seems the parks department would be open to having a John Jay student examine the remains.'

The slow turning of the pages paused. 'You already contacted them?'

'Yes. Just a feeler—'

'A feeler . . . You contacted another city agency without seeking prior permission?'

Uh-oh. 'Obviously I didn't want to bring you a project that might get shot down later by outside authorities. Um, was that wrong?'

A long silence, and then: 'Did you not read your undergraduate handbook?'

Corrie was seized with apprehension. She had in fact read it – when she'd been admitted. But that was over a year ago. 'Not recently.'

'The handbook is quite clear. Undergraduate students are not to engage other city departments except through official channels. This is because we're a city institution, as you know, a senior college of the City University of New York.' He said this mildly, almost kindly.

'I . . . Well, I'm sorry, I didn't recall that from the handbook.' She swallowed, feeling a rising panic – and anger. This was such unbelievable bullshit. But she forced herself to keep her cool. 'It was just a couple of phone calls, nothing official.'

A nod. 'I'm sure you didn't *deliberately* violate university regulations.' He began turning the pages again, slowly, one after the other, not looking up

17

at her. 'But in any case I find other problems with this thesis proposal of yours.'

'Yes?' Corrie felt sick.

'This idea that malnourishment leads to a life of crime . . . It's an old idea – and an unconvincing one.'

'Well, it seems to me worth testing.'

'Back then, almost everyone was malnourished. But not everyone became a criminal. And the idea is redolent of . . . how shall I put it? . . . of a certain philosophy that crime in general can be traced to unfortunate experiences in a person's childhood.'

'But malnourishment – severe malnourishment – might cause neurological changes, actual damage. That isn't philosophy; that's science.'

Carbone held up her proposal. 'I can already predict the outcome: you'll discover that these executed criminals *were* malnourished as children. The *real* question is why, of all those hungry children, only a small percentage went on to commit capital crimes. And your research plan does not address that. I'm sorry, this won't fly. Not at all.'

And, opening his fingers, he let her document drop gently to his desk.

CHAPTER 2

The famous – some might say infamous – 'Red Museum' at the John Jay College of Criminal Justice had started as a simple collection of old investigative files, physical evidence, prisoners' property, and memorabilia that, almost a hundred years ago, had been put into a display case in a hall at the old police academy. Since then, it had grown into one of the country's largest and best collections of criminal memorabilia. The crème de la crème of the collection was on display in a sleek new exhibition hall in the college's Skidmore, Owings & Merrill building on Tenth Avenue. The rest of the collection – vast rotting archives and moldering evidence from long-ago crimes – remained squirreled away in the hideous basement of the old police academy building on East Twentieth Street.

Early on at John Jay, Corrie had discovered this archive. It was pure gold – once she'd made friends with the archivist and figured out her way around the disorganized drawers and heaping shelves of stuff. She had been to the Red Museum archives many times in search of topics for papers and projects, most recently in her hunt for a topic for her Rosewell thesis. She had spent a great deal of time in the old unsolved-case files – those cold cases so ancient that all involved (including the possible perps) had definitely and positively died.

Corrie Swanson found herself in a creaking elevator, descending into the basement, one day after the meeting with her advisor. She was on a desperate mission to find a new thesis topic before it became too late to complete the approval process. It was mid-November already, and she was hoping to spend the winter break researching and writing up the thesis. She was on a partial scholarship, but Agent Pendergast had been making up the difference in tuition, and she was absolutely determined not to take one penny more from him than necessary. If her thesis won the Rosewell Prize, with its twenty-thousand-dollar grant, she wouldn't have to.

The elevator doors opened to a familiar smell: a mixture of dust and acidifying paper, underlain by an odor of rodent urine. She crossed the hall to a pair of dented metal doors, graced with a sign that said RED MUSEUM ARCHIVES, and pressed the bell. An unintelligible rasp came out of the antiquated speaker; she gave her name, and a buzzer sounded to let her in.

'Corrie Swanson? How good to see you again!' came the hoarse voice of the archivist, Willard Bloom, as he rose from a desk in a pool of light, guarding the recesses of the storage room stretching off into the blackness behind him. He presented a rather cadaverous figure, stick-thin, with longish gray hair, yet underneath was charming and grand-fatherly. She didn't mind the fact that his eyes often wandered over various parts of her anatomy when he thought she wasn't paying attention.

Bloom came around with a veined hand extended, which she took. The hand was surprisingly hot, and it gave her a bit of a start.

'Come, sit down. Have some tea.'

Some chairs had been set around the front of his desk, with a coffee table and, to the side, a battered cabinet with a hot plate, kettle, and teapot, an informal seating area in the midst of dust and darkness. Corrie flopped into a chair, setting her briefcase down with a thump next to her. 'Ugh,' she said.

Bloom raised his eyebrows in mute inquiry.

'It's Carbone. Once again he rejected my thesis idea. Now I have to start all over again.'

'Carbone,' Bloom said in his high-pitched voice, 'is a well-known ass.'

This piqued her interest. 'You know him?'

'I know everyone who comes down here. Carbone! Always fussing about getting dust on his Ralph Lauren suits, wanting me to play step-n-fetchit. As a result, I can never find anything for him, poor man . . . . You know the real reason he keeps rejecting your thesis ideas, right?'

'I figure it's because I'm a junior.'

Bloom put a finger to his nose and gave her a

21

knowing nod. 'Exactly. And Carbone is old school, a stickler for protocol.'

Corrie had been afraid of this. The Rosewell Prize for the year's outstanding thesis was hugely coveted at John Jay. Its winners were often senior valedictorians, who went on to highly successful law enforcement careers. As far as she knew, it had never been won by a junior – in fact, juniors were quietly discouraged from submitting theses. But there was no rule against it, and Corrie refused to be deterred by such bureaucratic baggage.

Bloom held up the pot with a yellow-toothed smile. 'Tea?'

She looked at the revolting teapot, which did not appear to have been washed in a decade. 'That's a teapot? I thought it was a murder weapon. You know, loaded with arsenic and ready to go.'

'Always ready with a riposte. But surely you know most poisoners are women? If I were a murderer, I'd want to see my victim's blood.' He poured out the tea. 'So Carbone rejected your idea. Surprise, surprise. What's plan B?'

'That *was* my plan B. I was hoping you might be able to give me some fresh ideas.'

Bloom sat back in his chair and sipped noisily from his cup. 'Let's see. As I recall, you're majoring in forensic osteology, are you not? What, exactly, are you looking for?'

'I need to examine some human skeletons that show antemortem or perimortem damage. Got any case files that might point to something like that?'

'Hmm.' His battered face screwed up in concentration.

'The problem is, it's hard to come by accessible human remains. Unless I go prehistoric. But that opens up a whole other can of worms with Native American sensitivities. And I want remains for which there are good written records. *Historic* remains.'

Bloom sucked down another goodly portion of tea, a thoughtful expression on his face. 'Bones. Ante- or perimortem damage. Historic. Good records. Accessible.' He closed his eyes, the lids so dark and veiny they looked like he might have been punched. Corrie waited, listening to the ticking sounds in the archives, the faint sound of forced air, and a pattering noise she feared was probably rats.

The eyes sprang open again. 'Just thought of something. Ever heard of the Baker Street Irregulars?'

'No.'

'It's a very exclusive club of Sherlock Holmes devotees. They have a dinner in New York every year, and they publish all sorts of Holmesian scholarship, all the while pretending that Holmes was a real person. Well, one of these fellows died a few years back, and his widow, not knowing what else to do, shipped his entire collection of Sherlockiana to us. Perhaps she didn't know that Holmes was a *fictional* detective, and we only deal in *nonfiction* here. At any rate, I've been dipping into it now and then. Lot of rubbish, mostly. But there was a copy in there of Doyle's diary – just a photocopy, unfortunately – and it made entertaining reading for an old man stuck in a thankless job in a dusty archive.'

'And what did you find, exactly?'

'There was something in there about a man-eating bear.'

Corrie frowned. 'A man-eating bear? I'm not sure—'

'Come with me.'

Bloom went to a bank of switches and struck them all with the flat of his palm, turning the archives into a flickering sea of fluorescent light. Corrie fancied she could hear the rats scurrying and squealing away as the tubes blinked on, one aisle after another.

She followed the archivist as he made his way down the long rows between dusty shelving and wooden cabinets with yellowed, handwritten labels, finally reaching an area in the back where library tables were piled with cardboard boxes. Three large boxes sat together, labeled BSI. Bloom went to one box, rummaged through it, hauled out an expandable folder, blew off the dust, and began sorting through the papers.

'Here we are.' He held up an old photocopy. 'Doyle's diary. Properly, of course, the man should be referred to as "Conan Doyle," but that's such a mouthful, isn't it?' In the dim light, he flipped through the pages, then began to read aloud:

. . . I was in London on literary business. Stoddart, the American, proved to be an excellent fellow, and had two others to dinner. They were Gill, a very entertaining Irish MP, and Oscar Wilde . . .

He paused, his voice dying into a mumble as he passed over some material, then rising again as he reached a passage he deemed important.

. . . The highlight of the evening, if I may call it that, was Wilde's account of his lecture tour in America. Hard to believe, perhaps, but the famed champion of aestheticism attracted huge interest in America, especially in the West, where in one place a group of uncouth miners gave him a standing ovation . . .

Corrie began to fidget. She had so little time to waste. She cleared her throat. 'I'm not sure Oscar Wilde and Sherlock Holmes are quite what I'm looking for,' she said politely. But Bloom continued to read, holding up his finger for attention, his reedy voice riding over her objections.

. . . Towards the close of the evening, Wilde, who had indulged a great deal in Stoddart's excellent claret, told me, sotto voce, a story of such singular horror, of such grotesque hideousness, that I had to excuse myself from the table. The story involved the killing and eating of eleven miners some years previous, purportedly by a monstrous 'grizzled bear' in a mining camp called Roaring Fork. The actual details are so abhorrent I cannot bring myself to commit them to paper at this time, although the impression left on my mind was indelible and one that will, unfortunately, follow me to the grave.

He paused, taking a breath. 'And there you have it. Eleven corpses, eaten by a grizzly bear. In Roaring Fork, no less.'

'Roaring Fork? You mean the glitzy ski resort in Colorado?'

'The very one. It started life as a silver boomtown.'

'When was this?'

'Wilde was there in 1881. So this business with the man-eating bear probably took place in the 1870s.'

She shook her head. 'And how am I supposed to turn this into a thesis?'

'Nearly a dozen skeletons, eaten by a bear? Surely they will display exquisite perimortem damage – tooth and claw marks, gnawing, crunching, biting, scraping, worrying.' Bloom spoke these words with a kind of relish.

'I'm studying forensic criminology, not forensic bearology.'

'Ah, but you know from your studies that many, if not most, skeletal remains from murder victims show animal damage. You should see the files we have on that. It can be very difficult to tell the difference between animal marks and those left by the murderer. As far as I can recall, no one has done a comprehensive study of perimortem bone damage of this kind. It would be a most original contribution to forensic science.'

Very true, Corrie thought, surprised at Bloom's insight. *And come to think of it, what a fabulous and original subject for a thesis.*

Bloom went on. 'I have little doubt at least some of the poor miners were buried in the historic Roaring Fork cemetery.'

'See, that's a problem. I can't go digging up some historic cemetery looking for bear victims.'

A yellow smile appeared on Bloom's face. 'My dear Corrie, the only reason I brought this up at all was because of the fascinating little article in the *Times* this very morning! Didn't you see it?'

'No.'

'The original "boot hill" of Roaring Fork is now a stack of coffins in a ski equipment warehouse. You see, they're relocating the cemetery on account of development.' He looked at her and winked, his smile broadening.

CHAPTER 3

Along the Côte d'Azur in the South of France, on a bluff atop Cap Ferrat, a man in a black suit, surrounded by bougainvillea, rested on a stone balcony in the afternoon sun. It was warm for the time of year, and the sunlight gilded the lemon trees that crowded the balcony and descended the steep hill to the Mediterranean, ending in a strip of deserted white beach. Beyond could be seen a field of yachts at anchor, the rocky terminus of the cape topped by an ancient castle, behind which ran the blue horizon.

The man reclined in a chaise longue covered with silk damask, beside a small table on which sat a salver. His silvery eyes were half closed. Four items sat on the tray: a copy of Spenser's *Faerie Queene*; a small glass of pastis; a beaker of water; and a single unopened letter. The salver had been brought out two hours ago by a manservant, who now awaited further orders in the shade of the portico. The man who had rented the villa rarely received mail. A few letters bore the return address of one Miss Constance Greene in New York; the rest came from what appeared to be an exclusive boarding school in Switzerland.

As time passed, the manservant began to wonder whether the sickly gentleman who had hired him at excessively high wages might have suffered a heart attack – so motionless had he been these past few hours. But no – a languid hand now moved, reaching for the beaker of water. It poured a small measure into the glass of pastis, turning the yellow liquid a cloudy yellowish green. The man then raised the glass and took a long, slow drink before replacing it on the tray.

Stillness returned, and the shadows of afternoon grew longer. More time passed. The hand moved again, as if in slow motion, again raising the cut-crystal glass to pale lips, taking another long, lingering sip of the liqueur. He then picked up the book of poetry.

More silence as the man appeared to read, turning the pages at long intervals, one after another. The afternoon light blazed its last glory on the façade of the villa. From below, the sounds of life filtered upward: a distant clash of voices raised in argument, the throbbing of a yacht as it moved in the bay, birds chattering among the trees, the faint sound of a piano playing Hanon.

And now the man in the black suit closed the book of poetry, laid it upon the salver, and turned his attention to the letter. Still moving as if under-water, he plucked it up and, with a long, polished nail, slit it open, unfolded it, and began to read.

29

Nov. 27

Dear Aloysius,

I'm mailing this to you c/o Proctor, in hopes he'll pass it along. I know you're still traveling and probably don't want to be bothered, but you've been gone almost a year and I figured maybe you were about ready to come home. Aren't you itching by now to end your leave of absence from the FBI and start solving murders again? And anyway, I just had to tell you about my thesis project. Believe it or not, I'm off to Roaring Fork, Colorado!

I got the most amazing idea for a thesis. I'll try to be brief because I know how impatient you are, but to explain I do have to go into a little history. In 1873, silver was discovered in the mountains over the Continental Divide from Leadville, Colorado. A mining camp sprang up in the valley, called Roaring Fork after the river flowing through it, and the surrounding mountains became dotted with claims. In May of 1876, a rogue grizzly bear killed and ate a miner at a remote claim in the mountains – and for the rest of the summer the bear totally terrorized the area. The town sent out a number of hunting teams to track and kill it, to no avail, as the mountains were extremely rugged and remote. By the time the rampage stopped, eleven miners had been mauled and horribly eaten. It was a big deal at the time, with a lot of local newspaper articles (that's how I learned these details), sheriff's reports, and such. But Roaring Fork was remote and the story died pretty quickly once the killings stopped.

The miners were buried in the Roaring Fork cemetery, and their fate was pretty much forgotten. The mines closed up, Roaring Fork dwindled in population, and in time it almost became a ghost town. Then, in 1946, it was bought up by investors and turned into a ski resort – and now of course it's one of the fanciest resorts in the world – average home price over four million!

So that's the history. This fall, the original Roaring Fork cemetery was dug up to make way for development. All the remains are now stacked in an old equipment shed high up on the ski slopes while everyone argues about what to do with them. A hundred and thirty coffins – of which eight are the remains of miners killed by the grizzly. (The other three were either lost or never recovered.)

Which brings me to my thesis topic:

A Comprehensive Analysis of Perimortem Trauma in the Skeletons of Eight Miners Killed by a Grizzly Bear, from a Historic Colorado Cemetery

There has never been a large-scale study of perimortem trauma on human bones inflicted by a large carnivore. Ever! You see, it isn't often that people are eaten by animals. Mine will be the first!!

My thesis advisor, Prof. Greg Carbone, rejected my two earlier topics, and I'm glad the bastard did, if you'll excuse my language. He would have rejected this one, too, for reasons I won't bore you with, but I decided to take a page out of your book. I got my sweaty hands on Carbone's personnel file. I knew the man was too perfect to be real. Some years back, he'd been boning an undergraduate student in one of his classes – and then was dumb enough to flunk her when she broke it off. So she complained, not about the sex, but the bad grade. No laws were broken (the girl was twenty), but the scumbag gave her an F when she deserved an A. It was all hushed up, the girl got her A and had her tuition 'refunded' for the year – a way of paying her off without calling it that, no doubt.

You can find anybody these days, so I

tracked her down and gave her a call. Her name's Molly Denton and she's now a cop in Worcester, Mass. – a decorated lieutenant in the homicide department, no less. Boy, did she give me the low-down on my advisor! So I went into the meeting with Carbone armed with a couple of nukes, just in case.

I wish you'd been there. It was beautiful. Before I even got into my new thesis idea, I mentioned all nice and polite that we had a mutual acquaintance: Molly Denton. And I gave him a big fat smirk, just to make sure he got the message. He went all pale. He couldn't wait to change the subject back to my thesis, wanted to hear about it, listened attentively, instantly agreed it was the most marvelous thesis proposal he'd heard in years, and promised he would personally shepherd it through the faculty committee. And then – this is the best part – he suggested I leave 'as soon as possible' for Roaring Fork. The guy was butter in my hands.

Winter break just started, and so I'm off to Roaring Fork in two days! Wish me well. And if you feel like it, write me back c/o your pal Proctor, who will have my forwarding address as soon as I know it.

Love,
Corrie

P.S. I almost forgot to tell you one of the best things about my thesis idea. Believe it or not, I first learned about the grizzly bear killings from the diary of Arthur Conan Doyle! Doyle heard it himself from no less than Oscar Wilde at a dinner party in London in 1889. It seems Wilde was a collector of horrible stories, and he'd picked up this one on a lecture tour of the American West.

The manservant, standing in the shadows, watched his peculiar employer finish reading the letter. The long, white fingers seemed to droop, and the letter slid to the table, as if discarded. As the hand moved to pick up the glass of pastis, the evening breeze gently lofted the papers and wafted them over the railing of the balcony, over the tops of the lemon trees; then they went gliding off into blue space, fluttering and turning aimlessly until they had vanished from view, unseen, unnoticed, and completely disregarded by the pale man in the black suit, sitting on a lonely balcony high above the sea.

CHAPTER 4

The Roaring Fork Police Department was located in a classic, Old West–style Victorian red-brick building, impossibly picturesque, that stood in a green park against a backdrop of magnificent snowy peaks. In front of it was a twelve-foot statue of Lady Justice, covered with snow, and – rather oddly – not wearing the traditional blindfold.

Corrie Swanson had loaded up with books about Roaring Fork and she had read all about this courthouse, which was noted for the number of famous defendants who had passed through its doors, from Hunter S. Thompson to serial killer Ted Bundy. Roaring Fork, she knew, was quite a resort. It had the most expensive real estate in the country. This proved to be annoying in the extreme, as she found herself forced to stay in a town called Basalt, eighteen winding miles down Route 82, in a crappy Cloud Nine Motel, with cardboard walls and an itchy bed, at the stunning price of $109 a night. It was the first day of December, and ski season was really ramping up. From her work-study jobs at John Jay – and money left over from the wad Agent Pendergast had pressed on her a year back, when he'd sent her away to stay with her father during a bad time – she had saved up almost four thousand dollars. But at a hundred and nine dollars a night, plus meals, plus the ridiculous thirty-nine bucks a day she was paying for a Rent-a-Junker, she was going to burn through that pretty fast.

In short, she had no time to waste.

The problem was, in her eagerness to get her thesis approved, she had told a little lie. Well, maybe it wasn't such a little lie. She had told Carbone and the faculty committee that she'd gotten permission to examine the remains: carte blanche access. The truth was, her several emails to the chief of the Roaring Fork Police Department, whom she determined had the power to grant her access, had gone unanswered, and her phone calls had not been returned. Not that anyone had been rude to her – it was just a sort of benign neglect.

By marching into the police station herself the day before, she'd finally finagled an appointment with Chief Stanley Morris. Now she entered the building and approached the front desk. To her surprise it was manned, not by a burly cop, but by a girl who looked to be even younger than Corrie herself. She was quite pretty, with a creamy complexion, dark eyes, and shoulder-length blond hair.

Corrie walked up to her, and the girl smiled.

'Are you, uh, a policeman?' Corrie asked.

The girl laughed and shook her head. 'Not yet.'

'What, then – the receptionist?'

The girl shook her head again. 'I'm interning at the station over the winter vacation. Today just happens to be my day to man the reception desk.' She paused. 'I would like to get into law enforcement someday.'

'That makes two of us. I'm a student at John Jay.'

The girl's eyes widened. 'No kidding!'

Corrie extended her hand. 'Corrie Swanson.'

The girl shook it. 'Jenny Baker.'

'I have an appointment with Chief Morris.'

'Oh, yes.' Jenny consulted an appointment book. 'He's expecting you. Go right in.'

'Thanks.' This was a good beginning. Corrie tried to get her nervousness under control and not think about what would happen if the chief denied her access to the remains. At the very least, her thesis depended on it. And she had already spent a fortune getting here, nonrefundable airplane tickets and all.

The door to the chief's office was open, and as she entered the man rose from behind his desk and came around it, extending a hand. She was startled by his appearance: a small, rotund, cheerful-looking man with a beaming face, bald pate, and rumpled uniform. The office reflected the impression of informality, with its arrangement of old, comfortable leather furniture and a desk pleasantly disheveled with papers, books, and family photographs.

The chief ushered her over to a little sitting area in one corner, where an elderly secretary brought in a tray with paper coffee cups, sugar, and cream. Corrie, who had arrived the day before yesterday and was still feeling a bit jet-lagged, helped herself, refraining from her usual four teaspoons of sugar only to see Chief Morris put no less than five into his own cup.

'Well,' Morris said, leaning back, 'sounds like you've got a very interesting project going here.'

'Thank you,' Corrie said. 'And thanks for meeting me on such short notice.'

'I've always been fascinated with Roaring Fork's past. The grizzly bear killings are part of local lore, at least for those of us who know the history. So few do these days.'

'This research project presents an almost perfect opportunity,' Corrie said, launching into her carefully memorized talking points. 'It's a real chance to advance the science of forensic criminology.' She waxed enthusiastic as Chief Morris listened attentively, his chin resting pensively on one soft hand. Corrie touched on all the salient points: how her project would surely garner national press attention and reflect well on the Roaring Fork Police Department; how much John Jay – the nation's premier law enforcement college – would appreciate his cooperation; how she would of course work closely with him and follow whatever rules were laid down. She went into a revisionist version of her own story: how she'd wanted to be a cop all her life; how she'd won a scholarship to John Jay; how hard she'd worked – and then she concluded by enthusing over how much she admired his own position, how ideal it was having the opportunity to work in such an interesting and beautiful community. She laid it on as thick as she dared, and she could see, with satisfaction, that he was responding with nods, smiles, and various noises of approval.

When she was done, she gave as natural a laugh as she could muster, and said she'd been talking way too much and would love to hear his thoughts.

At this Chief Morris took another sip of coffee, cleared his throat, praised her for her hard work and enterprise, told her how much he appreciated her coming in, and – again – how interesting her project sounded. Yes, indeed. He would have to think about it, of course, and consult with the local coroner's office, and with the historical society, and a few others, to get their views, and then the town attorney should probably be brought into the loop . . . And he finished off his coffee and put his hands on the arm of his chair, looking as if he was getting ready to stand up and end the meeting.

A disaster. Corrie took a deep breath. 'Can I be totally frank with you?'

'Why, yes.' He settled back in his chair.

'It took me ages to scrape together the money for this project. I had to work two jobs in addition to my scholarship. Roaring Fork is one of the most expensive places in the country, and just being here is costing me a fortune. I'll go broke waiting for permission.'

She paused, took a breath.

'Honestly, Chief Morris, if you consult with all those people, it's going to take a long time. Maybe weeks. Everyone's going to have a different opinion. And then, no matter what decision you make, someone will feel as if they were overridden. It could become controversial.'

'Controversial,' the chief echoed, alarm and distaste in his voice.

'May I make an alternative suggestion?'

The chief looked a bit surprised but not altogether put out by this. 'Certainly.'

'As I understand it, you have the full authority to give me permission. So . . .' She paused and then decided to just lay it out, completely unvarnished. 'I'd be incredibly grateful if you'd please just give me permission right now, so I can do my research as quickly as possible. I only need a couple of days with the remains, plus the option to take away a few bones for further analysis. That's all. The quicker this happens, the better for everyone. The bones are just sitting there. I could get my work done with barely anyone noticing. Don't give people time to make objections. Please, Chief Morris – it's *so* important to me!'

This ended on more of a desperate note than she intended, but she could see that, once again, she had made an impression.

'Well, well,' the chief said, with more throat clearings and hemmings and hawings. 'I see your point. Hmmm. We don't want controversy.'

He leaned over the edge of his chair, craned his neck toward the door. 'Shirley? More coffee!'

The secretary came back in with two more paper cups. The chief proceeded once again to heap an astonishing amount of sugar into the cup, fussing with the spoon, the cream, stirring the cup endlessly while his brow remained furrowed. He finally laid down the plastic spoon and took a good long sip.

'I'm very much leaning toward your proposal,' he said. 'Very much. I'll tell you what. It's only noon. If you like I'll take you over now, show you the coffins. Of course you can't actually handle the remains, but you'll get an idea of what's there. And I'll have an answer for you tomorrow morning. How's that?'

'That would be great! Thank you!'

Chief Morris beamed. 'And just between you and me, I think you can depend on that answer being positive.'

And as they stood up, Corrie had to actually restrain herself from hugging the man.

CHAPTER 5

C orrie slid into the passenger seat of the squad car, next to the chief, who apparently eschewed a driver and drove himself about. Instead of the usual Crown Vic, the vehicle was a Jeep Cherokee, done up in the traditional cop-car two-tone, with the city symbol of Roaring Fork – an aspen leaf – painted on the side, surrounded by a six-pointed sheriff's star.

Corrie realized she had lucked out, big-time. The chief appeared to be a decent, well-meaning man, and although he seemed to lack spine he was both reasonable and intelligent.

'Have you been to Roaring Fork before?' Morris asked as he turned the key, the vehicle roaring to life.

'Never. Don't even ski.'

'Good gracious. You need to learn. We're in the high season here – Christmas approaching and all – so you're seeing it at its finest.'

The Jeep eased down East Main Street and the chief began pointing out some of the historic sights – City Hall, the historic Hotel Sebastian, various famous Victorian mansions. Everything was done up in festive lights and garlands of fir, the snow lying on the roofs, frosting the windows, and hanging on the boughs of the trees. It was like something out of a Currier & Ives print. They passed through a shopping district, the streets thicker with upscale boutiques than even the gold mile of Fifth Avenue. It was amazing, the sidewalks thronging with shoppers decked out in furs and diamonds or sleek ski outfits, packing shopping bags. The traffic moved at a glacial pace, and they found themselves creeping down the street sandwiched among stretch Hummers, Mercedes Geländewagens, Range Rovers, Porsche Cayennes – and snowmobiles.

'Sorry about the traffic,' the chief said.

'Are you kidding? This is amazing,' Corrie said, almost hanging out the window as she watched the parade of stores slide by: Ralph Lauren, Tiffany, Dior, Louis Vuitton, Prada, Gucci, Rolex, Fendi, Bulgari, Burberry, Brioni, the windows stuffed with expensive merchandise. They never seemed to end.

'The amount of money in this town is off the charts,' said the chief. 'And frankly, from a law enforcement point of view, that can be a problem. A lot of these people think the rules don't apply to them. But in the Roaring Fork Police Department, we treat everyone – and I mean *everyone* – the same.'

'Good policy.'

'It's the only policy in a town like this,' he said,

43

not without a touch of pomposity, 'where just about everyone is a celebrity, a billionaire, or both.'

'Must be a magnet for thieves,' Corrie said, still staring at the expensive stores.

'Oh, no. The crime rate here is almost nil. We're so isolated, you see. There's only one road in – Route 82, which can be an obstacle course in the winter and is frequently closed due to snow – and our airport is only used by private jets. Then there's the cost of actually staying here – well beyond the means of any petty thief. We're too expensive for thieves!' He laughed merrily.

Tell me about it, Corrie thought.

They were now passing a few blocks of what looked like a re-creation of a western boomtown: bars with swinging doors, assay offices, general goods stores, even a few apparent bordellos with gaudily painted windows. Everything was spotlessly neat and clean, from the gleaming cuspidors on the raised wooden sidewalks to the tall false fronts of the buildings.

'What's all that?' Corrie asked, pointing at a family getting their picture taken in front of the Ideal Saloon.

'That's Old Town,' the chief replied. 'What remains of the earliest part of Roaring Fork. For years, those buildings just sat around, decaying. Then, when the resort business picked up, there was a move to clear it all away. But somebody had the idea to restore the old ghost town, make it into a kind of museum for Roaring Fork's past.'

Disneyland meets ski resort, Corrie thought, marveling at the anachronism of this scattering of old relics amid such a hotbed of conspicuous consumption.

As she stared at the well-maintained structures, a brace of snowmobiles roared past, throwing up billows of powder in their wakes.

'What's with all the snowmobiles?' she asked.

'Roaring Fork has an avid snowmobile culture,' the chief told her. 'The town's famous not only for its ski runs, but also for its snowmobile trails. There are miles and miles of them – mostly utilizing the maze of old mining roads that still exist in the mountains above the town.'

They finally cleared the shopping district and, after a few turns, passed a little park full of snow-covered boulders.

'Centennial State Park,' the chief explained. 'Those rocks are part of the John Denver Sanctuary.'

'John Denver?' Corrie shuddered.

'Every year, fans gather on the anniversary of his death. It's a really moving experience. What a genius he was – and what a loss.'

'Yes, absolutely,' Corrie said quickly. 'I love his work. "Rocky Mountain High" – my favorite song of all time.'

'Still brings tears to my eyes.'

'Right. Me, too.' They left the tight grid of down-town streets behind and continued up through a gorgeous stand of giant fir trees heavy with snow.

'Why was the cemetery dug up?' Corrie asked.

45

She knew the answer, of course, but she wanted to see what fresh light the chief could shed on things.

'There's a very exclusive development up ahead called The Heights – ten-million-dollar homes, big acreages, private access to the mountain, exclusive club. It's the most upscale development in town, and it carries a great deal of cachet. Old money and all that. Back in the late '70s, during the initial stage of its development, The Heights acquired "Boot Hill" – the hill with the town's original cemetery – and got a variance to move it. That was in the days when you could still do that sort of thing. Anyway, a couple of years ago, they exercised that right so they could build a private spa and new clubhouse on that hill. There was an uproar, of course, and the town took them to court. But they had some pretty slick lawyers, and also that 1978 agreement, signed and sworn, with ironclad provisions in perpetuity. So they won, the cemetery ultimately got dug up, and here we are. For now, the remains are being stored in a warehouse up on the mountain. There's nothing left but buttons, boots, and bones.'

'So where are they being moved to?'

'The development plans to rebury them in a nearby site as soon as spring comes.'

'Is there still controversy?'

The chief waved his hand. 'Once it was dug up, the furor died down. It wasn't about the remains, anyway – it was about preserving the historic cemetery. Once that was gone, people lost interest.'

The fir trees gave way to a broad, attractive valley, glittering in the noontime light. At the near end stood a plain, hand-carved sign, of surprisingly modest dimensions, which read:

The Heights
Members Only
Please Check In at Guard Station

Behind was a massive wall of river stones set with wrought-iron gates, beside which stood a fairy-tale guard house with a pointed cedar-shake roof and shingled sides. The valley floor was dotted with gigantic mansions, hidden among the trees, and the walls of the valley rose up behind, rooflines peeking above the firs – many with stone chimneys trailing smoke. Beyond that rose the ski area, a braid of trails winding up to the peaks of several mountains, and a high ridge sporting yet more mansions, all framed against a brilliant blue Rocky Mountain sky sprinkled with clouds.

'We're going in?' Corrie asked.

'The warehouse is to one side of the development, on the edge of the slopes.'

The chief was waved through by a security guard, and they headed along a winding, cobblestone drive, beautifully plowed and cleared. No, not cleared. The road was strangely free of ice and utterly dry, while the verges showed no signs of piled or plowed snow.

'Heated road?' asked Corrie as they passed what appeared to be the clubhouse.

'Not so uncommon around here. The ultimate in snow clearance – the flakes evaporate as soon as they touch down.'

Climbing now, the road crossed a stone bridge over a frozen stream – which the chief labeled Silver Queen Creek – then passed through a service gate. Beyond, screened by a tall fence, up hard against a ski run, stood several large equipment sheds built of Pro-Panel on a leveled area of ground. Ten-foot icicles hung down their sides, glittering in the light. The chief pulled up into a plowed area before the largest shed, parked, and got out. Corrie followed. It was a cold day but not desperately so, twenty or twenty-five perhaps, and windless. The great door to the shed had a smaller one set to the side of it, which Chief Morris unlocked. Corrie followed him into the dark space, and the smell hit her right away. And yet it was not an unpleasant odor, no scent of rot. Just rich earth.

The chief palmed a bank of switches and sodium lamps in the roof turned on, casting a yellow glow over all. If anything, it was colder inside the shed than outside, and she drew her coat more closely around her, shivering. In the front section of the shed, practically in the shadow of the large door, sat a line of six snowmobiles, almost all of identical make. Beyond, a row of old snowcats, some nearly antique looking, with huge treads and rounded

48

cabs, blocked their view toward the back. They threaded their way among the cats and came to an open area. Here was the makeshift cemetery, laid out on tarps: neat rows of baby-blue plastic coffins of the kind used by medical examiners to remove remains from a crime scene.

They walked over to the nearest row, and Corrie looked at the first box. Taped to the lid was a large card of printed information. Corrie knelt to read it. The card indicated where the remains had been found in the cemetery, with a photo of the grave in situ; there was space to record whether or not there had been a tombstone and, if so, room for the information printed on it, along with another photo. Everything was numbered, cataloged, and arranged. Corrie felt relief: there would be no problems with documentation here.

'The tombstones are over there,' said Chief Morris. He pointed to a far wall, against which was arrayed a motley collection of tombstones – a few fancy ones in slate or marble, but mostly boulders or slabs with lettering carved into them. They, too, had been cataloged and carded.

'We've got about a hundred and thirty human remains,' said the chief. 'And close to a hundred tombstones. The rest . . . we don't know who they are. They may have had wooden markers, or perhaps some tombstones were lost or stolen.'

'Did any identify bear victims?'

'None. They're traditional – names, dates, and sometimes a phrase from the Bible or a standard religious epitaph. The cause of death isn't normally put on tombstones. And being eaten by a grizzly would not be something you'd want memorialized.'

Corrie nodded. It didn't really matter – she had already put together a list of the victims from researching old local newspaper reports.

'Would it be possible to open one of these lids?' she asked.

'I don't see why not.' The chief grasped a handle on the nearest box.

'Wait, I've got a list.' Corrie fumbled in her briefcase and withdrew the folder. 'Let's look for one of the victims.'

'Fine.'

They spent a few minutes wandering among the coffins, until Corrie found one that matched a name on her list: Emmett Bowdree. 'This one, please,' she said.

Morris grabbed the handle and eased the lid off.

Inside were the remains of a rotten pine coffin that held a skeleton. The lid had disintegrated and was lying in pieces around and on top of the skeleton. Corrie stared at it eagerly. The bones of both arms and a leg lay to one side; the skull was crushed; the rib cage had been ripped open; and both femurs had been broken into pieces, crunched up by powerful jaws to obtain the marrow, no doubt. In her studies at John Jay, Corrie had examined many skeletons displaying perimortem violence, but nothing – *nothing* – quite like this.

'Jesus, the bear really did a number on him,' murmured Morris.

'You're not kidding.' As she examined the bones, Corrie noticed something: some faint marks on the broken rib cage. She knelt, looking closer, trying to make them out. Christ, what she needed was a magnifying glass. Her eyes darted about, and – on the crushed femur – she noticed another, similar mark. She reached out to pick up the bone.

'Whoa, there, no touching!'

'I need to just examine this a little closer.'

'No,' said the chief. 'Really, that's enough.'

'Just give me a moment,' Corrie pleaded.

'Sorry.' He slid the lid back on. 'You'll have plenty of time later.'

Corrie rose, perplexed, not at all sure about what she'd seen. It might have been her imagination. Anyway, the marks surely must be antemortem: no mystery there. Roaring Fork was a rough place back in those days. Maybe the fellow had survived a knife fight. She shook her head.

'We'd better get going,' the chief said.

They emerged into the brilliant light, the blaze off the glittering blanket of snow almost blinding. But try as she might, Corrie couldn't quite rid herself of the strangest feeling of disquiet.

CHAPTER 6

The call came the following morning. Corrie was seated in the Roaring Fork Library, reading up on the history of the town. It was an excellent library, housed in a modern building designed in an updated Victorian style. The interior was gorgeous, with acres of polished oak, arched windows, thick carpeting, and an indirect lighting system that bathed everything in a warm glow.

The library's historical section was state of the art. The section librarian, Ted Roman, had been very helpful. He turned out to be a cute guy in his midtwenties, lithe and fit, who had recently graduated from the University of Utah and was taking a couple of years off to be a ski bum. She had told him about her research project and her meeting with Chief Morris. Ted had listened attentively, asked intelligent questions, and showed her how to use the history archives. To top it off, he had asked her out for a beer tomorrow night. And she'd accepted.

The library's albums of old newspapers, broadsheets, and public notices from the silver boom days had been beautifully digitized in searchable PDF form. She'd been able, in a matter of hours, to pull up dozens of articles on the history of Roaring Fork and on the grizzly killings, obituary notices, and all kinds of related memorabilia – far more than she'd obtained in New York.

The town had a fascinating history. In the summer of 1873, a doughty band of prospectors from Leadville braved the threat of Ute Indians and crossed the Continental Divide, penetrating unexplored territory westward. There, they and others who followed made one of the biggest silver strikes in U.S. history. A silver rush ensued, with hordes of prospectors staking claims all through the mountains lining the Roaring Fork River. A town sprang up, along with stamp mills for crushing ore and a hastily built smelter for separating silver and gold from ore. Soon the hills were crawling with prospectors, dotted with mines and remote camps, while the town itself teemed with mining engineers, assayists, charcoal burners, sawmill workers, blacksmiths, saloonkeepers, merchants, teamsters, whores, laborers, piano players, faro dealers, con men, and thieves.

The first killing took place in the spring of 1876. At a remote claim high on Smuggler Mountain, a lone miner was killed and eaten. It took weeks for the man to be missed, and as a consequence his body wasn't discovered immediately, but the high mountain air kept it fresh enough to tell the gruesome tale. The body had been ripped open, obviously by a bear, then gutted, the limbs torn off. It appeared the bear had returned over the course of a week to continue feasting, with most of the bones stripped of their flesh, the tongue and liver eaten, the entrails and organs spread about and more or less consumed.

It was a pattern that would be repeated ten more times over the course of the summer.

From the beginning, Roaring Fork – and indeed much of Colorado Territory – had been plagued by aggressive grizzlies who were being driven to higher altitudes by settlements in the lower valleys. The grizzly bear – it was noted with relish in almost every newspaper report – was one of the few animals known to hunt and kill a human being for food.

During the course of that long summer, eleven miners and prospectors were killed and eaten by the rogue grizzly at a variety of remote claims. The animal had a large territory that, unfortunately, encompassed much of the upper range of the silver district. The killings caused widespread panic. But federal law required miners to 'work a claim' in order to maintain rights to it, so even at the height of the terror most miners refused to abandon their sites.

Hunting posses were formed several times to chase the grizzly, but it was hard to track the animal in the absence of snow, amid the rocky upper reaches of the mountains above the tree line. Still, the real problem, it seemed to Corrie, was that the hunting posses were none too eager to find the bear. They seemed to spend more time organizing in the saloons and making speeches than actually out in the field tracking the bear.

The killings stopped in the fall of 1876, just before the first snow. Over time, people began to think the bear had moved on, died, or perhaps gone into hibernation. There was some apprehension the following spring, but when the killings did not resume . . .

Corrie felt her phone vibrate, plucked it out of her handbag, and saw it was a call from the police station. Glancing around and noting the library was empty – save for the ski bum librarian, sitting at his desk reading Jack Kerouac – she figured it was okay to answer.

But it wasn't the chief. It was his secretary. Before Corrie could even get through the usual niceties, the lady was talking fast and breathily. 'The chief is so sorry, so very sorry, but it turns out he can't give you permission to examine the remains.'

Corrie's mouth went dry. 'What?' she croaked. 'Wait a minute—'

'He's tied up all day in meetings so he asked me to call you. You see—'

'But he said—'

'It's just not going to be possible. He feels very sorry he can't help you.'

'But *why*?' she managed to break in.

'I don't have the specifics, I'm sorry—'

'Can't I speak to him?'

'He's caught up in meetings all day and, um, for the rest of the week.'

'For the rest of the *week*? But just yesterday he said—'

'I'm sorry, I told you I'm not privy to his reasons.'

'Look,' said Corrie, trying to control her voice without much success, 'just a day ago he told me there wouldn't be any problems. That he'd approve it. And now he changes his mind, refuses to say why, and . . . and then dumps on you the job of giving me the bum's rush! It isn't fair!'

Corrie got a final, frosty *I wish I could help you, but the decision is final*, followed by a decisive click. The line went dead.

Corrie sat down and, banging her palm on the table, cried: 'Damn, damn, *damn*!'

Then she looked up. Ted was looking over at her, his eyes wide.

'Oh, no,' Corrie said, covering her mouth. 'I've disturbed the whole library.'

He held up his hand with a smile. 'As you can see, there's nobody here right now.' He hesitated, then came around his desk and walked over. He spoke again, his voice having dropped to a whisper. 'I think I understand what's going on here.'

'You do? I'd wish you'd explain it to me, then.'

Even though there was nobody around, he lowered his voice still further. '*Mrs Kermode.*'

'Who?'

'Mrs Betty Brown Kermode got to the chief of police.'

'Who is Betty Brown Kermode?'

He rolled his eyes and looked around furtively. 'Where to begin? First, she owns Town & Mount Real Estate, which is *the* real estate agency in town. She's the head of the Heights Neighborhood Association, and was the force behind getting the cemetery moved. She's basically one of those self-righteous people who run everything and everybody and brook no dissent. Fact is, she's the real power in this town.'

'A woman like that's got influence over the chief of police?'

Ted laughed. 'You met Morris, right? Nice guy. *Everyone* has influence over him. But especially her. I'm telling you, she's fearsome – even more so than that brother-in-law of hers, Montebello. I'm sure Morris had every intention of giving you permission – until he called Kermode.'

'But why would she want to stop me? What harm would it do?'

'That,' said Ted, 'is what you're going to have to find out.'

CHAPTER 7

At nine the next morning, Corrie pulled her Rent-a-Junker up to the gates of The Heights. There the guard – not nearly as friendly as the last time she'd passed through, with the chief of police – spent a long, insolent amount of time checking her ID and calling to verify her appointment, all the while casting disdainful looks at her car.

Corrie was careful to remain polite, and at length she was driving along the road toward the clubhouse and development offices. A cluster of buildings on the valley floor soon came into view: picturesque, snowcapped and icicled, their stone chimneys smoking. Beyond, well up on the far side of the snow-blanketed valley, Corrie could see a massive dirt scar of ongoing construction – no doubt the new club-house and spa. She watched backhoes and loaders busily at work digging footings. She couldn't help but wonder why they needed a new clubhouse when the old one looked pretty amazing.

She parked in the visitor's lot and entered the clubhouse, where the secretary pointed her toward the offices of Town & Mount Real Estate.

The reception area of Town & Mount was sumptuous – all wood and stone, with Navajo rugs on the walls, a spectacular chandelier made of deer antlers, cowboy-style leather-and-wood furniture, and a stone fireplace in which a real log fire burned. Corrie took a seat and settled in to wait.

An hour later, she was finally ushered into the office of Mrs Kermode, president of Town & Mount and director of the Heights Association. Corrie had dressed in her most corporate mode, a gray suit with a white blouse and low pumps. She was absolutely determined to keep her cool and win Mrs Kermode over with flattery, charm, and persuasion.

The previous afternoon, she had done her damnedest to dig up dirt on Kermode, heeding the Pendergastian dictum that if you want something from somebody, always have something 'ugly' to trade. But Kermode seemed to be a woman above reproach: a generous donor to local charities, an elder in the Presbyterian church, a volunteer at the local soup kitchen (it surprised Corrie that a town like Roaring Fork would even have a soup kitchen), and a businesswoman of acknowledged integrity. While she was not exactly loved, and was in fact heartily disliked by many, she was respected – and feared – by all.

Mrs Kermode surprised Corrie. Far from being the dowdy woman conjured up by the name Betty Brown Kermode, she was an extremely well-put-together woman in her early sixties, slender and fit, with beautifully coiffed platinum hair and understated makeup. She was dressed in high cowboy style with a beaded Indian vest, white shirt, tight jeans, and cowboy boots. A Navajo squash blossom necklace completed the ensemble. The walls of her office were covered with photographs of her riding a stunning paint horse in the mountains and competing in an arena, charging through a herd of cows. A water cooler stood in one corner. Another corner of the office was dominated by a magnificent western saddle, tooled all over and trimmed in silver.

In an easy, friendly way, Mrs Kermode came forward and shook Corrie's hand, inviting her to sit down. Corrie's irritation at being kept waiting for an hour began to dissipate in the warm welcome.

'Now, Corrie,' she began, speaking with a pronounced Texas accent, 'I want to thank you for coming in. It gives me a chance to explain to you, in person, why Chief Morris and I unfortunately can't grant your request.'

'Well, I was hoping to explain—'

But Kermode was in a hurry and overrode Corrie's attempt to present her talking points. 'Corrie, I'm going to be frank. The scientific examination of those mortal remains for a . . . college thesis is, in our view, disrespectful of the dead.'

This was not what Corrie expected. 'In what way?'

Kermode gave a poisonous little laugh. 'My dear

Miss Swanson, how can you ask such a question? Would you want some student pawing through your grandfather's remains?'

'Um, I would be fine with it.'

'Come, now. Of course you wouldn't. At least where I come from, we treat our dead with respect. These are *sacred* human remains.'

Corrie tried desperately to get back to her talking points. 'But this is a unique opportunity for forensic science. This is going to help law enforcement—'

'A college thesis? Contribute to forensic science? Aren't you exaggerating the importance of this project just a *teensy* little bit now, Miss Swanson?'

Corrie took a deep breath. 'Not at all. This could be a very important study and data collection of perimortem trauma caused by a large carnivore. When a skeleton of a murder victim is found, forensic pathologists have to distinguish animal tooth marks and other postmortem damage from the marks on the bones left by the perpetrator. It's a serious issue and this study—'

'So much Greek to me!' Mrs Kermode gave a laugh and waved her hand, as if she understood nothing.

Corrie decided to shift tack. 'It's important for me personally, Mrs Kermode – but it could be important for Roaring Fork, as well. It's doing something constructive, something positive with these human remains. It would reflect well on the community and the chief—'

'It's just not respectful,' said Kermode firmly.

'It's not *Christian*. There are many in this town who would find it deeply offensive. We are the guardians of those remains, and we take our responsibility seriously. I just can't under any circumstances allow it.'

'But . . .' Corrie could feel her temper rising despite her best efforts to keep it down. 'But . . . you dug them up to begin with.'

A silence, and then Kermode spoke softly. 'The decision was made long ago. Back in 1978, in fact. The town signed off on it. Here at The Heights we've been planning this new clubhouse and spa for almost a decade.'

'Why do you need it when you've already got a beautiful clubhouse?'

'We'll need a larger one to serve Phase III, as we open up West Mountain to a select number of custom home lots. Again, as I've repeatedly said to you, this has been in planning for years. We are responsible to our owners and investors.'

Our owners and investors. 'All I want to do is examine the bones – with the utmost respect – for valid and important scientific purposes. There's no disrespect in that, surely?'

Mrs Kermode rose, a bright fake smile plastered on her face. 'Miss Swanson, the decision has been made, it is final, and I am a very busy woman. It is now time for you to leave.'

Corrie rose. She could feel that old, horrible, blood-boiling sensation inside her. 'You dig up an entire cemetery so you can make money on a real

62

estate development, you dump the bodies in plastic boxes and store them in a ski warehouse – and then you tell me *I'll* be disrespecting the dead by studying the bones? You're a hypocrite – plain and simple!'

Kermode's face grew pale. Corrie could see a vein in her powdered neck throbbing. Her voice became very low, almost masculine. 'You little bitch,' she said. 'I'll give you five minutes to vacate the premises. If you ever – *ever* – come back, I'll have you arrested for trespassing. Now get out.'

Corrie suddenly felt very calm. This was the end. It was over. But she wasn't going to let anyone call her a bitch. She stared back at Mrs Kermode with narrowed eyes. 'You call yourself an elder in the church? You're no Christian. You're a goddamn phony. A fake, grasping, deceitful *phony*.'

On the way back to Basalt, it began to snow. As she crawled along at ten miles an hour in her car, windshield wipers slapping back and forth ineffectually, an idea came to her. Those anomalous marks she'd noticed on the bones . . . with a flash of insight, she realized there was possibly another way to skin this particular cat.

CHAPTER 8

Lying on the bed of her room at the Cloud Nine Motel in Basalt, Colorado, Corrie made her decision. If those marks on the bones were what she thought they might be, her problems would be solved. There wouldn't be any choice: the remains would have to be examined. Even Kermode couldn't stop it. That would be her trump card.

But only if she could prove it.

And to do that, she needed access to the bones one more time. Five minutes, tops – just long enough to photograph them with the powerful macro lens on her camera.

But how?

Even before she asked herself the question, she knew the answer: she would have to break in.

All the arguments against such an action lined themselves up before her: that B&E was a felony; that it was ethically wrong; that if she got caught, her entire law enforcement career would be flushed down the toilet. On the other hand, it wouldn't be all that difficult. During their visit two days before, the chief hadn't turned off any alarm systems or other security devices; he'd simply unlocked a padlock on the door and they had walked in. The shed was isolated from the rest of the development, surrounded by a tall wooden fence and screened by trees. It was partly open to one of the ski slopes, but nobody would be skiing at night. The shed was marked on trail maps of the area, and they showed a service road leading to it from the equipment yard of the ski area itself, bypassing The Heights entirely.

As she weighed the pros and cons, she found herself asking the question: what would Pendergast do? He never let legal niceties stand in the way of truth and justice. Surely he would break in and get the information he needed. While it was too late to achieve justice for Emmett Bowdree, it was never too late for the truth.

The snow had stopped at midnight, leaving a brilliantly clear night sky with a three-quarter moon. It was extremely cold – according to the WeatherBug app on her iPad, it was five degrees. Outside, it felt a lot colder than that. The service road turned out to be snowmobile-only, covered with hard-packed snow but still walkable.

Leaving her car at the very base of the road, by a tall stand of trees and as inconspicuous as possible, Corrie labored uphill, her knapsack heavy with gear: the Canon with tripod and macro, a portable light and battery pack, loupes, flashlight, bolt cutter, ziplock bags, and her iPad loaded with textbooks and monographs on the subject of osteological trauma analysis. The thin mountain air left her gasping, the smoke of her condensing breath blossoming in the moonlight as she hiked, her feet squeaking in the layer of fluff atop the hard-packed snow. Below, the lights of the town spread out in a magical carpet; above, she could see the warehouse, illuminated by lights on poles and casting a yellow glow through the fir trees. It was two o'clock in the morning and all was quiet. The only activity was some headlights high on the mountain, where the grooming equipment was being operated.

Again and again, she had choreographed in her head the exact series of steps she'd need to take, rearranging and refining them to ensure that she would spend as little time in the shed as possible. Five minutes, ten at most – and she'd be gone.

Approaching the shed, she did a careful recon to assure herself that she was alone. Then she stepped up to the fence gate and peered over it. To the left was the side door that she and the chief had used, illuminated in a pool of light, the snow well beaten down before it. The door was securely padlocked. By habit, she carried a set of lock picks. In high school, she had practically memorized the underground manual known as the *MIT Guide to Lockpicking*, and she took great pride in her skills. The padlock was a ten-dollar, hardware-store variety – no problem there. But she would have to cross the lighted area in order to reach the door.

And then she'd have to stand in the light while dealing with the lock. This was one of two elements of unavoidable danger in her plan.

She waited, listening, but all was quiet. The grooming machines were high up on the mountain and didn't look like they'd be passing by anytime soon.

Taking a deep breath, she vaulted the fence and darted across the lighted area. She had her set of lock picks ready. The lock itself was freezing, and her fingers quickly grew stupid in the cold. Nevertheless it took only twenty seconds for the padlock to spring open. She pulled the door ajar, ducked inside, and gently closed it behind her.

Inside the shed it was very cold. Fumbling a small LED light out of her backpack, she flicked it on and quickly moved past the rows of snowmobiles and antique snowcats to the rear of the structure. The coffins, laid out in neat rows, gleamed dully in her light. It only took a moment to find Emmett Bowdree's coffin. She removed the lid with care, trying to keep the noise to a minimum, then knelt, playing the light over the bones. Her heart was pounding in her chest, and her hands were shaking. Once again, a voice inside her pointed out that this was one of the dumbest things she'd ever done, and once again another voice responded that it was the only thing she could do.

Get a grip, she whispered to herself. *Focus.*

Following her mental script, Corrie pulled off

her gloves again, laid her backpack on the ground, and unzipped it. She quickly inserted a loupe to her eye, tugged the gloves back on, pulled out the broken femur she'd noticed before, and peered at it under the light. The bone showed several long, parallel scrapes in the cortical surface. She examined them carefully for any sign of healing, bone remodeling or periosteal uplifting, but there was none. The longitudinal marks were clean, fresh, and showed no sign of an osseous reaction. That meant the scraping had occurred perimortem: at the time of death.

No bear could have made a mark like this. It had been done with a crude tool, perhaps the blade of a dull knife, and – clearly – it had been done to strip the flesh from the bones.

But could she be sure? Her field experience was so limited. Removing her gloves again, she fumbled out her iPad and called up one of her school e-textbooks, *Trauma Analysis*. She looked through the illustrations of antemortem, perimortem, and postmortem injuries, including some with scrapes similar to these, and compared the illustrations with the bone in her hand. They confirmed her initial impression. She tried to warm her frozen fingers by breathing on them, but that didn't work and so she pulled her gloves back on and beat her hands together as quietly as she could. That brought back a little sensation.

Now she had to photograph the damaged bone. Once again the gloves had to come off. She hauled out the portable light, battery pack, and small tripod from her backpack. Next came her digital camera, with the massive macro lens attachment that had cost her a fortune. She screwed the camera into the mount and set it up. Placing the bone on the floor, she arranged things as best she could in the dark, then flicked on the light.

This was the second danger point – the light would be visible from outside. But it was absolutely indispensable. She had arranged things so that it would be on for the shortest possible amount of time, without a red flag of turning it off and on – and so that right afterward she could pack up and leave.

God, it was bright, casting a glow over everything. She quickly positioned the camera and focused. She took a dozen photos as quickly as she could, moving the bone a little bit each time and adjusting the light for a raking effect. As she did this, she noticed, under the strong glare, something else on the bone: apparent tooth marks. She stopped just a moment to examine them with the loupe. They were indeed tooth marks, but not those of a grizzly: they were far too feeble, too close together, and with too flat a crown. She photographed them from several angles.

She hurriedly put the bone back in the coffin, and moved on to the next anomalous mark she'd noticed on her first visit – the broken skull. The cranium showed massive trauma, the skull and face literally crushed. The biggest and, it seemed, first blow had occurred to the right of the parietal bone, shattering the skull in a star pattern and separating it along the sutures. These, too, were clearly perimortem injuries, for the simple reason that survival was impossible after such a violent blow. The green-bone nature of the fractures indicated they had occurred when the bone was still fresh.

The anomaly here was a mark at the point of the blow. She examined the point of fracture. A bear could certainly shatter a skull with the strike of a paw, or crush it with its jaws and teeth. But this mark did not look like either teeth or claws. It was irregular, with multiple indents.

Under the loupe, her suspicions were confirmed. It had been made by a rough, heavy object – almost certainly a rock.

Working even more quickly now, she took a series of photographs of the skull fragments with her macro. This was proof enough. Or was it? She vacillated a moment, then on impulse took out a couple of ziplock bags and slipped the fragment of femur and one of the damaged skull fragments into them. *That* was proof.

Done. She snapped off the light. Now she had incontrovertible evidence that Emmett Bowdree had not been killed and eaten by a bear. Instead, he had been killed and eaten by a human. In fact, judging from the extensive nature of the injuries, there might have been two or three, maybe more, who participated in the killing. They had first disabled him with a blow to the head, crushed his skull, smashed his bones, and literally ripped him apart with their bare hands. Then they had stripped the meat from the bones with a crude knife or piece of metal. Finally, they had eaten him raw – attested by the tooth marks and the absence of bone scorching and other evidence of cooking.

Horrible. Unbelievable. She had discovered a hundred-and-fifty-year-old murder. Which begged the next question: *Were the other ten miners killed in the same way, by humans?*

She glanced at her watch: eleven minutes. She felt a sudden shiver of fear: time to get the hell out. Quickly she began packing up her stuff, preparing to exit the shed.

Suddenly she thought she heard a noise. She flicked off the LED and listened. Silence. Then she heard it again: the faintest crunching sound of snow outside the door.

Jesus, someone was coming. Paralyzed with fear, her heart pounding, she continued to listen. A definite *crunch, crunch, crunch*. And then – across the warehouse, in a window high up in the eaves – she saw a beam of light flash quickly across the glass. More silence. And then the muffled sound of talk and the hiss of a two-way radio.

There were people outside. With a radio.

Heights security? Cops?

She zipped up her backpack with infinite care. The coffin lid was still off. Should she slide it back on? She began to move it back into place, but it made such a loud scraping noise that she stopped. She had to get it back on, though, so in one hasty movement she shoved it back in place.

Outside she could hear more activity: crunching, whispers. There were several people outside and they were trying, not very successfully, to be quiet.

She slid the knapsack over her shoulder and moved away from the coffins. Was there an exit door in the rear? She couldn't tell now – it was too dark – but she didn't recall seeing one. What she needed to do was find a secure hiding place and wait this out.

Tiptoeing across the floor, she headed for the rear of the warehouse, where the giant pieces of an old ski lift had been stored – pylons, chairs, and wheels. Even as she moved across the floor she heard the door open, and she ran the last few yards. Now hushed voices could be heard in the shed. More radio noise.

Reaching the stacks of old equipment, she burrowed her way in, getting down on her hands and knees and crawling as far back as she could, twisting and turning among the giant pieces of metal.

A sudden snapping noise, and then the fluorescent tubes came popping and clinking on, bathing the warehouse in brilliant light. Corrie crawled faster, throwing herself behind a huge coil of steel cable and balling herself up, hugging her backpack to her chest, making herself as small as possible. She waited, hardly daring to breathe. Maybe they thought the padlock had been accidentally left open. Maybe they hadn't noticed her car. Maybe they wouldn't find her . . .

Footsteps crossed the cement floor. And then Corrie heard a burst of whispering. Now she could distinguish individual voices and catch snatches of phrases. With a thrill of absolute horror she heard her own name spoken – in the Texas drawl of Kermode: querulous, inciting.

She buried her head in her gloved hands, reeling from the nightmare. She could feel her heart almost bursting with anxiety and dismay. Why had she done this? *Why?*

She heard a voice speak, loud and clear: the harsh twang of Kermode. 'Corrie Swanson?'

It echoed dreadfully in the cavernous room.

'Corrie Swanson, we know you're in here. We *know* it. You're in a world of trouble. If you come out and show yourself now, that would be the smart thing to do. If you force these policemen to have to find you, that won't be smart. Do you understand?'

Corrie was choking with fear. More sounds: additional people were arriving. She couldn't move.

'All right,' she heard the chief's unhappy voice say. 'You, Joe, start in the back. Fred, stay by the door. Sterling, you poke around those cats and snowmobiles.'

Still Corrie couldn't move. The game was up. She should show herself. But some crazy, desperate hope kept her hidden.

Burying her head deeper into her gloves, like a child hiding under the covers, she waited. She heard the tap of footsteps, the scrape and clank of equipment being moved, the hiss and crackle of radios. A few minutes passed. And then, almost directly above her, she heard, loudly: 'Here she is!' And then, aimed at her: 'This is the police. Stand up slowly and keep your hands in sight.'

She simply could not move.

'Stand up slowly, hands in sight. *Now.*'

She managed to raise her head and saw a cop standing just a few feet away, service revolver drawn and pointed. Two other cops were just arriving.

Corrie rose stiffly, her hands out. The cop came over, grasped her wrist, spun her around, pulled her arms behind her, and slapped on a pair of handcuffs.

'You have the right to remain silent,' she heard him say, as if from a great distance. 'Anything you say may be used against you in court . . .'

Corrie couldn't believe this was happening to her.

'. . . You have the right to consult with an attorney, and to have that attorney present during questioning. If you are indigent, an attorney will be provided at no cost to you. Do you understand?'

She couldn't speak.

'Do you understand? Please speak or nod your answer.'

Corrie managed to nod.

The cop said loudly: 'I make note of the fact the prisoner has acknowledged understanding her rights.'

Holding her by the arm, the cop led her out of the stacks of equipment and into the open. She blinked in the bright light. Another cop had unzipped her backpack and was looking through it. He soon extracted the two ziplock bags containing the bones.

Chief Morris watched him, looking exceedingly unhappy. Standing beside him and surrounded by several security officers of The Heights was Mrs Kermode, dressed in a slim, zebra-striped winter outfit trimmed in fur – with a look on her face of malice triumphant.

'Well, well,' she said, breathing steam like a dragon. 'The girl studying law enforcement is actually a criminal. I had you pegged the moment I saw you. I knew you'd try something like this – and here you are, predictable as clockwork. Trespassing, vandalism, larceny, resisting arrest.' She reached out and took a ziplock bag from the cop and waved it in Corrie's face. 'And *grave robbing.*'

'That's enough,' the chief said to Kermode. 'Please give that evidence back to the officer and let's go.' He took Corrie gently by the arm. 'And you, young lady – I'm afraid you're under arrest.'

CHAPTER 9

Five long days later, Corrie remained locked up in the Roaring Fork County Jail. Bail had been set at fifty thousand dollars, which she didn't have – not even the five-thousand-dollar surety – and the local bail bondsman declined to take her as a client because she was from out of state, with no assets to pledge and no relatives to vouch for her. She had been too ashamed to call her father, and anyway he sure didn't have the money. There was no one else in her life – except Pendergast. And even if she could reach him, she'd die before she took any more money from him – especially bond money.

Nevertheless, she'd had to write him a letter. She had no idea where he was or what he was doing. She hadn't heard from him in nearly a year. But he, or someone acting for him, had continued paying her tuition. And the day after her arrest, with the story plastered all over the front page of the *Roaring Fork Times*, she realized she had to write. Because if she didn't, and he heard about her arrest from someone else, saw those headlines . . . She owed it to him to tell him first.

So she had written a letter to his Dakota address, care of Proctor. In it she told the whole story, unvarnished. The only thing she left out was the bail situation. Writing everything down had really impressed on her what a brainless, overconfident, and self-destructive thing she had done. She concluded by telling him his obligation to her was over and that no reply was expected or wanted. He was no longer to concern himself with her. She would take care of herself from now on. Except that someday, as soon as she was able, she would pay him back for all the tuition he had wasted sending her to John Jay.

Writing that letter had been the hardest thing she had ever done. Pendergast had saved her life; plucked her out of Medicine Creek, Kansas; freed her from a drunken, abusive mother; paid for her to go to boarding school – and then financed her education at John Jay. And . . . for what?

But that was all over now.

The fact that the jail was relatively posh only made her feel worse. The cells had big, sunny windows looking out over the mountains, carpeted floors, and nice furniture. She was allowed out of her cell from eight in the morning until lockdown at 10:30 PM. During free time, the prisoners were allowed to hang around the dayroom and read, watch TV, and chat with the other inmates. There was even an adjacent workout room with an elliptical trainer, weights, and treadmills.

At that moment, Corrie was sitting in the

dayroom, staring at the black-and-white checkered carpet. Doing nothing. For the past five days she had been so depressed that she couldn't seem to do anything – read, eat, or even sleep. She just sat there, all day, every day, staring into space, and then spent each night in her cell, lying on her back in her cot, staring into darkness.

'Corrine Swanson?'

She roused herself and looked up. A detention guard was standing in the door of the room, holding a clipboard.

'Here,' she said.

'Your attorney has arrived for your appointment.'

She'd forgotten. She hauled herself to her feet and followed the guard to a separate room. She felt as if the air around her were thick, granular. Her eyes wouldn't stop leaking water. But she wasn't crying, exactly; it seemed like a physiological reaction.

She went into a small conference room to find the public defender waiting at the table, briefcase open, manila folders spread out in a neat fan. His name was George Smith and she had already met with him a few times. He was a middle-aged, slight, sandy-haired, balding man with a perpetually apologetic look on his face. He was nice enough, and he meant well, but he wasn't exactly Perry Mason.

'Hello, Corrie,' he said.

She eased down in a chair, saying nothing.

'I've had several meetings with the DA,' Smith

began, 'and, well, I've made some progress on the plea deal.'

Corrie nodded apathetically.

'Here's where we stand. You plead to breaking and entering, trespassing, and desecration of a human corpse, and they'll drop the petty larceny charge. You'll be looking at ten years, max.'

'Ten years?'

'I know. It's not what I'd hoped. There's a lot of pressure being brought to bear to throw the book at you. I don't quite understand it, but it may have something to do with all the publicity this case has generated and the ongoing controversy about the cemetery. They're making an example of you.'

'Ten *years*?' Corrie repeated.

'With good behavior, you could be out in eight.'

'And if we go to trial?'

The lawyer's face clouded. 'Out of the question. The evidence against you is overwhelming. There's a string of felonies here, starting with the B&E and going all the way to the desecration of a human corpse. That latter crime alone carries a sentence of up to thirty years in prison.'

'You're kidding – thirty years?'

'It's a particularly nasty statute here in Colorado because of a long history of grave robbing.' He paused. 'Look, if you don't plead, the DA will be pissed and he could very well ask for that maximum sentence. He's threatened as much to me already.'

Corrie stared at the scarred table.

'You've *got* to plead out, Corrie. It's your only choice.'

'But . . . I can't believe it. Ten years, just for what I did? That's more than some murderers get.'

A long silence. 'I can always go back to the DA. The problem is, they've got you cold. You don't have anything to trade.'

'But I *didn't* desecrate a human corpse.'

'Well, according to the way those statutes are written, you did. You opened the coffin, you handled the bones, you photographed them, and you took two of them. That's what they'll argue, and I'd be hard-pressed to counter. It's not worth the risk. The jury pool here is drawn from the entire county, not just Roaring Fork, and there are a lot of conservative ranchers and farmers out there, religious folk, who would not look kindly on what you did.'

'But I was just trying to prove that the marks on the bones . . .' She couldn't finish.

The attorney spread his thin hands, a pained look pinching his narrow face. 'It's the best I can do.'

'How long do I have to think about it?'

'Not long. They can withdraw the offer at any moment. If you could decide right now, that would be best.'

'I've *got* to think about it.'

'You have my number.'

Corrie rose and shook his limp, sweaty hand, walked out. The guard, who had been waiting

80

outside the door, led her back to the dayroom. She sat down and stared at the black-and-white carpet and thought about what her life would look like in ten years, after she got back out. Her eyes began leaking again, and she wiped at them furiously, to no avail.

CHAPTER 10

Jenny Baker arrived at the Roaring Fork City Hall lugging Chief Stanley Morris's second briefcase in both hands. The chief carried two bulging briefcases to every meeting he attended, it seemed, so as to be prepared to answer any question that might come up. Jenny had tried to persuade him to get a tablet computer, but he was a confirmed Luddite and refused even to use the desktop computer in his office.

Jenny rather liked that, despite the inconvenience of having to lug around two briefcases. So far, the chief had proven a pleasant man to work for, rarely made demands, and was always agreeable. In the two weeks she had interned in the police station, she'd seen him flustered and worried but never angry. Now he walked alongside her, chatting about town business, as they entered the meeting room. Big town meetings were sometimes held in the Opera House, but this one – on December thirteenth, less than two weeks from Christmas – was not expected to be well attended.

She took a seat just behind the chief in the town-official seating area. They were early – the chief was always early – and she watched as the mayor came in, followed by the Planning Board, the town attorney, and other officials whose names she did not know. Hard on their heels came a contingent from The Heights, led by Mrs Kermode, her coiffed, layered helmet of blond hair utterly perfect. She was followed by her brother-in-law, Henry Montebello, and several anonymous-looking men in suits.

The main item of the meeting – the agenda was routinely published in the paper – involved a proposal from The Heights regarding where the Boot Hill remains were to be reinterred. As the meeting opened, with the usual pledge of allegiance and the reading of minutes, Jenny's thoughts drifted to the woman she had met – Corrie – and what had happened to her. It sort of freaked her out. She had seemed so nice, so professional – and then to be caught breaking into a warehouse, desecrating a coffin, and stealing bones. You never could tell what some people were capable of doing. And a student at John Jay, too. Nothing like that had ever happened in The Heights, and the neighborhood was still up in arms about it. It was all her parents talked about at breakfast every morning, even now, ten days after the event.

As the preliminaries went on, Jenny was surprised to see just how many people were filing into the public seating area. It was already packed, and now the standing-room area in the back was filling up. Maybe the cemetery thing was going to erupt into controversy again. She hoped this wasn't going to make the meeting run late – she had a dinner date later that evening.

The meeting moved to the first item on the agenda. The attorney for The Heights rose and gave his presentation in a nasal drone. The Heights, he said, proposed to rebury the disinterred remains in a field they had purchased for just such a purpose on a hillside about five miles down Route 82. This surprised Jenny; she had always assumed the remains would be reburied within the town limits. Now she understood why so many people were there.

The attorney went through some legal gobble-dygook about how this was all perfectly legal, reasonable, proper, preferable, and indeed, unavoidable for various reasons she didn't understand. As he continued, Jenny heard a slow rising of disapproving sounds, murmurings – even a few hisses – from the public area. She glanced in the direction of the noise. The proposal was, it seemed, not being greeted with favor.

Just as she was about to turn her attention back to the stage, she noted a striking figure in a black suit appear in the very rear of the public area. There was something about the man that gave her pause. Was it his sculpted, alabaster face? Or his hair, so blond it was almost white? Or his eyes of such pale gray-blue that, even across the room, he looked almost like an alien. Was he a celebrity? If not, Jenny decided, he should be.

Now a landscape designer was on his feet and giving his spiel, complete with slide show, images on the portable screen displaying a plat of the proposed burial area, followed by three-dimensional views of the future cemetery, with stone walls, a quaint wrought-iron archway leading in, cobbled paths among the graves. Next came slides of the actual site: a lovely green meadow partway up a mountain. It was pretty – but it wasn't in Roaring Fork.

As he spoke, the murmurings of disapproval, the restlessness, of the gathered public grew in suppressed intensity. Jenny recognized a reporter from the *Roaring Fork Times* sitting in the front row of the public area, and the look of anticipatory delight on his face signaled that he expected fireworks.

And now, at last, Mrs Betty Brown Kermode rose to speak. At this, a hush fell. She was a commanding presence in town – even Jenny's father seemed intimidated by her – and those who had gathered to express their opinions were temporarily muted.

She began by mentioning the exceedingly unfortunate break-in of ten days earlier, the shocking violation of a corpse, and how this demonstrated the need to get those human remains back in the ground as soon as possible. She mentioned in passing the seriousness of the crime – so serious that the perpetrator had accepted a plea bargain that would result in ten years' incarceration.

The Heights, she went on, had been taking care of these remains with the utmost attention, deeply aware of their sacred duty to see that these rough miners, these pioneers of Roaring Fork, were given a burial site suitable to their sacrifice, their spirit, and their contribution to the opening of the American West. They had, she said, found the perfect resting place: on the slopes of the Catamount, with heartbreaking views of the Continental Divide. Surrounding the graveyard, they had purchased over a hundred acres of open space, which would remain forever wild. This is what these Colorado pioneers deserved – not being jammed into some town lot, surrounded by the hustle and bustle of commerce, traffic, shopping, and sport.

It was an effective presentation. Even Jenny found herself agreeing with Mrs Kermode. The grumbling was no longer audible when she returned to her seat.

Next to stand was Henry Montebello, who had married into Kermode's family and, as a result, gained instant power and respectability in the town. He was an older man, gaunt, reserved, and weathered looking. Jenny did not like him and was, in fact, afraid of him. He had a laconic mid-Atlantic accent that somehow caused every observation he made to sound cynical. Although he had been the master architect for The Heights way back when, unlike Kermode he did not live within the development, but rather had his home and office in a large mansion on the other side of town.

He cleared his throat. No expense had been spared, he told the gathered crowd, in developing The Heights – and not that alone, but also in ensuring that it conformed, not only with the spirit and aesthetic of Roaring Fork, but to the local ecology and environment, as well. He could say this, Montebello continued, because he had personally supervised the preparation of the site, the design of the mansions and clubhouse, and the construction of the development. He would, he said, oversee the creation of the new cemetery with the same close, hands-on attention he had given to The Heights. The implication seemed to be that the long-dead occupants of Boot Hill should be grateful to Montebello for his personal ministrations on their behalf. Montebello spoke with quiet dignity, and with aristocratic gravitas – and yet there was a steely undertone to his words, subtle but unmistakable, that seemed to dare anyone to challenge a single syllable of what he'd uttered. No one did, and he once again took his seat.

And now the mayor rose, thanked Mrs Kermode and Mr Montebello, and called for public comment. A number of hands went up, and the mayor pointed at someone. But as that person rose to speak, the man in the black suit – who had somehow slipped all the way to the front – held up his hand for silence.

'You are out of turn, sir,' said the mayor, sternly, rapping his gavel.

'That remains to be seen,' came the reply. The voice was as smooth as honey, an unusual Deep South accent Jenny could not place, but something about it gave the mayor just enough pause to allow the man to continue.

'Mrs Kermode,' the man said, turning to her, 'as you well know, permission from a qualified descendant is required to exhume human remains. In the case of historic burials, both Colorado and federal law state that a "good-faith effort" must be made to locate such descendants before any remains can be exhumed. I assume that The Heights made such an effort?'

The mayor rapped his gavel. 'I repeat, you are out of turn, sir!'

'I'm happy to answer the question,' Mrs Kermode said smoothly. 'We did indeed make a diligent search for descendants. None could be found. These miners were mostly transients without families, who died a century and a half ago, leaving no issue. It's all in the public documentation.'

'Very good,' said the mayor. 'Thank you, sir, for your opinion. We have many other people who wish to speak. Mr Jackson?'

But the man went on. 'That is strange,' he said. 'Because in just fifteen minutes of idle, ah, *surfing* on the Internet, I was able to locate a direct descendant of one of the miners.'

A silence, and then the mayor spoke. 'Just who are you, sir?'

'I'll get to that in a moment.' The man raised a piece of paper. 'I have here a letter from Captain Stacy Bowdree, USAF, just back from a tour in Afghanistan. When Captain Bowdree heard that you people had dug up her great-great-grandfather Emmett Bowdree, dumped his remains in a box, and stored them in a filthy equipment shed on a ski slope, she was exceedingly upset. In fact, she plans to press charges.'

This was greeted by silence.

The man held up another piece of paper. 'Colorado statute is very strict on the desecration of cemeteries and human remains. Allow me to read from Section Ninety-Seven of the Colorado Criminal Codes and Statutes: *Desecration of a Cemetery*.' And he began to quote aloud.

(2) (a) Every person who shall knowingly and willfully dig up, except as otherwise provided by law with the permission of an authorized descendant, any corpse or remains of any human being, or cause through word, deed or action the same to happen, shall upon conviction be guilty of a Class A felony and shall be imprisoned for not more than thirty (30) years or fined not more than Fifty Thousand Dollars ($50,000.00), or both, in the discretion of the court.

Now the mayor rose in a fury, hammering his gavel. 'This is not a court of law!' *Bang!* 'I will not have these proceedings co-opted. If you, sir,

89

have legal questions, take them up with the town attorney instead of wasting our time in a public meeting!'

But the man in the black suit would not be silenced. 'Mayor, may I direct your attention to the language? *Or cause through word, deed or action the same to happen.* That seems to apply to *you* quite specifically, as well as to Mrs Kermode and the chief of police. All three of you were responsible in *word, deed or action* for the illegal exhumation of Emmett Bowdree – were you not?'

'Enough! Security, remove this man from the premises!'

Even as two cops struggled to make their way to the man, he spoke again, his voice cutting the air like a razor. '*And are you not about to sentence someone to ten years in prison for violating this very statute that you, yourselves, have already so clearly violated?*'

Now the public was aroused, both pro and con. There were some murmurings and scattered shouts: 'Is it true?' and 'What goes?' along with 'Get rid of him!' and 'Who the hell is this guy?'

The two cops, pushing their way through the now-standing public crowd, reached the man. One took his arm.

'Don't give us any trouble, sir.'

The man freed himself from the cop's grasp. 'I would advise you not to touch me.'

'Arrest him for disturbing the peace!' the mayor cried.

'*Let him speak!*' someone shouted.

'Sir,' Jenny heard the cop say, 'if you won't cooperate, we'll have to arrest you.'

The man's response was drowned out by the hubbub. The mayor rapped his gavel repeatedly, calling for order.

'You're under arrest,' said the cop. 'Place your hands behind your back.'

Instead of obeying the order, Jenny saw the man remove his wallet with a single, smooth motion and flip it open. There was a flash of gold, and the two officers froze.

The hubbub began to die down.

'In response to your earlier question,' the man told the mayor in his dulcet southern voice, 'I am Special Agent Pendergast of the Federal Bureau of Investigation.'

Now the entire room went deathly silent. Jenny had never before seen the look she now saw on Mrs Kermode's face: shock and fury. Henry Montebello's face betrayed nothing at all. Chief Morris, for his part, looked paralyzed. *Paralyzed* wasn't the word – he looked wilted. Slumped. As if he wanted to melt into his chair and disappear. The mayor looked merely undone.

'Emmett Bowdree,' the man named Pendergast continued, 'is just one of a hundred and thirty human remains that the four of you – Mrs Kermode, the mayor, Mr Montebello, and the chief of police who signed the actual order – are responsible for desecrating, according to

91

Colorado statute. The criminal and civil liability is staggering.'

Mrs Kermode recovered first. 'Is this how the FBI operates? You come in here, interrupt our public meeting, and make threats? Are you even a real agent? Come down here and present your credentials to the mayor in the proper fashion!'

'Gladly.' The pale man slipped through the gate separating the public area from the official one and strolled down the aisle with a sort of insolent casualness. He arrived in front of the mayor and laid the shield down on the podium. The man examined it, his face reflecting growing consternation.

With a sudden, lithe movement, Agent Pendergast plucked the mayor's microphone out of its mount. Only then did Jenny realize that inviting the stranger to the front had probably not been the best idea. She could see the reporter from the *Roaring Fork Times* scribbling madly, a look of pure joy on his face.

Now the mayor spoke, raising his voice on account of having lost his amplification. 'Agent Pendergast, are you here in an official capacity?'

'Not yet,' came the answer.

'Then I move we adjourn this meeting so that our attorneys, the attorneys from The Heights, and you can address these issues in private.' A bang of the gavel sealed this statement.

Agent Pendergast's black-clad arm snaked out, took the gavel, and moved it out of reach of the mayor's hand. 'Enough of that uncivilized pounding.'

This brought a laugh from the public section.

'I am not yet finished.' Pendergast's voice, now amplified by the sound system, filled the hall. 'Captain Bowdree wrote me that, since her great-great-grandfather's remains have been so rudely disinterred, and nothing can remedy the insult to his memory, she believes that they should at least be examined for cause of death – for historical purposes, of course. Therefore, she has given permission for a certain Ms Corrine Swanson to examine those remains before they are reburied. In their *original* resting place, by the way.'

'What?' Kermode rose in a fury. 'Did that girl send you? Is *she* behind this?'

'She has no idea I'm even here,' the man said smoothly. 'However, it would seem that the most serious charge against her is now moot – but has instead redounded to the four of you. *You* are now the ones facing thirty years in prison – not on one count, but on one hundred and thirty.' He paused. 'Imagine if your sentences were to be served sequentially.'

'These accusations are outrageous!' the mayor cried. 'I hereby adjourn this meeting. Will security immediately clear the room!'

Chaos ensued. But Pendergast did nothing to prevent it, and the meeting room was finally cleared, leaving him alone with the town fathers, The Heights attorneys, Kermode, Montebello,

Chief Morris, and a few other officials. Jenny waited in her seat beside the chief, breathless. What would happen now? For the first time, Kermode looked defeated – haggard, her platinum hair undone. The chief was bathed in sweat, the mayor pale.

'It looks like there's going to be quite a story in the *Roaring Fork Times* tomorrow,' said Pendergast.

Everyone seemed to stagger at the thought. The mayor wiped his brow.

'In addition to that story,' said Pendergast, 'I'd like to see another one appear.'

There was a long silence. Montebello was the first to speak. 'And what might that be?'

'A story stating that you—' Agent Pendergast turned to Chief Morris – 'have dropped all charges against Corrine Swanson and released her from jail.'

He let that sink in.

'As I said before, the most serious charge is now moot. Ms Swanson has permission to examine the remains of Emmett Bowdree. The other charges – trespassing and B&E – are less grave and could be dismissed with relative ease. Everything can, in fact, be chalked up to an unfortunate miscommunication between Chief Morris here and Ms Swanson.'

'This is blackmail,' said Kermode.

Pendergast turned to her. 'I might point out it wasn't actually a miscommunication. My understanding is that Chief Morris indicated she would have access to the remains. He then withdrew that assurance, due to your own gross interference. It was unfair. I am merely rectifying a wrong.'

There was a pause while the others digested this. 'And what,' asked Kermode, 'will you do for us in return? That is, if the chief releases this lady friend of yours.'

'I'll persuade Captain Bowdree not to take her complaint *officially* to the FBI,' Pendergast said smoothly.

'I see,' said Kermode. 'It all depends on this Captain Bowdree. Provided, of course, this person even exists.'

'How unfortunate for you that Bowdree was an unusual name. It made my task so much easier. A phone call established that she was well aware of her Colorado roots and, in fact, quite proud of them. Mrs Kermode, you claimed The Heights made a good-faith effort to locate descendants. That is clearly a falsehood. Naturally, this is something the FBI would have to look into.'

Jenny noticed that under her makeup, Mrs Kermode's face was very pale. 'Let's get this straight. This Swanson girl – she's what, your girl-friend? A relative?'

'She's no relation to me.' Agent Pendergast narrowed his silvery eyes and looked at Kermode in a most unsettling way. 'I will, however, be remaining in Roaring Fork to take in the Christmas season – and to make sure you don't interfere with her again.'

As Jenny watched, Pendergast turned to the chief. 'I suggest you call the newspaper right away – I imagine their deadline is looming. I've already booked a room for Ms Swanson at the Hotel Sebastian, and I hope that – for your sake – she does not spend another night in your jail.'

CHAPTER 11

It was a few minutes before midnight when the silver Porsche 911 Turbo S Cabriolet pulled up to the elegant front door of 3 Quaking Aspen Drive. It did not stop there, however, but continued on into the shadow of the four-car garage beyond.

The young man at the wheel put the vehicle into park. 'Home,' he said. 'As you requested.' He leaned over the gear lever to nuzzle the girl in the passenger seat.

'Stop it,' she said, pushing him away.

The young man pretended to look hurt. 'I'm a friend, aren't I?'

'Yes.'

'Then bring on the benefits.' Another attempt at nuzzling.

'What a dork.' The girl got out of the car with a laugh. 'Thanks for dinner.'

'*And* the movie.'

'And the movie.' Jenny Baker slammed the door, then watched the car move off down the long, curving driveway until it reached the road leading to the gatehouse of The Heights, down in the valley half a mile away. For a lot of her girlfriends back at Hollywood High, losing one's virginity seemed like a badge of honor: the sooner the better. But Jenny didn't feel that way. Not on a first date, and certainly not with a dweeb like Kevin Traherne. Like so many of the male youth in Roaring Fork, he seemed to think that his father's dough was the only excuse he needed to get into a girl's pants.

She stepped up to the closest garage door, punched a code into the panel, and waited for the door to ascend. Then she walked past the row of gleaming, expensive cars, pressed the button to close the garage, and opened the door to the house. The security alarm was, as usual, off – there were few burglaries in Roaring Fork, and never a one in The Heights . . . unless you counted Corrie Swanson's breaking into the warehouse, of course. Her thoughts returned to the town meeting earlier in the day, and to the intimidating FBI agent in the black suit who'd descended on it like an avenging angel. She felt sorry for the chief: he was a decent guy, but he had a real problem with letting other people – like that witch Kermode – walk all over him. Nevertheless, she was glad the agent – Pendergast was his name, she remembered – had gotten Corrie out of jail. She hoped to run into her again, ask her about John Jay, maybe . . . as long as the chief wasn't around.

Jenny walked through the mudroom, through the pantry, and into the expansive kitchen of the vacation home. Through glass doors she could see the Christmas tree, all decked out and blinking. Her parents and her younger sister, Sarah, would be upstairs asleep.

She snapped on a bank of lights. They illuminated the long granite countertops; the Wolf oven and dual Sub-Zero refrigerator and freezer units; the three doors leading, respectively, into the laundry, the second kitchen, and the dining room.

She suddenly realized there had been no patter of nails on the floor, no shaggy, friendly dog wagging his misshapen tail in greeting. 'Rex?' she called out.

Nothing.

With a shrug, she got a glass from one of the cabinets, walked over to the fridge – decorated, as usual, with Sarah's stupid Nicki Minaj photos – poured herself a glass of milk, then took a seat at the table in the breakfast nook. There was a stack of books and magazines in the window seat, and she pushed a few aside – noting as she did so that Sarah had finally taken her advice and begun reading *Watership Down* – and plucked out her copy of Schmalleger's *Criminal Justice Today*. As she did so, she noticed that one of the chairs of the kitchen table had been knocked over.

Sloppy.

She found her page in the book and began to read, sipping her milk as she did so. It drove her father – a high-profile Hollywood lawyer – crazy that she wanted to go into law enforcement. He tended to look down on cops and prosecutors as lower forms of life. But in point of fact he was partly responsible for her interest. All the cop action movie premieres she'd attended – produced or directed by her father's clients – had left her fascinated with the job from an early age. And starting next fall, she'd be studying the subject full-time, as a freshman at Northeastern University.

Finishing her milk, she closed the book again, put her glass in the sink, and walked out of the kitchen, heading for the stairs up to her room. Her father had the connections to keep her from getting summer jobs with the California police, but there was nothing he could do to prevent her winter break internship here in Roaring Fork. The very idea of it made him nuts.

Which, of course, was part of the fun.

The huge, rambling house was very still. She ascended the curving staircase to the second floor, the landing above dark and silent. As she climbed, she thought once again about the mysterious FBI agent. *FBI*, she thought. *Maybe I should look into an internship in Quantico next summer . . .*

At the top of the stairs, she stopped. Something was wrong. For a moment, she wasn't sure what it was. And then she realized: Sarah's door was wide open, faint light streaming out into the dim hall.

At sixteen, Sarah had reached the age where adolescent privacy was all-important. These days her door was closed at all times. Jenny sniffed the air, but there was no smell of weed. She smiled:

her sister must have fallen asleep over a magazine or something. She'd take the opportunity to sneak in and rearrange her sister's stuff. That was sure to get a rise out of her.

Quietly, she crept down the hallway, approaching her sister's room on silent feet. She came up to the door frame, placed one hand upon it, then slowly leaned her head in.

At first, she could not quite process what she saw. Sarah lay on her bed, tied fast with wound wire, a dirty rag stuffed into her mouth, a billiard ball at its center – Jenny noticed a number, seven, engraved into its yellow-and-white surface – and secured behind her head with a bungee cord. In the faint blue light, Jenny saw that her sister's knees were bleeding profusely, staining the bedcovers black. As she gasped in horror and shock, Jenny saw Sarah's eyes staring back at her: wide, terrified, pleading.

Then Jenny registered something in her peripheral vision. She turned in mid-gasp to see a fearful apparition in the hall beside her: wearing black jeans and a tight-fitting jacket of dark leather. The figure was silent and utterly motionless. Its hands were gloved and gripped a baseball bat. Worst of all was the clown mask – white, huge red lips smiling maniacally, bright red circles on each cheek. Jenny stumbled backward, her legs going weak beneath her. Through the eyeholes on each side of the long pointed nose, she could see two dark eyes staring back at her, dreadful in their lack of expression, in awful counterpoint to the leering mask.

Jenny opened her mouth to scream, but the figure – springing into sudden, violent motion – reached forward and quickly stuffed an awful-smelling cloth over her mouth and nose. As her senses went black and she sank to the floor, she could just hear – as the darkness rushed over her – a faint, high-pitched keening coming through Sarah's gag . . .

Slowly, slowly, she regained her senses. Everything was fuzzy and vague. For a moment, she didn't know where she was. She was lying on something hard and smooth and that seemed to encircle her. Then, looking around in the darkness, she understood: she was in the tub of her private bathroom. What was she doing here? It felt as if she'd been asleep for hours. But no – the wall clock above her sink read ten minutes to one. She'd only been out for a couple of minutes. She tried to move – and realized she had been bound, hand and foot.

That was when the memory of what had happened came rushing back, falling upon her like a dead weight.

Instantly her heart accelerated, pounding hard in her chest. The rag was still in her mouth. She tried to spit it out, found she could not. The tight rope chafed at her wrists and ankles. Crime-scene photos she'd seen came into her mind, flashing quickly by in a terrible parade.

I'm going to be raped, she thought, shuddering at the recollection of that leering clown mask. But no – if rape was what he was after, he wouldn't have tied her up the way he did. This was a home invasion – and she'd walked right into the middle of it.

A home invasion.

Maybe he only wants money, she thought. *Maybe he only wants jewelry. He'll take what he can get, then leave, and then . . .*

But it was all so horribly stealthy – so diabolically calculating. First Sarah, now her . . .

. . . What about Mom and Dad?

At this thought, stark panic bubbled to the surface.

She struggled violently, jaw working, tongue pushing against the cloth wedged into her mouth. She tried to rise up, and an agonizing pain that almost caused her to faint lanced through her legs. She saw that her kneecaps had been beaten like her sister's, white edges of broken bone jutting up through torn, bloody flesh. She remembered the baseball bat clutched in one black-gloved hand, and she moaned in fresh panic, thrashing against the bottom of the tub despite the awful pain in her knees.

All of a sudden, sounds of fighting erupted from down the hall: her father yelling, her mother crying out in fear. Jenny listened in unspeakable horror. Furniture was overturned; there was the sound of breaking glass. Her mother's screams spiked in volume. A heavy thud. Abruptly, her father's shouts of anger and alarm changed to cries of pain. There was an ugly crack of what sounded like wood on bone, and his voice was abruptly cut off.

Jenny listened to the dreadful silence, whimpering under the gag, her heart beating even faster. And then, a moment later, came another sound: sobs, running feet. It was her mother, racing down the hall, trying to escape. Jenny heard her mother go into Sarah's room; heard her scream. And now a heavier tread came down the hall. It was not her father's.

Another cry of fear from her mother; the sound of feet pattering down the stairs. *She'll get away now*, Jenny thought, hope suddenly rising within her like white light. *She'll hit the alarm, she'll run out, call the neighbors, call the cops . . .*

The unfamiliar tread, faster now, went stomping down the steps.

Heart in her throat, Jenny listened as the sounds grew fainter. She heard her mother's step, running toward the kitchen and the master alarm panel. There was a cry as she was apparently cut off. The thunk of an overturned chair; the sound of glassware and dishes crashing to the floor. Jenny, struggling against her bonds, could hear it all, could follow the chase with dreadful articulation. She heard her mother's footsteps, running through the den, the living room, the library. A moment of silence. And then came a low, cautious sliding sound: it was her mother, quietly opening the door to the indoor pool. *She's going out the back*, Jenny thought. *Out the back, so she can get to the MacArthurs' house* . . .

All of a sudden there was a series of brutal crashes – her mother gave out a single, sharp scream – and then silence.

No . . . not quite silence. As Jenny listened, wide-eyed, whimpering, the blood rushing in her ears, she could make out the unfamiliar tread again. It was moving slowly now, deliberately. And it was getting closer. It was crossing the front hall. Now it was coming back up the stairs: she heard the squeak of the tread her father kept saying he'd get fixed.

Closer. Closer. The steps were coming down the hall. They were in her bedroom. And now a dark figure appeared in the doorway of her bath. It was silent, save for labored breathing. The clown mask leered down at her. There was no longer a baseball bat in one of the hands. It had been replaced by a plastic squeeze bottle, glowing pale gold in the faint light.

The figure stepped into the bathroom.

As it came closer, Jenny writhed in the tub, heedless of the pain in her knees. Now the invader was hovering over her. The hand holding the squeeze bottle came forward in her direction. As the figure began silently squeezing the liquid over her in long, arc-like jets, a powerful stench rose up: gasoline.

Jenny's struggles became frantic.

Painstakingly, Clown Mask sent the looping squirts of gasoline over and around her, missing nothing, dousing her clothes; her hair; the surrounding porcelain. Then – as her struggles grew ever more violent – the invader put down the bottle and took a step back. A hand reached into the pocket of the leather jacket, withdrew a safety match. Holding the match carefully by its end, the figure struck it against the rough surface of the bathroom wall. The head of the match flared into yellow life. It hovered over her, dangling, for an endless, agonizing second.

And then, with the parting of a thumb and index finger, it dropped.

. . . And Jenny's world dissolved into a roar of flame.

CHAPTER 12

Corrie Swanson entered the dining room of the Hotel Sebastian and found herself dazzled by its elegance. It was done up in Gay Nineties style, with red velvet flocked wallpaper, polished-brass and cut-glass fixtures, a pressed-tin ceiling, and Victorian-era mahogany tables and chairs trimmed in silk and gold. A wall of windowpanes looked across the glittering Christmas lights of Main Street to the spruce-clad foothills, ski slopes, and mountain peaks beyond.

Even though it was close to midnight, the dining room was crowded, the convivial murmur of voices mingling with the clink of glassware and the bustle of waiters. The light was dim, and it took her a moment to spy the solitary figure of Pendergast, seated at an unobtrusive table by one of the windows.

She brushed off the maître d's pointed inquiries as to how he could help her – she was still dressed from jail – and made her way to Pendergast's table. He rose, extending his hand. She was startled by his appearance: he seemed to be even paler, leaner, more ascetic – the word *purified* seemed somehow to apply.

'Corrie, I am glad to see you.' He took her hand in his, cool as marble, then held out her seat for her. She sat down.

She'd been rehearsing what she would say, but now it all came out in a confused rush. 'I can't believe I'm free – how can I ever thank you? I was toast, I mean, I was up shit creek, you know they'd already forced me to accept ten years – I really thought my life was over – thank you, *thank you* for everything, for saving my ass, for rescuing me from my incredible, unbelievable *stupidity*, and I'm so sorry, really, *really* sorry—!'

A raised hand stopped the flow of words. 'Will you have a drink? Wine, perhaps?'

'Um, I'm only twenty.'

'Ah. Of course. I shall order a bottle for myself, then.' He picked up a leather-bound wine list that was so massive, it could have been a murder weapon.

'This sure beats jail,' said Corrie, looking around, drinking in the ambience, the aroma of food. It was hard to believe that, just a few hours ago, she'd been behind bars, her life utterly ruined. But once again Agent Pendergast had swooped in, like a guardian angel, and changed everything.

'It took them rather longer than I'd hoped to complete the paperwork,' said Pendergast, perusing the list. 'Fortunately, the Sebastian's dining room is open late. I think the Château Pichon-Longueville 2000 will do nicely – don't you?'

'I don't know jack about wine, sorry.'

'You should learn. It is one of the true and ancient pleasures that make human existence tolerable.'

'Um, I know this may not be the time . . . But I just have to ask you . . .' She found herself coloring. '*Why* did you rescue me like this? And why do you go to all this trouble for me? I mean, you got me out of Medicine Creek, you paid for my boarding school, you're helping pay my tuition at John Jay – why? I'm just a screwup.'

He looked at her with an inscrutable gaze. 'The Colorado rack of lamb for two would go well with the wine. I understand it's excellent.'

She glanced at the menu. She was, it had to be admitted, starving. 'Sounds good to me.'

Pendergast waved over the waiter and placed the order.

'Anyway, getting back to what I was talking about . . . I would really like to know, once and for all, why you've helped me all these years. Especially when I keep, you know, effing up.'

Again that impenetrable gaze met hers. '*Effing*? I see your penchant for charming euphemisms has not abated.'

'You know what I mean.'

The gaze seemed to go on forever, and then Pendergast said: 'Someday, perhaps, you may make a good law enforcement officer or criminalist. That is why. No other reason.'

She felt herself coloring again. She wasn't quite

sure she liked the answer. Now she wished she hadn't asked the question.

Pendergast picked up the wine list again. 'Remarkable how many bottles of excellent French wine in rare vintages have found their way into this small town in the middle of the mountains. I certainly hope they are drunk soon; the altitude here is most unhealthy for Bordeaux.' He laid down the list. 'And now, Corrie, please tell me in detail what you noticed about the bones of Mr Emmett Bowdree.'

She swallowed. Pendergast was so damn . . . *closed.* 'I only had a few minutes to examine the bones. But I'm sure the guy was not killed by a grizzly bear.'

'Your evidence?'

'I took some photographs, but they confiscated the memory chip. I can tell you what I saw – or at least *think* I saw.'

'Excellent.'

'First of all, the skull showed signs of having been bashed in by a rock. And the right femur had scrape marks made by some blunt tool, with no signs that I could see of an osseous reaction or infectious response.'

A slow nod.

She went on with growing confidence. 'It looked to me like there were faint human tooth marks in some of the cancellous bone. They were pretty feeble and blunt, not sharp like a bear's. I think the corpse was cannibalized.'

In her zeal she'd raised her voice, and now she realized it had carried farther than she'd intended. The diners closest to them were staring at her.

'Oops,' she said, looking down at her place setting.

'Have you told anyone of this?' Pendergast asked.

'Not yet.'

'Very good. Keep it quiet. It will only create trouble.'

'But I need access to more remains.'

'I'm working on that. Of the other miners in question, I'm hoping we might find descendants in at least a few cases. And then, naturally, we'd have to get permission.'

'Oh. Thanks, but, you know, I could really do those things myself.' She paused. 'Um, how long do you plan to stay? A few days?'

'Such a lovely, self-indulgent, *rich* little town. I don't believe I've seen anything quite like it. And so charming at Christmastime.'

'So you're going to stay . . . a long time?'

'Ah, here's the wine.'

It had arrived, along with two big glasses. Corrie watched as Pendergast went through the whole routine of swirling the wine around in the glass, smelling it, tasting it, tasting it again.

'Corked, I'm afraid,' he told the waiter. 'Please bring another bottle. Make it an '01, to be on the safe side.'

With profuse apologies, the waiter hurried off with the bottle and glass.

'Corked?' Corrie asked. 'What's that?'

'It's a contaminant of wine, giving it a taste redolent of, some say, a wet dog.'

The new bottle came out and Pendergast went through the routine again, this time nodding his approval. The waiter filled his glass, motioned the bottle toward Corrie. She shrugged and the man filled her glass as well.

Corrie sipped it. It tasted like wine to her – no more, no less. She said, 'This is almost as good as the Mateus we all used to drink back in Medicine Creek.'

'I see you still enjoy provoking me.'

She took another sip. It was amazing, how quickly the memory of jail was fading. 'Getting back to my release,' she said. 'How did you do it?'

'As it happens, I was already on my way back to New York when I received your second letter.'

'You finally got sick of traveling the world?'

'It was your first letter, in part, that prompted my return.'

'Oh? Why's that?'

Instead of answering, Pendergast peered into the dark ruby of his wineglass. 'I was fortunate in locating Captain Bowdree so quickly. I explained everything to her frankly – how her ancestor had been rudely exhumed from his historic resting place to make way for a spa. I explained who you were, what your background was, how the chief promised you access and then withdrew it. I told her about your foolish break-in, how you got caught. And then I mentioned you were facing a ten-year prison sentence.'

He sipped his wine. 'The captain understood the situation immediately. She was most unwilling for you to be, as she put it, *fucked over* like that. She repeated that phrase several times with remarkable emphasis, and it led me to believe she may have had some experience in that line – perhaps in the military. At any rate, together we composed a rather effective letter, which on the one hand threatened to complain to the FBI and, on the other, gave you permission to study the remains of her ancestor.'

'Oh,' said Corrie. 'And that's how you got me out?'

'There was a rather boisterous town meeting this afternoon, at which I discussed the captain's letter.' Pendergast allowed himself the faintest of smiles. 'My presentation was singularly effective. You'll read all about it in tomorrow's paper.'

'Well, you saved my butt. I can't thank you enough. And please thank Captain Bowdree for me.'

'I shall.'

There was a sharp murmur in the dining room; a stir. Several patrons had begun looking toward the wall of windows, and some had stood up from their tables and were pointing. Corrie followed their gaze and saw a small, flickering yellow light on the side of a nearby ridge. As she watched, it rapidly grew in brightness and size. Now more restaurant patrons were standing, and some were walking toward the windows. The hubbub increased.

'Oh, my God, that's a house on fire!' Corrie said, standing up herself to get a better view.

'So it would seem.'

The fire blossomed with shocking rapidity. It appeared to be a huge house and the flames engulfed it with increasing violence, leaping into the night air, sending up columns of sparks and smoke. A fire siren began to go off in the town somewhere, followed by another. And now the entire dining room was on its feet, eyes glued to the mountain. A sense of horror had fallen on the diners, a hush – and then a voice rang out.

'That's the Baker house, up in The Heights!'

CHAPTER 13

Larry Chivers had seen many scenes of destruction in his career as a fire investigator, but he had never seen anything like this. The house had been gigantic – fifteen-thousand-plus square feet – and built with massive timbers, beams, log walls, and soaring, cedar-shake roofs. It had burned with a ferocity that left puddles of glass where the windows had been and even warped the steel I-beam stringers. The snow had completely vanished from within a five-hundred-yard perimeter of the house, and the ruin still radiated heat and plumes of foul steam.

Chivers, who ran a fire investigation consulting firm out of Grand Junction, had been called in at seven that morning. Most of his work was for insurance companies looking to prove arson so they didn't have to pay claims. But once in a while he got called in by the police to determine if a fire was an accident or a crime. This was one of those times.

It was a two-hour drive from Grand Junction, but he'd made it in ninety minutes, driving like hell in his Dodge pickup. Chivers liked traveling with the lightbar and siren going full blast, whipping past the poor speed-limit-bound schmucks on the interstate. Adding to the appeal of this case, the Roaring Fork Police Department paid well and didn't nickel-and-dime him to death like some of the other PDs he worked for.

But his exhilaration had been dampened by this scene of horror. Even Morris, the chief of police, seemed undone by it: stammering, inarticulate, unable to take charge. Chivers did his best to shake the feeling. The fact is, these were rich Hollywood types who used this colossal house as a second home – second home! – only a few weeks out of the year. It was hard to gin up a lot of sympathy for people like that. No doubt the homeowner could build five more just like it and barely dent his wallet. The man who owned this house, a fellow named Jordan Baker, hadn't been heard from, and nobody had been able to reach him yet to inform him of the fire. He and his family were probably off at some posh resort. Or maybe they had a *third* home. It wouldn't surprise Chivers.

He began preparing himself for the walk-through, checking and organizing his equipment, testing his digital recorder, putting on latex gloves. One good thing about the chief's apparent paralysis was that the fire scene hadn't been trampled over and messed up by all the forensic specialists who were still gathering around, waiting to do their thing. Morris had pretty much kept everyone out, waiting for his arrival, and for that he was grateful.

Although, as usual, there was considerable disturbance from firefighter activity – chopped-through floors and walls, shoveled and turned debris, everything soaked with water. The fire department had done a cursory structural integrity survey and had identified the areas that were unstable, taping them off.

Chivers shouldered his bag and nodded to Chief Morris. 'Ready.'

'Good,' the chief said absently. 'Fine. Rudy will take you through.'

The fireman named Rudy lifted the tape for him, and he followed the man down the brick walkway and through where the front door had been. The fire scene stank heavily of burnt and soggy plastic, wood, and polyurethane. There was still some residual heat – despite the freezing temperature the house itself was still sending plumes of steam into the cold blue sky. While he was required to wear a hard hat, he did not wear a respirator: Chivers saw himself as an old-fashioned fire-scene investigator, tough, no-nonsense, who relied more on intuition and left the science to the lab rats. He was used to the stench – and he needed his nose to sniff out any residual accelerants.

Inside the door, in what had been the entryway, he paused. The second floor had collapsed into the first, creating a crazy mess. A staircase ended in the sky. Puddles of glass and metal lay in the low spots, along with heaps of fire-shattered porcelain.

He walked from the entryway into what had obviously been the kitchen, observing the burn patterns. The first order of business was to determine if this was arson – if a crime had been committed. And Chivers was already sure one had. Only accelerants could have caused a fire to burn so hot and fast. This was confirmed as he looked around the kitchen, where he could see faint pour patterns on the remains of the slate floor. He knelt, removed a portable hydrocarbon sniffer from his bag, and took some air samples, moving it about. Moderate.

Still kneeling, he jammed a knife into the burnt, flaking floor and pried up a couple of small pieces, placing them in nylon evidence bags.

The kitchen was a mess, everything fused, scorched, melted. A second-floor bathroom had fallen into the middle of it, with the remains of a porcelain-covered iron claw-foot tub and bits of the sink, toilet, tiled floor, and walls all heaped and scattered about.

Using the sniffer, he got a big positive hit from the remains of the second-floor bathroom. Moving forward on hands and knees, keeping the sniffer low to the ground, Chivers swept it about, looking for a source. The hydrocarbon signature appeared to increase as he approached the tub itself. He rose, peered inside. There was a lot of stuff in the tub – and at the bottom, a layer of thick, black muck in which debris was embedded.

He sampled the muck, giving it a little stir

with a gloved finger. The sniffer went off the charts. And then Chivers stopped cold. Among the muck and debris he could see the fragments of bones poking up – and in the area he had stirred up, some teeth. Human teeth. He carefully probed with his gloved finger, exposing a small piece of a skull, a fragment of jaw, and the rim of an orbit.

Chivers steadied himself, lowered the sniffer. The needle shot up again.

He took out his digital recorder and began murmuring into it. The house had not been empty, after all. Clearly, a body had been placed in the bathtub and burned with accelerant. Putting aside the recorder, he removed another nylon evidence bag and took samples of the debris and muck, including a few small bone fragments. As he poked about in the black paste he saw the gleam of something – a lump of gold, no doubt once a piece of jewelry. He left that, but took samples from the grit and muck around it, including a charred phalange.

He stood up, breathing heavily, feeling a faint wave of nausea. This was a bit more than he was used to. But then again, this was clearly going to be a big case. A very big case. *Focus on that*, he told himself, taking another deep breath.

Chivers nodded to Rudy and continued to follow the fireman through the rest of the house, working the sniffer, taking samples, and speaking his observations into the handheld digital recorder. The charred corpse of what had once been a dog was fused to the stone floor at the back door of the house. Next to it lay two long, disordered piles of gritty ashes, which Chivers recognized as the much-burnt remains of two more victims, both adults judging by the length of the piles, lying side by side. More puddles of gold and silver.

Jesus. He took a sniffer reading but didn't come up with anything significant. Christ, no one had told him – and now he realized they probably didn't know – that the fire had claimed human victims.

Another couple of deep breaths, and Chivers moved on. And then, in what had been the living room, he came upon something else. Debris from the collapsed floor above lay in sodden heaps, and sitting in the center was a set of partly melted bedsprings. As he moved toward the twisted springs, he noted loops of baling wire affixed to them, as if something had been tied to the bed. Four loops – approximately where the ankles and hands would have been. And in one of those loops, he spied a fragment of a small, juvenile tibia.

Oh, Jesus and Mary. Chivers moved the sniffer to it, and again the needle pinned. It was all too clear what had happened. A kid had been wired to the bed, doused with accelerant, and set on fire.

'I need some air,' he said abruptly, rising and staggering. 'Air.'

The fireman grabbed his arm. 'Let me help you out, sir.'

As Chivers exited the fire scene and reeled down the walkway, he saw – out of the corner of his eye – a pale man, dressed in black, no doubt the local coroner, standing beyond the edge of the crowd, staring at him. He made a huge effort to pull himself together.

'I'm all right, thanks,' he said to the firefighter, shedding the embarrassing arm. He looked around, located Chief Morris at the makeshift command center, surrounded by the gathering forensic teams – photographers, hair and fiber, latent, ballistics, DNA. They were suiting up, preparing to go in.

Take it easy, he said to himself. But he could not take it easy. His legs felt like rubber, and it was hard to walk straight.

He approached the chief. Morris was sweating, despite the cold. 'What did you find?' he asked, his voice quiet.

'It's a crime scene,' said Chivers, trying to control the quaver in his voice. Faint lights were dancing in front of his eyes now. 'Four victims. At least, four so far.'

'Four? Oh, my God. So they were in there. The whole family . . .' The chief wiped his brow with a shaking hand.

Chivers swallowed. 'One of the remains is of a . . . a juvenile who was . . . tied to a bed, doused with accelerant . . . and set on fire. Another was burned in . . . in . . .'

As Chivers tried to get out the words, the chief's

face went slack. But Chivers barely noticed. His own world was getting darker and darker.

And then, as he was still trying to finish his sentence, Chivers folded to the ground, collapsing in a dead faint.

CHAPTER 14

Corrie had risen before dawn, gathered her equipment, and headed up to Roaring Fork. Now, as noon approached, she was ensconced in the warehouse at The Heights and well into her work. The remains of Emmett Bowdree were carefully arranged on a plastic folding table Corrie had bought at Walmart, under a set of strong studio lights. She had her stereo zoom in place, hooked to her laptop, the screen displaying the view from the microscope. Her Nikon stood on its tripod. It was like a little piece of heaven, being able to work carefully and thoroughly, without being half scared out of her wits and worrying about detection at any moment.

The only problem was, she was freezing her ass off. It had been below zero when she began the long drive from Basalt – having refused the free room at the Hotel Sebastian, courtesy of Pendergast. She had skipped breakfast to save money, and now she was starving as well as cold. She'd set up a cheap electric heater at her feet, but it was rattling and humming and the stream of warm air seemed to dissipate within inches of its grille. It was doing a good job of warming her shins, but that was about it.

Still, not even the cold and hunger could dampen her growing excitement at what she was finding. Almost all the bones showed trauma in the form of scrape marks, blunt cuts, and gouges. None of the marks showed signs of an osseous reaction, inflammation, or granulation – which meant the damage had been inflicted at the actual time of death. The soft, cancellous or spongy bone tissue showed unmistakable tooth marks – not bear but human, judging from the radius of the bite and the tooth profile. There were, in fact, no bear tooth or claw marks at all.

Inside the broken femur and inside the skull, she had discovered additional scraping and gouging marks, indicating that the marrow and brains had been reamed out by a metal tool. Under the stereo zoom, these defleshing marks disclosed some very faint parallel lines, close together, and what looked like iron oxide deposits – which suggested the tool was iron and, quite possibly, a worn file.

The initial blow to the cranium had definitely been inflicted by a rock. Under the microscope, she had been able to extract a few tiny fragments of it, which a cursory examination showed to be quartz.

The rib cage had been split open – also with a rock – and pulled apart, as if to get at the heart. The bones showed little evidence of trauma inflicted by a sharp edge – such as an ax or knife – nor

124

were there any injuries consistent with a gunshot wound. This puzzled her, as most miners of the time would no doubt have been armed with either a knife or a pistol.

The contemporary newspaper account of the discovery of Emmett Bowdree's body indicated that his bones had been found scattered on the ground a hundred yards beyond the door of a cabin; he had been 'almost entirely eaten' by the so-called bear. The newspaper article, perhaps for reasons of delicacy, didn't go into much detail on exactly what had been eaten or how the bones were disarticulated, except to note that 'pieces of the heart and other viscera were discovered at a distance from the body, partially consumed.' The article made no mention of a fire or cooking, and her examination of the remains showed no evidence of heat.

Emmett Bowdree had been eaten raw.

As she worked, she began to see, in her mind's eye, the sequence of injuries that had been inflicted on the body of Bowdree. He had been set upon by a group – no single person could have pulled a human body apart with such an extremity of violence. They struck him on the back of the head with a rock, causing a severe depressed fracture. While it may not have killed him instantly, it almost certainly rendered him unconscious. They gave the body a savage beating that broke almost every bone, and then proceeded to chop and pound at the body's major articulations – there was evidence of disorganized, haphazard hacking with broken rocks, followed by separation via a strong lateral force. After breaking the joints, they pulled the arms and legs from the torso, separated the legs at the knees, broke open the skull and removed the brains, stripped the flesh from the bones, broke up the larger bones and reamed out the marrow, and removed most of the organs. The killers appeared to have only one tool, a worn-out file, which they supplemented with sharp pieces of quartz rock, their hands, and their teeth.

Corrie surmised that the killing started out as a product of fury and anger, then evolved into – essentially – a cannibal feast. She stepped back from the remains for a moment, thinking. Who was the gang who did this? Why? Again, it seemed exceedingly strange to her that a gang of murderers would be roaming the mountains in the 1870s without guns or knives. And why didn't they cook the meat? It was almost as if they were a tribe of Stone Age killers, merciless and savage.

Merciless and savage. As she warmed herself in front of the heater, rubbing her hands together, Corrie's mind wandered once again to the terrible fire that had taken place the evening before – and the death of the girl, Jenny Baker. It was beyond horrible, the entire family perishing in the fire like that. A maintenance worker had stopped by the warehouse an hour earlier and given her the news. No wonder she'd managed to breeze through The Heights security at ten that morning with barely a nod, left to her own devices without a minder.

The horror of it, and the face of Jenny Baker – so earnest and pretty – haunted her. *Focus on your work*, she told herself, straightening up and preparing to place another bone on the stage for examination.

What she really needed was to get her hands on more sets of remains for comparison. Pendergast had said he was going to help her track down more descendants. She paused for a moment in her work, trying to figure out what it was about this that annoyed her. The force of his personality was such that he dominated any situation he was in. But this was *her* project – and she wanted to do it on her own. She didn't want to have people back at John Jay, especially her advisor, dismissing her work because of the help of a big-time FBI agent. Even the smallest amount of assistance from him might contaminate her achievement, giving them an opening to dismiss it all.

Then Corrie shook this thought away as well. The guy had just saved her career and maybe even her life. To get so possessive, so proprietary, was churlish. Besides, Pendergast always shunned credit or publicity.

She pulled off her gloves to position a tibia on the stereo zoom stage, moving it around until the light raked over it at just the right angle. It showed the same signs as the other bones: fracture damage with plastic response, no evidence of healing, scrape marks, and the clearest set of tooth marks yet. The people who had done this were freaks. Or had they just been really, really angry?

Her hands just about froze, but she managed to get a set of photographs before she had to stop and warm herself again at the heater.

Of course, it was possible this was an isolated case. The other victims might have indeed been killed by a rogue grizzly. The news reports quoted witnesses who had seen the animal, and in one instance a miner had been found in the process of being eaten – or, at least, his bones gnawed upon. Corrie was sorely tempted to check one of the other coffins, but resisted the impulse. From now on, she was going to do everything absolutely and totally by the book.

Able to feel her hands once again, she straightened up. If the other remains did prove to be the work of a gang of killers, her thesis would have to change. She would have a hundred-and-fifty-year-old serial killing on her hands to document. And it would be very cool – and a huge boost to her nascent career – if she could actually manage to solve it.

CHAPTER 15

Larry Chivers stood beside his truck, sealing the nylon evidence bags with a heat sealer and finishing up his notes and observations. He had recovered from his fainting spell, but not from his sense of furious embarrassment. Such a thing had never happened to him – ever. He imagined that everyone was looking at him, whispering about him.

With a grimace, he finished working on the final evidence bag, careful to make the seal complete. Already, he'd narrated the rest of his observations into the digital recorder while they were still fresh. He had to make absolutely sure he did everything just right. This was going to be a huge case – probably even national.

There was a sound behind him, and he turned to see Chief Morris approaching. The man looked utterly undone.

'Sorry about my reaction back there,' Chivers muttered.

'I knew the family,' the chief told him. 'One of the girls worked as an intern in my office.'

Chivers shook his head. 'I'm sorry.'

'I'd like to hear your reconstruction of the fire.'

'I can give you my first impressions. The lab results may take a few days.'

'Go ahead.'

Chivers took a deep breath. 'Point of origin of the fire, in my view, would be either the second-floor bath or the bedroom above the living room. Both areas were doused heavily with accelerant – so much so that the perp would have had to leave the house fairly quickly. Both areas contained human remains.'

'You mean, the Bakers . . . the victims . . . were burned with accelerant?'

'Two of them, yes.'

'Alive?'

What a question. 'That'll have to wait for the M.E. But I doubt it.'

'Thank God.'

'Two more victims were found by the back door – probably where the perp made his exit. There was the body of a dog there, too.'

'Rex,' said the chief to himself, wiping his brow with a trembling hand.

Chivers noted the same man in the black suit he'd seen before, floating in the background, eyes on them. He frowned. Why was the undertaker allowed inside the cordon?

'Motive?' asked the chief.

'Now I'm guessing,' Chivers continued, 'but from thirty years of experience I'd say pretty defin-itely we're looking at a home invasion and

130

robbery, combined with possible sex crimes. The fact that the entire family was subdued and controlled suggests to me there might have been more than one perp.'

'This was no robbery,' came a soft, drawling voice.

Chivers jerked his head around to find that the man in the black suit had somehow managed to approach without being noticed and was now standing behind them.

Chivers's scowl deepened. 'I'm talking to the chief. Do you mind?'

'Not at all. But if I may, I would like to offer a few observations for the benefit of the investigation. A mere robber would not have gone to the trouble to tie up his victims and then burn them alive.'

'*Alive?*' the chief said. 'How do you know?'

'The sadism and rage evident in the arc of this crime are palpable. A sadist wishes to see his victims suffer. That is how he derives his gratification. To tie someone to a bed, douse that person with gasoline, and light them on fire – where's the gratification in that, if the person is already dead?'

The chief's face went as gray as putty. His mouth moved but no sound came out.

'Bullshit,' said Chivers fiercely. 'This was a home invasion and robbery. I've seen it before. The perps break in, find a couple of pretty girls, have their way with them, load up on jewelry, and then burn down the place thinking they'll destroy the evidence – particularly the DNA inside the girls.'

'Yet they didn't take the jewelry, as you yourself noted in your taped observations a few minutes ago, regarding some lumps of gold you discovered.'

'Hold on, here. You were *listening* to me? Who the hell are you?' Chivers turned to the chief. 'Is this guy official?'

The chief passed a sopping handkerchief across his brow. He looked indecisive and frightened. 'Please. Enough.'

The man in the black suit regarded him a moment with his silver eyes, and then shrugged nonchalantly. 'I have no official role here. I am merely a bystander offering his impressions. I shall leave you gentlemen to your work.'

With that he turned and began to leave. Then he paused to speak over his shoulder. 'I should mention, however: there may well be . . . *more*.'

And with that he walked off, slipping under the tape and disappearing into the crowd of rubberneckers.

CHAPTER 16

Horace P. Fine III stopped, swiveled on his instep, and looked Corrie up and down, as if he had just thought of something.

'Do you have any experience house-sitting?' he asked.

'Yes, absolutely,' Corrie replied immediately. It was sort of true: she'd watched their trailer home overnight more than once when her mother went on an all-night bender. And then there was the time she'd stayed at her father's apartment six months before, when he'd gone to that job fair in Pittsburgh.

'Never anyplace this big, though,' she added, looking around.

Fine looked at her suspiciously – but then again, maybe it was just the way his face was put together. It seemed that every syllable she'd uttered had been greeted by distrust.

'Well, I don't have time to check your references,' he replied. 'The person I'd arranged to take the position backed out at the last minute, and I'm overdue in New York.' His eyes narrowed slightly.

'But I'll be keeping an eye on you. Come on, I'll show you to your rooms.'

Corrie, following the man down the long, echoing first-floor hallway, wondered just how Horace P. Fine planned to keep an eye on her from two thousand miles away.

At first it had seemed almost like a miracle. She'd learned of the opening by coincidence: a conversation, overheard at a coffee shop, about a house that needed looking after. A few phone calls led her to the mansion's owner. It would be an ideal situation – in Roaring Fork no less. No more driving eighteen miles each way to her fleabag motel room. She could even move in that very day. Now she'd be earning money instead of spending it – and doing so in style.

But when she'd dropped by the mansion to meet with the owner, her enthusiasm dimmed. Although the house was technically in Roaring Fork, it was way up in the foothills, completely isolated, at the end of a narrow, winding, mile-long private road. It was huge, to be sure, but of a dreary postmodern design of glass, steel, and slate that was more reminiscent of an upscale dentist's office than a home. Unlike most of the big houses she'd seen, which were perched on hillsides offering fantastic views, this house was built in a declivity, practically a bowl in the mountains, surrounded on three sides by tall fir trees that seemed to throw the place into perpetual gloom. On the fourth side was a deep, icy ravine that ended in a rockfall of snow-covered boulders. Ironically, most of the vast plate-glass windows of the house overlooked this 'feature.' The decor was so aggressively contemporary as to be almost prison-like in austerity, all chrome and glass and marble – not a straight edge to be found anywhere save the doorways – and the walls were covered with grinning masks, hairy weavings, and other creepy-looking African art. And the place was cold, too – almost as cold as the ski warehouse where she did her work. Corrie had kept her coat on during the entire walk-through.

'This leads down to the second basement,' Fine said, pausing to point at a closed door. 'The older furnace is down there. It heats the eastern quarter of the house.'

Heats. Yeah, right. 'Second basement?' Corrie asked aloud.

'It's the only part of the original house that still exists. When they demolished the lodge, the developer retained the basement for retrofitting into the new house.'

'There was a lodge here?'

Fine scoffed. 'It was called Ravens Ravine Lodge, but it was just an old log cabin. A photographer used it for a home base when he went out into the mountains to take pictures. Adams, the name was. They tell me he was famous.'

Adams. Ansel Adams? Corrie could just picture it. There had probably been a cozy, rustic little cabin here once, nestled in among the pines – until

135

it got razed for this monstrosity. She wasn't surprised that Fine was not familiar with Adams – only a Philistine, or his soon-to-be ex-wife, could have bought all this freaky art.

Horace Fine himself was almost as cold as the house. He ran a hedge fund back in Manhattan. Or maybe it was the U.S. branch of some foreign investment bank; Corrie hadn't really been listening when he told her. Hedge, branch – it was all so much shrubbery to her. Luckily, he seemed not to have heard of her or her recent stay in the local jail. He'd made it quite clear that he detested Roaring Fork; he hated the house; and he loathed the woman who had forced him to buy it and who was now making its disposal as difficult as she possibly could. 'The virago' was the way he had named her to Corrie over the last twenty minutes. All he wanted to do was get someone in the house and get the hell back to New York, the sooner the better.

He led the way down the corridor. The house was as strangely laid out as it was ugly. It seemed to be made up of a single endless hallway, which veered at an angle now and then to conform with the topography. All the important rooms were on the left, facing the ravine. Everything else – the bathrooms, closets, utility rooms – was on the right, like carbuncles on a limb. From what she could tell, the second floor featured a similar layout.

'What's in here?' she asked, stopping before a

partially open door on the right. There were no overhead lights on inside, but the room was nevertheless lit up with a ghostly gleam from dozens of points of green, red, and amber.

Fine stopped again. 'That's the tech space. You might as well see it, too.'

He opened the door wide and snapped on the light. Corrie looked around at a dizzying array of panels, screens, and instrumentation.

'This is a "smart" house, of course,' Fine said. 'Everything's automated, and you can monitor it all from here: the generator status, the power grid, the security layout, the surveillance system. Cost a fortune, but it ultimately saved me a lot in insurance charges. And it's all networked and Internet-accessible, too. I can run the whole system from my computers in New York.'

So that's what he meant by keeping an eye on me, Corrie thought. 'How does the surveillance system work?'

Fine pointed to a large flat panel, with a small all-in-one computer to one side and a device below that looked like a DVD player on steroids. 'There are a total of twenty-four cameras.' He pressed a button and the flat panel sprang to life, showing a picture of the living room. There was a number in the upper left-hand corner of the image, and time and date stamps running along the bottom. 'These twenty-four buttons, here, are each dedicated to one of the cameras.' He pressed the button marked DRIVEWAY and the image changed, showing a picture of, what else, the driveway, with her Rent-a-Junker front and center.

'Can you manipulate the cameras?' Corrie asked.

'No. But any motion picked up by the sensors activates the camera and is recorded on a hard disk. There – take a look.' Fine pointed to the screen, where a deer was now passing across the driveway. As it moved, it became surrounded by a small cloud of black squares – almost like the framing windows of a digital camera – that followed the animal. At the same time, a large red *M* inside a circle appeared on the screen.

'*M* for "movement,"' Fine said.

The deer had moved off the screen, but the red letter remained. 'Why is the *M* still showing?' Corrie asked.

'Because when one of the cameras detects movement, a recording of that video feed is saved to the hard disk, starting a minute before movement begins and continuing one minute past when it stops. Then – if there's no more movement – the *M* goes away.'

Movement. 'And you can monitor all this over the Internet?' Corrie asked. She didn't like the idea of being the subject of a long-distance voyeur.

'No. That part of the smart system was never connected to the Internet. We stopped the work on the security system when we decided to sell the house. Let the new owner pick up the cost. But it works just fine from in here.' Fine pointed to another button. 'You can also split the screen by repeatedly pressing this button.' For the first time, Fine seemed engaged. He demonstrated, and the image split in two: the left half of the monitor showing the original image of the driveway, with the right showing a view looking over the ravine. Repeated pressings of the button split the screen into four, then nine, then sixteen increasingly smaller images, each from a different camera.

Corrie's curiosity was quickly waning. 'And how do I operate the security alarm?' she asked.

'That was never installed, either. That's why I need someone to keep an eye on the place.'

He snapped off the light and led the way out of the room, down the hallway, and through a door at its end. Suddenly the house became different. Gone was the expensive artwork, the ultramodern furniture, the gleaming professional-grade appliances. Ahead lay a short, narrow hall with two doors on each side, ending in another door leading into a small bathroom with cheap fixtures. The floor was of linoleum, and the pasteboard walls were devoid of pictures. All the surfaces were painted dead white.

'The maid's quarters,' Fine said proudly. 'Where you'll be staying.'

Corrie stepped forward, peering into the open doors. The two on the left opened into bedrooms of almost monastic size and asceticism. One of the doors on the right led into a kitchen with a dorm-style refrigerator and a cheap stove; the other room appeared to be a minuscule den. It was barely a cut above her motel room in Basalt.

'As I said, I'm leaving almost immediately,' Fine said. 'Come back to the den and I'll give you the key. Any questions?'

'Where's the thermostat?' Corrie asked, hugging herself to keep from shivering.

'Down here.' Fine stepped out of the maid's quarters and went back down the hall, turning in to the sitting room. There was a thermostat on the wall, all right – covered in a clear plastic box with a lock on it.

'Fifty degrees,' Fine said.

Corrie looked at him. 'I'm sorry?'

'Fifty degrees. That's what I've set the house at and that's where it's going to stay. I'm not going to spend a penny more on this goddamn house than I have to. Let the virago pay the utilities if she wants to. And that's another thing – keep electricity use to a minimum. Just a couple of lights, as absolutely necessary.' A thought seemed to strike the man. 'And by the way, the thermostat settings and the kilowatt usage *have* been wired into the Internet. I'll be able to monitor them from my iPhone.'

Corrie looked at the locked thermostat with a sinking heart. *Great. So now I'm going to be freezing my rear off by night as well as by day.* She began to understand why the original applicant had decided against the job.

Fine was glancing at her with a look that meant

the interview was over. That left just one question.

'How much does the house-sitting job pay?' she asked.

Fine's eyes widened in surprise. 'Pay? You're getting to stay, free, in a big, beautiful house, right here in Roaring Fork – and you expect a *salary*? You're lucky I'm not charging you rent.'

And he led the way back toward the den.

CHAPTER 17

Arnaz Johnson, hairdresser to the stars, had seen a lot of unusual people in his day hanging out at the famous Big Pine Lodge on the very top of Roaring Fork Mountain – movie starlets decked out as if for the Oscars; billionaires squiring about their trophy girl-friends in minks and sables; wannabe Indians in ten-thousand-dollar designer buckskins; pseudo-cowboys in Stetson hats, boots, and spurs. Arnaz called it the Parade of the Narcissists. Very few of them could even ski. The Parade was the reason Arnaz bought a season pass and took the gondola to the lodge once or twice a week: that, and the atmosphere of this most famous ski lodge in the West, with its timbered walls hung with antique Navajo rugs, the massive wrought-iron chande-liers, the roaring fireplace so large you could barbecue a bull in it. Not to mention the walls of glass that looked out over a three-hundred-sixty-degree ocean of mountains, currently gray and brooding under a darkening sky.

But Arnaz had never seen anyone quite like the gentleman who sat at a small table by himself before the vast window, a silver flask of some unknown beverage in front of him, gazing out in the direction of snowbound Smuggler's Cirque, with its complex of ancient, long-abandoned mining structures huddled like acolytes around the vast rickety wooden building that housed the famous Ireland Pump Engine: a magnificent example of nineteenth-century engineering, once the largest pump in the world, now just a rusted hulk.

Arnaz had been observing the ghostly man with fascination for upward of thirty minutes, during which time the man had not moved so much as a pinkie. Arnaz was a fashionista, and he knew his clothes. The man wore a black vicuña overcoat of the finest quality, cut, and style, but of a make that Arnaz did not recognize. The coat was unbuttoned, revealing a bespoke tailored black suit of an English cut, a Zegna tie, and a gorgeous cream-colored silk scarf, loosely draped. To top off the ensemble – literally – the man wore an incongruous, sable-colored trilby hat of 1960s vintage on his pale, skull-like head. Even though it was warm in the great room of the lodge, the man looked as cold as ice.

He wasn't an actor; Arnaz, a movie buff, knew he had never seen him on the silver screen, even in a bit part. He surely wasn't a banker, hedge fund manager, CEO, lawyer, or other business or financial wizard; that getup would be entirely unacceptable in such a crowd. He wasn't a poseur,

143

either; the man wore his clothes casually, nonchalantly, as if he'd been born in them. And he was far too elegant to be in the dot-com business. So what the heck was he?

A gangster.

Now, that made sense. He was a criminal. A very, very successful criminal. Russian, perhaps – he did have a slightly foreign look about him, in those pale eyes and high cheekbones. A Russian oligarch. But no . . . where were his women? The Russian billionaires that came to Roaring Fork – and there were quite a few – always went about with a passel of spangled, buxom whores.

Arnaz was stumped.

Pendergast heard himself being addressed and turned, slowly, to see Chief Stanley Morris approaching him from across the vast room.

'May I?'

Pendergast opened his hand in a slow invitation to sit.

'Thank you. I heard you were up here.'

'And how did you hear that?'

'Well . . . You're not exactly inconspicuous, Agent Pendergast.'

A silence. And then Pendergast removed a small silver cup from his overcoat, and placed it on the table. 'Sherry? This is a rather indifferent Amontillado, but nevertheless palatable.'

'Ah, no thanks.' The chief looked restless, shifting his soft body in the chair once, twice. 'Look, I

144

realize I messed up with your, um, protégée, Miss Swanson, and I'm sorry. I daresay I had it coming there at the town meeting. You don't know what it's like being chief of police in a town like this, where they're always pulling you in five different directions at once.'

'I am indeed sorry to say this, but I fear your microscopic problems do not interest me.' Pendergast poured himself a small tot of sherry and tossed it back in one feral motion.

'Listen,' said the chief, shifting about again, 'I came to ask your help. We've got this horrific quadruple murder, a one-acre crime scene of unbelievable complexity. All my forensic people are arguing with each other and that fire expert, they're paralyzed, they've never seen anything like this before . . .' His voice cracked, then trailed off. 'Look, the girl – Jenny, the older daughter – was my intern. She was a *good* kid . . .' He managed to pull himself together. 'I need help. Informally. Advice, that's all I'm asking. Nothing official. I looked into your background – very impressive.'

The pale hand snaked out again, poured another tot; it was tossed off in turn. There was silence. Finally, Pendergast spoke. 'I came here to rescue my protégée – your term, not mine – from your incompetency. My goal – my *only* goal – is to see Miss Swanson finish her work without further meddling from Mrs Kermode or anyone else. And then I shall leave this perverse town and fly home to New York with all possible alacrity.'

'Yet you were up at the scene of the fire this morning. You showed your badge to get inside the tape.'

Pendergast waved away these words as one might brush off a fly.

'You were there. Why?'

'I saw the fire. I was ever so faintly intrigued.'

'You said there would be more. Why did you say that?'

Another casual wave-off.

'Damn it! *What made you say that?*'

No answer.

The chief rose. 'You said there would be more murders. I looked into your background and I realized that you, of all people, would know. I'm telling you, if there are more – and you refuse to help – then those murders will be on your head. I swear to God.'

This was answered by a shrug.

'Don't you shrug at me, you son of a bitch!' the chief shouted, losing his temper at last. 'You saw what they did to that family. How can you just sit there, drinking your sherry?' He gripped the side of the table and leaned forward. 'I have just one thing to say to you, Pendergast – fuck you, and thanks for nothing!'

At this, the smallest hint of a smile crossed the thin lips. 'Now, that is more like it.'

'More like what?' Morris roared.

'An old friend of mine in the NYPD has a

colorful expression that is appropriate for this situation. What was it again? Ah, yes.' Pendergast glanced up at the chief. 'I will help you, but only on the condition that you – as I believe he would put it – *grow a pair.*'

CHAPTER 18

Chief Stanley Morris stared at the ruined house. The residual heat from the previous day's fire was now gone and a light snow had fallen the night before, covering the scene of horror with a soft white blanket. Plastic tarps had been spread over the main areas of evidence, and now his men were carefully removing them and shaking off the snow in preparation for the walk-through. It was eight o'clock in the morning, sunny, and fifteen degrees above zero. At least there was no wind.

Nothing like this had ever happened to Morris, on either a personal or a professional level, and he steeled himself for the ordeal that lay ahead. He'd hardly slept the night before, and when he finally did a dreadful nightmare had immediately awakened him again. He felt like hell and still hadn't been able to fully process the depravity and horror of the crime.

He took a deep breath and looked around. To his left stood Chivers, the fire specialist; to his right, the figure of Pendergast, in his vicuña over-coat, incongruously pulled over an electric-blue down jacket. Puffy mittens and a hideous wool hat completed the picture.

The man was so pallid he looked like he'd already been stricken by hypothermia. And yet his eyes were very much alive, moving restlessly about the scene.

Morris cleared his throat and made an effort to project the image of a chief of police firmly in control. 'Ready, gentlemen?'

'You bet,' said Chivers, with a distinct lack of enthusiasm. He was clearly unhappy about the presence of the FBI agent. *Tough shit*, thought Morris. He was getting fed up with the disagreements, turf squabbles, and departmental infighting this case was generating.

Pendergast inclined his head.

The chief ducked under the tape, the others following. The fresh snow covered everything save where the tarps had been laid down, and those areas were now large dark squares in an otherwise white landscape. The M.E. had not yet removed the human remains. Forensic flags of various colors dotted the ruins, giving the scene an incongruously festive air. The stench of smoke, burnt electrical wiring, rubber, and plastic still hung heavy and foul.

Now Pendergast took the lead, moving lightly despite the bulky clothing. He darted forward, knelt, and with a small brush whisked away a patch of snow, examining the burnt slate floor. He did this at several apparently random spots as they continued moving through. At one point a glass tube made an appearance from under his coat, into which he put some microscopic sample with tweezers.

Chivers hung back, saying nothing, a frown of displeasure gathering on his thick face.

They finally reached the gruesome bathtub. Morris could hardly look at it. But Pendergast went right over and knelt beside it, bowing over it almost as if he were praying. Removing one glove, he poked around with his white fingers and the pair of long tweezers, putting more samples into tubes. At last he rose and they continued making their way through the ruined house.

They came to the burnt mattress with its loops of wire and bone fragments. Here Pendergast stopped again, gazing at it for the longest time. Morris began to shiver as the inactivity, cold, and a clammy sick feeling all began to penetrate. The agent removed a document from his coat and opened it, revealing a detailed plat of the house – where had he gotten that? – which he consulted at length before folding it up and putting it away. Then he knelt and examined with a magnifying glass the charred remains of the skeleton tied to the mattress, really just bone fragments, and various other things as well. Morris could feel the cold creeping deeper into his clothing. Chivers was becoming restless, moving back and forth and sometimes slapping his gloves together in an effort to keep warm – broadcasting through his body language that he considered this a waste of time.

Pendergast finally straightened up. 'Shall we move on?'

'Great idea,' said Chivers.

They continued through the burnt landscape: the ghostly standing sticks covered with hoarfrost, the scorched walls, the heaps of frozen ashes, the glistering puddles of glass and metal. Now the corpse of the dog could be seen to one side, along with the two parallel, crumbled piles of ash and bone representing Jenny Baker's mother and father.

Morris had to look away. It was too much.

Pendergast knelt and examined everything with the utmost care, taking more samples, maintaining his silence. He seemed particularly interested in the charcoaled fragments of the dog, carefully probing with his long-stemmed tweezers and a tool that looked like a dental pick. They moved into the ruins of the garage, where the burnt and fused hulks of three cars rested. The FBI agent gave them a cursory look.

And then they were done. Beyond the perimeter tape, Pendergast turned. His eyes startled Morris – they glittered so sharply in the bright winter sun.

'It is as I feared,' he said.

Morris waited for more but was greeted only with silence.

'Well,' said Chivers loudly, 'this just reinforces what I reported to you earlier, Stanley. All the evidence points toward a botched robbery with at least two perps, maybe more. With a possible sex-crime component.'

'Agent Pendergast?' Morris finally said.

'I'm sorry to say that an accurate reconstruction of the sequence of the crime may be impossible. So much information was taken by the fire. But I am able to salvage a few salient details, if you wish to hear them.'

'I do. Please.'

'There was a single perpetrator. He entered through an unlocked back door. Three members of the family were at home, all upstairs and probably sleeping. The perpetrator immediately killed the dog who came to investigate. Then he – or she – ascended the front staircase to the second floor, surprised a juvenile female in her bedroom, incapacitated and gagged her before she could make significant noise, and wired her to the bed, still alive. He may have been on his way to the parents' room when the second juvenile female arrived home.'

He turned to Morris. 'This would be your intern, Jenny. She came in through the garage and went upstairs. There she was ambushed by the perpetrator, incapacitated, gagged, and placed in the bathtub. This was accomplished with utmost efficiency, but nevertheless this second assault appears to have awakened the parents. There was a short fight, which began upstairs and ended downstairs. I suspect one of the parents was killed there, on the spot, while the other was dragged down later. They may have been beaten.'

'How can you know all this?' said Chivers. 'This is sheer speculation!' Pendergast went on, ignoring this outburst. 'The perpetrator returned upstairs, doused both juvenile victims with gasoline, and set them on fire. He then made a – by necessity – rapid exit from the premises, dragging the other parent down the stairs and spreading additional accelerant on his way out. He left on foot – not by car. A pity the snowy woods around the house were trampled by neighbors and firefighters.'

'No way,' said Chivers, shaking his head. 'No way can you draw all those conclusions from the information we have – and the conclusions you've drawn, well, with all due respect, most of them are wrong.'

'I must say I share Mr Chivers's, ah, skepticism as to how you can learn all this from a mere walk-through,' said Morris.

Pendergast replied in the tone of someone explaining to a child. 'It's the only logical sequence that fits the facts. And the facts are these: When Jenny Baker returned home, the perpetrator was already in the house. She came in through the garage – the boyfriend confirmed that – and if the parents had already been killed she would have seen their bodies at the back door. She didn't see the dog's body because it was behind a counter that once existed, here.' He pulled out the plat.

'But how do you know he was already upstairs when Jenny arrived home?'

'Because Jenny was ambushed upstairs.'

'She could have been attacked in the garage and forced upstairs.'

'If she was the first victim, and was attacked in the garage, the dog would be alive and would have barked, awakening the parents. No – the very first victim was the dog, killed at the back door, probably with a blow to the head by something like a baseball bat.'

'A *bat*?' Chivers said in disbelief. 'How do you know he didn't use a knife? Or gun?'

'The neighbors heard no shots. Have you ever tried to kill a German shepherd with a knife? And finally, the dog's burnt cranium showed green-bone fracture patterns.' He paused. 'One needn't be Sherlock Holmes to analyze a few simple details like these, Mr Chivers.'

Chivers fell silent.

'Therefore, when Jenny arrived home, the perpetrator was already upstairs and had already incapacitated the sister, as he would not have been able to subdue two at once.'

'Unless there were two perps,' said Chivers.

'Go on,' Morris told Pendergast.

'Using the bat or some other method, he immediately subdued Jenny.'

'Which is exactly why there must have been two perps!' said Chivers. 'It was a robbery gone bad. They broke into the house, but things spiraled out of control before they could commence the robbery. Happens all the time.'

'No. The sequence was well planned and the

perpetrator had everything under control at all times. The psychological hallmarks of the crime – the savagery of it – suggests a lone perpetrator who had a motive other than robbery.'

Chivers rolled his eyes at Morris.

'And as for your theory about a burglary gone wrong, the perpetrator was well aware there were at least three people at home. An organized burglar doesn't break into an occupied house.'

'Unless there are a couple of girls they might want to . . .' Chivers swallowed, glanced at the chief.

'The girls were not molested. If he intended to rape the girls he would have removed the threat of the parents by killing them first. And a rape fits neither the time line nor the sequence. I might point out that the elapsed time between the boyfriend dropping Jenny off and the fire appearing on the mountain was ten minutes or less.'

'And how do you know one of the parents was killed downstairs and the other dragged down later?'

'That is, admittedly, an assumption. But it is the only one that matches the evidence. We are dealing with a lone killer, and it seems unlikely he would have fought both parents, downstairs, simultaneously. This arranging of the parents is another staged element of the attack – a grisly detail, intended to sow additional fear and unrest.'

Chivers shook his head in disgust and disbelief.

'So.' The chief could hardly bring himself to ask the question he knew he had to. 'What makes you think there might be more killings like this?'

'This was a crime of hatred, sadism, and brutality, committed by a person who, while probably insane, was still in possession of his faculties. Fire is often the weapon of choice for the insane.'

'A revenge killing?'

'Doubtful. The Baker family was not well known in Roaring Fork. You yourself told me they appear to have no enemies in town and only spend a couple of weeks here a year. So if not revenge, what is the motive? Hard to say definitively, but it may not be one directed at this family specifically – but rather, *at what this family represents.*'

A silence. 'And what does this family represent?' Morris asked.

'Perhaps what this entire town represents.'

'Which is?'

Pendergast paused, and then said: 'Money.'

CHAPTER 19

Corrie entered the history section of the Roaring Fork Library. The beautiful, wood-paneled space was once again empty save for Ted Roman, who was reading a book at his desk. He looked up as Corrie entered, his lean face lighting up.

'Well, well!' he said, rising. 'Roaring Fork's most infamous girl returns in triumph!'

'Jeez. What kind of a welcome is that?'

'A sincere one. I mean it. You and that FBI agent really nailed Kermode. God, it was one of the best things I've ever seen in this town.'

'You were at the town meeting?'

'Sure as hell was. It's about time someone took down that . . . well, I hope you won't be offended if I use the word, but here goes: that *bitch.*'

'No offense here.'

'And not only did the man in black cut Kermode off at the knees, but he took on that cozy little triumvirate, her, the police chief, and the mayor. Your friend just about had the three of them soiling their drawers – Montebello, too!' He almost

157

cackled with glee, and his laugh was so infectious Corrie had to join in.

'I have to admit, it was satisfying to hear the story,' Corrie said. 'Especially after spending ten days in jail because of them.'

'I knew as soon as I read you'd been arrested that it was bullshit . . .' Ted tried to smooth down the cowlick that projected from his forehead. 'So. What are you working on today?'

'I want to find out all I can about the life of Emmett Bowdree – and his death.'

'The miner you've been analyzing? Let's see what we can find.'

'Is the library always this empty?' she asked as they walked over to the computer area.

'Yeah. Crazy, huh? The prettiest library in the West and nobody comes. It's the people in this town – they're too busy parading down Main Street in their minks and diamonds.' He aped a movie star, sashaying as if on a fashion runway, making faces.

Corrie laughed. Ted had a funny way about him.

He sat down at a computer terminal and logged on. He began various searches, explaining what he was doing while she peered over his shoulder.

'Okay,' he said, 'I've got some decent hits on your Mr Bowdree.' She heard a printer fire up behind her. 'You take a look at the list and tell me what you want to see.'

He fetched the printed sheets and she scanned them quickly, pleased – in fact, almost intimidated – by the number of references. It seemed that there was quite a lot on Emmett Bowdree: mentions in newspaper articles, employment and assay records, mining documents and claims, and other miscellanea.

'Say . . .' Ted began, then stopped.

'What?'

'Um, you know, considering how you stood me up for that beer last time . . .'

'Sorry. I was busy getting myself arrested.'

He laughed. 'Well, you still owe me one. Tonight?'

Corrie looked at him, suddenly blushing and awkward and hopeful. 'I'd love to,' she heard herself say.

CHAPTER 20

The chief had held press conferences before, usually when some bad-boy celebrity got in trouble. But this was different – and worse. As he observed the audience from the wings, he felt a rising apprehension. These people were seething, demanding answers. Because the old police station building only had a small conference room, they were back in the City Hall meeting room – site of his recent humiliation – and the reminder was not a pleasant one.

On the other hand, he had Pendergast on his side. The man who had started out as his nemesis was now – he might as well admit it – his crutch. Chivers was furious, and half his own department was in revolt, but Morris didn't care. The man was brilliant, even if he was a bit strange, and he was damn grateful to have him in his corner. But Pendergast wasn't going to be able to help him with this crowd. This was something he had to do on his own. He had to go in there looking like the Man in Charge.

He glanced at his watch. Five minutes to two – the hubbub of voices was like an ominous growl. *Grow a pair.* Fair enough: he would try his best.

Reviewing his notes one last time, he stepped out on stage, walking briskly to the podium. As the sound of voices dropped, he took another moment to observe the audience. The room was packed, standing-room only, and it looked like more were outside. The press gallery, too, was crammed. His eye easily picked out the black blot of Pendergast, sitting anonymously in the public area in front. And in the reserved section, he could see the ranks of officials, the mayor, fire chief, senior members of his department, the M.E., Chivers, and the town attorney. Conspicuously absent was Mrs Kermode. Thank God.

He leaned over, tapped the microphone. 'Ladies and gentlemen.'

The room fell silent.

'For those who may not know me,' he said, 'I'm Chief Stanley Morris of the Roaring Fork Police Department. I'm going to read a statement, and then I will take questions from the press and the public.'

He squared his papers and began to read, keeping his voice stern and neutral. It was a short statement that confined itself to the indisputable facts: the time of the fire, the number and identity of the victims, the determination it was a homicide, the status of the investigation. No speculation. He ended with an appeal for all persons to come forward with any information they might have, no matter how trivial. He of course did not mention Pendergast's suggestion that there might be more such events; that would be far too incendiary. Besides, there was no evidence for it – as Chivers had said, it was mere speculation.

He looked up. 'Questions?'

An immediate tumult from the press gallery. Morris had already decided whom he was going to call on and in what order, and he now pointed to his number one journalist, an old pal from the *Roaring Fork Times*.

'Chief Morris, thank you for your statement. Do you have any suspects?'

'We have some important leads we're following up,' Morris replied. 'I can't say more than that.' *Because we don't have shit*, he thought grimly.

'Any idea if the perp is local?'

'We don't know,' said Morris. 'We've gotten guest lists from all the hotels and rentals, we've got lift ticket sales, and we've enlisted the help of the National Center for the Analysis of Violent Crime, which is currently searching their databases for previous arson convictions.'

'Any possible motive?'

'Nothing concrete. We're looking into various possibilities.'

'Such as?'

'Burglary, revenge, perverted kicks.'

'Wasn't it true that one of the victims worked in your office?'

God, he had hoped to avoid that line of

questioning. 'Jenny Baker was an intern in my office, working over her winter break.' He swallowed, tried to go on despite the sudden fuzziness in his voice. 'She was a wonderful girl who had aspirations to a career in law enforcement. It was . . . a devastating loss.'

'There's a rumor that one of the victims was tied to a bed and doused with gasoline,' another reporter interjected.

Son of a bitch. Did Chivers leak that? 'That is true,' said the chief, after a hesitation.

This caused a sensation.

'And another victim was found burned to death in a bathtub?'

'Yes,' said the chief, without elaborating.

More uproar. This was getting ugly.

'Were the girls molested?'

The press would ask anything; they had no shame. 'The M.E. hasn't concluded his examination. But it may not be possible to know, given the state of the remains.'

'Was anything taken?'

'We don't know.'

'Were they burned alive?'

Rising furor.

'It'll be at least a week before most of the evidence has been analyzed. All right – please – enough questions from the press – we'll move on to the public.' The chief dearly hoped this would be easier.

The entire section was on its feet, hands waving.

Not a good sign. He pointed to someone he didn't know, a meek-looking elderly woman, but a person in front of her misunderstood – deliberately or not – and immediately responded in a booming voice. Christ, it was Sonja Marie Dutoit, the semi-retired actress, infamous in Roaring Fork for her obnoxious behavior in shops and restaurants and for her face, which had been lifted and Botoxed so many times it bore a perpetual grin.

'Thank you for choosing me,' she said in a smoke-cured voice. 'I'm sure I speak for everyone when I say how shocked and horrified I am about this crime.'

'Yes, indeed,' said Morris. 'Your question, please?'

'It's been thirty-six hours since this terrible, horrible, frightening fire. We all saw it. And judging from what you just said, you haven't made much progress – if any.'

Chief Morris said, calmly, 'Do you have a question, Ms Dutoit?'

'I certainly do. Why haven't you caught the killer yet? This isn't New York City: we've only got two thousand people in this town. There's only one road in and out. So what's the problem?'

'As I said, we've brought tremendous resources to bear, bringing in specialists from as far away as Grand Junction, as well as the involvement of the NCAVC. Now, I'm sure other people have questions—'

'I'm not done,' Dutoit went on. 'When's the next house going to get burned down?'

This led to a susurrus of muttering. Some people were rolling their eyes in reaction to Dutoit's questions; others were beginning to look ever so slightly nervous.

'There's not a shred of evidence that we're dealing with a serial arsonist,' the chief said, eager to cut off this avenue of speculation.

But Dutoit, it seemed, was not yet through. 'Which one of us is going to wake up in flames in their own bed tonight? *And what in the name of God are you doing about it?*'

CHAPTER 21

It was hard to believe the Mineshaft Tavern was part of Roaring Fork, with the sawdust on the floor, the basement rock walls hung with rusty old mining tools, the smell of beer and Texas barbecue, the scruffy working-class clientele – and above all, the talentless stoner at the mike strumming some tune of his own composition, his face contorted with excessive pathos.

As she walked in, Corrie was pleasantly surprised. This was much more her kind of place than the restaurant of the Hotel Sebastian.

She found Ted at 'his' table in the back, just where he'd said he would be, with an imperial pint in front of him. He stood up – she liked that – and helped her into her seat before sitting down again.

'What'd you like?'

'What are you drinking?'

'Maroon Bells Stout, made right down the road. Fantastic stuff.'

The waiter came over and she ordered a pint, hoping she wouldn't get carded. That would be embarrassing. But there were no problems.

166

'I didn't know a place like this could exist in Roaring Fork,' said Corrie.

'There are still plenty of real people in this town – ski lift attendants, waiters, dishwashers, handymen . . . *librarians*.' He winked. 'We need our cheap, low-down places of entertainment.'

Her beer arrived, and they clinked glasses. Corrie took a sip. 'Wow. Good.'

'Better than Guinness. Cheaper, too.'

'So who's the guy on stage?' Corrie kept her voice neutral in case he was a friend of Ted's.

Ted snickered. 'Open-mike night. Don't know him, poor fellow. Let's hope he hasn't quit his day job.' He picked up his menu. 'Hungry?'

She thought for a moment: could she spare the money? But the menu wasn't too expensive. If she didn't eat, she might get drunk and do something stupid. She smiled, nodded.

'So,' said Ted. 'How are things going in the charnel house up on the mountain?'

'Good.' Corrie contemplated telling him about what she'd discovered but decided against it. She didn't know Ted well enough. 'The remains of Emmett Bowdree have a lot to say. I hope to get permission to work on a few more skeletons soon.'

'I'm glad it's working out for you. I love to think of Kermode getting her knickers in a twist while you're up there doing your thing.'

'I don't know,' Corrie said. 'She's got worse things to worry about now. You know – the fire.'

'I'll say. Jesus, how awful was that?' He paused. 'You know, I grew up there. In The Heights.'

'Really?' Corrie couldn't hide her surprise. 'I never would have guessed that.'

'Thank you, I'll take that as a compliment. My dad was a television producer – sitcoms and the like. He palled around with a lot of Hollywood people. My mother slept with most of them.' He shook his head, sipped his beer. 'I had a kind of messed-up childhood.'

'Sorry to hear that.' In no way was Corrie ready to talk to Ted about her own childhood, however.

'No big deal. They got divorced and my dad raised me. With all the sitcom residuals, he never had to work again. When I came back from college I got my butt out of The Heights and found an apartment in town, down on East Cowper. It's tiny, but I feel better about breathing its air.'

'Does he still live up there in The Heights?'

'Nah, he sold the house a few years back, died of cancer last year – only sixty years old, too.'

'I'm really sorry.'

He waved his hand. 'I know. But I was glad to get rid of the connection to The Heights. It really frosts me the way they handled that Boot Hill thing – digging up one of the most historic cemeteries in Colorado to build a spa for rich assholes.'

'Yeah. Pretty ugly.'

Then Ted shrugged, laughed lightly. 'Well, stuff happens. What are you going to do? If I hated the place so much, I wouldn't still be here – right?'

Corrie nodded. 'So what did you major in at the University of Utah?'

'Sustainability studies. I wasn't much of a student – I wasted too much time skiing and snow-mobiling. I love snowmobiling almost as much as I do skiing. Oh, and mountain climbing, too.'

'Mountain climbing?'

'Yeah. I've climbed forty-one Fourteeners.'

'What's a Fourteener?'

Ted chuckled. 'Man, you really are an eastern girl. Colorado has fifty-five mountains over fourteen thousand feet – we call them Fourteeners. To climb them all is the holy grail of mountaineering in the U.S. – at least, in the lower forty-eight.'

'Impressive.'

Their food arrived: shepherd's pie for Corrie, a burger for Ted, with another pint for him. Corrie declined a refill, thinking about the scary mountain road up to her dentist's-office-on-the-hill.

'So what about you?' Ted asked. 'I'm curious about how you know the man in black.'

'Pendergast? He's my . . .' *God, how to put it?* 'He's sort of my guardian.'

'Yeah? Like your godfather or something?'

'Something like that. I helped him on a case a few years ago, and ever since he's kind of taken an interest in me.'

'He's one cool dude – no kidding. Is he really an FBI agent?'

'One of the best.'

A new singer took over the mike – much better

169

than the previous one – and they listened for a while, talking and finishing their meal. Ted tried to pay but Corrie was ready for him and insisted on splitting the check.

As they got up to leave, Ted said, his voice dropping low: 'Want to see my tiny apartment?'

Corrie hesitated. She was tempted – very tempted. Ted looked like he was all sinew and muscle, lean and hard, and yet charming and goofy, with the nicest brown eyes. But she had never quite been able to feel good about a relationship if she slept with the guy on the first date.

'Not tonight, thanks. I've got to get home, get my sleep,' she said, but added a smile to let him know it wasn't absolute.

'No problem. We'll have to do this again – soon.'

'I'd like that.'

As she drove away from the restaurant, heading toward the dark woods and thinking about crawling into a freezing bed, Corrie started to regret her decision not to 'see' Ted's tiny apartment.

CHAPTER 22

I n his suite of rooms on the top floor of the
Hotel Sebastian, Agent Pendergast laid aside
the book he was reading, drained the small
cup of espresso that sat on the side table, and then
– standing up – walked over to the picture window
on the far side of the sitting room. The suite was
perfectly silent: Pendergast disliked the clamor of
anonymous neighbors and had reserved the rooms
on both sides of his own to ensure he would remain
undisturbed. He stood at the window, absolutely
still, looking down over East Main Street and the
light snow that was falling onto the sidewalks,
buildings, and passersby, softening the evening
scene and bestowing a muted, dream-like quality
on the millions of Christmas lights stretching many
blocks. He remained there for perhaps ten minutes,
gazing out into the night. Then, turning away
again, he walked over to the desk, where a FedEx
envelope lay, unopened. It was from his factotum
in New York, Proctor, addressed to him in care of
the Hotel Sebastian.

Pendergast picked up the envelope, slit it open
with a smooth motion, and let the contents slip

onto the desk. Several sealed envelopes of various sizes fell out, along with an oversize card – embossed and engraved – and a brief note in Proctor's handwriting. The note said merely that Pendergast's ward, Constance Greene, had left for Dharamsala, India, where she planned to spend two weeks visiting the nineteenth rinpoche. The fancy card was an invitation to the wedding of Lieutenant Vincent D'Agosta and Captain Laura Hayward, which was scheduled for May twenty-ninth of the following spring.

Pendergast's gaze moved to the sealed envelopes. He glanced over them for a moment without touching any. Then he picked up an airmail envelope and turned it over thoughtfully in his hands. Leaving the others, he walked back to his sitting room chair, sat down, and opened the letter. A single sheet of thin paper lay inside, a letter in a childish hand, written in the old-fashioned German script known as Sütterlin. He began to read.

December 6
École Mère-Église
St Moritz, Switzerland

Dear Father,
It seems a long time since you last visited. I have been counting the days. They number one hundred and twelve. I hope you will again soon come.

I am treated well. The food here is very good. On Saturday suppers we have Linzer Torte for desert. Have you ever eaten Linzer Torte? It is good.

A lot of the teachers here speak German but I try always to use my English. They say my English is getting better. The teachers are very nice except for Madame Montaine who always smells of rose water. I like History and Science but not Mathematiks. I am not good at Mathematiks.

In the autumn I enjoyed walking on the hill sides after classes but now there is too much snow. They tell me that over the Christmas holidays I will be taught how to ski. I think I will like that.

Thank you for your letter. Please send me another. I hope we shall meet again soon.

Love,
Your son,
Tristram

Pendergast read the letter a second time. Then, very slowly, he refolded it and placed it back into its envelope. Turning off the reading lamp, he sat in the dark, lost in thought, book forgotten, as the minutes ticked by. Finally he stirred again, pulled a cell phone from his suit pocket, and dialed a number with a northern Virginia area code.

'Central Monitoring,' came the crisp, accentless voice.

'This is S. A. Pendergast. Please transfer me to South American Operations, Desk 14-C.'

'Very good.' There was a brief silence, a click, and then another voice came on the line. 'Agent Wilkins.'

'Pendergast speaking.'

The voice stiffened slightly. 'Yes, sir.'

'What's the status of Wildfire?'

'Stable but negative. No hits.'

'Your monitoring efforts?'

'All listening posts are active. We're monitoring national and local police reports and news media twenty-four seven, and we're electronically combing the daily NSA feeds as well. In addition, we continue to interface with CIA field agents in Brazil and the surrounding countries in search of any . . . anomalous activity.'

'You have my updated location?'

'In Colorado? Yes.'

'Very good, Agent Wilkins. As always, please inform me immediately if the status of Wildfire changes.'

'We'll do that, sir.'

Pendergast ended the call. Picking up the house phone, he ordered another espresso from room service. Then he used his cell phone to make another call: this one to a suburb of Cleveland called River Pointe.

The call was answered on the second ring. There

was no voice; just the sound of a connection being made.

'Mime?' Pendergast said into the silence.

For a moment, nothing. Then a high, thin voice wheezed: 'Is that my main man? My main Secret Agent Man?'

'I'd like an update, please, Mime.'

'All quiet on the Western Front.'

'Nothing?'

'Not a peep.'

'One moment.' Pendergast paused as a room service attendant brought in the espresso. He tipped the man, then waited until he was once again alone. 'And you're confident that you've cast your net widely, and finely, enough to spot the . . . target if he surfaces?'

'Secret Agent Man, I've got a series of AI algorithms and heuristic search patterns online that would make you stain your government-issue BVDs. I'm monitoring all official, and a goodly amount of unofficial, web traffic in and out of the target area. You can't imagine the bandwidth I'm burning through. Why, I've had to siphon off server farms from at least half a dozen—'

'I can't imagine. Nor do I want to.'

'Anyway, the objective's totally offline, no Facebook updates for this dude. But if the guy's as sick as you say, then the moment he surfaces – hoo, boy!' A sudden silence. 'Um, oops. I keep forgetting Alban's your son.'

'Just keep up the monitoring operations, please,

Mime. And let me know the instant you note anything.'

'You got it.' The phone went dead.

And Pendergast sat in the darkened room, unmoving, for a long time.

CHAPTER 23

Corrie parked her Rent-a-Junker Ford Focus in the sprawling driveway of 1 Ravens Ravine Road – aka, the Fine mansion – and got out. It was almost midnight, and a huge pale moon, hanging low in the sky, turned the pine trees blue against a creamy bed of white snow, striped with shadows. A light snow was falling, and here, in this bowl-like vale at the edge of a ravine, she felt like she was inside some child's overturned snow globe. Ahead, the row of six garage doors stood against the cement drive like big gray teeth. She killed the engine – for some obscure reason, Fine didn't want her to use the garage – and got out of the car. She walked up to the closest door, plucked off her glove, punched in the code. Then, as it rose on its metal rails, she turned suddenly, with a sharp intake of breath.

There, in the shadow of the side of the garage, was a shape. At first, Corrie couldn't make out what it was. But as the light from the garage door motor provided a faint illumination, she made out a small dog, shivering in the darkness.

'Well!' Corrie said, kneeling beside it. 'What are you doing out here?'

The dog came over, whining, and licked her hand. It was a mutt, looking like a cross between a small hound dog and a spaniel, with droopy ears, big sad brown eyes, and brown-and-white splotches of fur. It was not wearing a collar.

'You can't stay out here,' she said. 'Come on in.'

The dog followed her eagerly into the garage. Walking up to a bank of buttons, she pressed the one for the bay she'd entered. The garage was empty – a ludicrous expanse of concrete. Outside, she could hear the moaning of the wind as it shook the trees. Why on earth couldn't she park in here?

She glanced down at the dog, which was looking up at her and wagging its tail, a desperately hopeful look in its eyes. Screw Mr Fine – the pooch would stay.

Corrie waited until the garage door had closed completely before unlocking the door and stepping into the house. Inside, it was almost as cold as outdoors. She walked through a laundry room with machines big enough to service a battalion, past a pantry larger than her father's entire apartment, and then into the hallway that ran the length of the mansion. She continued on, dog at her heels, along the corridor as it bent once, then twice, following the contours of the ravine, past room after huge room filled with uncomfortable-looking avant-garde furniture. The corridor itself was filled with that African statuary, all big bellies and long angry faces and carven eyes that seemed to follow her as she passed by. The tall picture windows of the various rooms to her left had no curtains, and the bright moonlight threw skeletal shadows against the pallid walls.

The night before – her first night in the place – Corrie had checked out both the second floor and the basement, familiarizing herself with the rest of the layout. The upstairs consisted of a huge master bedroom, with dual bathrooms and walk-in closets, six other unfurnished bedrooms, and numerous guest bathrooms. In the main basement was a gym, a two-lane bowling alley, a mechanical room, a swimming flume – empty – and several storage areas. It seemed obscene that any house should be this big – or this empty.

She finally reached the end of the hallway and the door leading into her own small suite of rooms. She entered, closed the door behind her, and switched on the small space heater in the room she'd chosen as her own. Pulling a couple of bowls from the cabinet, she set out water and an improvised dinner of crackers and cereal for the dog – tomorrow, if she couldn't find the owner, she'd pick up some kibble.

She watched the little brown-and-white animal as it ate ravenously. The poor thing was starving. While a mutt, it was an endearing one, with a big shock of unruly hair that fell over its eyes. It reminded her of Jack Corbett, a kid she'd known in seventh grade back in Medicine Creek. His hair had flopped down over his face in just the same way.

'Your name is Jack,' she said to the dog, while it looked up at her, wagging its tail.

She thought for a moment about fixing a cup of herbal tea for herself, but she felt too tired to make the effort and instead washed up, changed quickly into her nightwear, then slipped between the chilly sheets. She heard the tick of claws as the dog came in and settled down on the floor at the foot of the bed.

Gradually, her body heat and the little space heater – cranked to maximum – blunted the worst of the cold. She decided against doing any reading, preferring to use the electricity for heat instead of light. She'd gradually increase the amount of juice she used, and see if Fine complained.

Her thoughts drifted back to the date she'd had with Ted. He was earnest, and funny, and nice, if a bit goofy – but then, ski bums were supposed to be goofy. Handsome and goofy and carefree. He was no lightweight, though – he had principles. Idealistic, too. She admired his independence in leaving his parents' grand house for a small apartment downtown.

She turned in the bed, slowly becoming drowsy. He was hot, and on top of it a nice guy, but she wanted to get to know him just a little better before . . .

. . . Somewhere, from the distant spaces of the house overhead, came a loud bump.

She sat up in bed, instantly wide awake. What the hell was that?

She remained motionless. The only light in the room came from the bright orange coils of the space heater. As she sat, listening intently, she could hear, faintly, the mournful call of the wind as it coursed through the narrow valley.

There was nothing else. It must have been a dead branch, broken loose by the wind and knocked against the roof.

Slowly, she settled back down into the bed. Now that she was aware of the wind, she listened to its faint muttering and groaning as she lay in the darkness. As the minutes passed, drowsiness began to return. Her thoughts drifted toward her plans for the next day. Her analysis of the Bowdree skeleton was just about complete, and if she was going to make any progress on her theory she'd need to get permission to examine some of the other remains. Of course, Pendergast had offered to do just that, and she knew enough of his meddling ways to believe that he would—

Meddling. Now, why had she used that word?

And come to think of it, why did the mere thought of Pendergast – for the first time ever, since she'd known him – cause an upwelling of annoyance? After all, the man had rescued her from a ten-year prison sentence. He'd saved her career. He'd paid for her education, basically put her life on track.

If she was honest with herself, she had to admit

181

it had nothing to do with Pendergast – and every-thing with herself. This cache of skeletons was a big project, and an incredible opportunity. She was wary at the thought of anyone else stepping in and stealing some of the limelight. And Pendergast – unintentionally – was capable of doing just that. If even a whiff got out that he'd helped her, everyone would assume that he'd done the real work and discount her own contribution.

Her mother had taken great relish in pointing out, again and again, what a loser she was. Her classmates back in Medicine Creek had called her a freak, a waste of space. She'd never realized, until now, just how much it meant to her to accomplish something important . . .

There it was: another sound. But this was no bump of a tree branch hitting the roof. This was a low scratching sound, coming from some spot not all that far away from her own bedroom: soft, even stealthy.

Corrie listened. Maybe it was the wind again, rubbing a pine branch back and forth against the house. But if it was the wind, it sounded awfully regular.

She pushed back the covers, got out of bed, and – heedless of the cold – stood in her darkened bedroom, listening.

Scratch. Scratch. Scratch. Scratch. Scratch.

At her feet, Jack whined.

She stepped out into the little hallway, turned on the light, opened the door into the mansion

182

proper, and paused again to listen. The sound seemed to have stopped. No: there it was again. It seemed to be coming from the ravine side of the house, maybe the living room.

Corrie walked quickly down the corridor, shadow-striped and echoing, and ducked into the security room. The various devices were on, humming and clicking, but the central flat panel was off. She turned it on. An image swam into view: camera one, the default, showing the front drive, currently empty.

She pushed the button that toggled the screen into a checkerboard of smaller images, looking at the feeds from various cameras. Two, four, nine, sixteen . . . and there, in the window of camera nine, she saw it: a red *M*, with a circle around it.

M for 'movement.'

Quickly she pressed the button dedicated to camera nine. Now its image filled the screen: it was the view out the back door, leading from the kitchen onto the vast deck overlooking the ravine. The *M* was much bigger now. But there was no movement, nothing she could see. She squinted at the pixelated image. Nothing.

What the hell had Fine said? When a camera registered movement, it recorded the video feed to hard disk: one minute prior to detecting the movement, and continuing for another minute after the movement ceased.

So what movement had triggered camera nine?

It couldn't be the wind, shaking the tree limbs:

there were no trees in view. Even as Corrie watched, the *M* disappeared from the screen. Now she saw only the back of the house, with the date and time stamps imprinted across the bottom of the feed.

She toggled it back to the checkerboard of cameras and looked at the computer, hoping to get a playback of camera nine. The machine was turned on, but when she moved the mouse a window popped open, demanding a password.

Shit. Now she cursed herself for not asking more questions.

Something red flashed in her peripheral vision. Quickly she turned back to the screen. There it was, in camera eight: something large and dark, creeping around the side of the house. Black rectangles hovered around it, tracking its progress. The *M* was once again flashing on the screen.

Maybe she should call nine-one-one. But she'd left her mobile in her car, and the cheap bastard Fine had of course disconnected the house phones.

Corrie looked closer, heart starting to pound. That section of the back deck was in shadow, the moonlight obscured by the house, and she couldn't make out exactly what she was seeing. Was it an animal? A coyote, maybe? No: it was too big to be a coyote. Something about the stealthy, deliberate way in which it moved sent a thrill of fear coursing through her.

Now it was off the screen. No alerts came up on the other images. But Corrie was not reassured.

Whatever she'd seen, it had been coming around the side of the house. Her side of the house.

She turned suddenly. What was that noise? The squeaking of a mouse? Or – maybe, just maybe – the soft protesting squeal of a window, being gingerly tried?

Heart in her mouth, she ran out of the security room and across the corridor into the den. The tall windows yawned dark before her.

'Get the fuck away from here!' she yelled at them. 'I've got a gun – and I'm not afraid to use it! Any closer, and I'm calling the cops!'

Nothing. Utter silence.

Corrie stood in the darkness, breathing hard. Still nothing.

At length she returned to the security room. The video feeds were quiet; no movement registered on any of them.

She stayed before the monitor, eyes glued to the various feeds, for fifteen minutes. Then she went through the entire house, dog at her heels, checking all the doors and windows to make sure they were locked. Finally she returned to her bedroom, lay down in the dark, and gathered the covers around her. But she did not fall asleep.

CHAPTER 24

The following morning was, if possible, even colder than it had been the day before. But for the time being, as she bustled around the ski shed, Corrie barely noticed. After a breakfast spent convincing herself she'd been imagining things the night before, she bundled up and went outside – only to find out there were very real, very human footprints in the snow all around the house. Someone apparently had been wandering around out there for a long time, perhaps hours. It scared the hell out of her, but she couldn't follow the confused welter of tracks or figure out where they'd come from.

Getting into her car and checking her cell phone, she played back a message from Pendergast announcing that he'd arranged the necessary permissions for her to examine three more skeletons from among the coffins in the shed. She drove down to the Hotel Sebastian to collect the necessary paperwork and thank Pendergast – only to learn that he was out, but had left everything for her at the front desk.

She almost forgot the cold as she tracked down the first of the three skeletons – Asa Cobb – carefully removed the remains from the rude coffin, and placed them on the examination table. Arranging her tools, she took a deep breath, then began a methodical analysis of the bones.

It was as she suspected. Many of the bones displayed damage from a tool: scrapes, gouges, cuts. Again, there were tooth marks: clearly human, not bear. And again, there was no sign of pot polishing, burning, or cooking of any kind – this man, too, had been eaten raw. Nor were there signs of bullet or knife wounds – death had been caused by a massive blow to the head with a rock, followed by the same brutal beating and dismemberment evidenced by the bones of Bowdree. The old brown bones told a graphic, violent tale of a man who was set upon, torn to pieces, and consumed raw.

She straightened up. There was no longer any doubt: these miners had fallen victim to a gang of serial killers.

'Is it as you expected?' came the honeyed drawl from behind her.

Corrie whirled around, heart suddenly pounding like mad in her chest. There was Pendergast, dressed in a black overcoat, a silk scarf around his neck. His face and hair were almost as white as the snow that clung to his shoes. The guy had the damnedest ability to sneak up on a person.

'I see you got my message,' Pendergast said. 'I

had tried calling you last night, as well, but you didn't pick up your phone.'

'Sorry.' As her heart returned to normal, she felt herself flushing. 'I was on a date.'

One eyebrow went up. 'Indeed? May I inquire as to whom with?'

'Ted Roman. A librarian here in Roaring Fork. Grew up in town. Nice guy, ex–ski bum, snow-mobile addict. Good researcher, too. He's helped me quite a bit.'

Pendergast nodded, then turned – significantly – toward the examination table.

'I've only had a chance to examine one of the skeletons,' she said, 'but it seems to have all the earmarks of the Bowdree killing.'

'So it's your opinion we're dealing with, how shall we call it, a *group* engaged in serial killing.'

'Exactly. I would think at least three or four, possibly more.'

'Interesting.' Pendergast picked up one of the bones and turned it over in his hands, giving it a perfunctory examination. 'Two murderers working together is uncommon, but not unheard of. Three or more, however, acting in concert, is a *rara avis* indeed.' He put the bone back on the table. 'Technically, three separate killings are necessary to establish a serial killer.'

'Eleven miners died. Isn't that enough to qualify?'

'Almost assuredly. I shall look forward to receiving your detailed reports on the other two miners, as well.'

Corrie nodded.

Hands in his pockets, Pendergast looked around the equipment shed before finally returning his pale gaze to her. 'When was the last time you read *The Hound of the Baskervilles?*'

This question was so unexpected, Corrie was certain she'd misheard. 'What?'

'*The Hound of the Baskervilles*. When did you last read it?'

'The Sherlock Holmes story? Ninth grade. Maybe eighth. Why?'

'Do you recall the initial letter you sent me regarding your thesis? In a postscript, you made reference to a meeting between Arthur Conan Doyle and Oscar Wilde. During that meeting, Wilde told Conan Doyle a rather dreadful story he'd heard on his American lecture tour.'

'Right.' Corrie stole a glance at the table. She was eager to get back to work.

'Would you find it interesting to know that one of the stops Oscar Wilde made on his lecture tour was right here in Roaring Fork?'

'I know all about that. It was in Doyle's diary. One of the Roaring Fork miners told Wilde the story of the man-eating grizzly, and Wilde passed on the story to Doyle. That's what gave me the idea for my thesis in the first place.'

'Excellent. My question to you is this: Do you believe Wilde's story might have inspired Doyle to write *The Hound of the Baskervilles?*'

Corrie hopped from one cold foot to the other.

'It's possible. Likely, even. But I'm not sure I see the relevance.'

'Just this: if you were to take a look through *The Hound*, there's a chance you might come across some clues as to what actually happened.'

'What actually happened? But . . . I'm sure Wilde heard the false story and told it to Doyle. Neither one could possibly have known the truth – that these miners weren't killed by a bear.'

'Are you sure?'

'Doyle wrote about the "grizzled bear" in his diary. He didn't mention a cannibalistic gang.'

'Consider for a moment: what if Wilde heard the *real* story and told it to Doyle? And what if Doyle found it too disturbing to put in his diary? What if Doyle instead concealed some of that information in *The Hound*?'

Corrie had to stop herself from scoffing. Was it possible Pendergast was serious? 'I'm sorry, but that's pretty far-fetched. Are you really suggesting that a Sherlock Holmes story could possibly shed light on my project?'

Pendergast did not reply. He simply stood there in his black overcoat, returning her gaze.

She shivered. 'Look, I hope you don't mind, but I'd really like to get back to my examination, if it's okay with you.'

Still Pendergast said nothing; he merely regarded her with those pale eyes of his. For some reason, Corrie got the distinct feeling that she had just failed some kind of test. But she couldn't help that; the answer lay not in fictional stories but right here, in the bones themselves.

After a long moment, Pendergast gave the slightest of bows. 'Of course, Miss Swanson,' he said coolly. Then he turned and left the equipment shed as silently as he had come.

Corrie watched until she heard the faint clunk of the door shutting. Then – with a mixture of eagerness and relief – she returned to the earthly remains of Asa Cobb.

CHAPTER 25

Chief Stanley Morris had shut his office door and given his secretary orders not to disturb him for any reason whatsoever while he updated his corkboard case-line. It was how the chief managed complex cases: reducing everything to color-coded three-by-five cards, each with a single fact, a piece of evidence, a photograph, or a witness. These he would organize chronologically, pin to a corkboard, and then – with string – connect the cards, looking for patterns, clues, and relationships.

It was a standard approach and it had worked well for him before. But as he surveyed the chaos on his desk, the corkboard overflowing with a rainbow of cards, the strings going in every direction, he began to wonder if he needed a different system. He felt himself growing more frustrated by the minute.

The phone buzzed and he picked it up. 'For heaven's sake, Shirley, I asked not to be disturbed!'

'Sorry, Chief,' said the voice, 'but there's someone here you really must see—'

'I don't care if it's the pope. I'm busy!'

'It's Captain Stacy Bowdree.'

It took a minute for the ramifications of this to sink in. Then he felt himself go cold. *This is all I need.* 'Oh. Jesus . . . All right, send her in.'

Before he could even prepare himself, the door opened and a striking woman strode in. Captain Bowdree had short auburn hair, a handsome face, and a pair of intense, dark brown eyes. She was all of six feet tall and somewhere in her midthirties.

He rose and held out his hand. 'Chief Stanley Morris. This is quite a surprise.'

'Stacy Bowdree.' She gave his hand a firm shake. Even though she was dressed in casual clothes – jeans, a white shirt, and a leather vest – her bearing was unmistakably military. He offered her a seat, and she took it.

'First,' said the chief, 'I want to apologize for the problems with the exhumation of your, ah, ancestor. I know how upsetting it must be. We here at the Roaring Fork PD believed the developers had done a thorough search, and I was dismayed, *truly* dismayed, when your letter was brought to my attention—'

Bowdree flashed the chief a warm smile and waved her hand. 'Don't worry about it. I'm not upset. Truly.'

'Well, thank you for your understanding. I . . . We'll make it right, I promise you.' The chief realized he was almost babbling.

'It's not a problem,' she said. 'Here's the thing.

I've decided to take the remains back for reburial in our old family plot in Kentucky once the research is complete. That's why I'm here. So you see, given the circumstances there's no longer any reason to rebury Emmett in the original location, as I originally requested.'

'Well, I'd be lying if I said I wasn't relieved. It makes things simpler.'

'Say . . . is that coffee I smell?'

'Would you like a cup?'

'Thank you. Black, no sugar.'

The chief buzzed Shirley and put in the order, with a second for himself. There was a brief, awkward silence. 'So . . .' he said. 'How long have you been in town?'

'Not long, a few days. I wanted to get the lay of the land, so to speak, before making my presence known. I realize my letter made quite a stir, and I didn't want to freak everyone out by storming into town like the Lone Ranger. You're the first person, in fact, that I've introduced myself to.'

'Let me then welcome you most warmly to Roaring Fork.' The chief felt hugely relieved by all she was saying – and also by her friendly, easygoing manner. 'We're glad to have you. Where are you staying?'

'I was in Woody Creek, but I'm looking for a place in town. Having a little trouble finding something I can afford.'

'I'm afraid we're in the high season. I wish I could give you some advice, but I think the town is pretty much full up.' He recalled the tumultuous, acrimonious press conference and wondered if things would stay that way.

The coffee arrived and Bowdree accepted it eagerly, took a sip. 'Not your usual police station coffee, I must say.'

'I'm a bit of a coffee aficionado. We've got a coffee roaster in town who does a mean French roast.'

She took another big sip, then another. 'I don't want to keep you – I can see you're busy. I just wanted to drop in to introduce myself and tell you about my plans for the remains.' She set down the cup. 'And I also wondered if you could help me. Where exactly are the remains now, and how do I get there? I wanted to see them and meet the woman who's doing the research.'

The chief explained, drawing her a little map of The Heights. 'I'll call Heights security,' he said. 'Tell them you're coming.'

'Thanks.' Captain Bowdree rose, once again impressing the chief with her stature. She was a damn fine-looking woman, supple and strong. 'You've been really helpful.'

Morris rose again hastily and took her hand. 'If there's anything I can do, anything at all, please let me know.'

He watched her leave, feeling like the week from

hell might finally be ending on a positive note. But then his gaze drifted to the corkboard, and the chaos of cards and strings on his desk, and the old feeling of dread returned. The week from hell, he realized, was far from over.

CHAPTER 26

Corrie heard the clang of the ski shed door and paused in her work, wondering if Pendergast had returned. But instead of a dark-suited figure, a tall woman strode into view wearing fleece winter warm-ups and a big knitted woolen hat with dangling pom-poms.

'Corrie Swanson?' she said as she approached.

'That's me.'

'Stacy Bowdree. I'd shake your hand, but I've got these coffees.' She handed Corrie a tall Starbucks cup. 'Venti skinny latte with four shots, extra sugar. I had to guess.'

'Wow. You guessed right.' Corrie accepted the cup gratefully. 'I had no idea you were coming to Roaring Fork. This is quite a surprise.'

'Well, here I am.'

'God, Stacy – can I call you that? – do I *owe* you. You saved my butt with that letter. I was looking at ten years in prison, I can't thank you enough—'

'Don't embarrass me!' Bowdree laughed, uncovered her own coffee, and took a generous swig. 'If you want to thank someone, you can thank your friend Pendergast. He explained the whole situation to

197

me, and what they'd done to you. I was only too happy to help.' She looked around. 'Look at all these coffins. Which one's Great-Great-Granddad Emmett?'

'Right over here.' Corrie led her to the man's remains, spread out on an adjacent table. If she'd known the woman was coming, she could have tried to put them in some modicum of order. She hoped Emmett's descendant would understand.

Corrie sipped her coffee a little nervously as Bowdree walked over, reached out, and gently picked up a piece of skull. 'Jeez, that bear really did a number on him.'

Corrie started to say something, then stopped herself. Pendergast, with excellent reason, had advised her against telling anyone – anyone – of the real cause of death until she had finished her work.

'I think this work is fascinating,' said Bowdree, gently putting down the piece of skull. 'So you really want to be a cop?'

Corrie laughed. She liked Bowdree immediately. 'Well, I think I'd like to become an FBI agent, actually, with a specialty in forensic anthropology. Not a lab rat, but a field agent with special skills.'

'That's great. I've sort of been thinking about law enforcement myself . . . I mean, it's logical after a career in the military.'

'Are you out, then? No longer a captain?'

She smiled. 'I'll always be a captain, but yes, I've been discharged.' She paused. 'Well, I'd better get a move on. I've got to find a cheaper place to stay if I'm going to hang around here much longer – the hotel I'm in now is bankrupting me.'

Corrie smiled. 'I know the feeling.'

'I just wanted to introduce myself and tell you that I think what you're doing here is great.' Bowdree turned to go.

'Just a minute.'

Bowdree turned back.

'Want to grab a coffee at Starbucks later?' She gestured with her cup. 'I'd like to return the favor – if you don't mind it being on the late side. I plan to make a long day of it – assuming I don't freeze first.'

Bowdree's face brightened. 'That would be great. How does nine o'clock sound?'

'See you then.'

CHAPTER 27

Mrs Betty B. Kermode sipped a cup of Earl Grey tea and looked from the picture window of her living room over the Silver Queen Valley. Her house on the top of the ridge – the best lot in the entire development of The Heights – commanded a spectacular view, with the surrounding mountains rising up and up toward the Continental Divide and the towering peaks of Mount Elbert and Mount Massive, the highest and second highest peaks in Colorado, which were mere shadows at this hour of the night. The house itself was quite modest – despite what people assumed, she was not by nature a showy woman – one of the smallest in the development, in fact. It was more traditional than the others, as well, built in stone and cedar on a relatively intimate scale: none of this ultra-contemporary, postmodern style for her.

The window also afforded an excellent view of the equipment shed. It had been from this same window that, not quite two weeks before, Mrs Kermode had seen the telltale light go on in the shed, very late at night. She immediately knew who was inside and had taken action.

The cup rattled in its saucer as she put it down and she poured herself another. It was difficult to make a decent cup of tea at eight thousand five hundred feet, where water boiled at one hundred ninety-six degrees, and she could never get used to the insipid flavor, no matter what kind of mineral water she used, how long she steeped it, or how many bags she put in. She pursed her lips tightly as she added milk and a touch of honey, stirred, and sipped. Mrs Kermode was a lifelong teetotaler – not for religious reasons, but because her father had been an abusive alcoholic and she associated drinking with ugliness and, even worse, a lack of control. Mrs Kermode had made control the centerpiece of her life.

And now she was angry, quietly but furiously angry, at the humiliating disruption of her control by that girl and her FBI friend. Nothing like that had ever happened to her, and she would never forget, let alone forgive, it.

She took another swallow of tea. The Heights was the most sought-after enclave in Roaring Fork. In a town filled with vulgar new money, it was one of the oldest developments. It represented taste, Brahmin stability, and a whiff of aristocratic superiority. She and her partners had never allowed it to grow shabby, as other 1970s-era ski developments tended to do. The new spa and clubhouse would be a vital part of keeping the development fresh, and the opening of Phase III – thirty-five two-acre lots, priced at $7.3 million and up – promised to bring a stupendous financial windfall to the original investors. If only this cemetery business could be resolved. The *New York Times* article had been an annoyance, but it was nothing compared with the bull-in-a-china-shop antics of Corrie Swanson.

That bitch. It was her fault. And she would pay.

Kermode finished her cup, put it down, took a deep breath, then picked up the phone. It was late in New York City, but Daniel Stafford was a night owl and this was usually the best time to reach him.

He picked up on the second ring, his smooth patrician voice coming down the line. 'Hello, Betty. How's the skiing?'

A wave of irritation. He knew perfectly well she didn't ski. 'They tell me it's excellent, Daniel. But I'm not calling to bandy civilities.'

'Pity.'

'We've got a problem.'

'The fire? It's only a problem if they don't catch the fellow – which they will. Trust me, by the time Phase III comes online he'll be heading to the electric chair.'

'The fire isn't what I'm calling about. It's that girl. And the meddling FBI agent. I hear he's managed to dig up three more descendants who've given permission to look at their ancestors' bones.'

'And the problem?'

'What do you mean, *and the problem*? It's bad enough that this Captain Bowdree has shown up in person – at least she wants to bury her ancestor's bones somewhere else. Daniel, what if those other descendants demand reburial in the original cemetery? We're five million dollars into construction!'

'Now, now, Betty, calm down. Please. That's never going to happen. If any so-called descendants take legal action – which they haven't yet – our attorneys will tie them up in knots for years. We've got the money and legal power to keep a case like this going forever.'

'It's not just that. I'm worried about where it could lead – if you know what I mean.'

'That girl's just looking at the bones, and when she's done, it ends. It isn't going to lead where you're worried it might lead. How could it? And if it does, trust me, we'll take care of it. Your problem, Betty, is that you're like your mother: you worry too much and you cherish your anger. Mix yourself a martini and let it go.'

'You're disgusting.'

'Thank you.' A chuckle. 'I'll tell you what. To ease your mind, I'll get my people to dig into their background, find some dirt. The girl, the FBI agent . . . anyone else?'

'Captain Bowdree. Just in case.'

'Fine. Remember, I'm only doing this to keep our powder dry. We probably won't have to use it.'

'Thank you, Daniel.'

'Anything for you, my dear cousin Betty.'

CHAPTER 28

They sat in comfortable chairs in the all-but-empty Starbucks. Corrie cradled her cup, grateful for the warmth. Across the small table, Stacy Bowdree stared into her own coffee. She seemed quieter, less effusive, than she had that morning.

'So why did you leave the air force?' Corrie asked.

'At first I wanted to make a career of it. After 9/11. I was in college, both my parents were dead, and I was looking for direction, so I transferred to the academy. I was really gung-ho, totally idealistic. But two tours in Iraq, and then two more in Afghanistan, cured me of that. I realized I wasn't cut out to be a lifer. It's still a man's game, no matter what they say, especially in the air force.'

'Four tours? Wow.'

Bowdree shrugged. 'Not uncommon. They need a lot of people on the ground over there.'

'What did you do?'

'On the last tour, I was the commanding officer of the 382nd Expeditionary EOD Bunker. Explosive Ordnance Disposal. We were stationed at FOB Gardez, Paktia Province.'

'You defused bombs?'

'Sometimes. Most of the time, we'd clear areas of the base or take munitions to the range and get rid of them. Basically, any time they wanted to put a shovel in the ground, we had to clear the area first. Once in a while, we had to go beyond the wire and clear IEDs.'

'You mean, with those big bomb suits?'

'Yeah, like in that film *The Hurt Locker.* Although mostly we used robots. Anyway, that's all in the past. I got my discharge a few months ago. I've sort of been drifting, wondering what to do with my life – and then Pendergast's bit of news came along.'

'And so you're here in Roaring Fork.'

'Yes, and you're probably wondering why.'

'Well, I am, a little.' Corrie laughed, still a little nervous. She had been afraid to ask the question.

'When you're done with him, I'm taking Great-Great-Granddad back to Kentucky and I'm going to bury him in the family plot.'

Corrie nodded. 'That's cool.'

'My parents are gone, I don't have any brothers or sisters. I've been getting interested in my family's past. The Bowdrees go back a long way. We've got Colorado pioneers like Emmett, we've got military officers going back to the Revolution, and then there's my favorite, Captain Thomas Bowdree Hicks, who fought for the South in the Army of Northern Virginia – a real war hero and a captain, just like me.' Her face glowed with pride.

'I think it's great.'

'I'm glad you think so. Because I'm not here to rush your work along. I don't have any burning agenda – I just want to reconnect with my past, with my roots, to make a personal journey of sorts, and in the end bring my ancestor back to Kentucky. Maybe by then I'll have a better idea of what to do next.'

Corrie simply nodded.

Bowdree finished her coffee. 'What a bizarre thing, getting eaten by a bear.'

Corrie hesitated. She'd been thinking about it all afternoon, and had decided she really couldn't in good conscience keep back the truth. 'Um, I think there's something you should know about your ancestor.'

Bowdree looked up.

'This has to remain confidential – at least until I've finished my work.'

'It will.'

'Emmett Bowdree wasn't killed and eaten by a grizzly bear.'

'No?'

'Nor were the other remains – at least the ones I've looked at.' She took a deep breath. 'They were murdered. By a gang of serial killers, it seems. Murdered and . . .' She couldn't quite say it.

'Murdered and . . .?'

'Eaten.'

'You've got to be kidding me.'

Corrie shook her head.

'And nobody knows this?'

'Only Pendergast.'

'What are you going to do about it?'

Corrie paused. 'Well, I'd like to stay here and solve the crime.'

Bowdree whistled. 'Good God. Any idea of who? Or why?'

'Not yet.'

A long silence ensued. 'You need any help?'

'No. Well, maybe. I've got a whole lot of old newspapers to comb through – I guess I could use a hand with that. But I need to do all the forensic analysis on my own. It's my first real thesis and . . . well, I want it to be my own work. Pendergast thinks I'm crazy and wants me to finish up and go back to New York with what I've got, but I'm not ready for that yet.'

Bowdree gave a big smile. 'I get it totally. You're just like me. I like doing things on my own.'

Corrie sipped her drink. 'Any luck finding a place to stay?'

'Nada. I've never seen such a gold-plated town.'

'Why don't you stay with me? I'm house-sitting an empty mansion on Ravens Ravine Road, just me and a stray dog, and to be honest the place is creeping me out. I'd love to have someone keep me company.' *Especially ex-military.* She'd been thinking about those footprints all afternoon, thinking how much better she'd feel with a roommate. 'All you'll have to do is avoid a few security cameras – the nonresident owner is a bit of a busybody. But I'd love to have you.'

'Are you serious? Really?' Bowdree's smile widened. 'That would be fantastic! Thank you so much.'

Corrie drained her drink and stood up. 'If you're ready, you can follow me up there now.'

'I was born ready.' And with that, Bowdree grabbed her gear and followed Corrie out into the freezing night.

CHAPTER 29

At five minutes to four in the morning, London time, Roger Kleefisch stepped into the large sitting room of his town house on Marylebone High Street and surveyed the dim surroundings with satisfaction. Everything was in its precise position: the velvet-lined easy chairs on each side of the fireplace; the bearskin hearth rug on the floor; the long row of reference works on the polished mantelpiece, a letter jammed into the wood directly below them by a jackknife; the scientific charts on the wall; the bench of chemicals heavily scarred with acid; the letters *V.R.* tattooed into the far wall with bullet holes – simulated bullet holes, of course. There was even a worn violin sitting in a corner – Kleefisch had been trying to learn how to play, but of course even discordant scrapings would have been sufficient. As he looked around, a smile formed on his face. Perfect – as close as he could possibly make it to the descriptions in the stories themselves. The only thing he'd left out had been the solution of cocaine hydrochloride and hypodermic needle.

He pressed a button beside the door, and the lights came up – gas, of course, specially installed at great expense. He walked thoughtfully over to a large mahogany bookcase and peered through the glass doors. Everything within was devoted to a single subject – *the* subject. The top three shelves were taken up with various copies of The Canon – of course he wasn't able to purchase the very first editions, even on his barrister's salary, but he nevertheless had some extremely choice copies, especially the 1917 George Bell edition of *His Last Bow*, with dust wrapper intact, and the 1894 George Newnes printing of *The Memoirs of Sherlock Holmes*, the spine still quite bright, with just the smallest amount of wear and foxing. The lower shelves of the bookcase were taken up by various volumes of scholarship and back issues of the *Baker Street Journal*. This last was a periodical issued by the Baker Street Irregulars, a group devoted to the study and perpetuation of Sherlockiana. Kleefisch had himself published several articles in the *Journal*, one of which – an exceedingly detailed work devoted to Holmes's study of poisons – had prompted the Irregulars to offer him a membership in the organization and present him with an 'Irregular Shilling.' One did not apply for membership in the Irregulars; one had to be asked. And becoming an Investiture was, without doubt, the proudest achievement of Kleefisch's life.

Opening the cabinet doors, he hunted around the lower shelves for a periodical he wanted to re-read, located it, closed the doors again, then walked over to the closest armchair and sat down with a sigh of contentment. The gaslights threw a warm, mellow light over everything. Even this town house, in the Lisson Grove section, had been chosen for its proximity to Baker Street. If it had not been for the infrequent sound of traffic from beyond the bow window, Kleefisch could almost have imagined himself back in 1880s London.

The phone rang, an antique 'Coffin' dating to 1879, of wood and hard rubber with a receiver shaped like an oversize drawer handle. The smile fading from his face, he glanced at his watch and picked up the receiver. 'Hallo.'

'Roger Kleefisch?' The voice was American – southern, Kleefisch noticed – coming in from a long distance, it seemed. He vaguely recognized it.

'Speaking.'

'This is Pendergast. Aloysius Pendergast.'

'Pendergast.' Kleefisch repeated the name, as if tasting it.

'Do you remember me?'

'Yes. Yes, of course.' He had known Pendergast at Oxford, when he had been studying law and Pendergast had been reading philosophy at the Graduate Centre of Balliol College. Pendergast had been a rather strange fellow – reserved and exceedingly private – and yet a kind of intellectual bond had formed between them that Kleefisch still remembered with fondness. Pendergast, he recalled, had seemed to be nursing some private sorrow, but Kleefisch's tactful attempts to draw him out on the subject had met with no success.

211

'I apologize for the lateness of the call. But I remembered your keeping, shall we say, unusual hours and hoped that the habit had not deserted you.'

Kleefisch laughed. 'True, I rarely go to bed before five in the morning. When I'm not in court, I prefer to sleep while the rabble are out and about. To what do I owe this call?'

'I understand you are a member of the Baker Street Irregulars.'

'I have that honor, yes.'

'In that case, perhaps you can assist me.'

Kleefisch settled back in the chair. 'Why? Are you working on some academic project regarding Sherlock Holmes?'

'No. I am a special agent with the FBI, and I'm investigating a series of murders.'

There was a brief silence while Kleefisch digested this. 'In that case, I can't imagine what possible service I could be to you.'

'Let me summarize as briefly as I can. An arsonist has burned down a house and its inhabitants at the ski resort of Roaring Fork, Colorado. Do you know of Roaring Fork?'

Naturally, Kleefisch had heard of Roaring Fork.

'In the late nineteenth century, Roaring Fork was a mining community. Interestingly, it is one of the places where Oscar Wilde stopped on his lecture tour of America. While he was there, he was told a rather colorful tale by one of the miners. The tale centered on a man-eating grizzly bear.'

'Please continue,' Kleefisch said, wondering just where this strange story was going.

'Wilde told this story, in turn, to Conan Doyle during their 1889 dinner at the Langham Hotel. It seemed to have had a powerful effect on Conan Doyle – powerful, unpleasant, and lasting.'

Kleefisch said nothing. He knew, of course, about the legendary dinner. He would have to take another look at the Conan Doyle diary entry about that.

'I believe that what Conan Doyle heard so affected him that he wove it – suitably fictionalized, of course – into his work, as an attempt at catharsis. I'm speaking in particular about *The Hound of the Baskervilles*.'

'Interesting,' Kleefisch said. To the best of his knowledge, this was a new line of critical thinking. If it proved promising, it might even lead to a scholarly monograph for the Irregulars. To be written by himself, of course: of late he had been searching for a new subject on which to focus. 'But I confess I still don't see how I can be of help. And I certainly don't understand what all this has to do with the arson case you're investigating.'

'On the latter point, I'd prefer to keep my own counsel. On the former point, I am becoming increasingly convinced that Conan Doyle knew more than he let on.'

'You mean, more than he alluded to in *The Hound of the Baskervilles*?'

'Precisely.'

Kleefisch sat up. This was more than interesting – this was downright exciting. His mind began to race. 'How do you mean?'

'Just that Conan Doyle might have written more about this man-eating bear, somewhere else – perhaps in his letters or unpublished works. Which is why I'm consulting you.'

'You know, Pendergast, there might actually be something in your speculations.'

'Pray explain.'

'Late in life, Conan Doyle supposedly wrote one last Holmes story. Nothing about it is known – not its subject, not even its name. The story goes that Conan Doyle submitted it for publication, but it was returned to him because its subject was too strong for the general public. What happened to it then is unknown. Most suspect it was destroyed. Ever since, this lost Holmes story has been the stuff of legends, endlessly speculated upon by members of the Irregulars.'

There was silence on the other end of the line.

'To tell you the truth, Pendergast, I'd rather suspected it of being just another Holmesian tall tale. They are legion, you know. Or, perhaps, a shaggy dog story perpetuated by Ellery Queen. But given what you've said, I find myself wondering if the story might actually exist, after all. And if it does, that it might . . .' His voice trailed off.

'That it might tell the rest of the story that always haunted Conan Doyle,' Pendergast finished for him.

'Exactly.'

'Do you have any idea how one might go about searching for such a story?'

'Not off the top of my head. But as an Irregular, and a Holmes scholar, there are various resources at my disposal. This could be an extraordinary new avenue of research.' Kleefisch's brain was working even faster now. To uncover a lost Sherlock Holmes story, after all these years . . .

'What's your address in London?' Pendergast asked.

'Five-Seventy-Two, Marylebone High Street.'

'I hope you don't mind if I call on you in the near future?'

'How near?'

'Two days, perhaps. As soon as I can break away from this arson investigation. I'll be staying at the Connaught Hotel.'

'Excellent. It will be a pleasure to see you again. In the meantime, I'll make some initial inquiries, and we'll be able to—'

'Yes,' Pendergast interrupted. His voice had changed abruptly; a sudden urgency had come into it. 'Yes, thank you, I'll do my best to see you then. But now, Kleefisch, I have to go; you'll excuse me, please.'

'Is something wrong?'

'There appears to be another house on fire.' And with that, Pendergast abruptly hung up and the line went dead.

CHAPTER 30

Even with liberal goosing of the siren and repeated yelling through the squad car's external megaphone, Chief Morris couldn't get closer than a block to the station, so thick was the press of cars, media, and people. And it wasn't even eight o'clock in the morning. With this second arson, the story had gone national – no surprise, given the identity of the victims – and the crime feeders were all there, along with the network news shows, CNN, and God only knew who else.

The chief now regretted he'd driven himself; he had no one to run interference, and his only option was to get out of the car and scrimmage his way through these jokers. They had surrounded his squad car, cameras rolling, microphones waving at him like clubs. He'd spent all night at the scene of the fire, which had started at eight in the evening, and he was now filthy, stinking of smoke, exhausted, coughing, and hardly able to think. What a state to face the cameras.

The chief's car was jostled and rocked by the unruly crowd of reporters. They were calling out questions, hollering at him, jockeying with each other for position. He realized he'd better think of something to say.

He took a deep breath, collected himself, and forced open the door. The reaction was instant, the crowd pushing forward, the cameras and mikes swinging dangerously, one even knocking his hat off. He stood up, dusted off his hat, replaced it, and held up his hands. 'All right. All right! Please. I can't make a statement if you keep this up. Give me some room, *please!*'

The crowd backed off a little. The chief looked around, acutely aware that his image was going to be broadcast on every nightly news show in the country.

'I will make a brief statement. There will be no questions afterward.' He took a breath. 'I've just come from the crime scene. I can assure you we are doing everything humanly possible to solve these vicious crimes and bring the perpetrators to justice. We have the finest forensic and crime-scene investigators in the state on this case. All our resources and those of the surrounding communities have been brought to bear. On top of that, we have brought in as a consultant one of the FBI's top agents specializing in serial killings and deviant psychology, as it appears we may be dealing with a serial arsonist.'

He cleared his throat. 'Now to the crime itself. The scene is of course still being analyzed. Two bodies have been recovered. They have been tentatively identified as the actress Sonja Dutoit and her

217

child. Our thoughts and prayers are with the victims, their families, and all of you who have been touched by this horrible event. This is a huge tragedy for our town and, truthfully, I can't find the words to express the depth of my shock and sorrow . . .' He found himself temporarily unable to continue, but quickly mastered the constriction in his throat and wrapped things up. 'We will have more information for you at a press conference later today. That is all I have to say for the moment. Thank you.'

He barreled forward, ignoring the shouted questions and the forest of microphones, and within five minutes managed to stagger into his office. There was Pendergast, sitting in the outer office, dressed in his usual impeccable style, sipping tea. The television was on.

Pendergast rose. 'Allow me to congratulate you on a most effective appearance.'

'What?' Morris turned to Shirley. 'I was on the tube already?'

'It was live, Chief,' she said. 'And you handled it very well. You looked like a hero, with that determined voice . . . and those streaks of soot on your face.'

'Soot? On my face?' Damn, he should have washed up.

'A Hollywood makeup artist couldn't have done a finer job,' said Pendergast. 'That, combined with the disheveled uniform, the windswept hair, and the evident emotion, made for a singular impression.'

The chief threw himself down in a chair. 'I

couldn't care less what they think. My God, I've never seen anything like this. Agent Pendergast, if you heard what I said on television, then you know I just elevated you to official consulting status.'

Pendergast inclined his head.

'So I hope to God in heaven you will accept. I need your help more than ever. How about it?'

The man responded by removing a slim envelope from his suit and dangling it in front of Morris by his fingertips. 'I'm afraid I beat you to it. I'm not just consulting – now I'm official.'

CHAPTER 31

As Corrie entered the empty library, it seemed less cheerful than before, more foreboding. Maybe it was because an atmosphere of doom seemed to have descended on the town – or perhaps it was simply due to the dark storm clouds that were gathering over the mountains, promising snow.

Stacy Bowdree, following her into the history section, whistled softly. 'Does this town have money, or what?'

'Yeah, but nobody ever comes in here.'

'Too busy shopping.'

She saw Ted, at his desk across the room, rising from his book to greet them. He was wearing a tight T-shirt and looking exceptionally good, and Corrie felt her heart flutter unexpectedly. She took a breath and introduced Stacy.

'What's on the program today, ladies?' Ted asked, giving Stacy an appreciative once-over. Corrie had to admit Stacy was striking and that any man would enjoy looking at her, but his attentive eye still concerned her.

'Murder and mayhem,' Corrie said. 'We want

all the articles you've got on murders, hangings, robberies, vigilantism, shootings, feuds – in short, everything bad – for the period of the grizzly killings.'

At this Ted laughed. 'Just about every issue of the old *Roaring Fork Courier* is going to have some kind of crime story. It was a hot town in those days – a real place, unlike now. What issues do you want to start with?'

'The first grizzly killing was in May 1876, so let's start with, say, April first, 1876, and go six months out from that.'

'Very good,' Ted replied.

Corrie noticed that his eyes were still straying regularly to Stacy – and not just to her face. But the captain seemed oblivious – or perhaps she was just used to it from her years in the military.

'The old newspapers are all digitized. I'll set you up at some terminals and show you what to do.' He paused. 'Sure is crazy in town today.'

'Yeah,' said Corrie. The truth was, aside from all the traffic she hadn't paid much attention.

'It's like *Jaws*.'

'What do you mean?'

'What was the name of that town – Amity? You know, the tourists leaving in droves. Well, that's what's happening here. Haven't you noticed? All of a sudden the ski slopes are deserted, the hotels are emptying out. Even the second-homers are making preparations to leave. In a day or two, the only people who'll still be here are the press. It's nuts.' He typed away at two side-by-side terminals, then straightened. 'Okay, they're all set up for you.' He showed them how to work the equipment. He paused. 'So, Stacy, when did you get here?'

'Four days ago. But I've been lying low, didn't want to cause a ruckus.'

'Four days. The day before the first fire?'

'I guess it must have been. I heard about it the following morning.'

'I hope you enjoy our little town. It's a fun place – if you're rich.' He laughed, winked, and, to Corrie's relief, went back to his desk. Was she jealous? She didn't have a lock on him – she'd even declined his offer to see his apartment.

They divided up the searching by date, Corrie taking the first three months while Stacy took the next three. Silence descended, broken only by the soft rapping of keys.

And then Stacy whistled softly. 'Listen to this.'

THEY WANTED THE SAME GIRL

And They Fought a Duel by Lantern Light on Her Account

BOTH MEN LITERALLY CUT TO RIBBONS

Two Ohio swains meet at midnight and, by the aid of a lantern, proceed to hack each other with swords and pocket knives until both are unconscious. One of the rivals, rousing himself, runs his adversary through with his sword, causing a fatal injury. The lady, Miss Williams, is prostrate with grief over the terrible affray.

'That's pretty bizarre,' said Corrie, hoping that Stacy wasn't going to read aloud every silly story she came across. It was only with a degree of soul searching that she'd accepted Stacy's offer of assistance.

'I like that. *Prostrate with grief.* I'll bet she just soaked her bloomers over the *affray*.'

The crudity of the comment shocked Corrie. But maybe that was the way women talked in the military.

As Corrie paged through the headlines, she realized Ted was right: Roaring Fork, at least in the summer of 1876, was a bloody town. There was practically a murder a week, along with daily stabbings and shootings. There were stagecoach robberies on Independence Pass, mining claim disputes, the frequent murder of prostitutes, stealing of horses, and vigilante hangings. The town was overrun with card sharps, shysters, thieves, and murderers. There was also a huge economic divide. Some few struck it rich and built palatial mansions on Main Street, while most lived in teeming boardinghouses, four or five to a room, and tent encampments overrun with filth, rats, and mosquitoes. A casual and pervasive racism infected everything. One end of town, called 'China Camp,' was populated with so-called coolies who were horribly discriminated against. There was also a 'Negro Town.' And the newspaper noted a squalid camp in a nearby canyon that was occupied by 'assorted drunken, miserable specimens of the Red Race, the sad remnants of the Utes of yore.'

In 1876, law had barely come to Roaring Fork. Most 'justice' was administered by shadowy vigilantes. If a drunken shooting or knifing occurred in a saloon the night before, the perpetrator would often be found the next morning hanging from a large cottonwood tree at the far end of town. The corpses were left up for days to greet newcomers. In a busy week there might be two, three, or even four bodies hanging on the tree, with 'the maggots dropping out of them,' as one reporter wrote with relish. The papers were full of colorful and outrageous stories: of a feud between two families that ended with the complete extermination of all but one man; of an obese horse thief whose weight was such that his hanging decapitated him; of a man who went berserk from what the newspaper called a 'Brain Storm,' thought he was Jesus, barricaded himself in a whorehouse, and proceeded to kill most of the ladies in order to rid the town of sin.

Work in the mines was dreadful, the miners descending before daybreak and coming up after sunset, six days a week, only seeing the light of day on Sundays. Accidents, cave-ins, and explosions were common. But it was even worse in the stamp mills and the smelter. There, in a large industrial operation, the silver ore was pulverized by gigantic metal 'stamps' weighing many tons. These literally smashed the ore, pounding day and night, producing a ceaseless din that shook the entire town. The resulting grit was dumped into immense iron tanks with mechanical agitators and grinding plates to further reduce it to a mush-like paste; then mercury, salt, and copper sulfate were added. The resulting witches' brew was cooked and stirred for days, heated by enormous coal-fired boilers that belched smoke. Because the town was in a valley surrounded by mountains, the coal smoke created a choking, London-style fog that blocked the sun for days on end. Those who worked in the mill and smelter had it worse than the miners, as they were often scalded to death by burst steam pipes and boilers, suffocated by noxious fumes, or horribly maimed by heavy equipment. There were no safety laws, no regulation of hours or pay, and no unions. If a man was crippled by machinery, he was immediately dismissed without even an extra day's wage, cast off to fend for himself. The worst and most dangerous jobs were given to the Chinese 'coolies,' whose frequent deaths were reported in the back of the paper in the same offhand tone one might use to describe the death of a dog.

Corrie found herself becoming increasingly indignant as she read about the injustice, the exploitation, and the casual cruelty in pursuit of profit perpetrated by the mining companies. What surprised her most, however, was to learn that it was the Staffords – one of the most respected philanthropist families in New York City, famous for the Stafford Museum of Art and the wealthy Stafford Fund – who had initially established their fortune during the Colorado silver boom as the financiers behind the mill and smelter in Roaring Fork. The Stafford family, she knew, had done a lot of good with their money over the years – which made the unsavory origin of their fortune all the more surprising.

'What a place,' said Stacy, interrupting Corrie's train of thought. 'I had no idea Roaring Fork was such a hellhole. And now look at it: the richest town in America!'

Corrie shook her head. 'Ironic, isn't it?'

'So much violence and misery.'

'True,' said Corrie, adding in a low voice: 'though I'm not finding anything that might point to a gang of cannibalistic serial killers.'

'Me neither.'

'But the clues are there, somewhere. They *have* to be. We just have to find them.'

Stacy shrugged. 'You think it might be those Ute Indians up in the canyon? They had a good motive: their land was stolen by the miners.'

Corrie considered this. Around that time, she'd read, the White River and Uncompahgre Utes had been fighting back against the whites who were pushing them westward through the Rocky Mountains. The conflict culminated in the White

River War of 1879, when the Utes were finally expelled from Colorado. It was possible that some Indians in the conflict had worked their way south-ward and taken revenge on the miners of Roaring Fork.

'I thought of that,' she said at length. 'But the miners weren't scalped – scalping leaves distinctive markings. And I learned that the Utes had a huge taboo against cannibalism.'

'So did whites. And maybe they didn't scalp them so as to conceal their identity.'

'Possible. But the killings were high-quality. What I mean is,' Corrie hastily added, 'they were not sloppy and disorganized. It can't be easy to ambush a wily, hardened Colorado miner guarding his claim. I don't think a sad camp of Utes could have perpetrated these killings.'

'What about the Chinese? I can't believe how terribly they were treated – it was as if they were considered subhuman.'

'I thought about that, too. But if the motive was revenge, why *eat* them?'

'Maybe they just faked the eating thing, to make it look like a bear.'

Corrie shook her head. 'My analysis shows they really did consume the flesh – raw. And another question: why did they suddenly stop? What goal had they accomplished, if any?'

'That's a really good question. But it's one o'clock, and I don't know about you, but I'm so hungry I could eat a couple of miners myself.'

'Let's get lunch.'

As they got up to leave, Ted came over. 'Say, Corrie,' he began. 'I meant to ask you. How about dinner tonight? Won't be any problems getting a reservation.' He ran his fingers through his curly brown hair and looked at her, smiling.

'I'd love to,' she said, gratified that Ted, despite his attention to Stacy, still was interested. 'But I'm supposed to have dinner with Pendergast.'

'Oh. Well. Some other time, then.' He smiled, but Corrie noticed he wasn't quite able to fully conceal a look of hurt. It reminded her of a puppy dog, and she felt a stab of guilt. Nevertheless, he turned gamely toward Stacy and gave her a wink. 'Good to meet you.'

As they bundled up in their coats and walked out into the winter air, Corrie wondered where another date with Ted might lead. The fact was, it seemed like a long time since she'd had a boyfriend, and her bed in the mansion up Ravens Ravine was so very, very cold.

CHAPTER 32

I
t was like a persistent nightmare, which terri-
fies you one night, then returns the next in an
even more malevolent form. At least, so it
seemed to Chief Morris as he walked through what
was left of the Dutoit house. The smoldering ruins
stood on the shoulder of a hill, with sweeping
views of the town below and the surrounding ring
of snowy mountains. He could hardly bear it:
walking along the same corridors of plastic tape;
smelling the same stench of burnt wood, plastic,
and rubber; seeing the charred walls and melted
puddles of glass, the scorched beds and heat-
shattered toilets and sinks. And then there were
the little things that had weirdly survived: a
drinking glass, a bottle of perfume, a sodden teddy
bear, and a poster of the movie *Marching Band*,
Dutoit's most famous film, still pinned to a gutted
wall.

It had taken most of the night to extinguish the
fire and beat it down to this damp, steaming pile.
The forensic specialists and the M.E. had gone in
at dawn, and had identified the victims as best they
could. They hadn't been burned quite as badly as

the Baker family – which only added to the horror. At least, the chief thought, he didn't have to deal with Chivers this time, who had already been through the crime scene and was now off preparing his report – a report that Chief Morris was doubtful of. Chivers was clearly in over his head.

He was, however, grateful for Pendergast's presence. The man was strangely reassuring to the chief, despite his eccentricities – and despite the fact that everyone else was put out by his presence. Pendergast wandered ahead of Morris, dressed in his inappropriate formal black coat and white silk scarf, with that same strange hat on his head, silent as the grave. The sun was obscured by heavy winter clouds, and the temperature outside the ruin was hovering in the low teens. Inside, though, the residual heat and plumes of steam created a humid, stinking microclimate.

They finally reached the first victim, which the M.E. had tentatively identified as Dutoit herself. The remains looked more or less like an oversize, blackened fetus nestled in a pile of springs, metal plates, screws, carpet tacks, and burnt layers of cotton batting, with bits of melted plastic and wire here and there. The skull was whole, the jaws gaping in a frozen scream, the arms burned to the bone, the finger bones clenched, the body curled in upon itself by the heat.

Pendergast halted and spent a long time just looking at the victim. He did not pull out test tubes and tweezers and take samples. All he did was look. Then, slowly, he circled the hideous thing. A hand lens came out, and he used it to peer at traces of melted plastic and other, obscure points of interest. While he was doing this, the wind shifted and the chief got a noseful of roasted meat, causing an instant gagging sensation. God, he wished Pendergast would hurry it up.

Finally the FBI agent rose and they continued their perambulation of the gigantic ruin, heading inexorably toward the second victim – the young girl. This was even worse. The chief had deliberately skipped breakfast in preparation, and there was nothing in his stomach to lose, but nevertheless he could feel the dry heaves coming on.

The victim, Dutoit's daughter, Sallie, had been ten years old. She went to school with the chief's own daughter. The two children had not been friends – Sallie had been a withdrawn child, and no wonder, with a mother like that. Now, as they approached the corpse, the chief ventured a glance. The girl's body was in a sitting position, burned only on one side. She had been handcuffed to the pipes under a sink.

He felt the first dry heave, which came like a hiccup, then another, and quickly looked away.

Again, Pendergast spent what seemed a lifetime examining the remains. The chief didn't even begin to understand how he could do it. Another heave came, and he tried to think of something else – *anything* else – to get himself under control.

'It's so perplexing,' Morris said, more to distract

himself than for any other reason. 'I just don't understand.'

'In what way?'

'How . . . well, how the perp selects his victims. I mean, what do the victims have in common? It all seems so random.'

Pendergast rose. 'The crime scene is indeed challenging. You are correct that the victims are random. However, the *attacks* are not.'

'How so?'

'The killer did not choose victims. He – or she, as the etiology of the attacks does not yet indicate gender – chose houses.'

The chief frowned. 'Houses?'

'Yes. Both houses share one trait: they are spectacularly visible from town. The next house will no doubt be equally conspicuous.'

'You mean, they were selected for show? In God's name, why?'

'To send a message, perhaps.' Pendergast turned away. 'Now back to the matter at hand. This crime scene is primarily interesting for the light it sheds on the mind of the killer.' Pendergast spoke slowly as he peered around. 'The perpetrator would appear to meet the Millon definition of a sadistic personality of the "explosive" subtype. He seeks extreme measures of control; he takes pleasure – perhaps sexual pleasure – in the intense suffering of others. This disorder presents violently in an individual who would otherwise seem normal. In other words, the person we seek might appear

232

to be an ordinary, productive member of the community.'

'How can you know that?'

'It is based on my reconstruction of the crime.'

'Which is?'

Pendergast looked around the ruins again before letting his eyes settle on the chief. 'First, the perpetrator entered through an upstairs window.'

The chief refrained from asking how Pendergast could determine this, especially since there was no second floor left.

'We know this because the house doors were massive and the locks were all engaged. To be expected, given the fear recently generated by the first fire and, perhaps, by the relative isolation of the structure. In addition, the first-floor windows are of massive, multi-light construction, glazed with expensive, high-R-value triple-paned glass with anodized aluminum cladding over oak. The ones I examined were all locked, and we can assume the rest were shut and locked as well, given the low temperatures and, as I said, the fear generated by the first attack. Such a window is extremely hard to break, and any attempt would be noisy and time consuming. It would alarm the house. Someone would have called nine-one-one or hit a panic button, with which this house was equipped. But the two victims were caught unawares – upstairs, probably while sleeping. The upstairs windows were less robust, double-paned, and furthermore not all locked – as is evident from this one, here.' Pendergast pointed at a tracery of ash and metal at his feet. 'Thus, I conclude that the killer came and left by an upstairs window. The two victims were subdued, then brought downstairs for the, ah, *denouement.*'

The chief found it hard to concentrate on what Pendergast was saying. The wind had shifted again, and he was breathing assiduously through his mouth.

'This tells us not only the killer's state of mind, but also some of his physical characteristics. He or she is certainly an athletic individual, perhaps with some rock climbing or other strenuous field experience.'

'Rock climbing experience?'

'My dear Chief, it follows directly from the fact there is no evidence of a ladder or rope.'

Chief Morris swallowed. 'And the, ah, "explosive" sadism?'

'The woman, Dutoit, was duct-taped to the downstairs sofa. The tape was wrapped all the way around the sofa – quite a job – rendering her immobile. She appears to have been doused with gasoline and burned alive. Most significantly, this occurred without the victim being gagged.'

'Which means?'

'The perpetrator wanted to talk to her, to hear her plead for her life, and then, after the fire began . . . to hear her scream.'

'Oh, dear Lord.' Morris remembered Dutoit's strident voice at the press conference. He felt another dry heave.

234

'But the sadism evident here—' Pendergast made a gentle gesture in the direction of the remains of the dead girl – 'is even more extreme.'

Morris didn't want to know more, but Pendergast went on. 'This girl was not doused with gasoline. That would have been too quick for our perpetrator. Instead, he started a fire to the right of her, there, and let it burn toward her. Now, if you will examine the pipes that the victim was handcuffed to, you will notice that they are bent. She was pulling on them with all her might in an effort to escape.'

'I see.' But the chief didn't even make a pretense of looking.

'But note the *direction* in which they are bent.'

'Tell me,' said Chief Morris, covering his face, no longer able to take it.

'They are bent in the direction of the fire.'

A silence fell. 'I'm sorry,' the chief said. 'I don't understand.'

'Whatever she was trying to get away from – it was even worse than the fire.'

CHAPTER 33

The last time Corrie was in the old Victorian police station, she'd been in handcuffs. The memory was fresh enough that she felt a twinge upon entering. But Iris, the lady at the reception desk, was almost too nice and happily directed her to Pendergast's temporary office in the basement.

She descended the stuffy staircase, walked past a dim, rumbling furnace, and came to a narrow corridor. The office at the end had no name on it, just a number; she knocked and Pendergast's voice invited her in.

The special agent stood behind an ancient metal desk covered by racks of test tubes, along with a chemistry setup of unknown function that was bubbling away. The office had no windows, and the air was stifling.

'Is this what they gave you?' Corrie asked. 'It's a dungeon!'

'It is what I requested. I did not wish to be disturbed, and this office is in a location where that is assured. No one comes to bother me here – no one.'

'It's hot as Hades in here.'

'It's no worse than a New Orleans spring. As you know, I am averse to cold.'

'Shall we go to dinner?'

'So as not to blight our meal with talk of corpses and cannibalism, perhaps we could spend a few moments catching up with your research first. Please sit down.'

'Sure thing, but can we please keep it short? *I'm* averse to heatstroke.' She took a seat and Pendergast did likewise.

'How are you progressing?'

'Great. I've finished examining four sets of remains, and they tell the same story: all victims of a gang of cannibalistic serial killers.'

Pendergast inclined his head.

'It's unbelievable, really. But there's no question. I did find something interesting in the last skeleton I looked at. The guy with the weird name, Isham Tyng. He was one of the first to be killed, and his bones do show extensive signs of perimortem damage from a large, powerful animal, no doubt a grizzly bear – along with the usual signs of beating, dismemberment, and cannibalism performed by human beings. I looked up the newspaper accounts of the killing, and in this case a bear was scared off the remains by the arrival of Tyng's partners. No doubt the bear was scavenging the victim *after* he'd been killed by the cannibal gang. But this sighting is clearly what cemented the idea in everyone's mind that

237

the killer was a grizzly. A reasonable assumption – but also, sheer coincidence.'

'Excellent. The story is now complete. I assume you don't need to examine any more remains?'

'No, four is plenty. I've got all the data I need.'

'Very good,' murmured Pendergast. 'And when will you be returning to New York?'

Corrie took a deep breath. 'I'm not going back yet.'

'And why is that?'

'I've . . . decided to expand the scope of my thesis.'

She waited, but Pendergast did not react.

'Because, I'm sorry, but the fact is the story *isn't* complete. Now that we know these miners were murdered . . .' She hesitated. 'Well, I'm going to do my damnedest to *solve* the murders.'

Another dead silence. Pendergast's silver eyes narrowed ever so slightly.

'Look, it's a fascinating case. Why not pursue it to its end? Why were these miners killed? Who did it? And why did the killings stop so abruptly? There are tons of questions, and I want to find the answers. This is my chance to turn a good thesis into a really great one.'

'If you survive,' said Pendergast.

'I don't think I'm in any danger. In fact, since the fires I've been ignored. And nobody knows about my most important discovery – everyone still believes a grizzly did it.'

'Nevertheless, I am uneasy.'

'Why? I mean, if you're worried about where I'm house-sitting, it's miles away from the houses that were burned. And I've got a new roommate – Captain Bowdree, as it happens. You couldn't ask for better protection than that. Let me tell you something: she's got a .45 and, believe me, she knows how to use it.' She didn't mention the footsteps she'd found circling the mansion.

'I have no doubt. But the fact is, I must leave Roaring Fork for several days, perhaps longer, and as a result I'll be unable to give you the benefit of my protection. I fear that your looking into this case may awaken the proverbial sleeping dog. And there is an ugly dog sleeping in this rich little town, of that I am sure.'

'Surely you don't believe the arson attacks are somehow linked to the miner killings? They were a hundred and fifty years ago.'

'I don't *believe* anything – yet. But I sense deep, strong water. I'm not in favor of your remaining in Roaring Fork any longer than necessary. I advise you to leave on the first plane out.'

Corrie stared at him 'I'm twenty, and this is *my* life. Not yours. I'm really thankful for all your help, but . . . you're not my father. I'm staying.'

'I will discourage it by withdrawing my financial support.'

'Fine!' Corrie's pent-up anger came bursting out. 'You've been interfering with my thesis from the beginning. You can't help interfering – it's the way you are – but I don't appreciate it. Can't you see

239

how important this is to me? I'm getting tired of you telling me what to do.'

Something flashed across Pendergast's face – something that, had she not been so angry, she would have recognized as dangerous. 'My only concern in the matter is your safety. And I must add that the risks you face are greatly augmented by your unfortunate tendency toward impetuousness and imprudence.'

'If you say so. But I'm done talking. And I'm staying in Roaring Fork whether you like it or not.'

As Pendergast began to speak again, she got up so abruptly she knocked over her chair and left the room without waiting to hear him out.

CHAPTER 34

It was one of the most prominent Victorian mansions on the main drag. Ted, who was a fountain of information on Roaring Fork, had told Corrie its story. The house had been built by Harold Griswell, known as the Silver King of Roaring Fork, who made a fortune and was then bankrupted by the Panic of 1893. He committed suicide by leaping into the main shaft of the Matchless Mine, leaving behind a young widow – a former saloon dancer named Rosie Ann. Rosie Ann spent the next three decades hiring and firing lawyers and bringing countless lawsuits, trying tirelessly to recover the repossessed mines and properties; eventually, when all her legal options ran out, she boarded over the windows of the Griswell Mansion and became a recluse, refusing even to shop for basic provisions and subsisting on the kindness of neighbors, who took it upon themselves to leave food at her door. In 1955, the neighbors complained of a bad smell coming from the house. When the police entered, they found an incredible scene: the entire house was packed floor-to-ceiling with tottering stacks of documents and other bric-a-brac, much of it amassed during the woman's endless lawsuits. There were bundles of newspapers, canvas bags full of ore samples, theater bills, broadsheets, ledgers, assay reports, mining certificates, depositions, trial transcripts, payroll records, bank statements, maps, mine surveys, and the like. They had found Rosie Ann's wizened body buried under a ton of paper; an entire wall of documents, undermined by gnawing mice, had toppled over and pinned her to the floor. Rosie Ann Griswell had starved to death.

She died intestate with no heirs, and the town acquired the building. The hoarded documents proved a historical treasure trove of unruly proportions. Over half a century later, the sorting and cataloging process was still going on, fitfully, whenever the impecunious Roaring Fork Historical Society could scrape together a grant.

Ted had warned Corrie about the state of the collection, which was very unlike the sleek, digitized newspaper archive that he ran. But after combing through the papers for evidence of a cannibalistic gang of killers and coming up empty-handed, Corrie decided to look into the Griswell Archive.

The archivist, it seemed, came in only two days a week. Ted had warned Corrie that he was an unqualified asshole. When Corrie arrived that gray December morning, with a few flakes drifting down from a zinc sky, she found the archivist in the mansion's parlor, sitting behind a desk, messing around with his iPad. While the parlor was free of paper, she could see, through the open doors leading off it, floor-to-ceiling metal shelves and filing cabinets packed with stuff.

The archivist rose and held out his hand. 'Wynn Marple,' he said. He was a prematurely balding, ponytailed man in his late thirties, with an incipient potbelly but retaining the confident, winking air of an aging Lothario.

She introduced herself and explained her mission – that she was looking for information on the year 1876, the grizzly killings, and also on crime and possible gang activity in Roaring Fork.

Marple responded at length, quickly segueing to what was evidently his favorite subject: himself. Corrie learned that he, Marple, had once been on the Olympic Ski Team that trained in Roaring Fork, which is why he had fallen in love with the town; that he was still a rad skier and a hot dude off piste as well; and that there was no way he could allow her into the archives without the proper paperwork and approvals, not to mention a much more specific and narrower scope of work.

'You see,' he said, 'fishing expeditions aren't permitted. A lot of these documents are private and of a confidential, controversial, or—' and here came another wink – 'scandalous nature.'

This speech was accompanied by several lickings of the lips and rovings of the eyes over Corrie's body.

She took a deep breath and reminded herself not to be her own worst enemy for once. A lot of guys just couldn't help being jerks. And she needed these archives. If the answer to the killings wasn't here, then it had probably been lost to history.

'You were an Olympic skier?' she asked, larding her voice with phony admiration.

That produced another gust of braggadocio, including the information that he would have won a bronze but for the course conditions, the temperature, the judges . . . Corrie stopped listening but kept nodding and smiling.

'That's really cool,' she said when she realized he was finished. 'I've never met an Olympic athlete before.'

Wynn Marple had a lot more to say on that point. After five or ten minutes, Corrie, in desperation, had agreed to a date with Wynn for Saturday night – and, in return, gained complete and unrestricted access to the archive.

Wynn tagged along after her as she made her way into the elegant yet decayed rooms, packed with paper. Adding to her woes, the papers had only been roughly sorted chronologically, with no effort made to arrange them by subject.

With the now-eager Wynn fetching files, Corrie sat down at a long baize-covered table and began to sort through them. They were all mixed up and confused, full of extraneous and misfiled material, and it became obvious that whoever had done the filing was either negligent or an idiot. As she sorted through one bundle after another, the smell of decaying paper and old wax filled the room.

The minutes turned into hours. The room was overheated, the light was dim, and her eyes started to itch. Even Wynn finally got tired of talking about himself. The papers were dry, and dust seemed to float off the pages with every shuffle. There were reams of impenetrable legal documents, filings, depositions, notices and interrogatories, trial transcripts, hearings, grand jury proceedings, commingled with plats, surveys, assay results, mining partnership agreements, payrolls, inventories, work orders, worthless stock certificates, invoices, and completely irrelevant posters and broadsides. Once in a while the tide of documents yielded a colorful playbill announcing the arrival of a busty burlesque queen or slapstick comedy troupe.

Infrequently, Corrie would turn up a document of faint interest – a criminal complaint, the transcript of a murder trial, WANTED posters, police records pertaining to undesirables and transients who were suspected of or charged with crimes. But there was nothing that stood out, no gang of crazies, no one with a motive to murder and consume eleven miners.

The name of Stafford turned up regularly, especially with respect to the smelting and refining personnel records. Those records were particularly odious, with ledger pages that listed killed workers like so much damaged equipment, next to sums paid to their widows or orphans, never amounting to more than five dollars, with the majority of the sums listed as $0.00 along with the notation 'no payment/worker error.' There were records of workers crippled, poisoned, or injured on the job who were then summarily dismissed with no compensation or recourse whatsoever.

'What a bunch of scumbags,' Corrie muttered to herself, handing over another batch of papers to Wynn.

At one point a handbill turned up that stopped Corrie.

THE AESTHETIC THEORY

A lecture by
MR OSCAR WILDE OF LONDON, ENGLAND

The practical application of the principles of the aesthetic theory, with observations upon the fine arts, personal adornment, and house decoration

TO BE GIVEN AT THE GRAND GALLERY OF THE SALLY GOODIN MINE

SUNDAY AFTERNOON, JUNE 2d

AT HALF-PAST TWO O'CLOCK

TICKETS SEVENTY-FIVE CENTS

Corrie almost had to laugh at the odd quaintness of it. This had to be the lecture where Wilde heard the story of the grizzly killings. And clipped to the handbill was a sheaf of news items, letters, and notes about the lecture appearance. It seemed ludicrous that the rough miners of Roaring Fork would have had any interest whatsoever in the aesthetic theory, let alone personal adornment or house decoration. But by all accounts the lecture had been a great success, resulting in a standing ovation. Perhaps it was the figure Wilde cut, with his outré dress and foppish mannerisms, or his preternatural wit. The poor miners of Roaring Fork had precious little entertainment beyond whoring and drinking.

She quickly leafed through the attached documents and came across an amusing handwritten note, apparently a letter by a miner to his wife back east. It was entirely without punctuation.

My Deere Wife Sun Day there was a Lektior by Mister Oscor Wild of London After the Lektior which was veery well Reseeved Mister Wild enjoyt talking to the Miners and Roufh Necks he was veery gray sheous while I was wating to speek to him that old drunk cogger Swinton button holt him pulld him asite and told him a storey that turnt the pore Man as Pail as a Gost I thot he wud drop and fent . . .

247

Wynn, reading over her shoulder, made a snorting laugh. 'Illiterate bastard.' He tapped the lecture handbill. 'You know, I'll bet this is worth money.'

'I'm sure it is,' she said, hesitating, and then clipping it all back together. As charming as the miner's letter was, it was too far afield to merit inclusion in her thesis.

She shuffled the papers aside and moved on to the next file. She noted that when Wynn carried the bundle back to the shelf, he slipped out the handbill and tucked it in another place. The guy was probably going to sell it on eBay or something.

She told herself what he did was none of her business. The next big bundle arrived, and then the next. Most of the papers dealt with milling and refining, and this time almost everything related to the Stafford family, which, by all indications, became more oppressive as their wealth and power increased. They seemed to have survived the silver panic of 1893 nicely, and even used the opportunity to pick up mines and claims at pennies on the dollar. There were plenty of faded maps of the mining districts, as well, with each mine, shaft, and tunnel carefully marked and identified. Strangely, though, there were precious few records of the smelting operations.

And then a document stopped her cold. It was a postcard dated 1933, from a family member named Howland Stafford to a woman named Dora Tiffany Kermode. It opened *Dear Cousin.*

Kermode. Cousin.

248

'Jesus!' Corrie blurted out. 'That bitch Kermode is *related* to the family who squeezed this town dry.'

'Who are you talking about?' Wynn asked.

She slapped the document with the back of her hand. 'Betty Kermode. That horrible woman who runs The Heights. She's related to the Staffords – you know, the ones who owned the smelter back in Roaring Fork's mining days. Unbelievable.'

It was only then that Corrie realized her mistake. Wynn Marple was drawing himself up. He spoke in a reproving, almost schoolmarmish tone. 'Mrs Kermode is one of the finest, most *gracious* people in this entire town.'

Corrie hastily backtracked. 'I'm sorry. I was just . . . I mean, she's responsible for putting me in jail . . . I didn't realize she was a friend of yours.'

Her stammered apology seemed to work. 'Well, I can appreciate how you might be upset with her for that, but I can vouch for her, I really can. She's *good people*.' Another wink.

Bully for you. In five hours, Corrie hadn't found anything, and now she was saddled with going on a date with this buffoon for nothing. She hoped it could be made short and in a place where Ted would never, ever see them. Or maybe she could beg off sick at the last moment. That's what she'd do.

She glanced at her watch. There was no way she was going to find what she needed in this hellhole of paper. For the first time, she began to feel that maybe she was overreaching. Perhaps Pendergast was right. She had enough for an excellent thesis already.

She got up. 'Look, this isn't working. I'd better be going.'

Wynn followed her to the front parlor. 'I'm sorry you weren't more successful. But at least . . .' He winked again. 'It resulted in our getting together.'

She would definitely have to call in sick.

She swallowed. 'Thanks for your help, Wynn.'

He leaned toward her, way too close. 'My pleasure.'

She suddenly paused. What was that she felt on her ass? His hand. She took a half step back and turned, but the hand followed like an octopus's sucker, this time giving her butt cheek a little squeeze.

'Do you *mind*?' she said acidly, brushing it away.

'Well . . . we *do* have a date coming up.'

'And that *justifies* you *groping* my *ass*?'

Wynn looked confused. 'But . . . I was just being friendly. I figured you'd like it. I mean, it isn't every day you get to go out with an Olympic skier, and I figured . . .?'

It was the final leering wink that did it. Corrie rounded on him. 'Olympic skier? When was the last time you looked at yourself in the mirror? Here's what you'll see – a balding, potbellied, mouth-breathing loser. I wouldn't go on a date with you if you were the last man alive.'

With that she turned, grabbed her coat, and left,

the cold air hitting her like a wall as she stepped outside.

Wynn Marple sat down at his desk. Both his hands were trembling and his breath was coming shallow and fast. He could hardly believe how that bitch had treated him, after all the help he'd given her. One of those feminazi types, objecting to a little innocent, friendly pat.

Wynn was so furious, so outraged, he felt the blood pounding in his head like a tom-tom. It took a few minutes, but then finally he was able to pick up the phone and dial.

CHAPTER 35

Betty Brown Stafford Kermode, sitting in the living room of her house at the top of The Heights, a piñon fire roaring in the fireplace, hung up the princess phone. She sat very still for some minutes, staring out the picture window at the mountains, considering the problem. Her brother-in-law, Henry Montebello, sat in a wing chair on the opposite side of the fire. He was dressed in a three-piece suit, a hand-knotted bow tie of dark paisley setting off a crisp white shirt. He was examining his nails with an air of patrician boredom. A weak winter sun filtered in.

Kermode considered the problem for another minute. And then she picked up the phone again and dialed Daniel Stafford.

'Hello again, my dear,' came the dry, sardonic voice. Kermode did not particularly enjoy talking to her cousin Daniel, but 'liking' and 'caring' did not figure in the bonds that held the Stafford family together.

Those bonds were made of money, and all family relationships were defined by it. As Daniel was not only the head of the Stafford Family Trusts, with assets of two billion dollars, but also one of two managing partners of the family investment company, with assets under management of sixteen billion dollars, she considered him close to her. Very close. It never occurred to her to wonder whether she actually liked the man or not.

'Am I on speakerphone?' Stafford asked.

'Henry is here with me,' Kermode replied. She paused. 'We have a problem.'

'If you're referring to the new fire, thank heaven it didn't occur in The Heights. This is wonderful, in fact – the impact on The Heights is now much diluted. What we need is a third fire even farther afield.' A dry chuckle followed.

'That's not amusing. In any case, I'm not calling about that. I'm calling because that girl – Corrie Swanson – made the connection between the Kermodes and the Staffords.'

'That's not exactly a state secret.'

'Daniel, she got into the Griswell Archive and hit a trove of documents related to the mines, mills, and smelter operations going way back. *All* the way back.'

A silence. And then she heard her cousin swear genteelly on the other end of the line. 'Anything, ah, *more* than that?' His voice was suddenly less flippant.

'No. At least, not yet.'

More silence. 'How good a researcher is she?'

'She's like a damn terrier, sinks her sharp little teeth in and never lets go. She doesn't seem to have made the connection yet, but if she keeps digging, she will.'

Another long silence. 'I was under the impression that the germane documents had been removed.'

'A mighty effort was made, but the archives are a complete mess. Anything might have slipped through.'

'I see. Well now, this *is* a problem.'

'Did you dig up any dirt on her and the others, as you promised?'

'I did. This fellow Pendergast has a checkered history, but he's untouchable. Bowdree's something of a war hero, with a raft of citations and medals, which makes her a tricky target. Except that she got a medical discharge from the air force.'

'Was she wounded?' Kermode asked. 'She looked healthy enough to me.'

'She spent a couple of months at the U.S. military hospital in Landstuhl, Germany. Her actual medical records are sealed, and the air force protects those files like the dickens.'

'And the girl, Swanson?'

'She's a little hellion. Grew up in a trailer park in a dreadful little town in Kansas. Parents were low, *low* working-class, split up after she was born. Mother's a raging alcoholic, father a ne'er-do-well, once accused of robbing a bank. She herself has a juvenile record as long as your arm. The only reason she got as far as she did is because this Pendergast fellow took her under his wing and financed her schooling. No doubt there's a quid pro quo there. The problem is, as long as Pendergast is around she'll be hard to get at.'

'The chief of police tells me he left for London last night.'

'That's lucky news. You'd better act fast.'

'And do what, exactly?'

'You're perfectly capable, my dear, of taking care of this problem before that FBI agent returns. I might just remind you what is at stake here. So don't play games. Hit hard. And if you decide to hire out, only hire the best. Whatever you do, I don't want to know about it.'

'What a coward you are.'

'Thank you. I'm quite willing to concede that you're the one in this family with the high testosterone, dear cousin.'

Kermode pressed the SPEAKERPHONE button with an angry jab, ending the phone call.

Montebello had remained silent throughout the conversation, his attention seemingly focused on his well-manicured nails. Now, however, he looked up. 'Leave this to me,' he said. 'I know just the person for the job.'

CHAPTER 36

Espelette, the upscale brasserie off the lobby of the Connaught Hotel, was a cream-and-white confection of tall windows and crisp linen tablecloths. The climatic change from Roaring Fork was most welcome. London had so far been blessed with a mild winter, and mellow afternoon sunlight flooded the gently curving space. Special Agent Pendergast, seated at a large table overlooking Mount Street, rose to his feet as Roger Kleefisch entered the restaurant. The figure was, Pendergast noted, a trifle stouter, his face seamed and leathery. Kleefisch had been practically bald even as a student at Oxford, so the shiny pate was no surprise. The man still walked with a brisk step, moving with his body thrust forward, nose cutting the air with the anxious curiosity of a bloodhound on a scent. It was these qualities – as much as the man's credentials as a Baker Street Irregular – that had given Pendergast confidence in his choice of partner for this particular adventure.

'Pendergast!' Kleefisch said, extending his hand with a broad smile. 'You look exactly the same. Well, almost the same.'

'My dear Kleefisch,' Pendergast replied, shaking the proffered hand. They had both fallen easily into the Oxbridge convention of referring to each other by their last names.

'Look at you: back at Oxford, I'd always assumed you'd been in mourning. But I see that was a misapprehension. Black suits you.' Kleefisch sat down. 'Can you believe this weather? I don't think Mayfair has ever looked so beautiful.'

'Indeed,' said Pendergast. 'And I noted this morning, with no little satisfaction, that the temperature in Roaring Fork had dropped below zero.'

'How dreadful.' Kleefisch shivered.

A waiter approached the table, laid out menus before them, and withdrew.

'I'm so glad you were able to catch the morning flight,' Kleefisch said, rubbing his hands as he looked over the menu. 'The "chic and shock" afternoon tea here is especially delightful. And they serve the best Kir Royale in London.'

'It is good to be back in civilization. Roaring Fork, for all its money – or perhaps because of it – is a boorish, uncouth town.'

'You mentioned something about a fire.' The smile faded from Kleefisch's face. 'The arsonist you spoke of struck again?'

Pendergast nodded.

'Oh, dear . . . On a brighter note, I think you'll be pleased with a discovery I've made. I'm hopeful your trip across the pond won't prove entirely in vain.'

The waiter returned. Pendergast ordered a glass of Laurent-Perrier champagne and a ginger scone with clotted cream, and Kleefisch a variety of finger sandwiches. The Irregular watched the waiter move away, then reached into his fat lawyer's briefcase, withdrew a slender book, and slid it across the table.

Pendergast picked it up. It was by Ellery Queen, and was titled *Queen's Quorum: A History of the Detective Crime Short Story As Revealed in the 106 Most Important Books Published in This Field Since 1845.*

'*Queen's Quorum,*' Pendergast murmured, gazing over the cover. 'I recall you mentioning Ellery Queen in our phone conversation.'

'You've heard of him, of course.'

'Yes. Them, to be more accurate.'

'Precisely. Two cousins, working under a pseudonym. Perhaps the preeminent anthologizers of detective stories. Not to mention being authors in their own right.' Kleefisch tapped the volume in Pendergast's hands. 'And this book is probably the most famous critical work on crime fiction – a collection, and study, of the greatest works in the genre. That's a first edition, by the way. But here's the odd thing: despite its title, *Queen's Quorum* has 107 entries – not 106. Have a look at *this.*'

And taking the book back, he opened it, turned to the contents page, and indicated an entry with his finger:

258

74. Anthony Wynne – *Sinner Go Secretly* – 1927

75. Susan Glaspell – *A Jury of Her Peers* – 1927

76. Dorothy L. Sayers – *Lord Peter Views the Body* – 1928

77. G.D.H. & M. Cole – *Superintendent Wilson's Holiday* – 1928

78. W. Somerset Maugham – *Ashenden* – 1928

78A. Arthur Conan Doyle – *The Adventure of* (?) – 1928 (?)

79. Percival Wilde – *Rogues in Clover* – 1929

'Do you see that?' Kleefisch said with something like triumph in his voice. '*Queen's Quorum* number seventy-eight A. Title uncertain. Date of composition uncertain. Even the existence uncertain: hence the *A*. And no entry in the main text – just a mention in the contents. But clearly, Queen had – most likely due to his preeminence in the field – heard enough about its rarity, secondhand, to believe it worth inclusion in his book. Or then again, maybe not. Because when the book was later revised in 1967, bringing the list up to one hundred twenty-five books, *seventy-eight A was left out.*'

'And you think this is our missing Holmes story.' Kleefisch nodded.

Their tea arrived. 'Uniquely, Conan Doyle has

a prior entry in the book,' Kleefisch said, taking a bite of a smoked salmon and wasabi cream sandwich. '*The Adventures of Sherlock Holmes. Queen's Quorum* number sixteen.'

'Then it would seem that the obvious next step should be to determine just what Ellery Queen knew about this Holmes story, and where he – they – learned it from.'

'Unfortunately, no. Believe me, the Irregulars have been down that path countless times. As you might imagine, *Queen's Quorum* seventy-eight A is one of the seminal bugbears of our organization. A special title has been created and is waiting to be conferred on the member who tracks down that story. The two cousins have been dead for decades and left behind no shred of evidence regarding either why seventy-eight A was in the first edition of *Queen's Quorum* or why it was later removed.'

Pendergast took a sip of champagne. 'This is encouraging.'

'Indeed.' Kleefisch put the book aside. 'Long ago, the Irregulars amassed a large number of letters from Conan Doyle's later life. To date, we have not allowed outside scholars to examine the letters – we wish to mine them for our own scholarly publications in the *Journal* and elsewhere. However, the late-in-life letters have for the most part been ignored, since they deal with that time in Conan Doyle's life when he was heavily involved in spiritualism, writing such nonfiction works as

The Coming of the Fairies and *The Edge of the Unknown* while Holmes was set aside.'

Kleefisch picked up another finger sandwich, this one of teriyaki chicken and grilled aubergine. He took a bite, then another, closing his eyes as he chewed. He wiped his fingers daintily on a linen napkin, and then – with a mischievous twinkle in his eye – he reached into the pocket of his jacket and pulled out two worn, faded letters.

'I am hereby swearing you to secrecy,' he told Pendergast. 'I have, ah, temporarily borrowed these. You wouldn't want to see me blackballed.'

'You have my assurance of silence.'

'Very good. In that case, I don't mind telling you that both of these letters were written by Conan Doyle in 1929 – the year before his death. Each is addressed to a Mr Robert Creighton, a novelist and fellow spiritualist that Conan Doyle befriended in his last years.' Kleefisch unfolded one. 'This first letter mentions, in passing: "I expect any day to receive news of the Aspern Hall business, which has been pressing on my mind rather severely of late."' He refolded the letter, returned it to his pocket, and turned to the other. 'The second letter mentions, also in passing: "Have learned bad news about Aspern Hall. I am now in a quandary about how to proceed – or whether I should proceed at all. And yet I cannot rest easy until I've seen the matter through."'

Kleefisch put the letter away. 'Now, all the Irregulars who've read these letters – and there

261

have not been many – assumed that Conan Doyle was involved in some sort of real estate speculation. But I spent all of yesterday morning going over the rolls of both England and Scotland . . . and there is no record of any Aspern Hall on the register. *It does not exist.*'

'So you're suggesting that Aspern Hall is not a place – but a story title?'

Kleefisch smiled. 'Maybe – just maybe – it's the title of Conan Doyle's rejected tale: "The Adventure of Aspern Hall."'

'Where could the story be?'

'We know where it isn't. It's not in his house. After being bedridden for months with angina pectoris, Conan Doyle died in July 1930 at Windlesham, his home in Crowborough. In the years since, countless Irregulars and other Holmes scholars have traveled down to East Sussex and explored every inch of that house. Partial manuscripts, letters, other documents were found – but no missing Holmes story. That's why I can't help but fear that . . .' Kleefisch hesitated. 'That the story's been destroyed.'

Pendergast shook his head. 'Recall what Conan Doyle said in that second letter: that he was in a quandary about how to proceed; that he couldn't rest until he'd *seen the matter through*. That doesn't sound like a man who would later destroy the story.'

Kleefisch listened, nodding slowly.

'The same cathartic urge that prompted Conan

Doyle to write the story in the first place would have prompted him to preserve it. If I had any doubts before, that entry in *Queen's Quorum* has silenced them. That story is out there – somewhere. And it may just contain the information I seek.'

'Which is?' Kleefisch asked keenly.

'I can't speak of it yet. But I promise you that if we find the story – you'll be the one to publish.'

'Excellent!' He brought his hands together.

'And so the game – to coin a phrase – is afoot.' With that, Pendergast drained his glass of champagne and signaled the waiter for another.

CHAPTER 37

Stacy was proving to be a big-time sleeper, often not rising until ten or eleven, Corrie thought as she dragged herself out of bed in the dark and eyed with envy the form through the open door, sleeping in the other bedroom. She remembered being like that before figuring out what she wanted to do with her life.

Instead of making coffee in her tiny kitchen, Corrie decided to drive into town and splurge on a Starbucks. She hated the freezing house, and even with Stacy Bowdree in residence she spent as little time there as she could.

She glanced at the outdoor thermometer: two degrees below zero. The temperature just kept dropping. She bundled up in a hat, gloves, and down coat, and made her way out to the driveway where her car was parked. As she dusted it off – a very light snow had fallen the night before – she once again regretted her outburst at Wynn Marple. It had been stupid to burn that bridge. But it was vintage Corrie, with her temper and her long-standing inability to suffer jerks. That behavior might have worked in Medicine Creek, when she was still a rebellious high-school student. But there was no excusing it anymore – not here, and not now. She simply *had* to stop lashing out at people – especially when she knew all too well that it was counterproductive to her own best interests.

She started the car and eased down the steep driveway to Ravens Ravine Road. The sky was gray, and the snow had started falling yet again. The weather report said a lot more was on the way – which in a ski resort like Roaring Fork was greeted as a farmer greets rain, with celebration and chatter. Corrie for her part was sick to death of it. Maybe it really was time to cash in her chips and get out of town.

She drove slowly, as there were often patches of ice on the hairpin road going down the canyon and her rental car, with its crappy tires, had lousy traction.

So what now? She had at most a day or two more of work on the skeletons – crossing the T's forensically, so to speak. Then that would be that. Even though it seemed unlikely, she would see if Ted had any more ideas about where she might find clues to the identity of the killers – tactfully, since of course he didn't know the truth about how the miners had really died. He'd asked her out again, for dinner tomorrow; she made a mental note to talk to him about it then.

Six days before Christmas. Her father had been begging her to come to Pennsylvania and spend it with him. He would even send her the money for airfare. Perhaps it was a sign. Perhaps . . .

A loud noise, a shuddering *BANG!*, caused her to jam on the brakes and scream involuntarily. The car screeched and slid, but didn't quite go off the road, instead coming to a stop sideways.

'What the *hell*?' Corrie gripped the steering wheel. What had happened? Something had shattered her windshield, turning it into an opaque web of cracks.

And then she saw the small, perfectly round hole at their center.

With another scream she ducked down, scrunching herself below the door frame. All was silent as her mind raced a mile a minute. That was a bullet hole. Someone had tried to shoot her. Kill her.

Shit, shit, shit . . .

She had to get out of there. Taking a deep breath and tensing, she swung herself back up, punched at the sagging window with her gloved hand, ripped a hole big enough to see through, then grabbed the wheel again and jammed on the gas. The Focus skidded around and she managed to get it under control, expecting more shots at any moment. In her panic she accelerated too fast; the car hit a patch of ice and slid again, heading for the guardrail above the ravine. The car ricocheted off it, slid back onto the road with a screech of rubber, and turned around another hundred eighty degrees. Corrie was shaken but – after a brief, panicked moment – realized she was unhurt.

'*Shit!*' she screamed again. The shooter was still out there, might even be coming down the road after her. The car had stalled and the passenger side was all bashed up, but it didn't seem to be a total wreck; she turned the key and the engine came to life. She eased the Focus back around, forcing herself to do a careful three-point turn, and drove down the road. The car still ran, but it made a nasty noise – a fender seemed to be scraping one of the tires.

Slowly, carefully, hands trembling on the steering wheel, she guided the vehicle down the mountain and into town, heading straight for the police department.

After Corrie had filled out an incident report, the sergeant behind the desk promptly showed her into the chief's office. Apparently, she was now a person of importance. She found Chief Morris behind his desk, which was heaped with three-by-five cards, photographs, string, pins, and glue. On the wall behind him was an incomprehensible chart that was no doubt related to the arson killings.

The chief looked like death warmed over. His cheeks hung like slabs of suet on his face, his eyes were sunken coals, his hair was unkempt. At the same time, there was a severe cast to his eye that hadn't been there before. That, at least, was an improvement.

He took the report and gestured for her to sit. A few minutes went by while he read it, then read it again. And then he laid it on the table. 'Is there any reason you can think of that someone might be unhappy with you?' he asked.

At this Corrie, shaken as she was, had to laugh. 'Yeah. Like just about everyone in The Heights. The mayor. Kermode. Montebello. Not to mention you.'

The chief managed a wan smile. 'We're going to open an investigation, of course. But . . . listen, I hope you won't think I'm trying to brush this off if I tell you we've been looking for a poacher up in that area for several weeks now. He's been killing and butchering deer, no doubt selling the meat. One of his wild shots went through the window of a house just last week. So what happened to you might – *might* – have been a stray shot from his poaching activity. This happened early in the morning, which is when the deer – and our poacher – are active. Again, I'm not saying that's what happened. I'm just mentioning it as a possibility . . . to ease your mind more than anything.'

'Thanks,' said Corrie.

They rose, and the chief held out his hand. 'I'm afraid I'll have to impound your car as evidence – do a ballistics analysis and see if we can recover the round.'

'You're welcome to it.'

'I'll have one of my officers drive you where you need to go.'

'No, thanks, I'm just going around the corner for a Starbucks.'

As Corrie sat sipping her coffee, she wondered if it really had been a poacher. It was true she had annoyed a lot of people early on, but that had blown over, especially with the start of the arson killings. Shooting at her car – that would be attempted murder. What kind of threat was she to merit that? Problem was, the chief was so overwhelmed – as was everyone else in the police department – that she had little faith he would be able to conduct an effective investigation. If the shooting was meant to intimidate her, it wasn't going to work. She might be frightened – but there was no way she'd be frightened out of town. If anything, it would make her want to stay longer.

Then again . . . it might be the poacher. Or it could be some other random crazy. It could even be the serial arsonist, switching M.O.'s. Her thoughts turned to Stacy up in the ravine, probably still asleep. She was eventually going to come into town, and she might also be in danger, get shot at, too.

She pulled out her cell phone and dialed Stacy. A sleepy voice answered. As soon as Corrie started telling her the story, she woke up fast.

'Somebody shot up your car? I'm going looking for the mother.'

'Wait. Don't do that. That's crazy. Let the police handle it.'

'His tracks will be out there, in the snow. I'll

follow the fucker back to whatever spider hole he crawled out of.'

'No, *please*.' It took Corrie ten minutes to persuade Stacy not to do it. As Corrie was about to hang up, Stacy said: 'I hope he shoots at *my* car. I've got a couple of Black Talon rounds just itching to explore his inner psyche.'

Next, she called Rent-a-Junker. The agent went on and on about how the chief of police himself had just called, how awful being shot at must've been, was she all right, did she need a doctor . . . And would an upgrade – a Ford Explorer? – be acceptable, at no extra charge, of course?

Corrie smiled as she hung up. The chief seemed to be acquiring, at long last, a bit of backbone.

CHAPTER 38

Roger Kleefisch sprawled in one of the two velvet-lined armchairs in the sitting room of his London town house, feet on the bearskin rug, his entire frame drinking in the welcome warmth from the crackling fire on the grate. Agent Pendergast sat in the other chair, motionless, his eyes gazing into the flames. When Kleefisch had let him in, the FBI agent had glanced around at the room, raising his eyebrows but making no other comment. And yet, somehow, Kleefisch felt that he approved.

He rarely let anyone into his sitting room, and he couldn't help but feel a little like Sherlock Holmes himself, here at home, partner in detection at his side. The thought managed to lift his spirits a little. Although, were he to be honest with himself, he should probably be assuming the role of Watson. After all, Pendergast was the professional detective here.

At last, Pendergast shifted, placed his whisky-and-soda on a side table. 'So, Kleefisch. What have you uncovered so far?'

It was the question Kleefisch had been dreading.

He swallowed, took a deep breath, and spoke. 'Nothing, I'm afraid.'

The pale eyes gazed at him intently. 'Indeed?'

'I've tried everything over these last twenty-four hours,' he replied. 'I've looked back through old correspondence, read and re-read Conan Doyle's diary. I've examined every book, every treatise on the man's last years that I could find. I've even tried picking the brains – circumspectly – of several of our most brilliant Investitures. I've found nothing, not even a trace of evidence. And I must say, despite my initial enthusiasm, it doesn't come as a surprise. All this ground had been covered so thoroughly by Irregulars in the past. I was a fool to think there might be something new.'

Pendergast did not speak. With the firelight flickering over his gaunt features, his head bowed, an expression of intense thought on his face, surrounded by Victorian trappings, he suddenly looked so much like Holmes himself that Kleefisch was taken aback.

'I'm truly sorry, Pendergast,' Kleefisch said, averting his gaze to the bearskin rug. 'I was so hopeful.' He paused. 'I fear you're on a wild goose chase – one that I may have encouraged. I apologize for that.'

After a moment, Pendergast stirred. 'On the contrary. You've already done a great deal. You confirmed my suspicions about the missing Holmes story. You showed me the evidence in *Queen's Quorum*. You made the connection, in Conan Doyle's letters, to Aspern Hall. Almost despite yourself, you've convinced me not only that "The Adventure of Aspern Hall" existed – but that it still exists. I must locate it.'

'For an Irregular like me, a Holmes scholar, that would be the coup of a lifetime. But again I have to ask – why is it so important to you?'

Pendergast hesitated a moment. 'I have certain ideas, conjectures, that this story might confirm – or not.'

'Conjectures about what?'

A small smile curled Pendergast's lip. 'You – a Holmes scholar – encouraging an investigator to indulge in vulgar speculation? My dear Kleefisch!'

As this Kleefisch colored.

'While I normally despise those who claim a sixth sense,' Pendergast said, 'in this case I *feel* that the lost story is at the center of all mysteries here – past and present.'

'In that case,' Kleefisch finally said, 'I'm sorry I've come up empty.'

'Fear not,' Pendergast replied. 'I haven't.'

Kleefisch raised his eyebrows.

Pendergast went on. 'I proceeded on the assumption that the more I could learn about Conan Doyle's final years, the closer I'd come to finding the lost story. I focused my efforts on the circle of spiritualists he belonged to in the years before he died. I learned that this group frequently met at a small cottage named Covington Grange, on the edge of Hampstead Heath. The cottage was owned by a spiritualist by the name of Mary Wilkes. Conan Doyle had a small room at Covington Grange where he would sometimes write essays on spirituality, which he would read to the group of an evening.'

'Fascinating,' Kleefisch said.

'Allow me to pose this question: is it not likely that, while writing his late texts on spiritualism at Covington Grange, he also wrote his final Sherlock Holmes story, "The Adventure of Aspern Hall"?'

Kleefisch felt a quickening of excitement. It made sense. And this was an avenue that had never, to his knowledge, been explored by a fellow Irregular.

'Given its incendiary nature, isn't it also possible that the author might not have hidden it somewhere in that little room he used for writing, or somewhere else in the Grange?'

'Might he not indeed!' Kleefisch rose from his chair. 'My God. No wonder the manuscript was never found at Windlesham! So what's next, then?'

'What's next? I should have thought that obvious. Covington Grange is next.'

CHAPTER 39

Teacup in hand, Dorothea Pembroke stepped back into her tidy alcove at the Blackpool headquarters of the National Trust for Places of Historic Interest or Natural Beauty. It was past ten forty-five, and Miss Pembroke was almost as serious about her elevenses as she was about her position, about which she was very serious indeed. A cloth napkin, placed daintily upon the desktop; a cup of Harrisons & Crosfield jasmine tea, one lump; and a wheatmeal biscuit dipped twice – not once, not three times – into the cup before being nibbled.

In many ways, Ms Pembroke felt, she *was* the National Trust. There were more important jobs than hers in the nonprofit association, of course, but nobody could boast a finer pedigree. Her grandfather, Sir Erskine Pembroke, had been master of Chiddingham Place, one of the more impressive stately homes in Cornwall. But his company had failed, and when the family realized they couldn't maintain either the taxes or the upkeep of the mansion, they entered into talks with the National Trust. The building's foundations and general fabric were restored, its gardens expanded, and ultimately Chiddingham Place was opened to visitors, while the family stayed on in modest rooms on the top floor. A few years later, her father had taken a position with the National Trust, as a development manager. As soon as she was out of school, Miss Pembroke had joined the Trust herself, rising over the past thirty-two years to the position of deputy administrator.

All in all, a most satisfactory rise.

As she put away the teacup and was folding the napkin, she became aware that a man was standing in the doorway. She was much too well bred to show surprise, but she paused just a moment before giving the napkin a final fold and placing it away in her desk. He was a rather striking-looking man – tall and pale, with white-blond hair and eyes the color of glacial ice, dressed in a well-cut black suit – but she did not recognize him, and visitors were usually announced.

'Forgive me,' he said in an American accent – southern – accompanied by a charming smile. 'I don't mean to intrude, Ms Pembroke. But the secretary in your outer office was away from her desk, and, well, we *did* have an appointment.'

Dorothea Pembroke opened her book and glanced at the current day's page. Yes, indeed: she did have an eleven fifteen appointment with a Mr Pendergast. She recalled that he had particularly asked to see her, as opposed to an administrator – most unusual. Still, he had not been announced, and she did not hold with such informality. But the man had a winning way about him, and she was prepared to overlook this breach of propriety.

'May I sit down?' he asked, with another smile.

Miss Pembroke nodded toward an empty seat before her desk. 'What, may I inquire, do you wish to speak with me about?'

'I wish to visit one of your properties.'

'Visit?' she said, allowing the faintest tinge of disapproval to color her voice. 'We have volunteers out in front who can assist you with that.' Really, it was too much, her being bothered with such a trivial request.

'I do apologize,' the man replied. 'I don't wish to take up your valuable time. I spoke about the matter with Visitor Services, and they referred me to you.'

'I see.' That did put another spin on things. And, really, the man had the most courtly manners. Even his accent spoke of breeding – not one of those harsh, barbarous American drawls. 'Before we get started, we have a little regulation here. We require visitor identification, if you please.'

The man smiled again. He had beautifully white teeth. He reached into his black suit and removed a leather wallet, which he laid open upon the table, exposing a brilliance of gold on top with a photo ID card below. Miss Pembroke was startled.

'Oh! Goodness! The Federal Bureau of Investigation? Is this . . . a criminal matter?'

The man gave a most winning smile. 'Oh, no, don't be the slightest bit alarmed. This is a personal matter, nothing official. I would have shown you my passport, but it's in the hotel safe.'

Miss Pembroke allowed her fluttering heart to subside. She had never been involved in a criminal matter and looked on such a possibility with abhorrence.

'Well, then, Mr Pendergast, that is reassuring, and I am at your service. Please tell me the property you'd like to visit?'

'A cottage named Covington Grange.'

'Covington Grange. Covington Grange.' Miss Pembroke was not familiar with the name. But then again, the Trust had hundreds of properties in its care – including many of England's greatest estates – and she could not be expected to remember all of them.

'Half a moment.' She turned to her computer, moused through a few menus, and entered the name into the waiting field. Several photos and a long textual entry appeared on the screen. As she read the entry, she realized she did have a faint recollection of the site. No wonder the people at Visitor Services recommended the man speak to an administrator.

She turned back. 'Covington Grange,' she said again. 'Formerly owned by Leticia Wilkes, who died in 1980, leaving it to the government.'

The man named Pendergast nodded.

'I'm very sorry to tell you, Mr Pendergast, that

a visit to Covington Grange is out of the question.'

At this news, a look of devastation crossed the man's face. He struggled to master himself. 'The visit needn't be a long one, Ms Pembroke.'

'I'm sorry, it's quite impossible. According to the file, the cottage has been shut up for decades, closed to the public while the Trust decides what to do with it.'

Poor man – he looked so desolated that even Dorothea Pembroke's hard and ever so correct heart began to soften. 'It's suffered serious damage from the elements,' she said, by way of explanation. 'It is unsafe and requires extensive conservation before we could ever allow anyone inside. And at present, our funds – as you might imagine – are limited. There are numerous other properties, more important properties, that also need attention. And, to be frank, it is of marginal historical interest.'

Mr Pendergast looked down, clasping and unclasping his hands. Finally, he spoke. 'I thank you for taking the time to explain the situation. It makes perfect sense. It's just—' And here, Mr Pendergast looked up again, meeting her gaze – 'It's just that I am Leticia Wilkes's last remaining descendant.'

Miss Pembroke looked at him in surprise.

'She was my grandmother. Of the family line, only I remain. My mother died of cancer last year, and my father was killed in a train accident the year before. My . . . sister was killed just three weeks ago, in a robbery gone bad. So, you see . . .' Mr Pendergast paused a moment to collect himself. 'You see, Covington Grange is all I have left. It is where I spent my summers as a boy, before my mother took us to America. It contains all the happy memories I have of my lost family.'

'Oh, I see.' This was a heartbreaking story indeed.

'I just wanted to see the place one last time, just once, before the contents go to wrack and ruin. And . . . in particular, there's an old family photo album I remember paging through as a boy, put up in a cupboard, which I'd like to take – if that's all right with you. I have nothing, *nothing*, of the family. We left everything behind when we went to America.'

Miss Pembroke listened to this tragic story, pity welling up in her heart. After a moment she cleared her throat. Pity was one thing, *duty* quite another.

'As I've said, I'm very sorry,' she said. 'But for all the reasons I've told you, it's simply out of the question. And in any case all the contents belong to the Trust, even the photographs, which might hold historic interest.'

'But they're just rotting away! It's been over thirty years and nothing's been done!' Pendergast's voice had taken on a wheedling tone. 'Just ten minutes inside? Five? Nobody would have to know besides you and me.'

This insinuation – that she might be privy to an underhanded scheme unbeknownst to the

Trust – broke the spell. 'That is out of the question. I am surprised you would make such an overture.'

'And that's your final word?'

Miss Pembroke gave a curt nod.

'I see.' The man's air changed. The forlorn expression, the faint tremor in the voice, vanished. He sat back in his chair and regarded her with quite a different expression than before. There was suddenly something in the expression – something Miss Pembroke could not quite put a finger on – that was ever so faintly alarming.

'This is of such importance to me,' said the man, 'that I will go to unreasonable lengths to achieve it.'

'I'm not sure what that means, but my mind is made up,' she said with absolute firmness.

'I greatly fear that your recalcitrance leaves me no choice.' And, reaching into his pocket, the FBI agent pulled out a quire of papers and held them up.

'What is this?' she demanded.

'I have information here that might prove of interest to you.' The man's tone of voice had changed, as well. 'I understand your family used to reside at Chiddingham Place?'

'Not that it can be of any interest to you, but they still do.'

'Yes. On the fourth floor. The material I think you'll find to be particularly interesting concerns your grandfather.' He placed the papers

281

on her desk with a courtly motion. 'I have here information – *incontrovertible* information – that during the final months of his business, just before he went bankrupt, he borrowed against the value of the stocks of his own shareholders in a desperate attempt to keep the company alive. To do so, he not only committed serious financial fraud, but he also lied to the bank, claiming the securities as his own.' He paused. 'His criminal actions left many of his shareholders penniless, among whom were a number of widows and pensioners who, subsequently, died in abject penury. I fear the story makes highly unpleasant reading.'

He paused.

'I'm sure, Ms Pembroke, you would not wish the good name of your grandfather – and of the Pembroke family by extension – to be sullied.' The man paused to display his white teeth. 'So wouldn't it be in your best interests to give me temporary access to Covington Grange? A small thing. I think it would work out best for everyone – don't you?'

It was that final, cold smile – those small, even, perfect teeth – that did it. Miss Dorothea Pembroke went rigid. Then, slowly, she rose from her chair. Just as slowly, she picked up the papers the man Pendergast had left on her desk. And then, with a disdainful motion, she tossed them at his feet.

'You have the effrontery to come into my office and attempt to blackmail me?' Her voice remained remarkably calm, surprising her. 'I have never in my life been subjected to such appalling behavior. You, sir, are nothing more than a confidence man. I wouldn't be surprised if that story you told me was as false as I suspect that badge is.'

'True or false, the information I have on your grandfather is rock-solid. Give me what I want or I hand it over to the police. Think of your family.'

'My duty is to my office and the truth. No less, no more. If you wish to destroy my family's name, if you wish to drag us through the muck, if you wish to take what little financial security we have – so be it. I shall live with that. What I shall *not* live with is a breach of my responsibility. And so I say to you, Mr Pendergast—' she extended her arm, pointing a steady finger at the exit, her voice quiet yet unyielding – 'leave this building at once, or I shall have you bodily ejected. Good day.'

Standing on the front steps of the National Trust for Places of Historic Interest or Natural Beauty, Agent Pendergast glanced around for a moment, the look of exasperation slowly giving away to a very different expression: admiration. True courage sometimes revealed itself in the most unlikely places. Few could have resisted such a thorough assault; Miss Pembroke, who was, after all, just doing her job, was one in a thousand. His thin lips twitched in a smile. Then he tossed the papers into a nearby trash can. And – as he descended the steps, heading for the station and the train back to London – he quoted under his breath: "'To Sherlock Holmes she is always *the* woman. I have seldom heard him mention her under any other name. In his eyes she eclipses and predominates the whole of her sex . . .'"

CHAPTER 40

Mockey Jones was smashed again and glad of it. Jones often thought of himself in the third person, and the little voice in his head was telling him that here was Mockey Jones, titubating down East Main Street, feeling no pain (or cold), with five expensive martinis and an eighty-dollar steak in his gut, his loins recently exercised, with a wallet full of cash and credit cards, no job, no work, and no worries.

Mockey Jones was one of the one percenters – actually one of the one-tenth of one-tenth of one percenters – and, while he hadn't actually earned a dime of his money, it didn't matter because money was money and it was better to have it than not have it, and better to have a lot of it than only some. And Mockey Jones had a lot of it.

Mockey Jones was forty-nine and had left three wives and as many children scattered in his wake – he gave a little bow as he proceeded down the street in homage to them – but now he was un-attached and totally irresponsible, with nothing to do but ski, eat, drink, screw, and yell at his invest-ment advisors. Mockey Jones was very happy to live in Roaring Fork. It was his kind of town. People didn't mind who you were or what you did as long as you were rich. And not just millionaire rich – that was bullshit. The country was lousy with cheap middle-class millionaires. Such people were despised in Roaring Fork. No – you had to be a billionaire, or at least a centimillionaire, to fit into the right circle of people. Jones was himself in the centi category, but while that was an embarrassment he had gotten used to, the two hundred million he had inherited from his jerk-off father – another bow to the memory – was adequate for his needs.

He stopped, looked around. Christ, he should have pissed back at the restaurant. This damn town had no public restrooms. And where the hell had he left his car? Didn't matter – he wasn't stupid enough to get behind the wheel in his condition. No way would there ever be the headline in the *Roaring Fork Times*: MOCKEY JONES ARRESTED FOR DUI. He would call one of the late-night drunk limo services, of which there were several, kept busy squiring home those like Mockey who had 'dined too well.' He pulled out his cell phone, but it slipped out of his gloved hands and landed in a snowbank; with an extravagant curse he bent down, picked it up, brushed it off, and hit the appropriate speed dial. In a moment he had arranged for the ride. Those martinis back at Brierly's Steak House had sure tasted good, and he was looking forward to another when he got home.

Standing at the curb, swaying slightly, waiting for the limo, Mockey Jones became vaguely aware of something rapidly intruding on his right field of vision. Something yellowish – and glowing unnaturally. He turned and saw, in the Mountain Laurel neighborhood on the eastern hillside just at the end of town, not even a quarter mile away, a large house literally exploding in flames. Even as he watched, he could feel the heat of it on his cheek, see the flames leaping ever higher into the air, the sparks rising like stars into the dark sky . . . And – oh, dear God – was that someone in an upstairs window, silhouetted by fire? Even as he watched, the window exploded and the body came tumbling out like a flaming comet, writhing, with a hideous scream that cut like a knife through the midnight air, echoing and re-echoing off the mountains as if it would never end, even after the burning body had disappeared below the fir trees. Almost immediately, within seconds it seemed, sirens were going off; there were police cars and fire trucks and bystanders in the streets; and – moments later – television vans with dishes on their roofs careening about. Last of all came the choppers, plastered with call signs, sweeping in low over the trees.

And then, with that hideous scream still echoing in his confused and petrified brain, Mockey Jones felt something first warm, then cool, between his legs. A moment later he realized he'd pissed his pants.

CHAPTER 41

Corrie Swanson eased the rented Explorer into the driveway, and looked up at the cold, dark house. Not a light was on, even though Stacy's car was in the driveway. Where was she? For some reason, Corrie found herself worrying about Stacy, feeling oddly protective toward her, when in fact she had hoped the opposite would happen – that Stacy would make her feel safe.

Stacy had probably gone to bed, even though she seemed to be a late-to-bed, later-to-rise person. Or maybe a date had picked her up in his car and they were still out.

Corrie got out of the car, locked it, and went into the house. The kitchen light had been turned off. That settled it: Stacy was asleep.

A helicopter flew low overhead, then another. During her drive up the canyon, there had been a lot of chopper activity, accompanied by the faint sound of sirens coming from the town. She hoped it wasn't another house burning down.

Her date with Ted hadn't quite ended as she'd hoped. She wasn't sure why, but at the last minute

288

she'd turned down his request to come back with her and warm her cold bed. She'd been tempted, exceedingly tempted, and she could still feel her lips tingling from his long kisses. Jesus, why had she said no?

It had been a wonderful evening. They'd eaten at a fancy restaurant in an old stone building that had been beautifully renovated, cozy and romantic, with candles and low lighting. The food had been excellent. Corrie, feeling famished, had consumed a gigantic porterhouse steak, rare, accompanied by a pint of ale, scalloped potatoes (her favorite), a romaine salad, and finished off with a brownie sundae that was positively obscene. They had talked and talked, especially about that jackass, Marple, and about Kermode. Ted had been fascinated – and shocked – to learn that Kermode was related to the infamous Stafford family. Having grown up in The Heights, he had known Kermode a long time and come to loathe her, but to learn she was part of the heartless family that had exploited and squeezed the town during the mining days really set him off. In turn, he told her an interesting fact: the Stafford family had originally owned the land The Heights had been built on – and their holding company still owned the development rights to the Phase III portion, slated to launch as soon as the new spa and clubhouse opened.

Putting away these thoughts, Corrie stepped out of the kitchen and into the central corridor.

Something made her uneasy – there was a foreign feeling she couldn't quite pinpoint, a strange smell. She walked through the house and headed to their rooms to check on Stacy.

Her bed was empty.

'Stacy?'

No answer.

Suddenly she remembered the dog. 'Jack?'

There hadn't been any barking, leaping, crazy little mutt to greet her. Now she was starting to freak out. She went down the little hall, calling the dog's name.

Still nothing.

She headed back into the main portion of the house. Maybe he was hiding somewhere, or had gotten lost. '*Jack?*'

Pausing to listen, she heard a muffled whine and a scratching sound. It came from the grand living room – a room that had been shut up and which she'd been strictly forbidden to enter. She went to the closed set of pocket doors. 'Jack?'

Another whine and bark, accompanied by more scratching.

She felt her heart pounding. Something was very, very wrong.

She placed her hand on the doors, found them unlocked, and slowly pulled them apart. Immediately, Jack rushed out from the darkness beyond, crouching and whining and licking her, tail clamped between his legs.

'Who put you in here, Jack?'

She looked about the dark room. It seemed quiet, empty – and then she saw a dark outline of a figure on the sofa.

'Hey!' she cried in surprise.

Jack cowered behind her, whining.

The figure moved a little, very slowly.

'Who are you and what are you doing here?' Corrie demanded. This was stupid. She should get out, now.

'Oh,' came a thick voice out of the blackness. 'It's you.'

'Stacy?'

No answer.

'Good God, are you all right?'

'Fine, no problem,' came the slurred voice again.

Corrie turned on the lights. And there was Stacy, slumped on the sofa, a fifth of Jim Beam half empty in front of her. She was still bundled up in her winter clothes – scarf, hat, and all. A small puddle of water lay at her feet, and watery tracks led to the sofa.

'Oh, no. Stacy!'

Stacy waved her arm, before letting it fall to the sofa. 'Sorry.'

'What have you been doing? Were you outside?'

'Out for a walk. Looking for that mother who shot up your car.'

'But I *told* you not to do that. You could have frozen to death out there!' Corrie noticed that Stacy was packing, a .45 holstered to her hip. Jesus, she would have to get that gun away.

'Don't worry about me.'

'I do worry about you. I'm *totally* worried about you!'

'Come on, siddown, have a drink. Relax.'

Corrie sat but ignored the offer of a drink. 'Stacy, what's going on?'

At this Stacy hung her head. 'I dunno. Nothing. My life sucks.'

Corrie took her hand. No wonder the dog had been freaked out. 'I'm sorry. I feel the same way myself sometimes. You want to talk about it?'

'My military career – shot. No family. No friends. Nothing. There's nothing in my life but a box of old bones to haul back to Kentucky. And for what purpose? What a fucked-up idea that was.'

'But your military career. You're a captain. All those medals and citations – you can do anything . . .'

'My life's fucked. I was discharged.'

'You mean . . . you didn't resign?'

Stacy shook her head. 'Medical discharge.'

'Wounded?'

'PTSD.'

A silence. 'Oh, Jesus. I'm sorry, I really am.'

There was a long pause. Then Stacy spoke again. 'You have *no* idea. I get these rages – no reason. Screaming like a fucking maniac. Or hyper-ventilation: total panic attack. Christ, it's awful. And there's no warning. I feel so *down* sometimes, I can't get out of bed, sleep fourteen hours a day. And then I start doing this shit – drinking. Can't get a job. The medical discharge . . . they see that on a job application, it's like, oh, we can't hire her, she's fucking mental. They've all got yellow ribbons on their cars, but when it comes to hiring a vet with posttraumatic stress disorder? Outta here, bitch.'

She reached out to take up the bottle. Corrie intercepted her and gently grasped it at the same time. 'Don't you think you've had enough?'

Stacy jerked the bottle out of her hand, went to take a swig, and then, all of a sudden, threw it across the room, shattering it against the far wall. 'Fuck, yeah. Enough.'

'Let me help you get to bed.' She took Stacy's arm. Stacy rose unsteadily to her feet while Corrie supported her. God, she stank of bourbon. Corrie felt so sorry for her. She wondered if she could slip the .45 out of its holster unnoticed, but decided that might not be a good idea, might set Stacy off. Just get her into bed and then deal with the gun.

'They catch the fuck shot your car?' Stacy slurred.

'No. They think it might have been a poacher.'

'Poacher, my ass.' She stumbled and Corrie helped right her. 'Couldn't find the bastard's tracks. Too much fresh snow.'

'Let's not worry about that now.'

'I *am* worrying!' She clapped her hand to the sidearm and yanked it out, waving it about. 'I'm gonna smoke that fucker!'

'You know you shouldn't handle a firearm when

you've been drinking,' Corrie said quietly and firmly, controlling her disquiet.

'Yeah. Right. Sorry.' Stacy ejected the magazine, which she fumbled and dropped to the floor, scattering bullets. 'You'd better take it.'

She held it out, butt-first, and Corrie took it.

'Careful, there's still one in the chamber. Lemme eject it for you.'

'I'll do it.' Corrie racked the round out of the chamber, letting it fall to the floor.

'Hey. You know what you're doing, girl!'

'I'd better, since I'm studying law enforcement.'

'Fuck, yeah, you're gonna make a good cop someday. You will. I *like* you, Corrie.'

'Thanks.' She helped Stacy along the hallway toward their rooms. Corrie could hear more choppers overhead, and, through a window, a spotlight from one of them trained on the ground, moving this way and that. Something was happening.

She finally got Stacy tucked under the covers, putting a plastic wastebasket next to the bed in case she puked. Stacy fell asleep instantly.

Corrie went back to the living room and started cleaning up, Jack trailing her. Stacy's drunkenness had freaked out the poor dog. It had freaked her out, as well. As she was straightening up she heard yet another chopper flying overhead. She went to the plate-glass windows and peered into the darkness. She could just see, over the ridge in the direction of town, an intense yellow glow.

CHAPTER 42

Just when things couldn't possibly get worse, they did, thought Chief Morris as he looked at the two wrecked cars blocking Highway 82 and the furious, desperate traffic jam piling up behind. The medevac chopper was just lifting off, rotor wash blowing snow everywhere, as if there weren't enough of it in the air already, carrying away the two victims to the advanced trauma unit at Grand Junction, where at least one of them, shot through the head, was probably going to die. What really infuriated the chief was that no one had been hurt in the accident; instead, it had generated a road-rage incident in which the driver of a BMW X5 had pulled a gun and shot the two occupants of the Geländewagen that had rear-ended him. He could hear the perp now, handcuffed in the back of his cruiser while waiting for the snowcat to arrive, yelling at the top of his lungs about 'self-defense' and 'standing my ground.' So if the victim died – and most people with a .38 round through the skull did – that would mean nine murders in little more than a week. All in a town that hadn't seen a murder in years.

What a nightmare – with no end in sight.

Four days before Christmas, and the snow was now falling heavily, with a prediction of twenty-four to thirty inches over the next three days, with accompanying high winds toward the tail end of the storm. Highway 82 – the only way out of town – was gridlocked because of the accident; the snowplows couldn't operate; the blizzard was quickly getting ahead of them; and in an hour or less the road would have to be closed and all these people sitting furiously in their cars, yelling and honking and screeching like maniacs, would have to be rescued.

McMaster Field had seen nonstop flights out as all the Gulfstreams and other private jets and planes fled the town, but it, too, would soon be closing. And when that happened, Roaring Fork would be bottled up, no way in or out except by snowcat.

He glanced in the rearview mirror, back in the direction of town. The third arson attack had been the worst of all. Not in terms of numbers of deaths, but in terms of the psychological effect it had on Roaring Fork. The burnt house stood just at the edge of town, on the first rise of the hill: a grand old Victorian belonging to Maurice Girault, the celebrity fund manager and New York socialite, number five on the Forbes list, a dashing older fellow with an ego as big as Mount Everest. The victims were himself and his fresh young wife, who looked as if she couldn't be a day over eighteen – and who had precipitated herself out an upper-story window while afire.

The entire town had seen it – and been traumatized. And this snarl of traffic, this road-rage shooting, this classic example of a FUBAR situation, was the result.

His thoughts returned, unwillingly, to Pendergast's now-prophetic words. *The next house will no doubt be equally conspicuous.* And his conclusion: *To send a message.*

But what message?

He returned his gaze to the mess. His idling squad car, with the shooter in the back, had its lights and sirens going – all for show. Idiots fleeing town had blocked both sides of the highway as well as the breakdown lanes, and high banks of snow on either side prevented cars from turning around – creating total gridlock. Even the chief was locked in; despite all his efforts to prevent cars from coming up behind and blocking him, they had.

At least they had managed to temporarily block the way out of town, preventing any more vehicles from adding to the mess. And, thank God, the RFPD had three snowcats, all of which were on their way. Even as he sat in his car, the wipers ineffectually swiping the snow back and forth, he heard the first one approaching. Immediately he grabbed his radio, directing the officer in the cat to get the perp out of there first. An angry crowd had started to gather around his squad car, yelling

297

at the shooter, cursing and threatening him, offering to string him up on the nearest tree, while the perp, for his part, was yelling back, taunting them. It was amazing, just like the days of the vigilantes. The veneer of civilization was thin indeed.

And on top of everything else, Pendergast had vanished, split, gone off to London at the worst possible moment. Chivers, the fire investigator, was now openly at war with the police department, and his own investigators were demoralized, angry, and disagreeing with each other.

Now the second snowcat had arrived, delivering a CSI team and a couple of detectives to document the accident and crime scene and to interview witnesses. The snow was beginning to fall more heavily, big fat flakes coming down fast. Getting out of his squad car, the chief walked back to the cat and climbed aboard, along with some of his other men who needed to get back to town and work the new arson attack. A number of desperate motorists wanted a ride back to town as well, and the chief allowed a few of them – a couple with a baby – to get on board, causing a ruckus among those left behind.

As the vehicle headed back to town through the deep snow on the side of the highway, the chief turned his thoughts again, for the thousandth time, to the central mystery of the arson attacks: what was the message? Was he completely insane? But if that was the case, how could the crimes be so carefully planned and executed?

As they entered the town, the chief was struck – after the chaos down on the highway – by the eerie emptiness of it. It had practically returned to ghost-town status, the streets hung with Christmas decorations and the shop windows stuffed with glittering, expensive merchandise adding a Twilight Zone element. It felt like the day after Armageddon.

The chief wondered if Roaring Fork would ever be the same.

CHAPTER 43

Later that afternoon, on her way back from the ski warehouse, Corrie decided to stop in town and warm up with a cup of hot chocolate while catching up on email. It was dark, the snow was falling, and she knew she should be getting home, but she did not want to face that horrible, cold mansion after spending most of the day freezing in the warehouse, which she had begun to refer to in her head as the 'Siberian torture chamber.'

The snow had lightened a bit as she parked her new Ford Explorer on the street. Since the arson attack of last evening, there was parking everywhere, when before you practically had to give up your firstborn to find a space. Despite the closing of the highway and the airport earlier in the day, an awful lot of people had managed to get out of town. She strolled into Ozymandias, one of the few ordinary, unpretentious cafés in town, with free Wi-Fi and a relaxed wait staff who didn't look down their noses at her.

The place was almost empty, but a friendly waitress came over and added a bit of cheer to Corrie's dreary mood. She ordered a hot chocolate and took out her iPad. There were quite a few emails, including one from her advisor asking for another update on her work, fishing for inside details on what was really going on in Roaring Fork, and complaining that she wasn't keeping him informed. It was true, she had been cagey in her reports; she didn't want him interfering or trying to shut her down, and she figured the less information he had to latch on to, the better. Once her thesis was completed and turned in, it would blow the committee away; her advisor would have no choice but to join in the general accolade; it would win the Rosewell Prize . . . or, at least, she hoped that's how it would happen. So to satisfy Carbone she composed a vague, ambiguous reply to his email, dressing it up as a report but saying essentially nothing, implying her work was getting off to a slow start and that she had little real information as yet. She hit the SEND button, hoping that would hold him for another few days.

Her hot chocolate arrived and she sipped it as she browsed through the last of the emails. Nothing from Pendergast – not that she'd expected it; he wasn't, apparently, an emailer. Email complete, she checked the *New York Times*, the *Huff Post*, and a few other sites. The *Times* had a front-page story on the arson attacks, which she read with interest. The story had gone national after the second attack, but this third one elevated it to one of those horrific, sensationalistic stories that captured the attention of the country. Ironic: now it was big news, just as the storm was about to hit and no reporters could get in to cover it.

Chocolate finished, she figured she really had better get home. Pulling her scarf tight, she exited the café and was surprised to see, walking down the far side of the street, just passing under a streetlamp, a couple she recognized as Stacy and Ted. She stared. While they weren't exactly walking hand in hand, they seemed pretty friendly, talking and chatting together. As she watched, they disappeared into a restaurant.

Corrie experienced a sudden sick feeling. Earlier, Stacy had claimed she was going to spend the day back at the Fine house, on account of her hangover. But the hangover didn't seem so bad that she couldn't go to dinner with Ted. Were the two of them cheating on her behind her back? It seemed unthinkable – and yet, suddenly, quite possible. Maybe this was some sort of payback on Ted's part for her refusal to sleep with him the previous night. Was he taking up with Stacy on the rebound?

. . . And what about Stacy? Maybe she was messed up enough to do something like that. After all, she sure hadn't turned out to be the supremely confident air force captain that Corrie had initially thought, but rather a confused and lonely woman. She hated the idea that all this had changed her feelings toward Stacy, but she couldn't help but think of her now as a different person. She wondered what the PTSD meant and how it might manifest itself. And then there was the odd fact that Stacy had arrived in town several days before revealing herself to anyone. What had she been doing during that time? Had she really just been 'getting a feel' for the place?

Corrie got into her car and started the engine. There was still some residual heat so it warmed up fast, which made her grateful. She drove out of town and headed up Ravens Ravine Road, taking the switchbacks very slow, the snow building up on her wipers. It was falling so thickly now that anyone waiting with a gun wouldn't even see her car on the road, let alone have a shot. So much the better. She thought ahead to her crappy meal of beans and rice – all she could afford – and another evening of freezing her ass in the house. The hell with it, she was going to pick the thermostat lock, turn up the heat, and let the owner howl. Ridiculous that a multimillionaire was so concerned about a few extra dollars.

The mansion emerged from the falling snow, dark and gloomy. Stacy's car was gone, as expected. Corrie hoped she wouldn't drink in the restaurant and try to drive home in this weather afterward.

She parked in the driveway. Her car would be plowed in the next morning, as it had been several times before, requiring her to shovel it out. All because the owner wouldn't let her use the garage. No wonder he was locked in a horrible divorce.

As she got out of the car, freezing already, it

abruptly occurred to her that Pendergast was right. It was time to get out of Roaring Fork. Her basic research was complete, and it was all too clear she wasn't going to solve the hundred-fifty-year-old serial killings. She'd exhausted all avenues without coming up with so much as a clue. As soon as the highway was opened, she'd split.

Decision made.

She stuck her key into the door of the house and opened it, expecting the usual flurry of barks and yips to greet her – only to be met with silence.

She felt a welling of apprehension. It was like last night all over again. 'Jack?' she called out.

No answer. Had Stacy brought the dog into town with her, in case he was lonely? But she hadn't shown much interest in Jack and professed to prefer cats.

'Jack? Here, *Jack*!'

Not even a whimper. Corrie tried once again to control her pounding heart. She flicked on all the lights – screw the electric bill – and called again and again. Making her way down the hall to her wing of the house, she found her bedroom door shut but unlocked. She pushed it open. 'Jack?'

The room was dark. There was a form at the foot of the bed, and a very dark area around it. She turned on the lights, and saw Jack's body – minus the head – lying on top of the rug, surrounded by a huge crimson stain.

She didn't scream. She couldn't scream. She simply stared.

And then she saw the head, propped up on the dresser, eyes open and staring, a cascade of congealing blood dripping down the fake wood front. Stuck between the jaws was a piece of paper. In an almost dream-like state, disconnected, as if it was happening to someone else, Corrie managed to pick up a letter opener, pry open the jaws, take out the paper, and read the message.

Swanson: Get out of town today or you're dead. A bullet through that sweet little head of yours.

Corrie stared. It was like some sick take on *The Godfather* . . . And what made it totally ridiculous was that, even if she wanted to get out of town, she couldn't.

The note snapped her out of her fog. Amid a sick wash of fear and disgust, she also felt a groundswell of rage so powerful it frightened her: fury at the crude attempt at intimidation, fury for what had been done to poor, innocent Jack.

Leave? No way. She was staying right here.

CHAPTER 44

Hampstead Heath, Roger Kleefisch remarked to himself, had changed sadly since the days when Keats used to traverse it on his way from Clerkenwell to the cottage of Cowden Clarke, there to read his poetry and chat about literature; or since Walter Hartright, drawing teacher, had crossed it late at night, deep in thought, only to encounter the ghostly Woman in White on a distant byroad. These days it was hemmed in on all sides by Greater London, NW3, with bus stops and Underground stations dotted along its borders where once only groves of trees had stood.

Now, however, it was almost midnight; the weather had turned chilly, and the heath was relatively deserted. They had already left Parliament Hill and its marvelous panorama of the City and Canary Wharf behind and were making their way northwest. Hills, ponds, and clumps of woodlands were visible as mere shadows beneath the pale moon.

'I brought a dark lantern along,' Kleefisch said, more to keep up his spirits than to be informative.

He brandished the device, which he'd kept hidden beneath his heavy ulster. 'It seemed appropriate to the occasion, somehow.'

Pendergast glanced toward it. 'Anachronistic, but potentially useful.'

Earlier, from the comfort of his lodgings, planning this little escapade had filled Kleefisch with excitement. When Pendergast had been unable to secure permission to enter Covington Grange, he had declared he would do so anyway, extralegally. Kleefisch had enthusiastically volunteered to help. But now that they were actually executing the plan, he felt more than a little trepidation. It was one thing to write scholarly essays on Professor Moriarty, the 'Napoleon of crime,' or on Colonel Sebastian Moran, the 'second most dangerous man in London.' It was quite another thing, he realized, to be actually out on the heath, with breaking and entering on the agenda.

'There's the Hampstead Heath constabulary, you know,' he said.

'Indeed,' came the response. 'What's their complement?'

'Maybe a dozen or so. Some use police dogs.'

To this there was no response.

They skirted South Meadow and passed into the heavy woods of the Dueling Ground. To the north, Kleefisch could make out the lights of Highgate.

'Then there's the National Trust groundskeepers to consider,' he added. 'There's always the chance one of them might be loitering about.'

307

'In that case, I would suggest keeping that lantern well concealed.'

They slowed as their objective came into sight over the lip of a small hill. Covington Grange was sited just at the far edge of the Dueling Ground, surrounded on three sides by woods. Stone Bridge and Wood Pond lay to the right. To the north, a green lawn ran away in the direction of sprawling Kenwood House. Beyond, late-night traffic hushed along Hampstead Lane.

Pendergast looked about him, then nodded to Kleefisch and made his way forward, keeping to the edge of the wood.

The Grange itself was an archaeological enigma, as if its builder could not decide which school, or even which era, he wished it to belong to. The low façade was half-timbered and Tudor, but a small addition to one side was a bizarre bit of neo-Romanesque. The long sloping wooden roof, bristling with exposed eaves, presaged the Craftsman era by a good half century. A greenhouse clung to the far side, its glass panels now cracked and covered with vines. The entire structure was enclosed by a hurricane fence, sagging and weathered, which appeared to have been erected as a security measure decades ago and long since forgotten.

Following Pendergast's lead, Kleefisch crept up to the front of the building, where a narrow gate in the fencing was held in place with a padlock. Beside it, a weather-beaten sign read: PROPERTY OF H. M. GOV'T. NO TRESPASSING.

'Shall we, Roger?' Pendergast asked, as calmly as if he were inviting Kleefisch in for cucumber sandwiches at the Ritz.

Kleefisch glanced uneasily around, clutched the dark lantern more closely to him. 'But the lock—' he began. Even as he spoke, there was a faint clicking noise and the padlock sprang open in Pendergast's hand.

They stepped quickly past the gate, and Pendergast closed it behind them. Clouds had drifted over the moon; it was now very dark. Kleefisch waited in the forecourt while Pendergast made a quick reconnoiter. He was aware of a variety of sounds: distant laughter; a faint staccato honk from the motorway; and – or so he imagined – the nervous beating of his own heart.

Pendergast returned, then gestured them toward the front door. This, too, yielded almost immediately to the FBI agent's touch. The two passed inside, Pendergast shut the door, and Kleefisch found himself in utter darkness. He was aware of several additional things now: the smell of mildew and sawdust; the pattering of small feet; the low squeaking of disturbed vermin.

A voice came out of the darkness. 'To aid us in our search, let us review again what we know. For over a decade, from about 1917 to 1929, Conan Doyle came here frequently, as a guest of Mary Wilkes, to further his study of spiritualism and to read his writings on the subject to like-minded friends. He died in 1930, bound for – in

309

his words – "the greatest and most glorious adventure of all." Mary Wilkes herself died in 1934. Her daughter, Leticia Wilkes, lived here – joined in the early years by her niece and nephew – until her own death in 1980, at which time she left the property to the government. It has not been lived in – indeed, it has apparently remained untouched – ever since.'

Kleefisch could add little to this, so he said nothing.

A small glow of red appeared. Pendergast was holding up a flashlight, a filter fixed to its end. The faint beam swept here and there, revealing a hallway leading back into what was obviously a furnished and, at one time, well-lived-in house, circa 1980. There were piles of books set along the wall in disorganized ranks, and various tiny gnomes and glass figurines sat on a brace of side tables, heavy with dust. The far end of the hallway gave onto a kitchen: to the left and right were openings leading to a parlor and dining room, respectively. The first floor seemed to be covered in shag carpet of a detestable orange color.

Pendergast sniffed the air. 'The odor of wood rot and decay is strong. My friend at the National Trust was correct: this house is in a state of dangerous decrepitude and may be structurally unsound. We must proceed with caution.'

They moved into the parlor, pausing in the doorway while Pendergast swept his muted light around the room. It was a scene of confusion. An upright piano stood in one corner, sheet music spilling from its music stand and overturned bench onto the floor; several card tables, furry with mold, held abandoned jigsaw puzzles and half-finished games of Monopoly and Chinese checkers. Magazines were spread haphazardly across the chairs and sofas.

'It would appear Leticia Wilkes allowed her charges to run wild,' Pendergast said with a disapproving sniff.

The rest of the first floor was the same. Toys, bric-a-brac, discarded jackets, swimming trunks, and slippers – and everywhere that same odious orange carpet, lit a dreadful crimson by Pendergast's hooded light. No wonder the National Trust had let the place fall to wrack and ruin, Kleefisch thought to himself. He could imagine some poor functionary, poking his head into the place for a minute, taking an exploratory glance around, and then closing the door again, despairing of renovation. He stared at the paisley-papered walls, at the worn and stained furniture, looking for some ghostly evidence of the enchanted cottage in which, once upon a time, Conan Doyle had worked and entertained. He was unable to find any.

The basement yielded nothing more than empty storage rooms, a cold furnace, and dead beetles. Pendergast led the way up the dangerously creaking stairs to the second floor. Six doors led off the central hallway. The first was a linen closet, its contents ravaged by time and moths. The second

311

was a common bathroom. The next three doors opened onto bedrooms. One, in somewhat decent order, had apparently been that of Leticia herself. The others had obviously been used by her niece and nephew, as attested to by the Dion and Frankie Valli posters in the first room and the numerous issues of the *Sun*, all opened to page three, in the other.

That left just the single, closed door at the far end of the hall. Kleefisch's heart sank. Only now did he realize how much he'd allowed himself to hope that, at long last, the missing Holmes story might actually be found. But he'd been a fool to believe he would succeed where so many of his fellows had already failed. And especially in this mess, which would take a week to search properly.

Pendergast grasped the knob, opened the final door – and as quickly as Kleefisch's heart had sunk, it leapt anew.

The room that lay beyond was as different from the rest of the house as day was from night. It was like a time capsule from a period that had vanished well over a hundred years before. The room was a study, sparsely but tastefully furnished. After the dreadful clutter of the rest of the house, it was to Kleefisch like a breath of fresh air. He stared, excitement overcoming his apprehension, as Pendergast moved his light around. There was a writing desk and a comfortable chair. Sporting prints and daguerreotypes hung on the walls in simple frames; nearby stood a bookcase, nearly empty. There was a single diamond-pane window, high up. Ornamental hangings, of austere design but nevertheless tasteful, were placed along the walls.

'I believe we might risk a little more light,' Pendergast murmured. 'Your lantern, please.'

Kleefisch brought the lantern forward, grasped its sliding panel, and slid it open a crack. Immediately, the room leapt into sharper focus. He noticed with admiration the beautiful wood floor, composed of polished parquet, laid out in an old-fashioned design. A small square carpet, of the kind once known as a drugget, lay in the middle of the room. Against a far wall, between the hangings, was a chaise longue that appeared to have also served in the capacity of a daybed.

'Do you think—?' Kleefisch asked, turning to Pendergast, almost afraid to ask the question.

As if in answer, Pendergast pointed to one of the daguerreotypes on the wall beside them.

Kleefisch took a closer look. He realized, with some surprise, that it was not a daguerreotype after all, but a regular photograph, apparently from early in the twentieth century. It showed a young girl amid a pastoral, sylvan scene, chin supported by one hand, gazing out at the camera with a look of bemused seriousness. In the foreground before her, four small creatures with slender limbs and large butterfly wings danced, cavorted, or played tunes on wooden reeds. There was no obvious evidence of trickery or manipulation of the image:

the sprites seemed to be an integral part of the photograph.

'The Cottingley Fairies,' Kleefisch whispered.

'Indeed,' Pendergast replied. 'As you well know, Conan Doyle firmly believed in the existence of fairies and in the veracity of these pictures. He even devoted a book to the subject: *The Coming of the Fairies.* Two Yorkshire girls, Elsie Wright and her cousin Frances Griffiths, claimed to see fairies and to have photographed them. These are some of their photographs.'

Kleefisch stepped back. He felt his heart accelerate. There could no longer be any doubt: this had been Conan Doyle's study away from home. And the Wilkes family had preserved it with loving care, even while allowing the rest of the house to go to wrack and ruin.

If the missing story was anywhere to be found, it would be in this room.

With sudden energy, Pendergast stepped forward, ignoring the fearful creaking of the floorboards, his flashlight arrowing here and there. He opened the desk and made an exhaustive search of its contents, removing drawers and tapping on the sides and back. Next he moved to the bookshelf, removing the few dusty tomes and looking carefully through each, going so far as to peer down the hinges of each spine. Then he took the pictures from the wall one at a time, looked behind each, and felt gently along the paper backings for anything that might be hidden within the frames.

Next, he approached each of the decorative hangings in turn, feeling carefully along their lengths.

He paused, his silvery eyes roaming the room. Taking a switchblade from one pocket, he stepped over to the chaise longue, made a small, surgical incision where the fabric met the wooden framing, inserted his light into it, and then his fingers, making a painstaking examination of the interior – obviously to no avail. Next, he applied himself to the walls, holding one ear to the plaster while knocking gently with his knuckles. In such a fashion, he circled the room with agonizing thoroughness: once, twice.

As he watched this careful search, done by an expert, Kleefisch felt the familiar sinking feeling return once again.

His eyes fell to the floor – and to the small rug that lay at its center. Something was familiar about it: very familiar. And then, quite abruptly, he realized what it was.

'Pendergast,' he said, his voice little better than a croak.

The FBI agent turned to look at him.

Kleefisch pointed at the carpet. '"It was a small, square drugget in the center of the room,"' he quoted. '"Surrounded by a broad expanse of wood-flooring in square blocks, highly polished."'

'I fear my knowledge of The Canon is not as nuanced as yours. What is that from? "The Musgrave Ritual"? "The Resident Patient"?'

Kleefisch shook his head. '"The Second Stain."'

315

For a moment, Pendergast returned his gaze. Then, suddenly, his eyes glittered in comprehension. 'Could it be so simple?'

'Why not recycle a good thing?'

In a moment, Pendergast was kneeling upon the floor. Pushing away the carpet, he began applying his fingertips as well as the blade of his knife to the floorboards, pushing here, probing gently there. Within a minute, there was the squeak of a long-disused hinge and one of the parquet squares flipped up, exposing a small, dark cavity beneath.

Pendergast gently reached into the hole. Kleefisch looked on, hardly daring to draw breath, as the agent withdrew his hand. When he did, it was clutching a rolled series of foolscap sheets, brittle, dusty, and yellowed with age, tied up with a ribbon. Rising to his feet, Pendergast undid the ribbon – which fell apart in his hands – and unrolled the quire, brushing off the topmost sheet with care.

Both men crowded around as Pendergast held his light up to the words scrawled in longhand across the top of the page:

The Adventure of Aspern Hall

Nothing more needed to be said. Quickly and silently, Pendergast closed the little trapdoor and pushed the rug back into place with his foot; then they stepped out of the room and made for the head of the stairs.

Suddenly there was a dreadful crash. A monumental billow of dust rose up to surround

Kleefisch, blotting out his lantern and plunging the hallway into darkness. He waved the dust away, coughing and spluttering. As his vision cleared, he saw Pendergast, his head, shoulders, and outstretched arms down at the level of Kleefisch's feet. The floor had given way beneath him and he had saved himself from falling through at just the last minute.

'The manuscript, man!' Pendergast gasped, straining with the effort of holding himself in place. 'Take the manuscript!'

Kleefisch knelt and plucked the manuscript carefully from Pendergast's hand. Snugging it into a pocket of his ulster, he grabbed Pendergast's collar and – with a great effort – managed to pull him back up onto the second-floor landing. Pendergast regained his breath, stood up and, with a grimace, dusted himself off. They maneuvered their way around the hole and had begun creeping down the stairs when a slurred voice sounded from outside:

'Oi! Who's that, then?'

The two froze.

'The groundskeeper,' Kleefisch whispered.

Pendergast gestured for Kleefisch to shutter his lantern. Then, raising his hooded light to reveal his face, he put a finger to his lips and pointed to the front door.

They moved forward at a snail's pace.

'Who's there!' came the voice again.

Silently, Pendergast drew a large handgun out of his jacket, turned it butt-first.

'What are you doing?' Kleefisch said in alarm as he grasped Pendergast's hand.

'The man's intoxicated,' came the whispered reply. 'I should be able to, ah, render him harmless with little effort.'

'Violence?' Kleefisch said. 'Good Lord, not upon one of Her Majesty's own!'

'Do you have a better suggestion?'

'Make a dash for it.'

'A dash?'

'You said it yourself – the man's drunk. We'll rush out of the gate and run south into the wood.'

Pendergast looked dubious but put away the weapon nevertheless. He led the way across the carpeting to the front door, opened it a crack, and peered out. Hearing nothing further, he motioned Kleefisch to follow him down the narrow walkway to the hurricane fence. Just as he opened the gate, the moon emerged from behind the clouds and a shout of triumph came from a nearby stand of hemlock:

'You, there! Don't go no further!'

Pendergast burst through the gate and took off at high speed, Kleefisch at his heels. There was the shattering blast of a shotgun, but neither paused in their headlong run.

'You've been hit!' Kleefisch gasped as he struggled to keep up. He could see droplets of blackish red liquid fly up from Pendergast's shoulder with every stride the man took.

'A few superficial pellet strikes, I suspect; nothing

more. I'll remove them with a tweezers back at the Connaught. What of the manuscript? Is it undamaged?'

'Yes, yes. It's fine!'

Kleefisch had not run like this since his Oxford days. Nevertheless, the thought of the drunken groundskeeper and his weapon brought vigor to his limbs, and he continued to follow Pendergast, past Springett's Wood to the Vale of Health, and from there – *Deo Gratias!* – to East Heath Road, a taxi, and freedom.

CHAPTER 45

It was still snowing when Corrie awoke in her room at the Hotel Sebastian, after a night full of restless, fragmentary nightmares. She got up and looked out the window. The town lay under a blanket of white and the snowplows were working overtime, rumbling and scraping along the downtown streets, along with front-end loaders and dump trucks removing the piles of snow and trucking them out of town.

She glanced at her watch: eight o'clock.

Last night had been awful. The police had come up immediately, to their credit, with the chief himself leading the way. They took away Jack's corpse and the note, asked questions, collected evidence, and promised to investigate. The problem was, they were clearly overwhelmed by the serial arsonist. The chief looked like he was on the verge of a nervous breakdown, and his men were so sleep-deprived they could have been extras in a zombie flick. There was no way they were going to be able to conduct a thorough investigation on this, any more than they were on the shooting at her car – the target of which she was no longer in any doubt.

And so Corrie had driven back into town and booked a room at the Hotel Sebastian. Including the stint in the jail, she'd been in Roaring Fork for three weeks now, and she'd been burning through her four thousand dollars with depressing speed. Lodgings at the Sebastian would take up a good portion of the money she had left, but she was so frightened by the murder of her dog that there was no way she could spend the night in that mansion – or any night, ever again.

She had called Stacy, telling her what had happened and warning her it was too dangerous to return to the Fine house. Stacy said she would make arrangements to spend the night in town – Corrie had a horrible feeling it might have been at Ted's place – and they'd agreed to meet that morning at nine in the hotel's breakfast room. In one hour. It was a conversation she was not looking forward to.

Adding to her woes, the police had contacted the owner of the mansion, and he had then called Corrie on her cell, waking her up at six, screeching and hollering, saying it was all her fault, that she had broken every house rule, turning up the heat and letting in squatters. As he got more and more worked up, he called her a criminal, speculated that she might be a drug addict, and threatened to sue her and her dyke friend if they went back into the house.

Corrie had let the man vent, and then given the bastard a royal licking of her own, telling him what

321

a despicable human being he was, that she hoped his wife took every penny he had, and concluding with a speculation on the relationship between the failure of his marriage and the inadequate size of his dick. The man had become inarticulate with rage, which gave Corrie a certain satisfaction as she hung up at the start of yet another foul-mouthed rant. The satisfaction was short-lived once she considered the problem of where she was going to stay. She couldn't even go back to Basalt, because of the closed road, and one more night in the Hotel Sebastian – or any hotel in town, for that matter – would bankrupt her. What was she going to do?

The one thing she did know was that she was not leaving Roaring Fork. Was she afraid of the bastards who'd shot at her, who'd killed her dog? Of course she was. But nobody was going to drive her out of town. How could she live with herself if she allowed that to happen? And what kind of law enforcement officer would she be if she backed down in the face of these threats? No: one way or another, she was going to stay right here and help catch the people responsible.

Stacy Bowdree was already seated with a big mug of coffee in front of her when Corrie entered the breakfast room. Stacy looked awful, with dark circles under her eyes, her auburn hair unkempt. Corrie took a seat and picked up the menu. Three dollars for an orange juice, ten for bacon and eggs, eighteen for eggs Benedict. She put the menu down: she couldn't even afford a cup of coffee. When the waitress came over she ordered a glass of tap water. Stacy, on the other hand, ordered the Belgian waffles with a double side of bacon and a fried egg. And then pushed her coffee mug forward. 'Go ahead,' she said.

With a grunt of thanks, Corrie took a sip, then a big drink. God, she needed caffeine. She drained the mug, pushed it back. She didn't quite know where to start.

Luckily, Stacy started it for her. 'We need to talk, Corrie. About this scumbag threatening your life.'

Okay. If you want to start there, fine. 'It makes me sick what they did to Jack.'

Stacy laid a hand on hers. 'Which is why this is no joke. The people who did this are bad, *bad* people, and they aren't fooling around. They see you as a huge threat. Do you have any idea why?'

'I can only assume I dug up a hornet's nest somewhere in my research. Came close to something somebody wants to keep hushed up. I wish I knew what.'

'Maybe it's the Heights Association and that bitch Kermode,' said Stacy. 'She looks like she's capable of anything.'

'I don't think so. All that's been resolved, the new location of the cemetery has been approved, they're busy tracking down various descendants and getting permission – and most important,

323

you're not insisting any more on having your ancestor reburied in the original Boot Hill.'

'Well then, do you think it might be the arsonist?'

'Not the same M.O. at all. The key is for me to figure out what information I have, or almost got, that spooked them so badly. Once I know that, maybe I'll be able to identify them. But I don't really think they're going to kill me – or they would've done it already.'

'Corrie, don't be naive. Anyone who would decapitate a dog is totally capable of killing a person. Which is why, from now on, I'm not leaving your side. Not me or . . .' Stacy patted the place where she carried her .45.

Corrie looked away.

'What's wrong?' Stacy said, looking at her anxiously.

Now Corrie saw no reason to hold back. 'I saw you with Ted last night. The least you could do was tell me you were going to date him. Friends don't do that to friends.' She sat back.

Stacy sat back herself. An unreadable expression crossed her face. 'Date him?'

'Well, yeah.'

'*Date* him? Jesus Christ, how the hell could you even think such a thing?' Stacy had raised her voice.

'Well, what was I supposed to think, seeing you two go into that restaurant—'

'You know why we went into that restaurant? Because Ted asked me to dinner to talk about *you*.'

Corrie looked at her, astonished. 'Me?'

'Yes, you! He's totally smitten with you, says he might be in love with you, and he's worried he's doing something wrong, thinking that he rubbed you the wrong way. He wanted to ask me about it – we spent the whole damn evening talking about you and nothing else. Do you think I enjoyed getting out of bed and driving into town, with a pounding head, to listen to some man spend the night talking about another *woman*?'

'I'm sorry, Stacy. I guess I was jumping to conclusions.'

'You're goddamn right!' Suddenly, Stacy was on her feet, her face a mixture of reproach and betrayal. 'It's the same old bullshit! Here, I befriend you, protect you, look after your best interests at the expense of my own – and what's my reward? Fucking accusations of two-timing with your boyfriend!'

Stacy's sudden upwelling of anger was scaring Corrie. The few other diners in the room were turning their heads. 'Look, Stacy,' Corrie said in a calming voice. 'I'm really, really sorry. I guess I'm kind of insecure about my relationships with guys, and you being so attractive and all, I just—'

But Stacy didn't let her finish. With a final, blazing glance, she turned on her heel and stalked out of the restaurant – leaving her breakfast unfinished and unpaid for.

CHAPTER 46

The familiar, silken voice invited her in. Corrie took a deep breath. He'd agreed to see her; that was a good first step. She'd been telling herself that he hadn't contacted her since leaving Roaring Fork only because he was too busy; she'd fervently hoped that was the case. The last thing she wanted to do, she now realized, was allow her relationship with Pendergast to be damaged by her own impetuousness and shortsightedness.

And now he was back just as abruptly as he had left.

That afternoon, the basement was, if possible, even stuffier than the last time Corrie had visited Pendergast's temporary office. He sat behind the old metal desk, which was now swept clear of the chemistry apparatus that had cluttered it before. A thin manila file was the only thing that lay on the scarred surface. It must have been eighty-five degrees in the room, and yet the special agent still had his suit jacket on.

'Corrie. Please take a seat.'

Obediently, Corrie sat. 'How did you get back into town? I thought the road was closed.'

'The chief kindly sent one of his men in a snowcat to pick me up in Basalt. He was, it seems, rather anxious to have me back. And in any case there is talk of the road being reopened – temporarily, at any rate.'

'How was your trip?'

'Fruitful.'

Corrie shifted uncomfortably at the small talk and decided to get to the point right away. 'Look. I wanted to apologize for the way I acted the other day. It was immature, and I'm embarrassed. The fact is, I'm incredibly grateful for all you've done for me. It's just that . . . you sort of overshadow everything you get involved in. I don't want my professors at John Jay saying, *Oh, her friend Pendergast did it all for her.*' She paused. 'No doubt I'm overreacting, this being my first big research project and all.'

Pendergast looked at her a moment. Then he simply nodded his understanding. 'And how did things go while I was gone?'

'Pretty well,' said Corrie, avoiding his direct gaze. 'I'm just finishing up my research.'

'Nothing untoward happened, I hope?'

'There was another awful fire, right up on the hill behind town, and a road-rage killing out on Highway 82 – but I suppose the chief must've told you all about that.'

'I meant untoward, directed at you.'

'Oh, no,' Corrie lied. 'I couldn't make any headway solving the crimes, so I've decided to drop that. I did stumble over a few interesting tidbits in my research, but nothing that shed light on the killings.'

'Such as?'

'Well, let's see . . . I learned that Mrs Kermode is related to the Stafford family, which owned the old smelter back during the silver boom and is still the force behind the development of The Heights.'

A brief pause. 'Anything else?'

'Oh, yes, something that might intrigue you – given your interest in Doyle and Wilde.'

Pendergast inclined his head, encouraging her to continue.

'While digging through some old files at the Griswell Archive, I came across a funny letter about a codger who buttonholed Wilde after his lecture and, it seems, told him a story that almost made him faint. I would bet you anything it was the man-eating grizzly tale.'

Pendergast went very still for a moment. Then he asked: 'Did the letter mention the old fellow's name?'

Corrie thought back. 'Only a surname. Swinton.'

Another silence, and then Pendergast said: 'You must be low on funds.'

'No, no, doing fine,' she lied again. Damn it, she was going to have to get a temporary job somewhere. And find another place to live. But no way was she going to take any more money from Pendergast after all he'd done for her

328

already. 'Really, there's no reason for you to worry about me.'

Pendergast didn't respond, and it was hard to read his expression. Did he believe her? Had he heard anything from the chief about the shot through her windshield or the dead dog? Impossible to tell. Neither had been covered in the local paper – everything was still about the serial arsonist.

'You haven't told me anything about your trip,' she said, changing the subject.

'I accomplished what I set out to do,' he said, his thin fingers tapping the manila folder. 'I found a lost Sherlock Holmes story, the last ever written by Conan Doyle and unpublished to this day. It is most interesting. I recommend it to you.'

'When I have time,' she said, 'I'll be glad to read it.'

Another pause. Pendergast's long fingers edged the file toward her. 'I should read this now, if I were you.'

'Thanks, but the fact is I've still got a lot on my plate, finishing things up and all.' Why did Pendergast keep pushing this Doyle business? First *The Hound of the Baskervilles*, and now this.

The pale hand reached out, took the edge of the folder, and opened it. 'There can be no delay, Corrie.'

She looked up and saw his eyes, glittering in that peculiar way she knew so well. She hesitated. And then, with a sigh of acquiescence, she took out the sheaves of paper within and began to read.

CHAPTER 47

THE ADVENTURE OF ASPERN HALL

Of the many cases of Sherlock Holmes for which I've had the privilege to act as his Boswell, there is one I have always hesitated to put to paper. It is not because the adventure itself presented any singularly grim or *outré* elements – no more so than Holmes's other investigations. Rather, I believe it due to the ominous, indeed baneful air that clung to every aspect of the case; an air that chilled and almost blighted my soul; and that even today has the power to vex my sleep. There are some experiences in life one might wish never to have had; for me, this was one. However, I will now commit the story to print, and leave it to others to judge whether or not my reluctance has merit.

It took place in March of '90, at the beginning of a drear and comfortless spring following hard on the heels of one of the coldest winters in living memory. At the time I was resident in Holmes's Baker Street lodgings. It was a dark evening, made more oppressive by a fog that hung in the narrow streets and turned the gaslights to mere pinpricks of yellow. I was lounging in an armchair before the fire, and Holmes – who had been striding restlessly about the room – had now placed himself before the bow window. He was describing to me a chemical experiment he had undertaken that afternoon: how the application of manganese dioxide as a catalyst accelerated the decomposition of potassium chlorate into potassium chloride and, much more importantly, oxygen.

As he spoke, I silently rejoiced at his enthusiasm. Bad weather had kept us very much shut in for weeks; no 'little problems' had arisen to command his attention; and he had begun to exhibit the signs of *ennui* that all too frequently led him to indulge his habit of cocaine hydrochloride.

Just at that moment, I heard a knock at the front door.

'Are you expecting company, Holmes?' I asked.

His only reply was a curt shake of the head. Moving first to the decanter on the sideboard, then to the gasogene beside it, he mixed himself a brandy and soda, then sprawled into an armchair.

'Perhaps Mrs Hudson is entertaining,' I said, reaching for the pipe-rack.

But low voices on the stairs, followed by footfalls in the passage, put the lie to this assumption. A moment later there came a light rap on the door.

'Come in,' cried Holmes.

The door opened and Mrs Hudson appeared. 'There's a young lady to see you, sir,' she said. 'I told her it was late, and that she should make an appointment for tomorrow, but she said it was most urgent.'

'By all means, show her in,' Holmes replied, rising once again to his feet.

A moment later, a young woman was in our sitting room. She was wearing a long travelling coat of fashionable cut, along with a veiled hat.

'Pray have a seat,' Holmes said, ushering her towards the most comfortable chair with his usual courtesy. The woman thanked him, undid her coat and removed her hat, and sat down. She was possessed of a pleasing figure and a refined carriage, and a decided air of self-possession. The only blemish of which I was aware was that her features seemed rather severe, but that may have been the result of the anxiety that was present in her face. As was my custom, I tried to apply Holmes's methods of observation to this stranger, but was unable to notice anything of particular value, aside from the Wellington travelling boots she wore.

I became aware that Holmes was regarding me with some amusement. 'Other than the fact that our guest comes from Northumberland,' he told me, 'that she is a devoted horsewoman, that she arrived here by hansom cab rather than the Underground – and that she is engaged to be married – I can deduce little myself.'

'I have heard of your famed methods, Mr Holmes,' said the young woman before I could answer. 'And I expected something like this. Allow me, please, to deduce your deductions.'

Holmes gave a slight nod, an expression of surprise registering on his face.

The woman held up her hand. 'First, you noted my engagement ring but saw no wedding band.'

An affirmative incline of the head.

She kept her hand raised. 'And you perhaps remarked on the half-moon callus along the outer edge of my right wrist, precisely where the reins cross when held by someone of good seat, with riding crop in hand.'

'A most handsome callus,' said Holmes.

'As for the hansom cab, that should be obvious enough. You saw it pull to the kerb. For my part, I saw you standing in the window.'

At this, I had to laugh. 'It looks as if you've met your match, Holmes.'

'As for Northumberland, I would guess you noted a trace of accent in my speech?'

'Your accent is not precisely of Northumberland,' Holmes told her, 'but rather contains a suggestion of Tyne and Wear, perhaps of the Sunderland area, with an overlay of Staffordshire.'

At this the lady evinced surprise. 'My mother's people were from Sunderland, and my father's from Staffordshire. I wasn't aware I had retained a hint of either accent.'

'Our modes of speech are bred in the bone, madam. We cannot escape them any more than we can the colour of our eyes.'

'In that case, how did you know I came from Northumberland?'

Holmes pointed at the woman's footwear. 'Because of your Wellingtons. I would surmise you began your journey in snow. We have not had rain in the last four days; Northumberland is the coldest county in England; and it is the only one presently with snow still on the ground.'

'And how would you know there is snow in Northumberland?' I asked Holmes.

Holmes gestured at a nearby copy of *The Times*, a pained expression on his face. 'Now, madam, do me the kindness of telling us your name and how we may be of assistance.'

'My name is Victoria Selkirk,' the woman said. 'And my impending marriage is, in large part, why I am here.'

'Do go on,' Holmes said, relapsing into his seat.

'Please forgive my calling on you without prior notice,' Miss Selkirk said. 'But the fact is I don't know who else to turn to.'

Holmes took a sip of his brandy and waited for the young lady to continue.

'My fiancé's estate, Aspern Hall, is situated a few miles outside Hexham. My mother and I have taken a cottage on the grounds in preparation for the wedding. Over the last few months, the region has been plagued by a ferocious wolf.'

'A wolf?' I remarked in surprise.

Miss Selkirk nodded. 'To date it has killed two men.'

'But wolves are extinct in Britain,' I said.

'Not necessarily, Watson,' Holmes told me. 'Some believe they still exist in the most remote and inaccessible locales.'

He turned back to Miss Selkirk. 'Tell me about these killings.'

'They were savage, as would be expected of a wild beast.' She hesitated. 'And – increasingly – the creature seems to be developing a taste for its victims.'

'A man-eating wolf?' I said. 'Extraordinary.'

'Perhaps,' Holmes replied. 'Yet it is not beyond the bounds of possibility. Consider the example of the man-eating lions of Tsavo. When other game is scarce – and you will recall the severity of last winter – carnivores will adapt in order to survive.' He glanced at Miss Selkirk. 'Have there been eyewitnesses?'

'Yes. Two.'

'And what did they report having seen?'

'A huge wolf, retreating into the forest.'

'What was the distance from which these observations were made?'

'Both were made across a blanket bog . . . I would say several hundred yards.'

Holmes inclined his head. 'By day or by night?'

'By night. With a moon.'

'And were there any particular distinguishing characteristics of this wolf, besides its great size?'

'Yes. Its head was covered in white fur.'

'White fur,' Holmes repeated. He put his fingertips together and fell silent for a moment. Then he roused himself and addressed the young woman again. 'And how, exactly, can we be of help?'

'My fiancé, Edwin, is the heir to the Aspern estate. The Aspern family is the most prominent in that vicinity. Given the fear that has gripped the countryside, he feels it necessary to take onto himself the task of destroying this beast before it kills yet again. He has been going out into the forest at night, often alone. Even though he is armed, I'm terrified for his safety and fear that some misfortune may befall him.'

'I see. Miss Selkirk—' Holmes continued, now a little severely – 'I fear that I am unable to assist you. What you need are the services of a game hunter, not a consulting detective.'

The anxiety on Miss Selkirk's features deepened. 'But I had heard of your successful close with that dreadful business at Baskerville Hall. That is why I came to you.'

'That business, my dear woman, was the work of a man, not a beast.'

'But . . .' Miss Selkirk hesitated. Her air of self-possession grew more tenuous. 'My fiancé is most determined. He feels it an obligation because of his station in life. And his father, Sir Percival, hasn't seen fit to prevent him. Please, Mr Holmes. There is no one else who can help me.'

Holmes took a sip of his brandy; he sighed, rose, took a turn round the room, then sat down again. 'You mentioned the wolf was seen retreating into

336

a forest,' he said. 'May I assume you are speaking of Kielder Forest?'

Miss Selkirk nodded. 'Aspern Hall abuts it.'

'Did you know, Watson,' Holmes said, turning to me, 'that Northumberland's Kielder Forest is the largest remaining wooded area in England?'

'I did not,' I replied.

'And that it is famed, in part, for housing the country's last large remaining population of the Eurasian red squirrel?'

Glancing over at Holmes, I saw that his look of cold disinterestedness had been replaced with one both sharp and keen. I of course knew of his great interest in *Sciurus vulgaris*. He was perhaps the world's foremost expert on the creature's behaviour and taxonomy, and had published several monographs on the subject. I also sensed in him an unusual admiration for this woman.

'In a population bed that large, there may well be opportunities to observe variances heretofore undiscovered,' Holmes said, more to himself than to us. Then he glanced at our guest. 'Do you have rooms in town?' he asked.

'I arranged to stay with relatives in Islington.'

'Miss Selkirk,' he replied, 'I am inclined to take up this investigation – almost in spite of the case rather than because of it.' He looked at me, and then – significantly – at the hat stand, upon which hung both my bowler and his cloth cap with its long ear-flaps.

'I'm your man,' I replied instantly.

'In that case,' Holmes told Miss Selkirk, 'we will meet you tomorrow morning at Paddington Station, where – unless I am much mistaken – there is an 8:20 express departing for Northumberland.'

And he saw the young woman to the door.

The following morning, as planned, we met Victoria Selkirk at Paddington Station and prepared to set off for Hexham. Holmes, normally a late riser, appeared to have regained his dubiousness concerning the case. He was restless and uncommunicative, and as the train puffed out it was left to me to make conversation with the young Miss Selkirk. To pass the time, I asked her about Aspern Hall and its tenants, both older and younger.

The Hall, she explained, had been rebuilt from the remains of an ancient priory, originally constructed around 1450 and partially razed during Henry VIII's dissolution of the monasteries. Its current owner, Sir Percival Aspern, had been a hatter by trade. In his youth he had patented a revolutionary method for making green felt.

Holmes paused in his perusal of the passing scenery. 'Green felt, you say?'

Miss Selkirk nodded. 'Beyond its use for gaming tables, the colour was most fashionable in millinery shops during the '50s. Sir Percival made his fortune with it.'

Holmes waved a hand, as if swatting away an insect, and returned his attention to the compartment window.

Sir Percival's specialty hats, Miss Selkirk informed

me, now held a royal warrant from Queen Victoria and formed the basis for his knighthood. His son Edwin – her fiancé – had gone into the army quite early, having held a commission in the light dragoons. He was now in temporary residence at the Hall, considering whether or not to make the military a lifelong career.

Although Miss Selkirk was the most tactful of her sex, I nevertheless sensed that, whilst Edwin's father wished him to take up the family trade, Edwin himself was of two minds on the subject.

As our journey lengthened, the rich grasses and hedgerows of the Home Counties began giving way to wilder vistas: moorlands, bogs, and skeletal trees, punctuated at intervals by rocky outcroppings and escarpments. At length we arrived at Hexham, an attractive country-town, consisting of a cluster of cottages fashioned of thatch and stone, huddled along a single High Street. A wagonette was waiting for us at the station, a dour-looking servant at the reins. Without a word, he loaded our valises and grips, then returned to his perch and directed his horses away from the station, along a rutted country lane in the direction of the Hall.

The road made its way down a gentle declivity, into an increasingly damp and dreary landscape. The snow – which Holmes had remarked on the day before – could still be seen in patches here and there. The sun, which had at last made its appearance during our train journey, once again slipped behind clouds, bestowing the vista round us with a sense of oppressive gloom.

After we had gone perhaps five miles, Holmes – who had not spoken since we alighted from the train – aroused himself. 'What, pray, is that?' he enquired, pointing off in the distance with his walking-stick.

Looking in the indicated direction, I saw what appeared to be a low fen, or marsh, bordered on its fringe by swamp grass. Beyond it, in the late-afternoon mist, I could just make out an unbroken line of black.

'The bog I spoke of earlier,' Miss Selkirk replied.

'And beyond it is the verge of Kielder Forest?'

'Yes.'

'And am I to infer, from what you mentioned, that the wolf attacks occurred between the one and the other?'

'Yes, that is so.'

Holmes nodded, as if satisfying himself on some point, but did not speak further.

The country lane ambled on, making a long, lazy bend in order to avoid the bog, and at length we could make out Aspern Hall in the distance. It was an old manor-house of a most unusual design, with unmatched wings and dependencies set seemingly at cross-angles to each other, and I attributed this architectural eccentricity to the fact that the manse had risen from the ruins of an ancient abbey. As we drew closer, I could make out additional details. The façade was rusticated and much dappled by lichen, and wisps of smoke rose from a profusion of brick chimneys. Sedge and stunte oaks surrounded the main structure as well as the various cottages and outbuildings. Perhaps it was the chill in the spring air, or the proximity of the bog and the dark forest, yet I could not help but form the distinct notion that the house had absorbed into itself the bleakness and foreboding of the very landscape in which it was situated.

The coachman pulled the wagonette up beneath the mansion's porte-cochère. He removed Miss Selkirk's travelling bag, then started for ours, when Holmes stopped him, asking him to wait instead. Following Miss Selkirk, we stepped inside and found ourselves in a long gallery, furnished in rather austere taste. A man, clearly the squire of Aspern Hall himself, was waiting for us in the entrance to what appeared to be a salon. He was gaunt and tall, some fifty-odd years of age, with fair thinning hair and a deep-lined face. He wore a black frock-coat, and held a newspaper in one hand and a dog-whip in the other. Evidently he had heard the wagonette draw up. Putting the newspaper and dog-whip aside, he approached.

'Sir Percival Aspern, I presume?' Holmes said.

'I am, sir; but I fear you have the advantage of me.'

Holmes gave a short bow. 'I am Sherlock Holmes, and this is my friend and associate, Doctor Watson.'

'I see.' Sir Percival turned to our female

341

companion. 'So this is the reason you went into town, Miss Selkirk?'

Miss Selkirk nodded. 'Indeed it is, Sir Percival. If you'll excuse me, I must see to my mother.' She departed the gallery rather abruptly, leaving us with the squire.

'I have heard of you, Mr Holmes,' Sir Percival said, 'but I fear that you have made a long journey to no purpose. Your methods, brilliant as I understand them to be, will have little application against a beast such as the one that plagues us.'

'That remains to be seen,' Holmes said shortly.

'Well, come in and have a brandy, won't you?' And Sir Percival led us into the salon, where a butler poured out our refreshment.

'It would appear,' Holmes said once we were seated round the fire, 'that you do not share your future daughter-in-law's concern for the safety of your son.'

'I do not,' Sir Percival replied. 'He's lately returned from India, and knows what he's about.'

'And yet, by all reports, this beast has already killed two men,' I said.

'I have hunted with my son in the past, and can vouch for his skill as both tracker and marksman. The fact is, Mr – Watson, was it? – Edwin takes his responsibilities as heir to Aspern Hall very seriously. And I might say that his courage and initiative have not gone unnoticed in the district.'

'May we speak with him?' Holmes asked.

'Certainly – when he returns. He is out in the forest at present, hunting the beast.' He paused. 'If I were a younger man, I would be at his side.'

This excuse seemed to me to betray a streak of cowardice, and I shot a covert glance at Holmes. However, his attention remained fixed on Sir Percival.

'Still, womanish fears or not, the fair sex must be humoured,' the man went on. 'I am certainly willing to give you free run of the place, Mr Holmes, and offer you all the assistance you might need, including lodgings, if you so wish.'

The invitation, generous as it was, was offered with a certain ill-grace.

'That won't be necessary,' Holmes said. 'We passed an inn back in Hexham – The Plough, I believe – which we will make our base of operations.'

As he was speaking, Sir Percival spilt brandy on his shirtfront. He set the glass aside with a mild execration.

'I understand, sir, that you are in the hat-making trade,' Holmes said.

'In years past, yes. Others look after the business for me now.'

'I've always been fascinated by the process of making felt. Purely a scientific curiosity, you understand: chemistry is a hobby of mine.'

'I see.' Our host dabbed absently at his damp shirtfront.

'The basic problem, as I understand it, is in

softening the stiff animal hairs to render them sufficiently pliable for shaping felt.'

I glanced again at Holmes, wondering where in the devil this particular tack could be leading.

'I recall reading,' Holmes continued, 'that the Turks of old solved this problem by the application of camel urine.'

'We have come a long way from those primitive methods,' Sir Percival replied.

Miss Selkirk entered the salon. She looked in our direction, smiled a trifle wanly, and took a seat. She was evidently much worried about her fiancé, and seemed to be at pains to maintain her self-command.

'No doubt your own process is much more modern,' Holmes said. 'I should be curious to hear its application.'

'I wish I could satisfy you on that score, Mr Holmes, but it remains a trade secret.'

'I see.' Holmes shrugged. 'Well, it is of no great consequence.'

At this point there was a commotion in the hall. A moment later, a young man in full hunting dress appeared in the doorway. This was clearly Sir Percival's son, and – with his determined features, his military bearing, and the heavy rifle slung over one shoulder – he cut a fine figure indeed. Immediately, Miss Selkirk rose and, with a cry of relief, flew to him.

'Oh, Edwin,' she said. 'Edwin, I beg of you – let this time be the last.'

'Vicky,' the young man said, gently but firmly, 'the beast must be found and destroyed. We cannot allow another outrage to occur.'

Sir Percival rose as well and introduced Holmes and myself. My friend, however, interrupted these civilities with some impatience in order to question the new arrival.

'I take it,' he said, 'that this afternoon's foray was unsuccessful.'

'It was,' Edwin Aspern replied with a rueful smile.

'And where, may I ask, did you undertake your stalk?'

'In the western woods, beyond the bog.'

'But was nothing discovered? Tracks? Scat? Perhaps a den?'

Young Aspern shook his head. 'I saw no sign.'

'This is a very devious, clever wolf,' Sir Percival said. 'Even dogs are hopeless to track it.'

'A deep business,' Holmes murmured. 'A deep business indeed.'

Holmes declined an invitation to supper, and after a brief survey of the grounds we rode the wagonette back into Hexham, where we took rooms at The Plough. After breakfast the following morning, we made application to the local police force, which, it turned out, comprised a single individual, one Constable Frazier. We found the constable at his desk, employed in jotting industriously into a small notebook. From my earlier adventures with Holmes, I had not formed a particularly high opinion of local constabulary. And at first sight, Constable Frazier – with his dark olive dustcoat and leather leggings – seemed to bear out my suspicions. He had heard of Holmes, however, and as he began to respond to the enquiries of my friend, I realized that we had before us – if not necessarily a personage of superior intellect – at the least a dedicated and competent officer with, it seemed, a laudable doggedness of approach.

The wolf's first victim, he explained, had been an odd, vaguely sinister individual, a shabbily-dressed and wild-haired man of advanced years. He had shown up abruptly in Hexham some weeks before his death, skulking about and frightening women and children with inarticulate ravings. He did not stay at the inn, seemingly being without ready funds, and after a day or two the constable was called in by concerned citizens to learn the nameless man's business. After a search, the constable discovered the man staying in an abandoned wood-cutter's hut within the borders of Kielder Forest. The man refused to answer the constable's enquiries or to explain himself in any way.

'Inarticulate ravings?' Holmes repeated. 'If you could be more precise?'

'He spoke to himself a great deal, gesturing frantically, quite a lot of nonsense, really. Something about all the wrongs that had been done him. Amongst other rot.'

'Rot, you say. Such as?'

'Mere fragments. How he had been betrayed. Persecuted. How cold he was. How he would go to law and get a judgement.'

'Anything else?' Holmes pressed.

'No,' replied the constable. 'Oh yes – one other very odd thing. He often mentioned carrots.'

'Carrots?'

Constable Frazier nodded.

'Was he hungry? Did he mention any other foods?'

'No. Just carrots.'

'And you say he mentioned carrots not once, but many times?'

'The word seemed to come up again and again. But as I said, Mr Holmes, it was all a jumble. None of it meant anything.'

This line of questioning struck me as a useless diversion. To dwell on the ravings of a madman seemed folly, and I could see no connection to his tragic end at the jaws of a wolf. I sensed that Constable Frazier felt as I did, for he took to looking at Holmes with a certain speculative expression.

'Tell me more about the man's appearance,' Holmes said. 'Everything that you can remember. Pray spare no details.'

'He was singularly unkempt, his clothes mere rags, his hair uncombed. His eyes were bloodshot, and his teeth black.'

'Black, you say?' Holmes interrupted with sudden eagerness. 'You mean, black as in unsound? Decayed?'

'No. It was more a dark, uniform grey that in

dim light almost looked black. And he seemed to be in a state of continual intoxication, though where he got the money for liquor I haven't the faintest idea.'

'How do you know he was intoxicated?'

'The usual symptoms of dipsomania: slurred speech, shaking hands, unsteady gait.'

'Did you come across any liquor bottles in the wood-cutter's hut?'

'No.'

'When you spoke with him, did you smell spirits on his breath?'

'No. But I've had to deal with enough drunkards in my time to know the signs, Mr Holmes. The matter is absolutely beyond question.'

'Very well. Pray continue.'

The constable took up again the thread of his narrative with evident relief. 'Well, opinion in town was strong against him, so strong that I was about to run him off, when that wolf did the job for me. The morning after I questioned him, he was found on the edge of the forest, his body dreadfully torn and mangled, with tooth marks on the arms and legs.'

'I see,' said Holmes. 'And the second victim?'

At this point, I confess I nearly objected to the line of enquiry. Holmes had questioned the constable closely on trivial matters, but was leaving the main points unbroached. Who, for example, had found the body? But I held my tongue, and Constable Frazier continued.

'That took place two weeks later,' the constable said. 'The victim was a visiting naturalist up from Oxford to study the red fox.'

'Found in the same location as the first?'

'Not far away. Somewhat nearer the bog.'

'And how do you know both killings were done by the same animal?'

'It was the look of the wounds, sir. If anything, the second attack was even more vicious. This time, the man was . . . partially eaten.'

'How did the town react to this second killing?'

'There was a lot of talk. Talk – and fear. Sir Percival took an interest in the case. And his son, who was recently returned from the Indian campaign, began roaming the woods at night, armed with a rifle, intent on shooting the beast. I opened an investigation of my own.'

'After the second killing, you mean.'

'Beg pardon, Mr Holmes, but there didn't seem to be any purpose to one before. You understand: good riddance to that ancient ruffian. But this time, the victim was a respectable citizen – and we clearly had a man-eater on our hands. If the wolf had killed twice, he would kill again . . . if he could.'

'Did you interview the eyewitnesses?'

'Yes.'

'And did their stories agree?'

The constable nodded. 'After the second killing, they saw the beast skulking back into the forest, a fearsome creature.'

'Seen from how far away?'

'At a distance, at night, but with a moon. Close enough to note the fur on its head having gone snow white.'

Holmes thought for a moment. 'What did the doctor who presided over the inquests have to say?'

'As I said, amongst other things he noted the fact that, whilst both victims were severely mauled, the second had been partially eaten.'

'Yet the first merely had a few tentative bite marks.' Holmes turned to me. 'Do you know, Watson, that that is the usual pattern by which beasts become man-eaters? So it was with the Tsavo lions, as we spoke of previously.'

I nodded. 'Perhaps this wolf's hunting range is deep within the forest, and it has been driven closer to civilization because of the long, cold winter.'

Holmes turned back to the constable. 'And have you made any further observations?'

'Lack of observations is more like it, I'm afraid, Mr Holmes.'

'Pray explain.'

'Well, it's strange.' Constable Frazier's face assumed a look of perplexity. 'My family farm is at the edge of the forest, and I've had opportunity to go out looking for traces of the animal half a dozen times, at least. You'd think a beast that large would be easy to track. But I only found a few tracks, just after the second killing. I'm no tracker, but I could swear there was something unusual in that beast's movements.'

'Unusual?' Holmes asked. 'In what way?'

'In the paucity of sign. It's as if the beast were a ghost, coming and going invisibly. That's why I've been out of an evening, searching for fresh track.'

At this, Holmes leaned forwards in his chair. 'Permit me to advise you right now, Constable, I want you to put a stop to that immediately. There are to be no more nocturnal ramblings in the forest.'

The constable frowned. 'But I have certain obligations, Mr Holmes. Besides, the person in true danger is young Master Aspern. He is out half the night, every night, looking for the creature.'

'Listen to me,' Holmes said severely. 'That is utter nonsense. Aspern is in no danger. But you, Constable, I warn you – look to yourself.'

This brusque dismissal, and the notion that Miss Selkirk's fears for her fiancé were unfounded, amazed me. But Holmes said nothing more, and had no further questions – save to again warn the constable to stay out of the woods – and, for the time being at any rate, our interview had ended.

It being Sunday, we were forced to confine our investigations to interviews with various inhabitants of Hexham. Holmes first tracked down the two eyewitnesses, but they had little to add to what Mr Frazier had already told us: they had both seen a large wolf, remarkably large in fact, loping off in the direction of the bog, the fur on the top of its head a brilliant white in the moonlight. Neither had investigated further, but instead had the good sense to return to their homes with all speed.

We then repaired to The Plough, where Holmes contented himself with asking the customers their opinion of the wolf and the killings. Everyone we spoke to was on edge about the situation. Some, as they lifted their pints, made brave statements about taking on the hunt themselves one day or another. The majority were content to let young Master Aspern track down the beast on his own and expressed much admiration for his courage.

There were only two dissenting opinions. One was a local grocer, who was of the firm belief that the killings were the result of a pack of feral dogs that lived deep within Kielder Forest. The other was the publican himself, who told us that the second victim – the unfortunate Oxford naturalist – had stated point-blank that the beast which committed these outrages was no wolf.

'No wolf?' Holmes said sharply. 'And to what erudition, pray tell, do we owe this unequivocal statement?'

'Can't rightly say, sir. The man simply stated that, in his opinion, wolves were extinct in England.'

'That's hardly what I would call an empirical argument,' I said.

Holmes looked at the publican with a keen expression. 'And what particular beast, then, did the good naturalist substitute for the wolf of Kielder Forest?'

'I couldn't tell you that, sir. He didn't offer

anything else.' And the man went back to polishing his glassware.

Save for the interview with the constable, it proved on the whole to be a day of rather fruitless enquiry. Holmes was uncommunicative over dinner, and he retired early, with a dissatisfied expression on his face.

Early the following morning, however, barely past dawn, I was awakened by a cacophony of voices from beneath my window. Glancing at my watch, I saw it was just past six. I dressed quickly and went downstairs. A cluster of people had gathered in the High Street, and were all talking and gesturing animatedly. Holmes was already there, and when he saw me emerge from the inn he quickly approached.

'We must hurry,' he said. 'There has been another wolf sighting.'

'Where?'

'In just the same spot, between the bog and the edge of the forest. Come, Watson – it is imperative we be the first on the scene. Do you have your Webley's No. 2 on your person?'

I patted my right waistcoat pocket.

'Then let us be off with all speed. That pistol may not bring down a wolf, but at least it will drive him away.'

Securing the same wagonette and ill-tempered driver we had employed before, we quickly left Hexham at a canter, Holmes urging the man on in strident tones. As we headed out into the desolate moorlands, my friend explained that he had already spoken to the eyewitness who had caused this fresh disturbance: an elderly woman, an apothecary's wife, who was out walking the road in search of herbs and medicinal flowers. She could add nothing of substance to the other two eyewitnesses, save to corroborate their observations about the beast's great size and the shock of white fur atop of its head.

'Do you fear—?' I began.

'I fear the worst.'

Reaching the spot, Holmes ordered the driver to wait and – without wasting a second – jumped from the wagonette and began making his way through the sedge- and bramble-covered landscape. The bog lay to our left; the dark line of Kielder Forest to our right. The vegetation was damp with a chill morning dew, and there were still patches of snow on the ground. Before we had gone a hundred yards, my shoes and trousers were soaked through. Holmes was far ahead of me already, bounding on like one possessed. Even as I watched, he stopped at the top of a small hillock with a cry of dismay, and abruptly knelt. As I made my way to him, my pistol at the ready, I was able to discern what he had discovered. A body lay amidst the swamp grass, not two hundred yards from the edge of the forest. A military rifle, apparently a Martini-Henry Mk IV, lay beside it. All too well I recognized the dustcoat and leather leggings, now torn and shredded in a most violent fashion. It was Constable Frazier – or, more precisely, what was left of him, poor fellow.

'Watson,' Holmes said in an imperious tone, 'touch nothing. However, I would appreciate, via visual observation only, your medical opinion of this man's condition.'

'He's obviously been savaged,' I said, examining the lifeless body. 'By some large and vicious creature.'

'A wolf?'

'That would seem most likely.'

Holmes questioned me closely. 'Do you see any specific and identifiable marks? Of fangs, perhaps, or claw marks?'

'It's difficult to say. The ferocity of the attack, the ruined condition of the body, render specific observation difficult.'

'And are any pieces of the body – missing?'

I took another look. Despite my medical background, I found this a most disagreeable undertaking. I had seen, more than once, native tribesmen of India who had been mauled by tigers, but nothing in my experience came close to the savagery under which Constable Frazier had fallen.

'Yes,' I said at length. 'Yes, I believe some few.'

'Consistent with the description of the second victim? The naturalist?'

'No. No, I'd say this attack was more extensive in that regard.'

Holmes nodded slowly. 'You see, Watson. It is again as it was with the man-eating lions of Tsavo.

With each victim, they grow more brazen – and more partial to their newfound diet.'

With this, he removed a magnifying glass from his pocket. 'The rifle has not been fired,' he announced as he examined the Martini-Henry. 'Apparently, the beast snuck up and struck our man from behind.'

After a brief inspection of the corpse, he began moving about in an ever-increasing circle, until – with another cry – he bent low, then started slowly forwards, eyes to the ground, in the direction of a distant farmhouse surrounded by two enclosed fields: the residence, I assumed, of the unfortunate constable. At some point, Holmes stopped, turned round, and then – still employing the magnifying glass – returned to the body and moved slowly past it, until he had reached the very edge of the blanket bog.

'Wolf tracks,' he said. 'Without doubt. They lead from the forest, to a spot near that farmhouse, and thence to the site where the attack took place. No doubt it emerged from the woods, stalked its victim, and killed him on open ground.' He applied his glass once more to the swamp grass along the verge of the marsh. 'The tracks go directly into the bog, here.'

Now Holmes undertook a circuit of the bog: a laborious activity, involving several halts, backtracks, and exceedingly close inspections of various points of interest. I stayed by the body, touching nothing as Holmes had instructed, watching him from a distance. The process took over an hour, by which time I was drenched to the skin and shivering uncontrollably. A small group of curious onlookers were by now standing back along the roadside, and the local doctor and the magistrate had come up – the latter being the titular authority, with the demise of Constable Frazier – just as Holmes completed his investigation. He said not a word of his discoveries, but simply stood there amongst the marsh grass, deep in thought, as the doctor, the magistrate, and myself wrapped up the body and carried it to the wagonette. As the vehicle rolled off in the direction of town, I made my way back out to where Holmes remained standing, quite still, apparently oblivious to his soaked trousers and waterlogged boots.

'Did you remark anything of further interest?' I asked him.

After a moment, he glanced at me. Instead of answering, he pulled a briar pipe from his pocket, lit it, and replied with a question of his own. 'Don't you find it rather curious, Watson?'

'The entire affair is mysterious,' I replied, 'at least insofar as that blasted elusive wolf is concerned.'

'I am not referring to the wolf. I am referring to the affectionate relationship between Sir Percival and his son.'

This *non sequitur* stopped me in my tracks. 'I'm afraid I don't see what you're driving at, Holmes. From my perspective, the relationship seems anything but affectionate – at least, with regard to the father's callous unconcern for his son's life and safety.'

Holmes puffed at his pipe. 'Yes,' he replied enigmatically. 'And *that* is the mystery.'

Being now rather closer to Aspern Hall than to Hexham, and having had our transportation commandeered by the magistrate, we made our way down the road to the Hall, arriving there in just under an hour. We were met by Sir Percival and his son, who had just finished breakfasting. The news of the latest attack had not yet reached them, and almost immediately the estate was thrown into an uproar. Young Edwin stated his intention of setting out directly to track the beast, but Holmes counselled him against it: in the wake of this latest attack, the animal had no doubt retreated to his lair.

Next, Holmes asked Sir Percival if he could have the use of his brougham; it was his intention to ride into Hexham without delay and catch the first train to London.

Sir Percival expressed astonishment but gave his consent. Whilst the coach was being called for, Holmes glanced in my direction and suggested we take a stroll round the garden.

'I think you should ride into Hexham with me, Watson,' he said. 'Gather up your things from The Plough and then return here to Aspern Hall for the night.'

'What on earth for?' I ejaculated.

'Unless I am much mistaken, I will be returning from London perhaps as soon as tomorrow,' he said. 'And when I do, I shall bring with me the confirmation I seek as to the riddle of this vicious beast.'

'Why, Holmes!'

'But until then, Watson, your life remains at grave risk. You must promise me that you will not leave the Hall until I return – not even for a turn about the grounds.'

'I say, Holmes—'

'I insist upon it. In this matter I shall not give way. Do not leave the main house – especially after dark.'

Although this request seemed eccentric in the last degree – especially given the fact that Holmes believed the much more aggressive Edwin Aspern to be in no danger – I relented. 'I must say, old man, that I don't see how you can be so certain of solving the case,' I told him. 'The wolf is here in Hexham – not in London. Unless you are planning to return with a brace of heavy-calibre rifles, I confess that in this matter I see nothing.'

'Quite the contrary – you see everything,' Holmes retorted. 'You must be bolder in drawing your inferences, Watson.' But just at that moment there was a clatter of horseshoes on the gravel drive and the brougham drew up.

I spent a dreary day at Aspern Hall. A wind came up, followed by rain: light at first, then rather heavier. There was little to do, so I occupied the hours with reading a day-old copy of *The Times*, jotting in my diary, and glancing through the books in Sir Percival's extensive library. I saw nobody but servants until dinner. During that meal, Edwin declared his intent of going out again that very evening in search of the wolf. Miss Selkirk, who was by now naturally even more concerned for her fiancé's well-being, protested violently. There was an ugly scene. Edwin, though not unmoved by Miss Selkirk's objections, remained determined. Sir Percival, for his part, was clearly proud of his son's courage and – when confronted by his daughter-in-law-to-be – defended himself with talk of the family honour and the high approval of the countryside. After Edwin had left, I took it upon myself to stay with Miss Selkirk and try to draw her into conversation. It was a difficult business, given her state of mind, and I was heartily glad when – at around half past eleven – I heard Edwin's footsteps echoing in the Hall. He had again been unsuccessful in the hunt, but at least he was safely returned.

It was very late the following afternoon when Sherlock Holmes reappeared. He had wired ahead to have Sir Percival's brougham meet him at the Hexham station, and he arrived at the Hall in high spirits. Holmes had brought the magistrate and the town doctor with him, and he wasted no time in assembling the family and servants of the Hall.

When all were settled, Holmes announced that he had solved the case. This caused no end of consternation and questioning, and Edwin demanded to know what he meant by 'solving' the case when everyone knew the culprit was a wolf. Holmes refused to be sounded further on the matter. Despite the late hour, he explained, he would return to his rooms at The Plough, where he had certain critical notes on the case, in order to put his conclusions into order. He had made use of the carriage ride to confer with the magistrate and the doctor, and had only come out to the Hall in order to bring me back to town with him to assist with the final details. Tomorrow, he declared, he would make his conclusions public.

Towards the end of this little speech, a coachman came in to make known that the rear axle of Sir Percival's carriage had broken and could not be repaired until morning. There was no way that Holmes – or the magistrate or town doctor, for that matter – could return to Hexham until the following day. There was nothing for it; they would all have to spend the night at Aspern Hall.

Holmes was dreadfully put out by this development. During almost the entire dinner that followed he said not a word, a peevish expression on his face, morosely pushing the food on his plate idly about with his fork, one elbow lodged on the damask tablecloth in support of his narrow chin. Just as dessert was served, he announced his intention of walking back to Hexham.

'But that's out of the question,' said Sir Percival in astonishment. 'It's over ten miles.'

'I shan't be taking the road,' Holmes replied. 'It's far too indirect. I shall make my way from Aspern Hall to Hexham in a direct line, as the crow flies.'

'But that will take you right past the blanket bog,' Miss Selkirk said. 'Where . . .' She fell silent.

'I will accompany you, then,' Edwin Aspern spoke up.

'You shall do nothing of the sort. The wolf's most recent attack occurred just the night before last, and I doubt its hunger will have returned so soon. No; I shall undertake the trip on my own. Watson, once I reach Hexham I will leave word for the wagonette to come for you and the others in the morning.'

And so the matter was settled – or so I thought. Shortly after the men had passed into the library for brandy and cigars, however, Holmes took me aside.

'Look here,' he told me *sotto voce*. 'As soon as you are able to effect it successfully, you will contrive to sneak out of the house, making sure your departure is undetected. That point is most vital, Watson – you *must* leave undetected. Remember that, for the time being, you remain in grave danger.'

Despite my surprise, I assured Holmes that I was his man.

'You are to make your way unobserved to the vicinity of that small hillock where we found Constable Frazier. Find a suitable hiding spot from which no approach can reveal your position – not the bog, not the forest, not the road. Be sure to be in position no later than ten o'clock. And there you are to wait for me to pass by.'

I nodded my understanding.

'When I come into sight, however, under no circumstances are you to call out, or stand, or in any manner betray your presence.'

'Then what am I to do, Holmes?'

'Depend upon it – when it comes time to act, you shall know. Now: do you still have your pistol about you?'

I patted my waistcoat pocket, where my Webley had been in residence ever since we had arrived at the Hall the previous day.

My friend nodded his satisfaction. 'Excellent. Keep it close at hand.'

'And you, Holmes?'

'I myself will spend some time here before I take my leave, engaging young Aspern in conversation, billiards, or whatever proves necessary to distract him. It is vital that he not indulge his penchant for wolf-hunting, tonight of all nights.'

Accordingly, I bided my time, waiting until the gentlemen were engrossed in a game of whist. Then, retiring to my room, I retrieved my cap and travelling coat, and – making sure I was observed by neither family nor servants – I left the house by way of the French doors of the morning room, slipped across the lawn, and from there out onto the Hexham road. The rain had stopped, but the moon remained partially obscured by clouds. Heavy tendrils of mist lay across the bleak landscape.

I followed the muddy lane as it curved leisurely to the northeast, anticipating in its course the expanse of bog that lay ahead. It was a chill night, and here and there patches of snow could still be seen amidst the brambles and swamp grass. After several miles, at the bend where the road reached its northernmost point and angled eastwards towards town, I struck off south through the low undergrowth in the direction of the bog itself. The moon had by now emerged from behind the clouds and I could just make out the bog ahead, shimmering with a kind of ghastly glow. Beyond it, and barely discernible in the darkness, was the black border of Kielder Forest.

Reaching the hillock at last, I glanced round, then set about following Holmes's instructions: to find a blind in which I could remain unseen from all directions. It took some doing, but at last I found a depression on the eastwards side of the hillock, partially surrounded by gorse and furze, which afforded excellent opportunities for concealment, whilst at the same time commanding a view of all approaches. And here I settled down to wait.

Over the next hour I held a most gloomy vigil. My limbs grew stiff from inactivity, and my travelling coat did little to keep out the damp and chill. From time to time, I examined the various approaches; on other occasions, from sheer force of nervous habit, I checked the state of my weapon.

It was past eleven o'clock when I at last heard the sound of footsteps, coming through the marsh grass from the direction of Aspern Hall. Carefully, I peered out from my place of concealment. It was Holmes, unmistakable in his cloth cap and long coat, his thin frame emerging out of the mists with its characteristic loping stride. He was walking along the very edge of the blanket bog, headed in my direction. Slipping the Webley out of my waistcoat pocket, I steeled myself for whatever action might now transpire.

I waited, motionless, as Holmes continued his approach, hands in his pockets, heading for Hexham with perfect equanimity, as if out for nothing more than an evening's stroll. Suddenly, from the direction of the forest, I saw another form appear. It was large and dark, almost black, and as I watched in horror it bounded directly towards Holmes on all fours. From his position on the far side of the hillock, my friend would not yet be able to catch sight of the creature. I tightened my grip on the Webley: it was beyond any doubt that here was the fearsome wolf itself, and that it was intent on bringing down a fourth victim.

I watched it draw near, ready with my pistol should the beast get too close to Holmes. But then – when the animal was some hundred yards from my friend, and just as it came into view of Holmes himself – the most peculiar thing happened. The beast stopped short, creeping forwards with savage menace.

'Good evening, Sir Percival,' Holmes said matter-of-factly.

The beast greeted this sally with a vicious bark. I was by now out of my blind and approaching the wolf from the rear. The wolf abruptly reared up on its hind legs. Drawing closer, whilst trying my best to conceal the sound of my approach, I saw to my astonishment that the creature was, in fact, human: Sir Percival, dressed in what appeared to be a heavy bearskin coat. The soles of his leather boots had been fitted out with makeshift claws, and wolf pads dangled by large buttons from his gloves. One hand appeared holding a pistol; the other a large, claw-like implement with a heavy handle and long, wicked tines. His fair, thinning hair shone a pale, unnatural white in the light of the rising moon. I found myself almost paralysed by this bizarre and wholly unexpected turn of events.

Sir Percival laughed again – a maniacal laugh. 'Good evening, Mister Holmes,' he said. 'You shall make an excellent repast.' And with a raving torrent of words that I could not begin to follow or understand, he cocked his pistol and raised it at Holmes.

This extremity broke my paralysis. 'Stand down, Sir Percival,' I cried from his flank, my own weapon raised. 'I have you in my sights.'

Caught off guard, Sir Percival wheeled towards

me, aiming in my direction. As he did so, I squeezed off a shot, catching him in the arm. With a cry of pain, the man clutched at his shoulder, then fell to his knees. In a moment, Holmes was at his side. He relieved Sir Percival of his weapon and the grotesque device – no doubt, I realized, used to simulate the lacerations of a wolf's claws – then turned to me.

'I should be glad, Watson, if you could head into town as quickly as you can,' he said calmly. 'Return with a dog-cart and several able-bodied men. I shall remain here with Sir Percival.'

The rest of the particulars can be summed up in short order. After Sir Percival was taken up by the authorities and remanded to the police-court, we returned to Aspern Hall. Holmes spoke briefly, in turn, with the magistrate; young Edwin Aspern; and Miss Selkirk, and then insisted on our returning to London by the very next train.

'I must confess, Holmes,' I told him as our carriage made its way along the road back towards Hexham just as dawn was breaking, 'that whilst I have often been in the dark in past cases, this is your most singular surprise yet. Without doubt it will prove your *coup-de-mâitre*. How on earth did you know that a human, not a wolf, was behind these outrages – and how in particular did you know it was Sir Percival, if in fact you knew that at all?'

'My dear Watson, you do me a disservice,' Holmes replied. 'Naturally I knew it was Sir Percival.'

'Then pray explain yourself.'

'Several clues presented themselves, for anyone with the discernment to sift the important from the mere coincident. To begin with, we have the madman – the first victim. When there is more than one killing to reckon with, Watson, you must always pay particular attention to the *first*. Frequently the motive, and therefore the entire case, rests upon that particular crime.'

'Yes, but the first victim was nothing but a mindless vagrant.'

'He might have been so in recent years, but he was not always thus. Recall, Watson, that in his ravings, a single word stood out again and again: *carrot*.'

I recalled this, and Holmes's fascination with it, all too well. How it could have any significance seemed to defy credibility. 'Go on,' I said.

'Carroting, you must understand, was a process by which animal fur is bathed in a solution of mercury nitrate, in order to render the hairs more supple, thus producing a superior *felt*.' At this last word, he threw a significant glance in my direction.

'Felt,' I repeated. 'You mean, for the making of hats?'

'Precisely. The solution is of an orange colour, hence the term *carroting*. However, this process had rather severe side effects on those who worked with it, which is why its use today is much reduced. When mercury vapours are inhaled over a long enough period of time – particularly, for our purposes, in the close quarters of a hat-making operation – toxic and irreversible effects almost inevitably follow. One develops tremors of the hands; blackened teeth; slurred speech. In severe cases, dementia or outright insanity can occur. Hence the term *mad as a hatter*.' Holmes waved a hand. 'I know all this, of course, due to my long-abiding interest in chemistry.'

'But what does all this have to do with Sir Percival?' I asked.

'Let us proceed in a linear fashion, if you please. You will recall that Constable Frazier believed our vagabond to be a drunkard, citing as evidence the man's slurred speech and impaired movement. And yet he detected no smell of alcohol on the man's breath. I immediately assumed that the real cause of the man's affliction was not drunkenness, but rather the effects of mercury poisoning. His mention of "carrots" explained how this poisoning had come about: as an occupational hazard of making felt, from working as a hatter. I naturally realized that there could be no coincidence between Sir Percival's former occupation and the sudden arrival of this curious fellow upon the scene. No: this man had clearly once been in business with Sir Percival. Recall, if you will, two things. First, how this man had raved about betrayal, about getting a judgement from a court of law. Second, how Sir Percival made his fortune by a unique felt-making process – a process, you may recollect, he refused to discuss with me when I broached the topic at Aspern Hall.'

The carriage continued its jostling way towards Hexham, and Holmes went on. 'Remarking on these facts, I began to consider the possibility that this man, now sadly reduced, had once been Sir Percival's business partner – and, perhaps, the true author of that revolutionary felt-making process. Now, years later, he had returned to square accounts with his former partner, to expose and ruin him. In other words, this whole matter began as a mere business dispute; one that Sir Percival solved in a traditional manner – by murder. It seemed to me highly likely that when this fellow appeared in Hexham, Sir Percival had promised him amends, and had agreed to meet with him in a lonely spot at the edge of the bog. There, Sir Percival murdered his former partner, and – to keep any suspicion from ever redounding upon him – tore the body cruelly, even going so far as to leave some tentative bite marks, so as to make it appear the work of a large and savage beast, most likely a wolf.'

'And in so doing, he seemed to have been entirely successful,' I said. 'Why, then, kill again?'

'The second person killed, you will recall, was a naturalist from Oxford. He was heard in the local inn debunking the rumours of a wolf, declaring that no wolves still survived in England. By killing this man, Sir Percival accomplished several goals. He silenced the man's insistence on the extinction of the English wolf – the very last thing Sir Percival would want was attention returning to the initial killing. Also, by this time he had of course heard the rumours in Hexham about a wolf being the culprit in his partner's murder. In case he was spotted, he had now had the opportunity to fit out a large bear coat, complete with wolf-paw gloves and boots that he – with his hatter's skill – could make entirely convincing. He used this disguise to run to and from the second murder scene on all fours. I believe, Watson, he was actually *hoping* for a witness this time, in order to inflame the rumours of a man-eating wolf. In this, at least, he was fortunate.'

'Yes, I can see a cruel logic in such a course of action,' I said. 'But what, then, of the constable?'

'Constable Frazier was, if not the world's most accomplished investigator, a man of great doggedness and persistence. No doubt Sir Percival perceived him to be a threat. Recall how the constable hinted at certain suspicions about the wolf's behaviour. Those suspicions, I would hazard, had to do with why the wolf tracks entered the bog *but never came out again.* The constable would have remarked on this after the second murder, if not before. I myself found this curious phenomenon to be the case after the constable's own death, when I made a circuit of the bog. Wolf tracks entered the region from the east; only human tracks emerged from the west. Sir Percival, you see, would have entered the bog on all fours, as a wolf; he would have used the concealing vegetation to come out from the bog as merely himself, should anyone encounter him. The constable must have mentioned his suspicions to Sir Percival – remember, Watson, his remarking he'd been to the Hall just the day before, to warn young Aspern to cease his hunting of the wolf – and in so doing, signed his own death warrant.'

Hearing these revelations, presented in Holmes's complacent tone, was nothing less than astounding. I could only shake my head.

'What clinched the case for me was Sir Percival's cavalier, indeed encouraging, attitude towards his son's hunting of the beast. He seemed to evince total unconcern for young Edwin's well-being. Why? At this point in the game, the answer was obvious to me: he knew his son was in no danger from the wolf, *because the wolf was himself.* Then, of course, there was the manner in which Sir Percival spilt his brandy.'

'What of it?'

'He was making great pains to hide his trembling hands. That incipient palsy demonstrated to my satisfaction that he himself was well on the road to madness brought on by mercury poisoning, and that he would soon be reduced to the same pitiable state as his former partner.'

By this time we had arrived at the Hexham station; we descended with our valises and mounted the platform, just in time for the 8:20 to Paddington.

'Armed with these suspicions,' Holmes went on, 'I went to London. It did not take me long to uncover the facts I was looking for: that, many years before, Sir Percival did indeed have a business partner. At the time, he accused Sir Percival of stealing a valuable patent, claiming it as his own. He was adjudged a lunatic, however, and was committed to an asylum – through the offices of Sir Percival himself. This poor unfortunate was released just days before the initial appearance of the raving madman in Kielder Forest.

'I returned from London, secure in the knowledge that, not only was there no man-eating wolf, but Sir Percival himself was the murderer of three men. The only question remaining was how to catch him up. I couldn't very well reveal the truth – that there was no wolf. No; I had to find a reason to manoeuvre Sir Percival into making me his next target, and to arrange it, so to speak, on home ground. Hence my dramatic announcement of having solved the case – and my nocturnal shortcut across the open countryside, between the bog and the forest edge, site of the previous killings. Unless I had made a mistake in my calculations, I felt certain Sir Percival would take the opportunity to make me his fourth victim.'

'But you undertook that walk only because Sir Percival's carriage broke an axle,' I said. 'How could you have anticipated such an eventuality?'

'I did not anticipate it, Watson. I precipitated it.'

'You mean—?' I stopped.

'Yes. I fear I committed an act of sabotage against Sir Percival's brougham. Perhaps I should send down a cheque for its repair.'

A faint whistle echoed out across the morning sky. A moment later, the express came into view. Within minutes we were boarding. 'I confess myself astonished,' I said as we entered our compartment. 'You are like the artist that outdoes his best work. There remains only one particular I do not understand.'

'In that case, my dear Watson, pray unburden yourself.'

'It is one thing, Holmes, to make a killing look like the work of an animal; quite another to actually devour portions of a body. Why did Sir Percival continue to do so – and, in fact, to an increasing extent?'

'The answer is quite simple,' Holmes replied. 'It would seem Sir Percival, in his growing madness, had begun acquiring a taste for his, ah, *prey.*'

The subject of the Hexham Wolf did not come up again until perhaps half a year later, when I came across a notice in *The Times* stating that the new owner of Aspern Hall and his fiancée were to be married in St Paul's the following month. It appeared that – in local opinion, at least – the atrocities of the father were more than compensated for by the son's military success, and by the courage he had displayed in his hunt for the would-be wolf. As for myself, I would have wished to have spent more time, had the circumstances been more pleasant, in the company of one of the handsomest young ladies of my acquaintance: Miss Victoria Selkirk.

On the lone occasion Holmes himself later referred to the case, he merely expressed a passing regret that the excursion had not furnished him with an opportunity to further his study of *Sciurus vulgaris* – the Eurasian red squirrel.

CHAPTER 48

Corrie finished the story and looked up to find Pendergast's silvery eyes upon her. She realized she had been holding her breath, and exhaled. 'Holy crap,' she said.

'One could say that.'

'This story . . . I can hardly get my head around it.' A thought struck her. 'But how did you know it was key?'

'I didn't. Not at first. But consider: Doyle was a medical man. Before starting his private practice, he had been the doctor on a whaling ship and ship's surgeon on a voyage along the West African coast. Those are among the most difficult postings a medical man could experience. He had surely seen a great deal of unpleasantness, to put it mildly, on these voyages. A story that would send him fleeing from the dining table had to be far more repugnant than a mere man-eating grizzly.'

'But the lost story? What led you to that in particular?'

'Doyle was so unsettled by the story he heard from Wilde that he did what many authors do to exorcise their demons: he incorporated it into his fiction. Almost immediately after the meeting in the Langham Hotel he wrote *The Hound of the Baskervilles*, which of course has a few parallels to Wilde's actual story. But *Hound*, while a marvelous story in its own right, was a mere ghost of the truth. Not much exorcism to be had there. One can surmise that Wilde's story continued to work on his mind for a long time. I began to wonder whether, in later years, Doyle finally felt compelled to write something closer to the bone, with much more of the truth in it, as a kind of catharsis. I made some inquiries. An English acquaintance of mine, an expert in Sherlockiana, confirmed to me a rumor of a missing Holmes story, which we surmised was titled "The Adventure of Aspern Hall." I put two and two together – and went to London.'

'But how did you know it was *that* story?'

'By all accounts the Aspern Hall story was soundly rejected. Never published. Consider that: a fresh Sherlock Holmes story, from the master himself, the first one in ages – and it is rejected? One might surmise it contained something unusually objectionable to Victorian taste.'

Corrie wrinkled her nose in chagrin. 'You make it sound so simple.'

'Most detection is simple. If I teach you nothing else, I hope you'll learn that.'

She colored. 'And I was so dismissive of this lead for so long. What an idiot I am. I'm sorry about that, really.'

Pendergast waved a hand. 'Let us focus on the matter before us. The famed *Hound of the Baskervilles* merely touched on the grizzly story. But this tale: this *incorporates* far more of what Doyle heard from Wilde, who had in turn heard it from this fellow you found, Swinton. A commendable discovery, that.'

'An accident.'

'An accident is only a puzzle piece that hasn't yet found its place in the picture. A good detective collects all "accidents," no matter how insignificant.'

'But we need to figure out what connection the story has to the real killings,' said Corrie. 'Okay: you have a bunch of cannibalistic murderers who are behaving somewhat like this guy Percival. They're killing and eating miners up on the mountain, trying to disguise what they're doing as grizzly killings.'

'No. If I may interrupt: the identification of the killings with a man-eating grizzly was originally made by chance, as you've probably learned for yourself. A grizzly bear passed by and masticated the remains of one of the early victims, and that clinched matters to the town's satisfaction. Later random sightings of grizzlies seem to confirm the connection. It is all about how human beings construct a narrative out of random events, baseless assumptions, and simple-minded prejudices. In my opinion, the gang of killers you mention *did not* set out to disguise their work as the result of a man-eating grizzly.'

'All right, so the gang wasn't trying to disguise their killings. But still, the story doesn't explain *why* they're killing. What's the motivation? Sir Percival has a motivation: he kills his partner to cover up the fact that he cheated him and stuck him in an insane asylum. I can't see how that has anything to do with what prompted the killers in the Colorado mountains.'

'It doesn't.' Pendergast looked at Corrie a long time. 'Not directly, at any rate. You're not focusing on the salient points. One should ask, first: why did Sir Percival *eat* portions of his victims?'

Corrie thought back to the story. 'At first, to make it look like a wolf. And then later, because he was going crazy and thought he was developing a taste for it.'

'Ah! And *why* was he going crazy?'

'Because he was suffering from mercury poisoning as a result of making felt.' Corrie hesitated. 'But what does hat making have to do with silver mining? I can't see it.'

'On the contrary, Corrie – you see everything. *You must be bolder in drawing your inferences.*' Pendergast's eyes gleamed as he quoted the line.

Corrie frowned. What possible connection could there be? She wished Pendergast would just tell her, rather than pulling the Socratic method on her. 'Can we dispense with the teachable moment? If it's obvious, why can't you just tell me?'

'This is not an intellectual game we are playing. This is deadly serious – particularly for you. I

379

am surprised that you have not already been threatened.'

He paused. In the silence, Corrie thought of the shot at her car, the dead dog, the note. She should tell him – clearly he would find out sooner or later. What if she confided in Pendergast? But that would only result in him putting more pressure on her to leave Roaring Fork.

'My first instinct,' Pendergast went on, almost as if reading her thoughts, 'was to spirit you away from town immediately, even if it meant commandeering one of the chief's snowcats. But I know you well enough to realize that would be futile.'

'Thank you.'

'The next best thing, therefore, is to get you thinking properly about this case – what it means, why you are in extreme danger, and from where. This is not, as you put it, a *teachable moment*.'

The seriousness of his tone hit her hard. She swallowed. 'Okay. Sorry. You've got my attention.'

'Let's return to the question you just asked, which I will rephrase in more precise terms: what does nineteenth-century English hat making have in common with nineteenth-century silver refining?'

It came to her in a flash. It *was* obvious. 'Both processes use mercury.'

'*Precisely.*'

All of a sudden, everything started to fall into place. 'According to the story, mercury nitrate was used to soften fur for the making of felt for hats. Carroting, they called it.'

'Go on.'

'And mercury was also used in smelting, to separate silver and gold from crushed ore.'

'Excellent.'

Now Corrie's mind was racing. 'So the gang of killers was a group of miners who must've worked in the smelter. And gone crazy, in turn, from mercury poisoning.'

Pendergast nodded.

'The smelter fired the crazy workers and hired fresh ones. Perhaps a few of those who were fired banded together. Without work, totally nuts, unemployable, they took to the hills, angry and vengeful, where they went progressively crazier. And, of course . . . they needed to eat.'

Another slow nod from Pendergast.

'So they preyed on isolated miners up at their claims, killing and eating them. And like the man-eating lions of Tsavo – and Sir Percival – they began to develop a taste for it.'

This was followed by a long silence. *What else?* Corrie asked herself. Where did the present danger come from? 'All this happened a hundred and fifty years ago,' she finally said. 'I don't see how this affects us now. Why am I in danger?'

'You have not put the last, crucial piece into place. Think of the "accidental" information you told me you'd recently uncovered.'

'Give me a hint.'

'Very well, then: who owned the smelter?'

'The Stafford family.'

'Go on.'

'But the history of labor abuses and the use of mercury at the smelter are already well known. It's a matter of historical record. It would be stupid for them to take steps to cover that up now.'

'Corrie.' Pendergast shook his head. 'Where *was* the smelter?'

'Um, well, it was somewhere in the area where The Heights is now. I mean, that's how the family came to own all that land to turn into the development.'

'And . . .?'

'And what? The smelter's long gone. It was shut in the 1890s and they tore down the ruins decades ago. There's nothing left of . . . *Oh, my God.*' She clasped one hand to her mouth.

Pendergast remained silent, waiting.

Corrie stared at him. Now she understood. 'Mercury. That's what's left of it. *The ground beneath the development is contaminated with mercury.*'

Pendergast folded his hands and sat back in his chair. 'Now you are starting to think like a true detective. And I hope you will live long enough to become that detective. I fear for you: you have always been, and still remain, far too rash. But despite that shortcoming, even you must see what is at stake here – and the grave danger you have placed yourself in by continuing this most unwise investigation. I would not have revealed any of this to you – not the lost Holmes story, not the Stafford family connection, not the poisonous groundwater – were it not, given your, ah, impetuous nature, necessary to convince you to leave this ugly place, as directly as I can make arrangements.'

CHAPTER 49

A. X. L. Pendergast surveyed the town of Leadville with tightly pursed lips. A sign announced its altitude, 10,150 feet, and stated it was the HIGHEST INCORPORATED TOWN IN THE UNITED STATES. It stood in stark contrast with Roaring Fork, across the Continental Divide. Its downtown strip was a single street bordered by Victorian buildings in various states of shabbiness and disrepair, with frozen heaps of snow along the verges. Beyond, forests of fir trees swept up to immense mountain peaks in almost all directions. The excessive Christmas decorations draped over every cornice, lamppost, streetlight, and parapet lent a sort of desperate air to the forlornness of the town, especially two days before Christmas. And yet despite the early-morning hour and the bitter cold, Pendergast was aware of a certain relief simply to be away from the oppressive wealth, entitlement, and smugness that hung like a miasma over Roaring Fork. Leadville, while impoverished, was a real place with real people – although it was nevertheless inconceivable why

384

anyone would want to live in this white Gehenna, this algid Siberian wasteland, this desert of frost buried in the mountains, far from the delights of civilization.

He had had the devil of a time tracking down any progeny of the aged Swinton, first name unknown, who had buttonholed Oscar Wilde after the Roaring Fork lecture and told him the fateful story. With the help of Mime, he had finally identified one remaining descendant: a certain Kyle Swinton, born in Leadville thirty-one years previously. He was an only child whose parents had been killed in a car accident around the time he dropped out of Leadville High. After that, his digital trail had vanished. Even Mime, Pendergast's shadowy and reclusive computer genius and information gatherer, had been unable to track the man beyond establishing the crucial fact that there was no record of his death. Kyle Swinton, it seemed, was still alive, somewhere within the borders of the United States; that was all Pendergast knew.

As soon as the snow had stopped in Roaring Fork – or rather paused, as the main event was still to come – the road had been cleared and Pendergast had made his way to Leadville to see if he could pick up a trace of the man. Weighed down by a sweater vest, heavy black suit, down vest, overcoat, two scarves, thick gloves and boots, and a woolen hat under his trilby, he exited his vehicle and made his way into what appeared to be the only five-and-dime drugstore in the town. He glanced around the store and selected the oldest employee: the pharmacist manning the prescription counter.

Unwrapping his scarves so he could speak, Pendergast said, 'I am trying to trace the where-abouts of a man named Kyle Swinton, who attended Leadville High School in the late '90s.'

The pharmacist looked Pendergast up and down. 'Kyle Swinton? What do you want with him?'

'I'm an attorney, and it's about an inheritance.'

'Inheritance? His family didn't have two nickels to rub together.'

'There was a great-uncle.'

'Oh. Well, good for him, I suppose. Kyle, he doesn't come into town very often. Maybe not till spring.'

This was excellent. 'If you could direct me to his house, I should be grateful.'

'Sure, but he's snowed in. Lives off the grid. You won't get up there except on a snowmobile. And . . .' The man hesitated.

'Yes?'

'He's one of those survivalist types. He's holed up in Elbert Canyon waiting for, I don't know, the end of civilization maybe.'

'Indeed?'

'He's got a bunker up there, stockpiles of food – and a big-time arsenal, or so they say. So if you go up there, you'd better be damn careful or he's liable to blow a hole in you.'

Pendergast was silent for a moment. 'Where, pray tell, may I rent a snowmobile?'

'There's a couple of places, it's a big sport in these parts.' He gave Pendergast another once-over, doubtfully. 'You know how to operate one?'

'Naturally.'

The druggist gave Pendergast the information and drew a map, showing him how to get to Kyle Swinton's place up in Elbert Canyon.

Pendergast exited the pharmacy and strolled down Harrison Avenue, as if shopping, despite the five-degree weather, the piles of snow, and the sidewalks so icy that even the salt froze to them. Finally he went into a gun-and-ammo store that also doubled as a pawnshop.

A man with a tattoo of an octopus on the shaved dome of his head strolled over. 'What can I do for you?'

'I would like to buy a small box of the Cor-Bon .45 ACP.'

The man placed the box on the counter.

'Does a Mr Kyle Swinton shop here?'

'Sure does, good customer. Crazy fucker, though.'

Pendergast considered for a moment the kind of person a man like this might think of as crazy.

'I understand he has quite a collection of firearms.'

'Spends every last penny on guns and ammo.'

'In that case, there must be quite a variety of ammo he buys from you.'

'Hell, yes. That's why we got all these rounds

here. He's got a collection of heavy-caliber hand-guns you wouldn't believe.'

'Revolvers?'

'Oh, yeah. Revolvers, pistols, all loads. Probably got a hundred K worth of firearms up there.'

Pendergast pursed his lips. 'Come to think of it, I'd like to also purchase a box of the .44 S&W Special, one of the .44 Remington Magnum, and another of .357 S&W Magnum.'

The man placed the boxes on the counter. 'Else?'

'That will suffice, thank you very much.'

The man rang the purchase up.

'No bag, I'll put them in my pockets.' Everything disappeared into his coat.

Business had not been good at the nearest snowmobile rental place. Pendergast was able to overcome their initial difficulty about renting him a machine for the day, despite his wildly inappropriate dress, southern accent, and lack of even minimal familiarity with its operation. They put a helmet and visor on his head and gave him a quick lesson in how to ride it, took him out for a five-minute practice spin, had him sign multiple disclaimers, and wished him luck. In so doing, Pendergast learned more about Kyle Swinton. He appeared to be known to all Leadville as a 'crazy fucker.' His parents had been alcoholics who finally went through the guardrail at Stockton Creek, drunk as skunks, and rolled a thousand feet down the ravine. Kyle had lived off the land ever since, hunting, fishing, and panning for gold when he needed ready cash to buy ammunition.

As Pendergast was leaving, the rental shop manager added: 'Don't go rushing up to the cabin, now, Kyle's liable to get excited. Approach real nice and slow, and keep your hands in sight and a friendly smile on your face.'

CHAPTER 50

The ride to Swinton's cabin was exceedingly unpleasant. The snowmobile was a coarse, deafening, stinking contraption, prone to jackrabbit starts and sudden stops, with none of the refinement of a high-performance motorcycle, and as Pendergast maneuvered it up the winding white road it threw up a steady wake of snow that plastered his expensive coat, building up layers. Pendergast soon looked like a helmeted snowman. He followed the advice he'd been given and slowed down as soon as he saw the cabin, half buried in snow, with a trickle of smoke curling from a stovepipe on top. Sure enough, as he came within a hundred yards a man appeared on the porch, small and ferret-like, with a gap between his two front teeth visible even at this distance. He was holding a pump-action shotgun.

Pendergast halted the snowmobile, which jerked to a stop. Plates of snow broke off and fell from his coat. He fumbled awkwardly with the helmet and finally managed to raise the visor with his bulky gloves.

'Greetings, Kyle!'

The response was a conspicuous racking of the pump. 'State your business, sir.'

'I'm here to see you. I've heard a lot about your outfit up here. I'm a fellow survivalist and I'm touring the country looking at what other people are doing, for an article in *Survivalist* magazine.'

'Where'd you hear about me?'

'Word gets around. You know how it is.'

A hesitation. 'So you're a journalist?'

'I'm a survivalist first, journalist second.' A cold gust of wind swirled the snow about Pendergast's legs. 'Mr Swinton, do you think you might extend me the courtesy of your hospitality so that we could continue this conversation in the confines of your home?'

Swinton wavered. The word *hospitality* had not gone unnoticed. Pendergast pressed his advantage. 'I wonder if keeping a man freezing in the cold at gunpoint is the kind of hospitality one should accord a kindred spirit.'

Swinton squinted at him. 'At least you're a white man,' he said, putting down the gun. 'All right, come on in. But see that you broom yourself off at the door; I don't want no snow tracked in my house.' He waited as Pendergast struggled through the deep snow to the porch. A broken broom stood next to the door and Pendergast swept himself as clean as he could while Swinton watched, frowning.

He followed Swinton in the cabin. It was surprisingly large, extending into a warren of rooms in the back. The gleam of gunmetal could be seen everywhere: racks of assault rifles, AK-47s and M16s illegally altered to fire on full-auto; a set of Uzis and TAR-21 bullpup assault rifles; another set of Chinese Norinco QBZ-97 rifles and carbines, again altered for fully automatic action. A nearby case contained a huge array of revolvers and pistols, just as the man in Leadville had said. Beyond, in one of the rooms, Pendergast glimpsed a collection of RPGs, including a pair of Russian RPG-29s – all quite illegal.

Other than the walls being completely covered with weaponry, the cabin was surprisingly cozy, with a fire burning in a woodstove with an open door. All the furniture was handmade of peeled logs and branches, draped with cowhides. And everything was neat as a pin.

'Shed that coat and seat yourself, I'll get the coffee.'

Pendergast removed the coat and draped it over a chair, straightened his suit, and sat down. Swinton fetched some mugs and a coffeepot off the woodstove and poured two cups. Without asking he heaped in a tablespoon of Cremora and two of sugar before handing it to Pendergast.

The agent took the mug and made a show of drinking. It tasted as if it had been boiling on the stove for days.

He found Swinton looking at him curiously. 'What's with the black suit? Somebody die? You come up here by snowmobile in that getup?'

'It was functional.'

'You sure as hell don't look like a survivalist to me.'

'What do I look like?'

'Some pussy professor from Jew York City. Or with that accent, maybe Jew Orleans. So what're you packing?'

Pendergast removed his .45 Colt and laid it on the table. Swinton picked it up, immediately impressed. 'Les Baer, huh? Nice. You know how to fire that?'

'I try,' said Pendergast. 'This is quite a collection you have. Do *you* know how to fire all those weapons?'

Swinton took offense, as Pendergast knew he would. 'You think I hang shit like that on my wall if I don't know how to fire it?'

'Anyone can pull the trigger on a weapon,' Pendergast said, sipping his coffee.

'I fire almost every weapon I own at least once a week.'

Pendergast pointed to the handgun cabinet. 'What about that Super Blackhawk?'

'That's a fine weapon. Updated Old West.' He got up, took it down from the rack.

'May I see it?'

He handed it to Pendergast. He hefted it, sighted, then opened the barrel and dumped out the ammo.

'What you doing?'

Pendergast picked up one of the rounds, inserted it back in the barrel, gave it a spin, then laid the revolver down.

393

'You think you're tough, right? Let's play a little game.'

'What the hell? What game?'

'Put the gun to your head and pull the trigger. And I'll give you a thousand dollars.'

Swinton stared at him. 'Are you stupid or something? I can see the fucking round isn't even in firing position.'

'Then you've just won a thousand dollars. If you pick the gun up and pull the trigger.'

Swinton picked the gun up, put it to his head, and pulled the trigger. There was a click. He laid it down.

Without a word, Pendergast reached into his suit-coat pocket, pulled out a brick of one-hundred-dollar bills, and peeled off ten of them. Swinton took the money. 'You're crazy, you know that?'

'Yes, I am crazy.'

'Now it's your own damn turn.' Swinton picked up the revolver, spun the barrel, laid it down.

'What will you give me?'

'I don't got no money, and I ain't giving you back the thousand.'

'Then perhaps you'll answer a question instead. Any question I choose to ask. Absolute truth.'

Swinton shrugged. 'Sure.'

Pendergast removed another thousand and put it on the table. Then he picked up the gun, placed it at his temple, and pulled the trigger. Another click.

'And now for the question.'

'Shoot.'

'Your great-great-grandfather was a miner in Roaring Fork during the silver boom days. He knew quite a bit about a series of killings, allegedly done by a man-eating grizzly bear, but in actuality done by a group of crazy miners.'

He paused. Swinton had risen from his chair. 'You're no damn magazine writer! Who are you?'

'I am the one who is asking you a question. Presuming that you're a man of honor, I will receive an answer. If you wish to know who I really am, that must await the next round of the game. Provided, of course, you have the fortitude to continue.'

Swinton said nothing.

'Your ancestor knew more than most people about those killings. In fact, I think he knew the truth – the entire truth.' Pendergast paused. 'My question is: What *is* the truth?'

Swinton shifted in his chair. The expression on his face went through several rapid changes. He exposed his ferrety teeth several times, his lips twitching. This went on for a while, then at last he cleared his throat. 'Why do you want to know?'

'Private curiosity.'

'Who are you gonna tell?'

'Nobody.'

Swinton stared hungrily at the thousand dollars sitting on the table. 'You swear to that? It's been a secret in my family for a long, long time.'

Pendergast nodded.

Another pause. 'It started with the Committee of Seven,' Swinton said at last. 'My great-great-granddaddy, August Swinton, was one of them. At least, that's what was passed down.' A tinge of pride edged into his voice. 'As you said, those were no grizzly killings. They was done by four crazy bastards, former smelter workers, who were living wild in the mountains and had turned cannibal. A man named Shadrach Cropsey went up to track the bear and discovered it wasn't a bear at all, but these fellers living in an abandoned mine. He figured out where they were holed up and then pulled together this Committee of Seven.'

'And then what happened?'

'That's a second question.'

'So it is.' Pendergast smiled. 'Time for another round?' He picked up the revolver, spun the cylinder, and laid it down.

Swinton shook his head. 'I can still see the round, and it ain't in the firing chamber. Another thousand bucks?'

Pendergast nodded.

Swinton picked up the gun and pulled the trigger again, put it down, held out his hand. 'This is the dumbest damn game I ever saw.'

Pendergast handed him a thousand dollars. Then he picked up the gun, spun the barrel, and without looking at it put it to his head and pulled the trigger. *Click.*

'You really are one crazy motherfucker.'

'There appear to be a great many like me in

this area,' Pendergast replied. 'And now for my question: What did Shadrach Cropsey and this Committee of Seven do then?'

'Back in those days, they handled problems the right way – they did it themselves. Fuck the law and all its bullshit. They went up there and smoked those cannibals. The way I heard it, old Shadrach got his ass killed in the fight. After that, there weren't no more "grizzly" killings.'

'And the place where they killed the miners?'

'Another question, friend.'

Pendergast spun the barrel, placed it on the table. Swinton eyed it nervously. 'I can't see the round.'

'Then it is either in the firing chamber or in the opposite chamber, hidden by the frame. Which means there is a fifty–fifty chance you will live.'

'I ain't playing.'

'You just said you would. I didn't imagine you were a coward, Mr Swinton.' He reached in his pocket and pulled out the brick of hundreds. This time he peeled off twenty. 'We'll double the stakes. You will receive two thousand – if you pull the trigger.'

Swinton was sweating heavily. 'I ain't gonna play.'

'You mean, you pass on your turn? I won't insist.'

'That's what I mean. I pass.'

'But I do not pass on my turn.'

'Go ahead. Be my fucking guest.'

Pendergast spun the barrel, held the revolver up, pulled the trigger. *Click.* He put it down.

'My final question: Where did they kill the miners?'

'I don't know. But I do have the letter.'

'What letter?'

'The one that got passed down to me. It sort of explains things.' He rose from his creaking chair and shuffled off into the dim recesses of the cabin. He returned a moment later with a dusty old piece of yellow paper sandwiched in Mylar. He eased himself back down and handed the letter to Pendergast.

It was a handwritten note, undated, with no salutation or signature. It read:

> mete at the Ideal 11 oclock Sharp to Night they are Holt Up in the closed Christmas Mine up on smugglers wall there are 4 of them bring your best Guns and lantern burn this Letter afore you set out

Pendergast lowered the letter. Swinton held out his hand, and Pendergast returned it. Swinton's brow was still beaded with sweat, but the look on his face was pure relief. 'I can't believe you played that game without ever looking at the cylinder. That's just crazy-ass dangerous.'

Pendergast dressed again in his coat, scarves, and hat, and then took up the revolver. He opened the cylinder and let the .44 magnum round drop into his hand. 'There was never any danger. I brought this round with me and substituted it for one of yours after I unloaded the gun.' He held it up. 'It's been doctored.'

Swinton rose. 'Mother*fucker*!' He came at Pendergast, drawing his carry, but in a flash Pendergast had shoved the round back in and rotated it into firing position, pointing the Blackhawk at Swinton.

'Or maybe I *didn't* doctor it.'

Swinton froze.

'You'll never know.' Pendergast picked up his own Les Baer, and – while covering Swinton with it – removed the round from the Blackhawk and put it in his coat pocket. 'And now I will answer your earlier question: I'm not a magazine writer. I'm a federal agent. And there's one thing I promise you: if you lied to me, I'll know it, sooner rather than later – and in that case, none of your weapons will save you.'

CHAPTER 51

That same day, at three o'clock in the afternoon, Corrie lounged in the room she had acquired at the Hotel Sebastian, wearing a terry-cloth bathrobe supplied by the hotel, first admiring the view, and then checking out the mini-bar (which she couldn't afford, but enjoyed rummaging through anyway) before moving into the marble bathroom. She turned on the shower, adjusted the water, and slipped out of the bathrobe, stepping in.

As she luxuriated in the hot shower, she considered that things were looking up. She felt badly about what happened at breakfast the day before, but even that paled in comparison with Pendergast's revelations. The Doyle story, the mercury-crazed miners – and the Stafford family connection – it was truly remarkable. *And* truly frightening. Pendergast was right: she had placed herself in grave danger.

Roaring Fork had now pretty much resumed the ghost-town status it once held, except it was all dressed up for Christmas with nowhere to go. Totally surreal. Even the press seemed to have packed up their cameras and microphones. The Hotel Sebastian had lost most of its guests and staff, but the restaurant was still going strong – stronger than ever, as those remaining in town, it seemed, all wanted to eat out. Corrie had managed to drive a hard bargain with the hotel manager, snagging room and breakfast free of charge in return for six hours of kitchen work every day. And although her arrangement with the hotel came with only one meal a day, Corrie had plenty of experience with all-you-can-eat deals and was confident she could scarf down enough food in one sitting to last twenty-four hours.

She got out of the shower, toweled off, and combed her hair. As she was drying it, she heard a knock at the door. Quickly donning the bathrobe again, she went to the door and peeked through the eyehole.

Pendergast.

She opened the door, but the agent hesitated. 'I'd be glad to return later—'

'Don't be silly. Sit down, I'll only be a moment.' She went back into the bathroom, finished blowing out her hair, wrapped the bathrobe a little tighter, and came back out, seating herself on the sofa.

Pendergast did not look well. His usual alabaster face was mottled with red and his hair looked like it had been in a wind tunnel.

'How did it go?' Corrie asked. She knew he had gone to Leadville to see if he could trace a Swinton descendant.

Instead of answering the question, he said, 'I am delighted to find you safely ensconced in the hotel. As for the cost, I'd be happy to help—'

'Not necessary, thank you,' Corrie said quickly. 'I managed to finagle free room and board in return for a few hours of kitchen work.'

'How enterprising of you.' He paused, his face growing more serious. 'I regret that you felt it necessary to deceive me. I understand from the chief that your car was shot at and your dog killed.'

Corrie colored deeply. 'I didn't want you to worry. I'm sorry. I was going to tell you eventually.'

'You didn't want me to take you away from Roaring Fork.'

'That, too. And I wanted to find the bastard who killed my dog.'

'You must not attempt to find out who killed your dog. I hope you now understand you're dealing with dangerous and highly motivated people. This is far bigger than a dead dog – and you're intelligent enough to realize that.'

'Of course. I understand that clearly.'

'There's a development worth two hundred million dollars at stake – but this isn't just about money. It will lead to heavy criminal indictments against those involved, some of whom happen to belong to one of the wealthiest and most powerful clans in this country, beginning with your Mrs Kermode and quite likely ending with members of the Stafford family as well. Perhaps now you can understand why they will not hesitate to kill you.'

'But I want them brought to justice—'

'And they will be. But not by you, and not while you're here. When you're safely back in New York, I will bring in the Bureau and all will be exposed. So you see, there's nothing left for you to do here except pack your bags and return to New York – as soon as the weather permits.'

Corrie thought about the coming storm. It would close the road again. She supposed she could start writing things up, get an outline of her thesis nailed down, before she had to leave.

'All right,' she said.

'In the meantime, I want you to stay within the confines of the hotel. I've spoken to the chief of security here, an excellent woman, and you'll be safe. You may be stuck here for a few days, however. The weather forecast is dire.'

'Fine with me. So . . . are you going to tell me about your trip to Leadville?'

'I am not.'

'Why?'

'Because the knowledge would only put you in more unnecessary danger. Please allow me to handle this from now on.'

Despite his kindly tone, Corrie felt irritated. She'd agreed to what he asked. She was going back to New York as soon as the weather cleared. Why couldn't he take her into his confidence? 'If you insist,' she said.

Pendergast rose. 'I would invite you to dine with me, but I have to confer with the chief. They have made little progress on the arsonist case.'

He left. Corrie thought for a moment, and then went over to the mini-bar. She was starving and had no money for food. Her breakfast deal didn't begin until the next morning. The can of Pringles was eight dollars.

Screw it, she thought as she tore off the lid.

CHAPTER 52

Three o'clock in the morning, December twenty-fourth. After flitting like a specter past the worn shopfronts and dark windows of Old Town, Pendergast took just seconds to break into the Ideal Saloon, picking the picturesque but ineffectual nineteenth-century lock.

He stepped into the dim space of the bar-*cum*-museum, its interior illuminated only by several strips of emergency fluorescent lighting, which cast garish shadows about the room. The saloon consisted of a large, central room, with circular tables, chairs, and a plank floor. A long bar ran the entire length of the far end. The walls consisted of wainscoting of vertical beadboard, gleaming with varnish and darkened by time, below flocked velvet wallpaper in a flowery Victorian pattern. The wall was decorated with sconces of copper and cut glass. Behind the bar and to the right, a staircase led up to what had been a small whorehouse. And farther off to the right, in an alcove partly under the staircase, stood some gaming tables. Velvet ropes just inside two swinging doors created a viewing area, preventing visitors from proceeding into the restored saloon.

Moving without noise, Pendergast ducked under the ropes and took a long, thoughtful turn about the room. A whisky bottle and some shot glasses stood on the bar, and several tables were also arrayed with bottles and glasses. Behind the bar stood a large mirrored case of antique liquor bottles filled with colored water.

He moved through the bar and into the gaming area. A poker table stood in one corner, covered with green felt, with hands of five-card stud laid out: four aces against a straight flush. A blackjack table, also artfully arranged with cards, stood beside a splendid antique roulette wheel with ivory, red jasper, and ebony inlay.

Pendergast glided past the gaming area to a door under the stairs. He tried to open it, found it locked, and swiftly picked the lock.

It opened into a small, dusty room, which remained unrestored, with cracked plaster walls and peeling wallpaper, some old chairs, and a broken table. Graffiti, some bearing dates from the 1930s, when Roaring Fork was still a ghost town, were scratched into the wall. A pile of broken whisky bottles lay in one corner. At the back of this room stood a door that led, Pendergast knew, to a rear exit.

He took off his coat and scarf and carefully draped them over one of the chairs, and looked around, slowly and carefully, as if committing everything to memory. He stood, quite still, for a long time, and then finally he stirred. Choosing a vacant spot on the floor, he lay down on the dirty boards and folded his hands over his chest, like a corpse in a coffin. Slowly, very slowly, he closed his eyes. In the silence, he focused on the sounds of the snow-storm: the muffled wind shaking and moaning about the exterior walls, the creaking of the wood, the rattling of the tin roof. The air smelled of dust, dry rot, and mildew. He allowed his respiration and pulse to slow and his mind to relax.

It was in this back room, he felt certain, that the Committee of Seven would have met up. But before he went down that avenue, there was another place he wished to visit first – a visit that would take place entirely within his mind.

Pendergast had once spent time in a remote Tibetan monastery, studying an esoteric medita-tive discipline known as Chongg Ran. It was one of the least known of the Tibetan mind techniques. The teachings were never put down in writing, and they could only be transmitted directly teacher-to-pupil.

Pendergast had taken the heart of Chongg Ran and combined it with several other mental discip-lines, including the concept of a memory palace as described in a sixteenth-century Italian man-uscript by Giordano Bruno titled *Ars Memoria*, Art of Memory. The result was a unique and highly complex form of mental visualization. With training, careful preparation, and a fanatical degree of intel-lectual discipline, the exercise allowed him to take a complex problem with many thousands of facts and surmises, and mentally stitch them together into a coherent narrative, which could then be processed, analyzed – and, especially, *experienced*. Pendergast used the technique to help solve elusive problems; to visualize places, via the force of his intellect, that could not be reached physically – far distant places, or even places in the past. The technique was extremely draining, however, and he employed it sparingly.

He lay for many minutes, as still as a corpse, first arranging a hugely complex set of facts into careful order, then tuning his senses to the surrounding environment while simultaneously shutting down the voice in his mind, turning off that incessant running commentary all people carry in their heads. The voice had been especially voluble of late, and it took a great deal of effort to silence it; Pendergast was forced to move his meditative stance from the Third Level to the Fourth Level, doing complex equations in his head, playing four hands of bridge simultaneously. At last, the voice was silenced, and he then began the ancient steps of Chongg Ran itself. First, he blocked every sound, every sensation, one after another: the creaking of the building, the rustling of the wind, the scent of dust, the hard floor beneath him, the seeming infinitude of his own corporal awareness – until at length he arrived at the state of *stong pa nyid*: the condition of Pure Emptiness. For a moment, there was only nonexistence; even time itself seemed to fall away.

But then – slowly, very slowly – something began to materialize out of the nothingness. At first it was as miniaturized, as delicate, as beautiful as a Fabergé egg. With that same lack of hurry, it grew larger and clearer. Eyes still shut, Pendergast allowed it to take on form and definition around him. And then, at last, he opened his eyes to find himself within a brightly lit space: a splendid and elegant dining room, refulgent with light and crystal, the clinking of glasses, and the murmur of genteel conversation.

To the smell of cigar smoke and the learned discourse of a string quartet, Pendergast took in the opulent room. His eyes traveled over the tables, finally stopping at one in a far corner. Seated at it were four gentlemen. Two of the men were laughing together over some witticism or other – one wearing a broadcloth frock coat, the other in evening dress. Pendergast, however, was more interested in the other two diners. One was dressed flamboyantly: white kid gloves, a vest and cutaway coat of black velvet, a large frilled necktie, silk knee breeches and stockings, slippers adorned with grosgrain bows. An orchid drooped in his button-hole. He was in deep descant, speaking animatedly, one hand pressed against his breast, the other pointing heavenward, index finger extended in a travesty of John the Baptist. The man beside him, who seemed to be hanging on his companion's every word, presented an entirely different appearance, a contrast so strong as to almost be comical.

He was a stocky fellow in a somber, sensible English suit, with big mustaches and an awkward bearing.

They were Oscar Wilde and Arthur Conan Doyle.

Slowly, in his mind, Pendergast approached the table, listening intently, as the conversation – or, more frequently, monologue – became audible.

'Indeed?' Wilde was saying, in a remarkably deep and sonorous voice. 'Did you think that – as one who would happily sacrifice himself on the pyre of aestheticism – I do not recognize the face of horror when I stare into it?'

There was no empty seat. Pendergast turned, motioned to a waiter, indicated the table. Immediately, the man brought up a fifth chair, placing it between Conan Doyle and the man Pendergast realized must be Joseph Stoddart.

'I was once told a story so dreadful, so distressing in its particulars and in the extent of its evil, that now I truly believe nothing I hear could ever frighten me again.'

'How interesting.'

'Would you care to hear it? It is not for the faint of heart.'

As he listened to the conversation taking place beside him, Pendergast reached forward, poured himself a glass of wine, found it excellent.

'It was told to me during my lecture tour of America a few years back. On my way to San Francisco, I stopped at a rather squalid yet picturesque mining camp known as Roaring Fork.' Wilde pressed his hand to Doyle's knee for emphasis. 'After my lecture, one of the miners approached me, an elderly chap somewhat the worse – or, perhaps, the better – for drink. He took me aside, said he'd enjoyed my story so much that he had one of his own to share with me.' He paused for a sip of burgundy. 'Here, lean in a little closer, that's a good fellow, and I'll tell it you exactly as it was told to me.'

Doyle leaned in, as requested. Pendergast leaned in, as well.

'I tried to escape him, but he would have none of it, presuming to approach me in a most familiar way, breathing fumes of the local *ubriacant*. My first impulse was to push past, but there was something about the look in his eye that stopped me. I confess I was also intrigued – in an anthropological fashion, Doyle, don't you know – by this leathern specimen, this uncouth bard, this bibulous miner, and I found myself curious as to what he considered a "good story." And so I listened, and rather attentively, as his American drawl was nigh indecipherable. He spoke of events that had occurred some years earlier, not long after the silver strikes that established Roaring Fork. Over the course of one summer, a grizzled bear – or so it was believed – had taken to roaming the mountains above the town, attacking, killing . . . *and* eating . . . lone miners working their claims.'

Doyle nodded vigorously, his face concentrated with the utmost interest.

411

'Naturally, the town fell into a state of perfect terror. But the killings went on, as there were many lone men upon the mountain. The bear was merciless, ambuscading the miners outside their cabins, killing and savagely dismembering them – and then feasting upon their flesh.' Wilde paused. 'I should have liked to have known whether the, ah, *consumption* commenced while consciousness was still present. Can you imagine what it would be like to be devoured alive by a savage beast? To watch it tear your flesh off, then chew and swallow, with evident satisfaction? That is a contemplation never even considered by Huysmans in his *À Rebours*. How sadly lacking the aesthete was, in hindsight!'

Wilde glanced over to see what effect his words were having on the country doctor. Doyle had grasped his glass of claret and taken a deep draught. Listening, Pendergast took a sip of his own glass, then signaled a waiter to bring him a menu.

'Many a fellow tried to track the grizzled bear,' Wilde continued, 'but none was successful – save for one miner, a man who had learned the fine art of tracking while living among Indians. He conceived a notion that the killings were not the work of a bear.'

'Not the work of a bear, sir?'

'Not the work of a bear, sir. And so, waiting until the next killing, this chap – his name was Cropsey – went a-tracking, and soon discovered that the perpetrators of this outrage were a group of men.'

412

At this, Doyle leaned back rather abruptly. 'I beg your pardon, Mr Wilde. Do you mean to say that these men were . . . cannibals?'

'Indeed I do. American cannibals.'

Doyle shook his head. 'Monstrous. Monstrous.'

'Quite so,' Wilde said. 'They have none of the good manners of your English cannibals.'

Doyle stared at his fellow guest in shock. 'This is no matter for levity, Wilde.'

'Perhaps not. We shall see. In any case, our Cropsey tracked these cannibals to their lair, an abandoned mine shaft somewhere on the mountain, at a place called Smuggler's Wall. There was no constabulary in the town, of course, and so this fellow organized a small group of local vigilantes. They cognominated themselves the Committee of Seven. They would scale the mountain in the dark of night, surprise the cannibals, and administer the rough justice of the American West.' Wilde toyed with his *boutonnière*. 'The very next night, at midnight, this group gathered at the local saloon to discuss strategy and no doubt fortify themselves for the coming ordeal. They then departed by a back door, heavily armed, and equipped with lanterns, rope, and a torch. This, my dear Doyle, is where the story turns . . . well, not to put too fine a point on it, rather ghastly. Do steady yourself, there's a good chap.'

The waiter brought over a menu, and Pendergast turned his attention to it. Three or four minutes later, he was jarred from his perusal by Doyle's

413

sudden violent rise from the table – knocking his chair over in his agitation – and subsequent flight from the dining room, his face a mixture of shock and disgust.

'Why, whatever's the matter?' Stoddart said, frowning, as Doyle disappeared in the direction of the gentlemen's lounge.

'I suspect it must be the prawns,' Wilde replied, and he dabbed primly at his mouth with a napkin . . .

. . . As slowly as it had come, the voice began to fade from Pendergast's mind. The sumptuous interior of the Langham Hotel began to waver, as if dissolving into mist and darkness. Slowly, slowly, a new scene materialized – a very different scene. It was the smoke-filled, whisky-redolent back room of a busy saloon, the sounds of gambling, drinking, and argument penetrating the thin wooden walls. A back room, in fact, remarkably similar to the one in which Pendergast was – in the Roaring Fork of the present – currently situated. After a brief exchange of determined voices, a group of seven men rose from a large table: men carrying lanterns and guns. Following their leader, one Shadrach Cropsey, they made their way out the back door of the little room and into the night.

Pendergast followed them, his incorporeal presence hovering in the cool night air like a ghost.

CHAPTER 53

The group of miners walked down the dirt main street of town, casually and without hurry, until they reached the far end, where settlement ceased and the forests mounted upward into the mountains. It was a moonless night. The scent of wood fires was in the air, and in the nearby corrals, horses were moving restlessly about. Silently, the group lit their lanterns and proceeded along a rough mining road, which made its way by switchbacks up, and then farther up, passing beneath the dark fir trees.

The night was cool and the sky was pricked with stars. A lone wolf howled somewhere in the great bowl of mountains, quickly answered by another. As the men gained altitude, the fir trees grew smaller, shorter, twisted into grotesque shapes by incessant winds and deep snows. Gradually the trees thinned out into matted thickets of krummholz, and then the cart path broached the tree line.

In his mind, Pendergast followed the group.

The line of yellow lanterns advanced up the barren, rock-strewn slopes approaching Smuggler's Cirque. They were now entering a recently abandoned mining zone, and around the men appeared ghostly tailings, like pyramids, spilling down the sides of the ridge, the gaping holes of the mines above, punctuated by rickety ore chutes, trestles, sluice boxes, and flumes.

Looming in the darkness to the right was an immense wooden structure, set into the flat declivity at the base of Smuggler's Cirque: the main entrance to the famed Sally Goodin Mine, still in operation now, in the early fall of 1876. The building housed the machines and pulley works used to raise and lower the cages and buckets; it also enclosed the two-hundred-ton Ireland Pump Engine, capable of pumping over a thousand gallons per minute, used to dewater the mine complex.

Now all the lanterns went out but one: a red-glass lamp that cast a bloody gleam in the murky night. The cart path divided into many winding tracks cut into the hillsides rising above the cirque. Their objective lay above, the highest of the abandoned tunnels high on the slope known as Smuggler's Wall, situated at an altitude close to thirteen thousand feet. A single track led in that direction, carved by hand out of the scree, switch-backing sharply as it climbed. It came over a ridge and skirted a small glacial tarn, the water black and still, its shore dotted with rusted pumping machinery and old flume gates.

Still the group of seven men climbed upward. Now the dark, square hole of the Christmas Mine became visible in the faint starlight against the upper scree slope. A trestle ran from the hole, and below it stood a tailings pile of lighter color. A jumble of wrecked machinery was strewn about the slope below.

The group paused, and Pendergast heard a low murmur of voices. And then they silently divided. One man made his way up, hiding among boulders above the entrance. A second took up a covered position among the scree just below the entrance.

Lookouts in place, the rest – four men led by Cropsey, now holding the lantern himself – entered the abandoned tunnel. Pendergast followed. The shutter on the red lamp was adjusted to produce only the faintest glow. Arms at the ready, the men walked single-file along the iron rails leading into the tunnel, making no noise. One carried a torch of pitch, ready to be lit.

As they proceeded, a smell came toward them, a smell that became ever more awful in the hot, moist, stifling atmosphere.

The Christmas Mine tunnel opened into a crosscut: a horizontal tunnel driven at right angles to the main tunnel. The group paused before the crosscut and readied their weapons. The torch was lowered, a match was struck, and the pitch set afire. In that moment, the men rounded the corner, weapons aimed down the tunnel. The smell was now almost overwhelming.

Silence. The flickering flames disclosed something in the darkness at the end of the tunnel. The group cautiously moved forward. It was an irregular, lumpy shape. When they drew close, the men saw that it was a heap of soft things: rotting burlap, old gunnysacks, leaves and pine needles, chunks of moss. Mingled into the material were pieces of gnawed bone, broken skulls, and strips of what looked like dried rawhide.

Skin. Hairless skin.

All around the heap lay a broad ring of human feces.

One of the men spoke hoarsely. 'What . . . *is this*?'

The question was initially answered with silence. Finally, one of the others replied. 'It's an animal den.'

'It ain't *animal*,' said Cropsey.

'God Almighty.'

'Where are they?'

Now their voices were rising, echoing, as fear and uncertainty began to set in.

'The bastards must be out. Killing.'

The torch sputtered and burned as their voices rose, discussing what to do. The guns were put away. There was disagreement, conflict.

Suddenly Cropsey held up his hand. The others fell silent, listening. There were sounds of shuffling, along with guttural, animalistic breathing. The noises stopped. Quickly the man carrying the torch doused it in a puddle of water, while Cropsey shut the lantern down. But now all was deathly silent: it seemed likely the killers had seen the light or heard their voices – and knew they were here.

'Give us some light, for Jesus's sake,' whispered one of the men, his voice tight with anxiety.

Cropsey opened the lantern a fraction. The others were crouching, rifles and pistols at the ready. The dim glow barely penetrated the gloom.

'*More* light,' someone said.

The lantern now threw light to the edge of the cross tunnel. All was silent. They waited, but nothing came around the corner. Nor were there sounds of flight.

'We go get 'em,' Cropsey announced. 'Afore they get away.'

No one moved. Finally Cropsey himself began stalking forward. The others followed. He crept to the crosscut. The rest waited behind. Holding up the lantern, he paused, crouched, then suddenly swung around the corner, wielding the rifle like a pistol in one hand, the lantern in the other. '*Now!*'

It happened with incredible speed. A flash of something darting forward; a gargling scream; and then Cropsey spun around, dropping his rifle and writhing in agony. A naked, filthy man was astride his back, tearing at his throat, more like a beast than a human being. None of the other four could fire; the combatants were too close together. Cropsey screamed again, staggering about, trying to shake off the man who tore at him with nails and teeth, ripping away anything he could reach: ears, lips, nose; there was a sudden spurt of arterial blood from the neck and Cropsey went down, the monster still on top of him, the lantern falling to the ground and shattering.

Simultaneously, as with a single mind, the other four began to shoot, aiming wildly into the darkness. From the muzzle flashes more figures could be seen, bellowing like bulls, running toward them from around the corner of the crosscut, a melee amid the wild eruption of gunfire. The two lookouts came charging down the tunnel, aroused by the din, and joined in with their own weapons. The guns roared again and again, the flashes of light blooming within clouds of ugly gray smoke – and then all went silent. For a moment, there was only darkness. Then came the sound of a match, scraping against rock; another lantern was lit – and its feeble light illuminated a splay of corpses, the four cannibals now just ruined bodies scattered about the tunnel, taken apart by heavy-caliber bullets, lying like so much ropy waste atop the sundered carcass of Shadrach Cropsey.

It was over.

Fifteen minutes later, Pendergast opened his eyes. The room was cool and quiet. He rose, brushed off his black suit, bundled himself up, and let himself out the back door of the saloon. The storm was in full blast, the fury of it thundering down Main Street and shaking the Christmas decorations like so many cobwebs. Bundling his coat around himself, wrapping his scarf tighter, and lowering his head against the wind, he made his way through the storm-shaken town back to his hotel.

CHAPTER 54

At eleven o'clock that morning – Christmas Eve day – after buttering two hundred pieces of toast, washing twice that number of dishes, and mopping the kitchen from wall to wall – Corrie went back to her room, bundled up in her coat, and ventured out into the storm. The idea that Kermode or her thugs might be out in this weather, waiting for her, seemed far-fetched; nevertheless, she felt an electric tickle of fear. She consoled herself with the thought that she was on her way to the safest place in town – the police station.

She had decided to confront Pendergast. Not so much confront him, exactly, but rather to make another pitch about why he should share with her the information he'd apparently gotten on his trip to Leadville. The way she saw things, it was unfair of him to withhold it. She had, after all, discovered the Swinton connection and shared the name with him. If he'd found information about the old killings, the least he could do would be to let her include it in her thesis.

The wind and flying snow came buffeting down the street as she turned onto Main. She leaned into it, holding her cap. The business district of Roaring Fork was relatively compact, but even so it proved a damn long journey in a blizzard.

The police station loomed up through the blowing snow, its windows glowing with yellow light, perversely inviting. All were apparently at work despite the storm. She walked up the steps, stomped off the snow in the vestibule, shook out her woolen hat and scarf, and went in.

'Is Special Agent Pendergast in?' she asked Iris, the lady at the reception desk, with whom she had gotten friendly over the past ten days.

'Oh, dear,' she sighed. 'He doesn't sign in and out, and he keeps the oddest hours. I just can't keep track.' She shook her head. 'Feel free to check his office.'

Corrie went down into the basement, grateful for once for the heat. His door was closed. She knocked; no answer.

Where could he be, in a storm like this? Not at the Hotel Sebastian, where he hadn't been answering his phone.

She turned the handle, but it was locked.

She paused for a moment, thoughtfully, still grasping the handle. Then she went back upstairs.

'Find him?' Iris asked.

'No luck,' said Corrie. She hesitated. 'Listen, I think I left something important in his office. Do you have a key?'

Iris considered this. 'Well, I do, but I don't think I can let you in. What did you leave?'

'My cell phone.'

'Oh.' Iris thought some more. 'I suppose I *could* let you in, so long as I stay with you.'

'That would be great.'

She followed Iris back down the stairs. In a moment the woman had opened the door and turned on the light. The room was hot and stuffy. Corrie looked around. The desk was covered with papers that had been carefully arranged. She scanned the surface with her eyes but it was all too neat, too squared away, to expose much information.

'I don't see it,' said Iris, looking about.

'He might have put it away in a drawer.'

'I don't think you should be opening up any drawers, Corrie.'

'Right. Of course not.'

She looked frantically around the desk, this way and that. 'It's got to be here somewhere,' she said.

And then Corrie caught a glimpse of something interesting. A page torn out of a small notebook, covered with Pendergast's distinctive copperplate handwriting, its top part sticking out of a sheaf of documents. Three underlined words jumped out: *Swinton* and *Christmas Mine*.

'Is it over here?' Corrie bent over the desk, as if looking behind a lamp, while 'accidentally' pushing the notebooks with her elbow, exposing a few more lines of the torn page, on which Pendergast had printed:

mete at the Ideal 11 oclock Sharp to Night
they are Holt Up in the closed Christmas
Mine up on smugglers wall there are 4 of

'*Really*, Corrie, it's time to go,' Iris said firmly,
with a frown on her lips at noticing Corrie reading
something on the desk.

'Okay. I'm sorry. Now, where *did* I leave that
darn phone?'

Back at the hotel, Corrie quickly wrote out the
lines from memory, then stared at them thoughtfully. It seemed obvious Pendergast had copied a
note or old document that mentioned the place
where the attack on the cannibals would take place:
the Christmas Mine. In the Griswell Mansion, she
had seen a number of maps of the mining district,
with each mine and tunnel marked and identified.
It would be simple to find the location, and maybe
even the layout, of this Christmas Mine.

This was interesting. This changed everything.
She'd suspected the mercury-crazed miners had
been hiding in some abandoned mine. If they were
killed in a tunnel or shaft, their remains could still
be there somewhere.

The Christmas Mine . . . if she recovered a few
bone and hair samples from the remains, she could
have them tested for mercury poisoning. Such a
test was cheap and easy; you could even send away
for a home kit. And if the tests were positive, it
would be the final feather in her cap. She would

have definitely solved the old murders and established a most unusual motivation.

She thought about her promise to Pendergast – to stay in the hotel, to abandon any attempt to find the person who'd shot at her and decapitated her dog. Well, she *had* abandoned the attempt. Pendergast shouldn't have withheld information from her – especially information of such crucial importance to her thesis.

She glanced out the window. The blizzard was still going strong. Since it was getting on toward Christmas Eve, everything was closed, and the town was almost completely deserted. Right now would be a perfect time to pay a little visit to the archives in the Griswell Mansion.

Corrie paused for a moment, then pocketed her small set of lock picks. The Griswell place would most likely have a period lock – no challenge at all.

Once again she bundled up and ventured out into the storm. Encouragingly, nobody except the snowplows was out and about as she made her way through the deserted streets. Some of the Christmas decorations, evergreen garlands and ribbons, had blown loose in the wind and were flapping and swinging forlornly from lampposts and street banners. Strings of bulbs had also come loose and were sputtering erratically. She couldn't see the outline of the mountains, but she could still hear, muffled by the snow, the hum and rumble of the lifts, which had been kept running

425

despite all that had happened and the almost complete absence of skiers. Perhaps skiing was such an ingrained part of Roaring Fork culture that the lifts and snow-grooming equipment simply never stopped operating.

As she turned the corner of East Haddam, she suddenly had the impression someone was behind her. She spun around and peered into the murk, but could see nothing except swirling snow. She hesitated. It might have been a passerby, or perhaps her imagination. Still, Pendergast's warning echoed in her mind.

There was one way to check. She retraced her steps – still quite visible in the snow. And indeed: there were additional footprints. The footprints had apparently been tracing hers, but they had suddenly veered away and gone off into a private alley – at just about the point where she had spun around.

Corrie suddenly found her heart beating hard. Okay, someone *was* following her. Maybe. Was it the thug who'd been trying to drive her out of town? Of course it might also be coincidence, paired with her justified sense of paranoia.

'Screw this,' she said out loud, turned back, and hurried down the street. Another corner and she found herself in front of the Griswell Mansion. The lock, as she figured, was old. It would be a simple matter to get inside.

But was the place alarmed?

A gust of wind buffeted her as she peered inside

the door panes for signs of an alarm system. She couldn't see anything obvious like infrared sensors or motion detectors mounted in the corners; nor was the building posted with an alarm warning. The place had an air about it of neglect and penny pinching. Maybe no one felt the piles of paper inside had any value or needed to be protected.

Even if the place *was* alarmed, and she set it off, were the police really going to respond? Right now they had bigger fish to fry. And in a storm like this, with high winds, falling branches, and ice, alarms were probably going off all over town.

Looking around, she removed her gloves and quickly picked the lock. She slipped inside, shut the door, took a deep breath. No alarm, no blinking lights, nothing. Just the shudder of the wind and snow outside.

She rubbed her hands together to warm them. This was going to be a piece of cake.

CHAPTER 55

Half an hour later, hunched over a pile of papers in a dim back room, Corrie had found what she needed. An old map showed her the location and layout of the Christmas Mine. According to the information she had dug up, the mine was a bust, one of the first to become played out and be abandoned, way back in 1875, and as far as she could tell never again reopened. That was probably why the crazed miners had used it as a home base.

She took another, more careful, look at the map. While the mine was high up on Smuggler's Wall, at nearly thirteen thousand feet in altitude, it was readily accessible by the web of old mining roads on the mountain, now used by four-wheelers in the summer and snowmobilers in the winter. The mine stood above a well-known complex of old structures situated in a natural bowl known as Smuggler's Cirque, which was a popular tourist destination in the summertime. One of the buildings, by far the tallest, was famous for holding the remains of the Ireland Pump Engine, supposedly the largest pump in the world when it was constructed, which had been used to dewater the mines as the shafts were dug below the water table.

The Christmas Mine would surely be sealed – all the old mines and tunnels in Roaring Fork, Corrie had learned, had been bricked up or, in some cases, plated with iron. The mine might be difficult or even impossible to break into, especially considering the snow. But it was worth a try. She had every reason to believe the remains of the cannibals would still be there, perhaps secreted away someplace by the vigilantes who killed them.

As she looked over the papers, maps, and diagrams, she realized that – quite subconsciously – a plan had already formed in her mind. She'd go up to the mine, locate the bodies, and take her samples. And she'd do it now – while the routes out of town were still impassable, and before Pendergast could force her to return to New York.

But how to get up there, way up the side of a mountain in a furious storm? Even as she posed the question, she realized the answer. There were snowmobiles up at the ski shed. She would simply go up to The Heights, borrow a snowmobile . . . and pay a quick visit to the old Christmas Mine.

And now really was the perfect time: Christmas Eve day, when ninety percent of the town had left and everyone else was hunkered down at home. Even if somebody *was* tailing her, they'd never follow her to the mine – not in weather like this. Just a brief reconnaissance up to the mountain and back . . . and then she'd hole up in the hotel until she could make arrangements to leave town.

It occurred to her that it wasn't just Kermode's thugs she should be aware of, but the weather as well. If anybody else would be crazy going out in this storm, then wasn't she acting a little crazy, too? She told herself she'd take it one step at a time. If the storm got too bad, or if she felt she was getting into a situation she couldn't handle, she'd abandon the recon and head back.

Pocketing the old map of the mine and another map of the overall mining district showing all the connecting tunnels, she made her way back to the Hotel Sebastian, keeping an eye out for the suspected stalker but seeing no sign. In her room she began to prepare for the task ahead. She packed her backpack with a small water bottle, sampling bags, headlamp with extra batteries, extra gloves and socks, matches, canteen, Mars Bars and Reese's Pieces, her lock-picking tools, a knife, Mace (which she carried everywhere), and her cell phone. She took another look at the Christmas Mine map she'd liberated from the archives, noting with satisfaction that the underground courses of the tunnels were clearly delineated.

The hotel concierge was able to provide – most useful of all – a snowmobile route map of the surrounding mountains. She also managed to 'borrow' from hotel maintenance a claw hammer, bolt cutter, and wrecking bar.

She bundled up, loaded her car, and headed

down Main Street in the storm, windshield wipers slapping. The snow was lightening a bit, the wind dropping. The snowplows were still out in force – snow clearing was amazingly efficient in this town – but even so the storm had gotten ahead of the clearing and there were three to four inches of snow on most of the roads. Nevertheless, the Ford Explorer handled well. As she approached The Heights, she rehearsed what she would say to the guard on duty; but when she actually arrived at the gate she found it open and the guardhouse empty. And why not? The workers would want to be home on Christmas Eve – and who in their right mind would be out in this storm anyway?

The heated road beyond was not bad, even though the snow was overwhelming the ability of the heating system to keep up. She almost got stuck a few times. But she shifted into 4L and managed to keep going. At least on the way out it would be mostly downhill.

The clubhouse came into view through the blowing snow, its lights on, the big plate-glass windows casting an inviting yellow glow. But the parking lot was empty, and Corrie pulled up close to the side of the building, got out of the car. In a storm like this, she doubted anyone would be inside. Nevertheless, she didn't want any prying eyes observing her taking one of the snowmobiles from the ski shed. After stamping and brushing the snow off herself, she walked around to the front and tried the door.

Locked.

She peered in the little row of panes to the right of the door. Inside, the place was lit up and festooned with decorations. A gas fire burned merrily in a fireplace. But nobody could be seen.

Just to be safe, she walked around the rest of the building, staring through windows, the wind, though abating, still crying in her ears. It was the work of five slow, careful minutes to satisfy herself that there was no one home.

She headed back to the side of the building, ready to continue up toward the ski shed. As she walked across the parking lot, she noticed that the snow had almost ceased. The unpaved road leading to the shed would still be passable. She got into the Explorer, started the engine. Everything was going her way. She'd have her pick of snowmobiles to choose from . . . and she still had the key to the shed padlock.

But then, as she was pulling around the circular driveway to the clubhouse and back toward the main, heated road, she noticed a second set of tire tracks in the snow, lying on top of hers.

CHAPTER 56

Coincidence? It was certainly possible. Corrie told herself that the tracks might be from someone in the development – after all, there were dozens of houses up there. Perhaps it was just some resident, hurrying home before the storm got worse. On the other hand, she'd been followed earlier, back in town. And why had the car pulled in to the parking lot? She felt a surge of apprehension and looked around, but there were no other vehicles in sight. She glanced at her watch: two o'clock. Three hours of daylight left.

The Explorer fishtailed up the road, Corrie gunning its engine. She skidded around the last bend and pulled the car up to the fence surrounding the shed. The snow had slacked off even further, but looking up she could see thick gray clouds that promised more on the way.

Keeping the car running, she double-checked her backpack – all was there, in good order. She didn't have a snowmobile suit, but had put on practically all her layers of winter clothes, along with two pairs of gloves, a balaclava, and heavy Sorel snow boots.

She got out of the car and hefted the heavy backpack, slinging it over one shoulder. It was strangely still. Everything was bathed in a cold, gray light; the air was frosty, her breath condensing. It smelled like evergreens. The tree boughs were laden with snow and drooping, the roofline of the shed piled deep, the rows of icicles dull and cold in the half light.

She unlocked the padlock with her key and entered the shed, turning on the light. The snow-mobiles were all there, neatly lined up, keys in the ignitions, helmets hung on a nearby pegboard. She walked down the line, looking them over, checking the gas gauges. While she had never driven a snow-mobile, as a teenager back in Kansas she had spent a fair amount of time on dirt bikes, and the snow-mobiles seemed to work the same way, with the throttle on the right handlebar and the brake on the left. It looked straightforward enough. She picked out the cleanest-looking one, made sure it had a full tank of gas, selected a helmet, and stowed her backpack in the under-seat storage compartment.

Stepping over to the main door of the shed, she unlocked it from the inside and slid it open with difficulty. Snow piled up against the door avalanched inside. Starting the snowmobile, she sat on the seat and looked over the controls, throttle, brakes, and shift, then turned the lights on and off a few times.

Despite the fear and anxiety that gnawed at her,

she couldn't help but feel a sense of excitement welling up. She should be looking at this as a sort of adventure. If someone was following her, would they follow her up the mountain? It seemed unlikely.

She put on the helmet and gave the machine a little gas, edging it cautiously through the doorway. Once outside she tried to shut the shed door, but the snow that had fallen inside prevented it from sliding.

It occurred to her that she was, in fact, stealing a snowmobile, which was probably a felony. But with the holiday, the snowstorm, and the police occupied with the arsonist, the chances of getting caught seemed nil. According to the map, the Christmas Mine entrance was about three miles away, up old mining roads that were now established snowmobile trails. If she proceeded cautiously, she could be there in, say, ten to fifteen minutes. Of course, a lot of things could go wrong. Maybe she wouldn't be able to break into the tunnel, or would find it caved in; perhaps the remains would have been buried or hidden. Or – God forbid – she might find Pendergast there ahead of her. After all, she'd indirectly learned the location from him. But at least she'd feel she'd done her best. Regardless, she could be up and back in less than an hour.

She took a long look at her maps, trying to memorize the route, then tucked them into the glove box below the small windshield. She eased the machine farther into the snow, where it began to sink alarmingly. With a little more gas, however, it rode higher and more securely. Gingerly goosing the throttle, she accelerated up the service road that, according to her map, joined the network of snowmobile trails into the mountains, eventually leading to the old mining road that would take her to Smuggler's Cirque and the mine entrance above.

Pretty soon she had the feel of the controls and was moving at a good clip, twenty miles per hour, the machine throwing up a wake of snow behind. It was unexpectedly exhilarating, flashing through the spruce trees, the frosty air rushing by, magnificent mountain peaks all around. She was plenty warm in her many layers.

As she attained the ridge, she came to the main snowmobile trail, conveniently marked with a sign. The heavy snow had obliterated any snowmobile tracks that might have been there, but the road cut itself was clearly visible as it went up Maroon Ridge, marked by tall posts with Day-Glo orange cards.

She continued on. As the altitude increased, the trees became smaller and stunted, some mere lumps of snow – and then, quite suddenly, she emerged above the tree line. She stopped to check her map – all good. The views were outstanding: Roaring Fork itself was spread out in the valley below, a miniature village, doll-like, cloaked in white. To her left, the ski area rose into the mountains in ribbons of white trails. The lifts were still running, but only the most hard-core skiers seemed to be out. Behind her stood the awe-inspiring peaks of the Continental Divide, fourteen thousand feet high.

According to the map, she was already halfway to the area of old mining buildings in the cirque.

She suddenly heard a distant buzzing sound coming up from below and halted to listen better. It was a snowmobile engine. Looking back down the route she had come up, she caught a glimpse of a black dot coming around one of the hairpin turns of the trail before vanishing into the trees.

She felt a wave of panic. Someone *was* following her. Or could it be just another snowmobiler? No – coincidence was one thing, but this was the third time that day she'd had the feeling she was being followed.

It *had* to be the stalker – Kermode's hired thug, she was certain, the person who had menaced her, killed her dog. At the thought a fresh surge of fear swept over her. This wasn't an adventure. This was sheer foolhardiness: she'd placed herself in a vulnerable position, alone on the mountain, far from help.

She immediately took out her cell phone. No service.

The sound of the engine grew rapidly. She didn't have much time.

Her mind raced. She couldn't turn around and go back – there was only one trail down, unless she went straight down the almost vertical ridge. She couldn't pull off the trail and hide – the machine made such obvious tracks. And the snow was too deep for her to abandon the snowmobile and go on foot.

It began to sink in that she had put herself in real trouble. The best thing, she decided, would be to continue on up to the mine, break in if she could, and get away from the stalker in there. She had a map of the Christmas Mine and he surely did not.

Even as she started up the trail again, she saw the snowmobile come around the final bend before the tree line, accelerating toward her.

Goosing the throttle, she tore up the trail, notching the snowmobile up to thirty miles an hour, then thirty-five, then forty. The machine practically flew, an almost sheer cliff to one side of the trail, on the other a steep wall of snow. In another five minutes the trail came over the lip of a hanging valley and she found herself in the old mining complex, nestled in the broad hollow marked on the map as Smuggler's Cirque: surrounded by high ridges, with derelict mining buildings scattered about, their sagging rooflines mantled with snow, some mere piles of broken boards. She paused briefly to orient herself with the map. The Christmas Mine was higher still, on a steep slope halfway up the mountainside, directly above the old buildings. Smuggler's Wall. Map in hand, she squinted upward in the gray light, locating the entrance. The official snowmobile trail ended here, but the map showed an old mining road, still extant, that led up to the mine. As she looked at the steep wall of the cirque she made out the road cut, switchbacking up in a series of terrifying hairpin turns, with heavy drifts of snow lying across it.

Again, she could hear the snowmobile closing in behind her.

Stuffing away the map, she gunned the engine, riding past the old buildings and heading for the far side of the bowl, where the slope climbed upward again. She was surprised to see fresh snowmobile tracks among the buildings, somewhat snowed over but clearly made earlier in the day.

She reached the base of the road cut. This was going to be scary. But even as she contemplated the almost vertical wall above her, the sound of the pursuing snowmobile grew louder and she turned to see it coming over the rim of the cirque, not half a mile away.

Revving the throttle, she started up the trail, keeping as much to the inside edge as she could, blasting through drifts and fins of snow. The first hairpin turn was so steep and narrow, it just about stopped her heart. As she crawled around it, decelerating sharply, she almost became stuck in a drift and her efforts to get loose sent snow cascading down in a plume, the snowmobile tipping. She gunned it hard, spewing snow, and just managed to get back on the track. She paused, breathing hard, terrified by the yawning white space below her. It occurred to her that the avalanche danger on this steep slope must be high. She could see her pursuer was now riding through the old mining complex, following in her tracks. He was close enough for her to see the rifle slung over his shoulder.

She realized she had allowed herself to become cornered on the mountain. The road ended at the mine, and there was nothing but vertical cliffs above. And a killer below.

She made it past another half a dozen terrifying turns, driving recklessly through the deep snow, not letting the machine stop and settle. She finally reached the entrance to the Christmas Mine, marked by a rickety trestle and a square opening of massive, rotten timbers. She pulled the snow-mobile right up to the opening, tore off her helmet, pulled up the seat, and hauled out her backpack. As soon as the engine was off she could hear the roar of the other snowmobile, much closer.

The door was set back into the tunnel about ten feet, which meant it was not drifted up with snow. The entrance had a rusted door set into a plate of riveted steel, deeply pitted by age, fixed with a heavy, ancient padlock.

The engine sound got louder. Corrie began to panic. She stripped off her gloves, grabbed her lock-pick tools, and tried to insert a bump key, but it was immediately apparent the lock was frozen with rust and unpickable. Even as she fumbled around she could hear the approaching roar of the snowmobile.

She grabbed the bolt cutters from her pack, but they were not heavy enough for the jaws to fit over the thick bar of the lock. They did, however, fit partway across the hasp. She jammed the jaws of the cutter over the hasp and drew down hard, the jaws closing with much effort. Taking the hammer, she gave the partially cut hasp a tremendous blow, then another, bending it enough for her to cut it the rest of the way through. Even so, everything was so solid with rust she had to pound the pieces with the hammer to shake them loose.

She threw herself against the iron door but it hardly budged, letting out a great screech of protesting metal.

The approaching snowmobile engine gave a sudden roar; she saw a flurry of snow; and then it appeared at the mouth of the mine, driven by a man in a black helmet and puffy snowsuit. He rose from the machine, undoing his helmet and unshipping his rifle at the same time.

With an involuntary cry she threw herself against the door, almost dislocating her shoulder in the process, and with a loud *scree* it budged open just enough for her to squeeze through. Grabbing her backpack she rammed herself through the opening, then turned and threw herself back against the iron, thrusting the door shut again – just as there came a deafening boom from the rifle, with a round clanging off the door and ricocheting into the mine, sending up sparks as it splintered on the rocks behind her.

A second push shut the door completely. Bracing against it, Corrie fumbled out her headlamp, pulled it on over her balaclava, and turned it on. A pair of rounds smacked into the door with a deafening noise, but it was made of thick iron and they left only dents. And now she felt a person slam into the door on the other side, pushing it open a few inches. Once more, she threw herself against it hard, slamming it shut again, and then she yanked the wrecking bar out of her pack and wedged it under the door edge, giving it a blow with a hammer, then another blow, until it held, even as she felt the man on the other side shouldering the door, trying to force it open.

He pounded furiously on the door, the bar sliding back just a little. It would hold only so long. She cast about. Broken rocks lay everywhere, along with old pieces of iron and ancient equipment.

Wham! The man was now throwing himself against the door, jarring the wrecking bar loose.

She hammered it back into place and began piling rocks and iron against the door. Down the tracks she could see an old ore cart, and with great difficulty she got it moving, levering it off the tracks so that it tipped over against the door. She rolled some larger rocks in place. Now the door would hold – at least for a while. She sagged against the rock wall, panting hard, trying to recover her breath and figure out what to do next.

More shots were fired against the door, producing a series of deafening clangs in the enclosed space and causing her to jump. Grabbing her pack, she turned and retreated down the tunnel. For the first time she could see the space she was in. The air was cold, but not so cold as outside, and it smelled of mold and iron. The tunnel ran straight ahead through solid rock, supported every ten feet or so by heavy wooden timbers. A set of ore tracks led into darkness.

She started down the tunnel at a jog. The sounds of the stalker trying to break in echoed down the passageway. Corrie came to a cross tunnel, turned in to it, and then, at a cul-de-sac, finally had to stop to rest. And think.

She had bought some time, but eventually the man would manage to wedge open the door. The old map she had indicated that a section of the Christmas Mine connected to other, lower mines, forming a maze of tunnels and shafts – assuming they were all still passable. If she could reach them, find her way out . . . but what good would that do? The snow outside was several feet deep, impossible to walk through. There was only one way off the mountain – via snowmobile.

And nobody knew she was up here. She hadn't told anyone. *My God*, she thought, *what a mess I've gotten myself into.*

At that moment she heard a shriek of metal,

then another. She looked around the corner of the passage, back toward the distant door, and saw a wedge of light. Another screech and the wedge grew wider.

The man was prying open the door. She made out a shoulder, a cruel-looking face – and an arm with a handgun.

She ran as the shot was fired.

CHAPTER 57

The shots came screaming past her, sparking off the stone floor of the main tunnel ahead, the ricocheting fragments whining away like bees. She ran in terror, leaping the old car rails, expecting any moment to feel a round slam into her back and knock her to the ground. The tunnel ended in another cross tunnel, a wall of rock. Another fusillade of shots came booming down the tunnel, smacking the timbers above her with a burst of splinters and dust, flashing against the rock face before her.

She skidded around the corner and kept running. She desperately tried to remember the layout of tunnels she'd seen on the map, but her mind had shut down in panic. The shots had temporarily stopped after she turned the corner, and now she saw another, much narrower tunnel going off to the right, sloping steeply downward in a series of crude steps like a gigantic stone staircase. She flew down them, two steps at a time, to find herself in a lower tunnel, a trickle of water flowing along its bottom. It was warmer here, maybe even above freezing, and she was sweating in her bulky winter outfit.

'You can't escape,' came a yell from behind. 'It's all dead ends in here!'

Bullshit, she told herself with a bravado she didn't feel, *I've got a map.*

Another pair of shots came, but they struck to the rear and she felt the spray of rock pepper her jacket. She looked around. Another tunnel branched off to the left – also headed downward at an even steeper angle, the steps slick with water, with a rotting rope strung along as a kind of banister.

She took it, running at a reckless speed. Partway down she slipped and grasped frantically for the rope, which came apart like dust in her hands. She pitched forward, breaking her fall with her shoulder and rolling hard downhill, finally crashing into the bottom and sprawling on the wet stone. Her bulky winter clothes and woolen hat cushioned the fall – but not by much.

She staggered to her feet, her limbs aching, a burning cut on her forehead. She was in a broad, low seam, barely five feet high, with pillars of rock holding up the ceiling. It extended in two dimensions as far as the beam of her headlamp could penetrate. She ran at a crouch, zigzagging past the pillars, briefly shining the light ahead to see where she was going, and then turning it off again and running onward into the dark. She did this two more times, and then on the third time, while the light was off, she took a sharp right angle, slowing down and moving as silently as she could.

The flashlight beam of her pursuer lanced

through the darkness behind her, wobbling as he ran, probing this way and that. She moved behind a pillar and pressed herself against it, waiting. He was now off course and heading past her. In a moment she could see him slow down and look around, a pistol in his right hand. Clearly, he realized he had lost her.

She slipped from behind the pillar and went back the way they had come, then veered off into a new passage, creeping ahead in the dark, not daring to turn on the headlight but rather feeling her way with her hands. She blinked, wiped her eyes – blood was running freely from the cut on her forehead. After a while she saw a flicker of light behind her and realized he, too, had turned around and was coming back. She hurried faster now, pulling the headlamp off her head and holding it down low, just flicking the beam on for a second to see ahead so she could move faster.

Bad move: a pair of shots boomed out and then she heard him running, his light beam flashing around, illuminating her. Another shot. But the idiot was firing while running, which only worked on TV, and she took the opportunity to sprint like mad.

She almost didn't see it in time – a vertical shaft yawning directly ahead. She stopped so fast that she slid on her side like a base runner. Even so, one leg went over the edge. She scrambled and clawed her way back from the gaping chasm with an involuntary yelp of fear. An iron catwalk crossed the chasm, but it looked rotten as hell. An iron ladder went down into the blackness – also corroded.

It was either one or the other.

She chose the ladder, grasped the rung, and swung around, her foot finding a rung below, then another. The thing groaned and shook under her weight. A stale draft of still-warmer air came up from below. No going back now: she started down as fast as she could, the entire ladder shuddering and swaying. There was a loud snapping sound, then a second, as bolts holding the ladder to the stone broke free, and the ladder jerked violently down. She clung to it, tensing for a horrible, fatal fall – but with a screech of metal it came to an uneasy stop.

A light shone down from above, along with the gleam of a gun. Grabbing the edges of the ladder with her gloves, and taking her feet from the rungs and pressing them against the vertical sides of the ladder, she slid down – faster, faster, the rust coming off in a stream, until she hit the bottom hard, tumbling away, just as the shots came, gouging holes into the stone floor where she had just been.

Damn, she'd done something to her ankle.

Did he have the guts to descend the precarious ladder? Right at its base was a pile of rotting canvas and a stack of old planking. Limping over, she half dragged, half hauled the canvas underneath the ladder. The material was dry as dust and practically falling apart in her hands. The ladder was shaking now, groaning – her pursuer was descending.

Which meant he wouldn't be able to fire his weapon.

She shoved the heap of canvas against the base of the ladder and piled on the planks, pulled out her lighter, and lit the makeshift pyre. It was so desiccated, it went up like a bomb.

'Burn in hell!' she screamed as she dragged herself down the tunnel, trying to ignore the pain in her ankle. God, it felt like it was broken. Limping, the pain excruciating, she continued along another tunnel and then another, taking turns at random, now completely lost. Clearly, though, she was well out of the Christmas Mine and deep into the labyrinths of the Sally Goodin or one of the other, lower mines that honeycombed the mountain. She could hear sounds from behind, which seemed to indicate her pursuer had somehow gotten past the fire, or perhaps he'd just waited until it burned out.

Ahead, her headlight disclosed a cave-in, a bunch of jagged boulders strewn about on the floor of the tunnel, with some crossed beams lying atop. A narrow path, however, could be seen twisting through the rubble. Cold air streamed down from above. She climbed painfully over the piles of rock and broken timbers, then looked up. A crack disclosed a piece of dark, gray sky – but that was all. There was no way out, no way to reach it.

She continued picking her way through the rubble and came at last to a flat area on the far side. Suddenly, she heard a buzzing noise. She stopped, shone her light ahead, then gave a little cry and shrank back. Nestled among the fallen boulders, blocking the way, was a huge, ropy mass of hibernating rattlesnakes. They were half asleep in the cold air, but the twisted clump still moved in a kind of horrible slow motion, pulsing, rotating, almost like a single entity. Some were awake enough to be rattling in warning.

She shone the light around and saw that other rattlers were coiled up into the various small spaces between the rocks. They were everywhere – seemingly hundreds of them. Even – she realized with a sickening sensation – behind her.

Suddenly the boom of the gun sounded, and she felt one hand jerk in response to an impact. Instinctively, she leapt over the mass of snakes, scrambling among the boulders, the pain in her ankle even more excruciating. Another shot followed, then another, and she took refuge behind a large boulder – right next to a fat, sleeping rattler. There were some stones nearby – this was an opportunity she couldn't pass up. She picked up a heavy stone in her right hand – something was wrong with her left hand but she'd worry about that later – and jumped onto the large boulder, letting the rock fly with great violence at the main mass of snakes.

The rock smacked into the bolus of reptiles, and

the reaction was immediate and terrifying – an eruption of buzzing that filled the tunnel with a sound like a thousand bees, accompanied by an explosive writhing of movement. The lazy mass of snakes suddenly turned into a whirlwind, coiling, striking, sliding off in all directions – several coming straight at her.

She scrambled backward. Another shot struck the rocks around her, ricocheting about, and she fell in between two boulders. The buzzing filled the cave like a vast humming dynamo. She got up and ran, dragging her injured ankle. Half a dozen snakes struck at her and she jumped away. Two got hung up by their fangs on the thick fabric of her snow pants. With a scream she whacked them off, fairly dancing among the striking snakes, as another pair of shots whined among the rocks. A few moments later she was beyond the furious mass, limping away, until she could stand it no longer and finally collapsed in pain. She lay there, gasping, the tears running down her face. Her ankle was certainly broken. And then there was her hand: even in the dark she could see that her glove was soaked with warm liquid. She removed it gingerly, held her hand up to the light, and was amazed by what she saw: her pinkie finger was dangling by a mere thread of skin, blood welling out.

'Fuck!'

She shook off the useless finger, almost passing out from a combination of dizziness and disgust.

Unwrapping her scarf, she cut a strip of it off with a knife and wrapped it around her hand and the stump of the finger, tightening it to stem the flow of blood.

My finger. Jesus. In a dream, almost in shock from disbelief, she pulled the glove back over the wadded scarf as best she could to hold it in place. As she did so, she heard a shout from behind, then a scream, and the wild firing of the gun. But this time the shots were not directed at her. A rattling noise filled the tunnel with an unholy sound of reptilian fury. More shots and yells.

She had to keep going – eventually he would get through the snakes, unless by great good luck he was bitten. She hauled herself to her feet, fighting the dizziness and, now, a growing nausea. Christ, she needed a crutch, but there was nothing at hand. Limping badly, she continued along the tunnel, which descended steadily for some distance, passing several crosscuts. In time she came to a small side alcove, blocked up with rocks that formed a makeshift wall, now half collapsed. A place to hide? She dragged herself to it, pulled out some more stones, and looked in.

The beam of light fell upon a horde of rats, which erupted in excitement and went scurrying every which way with a chorus of squeals – exposing the remains of several bodies.

She stared with something like stupefaction. There were four in all, laid out in a row of skeletons – or rather, partial mummies, as they still had dried flesh on their bones, rotten clothes, old boots, and hair. Their dried-up heads were tilted back, their jaws wide open as if screaming, exposing mummified mouths full of black, rotten teeth.

As she crawled in to look more closely, she could see all the signs. They had been shot – she could see numerous holes in their skulls, many other bones broken by what looked like bullet impacts. A firing-squad attack far in excess of what would have been necessary to kill them – a display of violent, homicidal fury.

The four mercury-crazed miners. They'd been killed somewhere in this tunnel system, probably the Christmas Mine, and their bodies dragged down here and hidden.

Near the corpses lay a long, heavy stick – a cudgel, really, perhaps carried by one of the killers. It would do for an improvised crutch.

As quickly as she could without compromising the integrity of the evidence, Corrie took off her knapsack, removed the specimen bags, and laid them out. Removing the glove from her good hand and dropping to her knees, she crawled from body to body, taking from each a sample of hair, a fragment of papery dried flesh, and a small bone. She sealed them in the bags and put them back in her backpack. She photographed the bodies with her cell phone, then put the pack back on.

With a gasp of pain, she managed to get to her feet, leaning on the cudgel. Now she had to figure out where she was and find her way out – without getting shot in the process.

As if on cue, she could hear, way back near the cave-in, additional firing. She almost imagined she could hear the buzzing of the rattlers, a soft hiss in the distance: pleasant, like the ocean.

She made her way farther down the tunnel, gasping with pain, trying to find some distinctive landmark that she could in turn locate on the map, and thus orient herself toward an exit. And to her great relief, ten minutes of slow wandering brought her to a junction of tunnels – three horizontal ones and a vertical shaft coming together. She collapsed, took out the map, and scrutinized it.

And there it was.

Thank God. A break, at last. According to the map, she was now in the Sally Goodin Mine, not far from a lower exit. A dewatering tunnel, containing a large pipe, lay a few hundred yards from where she was, and it led directly to the Ireland Pump Engine, in the cirque below the Christmas Mine. Folding up the map, she tucked it away and took the indicated tunnel.

Sure enough: after a few more minutes of excruciating travel she finally came to a low stream of water that covered the rock floor, and then to the opening of an ancient pipe, nearly three feet in diameter, that ran along one side of the tunnel. She stooped and crawled into its mouth, grateful to be off her feet, and began making her way down its length.

It was dark and close, and her bulky suit kept catching and tearing on rusted areas of the pipe. But the going was relatively clear, with no cave-ins or narrowings. Within ten minutes she could feel the flow of air growing colder and fresher, and she fancied she could smell snow. In another few minutes she made out the dimmest of lights ahead, and soon she emerged, first through a shunt, and then a partially open wooden door, into a dark, dingy space, thick with rusted pipes and giant valves. It was now very cold, and a dim gray light filtered in through gaps and cracks in the wooden ceiling. She figured she must be somewhere in the depths of the old Ireland Pump building.

Giving a sob of relief, she looked around and saw an old staircase leading upward. As she limped toward it, she saw, out of the corner of her eye, a dark, moving shape. A human shape – coming at her fast.

He's gotten through the snakes. Somehow he's gotten through the snakes and flanked me . . .

One arm wrapped around her waist; another around her neck, covering her mouth, stifling her scream and pulling her head back. Then a face appeared, in the dimness – a face that was just recognizable.

. . . Ted.

'You!' Ted cried, suddenly loosening his grip and uncovering her mouth. 'It's *you*! What on earth are you doing here—?'

'Oh, my God,' she gasped, 'Ted! There's a man.

Back there . . . he tried to kill me . . .' She gasped, unable to continue, as he held her.

'You're bleeding!' he exclaimed.

She started to sob. 'Thank God, Ted, thank God you're here. He's got a gun . . .'

Ted's grip tightened again as he held her up. 'He's fucked if he comes here,' he said quietly, in a dark voice.

She sobbed, gasped. 'I'm so glad to see you . . . My finger's been shot off . . . I need to get to a hospital . . .'

He continued to hold her. 'I'm going to take care of you.'

CHAPTER 58

At half past two o'clock in the afternoon, a man wearing an enormous greatcoat, bundled up in gloves, silk scarf, and a trilby hat, carrying a bottle of champagne, rang the doorbell of the large Italianate mansion at 16 Mountain Trail Road. A maid, dressed in a starched black uniform with a white apron and cap, answered the door.

'May I help—?' she began, but the man came striding in with a cheery Christmas greeting, overriding her voice. He handed her his hat, scarf, and coat, revealing himself to be dressed in a severe black suit.

'The storm seems to be letting up!' he said to no one in particular, his voice loud in the echoing marble foyer. 'My goodness, it's cold out there!'

'The family is at Christmas Eve dinner—' the maid began again, but the man in black didn't seem to hear as he strode across the foyer and past the great curving staircase into the long hall leading to the dining room, the maid hurrying after him, burdened with his outerwear. 'Your name, please, sir?'

But the man paid no attention.

'I'm supposed to announce you—'

She could hardly keep up with him. He arrived at the great double doors to the dining room, grasped the handles, and threw them open, to reveal the entire family, a dozen or more, seated around an elegant table gleaming with silver and crystal, the remains of a suckling pig on a giant platter in the center. The pig had been reduced to a rib cage surrounded by greasy gobbets and bones, the only thing remaining intact being its head, with its crispy curled ears and the requisite baked apple in its mouth.

Everyone at the table stared at the man in surprise.

'I tried to—' the maid began, but the gentleman in black interrupted her as he held up the bottle of champagne.

'A bottle of Perrier-Jouët Fleur de Champagne and a Merry Christmas to each and every one of you!' he announced.

A shocked silence. And then Henry Montebello, sitting at the head of the table, rose. 'What is the meaning of this interruption?' His eyes narrowed. 'You – you're that FBI agent.'

'Indeed I am. Aloysius Pendergast, at your service! I'm making the rounds of all my friends, bringing season's greetings and gifts of cheer!' He sat down in the only empty chair at the table.

'Excuse me,' Montebello said coldly. 'That chair is reserved for Mrs Kermode, who should be here momentarily.'

'Well, Mrs Kermode's not here yet, and I am.' The man plunked the champagne down on the table. 'Shall we open it?'

Montebello's patrician features hardened. 'I don't know who you think you are, sir, bursting into a private family dinner like this. But I must ask you to leave this house at once.'

The agent paused, swaying slightly in the chair, a hurt expression gathering on his face. 'If you're not going to open the champagne, fine, but don't send me away without a little glass of *something*.' He reached over the table and picked up a half-full bottle of wine, examining the label. 'Hmmm. A 2000 Castle's Leap Cabernet.'

'What are you doing?' Montebello snapped. 'Put that down and leave at once, or I shall call the police!'

Ignoring this, the man plucked a nearby glass off the table, poured a measure of the wine, and made a huge production of swirling it about, sticking his nose in the glass, sipping, noisily drawing in air, puffing his cheeks, sipping again. He put the glass down.

'Some good berry notes, but no body and a short finish. Dull, I'm afraid; very dull. What sort of wine is this to serve at a Christmas Eve dinner? Are we but barbarians, Squire Montebello? Philistines?'

'Lottie, call nine-one-one. Report a home invasion.'

'Ah, but I was invited in,' said Pendergast. He turned to the maid. 'Wasn't I, dear?'

'But I just opened the door—'

'And what is more,' Montebello said, his voice crackling with fury as the rest of the family looked on with blank consternation, 'you are *drunk*!'

In that moment, as if on cue, a cook entered from the kitchen, flanked by attendants, carrying a huge flambé, the flames leaping up from the silver server.

'Cherries jubilee!' Pendergast cried, jumping to his feet. 'How marvelous!' He surged forward. 'It's too heavy for you – let me help. That fire could be dangerous – especially here, in Roaring Fork!'

The cook, alarmed at the drunken man coming at her, took a step backward, but she was too slow. The FBI agent seized the great flaming platter; there was a sudden moment of imbalance; and then it overturned, the platter, cherries, ice cream, and burning brandy all crashing to the table and splattering over the remains of the pig.

'Fire! Fire!' Pendergast cried, aghast as the flames leapt up, his face a mixture of dismay and panic. 'This is dreadful! Run! Everyone outside!'

A chorus of cries and shrieks went up around the table as everyone scrambled backward, knocking over chairs, spilling wine.

'Out, quickly!' shouted Pendergast. 'Pull the alarm! The house is burning down! We'll be burned alive *just like the others*!'

The sound of terror in his voice was infectious. There was instant pandemonium. A smoke alarm

460

went off, which only increased the mindless panic to get out, to get away at all costs from the fire. In mere seconds the diners, cook, and wait staff had all cleared the room, some pushing others away in their panic, and stampeded down the hall and across the foyer. One after another, they burst out the front door and into the night. The man in black was left alone in the house.

With sudden calm, he reached out, picked up an enormous gravy boat, and poured it over the alcohol flames, which were largely sputtering out anyway due to the melting ice cream and juices of the roasted carcass. A dash of wine from the bottle of inferior Cabernet completed the fire suppression. And then, with great aplomb and rapid efficiency of movement, he strode through the dining room, into the living room, and through it to a series of formally decorated rooms in the back, where Henry Montebello maintained his home legal office. There, Pendergast went straight to a cluster of filing cabinets. Perusing the labels on the front of each, he chose one, jimmied it open with a swift, sure motion, flipped through the papers, removed a fat accordion file, shut the cabinet, and carried the file back through the house to the front hall, plucking his bottle of champagne from the dining table in the process. In the front hall, he retrieved his greatcoat, scarf, hat, and gloves from where the maid had dumped them on the floor in her panic, secreted the file in the bulk of his coat, and stepped outside.

'Ladies and gentlemen,' he announced, 'the fire is out. It's safe to return now.'

He strode off into the snowy afternoon, to his waiting car, and drove away.

CHAPTER 59

Corrie felt Ted's powerful arms around her, holding her tight. The tightness of it made her feel safe. Relief flooded through her. She relaxed and took the pressure off her broken ankle as he continued to hold her up. 'I'm going to take care of you,' he said again, a little louder.

'I can't believe you're here,' she sobbed. 'That guy in the mine – he's a goon, hired by Kermode to run me out of town. He's the one who killed my dog, shot up my car . . . and now he's trying to kill me.'

'Kermode,' Ted said, his voice taking on an edge. 'Figures. That bitch. I'm going to take care of her as well. Oh, God, will I take care of *that* bitch.'

She was a little taken aback by his vehemence. 'It's okay,' she said. 'God, I'm so light-headed. I think I need to lie down.'

He didn't seem to have heard. The arms tightened even more.

'Ted, help me sit down . . .' She twisted a little because he was gripping her so hard it was beginning to hurt.

'Fucking bitch,' he said, louder.

463

'Forget Kermode . . . Please, Ted – you're hurting me.'

'Not talking about Kermode,' he said. 'Talking about you.'

Corrie was sure she hadn't heard right. She was so dizzy. His arms tightened even more, to the point where she could hardly breathe. 'Ted . . . That hurts. Please!'

'Is that all you've got to say for yourself, *bitch*?'

His voice was different now. Rough, hoarse.

'Ted . . . *what*?'

'*What, Ted, what?*' He mimicked her in a high, squeaky voice. 'What a piece of work you are.'

'What are you talking about?'

He squeezed so hard she cried out. 'You like that? 'Cause you *know* what I'm talking about. Don't play the innocent little girl.'

She struggled, but had almost no strength left. It was like a nightmare. Maybe it *was* a nightmare – maybe all of this was. 'What are you saying?'

'What are you *say*-ing?' he mimicked.

She twisted, trying to break free, and he roughly spun her around, his face almost touching hers. The red, sweaty, misshapen, furious look that disfigured his face frightened her terribly. Both his eyes were bloodshot and leaking water. 'Look at you,' he said, lowering his voice, his lips warped with anger. 'Leading me on, always teasing, first promising and then saying no, making a fool of me.'

He gave her a sudden, violent squeeze with his powerful arms and she felt a rib crack under the pressure, pain lancing through her chest. She screamed, gasped, tried to speak, but he squeezed her again, forcing the air from her lungs. 'The cocktease stops right here, *right now*.' Spittle splattered her face. His lips, covered with a white film, were now brushing hers, his strangely foul breath washing over her like fumes from a rotting carcass.

She tried to breathe but couldn't. The combined pain of her ankle, her hand, and now her ribs was so excruciating she was unable to think straight. Fear and shock sent her heart, already racing from the pursuit through the mines, into overdrive. She had never seen a face so twisted and so terrifying. He was completely mad.

Mad. Mad . . . She didn't want to think of the ramifications of that – she would not, *could* not, follow that thought to its natural conclusion.

'Please—' she managed to gasp.

'Isn't this perfect? You just running into my arms like this. It's karma. It saves me all the usual kinds of preparation. The universe wants to teach you a lesson, and I'll be the teacher.'

With that he threw her to the ground. She fell sprawling, with a cry of pain. He followed up with a kick to her injured ribs. The pain was unbearable and she cried out again, gasping for air. She felt the world swirling around, a strange ethereal floating sensation, pain and fright and disbelief overpowering all rational thought. A mist passed before her eyes, and consciousness shut down.

A long, dark time seemed to pass before another

465

searing lance of pain brought her back to herself. She was still in the dingy room. Mere moments must have ticked by. Ted stood over her, his face still grotesquely distorted, eyes watering, lips covered with a sticky bloom of white. He reached down, seized her leg, spun her around, and began dragging her over the rough floorboards. She tried to scream but couldn't. Her head banged roughly against the floor and once again she felt herself on the verge of passing out.

He dragged her from the back room into the main section of the structure. The vast pump rose above her, a monstrous juggernaut of giant pipes and cylinders. The tall building creaked in the wind. He pulled her alongside a horizontal pipe, yanked off her gloves, took notice of her damaged hand – lips curling into a malevolent smile at the sight – then lifted the other arm and roughly cuffed her wrist to the pipe.

She lay there, gasping, swimming in and out of consciousness.

'Look at you now,' he said, and spat on her.

As she struggled weakly to sit up, gasping in pain, part of her mind seemed to sense that this was happening, not to her, but to somebody else, and that she was watching from someplace far, far away. But there was another part of her mind – cold and relentless – that kept telling her exactly the opposite. This was real. Not only that – Ted was going to kill her.

Having shackled her to the pipe, Ted stepped

466

back, crossed his arms, and surveyed his handi-work. The dark mist that hovered around her seemed to clear slightly, and she grew more aware of her surroundings. Old pieces of lumber littered the floor. A couple of kerosene lanterns were hung nearby, casting a feeble yellow light. In one corner was a cot with a sleeping bag on it, a box of hand-cuffs, a couple of balaclavas, and several large cans of kerosene. A table held several hunting knives, coils of rope, duct tape, a glass-stoppered vial with some clear liquid within, wadded piles of wool socks and heavy sweaters, all black. There was a gun, too, that looked to Corrie like a 9mm Beretta. Why would Ted have a handgun? Pegs on the walls held a dark leather coat and – perversely – assorted clown masks.

This seemed to be a hideout of some sort. A lair – *Ted's* lair. But why should he need one? And what were all these things for? An old woodstove was burning to one side, the light shining between the cracks in the cast iron, throwing out heat. And now she noticed an odor in the air – a vile odor.

Ted pulled up a chair, turned it around, and straddled it, balancing his arms on the chair back. 'So here we are,' he said.

Something was terribly wrong with him. And yet the furious, violent, half-demented Ted of the last few minutes had changed. Now he was calm, mocking. Corrie swallowed, unable to take all this in. Maybe if she talked to him, she could learn what was troubling him, bring him back from whatever dark place he was in. But when she tried, all that came out was a pathetic garble of sound.

'When you first arrived in town, I thought maybe you were different from the others around here,' he said. His voice had changed again, as if his rage had buried itself deep in ice. It was remote, cold, detached, like someone speaking to himself – or, perhaps, to a corpse. 'Roaring Fork. Back when I was young, it used to be a real town. Now the ultra-high-net-worth bastards have taken over, the assholes with their social-climbing bimbos, the movie stars and CEOs and Masters of the Universe. Raping the mountains, clear-cutting the forests. Oh, they talk a good line about the environment! About going organic, about reducing their carbon footprints by buying offsets for their Gulfstream jets, about how "green" their ten-thousand-square-foot mansions are. Mother*fuckers*. That's just sick. They're parasites on our society. Roaring Fork is where they all gather, flattering each other, grooming each other of their lice like fucking chimpanzees. And they treat the rest of us – the real folk, the native-born residents – as scum fit only to sweep their palaces and stroke their egos. There's only one cure for all that: fire. This place should burn. It *needs* to burn. And it *is* burning.' He grinned, another fleshy, demonic distortion, frighteningly close to the face he'd shown her before.

Kerosene. Handcuffs. Rope. *It needs to burn.* Now, through the fog in her head, Corrie understood: Ted was the arsonist. A huge shudder of

468

fear coursed through her, and she struggled against the cuffs despite the pain that racked her body.

But then, as soon as she started to struggle, she stopped again. He cared for her – she knew he did. Somehow, she had to reach him.

'Ted,' she croaked, managing to speak. 'Ted. You know I'm not one of them.'

'*Oh, yes you are!*' he screamed, leaning toward her, the white scum flying off his lips in droplets. As quickly as it had come, the icy, methodical veneer fell away, replaced by a mad, bestial rage. 'You faked it for a while, but no – you're just like them! You're here for the same reasons they are: *money.*'

His eyes were so bloodshot, they were almost red. His hands were trembling with rage. His whole body was trembling. And his voice was so strange, so different. Looking at him was like looking into the maw of hell. It was so awful, so inhuman an expression, Corrie had to avert her eyes.

'But I don't have any money,' she said.

'Exactly! Why are you here? To find some rich asshole. *I* wasn't rich enough for you! That's why you *played* with me. Leading me on the way you did.'

'No, no, that wasn't it at all . . .'

'*Shut* the *fuck* up!' he screamed at a larynx-shredding volume, so loud that Corrie felt her eardrums tremble at the pressure. And then, just as abruptly as it had left, the icy control returned. The fluctuation – from homicidal, brutish, barely

469

controlled rants to a cold and calculating distance – was unbearable. 'You should be grateful,' he said, turning away, sounding for a minute like the Ted of old. 'I have conferred wisdom onto you. Now you understand. The others – the others that I've taught – they learned nothing.'

Then, suddenly, he spun back, staring at her with a hideous, speculative grin. 'You ever read Robert Frost?'

Corrie couldn't bring herself to speak.

He began to recite:

Some say the world will end in fire;

Some say in ice.

From what I've tasted of desire

I hold with those who favor fire.

He reached out, grasped a long, dry stick of old lumber from the many that littered the floor, and used the end of it to toggle the latch on the wood-stove door open. The flames inside threw a flickering yellow light about the room. He shoved the stick into the fire and waited.

'Ted, *please.*' Corrie took a deep breath. 'You don't have to do this.'

He began to whistle a tuneless melody.

'We're friends. I didn't reject you.' She sobbed a moment, gathered her wits as best she could. 'I just didn't want to rush things, that's all . . .'

'Good. That's very good. I haven't rejected you, either. And – I won't rush things. We'll just let nature take its course.'

He withdrew the stick, the end burning brightly

470

now, dropping sparks. His eyes, reflecting the dancing light of the fire, rolled slowly toward her, their bloodshot whites shockingly large. And Corrie, looking from him to the burning brand and back again, realized what was about to happen.

'Oh, my God!' she said, voice rising into a shriek. 'Please don't. *Ted!*'

He took a step toward her, waving the burning stick before her face. Another step closer. Corrie could feel the heat of the flaming brand. 'No,' was all she could manage.

For a minute, he just stared at her, the stick sparking and glowing in his hand. And when he spoke, his voice was so quiet, so controlled, it nearly drove her mad.

'It's time to burn,' he said simply.

CHAPTER 60

Pendergast arrived in his office in the basement of the police station and placed the accordion file on his desk. It contained the documents he had earlier sought in the town's public records office but which had, according to the archivist, mysteriously disappeared some years back. As he expected, he found them – or copies of them – in the filing cabinet in the home office of Henry Montebello, the architect who had prepared them in the first place. The file contained all the records relating to the original development of The Heights – documents that, by law, were supposed to be a matter of public record: plats, surveys, permit applications, subdivision maps, and terrain management plans.

Delving into the accordion file, Pendergast removed several manila folders and laid them out in rows, their tabs lined up. He knew exactly what he was looking for. The first documents he perused involved the original survey of the land, done in the mid-1970s, with corresponding photographs. They included a detailed topographic survey of the terrain, along with a sheaf of photos depicting exactly how the valley and ridges looked before the development began.

It was most revealing.

The original valley had been much narrower and tighter, almost a ravine. Along its length, carved into a benchland a hundred feet above the stream known as Silver Queen Creek, stood the remains of an extensive ore-processing complex first built by the Staffords in the 1870s – the fountainhead of much of their wealth. The first building to be erected housed the 'sampler' operation, to test the richness of the ore as it came from the mine; next came a much larger 'concentrator' building, containing three steam-powered stamp mills, which crushed the ore and concentrated the silver tenfold; and finally, the smelter itself. All three operations generated tailings, or waste piles of rock, and those tailings were clearly visible on the survey as enormous piles and heaps of rubble and grit. The tailings from all of the operations contained toxic minerals and compounds that leached out into the water table. But it was the last set of tailings – from the smelter – that were truly deadly.

The Stafford smelter in Roaring Fork used the Washoe amalgamation process. In the smelter, the crushed, concentrated ore was further ground up into a paste, and various chemicals were added . . . including sixty pounds of mercury for each ton of ore concentrate processed. The mercury dissolved the silver – amalgamated with it – and the resulting heavy paste settled to the bottom of

473

the vat, with the waste slurry coming off the top to be dumped. The silver was recovered by heating the amalgam in a retort and driving off the mercury, which was recaptured through condensation, leaving behind crude silver.

The process was not efficient. About two percent of the mercury was lost in each run. That mercury had to end up somewhere, and that somewhere was in the vast tailings dumped into the valley. Pendergast did a quick mental calculation: a two percent loss equaled about a pound of mercury for each ton of concentrate processed. The smelter processed a hundred tons of concentrate a day. By inference, that meant a hundred pounds of mercury had been dumped into the environment on a daily basis – over the nearly two decades during which the smelter operated. Mercury was an exceedingly toxic, pernicious substance, which over time could cause severe and permanent brain damage in people who were exposed to it – especially in children and, to an even greater extent, to the unborn.

It all added up to one thing: The Heights – or at least, the portion of the development that had been erected in the valley – was essentially sitting atop a large Superfund site, with a toxic aquifer underneath.

As he replaced the initial documents, everything came together in Pendergast's mind. He understood everything with great clarity – everything – including the arson attacks.

Moving more rapidly now, Pendergast glanced through documents relating to the early development itself. The terrain management plan called for using the vast tailing piles to fill the narrow ravine and create the broad, attractive valley floor that existed today. The clubhouse was built just downstream from where the old smelter had been, and a dozen large homes were situated within the valley. Henry Montebello, the master architect, had been in charge of it all: the demolishment of the smelter ruins, the terrain alterations, the spreading of tailings into a nice broad, level area for the lower development and the clubhouse. And his sister-in-law, Mrs Kermode, had also been an integral player.

Interesting, Pendergast thought, that Montebello's mansion was on the far side of town, and that Kermode's own home was built high up on the ridge, far from the zone of contamination. They, and the other members of the Stafford family who were behind the development of The Heights, must have known about the mercury. It occurred to him that the real reason they were building a new clubhouse and spa – which had seemed the very essence of needless indulgence – and situating it on the old Boot Hill cemetery was, in fact, to get it out of the area of contamination.

Pendergast moved from one manila folder to the next, paging through documents relating to the original subdivisions and association planning.

The lots were large – minimum two-acre zoning – and as a result there was no community water system: each property had its own well. Those houses situated in the valley floor, as well as the original clubhouse, would have obtained their water from wells sunk directly into the mercury-contaminated aquifer.

And, indeed, here was a file of the well permits. Pendergast looked through it. Each well required the testing of water quality – standard procedure. And every single well had passed: no mercury contamination noted.

Without question, falsified results.

Now came the sales contracts for the first houses built in The Heights. Pendergast selected those dozen properties in the contaminated zone in the valley for special scrutiny. He examined the names of the purchasers. Most appeared to be older, wealthy individuals in retirement. These houses had changed hands a number of times, especially as real estate values skyrocketed in the 1990s.

But Pendergast did recognize the name of one set of purchasers: a 'Sarah and Arthur Roman, husband and wife.' No doubt the future parents of Ted Roman. The date of purchase: 1982.

The Roman house was built directly on the site of the smelter, in the zone of greatest contamination. Pendergast thought back to what Corrie had told him about Ted. Assuming he was her age, or even a few years older, there was little doubt that Ted Roman had been exposed to toxic mercury

476

in his mother's womb, and raised in a toxic house, drinking toxic water, taking toxic showers . . .

Pendergast put the records aside, a thoughtful expression on his face. After a moment, he picked up the phone and called Corrie's cell phone. It went directly over to her voice mail.

He then called the Hotel Sebastian and, after speaking to several people, learned that she had left the hotel shortly after her work shift ended at eleven. In her car, destination unknown. However, she had asked the concierge for a snowmobile map of the mountains surrounding Roaring Fork.

With somewhat more alacrity, Pendergast dialed the town library. No answer. He looked up the head librarian's home number. When she answered, she explained to him that December twenty-fourth was normally a half day at the library, but she had decided not to open at all because of the storm. In response to his next question, she replied that Ted had, in fact, told her he was going to take advantage of the free day by engaging in one of his favorite activities: snowmobiling in the mountains.

Again, Pendergast hung up the phone. He called Stacy Bowdree's cell, and it, too, went over to voice mail.

A furrow appeared on his pale brow. As he was hanging up, he noticed something he normally would have seen immediately had he not been preoccupied: the papers on his desk were disarranged.

He stared at the papers, his near-photographic

mind reconstructing how he had left them. One sheet – the sheet on which he'd copied the message of the Committee of Seven – had been pulled partway out and the papers surrounding it displaced:

> mete at the Ideal 11 oclock Sharp to Night they are Holt Up in the closed Christmas Mine up on smugglers wall

Pendergast quickly left his office and went upstairs, where Iris was still dutifully manning the desk.

'Has anyone been in my office?' he asked pleasantly.

'Oh, yes,' the secretary said. 'I brought Corrie down there for a few minutes, early this afternoon. She was looking for her cell phone.'

CHAPTER 61

The vile, rotting odor in the air seemed to intensify as Ted waved the burning stick about. The flames licking at its end began to die back into coals, and he pushed it back into the stove.

'Love is the Fire of Life; it either consumes or purifies,' he quoted as he slowly twirled the stick among the flames, as if roasting a marshmallow. There was something awful – after his fierce and passionate ranting – about the calm deliberation with which he now moved. 'Let us prepare for the purification.' He pulled the stick from the stove and passed it again before Corrie's face, with a strangely delicate gesture, gingerly, tentative now – and yet it hovered so close that, although she twisted away, it singed her hair.

Corrie tried to gain control of her galloping panic. She had to reach him, talk him out of this. Her mouth was dry, and it was hard to articulate words through her haze of pain and fear. 'Ted, I liked you. I mean I *like* you. I really do.' She swallowed. 'Look, let me go and I'll forget all about this. We'll go out. Have a beer. Just like before.'

'Right. Sure. You'd say anything now.' Ted began to laugh, a crazy, quiet laugh.

She pulled against the cuff, but it was tight around her wrist, securely fastened to the pipe. 'You won't get in trouble. I won't tell anyone. We'll forget all about this.'

Ted did not reply. He pulled the burning brand away, inspected it closely, as one would a tool prior to putting it to use.

'We had good times, Ted, and we can have more. You don't have to do this. I'm not like those others, I'm just a poor student, I have to wash dishes at the Hotel Sebastian just to pay for my room!' She sobbed, caught herself. 'Please don't hurt me.'

'You need to calm down, Corrie, and accept your fate. It will be by fire – purifying fire. It will cleanse you of your sins. You should thank me, Corrie. I'm giving you a chance to atone for what you did. You'll suffer, and for that I'm sorry – but it's for the best.'

The horror of it, the certainty that Ted was telling the truth, closed her throat.

He stepped back, looked around. 'I used to play in all these tunnels as a kid.' His voice was different now – it was sorrowful, like one about to perform a necessary but distasteful service. 'I knew every inch of these mine buildings up here. I know all this like the back of my hand. This is my childhood, right here. This is where it began, and this is where it will end. That door you came out of? That was the entrance to my playground. Those mines – they were a *magical* playground.'

His tone became freighted with nostalgia, and Corrie had a momentary hope. But then, with terrible rapidity, his demeanor changed utterly. 'And *look what they did!*' This came out as a scream. 'Look! This was a nice town once. Friendly. Everyone mingled. Now it's a fucking tourist trap for billionaires . . . billionaires and all their toadies, bootlickers, lackeys. People like you! *You . . .!*' His voice echoed in the dim space, temporarily drowning out the sound of the storm, the wind, the groaning timbers.

Corrie began to realize, with a kind of awful finality, that nothing she could say would have any effect.

As quickly as it had come, the fit passed again. Ted fell abruptly silent. A tear welled up in one eye, trickled slowly down his cheek. He picked up the gun from the table and snugged it into his waistband. Without looking at her, he turned sharply on his heel and strode away, out of her vision, into a dark area behind the pump engine. Now all she could see was the burning end of his stick, dancing and floating in the darkness, slowly dwindling, until it, too, disappeared.

She waited. All was silent. Had he left? She could hardly believe it. Hope came rushing back. Where had he gone? She looked around, straining to see in the darkness. Nothing.

But no – it was too good to be true. He hadn't really left. He had to be around somewhere.

And then she smelled a faint whiff of smoke. From the woodstove? No. She strained, peering this way and that into the darkness, the pain in her hand, ribs, and ankle suddenly forgotten. There was more smoke – and then, abruptly, a whole lot more. And now she could see a reddish glow from the far side of the pump engine.

'Ted!'

A gout of flame suddenly appeared out of the blackness, and then another, snaking up the far wall, spreading wildly.

Ted had set the old building on fire.

Corrie cried out, struggled afresh with the handcuffs. The flames mounted upward with terrible speed, great clouds of acrid smoke roiling up. A roar grew in intensity, until it was so ferocious it was a vibration in the air itself. She felt the sudden heat on her face.

It had all happened in mere seconds.

'No! *No!*' she screamed. And then, through her wild cries, she saw Ted's tall figure framed in the doorway to the dingy room from which she'd first emerged. She could see the open door to the Sally Goodin Mine, the dewatering tunnel running away into darkness. He was standing absolutely still, staring at the fire, waiting; and as it grew brighter and stronger she could see the expression on his face: one of pure, unmitigated excitement.

Corrie squeezed her eyes closed for a moment,

prayed – prayed for the first time in her life – for a quick and merciful end.

And then, as the flames began to lick up all around, consuming the wooden building on all sides, bringing with them unbearable heat, Ted turned and vanished into the mountain.

The flames roared all around Corrie, so loudly that she couldn't even hear her own screams.

CHAPTER 62

At three o'clock in the afternoon, Mike Kloster had pulled his VMC 1500 snowcat with its eight-way hydraulic grooming blade out of the equipment shed, getting it ready for the night ahead. Twenty inches of snow had fallen over the last forty-eight hours, and at least another eight were on the way. This was going to be a long night – and it was Christmas Eve, no less. Turning up the heat in the cab, he let the machine warm up while he pulled over the tow frame and began bolting it on to the rear. As he bent over the hitch, he sensed a presence behind him. Straightening up again, he turned to see a bizarre figure approaching, bundled up in a black coat and trilby hat, wearing heavy boots. He looked almost clown-like.

He was about to make a wisecrack when his gaze fell on the man's face. It was as cold and pale as the surrounding landscape, with eyes like chips of ice, and the words died in Kloster's throat.

'Um, this is a restricted area—' he began, but the man was already removing something from his coat, a worn alligator wallet, which fell open to reveal a badge.

'Agent Pendergast. FBI.'

Kloster stared at the badge. FBI? For real? But before he could even answer, the man went on.

'Your name, if you please?'

'Kloster. Mike Kloster.'

'Mr Kloster, unbolt that device immediately and get in the cab. You are going to take me up the mountain.'

'Well, I've got to, you know, get some kind of authorization before—'

'You will do as I instruct, or you will be charged with impeding a federal officer.'

The tone of voice was so absolute, and so convincing, that Mike Kloster decided he would do exactly as this man said. 'Yes, sir.' He unhitched the tow frame and climbed into the cab, sliding behind the wheel. The man got into the passenger side, his movements remarkably agile given the ungainly dress.

'Um, where are we going?'

'To the Christmas Mine.'

'Where's that?'

'It is above the old Smuggler's Cirque mine complex where the Ireland Pump building is situated.'

'Oh. Sure. I know where that is.'

'Then proceed, if you please. Quickly.'

Kloster engaged the gears, raised the front groomer blade, and started up the slopes. He thought of radioing his boss to tell him what was going on, but decided against it. The guy was a pain in the ass and he might just put up a fuss. Better to tell him after the fact. His passenger was FBI, after all, and what better excuse was there?

As they climbed, curiosity began to get the better of Kloster. 'So, what's this all about?' he asked in a friendly way.

The pale-faced man did not answer. He didn't appear to have heard.

The VMC had an awesome sound system, and Kloster had his iPod all docked and ready to go. He reached out to turn it on.

'No,' said the man.

Kloster snatched back his hand as if it had been bitten.

'Make this machine go faster, please.'

'Well, we're not supposed to take it over three thousand rpms—'

'I'll thank you to do as I say.'

'Yes, sir.'

He throttled up, the groomer crawling a little faster up the mountain. The snow had started again and now the wind was blowing as well. The flakes were of the tiny, BB-pellet variety – from long experience, Kloster knew every variety of snowflake there was – and they bounced and ticked noisily off the windscreen.

Kloster put on the wipers and flicked the lights to high. The cluster of beams stabbed into the grayness, the pellets of snow flashing through. At three thirty it was already starting to get dark.

'How long?' the man asked.

486

'Fifteen minutes, maybe twenty, to the mine buildings. I don't think this machine'll get any higher than that – the slopes are too steep above Smuggler's Cirque. The avalanche danger is pretty extreme, too. They're gonna be setting off avalanche charges all Christmas Day, I bet, with this new snow.'

He realized he was babbling – this man sure made him nervous – but again the agent didn't even acknowledge having heard.

At the top of the ski slope, Kloster took the service road that led to the top of the ridge, where it joined the network of snowmobile trails. Arriving at the trails, he was surprised to see fresh snowmobile tracks. Whoever it was, they were hard-core, venturing out on a day like this. He continued on, wondering just what the heck his passenger was after . . .

And then, above the dark spruce trees, he saw something. A glow, up on the mountain. Instinctively he slowed, staring.

The FBI agent saw it, too. 'What is that?' he asked sharply.

'I don't know.' Kloster squinted upward. He could make out, beyond and above the trees, the upper part of Smuggler's Cirque. The steep slopes and peaks were bathed in a flickering yellow glow. 'Looks like a fire.'

The pale man leaned forward, gripping the dashboard, his eyes so bright and hard they unnerved Kloster. 'Where?'

487

'Damn, I'd say it's in that old mine complex.'

Even as they watched, the glow grew in intensity, and now Kloster could see dark smoke billowing upward into the snowstorm.

'Fast. *Now.*'

'Right, sure.' Kloster really gunned it this time, the VMC churning across the snow at top speed – only twenty miles an hour, but plenty fast for an unwieldy groomer.

'Faster.'

'It's pegged, sorry.'

Even as he made the last turn before the tree line, he could see that the fire in the cirque was big. Huge, in fact. Flames were shooting up at least a hundred feet, sending up towering pillars of sparks and black smoke, as thick as a volcanic eruption. It had to be the Ireland Pump Engine building itself – nothing else up there was big enough to produce that kind of inferno. Even so, it couldn't be a natural fire – nothing natural could spread so fast and so fiercely. It occurred to Kloster that this must be the work of the arsonist, and he felt a stab of fear, which was not reassured by the strange intensity of the man next to him. He kept the pedal to the metal.

The last stubby trees slid past them and they were now on the bare ridge. The snow was shallower here, due to wind scouring, and Kloster was able to eke out a few more miles per hour. God, it was like a firestorm up there, mushroom clouds of smoke and flame pummeling the sky, and he fancied he could even hear the sound of it above the roar of the diesel engines.

They crossed the last part of the ridge and headed up the lip to the hanging valley above. The snow grew deeper again and the VMC churned its way forward. They cleared the lip and, instinctually, Kloster stopped. It was indeed the Ireland building, and it had burned so fast, so furiously, that all that remained was a burning skeleton of timbers – which even as they watched collapsed with a thunderous cracking noise, sending up a colossal cascade of sparks. It left the Ireland Pump itself standing alone, naked, the paint peeling and smoking. The fire began to die as quickly as it had exploded: when the building collapsed, huge piles of snow had fallen from the roof into the burning rubble, sending up volatile plumes of steam.

Kloster stared, stunned by the violence of the scene, the utter suddenness of the building's immolation.

'Move closer,' the man ordered.

He eased the groomer forward. The wooden frame had been consumed with remarkable speed, and the cascade of snow from the collapsing roof and the continuing blizzard were damping down what remained of the fire. None of the other buildings had burned – their snow-laden roofs were protecting them from the incredible shower of sparks that rained downward all around them like the detritus of countless fireworks.

Kloster eased the cat among the old mining

structures. 'This is as far as I'd better go,' he said. But instead of the argument he expected, the pale man simply opened the door and got out. Kloster watched, first in amazement, and then horror, as the man walked toward the smoking, fire-licked remains of the structure and circled it slowly, like a panther, close – way too close.

Pendergast stared into the hellish scene. The air around him was alive with falling sparks mingled with snowflakes, which dusted his hat and coat, hissing out in the dampness. The engine and all its pipework had survived intact, but the building was utterly gone. Plumes of smoke and steam billowed up from hundreds of little pockets of heat, and timbers lay scattered about, hissing and smoking, with tongues of fire flickering here and there. There was an acrid stench, along with the whiff of something else: singed hair and burnt meat. All that could be heard now was the low hiss of steam, the crackle and pop of isolated fires, and the sound of the wind moaning through the ruins. He made a circuit around the perimeter of the fire. There was enough light from the many dying fires to see everything.

At a certain point he paused abruptly.

Now, moving ever so slowly, he stepped deeper into the fire zone, raising the scarf to cover his mouth against the acrid smoke. Winding his way among pipes and valves, his feet crunching on the cracked cement floor littered with nails and glass, he approached the thing that had stopped him in his tracks. It resembled a long, black log, and it, too, was hissing and smoking. As he got closer he confirmed it was the remains of a human body, which had been handcuffed to a set of pipes. Even though the arm had burned off, and the body had dropped to the floor, a carbonized hand remained in the cuffs, the fingers curled up like the legs of a dead spider, blackened bones sticking out from where the wrist should have been.

Pendergast sank to his knees. It was an involuntary motion, as if all the strength was suddenly drained from his body, forcing him down against his will. His head fell forward and his hands clasped together. A sound came from his mouth – low, barely audible, but undeniably the by-product of a grief beyond words.

CHAPTER 63

Pendergast did not linger long over the charred body. He rose, a tall figure among the smoking ruins, his cold gaze surveying the burnt remains of the pump building. For a moment, he remained as immobile as a statue, only his two pale eyes exploring the scene, pausing here and there to take in some invisible detail.

A minute passed. And then his eyes turned back to the corpse. He reached into his coat, slid out his custom Les Baer 1911 Colt, ejected the magazine, checked it, slid it back into place, and racked a round into the chamber. The firearm remained in his right hand.

Now he began to move forward, a small flashlight appearing in his other hand. The heat of the fire had melted much of the snow in the immediate vicinity of the area, leaving puddles of water and even, here and there, exposed brown grass, now quickly being reblanketed with snow. He made a circuit of the ruined building, peering through the falling snow, stepping over the innumerable piles of charred and smoking debris. Darkness was falling, and the snow thickened on his shoulders and hat, making him appear like a wandering ghost.

At the far side of the devastation, where the flanks of the mountainside began to rise up, he paused to examine a small, scorched wooden door, which covered what appeared to be a tunnel entrance. After a moment he knelt and examined the handle, the nearby ground, and then the door itself. He grasped the handle and tested the door, finding it locked from the inside – padlocked, apparently.

Pendergast rose and – with a sudden explosion of movement – stove in the door with a massive kick. He grasped the broken pieces and ripped them out by main force with his hands, throwing them aside. As quickly as it had come, the furious violence passed. He knelt, shining the light inside. The beam revealed an empty dewatering tunnel running straight into the mountain.

He turned the light to the ground. There were fresh scuffs and various confused marks in the dust, both coming and going. A moment of stasis . . . and then he was suddenly in motion, trotting alongside the pipe as smoothly as a cat, his coat billowing behind him, the Colt in his hand gleaming faintly in the dimness.

The pipe ended in a low stream of water that interrupted the tracks. Moving forward, Pendergast came to an intersection; continued on; reached another, and then – trying to think like his quarry – took a right, where the tunnel abruptly changed slope and ascended steeply to a higher level.

The tunnel continued for a quarter mile, deep into the mountain, until it struck what had once been a complex mineral seam, perhaps a dozen feet wide. This seam almost immediately divided the tunnel into a warren of shafts, crawl spaces, and alcoves, the spaces that remained after the ancient mining operation had cleared out every vein and pocket of a complex ore body that had once threaded this way and that through the heart of the mountain.

Pendergast paused. He understood that his quarry would have anticipated pursuit, and as a result had led his presumed pursuer to this very place: this maze of tunnels, where he, with his undoubtedly superior knowledge of the mine complex, would have the advantage. Pendergast sensed it was very likely his presence had already been noted. The prudent course of action would be to retreat and return with additional manpower.

But that would not do. Not at all. His quarry might use such a delay to escape. And besides, it would deprive Pendergast of what he needed to do so very badly that he could taste the bile of it in his mouth.

He doused the light and listened. His preternaturally acute sense of hearing picked up many sounds – the steady drip of water, the faint movement of air, the occasional *tick-tick* of settling rock and wooden cribbing.

But there was no light, no telltale sound or scent.

And yet he sensed, he *knew*, that his quarry – Ted Roman – was near and well aware of his presence.

He turned the light back on and examined the surrounding area. Much of the rock in this section of the mine was rotten, shot through with cracks and seams, and extra cribbing had been placed to hold it up. He stepped over to a vertical member, removed a knife from his pocket, and pushed it into the wood. It sank into the cribbing like butter, all the way to the hilt. He pulled it out and pried away at the wood, pulling off big, dusty pieces.

The wood was thoroughly weakened by dry rot. It might not be hard to bring it down . . . but that would lead to unpredictable consequences.

He ceased moving and paused, frozen in place, listening. He heard a faint sound, the tiny drop of a pebble. It was impossible, in the echoing spaces, to tell whence it came. It almost seemed to him deliberate, a tease. He waited. Another ping of rock against rock. And now he knew for certain that Ted Roman was playing with him.

A fatal mistake.

With the light on, acting as if he had heard nothing, unsuspecting, Pendergast chose a tunnel at random and passed down it. After a few steps he halted to discard his bulky coat, gloves, and hat, and stuff them into an out-of-the-way alcove. It was much warmer here, deep in the mine – and the coat was too constricting for the work that lay ahead of him.

The tunnel twisted and turned, dipped and rose, dividing and redividing. Many small tunnels, stopes, and shafts branched off in odd directions. Old mining equipment, pulleys, cages, cables, buckets, carts, and rotting ropes were strewn about in various stages of decay. At several points, vertical shafts sank down into darkness. Pendergast examined each one of these carefully, shining his light on the descending walls and testing the depths with a dropped pebble.

At one shaft, he lingered somewhat longer. It took two seconds for the pebble to hit bottom; a quick mental calculation indicated the distance would be twenty meters, or about sixty feet. Sufficient. He examined the rock making up the wall of the shaft and found it rough, solid, with enough adequate footholds: suitable for the purpose he had in mind.

Now, making a detour around the shaft, he stumbled and fell hard, the flashlight dropping to the ground with a clatter and going out. With a curse, Pendergast lit a match and tried to edge around the shaft, but the match went out, burning his fingers, and he dropped it with another muttered deprecation. He got up and tried to light another match. It sputtered to life and he took several steps, but he was moving too fast now and the light went out again, right at the edge of the deep pit; he slipped and, in the process, swept a loose rock off the edge, giving a loud cry as he himself went over. His powerful fingers grasped a fissure just below the edge of the shaft, and he swung his body down so that he was dangling into the dark void, out of sight of the tunnel above. He abruptly cut off his cry when the rock he had dislodged crashed into the bottom.

Silence. Dangling, he found a purchase for his toes, his knees well flexed, giving him the leverage he needed. He waited, clinging to the edge of the shaft, listening intently.

Soon he could hear Roman cautiously making his way down the tunnel. The beam of a flashlight flickered over the lip of the shaft as the sound of movement paused. Then, ever so slowly, he heard the man advance toward the pit. Pendergast's muscles tensed as he sensed the man creeping toward the edge he hid beneath. A moment later, Roman's face appeared, bloodshot eyes wild, flashlight in one hand, handgun in the other.

Uncoiling like a snake, Pendergast leapt up and grabbed Roman's wrist, yanking him forward and pulling him toward the void. With a scream of surprise and dismay, Roman reared back, his gun and flashlight skittering off across the rocky ground as he used both hands to fend off the attack and counteract the pull. He was immensely strong and quick, surprisingly so, and he managed to correct the sudden imbalance and dig in his heels, striking at Pendergast's forearm with a bear-like roar of rage. But Pendergast was up and over the edge in a flash, Roman scrabbling backward. Pendergast raised his own gun to fire, but it was now black and Roman, anticipating the shot, threw himself sideways. The bullet ricocheted harmlessly off the rock floor, but the flash of the discharge betrayed Roman's position. Pendergast fired again, but now the muzzle flash revealed nothing: Roman had vanished.

Pendergast dug into his suit and pulled out his backup light: a handheld LED. Roman had apparently launched himself into a narrow, low-ceilinged seam that angled down steeply from the main tunnel. Dropping to his knees, Pendergast crawled into the seam and followed. Ahead, he could hear Roman in panicked flight, scrabbling along the low passage, gasping in fear. He, too, it seemed, had a second light: Pendergast could make out a jerky glow in the darkness of the seam ahead.

Relentlessly, Pendergast pursued his quarry. But as hard as he pushed, Roman stayed well ahead. The young man was in peak physical condition and had the advantage of knowing the tunnels, their fantastic complexity only adding to his edge. Pendergast was doing little more than moving blind, following the sound, the light, and – occasionally – the tracks.

Now Pendergast entered an area of large tunnels, cracks, and yawning, vertical chimneys. Still he pursued with monomaniacal intensity. Roman, Pendergast knew, had lost his weapon and was in a state of panic; Pendergast retained his weapon and his wits. To heighten Roman's terror and keep him off balance, now and then Pendergast would fire a round in the direction of the fleeing man, the bullet cracking and zinging as it tore through the tunnels ahead. There was little chance he would hit Roman, but that was not his intention: the deafening roar of the gun, and the terrifying ricochet of the rounds, was having the desired psychological effect.

Roman seemed to be going somewhere, and it soon became clear – as the air in the tunnels grew steadily fresher and colder – that he was heading outside. Into the storm . . . where Pendergast, having jettisoned his outerwear, would be at an additional disadvantage. Ted Roman might be beside himself with fear – but he was still able to think ahead and strategize.

A few minutes later, Pendergast's suspicions were confirmed: he rounded a corner and saw, directly ahead, a rusty steel wall with a door in it, open, swinging in the wind, the sound of the storm filling the entranceway. Rushing to the door, Pendergast shone his flashlight out into the murk. All was black; night had settled. The dim light disclosed a mine entrance, broken trestle, and the plunging slope of the cirque, falling away at a fifty-degree angle. The beam did not penetrate far, but nevertheless he could make out Roman's footprints in the deep snow, floundering off into the storm. Farther below, through the murk, he could see a cluster of glowing pinpoints – the smoldering remains of the pump building – and the lights of the idling snowcat nearby.

He turned off his light. He could just see the faint, bobbing glow of Roman's flashlight, descending the steep slope, about a hundred yards to one side. The man was moving slowly. Pendergast raised his weapon. It would be an exceptionally difficult shot, due to the high winds and the added complication of altitude. Nevertheless, Pendergast took a careful bead on the wavering light, mentally compensating for windage and drop. Very slowly, he squeezed the trigger. The firearm kicked with the shot, the report loud against the mountainside, the rolling echoes coming back from several directions.

A miss.

The figure kept moving, faster now, floundering downhill, getting ever farther out of range. Pendergast, without winter clothing, had no hope of catching him.

Ignoring the snow that stung his face and the vicious wind that penetrated his suit, Pendergast took another bead and fired, missing again. The chance for a hit was becoming nil. But then – as he took aim a third time – he heard something: a muffled *crack*, followed by a low-frequency rumble.

Above and ahead of Pendergast, the heavy snow surface was fracturing into large plates, the plates detaching and sliding downward, slowly at first, then faster and faster, breaking up and tumbling into chaos. It was an avalanche, triggered by the noise of his shots and, no doubt, Roman's own floundering about. With a growing roar the churning front of snow blasted past the mine entrance. The air was suddenly opaque, full of roiling, violent snow, and the gust of its passing knocked Pendergast backward as it thundered by him.

Within thirty seconds the roar had subsided. It had been a small slide. The slope before Pendergast was now swept clean of deep snow, the residual, trickling streams of it sliding down the mountain in rills. All was silent save for the cry of the wind.

Pendergast glanced downward to where Roman's bobbing flashlight had been. There was nothing now but a deep expanse of snow rubble. There were no signs of movement; no calls for help – nothing.

For a moment, Pendergast just stared down into the darkness. For the briefest of moments – as the blood rage that had taken possession of him still pulsed through his veins – he grimly contemplated the justice of the situation. But even as he stared, his fury ebbed. It was as if the avalanche had scoured his mind clear. He paused to consider what, subconsciously, he'd already understood until the sight of Corrie's burnt corpse swept all logic from his mind: that Ted Roman was as much a victim as Corrie herself. The true evil lay elsewhere.

With a muffled cry, he sprang from the mine entrance into the snow and struggled down the slope, coatless, sliding and floundering to where the avalanche had piled up along the top of the cirque. It took a few minutes to get there, and by the time he reached the spot he was half frozen.

'Roman!' he cried. 'Ted Roman!'

No reply but the wind.

Now Pendergast jammed one ear into the snow to listen. Just barely, he could hear a strange, muffled, horrifying sound, almost like a cow bawling: *Мииииииии тииииии, тиии тиии.*

It seemed to be coming from the edge of the snow rubble. Moving toward it in the bitter cold, Pendergast began to dig frantically, with his bare hands. But the snow was compacted by the pressure of the avalanche, his hands inadequate to the task. Without jacket or hat, the cold had penetrated to his skin, and he weakened, his hands numbing to uselessness.

Where was Roman? He listened again, placing his ear against the hard-packed snow, trying to warm his hands.

Миии . . . тиии . . .

It was rapidly growing fainter. The man was suffocating.

He dug and dug, and then paused to listen again. Nothing. And now he saw, out of the corner of his eye, a light coming up the slope. Ignoring it, he kept digging. A moment later a pair of strong hands grasped him and gently pulled him away. It was Kloster, the snowcat operator, with a shovel and a long rod in his hands.

'Hey,' he said. 'Hey, easy. You're going to kill yourself.'

'There's a man down there,' Pendergast gasped. 'Buried.'

'I saw it. You go down to the cat before you freeze to death. There's nothing you can do. I'll take care of it.' The man began probing with the rod across the rubble of the avalanche, sliding it into the snow, working fast and expertly. He had done this kind of thing before. Pendergast did not go to the cat but stood nearby, watching and shivering. After a few moments Kloster paused, probing more gingerly in a tighter area, and then he began to dig with the shovel. He worked with energy and efficiency, and within minutes had exposed part of Roman's body. A few more minutes of extremely rapid work uncovered the face.

Pendergast approached as the man's light played over it. The snow was soaked with blood all around the head, the skull partly depressed, the mouth open as if in a scream but completely stoppered with snow, the eyes wide open and crazy.

'He's gone,' said Kloster. He put an arm on Pendergast to steady him. 'Listen, I'm going to take you back to the cat now so you can warm yourself up – otherwise, you're going to be following him.'

Pendergast nodded wordlessly and allowed himself to be helped through the deep snow to the cab of the idling machine.

CHAPTER 64

Half a mile away, on the lower, eastern slope of the cirque, a metal door opened at the entrance to a mine tunnel. Moments later a figure came staggering out, dragging one leg, leaning on a stick and coughing violently. The figure paused in the mine opening, swayed, leaned against a bracing timber, then doubled over with another coughing fit. Slowly, the figure slid down, unable to support itself, and ended up in the snow, propped against the vertical timber.

It was her. Just as he'd expected. He knew she had to come out sometime – and what a perfect target she made. She wasn't going anywhere, and he had all the time in the world to set up his shot. The sniper, crouched in the doorway of an old mining shack, unshouldered his Winchester 94, worked the lever to insert a round into the chamber, then braced the weapon against his shoulder, sighting through the scope. While it was dark, there was still just enough ambient light in the sky to place the crosshairs on her dark, slumped form. The girl looked like she was in pretty bad shape already: hair singed, face and clothes black with smoke. He believed at least one of his earlier shots had hit home. As he'd pursued her through the tunnels, he had seen copious drops of blood. He wasn't sure where she'd been hit, but a .30-30 expanding round was no joke, wherever it connected.

The sniper did not understand why she was up here, why the snowcat had raced by on its way up the mountain, or why the pump building had burned. He didn't need to know. Whatever crazy shit she was involved in was none of his business. Montebello had given him an assignment and paid him well to do it – extremely well, in fact. His instructions had been simple: scare the girl named Corrie Swanson out of town. If she didn't leave, kill her. The architect hadn't told him anything more, and he didn't want to know anything more.

The shot through the car window hadn't done it. Decapitating the mutt hadn't done it – although he recalled the scene with a certain fondness. He was proud of the tableau he'd arranged, the note in the dead dog's mouth – and he was disappointed and surprised it hadn't scared her off. She had proven to be one feisty bitch. But she didn't look so feisty now, slumped against the timber, half dead.

The moment had come. He'd been following her almost continuously now for thirty-six hours, waiting for an opportunity. As an expert hunter, he knew the value of patience. He had not had a good shot either in town or at the hotel. But when she had gone to The Heights, stolen a snowmobile, and taken it up the mountain on whatever insane errand she was on, the opportunity was placed in his hands, like a gift. He had borrowed another snowmobile and followed her. True, she had proven unusually resourceful – that business with the rattlesnakes back in the tunnel had seriously put him out. But he had found another way out of the mine and – when he discovered her snow-mobile was still there – decided to stick around: He positioned himself a little way down the moun-tain, in the darkness of a mining shack, a blind that commanded an excellent view of most of the old adits and tunnel entrances up on the cirque. If she was still inside the mountain, he'd reasoned, she would eventually come out one of those. Or, perhaps, from the Christmas Mine, where she'd left her snowmobile. In any case, she'd have to pass by him on the way down.

And now, here she was. And in a good location, away from the activity around and above, where the pump building had burned and where the snowcat was parked. Someone had fired shots, which, it seemed, had in turn triggered an avalanche. From his hiding place, through the magnification of the scope, he watched the frantic digging and the discovery of the body. Something crazy-big was going down – drugs, he figured. But it had nothing to do with him, and the sooner he killed the target and got his ass out of there, the better.

Easing out his breath, finger on the trigger, he aimed at the slumped girl. The crosshairs steadied, his finger tightened. Finally, the time had come. He'd take her out, climb on his snowmobile parked behind the shack, and go collect his pay. One shot, one kill . . .

Suddenly the rifle was knocked brutally from behind, and it went off, discharging the round into the snow.

'What the—?' The sniper grasped the rifle, tried to rise, and as he did so felt something cold and hard pressed against his temple. The muzzle of a pistol.

'So much as blink, motherfucker, and I'll make a snow angel with your brains.'

A woman's voice – full of authority and seriousness.

A hand reached out, seized his rifle by the barrel. 'Let go.'

He let go the rifle and she flung it out into the deep snow.

'All your other weapons – toss them into the snow. *Now.*'

He hesitated. He still had a handgun and knife, and if he forced her to search him there might be an opportunity . . .

The blow against the side of his head was so hard it knocked him to the ground. He lay dazed on the wooden floor for a moment, wondering why the heck he was lying here and who this woman was standing over him. Then it all started to come back as she bent over him, searched him roughly, removed the knife and pistol, and threw them far out into the snow as well.

'Who . . . who the fuck are you?' he asked.

The answer came with another stunning blow to his face from the butt of her gun, leaving the inside of his lips torn and bloody and his mouth full of broken fragments of teeth.

'My name,' she said crisply, 'is Captain Stacy Bowdree, USAF, and I am the very worst thing that's happened to you in your entire shitty life.'

CHAPTER 65

Corrie Swanson saw the tall, handsome figure of Stacy Bowdree emerge out of the swirling snow, leading a man with his hands tied together and his shaggy head bowed. She dimly wondered if it was all a dream. Of course it was a dream. Stacy would never be up here. As Stacy stopped before her, Corrie managed to say, 'Hello, dream.'

Stacy looked aghast. 'My God. What happened to you?'

Corrie tried to think back on all that had happened, and couldn't quite bring it into focus. The more she tried to remember, the stranger everything became. 'Are you for real?'

'You're damn right!' Stacy bent forward, examined Corrie closely, her blue eyes full of concern. 'What are you doing with these handcuffs fastened to your wrist? And your hair is burned. Jesus, were you in that fire?'

Corrie tried to form the words. 'A man . . . tried to kill me in the tunnels . . . but the rattle-snakes . . .'

'Yeah. This is him.' Stacy shoved the man facedown

509

into the snow before Corrie and put her booted foot on his neck. Corrie noticed the .45 in Stacy's hand. She tried to focus on the man lying on the ground but her eyes were swimming.

'This is the guy hired to kill you,' Stacy went on. 'I caught him just as he was about to pull the trigger. He won't tell me his name, so I'm calling him Dirtbag.'

'How? How . . .?' It all seemed so confusing.

'Listen. We've got to get you to a hospital and Dirtbag to the police chief. There's a snowcat about half a mile away, near the burnt pump building.'

Pump building. 'Burn . . . He tried to burn me alive.'

'Who? Dirtbag here?'

'No . . . Ted. I had my bump key . . . picked the cuffs . . . just in time . . .'

'You're not making much sense,' Stacy said. 'Let me help you up. Can you walk?'

'Ankle's broken. Lost . . . a finger.'

'Shit. Let's take a look at you.'

She could feel Stacy examining her, gently touching her ankle, asking questions and probing for injuries. She felt comforted. A few minutes later Stacy's face came back in focus, close to her own. 'Okay, you've got a few second-degree burns. And you're right: your ankle's broken and a little finger's gone. That's bad enough, but luckily it seems to be all. Thank God you were bundled up in winter clothes, otherwise you'd be a lot more burned than you are.'

Corrie nodded. She couldn't quite understand what Stacy was saying. But was it really Stacy, and not some vision? 'You disappeared . . .'

'Sorry about that. When I cooled off I realized those assholes had hired some thug to drive you out of town, and so I shadowed you for a while and pretty soon saw Dirtbag, here, skulking after you like a dog sniffing for shit. So I followed him. In the end, I stole a snowmobile back there in the equipment shed – just as the two of you did – followed your tracks up here just in time to see Dirtbag vanish into the mine entrance. I lost you in the mines but figured he had, as well, and I managed to backtrack in time.'

Corrie nodded. Nothing was making any sense to her. People had been trying to kill her – that much she knew. But Stacy had saved her. That's all she needed to know. Her head was spinning and she couldn't even seem to hold it up. Black clouds gathered in front of her eyes.

'Okay,' Stacy continued, 'you stay here, I'll take Dirtbag to the cat and then we'll drive back to get you.' She felt Stacy's hand on her shoulder, giving it a squeeze. 'Hang in there just a minute more, girl. You're dinged up, but you're going to be okay. Trust me, I know. I've seen . . .' She paused. 'Much worse.' She turned away.

'No.' Corrie sobbed, reaching out for Stacy. 'Don't go.'

'Have to.' She gently put Corrie's hand to her side. 'I can't keep Dirtbag under control and help you, too. It's better if you don't walk. Give me ten minutes, tops.'

It seemed a lot shorter than ten minutes. Corrie heard the roar of a diesel, then saw a cluster of moving headlamps stabbing through the murk, approaching fast, pulling up to the mine entrance in a swirling cloud of snow. A strange, pale figure emerged – Pendergast? – and she felt herself suddenly in his arms, lifted bodily as if she were a child again, her head cradled against his chest. She felt his shoulders began to convulse, faintly, regularly, almost as if he was weeping. But that was, of course, impossible, as Pendergast would never cry.

EPILOGUE

The brilliant winter sun streamed in the window and lay in stripes across Corrie's bed at the Roaring Fork Hospital. She had been given the best room in the hospital, a corner single on a high floor, the large window overlooking most of the town and the mountains beyond, everything wreathed in a magical blanket of white. This was the view Corrie had awoken to after the operation on her hand, and the sight had cheered her considerably. That was three days ago, and she was set to be discharged in two more. The break in her foot had not been serious, but she had lost her little finger. Some of the burns she'd suffered might scar, but only slightly, and only, they had told her, on her chin.

Pendergast sat in a chair on one side of the bed and Stacy sat in another. The foot of the bed was covered in presents. Chief Morris had been in to pay his respects – he'd been a regular visitor since her operation – and after inquiring about how Corrie was feeling and thanking Pendergast profusely for his help in the investigation, he'd added his own gift (a CD of John Denver's greatest hits) to the pile.

513

'Well,' said Stacy, 'are we going to open them, or what?'

'Corrie shall go first,' said Pendergast, handing her a slim envelope. 'To mark the completion of her research.'

Corrie tore it open, puzzled. A computer printout emerged, covered with columns of crabbed figures, graphs, and tables. She unfolded it. It was a report from an FBI forensic lab in Quantico – an analysis of mercury contamination in twelve samples of human remains – the crazed miners she'd found in the tunnels.

'My God,' Corrie said. 'The numbers are off the charts.'

'The final detail you require for your thesis. I have little doubt you will be the first junior in the history of John Jay to win the Rosewell Prize.'

'Thank you,' Corrie said, and then hesitated. 'Um, I owe you an apology. *Another* apology. A really big one this time. I messed up, well and truly. You've helped me so much, and I just never really appreciated it the way I should have. I was an ungrateful—' she almost said a bad word but amended it on the fly – 'girl. I should have listened to you and never gone up there alone. What a stupid thing to do.'

Pendergast inclined his head. 'We can go into that some other time.'

Corrie turned to Stacy. 'I owe a big apology to you, too. I'm really ashamed that I suspected you and Ted. You saved my life. I really don't have the words to thank you . . .' She felt her throat close up with emotion.

Stacy smiled, squeezed her hand. 'Don't be hard on yourself, Corrie. You're a true pal. And Ted . . . Jesus, I can hardly believe he was the arsonist. It gives me nightmares.'

'On one level,' Pendergast said, 'Roman wasn't responsible for what he did. It was the mercury in his brain, which had been poisoning his neurons since he was in his mother's womb. He was no more a criminal than were those miners who went mad working in the smelter and ultimately became cannibals. They are all victims. The true criminals are certain others, a family whose malevolent deeds go back a century and a half. And now that the FBI is on it, that family will pay. Perhaps not as brutally as Mrs Kermode did, but they will pay nonetheless.'

Corrie shuddered. Until Pendergast had told her, she hadn't any idea that, the whole time she'd been shackled to the pump, Mrs Kermode had been in the building as well, out of sight, hand-cuffed to the far side of the engine – probably unconscious after being beaten up by Ted. *Oh, God, will I take care of that bitch*, he'd said . . .

'I was in such a hurry to escape the flames, I never even saw her,' Corrie said. 'I'm not sure anyone deserves to be burned alive like that.'

The expression on Pendergast's face indicated he might disagree.

'But there's no way Ted could have known that

515

Kermode and the Staffords were responsible for his own madness – was there?' Corrie asked.

Pendergast shook his head. 'No. Her end at his hands was poetic justice, nothing more.'

'I hope the rest of them rot in prison,' said Stacy.

After a silence, Corrie asked, 'And you really thought Kermode's burnt body was mine?'

'There was no question in my mind,' Pendergast replied. 'If I'd been thinking more clearly, I might have realized that Kermode was potentially Ted's next victim. She represented everything he despised. That entire *auto-da-fé* up on the mountain was arranged for her, not for you. You just fell into his lap, so to speak. But I do have a question, Corrie: how did you undo the handcuffs?'

'Aw, they were crappy old handcuffs. And I'd tucked my picks into the space between the inner and outer glove when I was trying to pick the lock into the mine – because, as you of all people know, you have to use several tools simultaneously.'

Pendergast nodded. 'Impressive.'

'It took me a while to remember I even had the tools, I was so terrified. Ted was . . . I've never seen anything like it in my life. The way he shifted from screaming rage to cold, calculated precision . . . God, it was almost more frightening than the fire itself.'

'A common effect of mercury-induced madness. And that perhaps explains the mystery of the bent pipes in the second fire—'

Stacy said hastily, 'Um, let's open the rest of the presents and stop talking about this.'

'I'm sorry I don't have anything for anyone,' said Corrie.

'You were otherwise engaged,' said Pendergast. 'And while I'm on the subject, given what also happened to you in Kraus's Kaverns back in Medicine Creek, in the future I would advise you to avoid underground labyrinths, especially when they are tenanted by homicidal maniacs.' He paused. 'Incidentally, I'm very sorry about your finger.'

'I suppose I'll get used to it. It's almost colorful, like wearing an eye patch or something.'

Pendergast took up a small package and examined it. There was no card, just his name written on it. 'This is from you, Captain?'

'Sure is.'

Pendergast removed the paper, revealing a velvet box. He opened it. Inside, a Purple Heart rested on satin.

He stared at it for a long time. Finally he said: 'How can I accept this?'

'Because I've got three more and I want you to have it. You deserve a medal – you saved my life.'

'Captain Bowdree—'

'I mean it. I was lost, confused, drinking myself into oblivion every evening, until you called out of the blue. You got me here, explained about my ancestor, gave me purpose. And most of all . . . you respected me.'

Pendergast hesitated. He held up the medal. 'I will treasure this.'

'Merry Christmas – three days late.'

'And now you must open yours.'

Stacy took up a small envelope. She opened it and extracted an official-looking document. She read it, her brow furrowing. 'Oh, my God.'

'It's nothing, really,' said Pendergast. 'Just an appointment for an interview. The rest is up to you. But with my recommendation, and your military record, I feel confident you will pass muster. The FBI needs agents like you, Captain. I've rarely seen a finer candidate. Corrie here may rival you, one day – all she lacks is a certain seasoning of judgment.'

'Thank you.' It looked for a moment like Bowdree might hug Pendergast, but then she seemed to decide the gesture might not be welcome. Corrie smiled inwardly; this entire ceremony, with its attendant displays of affection and emotion, seemed to be making him a little uncomfortable.

There were two more presents for Corrie. She opened the first, to find within the wrapping a well-worn textbook: *Techniques for Crime Scene Analysis and Investigation: Third Edition.*

'I know this book,' she said. 'But I already have a copy – a much later edition, which we use at John Jay.'

'I'm aware of that,' Pendergast said.

She opened it, suddenly understanding. Inside, the text was heavily annotated with marginalia:

comments, glosses, questions, insights into the topic being discussed. The handwriting was precise, and she recognized it immediately.

'This . . . this was your copy?'

Pendergast nodded.

'My God.' She touched the cover, caressing it almost reverentially. 'What a treasure trove. Maybe by reading this I'll be able to think like you someday.'

'I had considered other, more frivolous gifts, but this one seemed – given your evident interest in a law enforcement career – perhaps the most useful.'

There was one gift left. Corrie reached for it, carefully removed the expensive-looking wrapping paper.

'It's from Constance,' Pendergast explained. 'She just returned from India a few days ago, and asked me to give you this.'

Inside was an antique Waterman fountain pen with a filigreed overlay of gold, and a small volume in ribbed leather, with cream-colored, deckle-edged pages. It was beautifully handmade. A small note fell out, which she picked up and read.

Dear Miss Swanson,

I have read with interest some of your online 'blogs' (hateful word). I thought that perhaps you might find indulging in a more permanent and private expression of your observations to be a useful occupation. I myself have kept a diary for many years. It has always been a source to me of interest, consolation, and personal insight. It is my hope this slight volume will help confer those same benefits on you.

Constance Greene

Corrie looked at the presents scattered around her. Then she glanced at Stacy, seated on the edge of the bed, and Pendergast, relaxing in his chair, one leg thrown lightly over the other. All of a sudden, to her great surprise, she burst into tears.

'Corrie!' Stacy said, leaping to her feet. 'What's wrong? Are you in pain?'

'No,' Corrie said through her tears. 'I'm not in pain. I'm just happy – so happy. I've never had a happier Christmas.'

'Three days late,' Pendergast murmured, with a twitch of his facial features that might have indicated a smile.

'And there's nobody on earth I'd rather share it with than you two.' Corrie furiously brushed away the tears and, embarrassed, turned to look out the window, where the morning sun was gilding Roaring Fork, the low flanks of the mountains, and – farther up – the bowl-like shape of Smuggler's Cirque and the small, dark smudge against the snow where a fire had almost ended her life.

She tapped the journal. 'I already know what my first entry will be,' she said.

ANGELS

ANGELS

Marian Keyes

MICHAEL JOSEPH
an imprint of
PENGUIN BOOKS

MICHAEL JOSEPH

Published by the Penguin Group
Penguin Books Ltd, 80 Strand, London WC2R 0RL, England
Penguin Putnam Inc., 375 Hudson Street, New York, New York 10014, USA
Penguin Books Australia Ltd, 250 Camberwell Road,
Camberwell, Victoria 3124, Australia
Penguin Books Canada Ltd, 10 Alcorn Avenue, Toronto, Ontario, Canada M4V 3B2
Penguin Books India (P) Ltd, 11 Community Centre,
Panchsheel Park, New Delhi – 110 017, India
Penguin Books (NZ) Ltd, Cnr Rosedale and Airborne Roads,
Albany, Auckland, New Zealand
Penguin Books (South Africa) (Pty) Ltd, 24 Sturdee Avenue,
Rosebank 2196, South Africa

Penguin Books Ltd, Registered Offices: 80 Strand, London WC2R 0RL, England

www.penguin.com

First published 2002
1

Set in 12/16.5 pt Monotype Minion
Typeset by Rowland Phototypesetting Ltd,
Bury St Edmunds, Suffolk
Printed in Great Britain by Clays Ltd, St Ives plc

A CIP catalogue record for this book is available from the British Library

ISBN 0-718-14466-X
Trade paperback ISBN 0-718-14513-5

For Tony

Acknowledgements

I'd like to thank the following people:

My editor Louise Moore for her clever, intuitive input, Harriet Evans for her meticulous work, and all at Penguin.

Everyone at Poolbeg, with special thanks going to Paula Campbell for the snooker story.

Jonathan Lloyd, Tara Wynne and Nick Marston at Curtis Brown.

The wonderful Ricardo Mestres, Danny Davis and Heij at Touchstone Pictures for my first LA adventure.

The equally wonderful Bob Bookman, Sharie Smiley and Jessica Tuchinsky at CAA for my second LA adventure.

And the following, for generously providing information, encouragement and/or confectionery: Guy and Julie Baker, Jenny Boland, Ailish Connelly, Siobhan Coogan, Emily Godson, Gai Griffin, Dr Declan Keane at Holles St Hospital, Caitríona Keyes, Mammy Keyes, Rita-Anne Keyes, Julian Plunkett-Dillon, Deirdre Prendergast, Eileen Prendergast, Suzanne Power, Morag Prunty, Jason Russell, Anne-Marie Scanlon, Emma Stafford, Louise Voss, Amy Welch and Varina Whitener. Thanks to all of you.

Finally, thanks to my beloved Tony, to whom this book is dedicated.

Prologue

'We will shortly be landing at Los Angeles International Airport. Please ensure your seat is in the upright position, that you weigh less than a hundred pounds and that you have excellent teeth.'

1

I'd always lived a fairly blameless life. Up until the day I left my husband and then ran away to Hollywood, I'd hardly ever put a foot wrong. Not one that many people knew about, anyway. So when, out of the blue, everything just disintegrated like wet paper, I couldn't shake a wormy suspicion that this was long overdue. All that clean living simply isn't natural.

Of course, I didn't just wake up one morning and skip the country, leaving my poor sleepy fool of a husband wondering what that envelope on his pillow was. I'm making it sound much more dramatic than it actually was, which is strange because I never used to have a penchant for dramatics. Or a penchant for words like 'penchant', for that matter. But ever since the business with the rabbits, and possibly even before that, things with Garv had been uncomfortable and weird. Then we'd suffered a couple of what we chose to call 'setbacks'. But instead of making our marriage stronger – as always seemed to happen to the other luckier setback souls who popped up in my mother's women's magazines – our particular brand of setbacks did exactly what it said on the tin. They set us back. They wedged themselves between myself and Garv and alien- ated us from one another. Though he never said anything, I knew Garv blamed me.

And that was OK, because I blamed me too.

*

His name is actually Paul Garvan, but when I first got to know him we were both teenagers and nobody called anybody by their proper names. 'Micko' and 'Macker' and 'Toolser' and 'You Big Gobshite' were some of the things our peers were known as. He was Garv, it's all I've ever known him as, and I only call him Paul when I'm extremely pissed off with him.

Likewise, my name is Margaret but he calls me Maggie, except when I borrow his car and scrape the side against the pillar in the multi-storey car park (something that occurs more regularly than you might think).

I was twenty-four and he was twenty-five when we got married. He'd been my first boyfriend, as my poor mother never tires of telling people. She reckons it demonstrates what a nice girl I was, who never did any of that nasty sleeping-around business. (The only one of her five daughters who didn't, who could blame her for parading my suspected virtue?) But what she conveniently omits to mention when she's making her proud boast is that Garv might have been my first boyfriend, but he wasn't my only one.

However.

We'd been married for nine years and it would be hard to say exactly when I'd started to fantasize about it ending. Not, let me tell you, because I wanted it to be over. But because I thought that if I imagined the worst possible scenario, it would somehow be insurance against it actually happening. However, instead of insuring against it, it conjured the whole bloody thing into existence. Which just goes to show.

The end came with surprising suddenness. One minute my marriage was a going concern – even if I was doing strange stuff like drinking my contact lenses – the next minute it was entirely finito. Which caught me badly on the hop, as I'd always thought there was a regulation period of crockery-throwing and name-calling before the white flag could be waved. But everything caved in without a single cross word being exchanged, and I simply wasn't prepared for it.

God knows, I *should* have been. A few nights previously I'd woken in the darkness for a good worry. Something I often did, usually fretting about work and money. You know, the usual. Having too much of one and not enough of the other. But recently – probably longer than recently, actually – I'd been worrying about me and Garv instead. Would things ever get better? Were they better already and I just wasn't seeing it?

Most nights I didn't come to any conclusions and lapsed back into an unreassured sleep. But this time I was afflicted with sudden, unwelcome x-ray vision. I could see straight through the padding of the daily routine, the private language and the shared past, right into the heart of me and Garv, into all that had happened over the last while. Everything was stripped away and I had a horrible, too-clear thought: *We're in big trouble here.*

It literally made me cold. All the little hairs on my skin lifted and a chill settled somewhere between my ribs. Terrified, I tried to cheer myself up by having a little fret about the amount of work I'd have to do the following day, but no dice. So then I reminded myself that my parents were getting older and that I'd be the one who'd end up having to take care of them, and tried to scare myself with that instead.

After a while I went back to sleep, scratched my right arm raw, ground my teeth with gusto, awoke to the familiar sensation of a mouth coated with bits of grit, and carried on as normal.

I was to remember that *We're in big trouble here* when it transpired that we actually were. On the evening in question we were meant to be going out for dinner with Elaine and Liam, friends of Garv's. And who knows, if Liam's new flatscreen television hadn't fallen off the wall and on to his foot, breaking his big toe in the process, so that I'd gone out instead of going home, maybe Garv and I would never have split up.

The irony is, I was *praying* that Elaine and Liam would cancel. The chances were good – the last three times we were supposed to meet up, it hadn't happened. The first time, Garv and I had bowed out because we were getting our new kitchen table delivered. (No, of course it didn't come.) The next time, Elaine – who's some bigwig in pensions – had to drive to Sligo to make a load of people redundant. ('The new Jag arrived just in time!') Then the last time I'd managed to come up with some spurious excuse which Garv had agreed with all too readily. This time it was their call.

Not that I didn't like them. Well, actually I didn't. Like I said, she's a bigwig in pensions and he's a stockbroker. They're good-looking, earn *tons* of money and are unkind to waiters. They're the sort of people who always seem to be getting new cars and going on holiday.

Most of Garv's mates were lovely, but Liam was a glaring exception: the problem was that Garv was one of those types who went around seeing the good in people – most people, anyway. This is a great quality in theory, and I'd no objection to him seeing the good in people I liked myself, but it was a bit of a pain when he persisted with the ones I didn't. Himself and Liam had been friends since junior school, in the days when Liam had been a lot nicer, and, even though Garv had tried very hard for my sake, he'd been unable to shake his residual affection for him.

But even Garv agreed that Elaine was terrifying. Shespokerealfast. Firingquestionsfromamachinemouth. How'swork? Whenareyougettinglisted? Her dynamic glamour reduced me to stammering inadequacy, and by the time I'd cobbled together an answer, she'd have lost interest and moved on.

But even if I had liked Liam and Elaine, I still wouldn't have wanted to go out that particular night – putting on a big, fat, happy head is that much harder if you've an audience. Also there was a pile of scary manila envelopes to be dealt with at home. (Plus two soaps eager to tend to my needs and a couch that couldn't do enough for me.) Time was too precious to waste an entire evening out enjoying myself.

And I was *so* tired. My work – like most people's, I would imagine – was very demanding. I guess the clue is in the name: 'work'. Otherwise they might call it 'flat on your back on a sunlounger' or 'having a deep-tissue massage'. I worked in a legal firm which had a lot of dealings with the US. Specifically, entertainment law. (After we'd got married, Garv, on account of his general fabulousness, had been seconded for five years to his company's Chicago office. I'd worked for one of the big legal firms there, so when we returned to Ireland three years ago I claimed to be well versed in US entertainment law. The kicker was that even though I'd done night classes and got some qualifications in Chicago, I wasn't a proper lawyer. Which meant I got tons of the work, most of the abuse, but only a fraction of the moola. I was more of an interpreter, I suppose; a clause which meant one thing in Ireland could mean something different in the States, so I translated US contracts into Irish law and drafted contracts that should – hopefully – stand in both jurisdictions.)

I lived in vague but constant fear. Sometimes I had dreams where I'd left out a vital clause and my firm got sued for four trillion dollars, which they deducted from my wages at the rate of seven pounds fifty a week, and I had to work there for all eternity paying it back. Sometimes, in those dreams all my teeth fell out as well. Other times, I'm sitting in the office and I look down to find that I'm naked and that I need to get up and use the photocopier.

Anyway, the day the balloon went up, I was very busy. So busy that my new fitness regime had gone by the board. I'd recently realized that biting my nails was the only exercise I was getting so I'd hatched a cunning plan – rather than ring Sandra, my assistant, to come and collect my dictaphone tapes, I'd walk the twenty yards to her office and hand-deliver them instead. But no time for such self-indulgence that particular day. A deal with a film studio was about to fall apart: if the contract wasn't finalized that week, the actor who'd attached himself to the project was going to walk.

For a minute there my job sounded glamorous. Take my word for it, it was as glamorous as a cold sore. Even the business lunches I occasionally had to go to at expensive restaurants weren't all that. You could never truly relax – people always asked a question requiring a long and detailed answer just after I'd put a forkful of food into my mouth, and whenever I laughed I was haunted by an irresistible fear that I had green food stuck in my teeth.

Anyway, the scriptwriter – my client – was desperate to get the contract all sorted out so that he could get his fee and his family could eat. (And so his father might finally be proud of him, but I digress.) The US lawyers had come to work at three in the morning, their time, in order to try and close the deal, and all day e-mails and phone calls zipped back and forth. Late in the day we dotted the final 'i' and crossed the final 't', and even though I was wrecked I felt light and happy.

Then I remembered that we were supposed to be going out with Liam and Elaine and a cloud passed over the sun. It wasn't so bad, I consoled myself; at least I'd get a nice dinner out of it – they were fond of fancy-dan restaurants. But God, I was exhausted. If only it was *our* turn to cancel!

And then, just when it seemed that we were beyond all hope, the call came.

'Liam's broken his toe,' Garv said. 'His new flatscreen telly fell on it.' (Liam and Elaine had every consumer durable known to man – and I stress *man*, not woman. Give me a mobile phone and a hair-curler and I'm happy. But Garv, being a man, yearned after digital this and Bang & Olufsen that.) 'So tonight's off.'

'Great!' I exclaimed. Then I remembered myself; they were his friends. 'Well, not great for him and his toe, but I've had a tough day and –'

'It's OK,' Garv said. 'I didn't want to go either. I was just about to ring them and pretend our house had been burnt down or something.'

'Dandy. Well, see you back at the ranch.'

'What'll we do about food? Will I pick up something?'

'No, you did it last night. I'll do it.'

I had just launched into an orgy of switching stuff off when someone said, 'Going home, Maggie?' It was my boss, Frances, and her *already?* might have been silent but I still heard it.

'That's right.' Lest there be any confusion. 'Going home.' Polite but firm. Trying to keep my prone-to-quaver-under-pressure voice free of tell-tale traces of fear.

'That contract ready for tomorrow morning's meeting?'

'Yes,' I said. No, actually it wasn't. She was talking about a different contract, one I hadn't even started on. There was no point whinging to Frances that all day I'd been frantically sewing up a great deal. She was an über-achiever, well on her way to being made a partner, and she'd made hard work into a performance art. She rarely left the office and popular opinion (not that she *was* popular, of course) had it that she slept under her desk and washed, like a bag lady, in the staff toilets.

'Can I take a quick look?'

'It's not really laid out properly yet,' I said awkwardly. 'I'd rather wait until it's all done before I show you.'

She gave me a watchful, too-long look. 'Make sure it's on my desk by nine-thirty.'

'Right!' But the good spirits engendered by being let off the hook for the evening had all leached away. As she hammered her heels back to her office, I looked appraisingly at the computer I'd just switched off. Should I stay and do a couple of hours on it there and then? But I couldn't. I was all out. Of enthusiasm, of work-ethic, whatever. Instead I'd get up very early and come in and do it then.

I hadn't eaten much all day. At lunch-time, instead of stopping work, I'd foraged in my desk drawer for a half-eaten Mars bar that I'd vaguely remembered abandoning some days earlier. To my delight, I found it. I dashed off the paper clips and the worst of the fluff and, I must say, it was delicious.

So as I drove home I was hungry, and I knew there would be shag-all in the house. Food was a big problem for Garv and me. We subsisted, like most people we knew, on microwaved stuff, takeaways and meals out. Now and again – at least, before things had gone weird on us – when we'd cleared our backlog of ordinary worries, we'd spend a bit of time worrying that we weren't getting enough vitamins. So we'd vow to embrace a new, healthier way and buy a jar of multivitamins, which we'd take for a day or so, then forget about. Or else we'd go on a mad splurge in the supermarket, pulling our arms out of their scurvied sockets lugging home heads of broccoli, suspiciously orange carrots and enough apples to feed a family of eight for a week.

'Our health is our wealth,' we'd say, pleased as punch, because it seemed that *buying* raw foodstuffs was an effective thing to do in itself. It was only when it became clear that the food had to be eaten that the trouble would begin.

Immediately events would set about conspiring to thwart our cooking plans: we'd have to work late or go out for some-one's birthday. The ensuing week was usually spent in edgy awareness of all the fresh fruit and vegetables clamouring for our attention. We could hardly bear to go into the kitchen. Visions of cauliflowers and grapes constantly hovered on the corner of our consciousness, so that we were never truly at peace. Slowly, day by day, as the food went off, we'd furtively throw it out, never acknowledging to each other what we were doing. And only when the final kiwi fruit had been bounced off the inside of the bin did the black shadow lift and we could relax again.

Give me a frozen pizza any time, far less stressful.

Which is precisely what I bought for that evening's meal. I mounted the pavement, ran into the Spar and flung a couple of pizzas and some breakfast cereals into a basket. And then Fate intervened.

I can go without chocolate for weeks at a time. OK, days. But once I have a bit I want more, and the fluff-covered, lunch-time Mars bar had roused the hungry beast. So when I saw the boxes of handmade truffles in a chilled compartment I decided in a mad splurge of go-on-you-divil justification to buy myself one.

Who knows what would have happened if I hadn't? Did something as benign as a box of chocolates alter the entire course of my life?

Garv was already home and we greeted each other a little warily. We hadn't expected that this evening would be just the two of us; we'd been kind of depending on Liam and Elaine to dilute the funny atmosphere between us.

'You just missed Donna,' he said. 'She'll call you at work tomorrow.'

'So what's the latest?' Donna had a messy, high-concept love life and, as one of her best friends, it was my duty to provide advice. But she often consulted Garv to get what she called 'the male perspective', and he'd been so helpful that she'd rechristened him Doctor Love.

'Robbie wants her to stop shaving under her arms. Says he thinks it's sexy, but she's afraid she'll look like a gorilla.'

'So what did you advise?'

'That there's nothing wrong with women having hair –'

'Right on, sister.'

'– but that if she really doesn't want it, she should say that she'll stop shaving under her arms if he'll start wearing girls' knickers. Sauce for the goose and all that.'

'You're a genius, you really are.'

'Thanks.'

Garv pulled off his tie, flung it over the back of a chair, then raked his fingers through his hair, shaking away the vestiges of his work persona. For the office his hair was Ivy League neat:

shorn close at the neck and sleeked back off his face, but off-duty, it flopped down over his forehead.

There are some men who are so good-looking that meeting them is like being hit on the head with a mallet. Garv, however, isn't one of them; he's more the sort of man you could see day-in, day-out for twenty years, then just wake up one morning and think, 'God, he's nice, how come I never noticed him before now?'

His most obvious attraction was his height. But I was tall, too, so I'd never gone around saying, 'Ooh, look at how he towers over me!' All the same, I was able to wear heels with him, which I appreciated – my sister Claire had been married to a man who was the same height as her, so she'd had to wear flats in order that he wouldn't feel inadequate. And she really *loves* shoes. But then he had an affair and left her, so everything works out for the best in the end, I suppose.

'How was work?' Garv asked.

'Mostly awful. How was yours?'

'Bad for most of the day. I had a nice ten minutes between four-fifteen and four-twenty-five when I stood on the fire escape and pretended I still smoked.'

Garv works as an actuary, which makes him a cheap target for accusations of being boring – and on first meeting him you might confuse his quietness with dullness. But in my opinion it's a mistake to equate number-crunching with being boring; one of the most boring men I ever met was this gobshite novelist boyfriend of Donna's called John – you couldn't get more creative. We went out for dinner one night and he BORED us into the ground, loudly monologuing about other writers and what overpaid, meretricious bastards they were. Then he began questioning me about how I'd felt about something or other;

probing and delving with the intimacy of a gynaecologist. 'How did you feel? Sad? Can you be more specific? Heartbroken? Now we're getting someplace.' Then he hurried to the gents' and I just *knew* that he was writing everything I'd said into a notebook, to use in his novel.

'You're not to be jealous about Liam's flatscreen telly,' I said to Garv, happy to pretend that his subdued mood was down to his mate having more consumer durables than him. 'Didn't it attack him? It might have to be put down.'

'Ah,' Garv shrugged the way he always does when he's bothered, 'I'm not bothered.' (Though happy to discuss Donna's problems with her, you'll note his reluctance to talk about his own feelings, even when they're only about a telly.) 'But do you know how much it cost?' he blurted.

Of course I knew. Every time I went into town with Garv we had to call into the electrical department in Brown Thomas and stand before said telly, admiring it in all its twelve thousand pounds' worth of glory. Though Garv was well paid, he didn't earn anything like Liam's telephone-number wedge. And what with our high mortgage, the cost of running two cars, Garv's addiction to CDs and my addiction to face creams and hand-bags, funds just didn't run to flatscreen tellies.

'Cheer up, it probably broke when it fell off the wall. And one day soon you'll be able to afford one of your own.'

'Do you think?'

'Sure I do. As soon as we finish furnishing the house.' This seemed to do the trick. With a slight spring in his step, he helped unload the shopping. And that was when it happened.

He lifted out my box of go-on-you-divil truffles and exclaimed, 'Hey, look!' His eyes were a-sparkle. 'Those sweets again. Are they following us?'

I looked at him, looked at the box, then back at him. I hadn't a clue what he was on about.

'You *know*,' he insisted skittishly. 'The same ones we had when –'

He stopped abruptly and, my brow furrowed with curiosity, I stared at him. He stared back at me and, quite suddenly, several things occurred at once. The playful light in his eyes went out, to be replaced with an expression of fear. Horror, even. And before the thoughts had even formed themselves into any order in my consciousness, I *knew*. He was talking about someone else, an intimate moment shared with a woman other than me. And it had been recently.

I felt as if I was falling, that I would go on falling for ever. Then, abruptly, I made myself stop. And I knew something else: I couldn't do this. I couldn't bear to watch the downward spiral of my marriage begin to catch other people and spin them into the vortex too.

Shocked into stillness, our eyes locked, I silently beseeched him, desperate for him to say something to explain it, to make it all go away. But his face was frozen in horror – the same horror that I felt.

'I –' he managed, then faltered.

A sudden stab of agony shot up into my back tooth and, as though I was dreaming, I left the room.

Garv didn't follow me; he remained in the kitchen. I could hear no sound and I presumed he was still standing where I'd left him. This, in itself, seemed like an admission of guilt. Still in my waking nightmare, I was picking up the remote and switching on the telly. I was waiting to wake up.

2

We didn't exchange a word for the rest of the evening. Perhaps I should have been shrieking for details – who was she? How long? But at the best of times that wasn't my way and after all we'd gone through over the past while, I'd no fight left in me.

If only I was more like my sisters, who were great at expressing pain – experts at slamming doors, crashing phones back into cradles, throwing things at walls, screeching. The whole world got to hear of their anger/disappointment/double-crossing man/chocolate mousse missing from the fridge. But I'd been born without the diva gene, so when devastation hit me I usually kept it inside, turning it over and over, trying to make sense of it. My misery was like an ingrowing hair, curling further and further into me. But what goes in must come out and my pain invariably re-emerged in the form of scaly, flaking, weeping eczema on my right arm – it was a cast-iron barometer of my emotional state and that night it tingled and itched so much that I scratched until it bled.

I went to bed before Garv and, to my surprise, actually managed to fall asleep – the shock, perhaps? Then I awoke at some indeterminate time and lay staring into the blanket of darkness. It was probably four a.m. Four in the morning is the bleakest time, when we're at our lowest ebb. It's when sick people die. It's when people being tortured crack. My mouth tasted gritty and my jaw ached: I'd been grinding my teeth again. No wonder my back tooth was clamouring for attention – making a last desperate plea for help before I ground it into nothingness.

Then, wincing, I faced the repulsive revelation full-on. This truffle woman – was Garv really having a thing with her?

In agony, I admitted that he probably was; the signs were there. Looked at from the outside I'd conclude that he definitely was, but isn't it always different when it's *your* life that's under scrutiny?

I'd been afraid of something like this happening, so much so that I'd half-prepared myself for it. But now that it seemed it had come to pass, I wasn't at all ready. He'd got such a glow on when he'd noticed 'their' chocolates . . . It had been dreadful to witness. He *must* be up to something. But that was too much to take on and I was back to not believing it. I mean, if he'd been messing around, surely I'd have noticed?

The obvious thing would be to ask him straight out and put an end to the speculation, but he was bound to lie like a rug. Worse still, he might tell me the truth. Out of nowhere, lines came to me from some B-movie. *The truth?* (Accompanied by a curled lip.) *You couldn't HANDLE the truth!*

The thoughts kept coming. Could she be someone he worked with? Might I have met her at their Christmas party? I shuffled through my memories of that night, endeavouring to locate a funny look or a loaded comment. But all I could remember was dancing the hora with Jessica Benson, one of his colleagues. Could it be her? But she'd been so nice to me. Mind you, if I'd been having sex with someone's husband, maybe I'd be nice to her, too . . . Apart from the women Garv worked with, there were the girlfriends and wives of his mates – and then there were my friends. I was ashamed even to have that thought, but

I couldn't help myself; suddenly I trusted no one and suspected everyone.

What about Donna? Herself and Garv always had a great laugh *and* she called him Doctor Love. I went cold as I remembered reading somewhere that nicknames were a cast-iron indication that people were up to high jinks.

But then, with a silent sigh, I released Donna without charge: she was one of my best friends, I truly couldn't believe she'd do that to me. Plus, for reasons best known to herself, she was mad about Robbie the flake. Unless he was an elaborate red herring, of course. But there was one thing that convinced me totally that Garv wasn't having an affair with Donna, and that was the fact that she'd told him about her verruca. In fact, she'd pulled off her boot and sock and thrust the sole of her foot at him so that he could see for himself just how gross it was. If you're having a passionate fling with someone, you don't own up to things like verrucas. It's all about mystique and impractical bras and round-the-clock upkeep on hairy legs – or so I'm told.

What about my friend Sinead? Garv was so kind to her. But it was only three months since she'd been given the road by her boyfriend, Dave. Surely she was far too fragile for an affair with her friend's husband – and far too fragile for any normal man to try it on? Unless it was her fragility that Garv liked. But wasn't he getting enough of that from me? Why go out for broken crockery when you've got it in absolute smithereens at home?

Beside me, I realized that Garv was awake too – his fake deep-breathing was the giveaway. So we could talk. Except we couldn't, we'd been trying for months. I didn't hear the intake of breath that precedes speech, so I was startled when the ink-dark silence was violated by Garv's voice. 'Sorry.'

Sorry. The worst thing he could have said. The word hung in the darkness and wouldn't go away. In my head I heard it echo again, then again. Each time fainter, until I wondered if I'd just imagined hearing it. Minutes passed. Without ever replying, I turned my back to him and surprised myself by falling asleep again.

In the morning, we woke late, and there was blood under my nails from scratching my arm. My eczema was back in force – I'd have to start wearing gloves in bed again if this continued. But would it continue? Again I got that falling sensation.

I busied myself with showers and coffee, and when Garv said, 'Maggie,' and tried to stop my incessant motion, I neatly sidestepped him and said, without eye contact, 'I'll be late.' I left, carrying that empty, four-in-the-morning feeling with me.

Despite sidestepping Garv, I was late for work and the contract wasn't on Frances's desk by nine-thirty. She sighed, 'Oh Maggie,' in an I'm-not-angry-with-you-I'm-disappointed way. It's meant to reach the parts a bollocking doesn't and make you feel shitty and ashamed. However, I appreciated not being shouted at. Not the reaction Frances was looking for, I suspect.

I felt entirely lost, but at the same time unnaturally calm – almost as if I'd been waiting for a catastrophe and it was a weird sort of relief that it had finally happened. Because I had no idea how to behave in these circumstances, I decided to mimic everyone else there and immerse myself in work. Wasn't it strange, I thought, that after such a dreadful shock I was still functioning as normal? Then I noticed I kept botching the double-click on my mouse because my hand was trembling.

For seconds, I'd manage to lose myself in a contract clause, but all the time the knowledge surrounded me: *Something is very wrong.* Over the years, like every couple, Garv and I had had our rows, but not even the most vicious of those had ever felt like this. The worst scrap had been one of those odd ones which had started out as a muscular discussion over whether a new skirt of mine was brown or purple, and had unexpectedly disintegrated into a bitter stand-off, with accusations of colour-blindness and hyper-sensitivity flying about.

(*Garv:* 'What's wrong with it being brown?'

Me: 'Everything! But it's not brown, it's purple, you stupid colour-blind fucker.'

Garv: 'Look, it's only a skirt. All I said was I was *surprised* at you buying a brown one.'

Me: 'But I DIDN'T! It's PURPLE!'

Him: 'You're overreacting.'

Me: 'I'm NOT. I would NEVER buy a brown skirt. Do you know the first thing about me?')

At the time I'd thought I'd never forgive him. I'd been wrong. But this time was different, I was horribly sure of it.

At lunch-time, I just couldn't find it in me to care about my urgent piles of work, so I went to Grafton Street, looking for comfort. Which took the form of spending money – again. Unenthusiastically, I bought a scented candle and a cheapish (relatively speaking) copy of a Gucci bag. But neither of them did anything to fill the void. Then I stopped into a chemist to get painkillers for my tooth and got intercepted by a white-coated, orange-faced woman who told me that if I bought two Clarins products – one of which had to be skincare – I'd get a free gift. Listlessly I shrugged, 'Fine.'

She couldn't believe her luck, and when she suggested the dearest stuff – serums in 100 ml bottles – again I lifted and slumped my shoulders. 'Sure.'

I liked the sound of a free gift – I found the idea of a present very consoling. But back at work, when I opened my present, it was a lot less exciting than it had looked on the picture: funny-coloured eyeshadow, a mini-mini-mini tube of foundation, four drops of eye-cream and a thimble of vinegary perfume. Anti-climax set in, and then, in an unexpected reprieve of normality, came guilt, which swelled big and ugly as the afternoon lengthened. *I had to stop spending money.* So as soon as I could reasonably leave, I hurried back to Grafton Street to try to return the handbag – I couldn't return the Clarins stuff because I'd already tried the free gift – but they wouldn't give me a refund, only a credit note. And before I'd made it back to the car, my eye was caught by yellow flowery flip-flops in a shoe-shop window and, like an out-of-body experience, I found myself inside, handing over my card and spending another thirty quid. It wasn't safe to let me out.

That evening I went to a work thing and did something I don't usually do at work things – I got drunk. Messy drunk, so bad that on one of my many trips back from the loo, when I met Stuart Keating, I ended up lunging at him. Stuart worked in another department and he'd always been nice to me; I can still see the surprise on his face as I zoomed in on him. Then we were kissing, but only for a second before I had to disengage. *What was I doing?* 'Sorry,' I exclaimed and, appalled at myself, I returned to the party, picked up my jacket and left without saying goodbye to anyone. From across the room Frances watched me, her expression unreadable.

When I came home, Garv was waiting bolt upright, like an anxious parent. He tried to talk to me, but I mumbled drunkenly that I had to go to sleep and lurched to the bedroom, Garv in hot pursuit. I stripped off my clothes, letting them lie where they fell, and climbed between the sheets. 'Drink some water.' I heard the clatter as Garv put a glass on my bedside table. I ignored it and him, but just before I sank into the merciful oblivion of sleep, I remembered I hadn't taken out my contact lenses. Too tired, drunk, whatever to get on my feet and go to the bathroom, I slipped them out and plopped them into the handily placed glass of water, promising myself I'd rinse them good and proper in their solution in the morning.

But when morning came, my tongue was superglued with dryness to the roof of my mouth. Automatically, I stretched out my hand for my glass of water and gulped it in one go. Only when the last of it was racing down my throat did I remember. My contact lenses. I'd drunk my contact lenses. *Again*. The third time in six weeks. They were only monthly disposables, but all the same.

And the following day, as luck would have it, I lost my job.

I wasn't exactly sacked. But my contract wasn't renewed. It was a six-month contract and since I'd moved back to Dublin from Chicago it had already been renewed five times. I had thought renewing it again was a mere formality.

'When you first started here,' Frances said, 'we were im- pressed with you. You were hard-working and reliable.'

I nodded. That sounded like me all right. On a good day.

'But in the last six months or so, the standard of your work and commitment has dropped dramatically. You're often late, you leave early . . .'

I listened, almost in surprise. Of course, I'd known that in my *head* stuff hadn't been great, but I'd thought I'd done a pretty good job of presenting a convincing business-as-usual façade to the outside world.

'. . . you've been clearly distracted and you've taken ten days' sick leave.'

I could have leapt to my feet and given a speech telling Frances why I'd been distracted and where I'd been on my ten days' sick leave, but I remained sitting like a plank, my face closed. It was no one's business but mine. Yet, paradoxically, I felt she should have seen that something had been very wrong over the past months and made allowances for me. I've been more rational, I suspect.

'We want people who care about their work –'

I opened my mouth to protest that I did care, until I realized, with a shock, that actually I didn't give a damn.

'– and it's with regret that I have to tell you that we are unable to renew your contract with us.'

It was years since I'd been sacked. In fact, the last time had been when I was seventeen and babysitting for a neighbour. I'd smuggled my boyfriend in when the children had gone to bed, because a house with no adults in had been too much to resist. But the horrible son – appropriately enough called Damian – spotted me smuggling my boyfriend back out. I'll never forget it: Damian was standing at the top of the stairs, and his expression was so malevolent that the Old Spice music began playing spontaneously in my head. I was never asked to babysit there again. (To be honest, it was nearly a relief.)

But since then I had never been fired. I was a pretty good worker – not so good that I was ever in danger of winning the Employee of the Month Award, but fairly reliable and productive.

'You want me to go?' I asked faintly.

'Yes.'

'When?'

'Now would be good.'

Oddly enough, it was losing my job that finally made me decide to leave Garv. I don't really understand why. Because, you know, it's not easy to leave someone. Not in real life. In fiction it's all so cut and dried and clear: if you can see no future together, then of *course* you leave. Simple. Or if he's having an affair, then you'd be a total idiot to stay, right? But in real life it's amazing the things that conspire to keep you together. You might think, OK, so we can't seem to make each other happy any more, but I get on so well with his sister and my friends are so fond of him, and our lives are too interwoven for us to be able to extricate ourselves. And this is our house, and see those lupins in our little back garden? – I planted them. (Well, not planted *planted*, I didn't actually put them in the ground with my own hands, it was a narky old man called Michael who did, but I masterminded the whole thing.)

Leaving someone is a big deal. I was walking away from a lot more than a person, it was an entire life I was saying goodbye to.

But the shock of losing my job had triggered the conviction that everything was falling apart. Once the door to one disaster had opened, the possibilities for catastrophe seemed open-ended and I felt I'd no choice but to go along with my life as it unravelled. Losing a job? Why not go for broke and lose a marriage as well? It had suffered so many body blows during the past months, it was over in all but name anyway.

By the time Garv came home from work, I was in the bedroom, waist-high in a pathetic attempt at packing. How anyone manages to do a midnight flit is beyond me. Most people (if they're anything like me) accumulate so much *stuff*.

He stood and looked at me, and it was like I was dreaming the whole thing.

He seemed surprised. Or maybe not. 'What's going on?'

This was my cue for the dramatic exit lines people always deliver in fiction. *I'm LEAVING you! It's OVER.* Instead, I hung my head and mumbled, 'I think I'd better go. We've tried our best with this and . . .'

'Right,' he swallowed. 'Right.' Then he nodded, and the nod was the worst bit. Such resignation in it. He agreed with me.

'I lost my job today.'

'Christ. What happened?'

'I've been distracted and taken too much sick leave.'

'Bastards.'

'Yeah, well.' I sighed. 'The thing is, I mightn't make this month's mortgage, so I'll give it to you from my Ladies' Nice Things account.'

'Forget it, forget it. I'll take care of it.'

Then we lapsed into silence and it became clear that the mortgage was all he was planning to take care of.

Maybe I should have been angry with him and Truffle Woman. Perhaps I should have despised him for not jumping into the breach and promising me passionately that he wouldn't let me go and that we could work it out.

But the truth was, right then, I *wanted* to go.

3

Maintenance level dysfunctional. That's how I'd like to describe my family, the Walshes. Well, actually, that's not how I'd *like* to describe my family. I'd *like* to describe my family as the prototype for the Brady Bunch. I'd *like* to describe my family as the Waltons of Waltons' Mountain, only more lickarsey. But alas, maintenance level dysfunctional is as good as it gets.

I have four sisters, and the credo that each of them seems to live by is: The More Dramas the Better. (Sample thereof: Claire's husband left her the day she'd given birth to their first child; Rachel is a (recovered) addict; Anna doesn't really *do* reality; and Helen, the youngest – well, it's kind of hard for me to describe . . .) But I've never been fond of chaos and I couldn't figure out why I was so different. In my lonelier moments I used to entertain a fantasy that I was adopted. Which I could never truly relax into, because it was obvious from my appearance that I was *one of them*.

My sisters and I come in two versions: Model A and Model B. Model As are tall, wholesome-looking and, if left unchecked, have brick-shithouse tendencies. I am a textbook Model A. My eldest sister, Claire, and the sister next in line to me, Rachel, are also Model As. Model Bs, on the other hand, are small, kitten-cute and gorgeous looking. With their long, dark hair, slanty green eyes and slender limbs, the two youngest sisters, Anna and Helen, are both clear-cut examples of the genre.

Though Anna is nearly three years older than Helen, they look almost like twins. Sometimes even our mother can't tell them apart – although that's probably as much to do with her not wearing her glasses as their appearance, now that I come to think of it. To make it easy, Anna – a neo-hippy – dresses as though she's been rummaging through the dressing-up box, and Helen is the one with the air of psychosis.

Model As share the common characteristics of being tall and strong. Not necessarily fat. Not *necessarily*. Indeed, Model As have been known to look willowy and slender. If they're in the grip of anorexia, that is – not as unlikely as it sounds. It's certainly happened, although not, sadly, to me. I've never had an eating disorder – apparently I didn't have the imagination, Helen told me.

I mightn't have had an eating disorder, but I suspected I had a mild problem with another form of bulimia – shopping bulimia. It seemed like I was always splurging on stuff, then trying to return it. In fact, it had recently caused a huge row that involved most of my family. Helen had been lamenting on how hard it was to live on what she got paid as a make-up artist, and she suddenly rounded on me and accused, 'You're good with money.' This happened a lot; they referred to me as clean-living and sporty – even though I hadn't played any sport since living in Chicago – and painted a picture of me that was years, probably decades, out of date. My parents were wholly in approval of this sepia-tinted version of me, but my younger sisters – affectionately, mind – treated me as a figure of fun. Most of the time I humoured them, but that particular day I suddenly baulked at being – albeit affectionately – depicted as life-crushingly dull.

'In what way am I good with money?'

'Not living beyond your means. Thinking carefully before you buy stuff, that sort of thing,' Helen said, scathingly. 'Neither a borrower nor a lender be, hahaha.'

'I'm not good with money,' I said sharply.

'You are!' they chorused – my parents with admiration, Helen without.

'She's not,' Garv said.

'Thank you,' I turned briefly to him.

'You are so! I bet you've a huge stash of used fivers in a biscuit tin under your bed.'

'She wouldn't keep it in a biscuit tin,' Dad defended me against Helen. 'You don't get any interest in biscuit tins. She has her savings in a high-interest account.'

'What savings? I don't have any savings!'

'Don't you?' Mum sounded confused. Upset even. 'Didn't you used to have a post-office book? Didn't you pay in 50p a week?'

'Yes, when I was *nine.*'

'But you've a pension fund?' Dad asked anxiously.

'That's different, that's not savings and you don't get it till you're sixty. And I'm *always* buying things I don't need.'

'Then you bring them back.'

'But they don't always give refunds. Sometimes they only give credit notes, so that's the same as spending money.' My voice was rising. 'And sometimes they go out of date before I use them.'

'No!' Mum was appalled.

'Well, I bet you pay your credit card off in full every month,' Helen persisted.

'I DON'T pay my credit card off in full every month.' They were all slightly open-mouthed at my unexpected fury. 'Only SOME MONTHS!'

'Oh, rock'n'*roll*.'

I knew it was a little strange to be having this argument. I knew people argued about money – but usually they were being accused of spending too much and insisting that they didn't, not the other way round. So overwrought was I that eventually Mum made Helen apologize. Then she murmured to me, 'It's nothing to be ashamed of, earning good money and putting some by.'

It was at that point that Garv made me leave, raging that they'd upset me so. (You know the way Garv sees the good in most people? Well, he suspends such altruism around most of my family.)

On the drive home, I said anxiously, 'I know everything is relative and I know I'm not in their league, but I *am* neurotic, aren't I?'

'You are, of course,' he said stoutly. 'Don't mind them!'

However, I'm not dwelling on my family in this manner to provide background colour, there's actually a reason for it: it's because I'm about to resume living with them. I *could* have moved in with Donna, except she'd recently managed to get on-again-off-again-I'll-just-get-my-head-out-of-my-arse-if-you'll-give-me-a-second Robbie to live with her, so I wasn't sure she'd welcome the presence of a third party. Or I could have asked Sinead, except Dave had kicked her out and she was currently even more homeless than me. And I could have tried my best friend Emily, who has *plenty* of room. The only problem is that she lives in Los Angeles. Not exactly handy.

So, cap in hand, I've to return to the bosom of my family. First, though, I have to tell them, and I'm dreading it.

Perhaps it's never easy to disappoint your mum and dad, but in my case it feels extra difficult. I'm the one who married her first boyfriend, and they've been so heartbreakingly proud of me and of the ticks beside almost every item on the checklist: the marriage, the house, the car, the job, the pension plan, the robust mental health.

'You've never given us a moment's worry,' they've often said. 'The only one who hasn't.' Then would follow a baleful look at whichever of my sisters was giving them grief at the time. Now, after successfully avoiding them all those years, it was *my* turn for the baleful looks.

I paused at the front door before letting myself in. Just taking a moment. Filled with a fierce need to run away, leave the country, avoid facing my atrocious failure. Then, with a sigh, I shoved my key in the lock. I couldn't run away – I'm responsible and conscientious. In a family where several black sheep are jockeying for position, being the sole white sheep isn't much fun.

There was a racket coming from the television room and it sounded like all those currently domiciled in the house – Mum, Dad, Helen and Anna – were actually present. Helen, at twenty-five, still lived at home because of her on-off relationship with gainful employment – she's had many career changes. Two or three years were spent wasting time at university, and after a spell of unemployment she'd tried to be an air hostess, but couldn't manage to be pleasant enough. ('Stop ringing that fucking call-bell, I heard you the first time,' was, I believe, the sentence that ended her high-flying career.) More unemployment followed, then she did an expensive course as a make-up artist. She'd hoped to work in theatre and film, but instead ended up doing wedding after wedding after wedding – mostly the daughters of my parents' friends. But Mum's efforts to drum up work for Helen weren't appreciated and, in high dudgeon,

Mum told me that Helen had sworn that if she ever had to make up another six-year-old flower-girl she'd gouge her eyes out with her taupe eyeliner. (It wasn't clear whether she was talking about her own eyes or the flower-girl's.)

Helen's problem is that she's burdened with high intelligence coupled with an unfeasibly short attention span, and she has yet to find her true calling.

Unlike Anna, who has yet to find *any* calling, true or otherwise. She's resisted any encouragement to embark on a career path and has eked out a living waitressing, bartending and reading tarot cards. Never for any sustained period, mind; her CV is probably as long as *War and Peace.* Until she and her ex-boyfriend, Shane, split up they'd lived a hand-to-mouth, free-spirited existence. They were the type who'd pop out for ten minutes to buy a KitKat and the next time you'd hear from them they'd be in Istanbul, working in a tannery. Their motto was 'God will provide,' and even if God wouldn't, the dole did. I'd envied them their devil-may-care existence. Actually, that's a complete lie. I'd have hated it – the insecurity, never knowing if you could eat, buy exfoliator, that sort of thing.

The thing about Anna is that she can be acutely, almost shockingly perceptive, but she's not great on practical things. Like remembering to get dressed before leaving the house. There was a time when we felt her sweet, absent nature was down to her fondness for recreational drugs, but she knocked that on the head about four years ago, around the same time that Rachel did. And although she's possibly a little more lucid than she used to be, I couldn't say for sure.

She'd moved back in with my parents a few months before, when she'd broken up with Shane – though she hadn't been given the same sort of grief as I expected to get. One, because she hadn't been married and two, because they seemed to expect her to be unreliable.

Cautiously, I opened the lounge door. They were clustered on the couch watching *Who Wants to Be a Millionaire?* and pouring scorn on the candidates.

'Any thick knows the answer to that,' Helen threw at the screen.

'What is it, then?' Anna asked.

'I don't know. But I don't HAVE to know. I'm not about to lose ninety-three thousand pounds. Oh, go on then, phone your friend, for all the good it'll do, if he's as thick as you –'

Why did they all have to be in? Why couldn't it just have been, say, Anna? I could have told her, then slunk off to bed like a coward, leaving her to break the news to everyone else.

Then Mum spotted me at the door.

'Margaret!' she exclaimed. For years I've been telling her that my name is Maggie, but she's in denial. 'Come in. Sit down. Have a Cornetto.' She elbowed Dad. 'Get her a Cornetto.'

'Chocolate? Strawberry? Or . . .' Dad paused, before triumphantly delivering his *pièce de résistance*. 'Or M&M? They're new!'

There is always a wonderful selection of confectionery available at my parents' house. Unlike most houses, though, this isn't in addition to the usual foodstuffs, it's *instead* of. It wasn't so much that my mother didn't enjoy cooking meals, it was more that we didn't enjoy eating them. Some time in the early eighties she stopped preparing meals altogether. 'What's the point if you ungrateful brats never eat them?'

'I eat them,' Dad bleated, a voice in the wilderness.

But it made no difference. Convenience foods were ushered

in and it made me sad. I'd always yearned for an Italian-style family who gathered for their evening meal, passing platters and bowls of steaming homemade food along the scrubbed pine table while the roundy mama beamed from the stove.

All the same, unlimited ice-cream was not to be sniffed at. Graciously, I accepted a Cornetto (an M&M one, of course) and watched the end of the programme. I might as well, there was no way I'd get their attention until it was over. Besides, it suited me to defer the moment when I had to spill the words *Garv and I have split up*. I was afraid that saying it out loud would mean that it had actually happened.

And then it was time.

I sighed, swallowed away the nausea and began. 'I've something to tell you all.'

'Lovely!' Mum rearranged her features into her I'm-going-to-be-a-granny-again expression.

'Garv and I have split up.'

'Ah, here!' With a sharp rustle my father promptly disappeared behind his paper. Anna flung herself upon me, even Helen looked startled, but my poor mother . . . She looked as though she'd been hit on the head by a flying brick. Stunned and stricken and shocked beyond belief.

'In a minute you'll tell me you're joking,' she gasped.

'In a minute I won't,' I said stoutly. I hated doing this to her, especially because I was the second of her daughters to have a failed marriage, but it was important not to mislead her. False hope was worse than no hope.

'But,' she struggled for breath, 'but you've always been the good one. Say something,' she angrily urged my father.

He appeared reluctantly from behind the newspaper shield. 'Seven-year itch,' he offered tentatively.

'*Gentlemen Prefer Blondes*,' Helen countered, then elbowed Anna, who thought for a moment, then said, '*The Misfits*.'

'You're describing yourself,' Helen replied scathingly, then curled her lip at the wall of newspaper. 'See, Dad? We can all name Marilyn Monroe films, but how does it help?'

'It's actually *nine* years I've been married,' I quietly told Dad's newspaper. He meant well.

'This has come as an awful shock to me,' Mum reiterated.

'I thought you'd be glad, seeing as you all hate Garv.'

'I know, but –' Abruptly Mum collected herself. 'Stop that nonsense, we don't all hate him.'

But they did – all apart from Claire, who'd got to know him when she had a teenage fling with his big brother (also confusingly known as Garv). She'd always thought *my* Garv was sweet, especially since he'd fixed her tapedeck for her. (You wouldn't want to get her on the subject of the elder Garv, mind.) But despite Claire's stamp of approval, *my* Garv had somehow – through no fault of his own – acquired a reputation for tight-fistedness and old-before-his-time fustiness with the rest of the family.

The stinginess allegation had raised its ugly head the first night I'd ever officially brought him out with my family. He'd been knocking around on the fringes for a good while before that, but I'd realized I was serious about him and that it was time he met my family properly. With a sense of occasion we repaired to Phelan's, the local pub, and the salient fact is that Garv didn't stand his round.

Not Standing Your Round is a mortal sin in my family, and there's always great competition to out-give and out-convivialize all the others. Hand-to-hand combat almost breaks out as people try to be the first to get to the bar.

On the night in question, Garv was more than willing to buy drinks for my family, but he was nervous and way too mild-mannered to stand up to them. As soon as anyone's drink had passed the halfway mark, he'd leap to his feet, fumbling for his money, asking, 'Same again?' But each time he did so the table erupted like a dealing-room floor, with everyone yelling at him to sit down and put his money away, that he was insulting us. Even I joined in, getting carried away in the heat of the moment. Beaten back by a hail of words, Garv reluctantly lowered himself back on to his bar stool.

The net result of the evening was that Dad bought a round, Rachel bought a round, I bought a round, Anna bought a round, then Dad bought another round. And Garv gained a reputation as a tight-arse.

Hot on the heels of that miscarriage of justice came the polo-shirt incident. A story that begins happily and ends tragic-ally. One Saturday afternoon, Garv and I were traipsing around town, half-heartedly going in and out of clothes shops. Because Garv was still only a trainee and he'd just bought a car, money was tight, so we were on the lookout for bargains. Free things, preferably. When by pure chance we found a polo shirt in the bottom of a clearance bin. To our great surprise, it had none of the characteristics you normally associate with things found in clearance bins, like three sleeves, no neck-hole or indelible, bile-coloured stains. In fact, it was perfect – the right size, the right price and a pale, icy colour that made his eyes look blue when normally they look grey.

It was only when we got it home that we realized there was a small logo above the breast pocket. A tiny outline of a man swinging a golfclub which, somehow in the euphoria of discovering the garment only had two sleeves, we'd missed.

Naturally enough, we were both dismayed, but concluded that it was so small it was barely visible. Besides, we were too skint for him not to wear it. So he wore it. And the next thing I hear is that Garv wears the same kind of jumpers as Dad. Then a rumour started up that he played golf, which was not only untrue but very, very unfair.

Garv is no fool and he was aware of my family's antipathy. Well, it was hard to be *un*aware, when every time he appeared at the house, Helen would bellow, 'For God's sake, don't let him in!'

While he never responded to their discourtesy with rudeness of his own, nor did he launch a charm offensive to try and win them over either. And he *could* have – he had a nice, easy manner most of the time. Instead, he became very protective of me around them, which they interpreted variously as stand-offishness or downright hostility. And *responded* with stand-offishness or downright hostility. All in all, it hasn't been that easy, especially at Christmas times . . .

'You're just going through a bad patch,' Mum tried valiantly.

Wretchedly, I shook my head. Did she think I hadn't thought of that? Did she think that I hadn't clung on to that, hoping with gritted teeth that that was all that was wrong?

'Was he, ah . . . ?' My father was clearly trying to frame a delicate question. 'Was he dipping his wick where he shouldn't have been?'

'No.' Perhaps he had been, but that wasn't the cause. It was a symptom of what was wrong.

'Things haven't been easy for you, for either of you.' Mum was off again. 'You've had a couple of –'

'– setbacks,' I said quickly, before she used another word.

'Setbacks. Would you not have a holiday?'

34

'We've had a holiday, remember? It was a disaster, it did more harm than good.'

'What about going for counselling?'

'Counselling? Garv?' If I'd been capable of laughter, this would have been a good opportunity. 'If he won't talk to me, he's hardly likely to talk to a total stranger.'

'But you love each other,' she said, with desperation.

'But we're making each other miserable.'

'Love conquers all,' Mum coaxed, like I was five.

'No. It. Doesn't,' I spelt out, an edge of hysteria to my voice. 'Do you think I'd do something as awful as leave him if it was that easy?'

That plunged her into sulky, that's-no-way-to-talk-to-your-mother silence.

'So you're not going to tell us what's going on?' Helen concluded.

'But you know everything that's happened.' OK, not quite everything, but Truffle Woman was not the cause, she was simply the final nail.

Scornfully, Helen flicked her eyes upwards. 'This is like your driving test all over again.'

I might have known someone would bring that up. The bitterness still ran deep.

When I was twenty-one, I did a course of driving lessons, then sat my test and passed it. Only then did I tell any of my family, but instead of being delighted for me, they were hurt and confused. They felt left out, short-changed, deprived of a drama, and they couldn't understand why I hadn't involved them.

'I could have given you a St Christopher's medal for your test,' Mum had protested.

'But I didn't need it, I passed anyway.'

'I could have taken you out to practise in my car,' Dad had said wistfully. 'I see Maurice Kilfeather takes Angela out.'

'We could have waved you off from the test centre,' Claire had pointed out.

Which was precisely the kind of thing I'd wanted to avoid. Doing my driving test was just something I'd wanted to do on my own. I didn't think it was anyone else's business. And if I was being brutally honest, I'd have to acknowledge the issue of failure – if I'd failed my test I'd never have been let forget about it.

Finally Dad spoke. 'How's work?'

4

I was dreading the first night away from Garv (and all the subsequent nights, but first things first). I was sure I wouldn't sleep, because wasn't that what happened to people in distress? But I needn't have worried: I slept like I was dead and woke up in a bed and a room that I didn't recognize. *Where's this?* For a moment my curiosity was almost pleasant, then reality tumbled down on to me.

That day was one of the most dislocated of my life. With no job to show up at, my time was spent mostly in my bedroom, keeping out of Mum's way. Even though she was very vocal about how this was just a phase I was going through and that I'd be back with Garv in no time, my popularity with her was enjoying an all-time low.

Helen, on the other hand, was treating me like a visiting freak show and dropped by to torment me before she went to work. Anna came too, in an attempt to protect me.

'God, you're still here,' Helen marvelled, marching into the room. 'So you've really left him? But this is all wrong, Maggie, you don't do this sort of thing.'

I was reminded of a conversation I'd had with my sisters the previous Christmas – we were trapped in the house without even a Harrison Ford film to take our minds off things and were driven to wondering what each of us would be if we were food instead of people. It was decided that Claire would be a green curry because they were both fiery, then Helen decreed that Rachel would be a jelly baby, which pleased Rachel no end.

'Because I'm sweet?'

'Because I like to bite your head off.'

Anna – 'this is nearly too easy,' Helen had said – was a Flake. And I was 'plain yoghurt at room temperature'.

OK, so I knew I'd never been in with a shout of being, say, an After Eight ('thin and sophisticated'), or a Ginger Nut biscuit ('hard and interesting'). But I saw nothing wrong with me being a trifle ('has hidden depths'). Instead, I was the dullest thing, the most flavourless thing anyone could think of – plain yoghurt at room temperature. It cut me deep, and even when Claire said that Helen was a human durian fruit because she was offensive and banned in several countries, it wasn't enough to lift my spirits.

Back in the present, Helen continued jibing me. 'You're just not the type to leave her husband.'

'No, having a broken marriage isn't the sort of thing that plain yoghurt at room temperature does, does it?'

'What?' Helen sounded confused.

'I *said*, having a broken marriage isn't the sort of thing that plain yoghurt at room temperature does, does it?'

She gave me a funny look, muttered something about brides-maids who looked like the elephant man and what was she supposed to do about it, then finally left.

Anna got into bed beside me and linked her arm through mine. 'Plain yoghurt can be delicious,' she said quietly. 'It's perfect with curry. And . . .' After a long, searching pause, she added, 'And they say it's very good for thrush.'

*

I languished in the house, with no real idea of what I was doing there. I let telly programmes wash over me: 'Smokin' crack ain't so all that'; 'Girlfrien', your butt is bigger than my car'. Whenever they finished, I'd find myself looking around, confused to find myself no longer in the Chicago projects, but in a flowery-curtained, befigurine'd, suburban Dublin house. And not just any flowery-curtained, befigurine'd, suburban Dublin house. *How have I ended up back here? What happened?*

I felt like such a failure that I was afraid to leave the house. And I thought about Garv and the girl – a lot. So much that I had to go back to using my much-hated steroid cream on my unbearably itchy arm. I was tormented by her identity. Who was she, anyway? How long had it been going on? And – God forbid – was it serious? The questions scurried incessantly; even as I watched two obese girls punching each other and Jerry Springer pretending to be appalled, another part of my brain was panning over the past few months with a magnifying glass, searching for clues and discovering nothing.

But I felt I'd no right to mind about the girl and that it didn't make any difference anyway. With or without her, the game was up.

I'd been back at my parents' about twenty-four hours when the reaction set in. As I listlessly watched telly, my temperature abruptly plummeted. Though the room was warm (far *too* warm), the skin on my arms had contracted like cling-wrap before heat, and the hairs were standing to attention from goosepimpled follicles. I blinked, only to discover that my eyes hurt. Then I noticed that my head was packed tight with cotton wool and my bones ached, and I was unable to find enough energy even to pick up the remote control. Muzzy and spaced,

I watched *Animal Hospital*, wishing I could do something to make it stop. What was wrong with me?

'What's wrong with you?' Mum had come into the room. 'Lord above! What are they doing to that poor Alsatian?'

'He's got piles.' My tongue belonged to someone else, someone with a much bigger mouth. 'And I think I've got the flu.'

'Are you sure?'

'I'm cold and everything hurts.' Me, hardy Maggie, who never got sick.

'I didn't know dogs could even *get* piles.' She was still glued to the screen.

'Maybe he sat on a cold step. I think I've got the flu,' I repeated, slightly louder this time.

Finally I had her attention. 'You don't look the best,' she agreed. She looked concerned. Almost as concerned as she had been about the aller. She placed her hand on my forehead. 'I wonder if you've a temperature.'

'Course I have,' I croaked. 'I've the flu.'

She located a thermometer and gave it several of those violent flicks that people always do before they take someone's temperature. An energetic throw, as if they're about to fling the glass stick across the room, but change their mind at the last minute. But despite her adherence to protocol, my temperature was normal.

'Though it's hard to be sure,' she added, casting a jaundiced eye at the thermometer. 'Thirty years we've had it and that yoke has never worked.'

I went to bed at nine-thirty and didn't come round until two the following afternoon. I was lying in exactly the same position I'd been in before I went to sleep, as though I hadn't moved once in any of that time. Instead of feeling better I actually felt worse: lethargic and hopeless. And I continued to feel wretched.

I'd never believed it was possible to become sick from sadness. I'd thought that was a nonsense concept confined to melodramatic Victorian novels. But sometime over the course of the following week I understood that there was nothing wrong with me – nothing physical, in any case. My temperature was normal, and how come no one else had caught my flu? Whatever was wrong with me, it was emotional. Mourning sickness. My body was fighting my separation from Garv as though it was a hostile organism.

I couldn't stop sleeping. Deep, druggy sleeps from which I never fully woke up. Once conscious, I could barely manage the smallest things. I knew I was supposed to be getting on with stuff. Getting another job. Tidying up the loose ends of my old life. Sorting out my new one. But I felt as though I was walking underwater. Moving too slowly through an unwieldy world.

When I got beneath the shower, the water felt like a hail of sharp gravel being hurled at my tender skin. The house was too noisy – every time a door slammed my heart pumped too hard. When Dad dropped a saucepan with a clatter on the floor, I got such a fright my eyes filled with tears. I carried a permanent oppression, as though a dirty grey sky had been nailed in place two inches above my head.

I continued to perform poorly in the opinion polls. Mum was still vacillating between sharper-than-a-serpent's-tooth-it-is-to-have-a-thankless-child chilliness and would-you-not-cop-on-and-go-home-to-your-husband cajolery. I wasn't getting the same degree of grief from Dad, but then again I've always been his pet. What with once having played in team sports and going to the snooker championship with him, he's nearly managed to convince himself that I'm his son.

Outside of my immediate family, I spoke to no one. People were keen to speak to me, however. Nothing like a disaster to get those phone lines a-hopping. Close friends like Donna and Sinead rang, but I mumbled, 'Tell her I'll call her back,' and never managed it. Coffin-chasers like Elaine also called. (Mum thought she sounded like 'a lovely girl'.) Claire rang from London and begged me to go and stay with her. Rachel rang from New York and we had much the same conversation. But there wasn't a hope of me visiting either of them – walking from the telly to the kettle was about the only journey I could manage.

I didn't call Garv – and to the great disappointment and confusion of my parents, he didn't call me either. In a way it was a relief, but a relief that somehow managed to be an unpleasant one.

Anna was also in the house a lot – she was devastated about Shane. We hung out furtively, because when Mum saw us together her mouth would squinch like a cat's bottom and she'd enquire, 'Is it a rest home for fallen women I'm running here?' As best we could, we talked about our respective break-ups. What had happened for her was that Shane had set up a computer business making on-line music, and out of nowhere he became a bread-head. 'He got his hair cut. At a hairdresser's. He bought styling wax, then I knew it was all over. I suppose,' Anna sighed, 'he wants to grow up and I don't. So what about you and Garv?'

'Oh, you know . . .' I couldn't tell her about Truffle Woman. Whatever energy would have been required to pull those words out of my gut and into the open just wasn't there. 'Mostly I feel nothing,' I managed. 'It's a horrible sort of nothing, but . . . you know . . . that can't be right. Shouldn't I be roaring crying?'

Shouldn't I be breaking into Truffle Woman's house and planting grass in her carpets and prawns in her curtain rails? Shouldn't I be making plans to cut the arms and legs off all Garv's clothes?

'I haven't even rung Garv to say I miss him.' Even though a spasm of longing for him jack-knifed me roughly once every waking hour. 'My life is ruined and all I feel is nothing.' My future was a roped-off area – I managed occasional fleeting glimpses of the sadness, but they didn't stay. It was as if a door into a noisy room opened and immediately slammed shut again.

'You're depressed,' Anna said. 'You're very depressed. Is it any surprise, after all you've been through?'

But that didn't sit comfortably. 'I'm not a depressive.' (I know because I did a quiz in *Cosmopolitan*.)

'You are now. And Garv probably is too.'

She'd said something interesting, maybe even important, but I couldn't hold the thought. I was too weary.

Unlike me, Anna couldn't sleep. At least, not in her own bed, so she wandered the house at night, moving from bed to bed. She often got in beside me, but was usually gone when I woke, leaving the faint residue of a wraith-like creature who sighed a lot and smelt of Bacardi Breezers. It was like being haunted by a benign ghost.

Occasionally she was still there when I woke. One morning I came to to find one of her feet resting on my ear and the other in my mouth; for reasons best known to herself, Anna had decided to get into bed upside-down.

Another night I emerged from sleep feeling absurdly happy: warm, safe, cherished. Then, going into hollow freefall, I realized what it was – Anna was snuggling into me, nuzzling and mewing, 'Oh Shane.' Deep in sleep, her arm tight around me, I'd thought she was Garv.

Sometimes Anna and I could provide comfort for each other. She developed a theory that our lives were so awful because our guardian angels had gone on sabbaticals, and that currently we were being minded by temps who took no pride in their work.

'They do the bare minimum. We won't get our hands caught in a mincing machine, but that's all they'll do for us.'

'What's my real angel called?'

'Basil.'

'*Basil?*'

'Henry, then.'

'Henry?'

'How about Clive?'

'He's a boy angel?'

'Oh no, they're neutral.'

'What's he like?'

'He smells of Turkish Delight and he's pink.'

'Pink?'

'With green spots.'

'You're not taking this seriously.'

'Sorry. What's mine called?'

'Penelope.'

'Favourite food?'

'Carrots and parsnips mashed together.'

'Best bit about being a guardian angel?'

'Helping people find the right dress and shoes for their Christmas party. What's Clive's best bit?'

'Finding lost earrings.'

. . . And sometimes we couldn't provide comfort for each other.

One bad morning, Anna got in beside me and we both lay on our backs, staring miserably at the ceiling. After some time she said, 'I think we're making each other worse.'

'I think we are,' I agreed.

'I'll go back to my own bed, will I?'

'OK.'

Unlike me, Anna occasionally left the house – if only in response to a request from Shane.

'He says he wants "to talk".'

'And what's wrong with that?'

'He really means he wants to have sex. That's what's happened the last three times. It gets my hopes up, then leaves me feeling even worse.'

'Maybe you shouldn't sleep with him any more,' I suggested.

'Maybe,' she said vaguely, unconvinced.

'Maybe you shouldn't even meet him.'

But the next time he rang and said he wanted to see her, she agreed. 'Don't worry,' she promised me. 'I'm not going to sleep with him.'

But as I went to bed that night she wasn't back. Mind you, it was barely nine-fifteen and she'd only been gone half an hour.

Some unknown time that night, I woke into darkness. I wondered what had disturbed me – and then I heard it, a noise I remembered well from my teenage years: a scraping and scratching from the front door. One of my sisters – Anna in this case – was having trouble getting her key in the lock. It went on for so long that I was just about to get up and let her in when the door was finally pushed open, then I heard the reassuring crash as she bumped into and knocked over the hall table, followed, a few minutes later, by the disgusting smell of baked beans heating in a saucepan. Just like the old days, I thought dreamily, as I sank back into sleep. It's yesterday once more . . .

Some time later I jumped awake again. The fire alarm was beeping in a fussy frenzy and Dad was hopping about the landing in a wild-eyed, pyjama'd panic. 'How do I turn this shagging thing off?' Grey smoke was swirling around the hall, the beans and saucepan were burnt to a crisp and Anna was slumped over the kitchen table, deep in sweet slumber.

We put her to bed, but sometime later she got in beside me, reeking so strongly of drink that if I'd been awake, I'd have passed out. As it was, her incendiary breath had the effect of smelling salts, and woke me up.

Later that same night, the whole house was once again woken – this time by an almighty thump; it sounded like a ceiling had fallen in. Closer investigation revealed that it was nothing quite so exciting. All that had happened was that Anna had tried to get into bed beside Helen, and Helen, who objected to sleeping with 'a one-woman brewery', had pushed her out on to the floor.

'But at least I didn't sleep with him,' Anna said the following morning, as she inspected her bruises. 'OK, I drank myself into a coma and nearly burnt the house down, but at least I didn't sleep with him.'

'It's progress,' I agreed.

At some stage during the second dreadful week, I needed *something*, but there were so few options open to me.

'Go for a walk,' Dad suggested. 'Get some fresh air.'

I've never really understood the concept of Going for a Walk. And not even at my sportiest did I get the appeal of Going for a Walk in suburbia. But I was bad enough to give it a try.

'Take a coat,' he advised. 'It might rain.'

'It's June.'

'It's Ireland.'

'I haven't got a coat.' Well, I had, but it was in my house, Garv's house, you know the one I mean. I was afraid to go there in case he'd moved the girl in. Perhaps that sounds like a wild overreaction, but my instinct was warning me that anything was possible.

'Take mine.' Dad's anorak was red, nylon, awful, but I longed for affection and I couldn't resist letting him help me into it.

Off I went. Nothing too ambitious. I walked a couple of hundred yards to the green and sat on a wall, watching some kids do whatever kids do on greens: surreptitious smoking; trading inaccurate information on sex; whatever. I felt horrible. The sky was mushroom grey and stagnant, even the bits that weren't directly over me. After a while, when I didn't feel any better, I decided I might as well go home again. It was bound to be time for some version of 'Girlfrien', you ain't so all that.' No point in missing it.

I was traipsing back down the hill when someone flickered across my vision and vaguely alerted me. I looked properly. It was a man about fifty yards away, lifting things out of a car boot. Oh my ... God. Shay Delaney. Well, for a second I thought it was him, then it was clear that it wasn't. There was just something about the man that reminded me slightly of Shay and even that was enough to unsteady me.

But as I continued, with a whoosh of dizziness I saw that it *was* him. Different, but still the same. The change was that he looked older and this gave me some pleasure, until it dawned on me that if he looked older, then so would I.

He was lifting stuff from the boot of a car and stacking it at the gate of his mother's house. How could I not have instantly known it was him? He was outside his own house. Well, the house he'd lived in until he'd left to go away to college fifteen years ago. *Fifteen years.* How? I'm young now and I was grown-up then, there isn't *room* for fifteen years. Dizzy again.

I *couldn't* meet him. Not now, not with all this shame. A powerful impulse almost had me marching away in the direction I'd just come from and, after a frantic, weighing-up session, only the fear that he might notice stopped me.

But of all the times to bump into him, I thought wildly. Of all the times to have to play the game of How Did Your Life Turn Out? Why couldn't I have met him when I'd had a marriage I was proud of, when I'd been happy? Of course, I didn't have to tell him how wrong everything had gone. But wouldn't he guess, wasn't it obvious. . . ?

My hollow legs continued leading me down the hill, straight into his path.

For years I used to fantasize about meeting him again. Time after time I comforted myself with meticulous plans. I'd be thin, beautiful, trendily dressed, expertly lit. I'd be poised, confident, on top of my game. And he'd have lost his appeal. Somehow he'd have shrunk to about five five, his dark-blond hair would have fallen out and he'd have put on a ton of weight.

But from what I could see, he still had his hair and his height, and if he'd bulked out a bit, it had the unfortunate effect of suiting him. Meanwhile, look at me – the trackie bottoms, the air of failure, the way my face had gone a bit funny and immobile. It was nearly laughable. The only thing I had going for me were the floodlights in my hair – I'd been uncertain when the 'dresser first suggested it, but now it was clear it was a godsend.

Closer I got. Closer. He'd no interest in me, not at all. It seemed as if I could escape with my raw, white face, my dad's anorak, my air of recently separated bleakness. Then I was right up beside him, passing him by and still he wasn't looking. And with a strange defiance I decided that if he wasn't going to speak, then I would.

'Shay?'

He looked, I have to say, gratifyingly shocked.

'Maggie?' He froze in the act of lifting something from the boot, then stood up. 'Maggie Walsh?'

'Garvan,' I corrected shyly. 'Maggie Garvan now, but yeah.'

'That's right,' he agreed warmly. 'I heard you got married. So, ah, how's Garv?'

'Fine.' A little defensively.

All was still – and mildly uncomfortable. Then he rolled his eyes playfully to indicate shock. 'Wooh, Maggie Walsh. Long time. So!' Before he even asked it, I knew he was going to. 'Any kids?'

'No. You?'

'Three. Little monkeys.' He made a face.

'I bet. Hahaha.'

'You look fantastic!' he declared. He was either blind or insane, but such was his enthusiasm that I tentatively began to half-believe him.

'How's your mum?' As if he was genuinely interested. 'How's the cooking?'

'Ah, she gave up on it.'

'She's some gal,' he said admiringly. 'And your dad? Still driven mad by the lot of you?'

'Oh, yes.'

'And what are you up to these days?'

'Paralegal stuff.'

'Yeah? Great.'

'Yeah, great. You?'

'Working for Dark Star Productions.'

'I've heard of them.' I'd read something about them in the paper, but couldn't remember what exactly, so I said, 'Yeah, great,' a bit more.

And then he said, 'Well, *great* to see you,' and stuck out his hand. I looked dumbly at it – only for a second: he was expecting me to shake it. Like we were business colleagues. As I rubbed my palm against his, I remembered that he used to hold that hand over my mouth. To muffle the sounds I was making. When we were having sex.

How weird life is.

Already he was moving off. 'Tell your mum and dad I was asking for them.'

'And Garv?' I couldn't help it.

'Sure. And Garv.'

As I walked away I was fine. I couldn't believe it. I'd finally met him, and spoken to him, and I was fine. All those years wondering about it and I was fine. *Fine.* On a huge high, I danced towards home.

The minute I was inside the house I started to shake. So badly I couldn't get my fingers to undo the zip of the anorak. Too late, I remembered that I shouldn't have been nice to him. I should have been cold and unpleasant, after the way he'd treated me.

Mum appeared in the hall. 'Did you meet anyone?' she asked, her antipathy to me wrestling with her social curiosity.

'No.'

'No one at all?'

'No.'

She'd loved Shay Delaney. He'd been a mother's dream, already manly looking and with a golden-stubbled jaw while the other youths were still raw and unformed. This she put down to the fact that Shay's father had left them, and Shay had to be the man of the house. The other lads in the gang – Micko, Macker, Toolser, even Garv – were sullen around adults; they found it impossible to maintain eye contact with anyone more than a year older than them. But Shay, the only one of his contemporaries to be called by his real name, as I recall, was perpetually good-humoured. Almost, at times, flirtatious. Claire, who was a couple of years older than him, used to say wryly, 'I'm Shay Delaney and I always get what I want.'

But I was too busy for one of Mum's avid interrogation sessions. ('Had he a big car?' 'I believe his wife's very glamorous?' 'Did the father ever leave the floozie and come home?') I had to lie on my bed and tremble and think about Shay.

He'd been in the same year in school as Micko, Macker, Toolser and Garv, but he wasn't fully part of their gang; his choice, not theirs, they'd have been delighted to be first best friends with him. He'd seemed to float between several factions and was welcomed by all. He was just one of those people who had – although I wouldn't have known the word for it in those days – charisma. Claire had articulated it best by saying, 'If Shay Delaney fell into a pit of shite he'd come out smelling of Chanel No. 5.'

Not only was he noticeably good-looking, but he had the

51

decency not to rub people's noses in it, so he got a rep as a nice person into the bargain. And of course, the tragedy of his father having walked out on the family generated a lot of sympathy for him. Because he looked older and had the confidence and charm to blag his way past doormen, he went places that we didn't and inhabited different worlds to ours. But he chose to return to us, and he managed never to sound like he was boasting when he regaled us with stories of drinking crème de menthe in a nurses' residential or going to some horsey girl's twenty-first party in Meath. Of course, he'd always had lots of girlfriends; they'd usually left school and were either working or in college, which impressed the other lads no end.

Anyway, I'd been going out with Garv for about six months and I was perfectly happy with him – then Shay Delaney began to pay me attention. Giving me warm smiles and one-on-one conversations so low they excluded everyone else. And it seemed like he was always *watching* me. We'd all be there, hanging around a wall, smoking, pushing each other – the usual messing – and I'd look up to find his gaze upon me. If he'd been anyone else I'd have assumed that he was flirting, but this was Shay Delaney, he was way out of my price range. And then, after a week when he'd cranked up the intensity of his smiles and intimate conversations, there was a party. A fluttering in my gut let me know that something was going to happen and sure enough, when Garv had been sent out to buy more drink, Shay headed me off as I emerged from the kitchen, then pulled me into the cupboard under the stairs. I protested breathlessly but he laughed and shut the door behind us and, after some half-teasing compliments about how I was driving him mad, tried to kiss me. Squashed up against his bigness in the dark, confined space, finally knowing that I hadn't imagined his interest in me, I felt him move his face down to mine, and it was like every dream I'd ever had had come true.

'I can't,' I said, turning my head away.

'Why not?'

'Because of Garv.'

'If you weren't with Garv would you let me?'

I couldn't answer. Surely it was obvious?

'Why me?' I asked. 'Why are you bothered with me?'

'Because I am. Big time,' he said, pulling his thumb along my mouth and making me dizzy.

I never really got to the bottom of why he wanted me. I was nothing like as good-looking as his other girlfriends, or as sophisticated. The best I could come up with myself was that as his father had left them and his home-life was a bit chaotic, I represented stability. That my normalness was the most attractive thing about me.

So, shallow cow that I was, I broke it off with poor Garv. We kind of pretended that it was a mutual thing and insisted that we'd stay friends and all that other crap you talk when you're a teenager, but the truth of the matter was that I dumped Garv for Shay. Garv knew it as much as I did. From the moment Shay had decided he wanted me, Garv hadn't stood a chance.

Later that evening, Dad sidled into my room, a brown paper bag under his arm.

'McDonald's!' he declared. 'Your favourite.'

When I'd been eleven, perhaps, but I welcomed the company. 'Chicken nuggets,' he announced proudly. 'With two different dips.'

'What's this in aid of?'

'You have to eat. And your mother . . .' he paused and sighed, his expression wistful, '. . . well, she tries her best.'

Since the night I'd left Garv, the mere thought of food had been anathema – it didn't make me feel sick, just amazed. But this evening I was going to have to try, because as well as the chicken nuggets, Dad had also got me a large fries and a coke and, by the look of things, a Happy Meal for himself. It came with a free robot.

'Eat a fry yoke,' he tempted. (He feels silly calling them 'fries'. The real name, he feels, is 'chips'.)

I'd almost have preferred to eat the robot, but because I felt sorry for him, I tried. The chip (or fry, if you prefer) sat in my mouth like a foreign body. He watched me anxiously and I attempted to choke it down my closed throat.

'Do you want a drink?' he asked. 'Brandy, vodka, cider?'

I was stunned. That was one of the strangest questions I'd ever been asked in my entire life, bar none. The only time my parents ever have drink with their meals is on Christmas Day, when the bottle of warm Blue Nun is wheeled out – always assuming that it hasn't been discovered and drunk the night before. Besides, there wasn't any – what had he suggested? – brandy, vodka or cider in the house. Then I realized Dad wasn't *offering* me a drink. He was simply curious, trying to gauge how bad I was.

I shook my head. 'I don't want a drink.' That would be a huge mistake. When I was depressed, alcohol never cheered me up. In fact, it probably made me worse – maudlin and self-pitying. 'If I got drunk I'd probably kill myself.'

'Good then. Marvellous.' Suddenly he was as happy as his meal. He ate with relieved gusto, attempted to play with his robot – 'What does this yoke do?' – then departed.

A few minutes later he was back. 'Emily's on the phone.'

5

Emily is my best friend. Best *girl*friend, that is, and actually, since Garv and I have gone weird on each other, probably best friend.

Gawky twelve-year-olds, we met at secondary school and instantly recognized in each other a kindred spirit. We were outsiders. Not total pariahs, but we were a long way from being the most popular girls in the class. Part of the problem was that we were both good at sport: genuinely cool girls smoked and faked letters from their parents saying they had verrucas. Another black mark against us was that we'd no interest in the usual teenage experimentation with cigarettes and alcohol. I was too terrified of getting into trouble and Emily said it was a waste of money. Together we pronounced it 'stupid'.

At school, Emily was small, skinny and looked like ET with a bad perm. A far cry from how she looks today. She's still small and skinny, which we now know to be a Good Thing, right? Especially the skinny bit. But the bad perm (which wasn't a perm at all, but the real thing) is just a distant memory. Her hair is now swishy and glossy – very, very impressive, even though she says that in its natural state she could still double for a member of the Jackson Five and that to get her hair fully frizz-free, her hairdresser sometimes has to put his foot on her chest and tug hard.

Her look is very pulled together and confident. When a

certain style is in vogue, I usually buy something from the 'new-look' and team it with the rest of my 'old-look' wardrobe and think I'm doing pretty well. But not Emily. For instance, remember when the rock-chick look was in? I bought a T-shirt that said 'Rock Chick' in pink, shiny letters and I thought I was it. Emily, however, appeared in bandage-tight snakeskin jeans, purple stiletto-heeled cowboy boots and a pink leather stetson. But instead of looking preposterous – and she could have done, that pink leather stetson was borderline – I wanted to applaud. She's also a woman who knows how to accessorize. Coloured shoes (a colour other than black, that is), handbags shaped like flower-pots, kooky barettes in her hair if the occasion demands it.

I'm not a total klutz. I read magazines, I'm an enthusiastic shopper and I take a keen interest in skirt lengths, heel shapes and the light-diffusing qualities of foundation. But you only have to look at my single friends to see that they're all thinner and more glamorous than me and their make-up bags are cornucopias of breaking-news wondrousness. While I'm still reading about something, they're already wearing it. (Do you know how long it took me to realize that blue shimmer shadow was back in? Honestly, I'd be too ashamed to tell you, and even though it's a cliché, it *is* something to do with having a man and not being 'out there'.)

Despite our divergent lifestyles and living several thousand miles apart, my friendship with Emily has endured. We'd e-mail each other twice or three times a week. She'd tell me about all her disastrous relationships, then she'd debrief me on my dull, married life, then we'd both go home happy.

It was a great source of sadness to me that we couldn't seem to manage to live on the same continent. Garv and I had only been married a few months before we moved to Chicago for five years. Then less than four weeks before we returned to Ireland, Emily departed for Los Angeles.

What happened was, Emily had always wanted to be a writer. She'd tried her hand at short stories and novels and got nowhere. Her stuff always seemed good to me, but what would I know? Like Helen says, I've no imagination.

Then, five or so years ago, Emily wrote a short film called *A Perfect Day* which was picked up by an Irish production company and got shown on RTE. It was whimsical and charming, but what normally happens with a 'short' is that it gets shown once, then disappears. It's regarded as a type of practice run for wannabe film-makers. But something unprecedented happened with *A Perfect Day*, because it was a very odd length: fourteen and a half minutes. Whenever Ireland had some sort of corruption scandal (every other week), the nine o'clock news would run over and a 'filler' item would be needed to occupy the airwaves until ten o'clock, when things could get back on schedule. Three times over a four-month period *A Perfect Day* was that filler, and it began to work its way beneath the skin of the nation. Suddenly at water-coolers and photocopying machines and bus-stops throughout the land people were asking each other, 'Did you see that lovely thing that was on after the news last night?'

Overnight, in Ireland at least, Emily became a householdish name – people didn't exactly know who she was, but they knew that they'd heard of her, and they had definitely heard of her film. She could have made a decent enough living in Ireland, if she'd been prepared to be flexible, and do sit-coms, plays, ads – apparently they pay very handsomely – as well as films. But she decided to go for broke, left her dreary day-job and departed for Los Angeles.

Time passed, then news came back that she'd been taken on by one of the big Hollywood agencies. Not long after that came the announcement that she'd sold a full-length script to Dreamworks. Or was it Miramax? One of the big ones, anyway. The film was called *Hostage* (or it might be *Hostage!*), and was about a tiny, honeymooners' island in the South Pacific, which is invaded by terrorists who kill the few locals and take several of the honeymooners hostage. Others escape into the under-growth, survive castaway-style on twigs etc., and plot a rescue mission. It was described as 'an action movie, with a love story and comic overtones'.

The *Sunday Independent* did a feature about the deal, RTE ran *A Perfect Day* again, and Emily's mother bought a long, navy, spangledy dress for the première. (She got it in the sales, at 40 per cent off, but it was still fairly pricey.)

More time passed, and not much happened. No one got cast and whenever I asked what stage they were at, Emily said tersely, 'We're still fine-tuning the script.' I stopped asking about it.

Eventually, Emily's mother rang and asked Emily would she mind if she wore the long, navy, spangledy dress to Mr Emily's Christmas work do? Only it was nearly a year since she'd bought it, and though it had been in the sales, at 40 per cent off, it had still been fairly pricey. She'd like to get some use out of it.

Work away, Emily advised.

Then, lo and behold, a rival studio brought out a film. It was about a group of eight couples who go on a golfing holiday on a tiny island off Fiji. The island is invaded by terrorists, who kill the few locals and take several of the golfers hostage. Some escape into the undergrowth, survive castaway-style on twigs etc., and plot a rescue mission. It was an action movie, with – you'll never guess – a love story. And even, would you believe,

58

one or two laughs. I'd worked on the fringes of the film business long enough not to be surprised when news filtered back that the studio had decided to 'pass' on making Emily's movie. 'Pass' was Hollywood-speak for 'turn down', 'reject' or 'want nothing further to do with'. I rang Emily to tell her how sorry I was. She was crying. 'But I'm working on a new script,' she told me. 'You win some, you lose some, right?'

That was a year and a half ago. Soon afterwards, she came home to Ireland for Christmas and persuaded me to go out on the town with her, just the two of us.

Garv begged to be allowed to come, but sorrowfully Emily told him it was a girls' night out and he wouldn't be able for it. And she was right – at the best of times, she was a dangerous person to go out with, and when she was feeling raw, humiliated and disinclined to talk about it, she was even worse.

It was the pink stetson night: the rock-chick look was reaching critical mass and was about to collapse under the weight of its own silliness. But it hadn't yet happened and she looked sensational.

I jumped all over her, so happy to see her, but despite our delight in each other's company, it was a strange night. At the time I thought I was having the time of my life, but in retrospect I'm not so sure. Emily drank an awful lot at high speed – since she'd started drinking she'd become very good at it. Normally I didn't even attempt to keep up, but on this particular night I did. Obviously I got very drunk, but strangely I didn't realize it. I felt perfectly sober. The only indication that anything was amiss was the fact that everyone I came into contact with seemed to do something to insult or annoy me. It never occurred to me that the fault might be mine.

We were in a bar in the Hayman, a new fancy-dan hotel,

where everything from the roof tiles right down to the ashtrays had been 'created' by some celebrated New York designer. I'd heard about the place – it had been all over the papers, not least because most of its *objets* were for sale – but had never been there, whereas Emily had only been home three days and had already been there twice.

We settled down at a corner table, ordered a bottle of wine, and Emily launched into the story of her life since we'd last seen each other. She refused to talk about her writing – 'Don't mention the war,' she'd groaned, and instead told me about her love life. The dates she'd gone on with the gay man who insisted he wasn't and the straight man who insisted he was gay. She was a great raconteur, with impeccable attention to detail. No broad brushstrokes. Gripping stuff.

She always seemed to do a lot more talking than me. But then again she had a lot more to talk about. By the time we were finally up to speed on her life we'd almost finished our second bottle of wine.

'Now you,' she ordered. 'What's the story with the rabbits?' She frowned. 'And what does a girl have to do to get a drink around here?'

I sighed and began my sorry tale, then through the throng spotted my sister Claire.

'What are you doing here?' she exclaimed. Then she saw Emily and understood. She spent a bit of time chatting to us, then noticed the people she was meant to be meeting, so off she went. No sooner was she out of earshot than Emily muttered darkly, 'Oh yeah? You go on off and have a nice time with the people at the BIGGER table.'

She looked at me levelly – or so I thought at the time, but clearly we were just swaying in time with each other. 'I've taken agin your sister . . . And,' she appended grandly, 'her friends.'

I looked over at the table that Claire had just joined. At her arrival it had blown up with laughter and talk. I was pierced with a peculiar sense of exclusion. 'I've taken against them too!'

'You haven't taken against them.'

Hadn't I?

Emily leant her head back and tipped the last of her wine down her throat. 'You've taken *agin* them.'

Fair enough. I'd taken agin them.

We managed to procure another bottle of wine, then decided to go somewhere else, where the people weren't quite so annoying. As we beat our way out, we passed Claire and her friends.

'We're leaving now,' Emily said haughtily. 'No thanks to you.'

Cryptic, I know, but at the time it made perfect sense.

In the hotel lobby, by the front door, we decided to have a little dance before we left. I'm not sure whose idea it was, but we were both agreed that it was a good one. We actually put our handbags down and had a brief dance around them before cackling off into the night. To this day I can still see the astonished expressions of the three considerably more sober men standing near us.

Outside, we hailed a taxi and asked – demanded, more likely – to be taken to Grafton Street. Within seconds we'd taken agin the driver, paranoid that he was taking the long and lucrative way round.

'You can't turn right on that bridge,' he defended himself.

'Sure,' Emily scorned. 'You can't swizz me, I live here,' she lied aggressively. 'I'm not a tourist.'

Then she poked me with her small, sharp elbow and giggled hoarsely, 'Maggie, look.' She opened wide her handbag – like a dentist trying to reach the furthest molars – where, in amongst her LV wallet (fake) and Prada make-up bag (real), nestled one of the ashtrays from the hotel. If I remembered correctly it had carried a price tag of thirty pounds.

'Where did you get that?!'

A rhetorical question. When Emily is under stress she nicks things and I hate it. Why can't she be more like me? My way of dealing with stress is to get an outbreak of eczema on my right arm. I'm not saying it's pleasant but at least you can't get arrested for it.

'Stop stealing things,' I scowled, low and fierce. 'Sometime you'll get caught and you'll be in terrible trouble!'

But answer came there none, because she was berating the driver again.

We went to a nightclub that we were really far too old for and had a great time taking agin more people – the doorman, who didn't summon us to the top of the queue quickly enough for Emily's liking, barmen who didn't serve us instantly, sundry merry-makers who didn't leap to their feet and give us their seats as soon as they saw us.

Basically, we had a blast, and the following day Garv was not unsympathetic. He speedily vacated the bathroom when I had to vomit, and stood patiently on the landing, his face covered in shaving cream, his razor in his hand.

By six that evening I was well enough to talk, so I rang Emily. I was quite giddy – almost proud of our wild behaviour the night before, but Emily sounded subdued.

'Did we dance around our handbags in the Hayman?' she asked.

'We did.'

'Do you know?' she said fake-casually. 'I have a horrible feeling there was no dance-floor.'

'Never mind no dance-floor,' I exclaimed. 'There was no music. And wasn't it great the way we took agin all those people?'

Emily made a funny noise. A whimper crossed with a groan. 'Don't tell me I was taking against people.'

'Agin,' I corrected. 'We took *agin* people. It was great.'

'Oh God.'

I picked up the phone. 'Emily?'

'Are you OK?'

'I'm fine,' I croaked. 'I just think I've a touch of the flu.'

'Your mum says you've split up with Garv.'

'Oh . . . yeah.'

'And that you've lost your job.'

'Yes,' I sighed, 'I have.'

'But . . .' She sounded both astonished and helpless, 'I've been e-mailing you at work. Whoever has taken over from you will have got the finer details of Brett and his penis enlargement.'

I managed to say, 'Sorry. I haven't really been in touch with anyone.'

A silence while static hopped and blew on the line. I knew she was dying to ask questions, but she satisfied herself with, 'Are you sure you're OK?'

'I'm fine.'

More static. 'Look,' she said slowly, 'if you're not working and . . . stuff, why don't you just hop on a plane and come out here for a while?'

'What's out there?'

'Sunshine,' she cajoled. 'Fat-free Pringles, *me*.'

It was a measure of how far gone I was that I suspected she didn't mean it. That she was only saying it because she felt she had to, that it was what a good friend *should* say. But all the same, something sparked in my deadness. Los Angeles. City of Angels. I wanted to go.

6

We were spending an alarming amount of time flying over the suburbs of Los Angeles. They just kept unscrolling beneath me, grid after grid of dusty, single-level houses, the neat squares occasionally interrupted by a huge concrete freeway snaking violently through them. From far away in the distance came the diamond glint of the ocean.

It was barely a week since the phone call from Emily and I could hardly believe I was here. *Almost* here – were we ever going to land?

There had been strong opposition to me making the journey. Especially from my mother. 'Los Angeles? *What* Los Angeles?' she had demanded. 'Didn't Rachel say you could stay with her in New York? And didn't Claire say you could go to London and live with her for as long as you wanted? And what if there's an earthquake in that Los Angeles place?' She turned on Dad. 'Say something!'

'I've two tickets for the Hurling semi-final,' Dad said sadly. 'Now who'll come with me?'

Then Mum remembered something and addressed Dad. 'Isn't Los Angeles the place where you hurt your neck?'

About twenty years ago, Dad had gone with a load of other accountants on some junket to Los Angeles, and had come back with a gammy neck from the Log Flume at Disneyland.

'It was my own fault,' he insisted. 'There were signs saying I shouldn't stand up. And it wasn't just me, the whole seven of our necks got dislocated.'

'Oh, mother of God!' Mum clapped a hand over her mouth. 'She's taken off her wedding ring!'

I'd been kind of experimenting, to see what it felt like. The missing rings (the engagement ring went too) left a very obvious indent and a circle of white skin like uncooked dough. I don't think in the nine years I'd been married I'd ever taken them off: being without them felt strange and bad. But so did wearing them. At least this way was more honest.

Next to register his displeasure at my departure was Garv. I'd phoned to tell him I was off for a month or so and he'd come hot-footing it round. Mum ushered him into the sitting-room. 'Now!' she declared triumphantly, her entire demeanour saying, 'Time for this nonsense to stop, young lady.'

Garv said hello, and we both looked at each other for far too long. Maybe that's what you do when you split up with someone: try to remember what once welded you together. He'd gone slightly bitty and unkempt. Even though he was in his work clothes, he was wearing his off-duty hair and his expression was grim – unless it was always grim? Maybe I was reading more into this than I should.

Indeed, he didn't look like he was fading away through sorrow; he was still, to use a phrase of my mother's (except she never said it about Garv), 'a fine figure of a man'. Hazily, I suspected that these weren't the right thoughts to be thinking in the circumstances; they didn't seem weighty enough. But they were all I could manage. Why? Shock, maybe? Or could it be that Anna was right and *Cosmopolitan* was wrong – perhaps I *was* depressed.

'Why LA?' Garv asked stiffly.

'Why not? Emily's there.'

He gave me a look which I didn't understand.

'I've no job and . . . you know . . .' I explained. 'I might as well. I know we've a lot of stuff to sort out, but . . .'

'When will you be back?'

'Don't know exactly, I've an open-ended ticket. In about a month.'

'A month.' He sounded weary. 'Well, when you come back, we'll talk.'

'That'd make a change.' I hadn't meant to sound so bitter.

Rancour mushroomed between us, like a cloud of poison. Then – poof! – it was gone again and we were back to being polite adults.

'We do need to talk,' he stressed.

'If I'm not back in a month you can come and get me.' I strove to sound pleasant. 'Then we'll get solicitors and all that.'

'Yes.'

'Don't you go jumping the gun and getting one before me.' It was meant to sound light-hearted, but instead emerged sounding spiteful.

He looked at me, without expression. 'Don't worry, I'll wait until you're back.'

'I won't be working so I'll pay the mortgage from my Ladies' Nice Things account.'

I had a separate bank account from my joint one with Garv, into which I put a small amount every month – just enough to cover impractical sandals and unnecessary lip-glosses without feeling riddled with guilt at spending our mortgage money. Some of my friends – specifically Donna – wondered how I'd conned Garv into agreeing to it, but in fact it had been his idea and he was the one who'd come up with the jokey name.

'Forget the mortgage,' he sighed. 'I'll cover it. You'll need your Ladies' Nice Things money to buy ladies' nice things.'

'I'll pay you back.' I was relieved to have a bit more money for Los Angeles. 'Is it OK for me to go to the house to get some of my stuff?'

'Why wouldn't it be?' Something guilty and defensive flickered. He knew exactly what I was talking about, but he pretended not to. And I didn't bother to elucidate. There was a funny complicity between us, and an awful lot not being said. It was the way I wanted it: if he had someone else I *so* did not want to know. 'It's your house,' he said. 'You own half of it.'

It was then that I had the first normal thought that a person whose marriage has just broken up should have – we'd have to sell the house. The mist cleared and my future unspooled like a film. Selling the house, having nowhere to live, searching for somewhere else, trying to make a new life, being alone. *And who would I be?* So much of my sense of self was tied up in my marriage that, without it, I hadn't a clue who I was.

I felt dislocated from everything, floating in empty time and space, but I couldn't think about it now.

'All in all, how are you? Are you OK?' Garv asked.

'Yeah. Considering. You?'

'Yeah.' A breathless little laugh. 'Considering. Keep in touch,' he said, and made a funny move towards me. It began as a hug, but ended up being a pat on my shoulder.

'Sure.' I slid away from his heat and familiar smell. I didn't want to get too near to him. We said goodbye like strangers.

Through the window I watched him leave. That's my husband, I told myself, marvelling at how unreal it seemed. Soon to be *ex*-husband, and more than a decade of my life is going with him. As he walked out of the short drive and became

68

hidden by the hedge, I was ambushed by an inferno of white-hot fury. *Go on*, I wanted to empty my lungs and bellow, *fuck off back to Truffle Woman*. As quickly as it had appeared, the rush of rage receded, and once again I felt heavy and kind of dead.

Helen was the only one who approved of me going to LA.

'Smart work,' she said. 'Just think of the men. Lovely ridey surfey types.' She groaned. '*Christ*. Tanned, sun-bleached hair all tangled and salty, six-pack stomachs, muscly thighs from staying up on the surfboards –' She paused and announced, 'Jesus, I might come with you!'

And then it hit me: I was single. I was a single woman in my thirties. I'd spent my twenties in the safe cocoon of marriage and I had no idea what it was like to be on my own. Of course I knew about singletons, about the culture of the thirty-something single person. I'd heard the statistics: a thirty-something woman had a better chance of being abducted by aliens (I think) than receiving a proposal of marriage. I had watched my single sisters and friends pursue true love, and had joined in wondering where all the good men were when things didn't work out. But the interest I'd taken had been purely theoretical. I'd *wondered* where all the good men were, but I hadn't really cared. I hadn't been smug – at least, not consciously – but there's no doubt that pride comes before a fall.

I had no man now. I was no different from Emily or Sinead or anyone. Although, in fairness, I didn't want a man. I no longer wanted to be with Garv, but I was blocked. I couldn't make the necessary leap of imagination to being with anyone else.

It was then that I had my second normal thought: *My life is over*. That was the only thing I was sure of, the one fixed fact in an uncertain world. I clung on to this knowledge because, strangely, it gave me comfort.

Immigration took for ever. Finally, it was my turn to hand my passport over to the big, unpleasant guy at the desk. (And it made no difference which desk you picked: somewhere there must be a factory where they manufacture these men.) As he ran a disgusted eye over me, I found myself wondering if he was married or divorced. Not – let me hasten to add – because I fancied him. I'd wondered it about the woman I was sitting next to on the plane, too, and I'm fairly sure I didn't fancy her. I just didn't want to be the only one . . .

My speculation came to an abrupt halt when he barked, 'Reason for visiting the United States?'

'Vacation.'

'Where are you staying?'

'With a friend in Santa Monica.'

'And your friend in Santa Monica? What does he do?'

'*She* is a scriptwriter.'

And I swear to God, Mr Narky changed before my eyes. He sat up straight, stopped narrowing his eyes contemptuously, and suddenly he was as sweet as candy.

'Oh yeah? Someone buy her script?'

'Universal.' Or was it Paramount? But then they'd sidelined it . . .

'So is there a part for me in this movie?' he joked. Only thing is, I'm not sure he was joking.

'Dunno,' I said nervously.

'You dunno,' he sighed, reaching for his stamp and giving my passport a good thump with it.

I was in!

*

And there was Emily, tapping her (beautiful, Japanese-style besandalled) foot impatiently. God, it was so good to see her.

'How are you? Psychotic with jet lag?' she asked sympathetically.

'Certifiable. I believe I watched three films on the plane and I couldn't tell you the first thing about any of them. One of them might have been about a dog.'

'Gimme that.' Emily positioned herself at the helm of my trolley – or should I say 'cart'? – and pushed it briskly towards the airport car park.

The heat hit like God had opened a huge oven door. 'Lord,' I reeled.

'Not far,' she encouraged.

'Hey, look!' I was distracted from the faint-making heat by a bunch of holy-roller, culty types, clustered on a patch of grass, wearing turquoise robes, shaking tambourines and chanting away goodoh. I half-suspected they'd been laid on specially for me – Welcome to LA – the way in Hawaii they get some girl to put one of those garlands of flowers around your neck.

Emily was unimpressed. 'Plenty more where they came from. Get in.' She opened the car door. 'The air-con will be on in a minute.'

I'd never been to Los Angeles before, but I'd have known it anywhere. It was all so familiar – the sixteen-lane freeways, the tall, skinny palm trees, the adobe-style houses. The skyline was low and extended for ever – it was nothing *at all* like Chicago.

Every few blocks we passed mini-malls which advertised pet-grooming, nail salons, gun shops, surveillance equipment, dentists, tanning salons, more pet-grooming . . .

'You could groom a lot of pets in this town,' I remarked dreamily. It was the jet lag. I was gone a bit mental from it.

Emily had no time for such nonsense. There was a story and she wanted to hear it. 'So what's up with you and Garv?'

I had a very real urge to jump from the speeding car. I plumped for, 'We were making each other miserable, so we've called it a day.'

'Yeah, but –' I could hear fear in her voice. 'You haven't actually *split up*? You're just taking a break from each other? 'Cos of everything?'

What was this conspiracy? Why would nobody accept it was finished?

'We *have* split up.' My right arm began to tingle. 'It's all over.'

'God.' She sounded terribly upset. 'But you're not going to . . . get divorced?'

A wash of shame hit me. 'What else would we do?'

'Have you actually started proceedings?'

'Not yet. We're waiting until I get back.' With those words, a fact I'd known intellectually transformed itself into something personal. 'I'll be a divorcee!'

'Um . . . if you get divorced, you probably will.' Emily threw me an anxious glance. 'Is that a shock?'

'No, it's just . . . It's just hit home.' All the same, it had hardly been part of my life plan. 'A divorcee.' I tried out the word again and my ever-present sense of failure intensified. Striving for humour, I said, 'You know what that means? I'll have brassy blonde hair and make a show of myself at family parties, drinking too much and dancing provocatively with younger men.'

'That's me now,' Emily said. 'And, you know, it's not so bad.'

Silence descended, and I could almost hear the turning of the cogs in her overtaxed brain.

'But I still can't believe it,' she breathed. 'Like, what *happened*? Did he end it or did you . . . ?'

I didn't want to discuss it. I wanted to forget it and enjoy myself. 'Neither of us. Both of us, I mean.' Then, like a grenade, I lobbed into the conversation, 'I think he's met someone else.'

'Who? *Garv!*' she shrieked, nearly so high-pitched that only bats could hear her.

'He's an attractive man.' I felt oddly defensive.

'That's not what I meant.' With a volley of well-targeted questions she extracted the story of Truffle Woman, and she took it almost worse than I had done. Driving into the sun, she muttered, 'I thought the decent behaviour of Garv Garvan was the one thing I could depend on. I thought he was one of the few good ones out there. Maggie, I'm devastated.'

'I'm not exactly jumping for joy myself.'

'And who is this girl?'

'Could be anyone. Someone he works with. Could be . . .' I made myself say it. 'Could be Donna. Or Sinead. He gets on well with both of them.'

'It's not Donna or Sinead. They wouldn't do that. And if they did I'd have heard. Men,' she said bitterly, 'they're all the same. The few brains they have are in their mickeys. How much do you hate him?'

'Lots. When I have the energy.' The thing was that even though I was raging with Garv, in a way I didn't blame him.

Emily gave me a sharp look. She knows me very well, I have no secrets from her. But before she could explore further I tried to head her off at the pass.

'It could be worse,' I said with grisly cheer. 'At least it's amicable . . . Amicable*ish*,' I added, less certainly. 'The money and house will be sorted out properly.'

'Of course they will. Garv is nothing if not decent. At least you don't have –' She stopped, aghast.

'Children,' I finished for her.

'I'm sorry,' she whispered.

'It's OK,' I reassured. It wasn't really, but I wasn't going to think about it.

'Do you –' she started, at the same time as I said, '*Any*way! So what road is this we're on?'

Emily ignored my attempt to change the conversation. Instead she warned, 'Amicable or not, you're going to have to talk about you and Garv.'

I sagged with reluctance, and all of a sudden I knew what this reminded me of. When I was sixteen I'd slipped coming down the stairs and my knee accidentally went through the glass front door. I'd ended up with hundreds of slivers of glass embedded in my knee, each one having to be removed individually with tweezers. Pain relief hadn't been on the agenda, and I'd been rigid and sweating with pain and the anticipation of more to come. Every word about me and Garv was like another sliver being picked from my raw flesh. 'I will talk about it,' I said. 'But not now. Please.'

'OK.'

Eventually, the character of the roads began to change until we were in a modest residential area. All the houses looked like one-offs – some adobe style, some New England, some deco, painted in low-key pastel shades. There was a general air of kemptness. Everywhere there were flowers.

'We're nearly there. Nice, isn't it?'

'Lovely.' It was just that I'd expected something a little edgier from Emily.

'When I first moved to LA I had to live in a rotting – literally, it was rotting in the heat – apartment building in East LA, and people kept getting shot and killed outside my window.'

OK, maybe edgy wasn't so great.

'The murder rate in Santa Monica is way low,' she reassured.

Marvellous!

We pulled up outside a white clapboard bungalow, with a small lawn on to the pavement. Water sprinklers worked like searchlights back and forth on the grass.

'Keep an eye out for them fecking sprinklers,' Emily advised. 'They're on a timer, and they're always surprising me and destroying my hair. And keep an eye out for the neighbours on that side, they're the kind of people who give LA a bad name.'

'Serial killers?'

'New Agers; they'd read your aura as soon as look at you. The neighbours on the other side aren't much better. Boys. College students, doing computer programming or something. They're handy if ever you want to buy drugs, not that you'd want to, I know.'

This gave me a little breathing space of relief; I didn't want to be surrounded by married couples. Drug-dealing students were far preferable.

Flowers blazed shocking pink against the dazzling white of Emily's house. It was all very pretty. Then I noticed the 'Armed Response' sign in the front garden and my delight with my surroundings dimmed somewhat. What happened around here that an armed response was necessary?

We hoicked my stuff into the cool, shady house. While I oohed and aahed over the hardwood floors, white blinds and pretty back garden, Emily made straight for her answering machine. 'Gaaaaaargh,' she groaned. 'Ring, you bastard.'

'A man?' I asked, with as much compassion as I could muster.

'I wish.'

'Oh?'

'Maggie,' she slumped on to a chair. 'I'm officially Down on My Luck.'

'Are you?' I asked faintly, suddenly aware that I wasn't the only person in the world who was mid-crisis.

'I'm so glad you're here.'

'Are you?' How had I suddenly mutated from comfortee to comforter?

Emily sighed, then her whole sorry story unravelled.

After the studio had passed on *Hostage* (or was it *Hostage!?*) her agent had fired her, which was nothing less than catastrophic. Studios never, but *never* looked at work which hadn't been submitted by an agent; and it was almost impossible to get an agent, she explained. Every day, literally thousands of screenplays arrived at the mail rooms of the big agencies and had to go through a savage screening process. If the mail-room kids didn't like it, it was out. If it made it past them, it had to pass muster with a reader. In the unlikely event of that happening, it got read by an agent's assistant. And only if they raved about it would an agent deign to look at it.

Emily had spent the past year and a half writing several new scripts, and every time she tried to get an agent, she got knocked back.

'But you've a name.'

'I've a *bad* name,' she corrected. 'Everyone remembers that the studio passed on *Hostage*. I'm in a worse position than a total newcomer. It's an unforgiving town.'

'Why didn't you tell me?'

'Dunno. Too ashamed. Me, the big success story. And I kept hoping things would improve. You know?'

I did, as it happened.

Only ten days ago, Emily had managed to place her most recent script with a new agent. But he was with a much smaller agency which didn't carry the same clout with the studios.

'His name is David Crowe. He's gone out with my script. He's trying to get a buzz going and see if he can kickstart a bidding war. And I've heard nothing.'

'But he's only just gone out with it.'

'Things happen very fast in this town, or they don't happen at all. It's working my last nerve,' she said. 'If this doesn't take off, it's over for me.'

'Don't be mad. You'll just pick yourself up and try again.'

'I fucking won't, you know,' she said grimly. 'I'm burnt out. This city has me in shreds. The casualties are everywhere. You'll see . . . And I'm skint,' she added.

'How?' I was shocked. She'd got a huge fee for *Hostage*, which she didn't have to return when the studio passed on making the film.

'I got paid nearly three years ago and two hundred grand, after taxes and agents' commission, doesn't last so long. And don't think I was too high and mighty to look for commissions writing B-movie, straight-to-video crap. I even pitched for a porn film!'

'To be *in* it?' Were things really that bad?

'No, to write it. But now that you mention it, I'd probably have had more luck if I'd auditioned to star in it. Even they turned me and my studio pedigree down. I couldn't get arrested.'

'Oh, my God.'

'It's been a horrible eighteen months,' she admitted. 'The day that Beam Me Up Productions –'

'Who?'

77

'Exactly. Some C-list, outer-space merchants operating out of a Portakabin in Pasadena. The day they passed on my pitch to do the fourth sequel to *Squelch Beings from Gamma 9* was my blackest day so far.'

I was crippled by the magnitude of her problems. It was too hot, I was too tired, and I wanted to go home. But home no longer existed.

'Oh Christ, Christ, Christ.' She looked suddenly stricken. 'I'm sorry, Maggie. I'm terribly sorry . . . What a thing to be doing to you! Let me make you something to eat.'

She flung together a salad and opened a bottle of white wine. Mercifully, she seemed to cheer up.

'Things aren't so bad. I can always go back to Ireland and get some film work there, now that I have a lot of contacts,' she chattered.

She paused. 'Do you know who I see the odd time in the course of work?'

Something in her tone alerted me.

'Who?'

A beat. 'Shay Delaney.' It was clear that she'd been waiting for the right time to tell me.

'How?'

'He's a producer with Dark Star Productions. An –'

' – independent film company,' I finished for her. I'd suddenly remembered what the name had meant to me when he'd told me who he worked for.

'He has to spend a lot of time over here.' She sounded almost defensive.

'I suppose he does. People who work in movie-production companies tend to.' She looked puzzled and I said, 'I met him. Last week.'

'No way!' As Emily marvelled at what a coincidence that was, I hunched over my salad. Was that why I'd been so keen to come to Los Angeles?

7

I awoke in darkness to the rattle of machine-gun fire. My blood was pounding. I listened for more sounds – shouts, moans, police sirens – but nothing.

We're not in Kansas any more, Toto.

Lying in the blackness, I admitted the bitter truth. I was sorry I'd come. I'd expected to feel magically better, but how could I when I'd brought myself and my failed life with me? And living in someone else's house – even a good friend's – was tougher than I'd expected. Despite the eight-hour time difference, I hadn't got to sleep for ages because Emily had the telly on so loud. I'd seethed in my bedroom (which was actually her office), wishing she'd turn it down. But there was nothing I could do – it wasn't my house. When a raucous blast of canned laughter had exploded through the thin walls, I'd experienced a violent longing for my life with Garv. I couldn't live like this. All at once, I was ready to admit that splitting up had been a terrible mistake and that business as usual could resume with immediate effect. I was used to harmony and being able to turn off the telly whenever it suited me.

But was that a good enough reason to try again? Probably not, I decided reluctantly.

I did eventually go to sleep, but now I was awake.

Another crackle of machine-gun fire caused my heart to burst against my ribs. What was going *on* out there?

If only I could go home, I yearned. But I suspected I had to stick it out. Everyone would think I'd cracked up if it came out that I went to Los Angeles and only stayed a day. And this wasn't just about me – it was clear that Emily needed someone around. Christ, maybe we'd be going home together, a duo of failures. We'd have to sit in a special cordoned-off area on the plane in case we infected the other passengers.

A noise at the window made me jerk about three feet off the bed. What was it? The branch of a tree banging against the glass? Or a roaming madman on the lookout for a girl to torture and murder? My money was on the roaming madman. After all, this was Los Angeles, full, by all accounts, of pathological killers. I'd read one or two Jackie Collins novels in my time and I knew all about psychos who think in italics.

Not long now. Not long before revenge would be his. And then they'd be sorry they'd laughed at him and refused to return his calls. He was strong now. He'd never been stronger. And he had his knife. The knife that would do his deft bidding. First he'd cut off her hair, then he'd cut off her jewellery, then he'd start opening her skin. She'd beg, she'd plead for mercy, for the agony to stop. But it wouldn't stop, because this time it was her turn for the pain, this time it was her turn . . .

I began to sweat. These clapboard Californian houses were so flimsy and I felt the vulnerability of being on the ground floor very keenly.

Slick with fear, I had to turn on the lamp and look on Emily's bookcase for something to read. Preferably something light, to take my mind off my imminent dismemberment. But because I was in her office, all I could find were textbooks on the art of scriptwriting. Then I saw the bundle of pages on the desk. *Plastic Money*, her new screenplay. That'd do.

Two pages in, I was gripped, the roaming madman forgotten. The story was about two women who pull off a jewellery heist to pay for plastic surgery for their daughters, so that they'll have better luck with men than they did. It was a comedy, a thriller, a love story and, most importantly for Hollywood, it had the requisite schmaltzy bit. ('But I love you, Mom. You don't have to buy me new boobs.')

Just before I fell back to sleep, I thought fuzzily, *I'd option it . . .*

When I woke up again, I got the fright of my life – the sun was shining, pouring lemon light into the room. With a pounding heart I wondered, *Where the hell am I?* The last nine months galloped towards me, gathering up awful memories and whooshing them at me, until I remembered why I was in this strange sunny place. Oh yeah . . .

Emily was in the kitchen, clicking away at her laptop.

'Morning,' I said. 'Are you working?'

'Yes, on a new script.'

'A *new* new one?'

'Yeah.' She laughed, then got up and began making herself what I would later come to know as a protein shake. 'I don't know if it's any good, but I've got to keep pressing on with it just in case *Plastic Money* doesn't work out.'

What a nightmare, I thought. To cheer us both up, I said, 'Isn't it a gorgeous day?'

'Yes, I suppose.' She sounded surprised. 'But they're all like this. So did you hear the fireworks last night?'

'Fireworks?'

'Yeah, for the Santa Monica festival. But you were probably out for the count.'

'No, I heard them.' Then in a mortified rush I blurted, 'But I thought they were machine guns.'

'Why would you think they were *machine* guns? Christ in the marketplace!' Her face was stamped with distress and concern. 'You *are* in a bad way.'

She was behind the table and wrapping her wiry little Emily body around mine, and I was so touched by the contact that for the first time since I'd left him, I was able to cry. All my tears had been packed tight inside me, frozen and out of reach until now.

'I'm so sad,' I choked. 'I'm so sad. I'm just so sa-aa-aaad.'

'I know, I know, I know.' On a loop.

The grief that, until then, I'd only caught out-of-the-corner-of-my-eye glimpses of suddenly revealed itself to me, and I felt the full weight of all our blunted hopes. The end of a marriage is the saddest thing in the whole world. Surely no one gets married thinking that theirs mightn't make it? I had an image of a twenty-four-year-old me and a twenty-five-year-old Garv and our innocent trust in the future, and it was killing me.

'All the hope we had and it did us no good.' I pressed a lump of kitchen paper to my leaking face. 'I had to go, Emily, I didn't have any choice, it was so awful. He would have left if I hadn't. But now it's all go-onnnne.'

'I know, I know, I know,' Emily murmured. 'I know.'

'I thought I could never again feel as sad as I did last February,' I coughed with tears. 'But I doo-hoo. It's sadder than the hungry babies in *Angela's Ashes*.'

'Sadder than Mary going blind in *Little House on the Prairie*?'

'Yeah. Sadder.'

But the damage was done. She'd made me smile. After she'd mopped me up a bit and got me to blow my nose, she tempted, 'Will you have a protein shake? It's a local delicacy.'

'Go on then.'

Emily whipped me up a (frankly, delicious) shake and we sat outside in the tiny, sun-drenched back garden, and I was feeling a little bit calmer until she decided to have another go at making sense of me and Garv.

'The thing is, it all feels a bit premature. Too sudden.'

I sat in silence while my arm got hotter and itchier.

'Nothing ends this cleanly,' she insisted.

'It's not clean.'

She tried to jolly me into engaging. 'You've missed out vital parts of the breaking-up process. What normally happens is you go for counselling, you have to have at least two attempts at a reunion. They've got to fail really horribly, and if you think you're bitter now, it's nothing compared to how you'll be then. *Then* it's allowed to be over.'

'It couldn't be more over now because he's . . . with . . .' – I couldn't bring myself to say 'sleeping with' – 'someone else. I could never trust him again. Or forgive him.'

'I understand,' she started. 'But it's because of the –'

'Please, Emily!' I started out sounding snappy but quickly moved to desperation. 'It's over and I need you to believe me because I can't keep going through this.'

'OK. Sorry.' She seemed glad to stop. She looked exhausted. 'So what would you like to do today?'

'Dunno.'

'I've to see my accountant about my IRS returns this morning,' she said. 'You're welcome to come with me, or I could drop you to the beach.'

I didn't want to be on my own. But how stupid would it be to sit in an accountant's office while Emily went through her tax returns? The sun was splitting the stones and I was a big girl now.

'I'll go to the beach,' I swallowed.

'How are you fixed for money?' Emily asked. 'Not that I'm looking for any,' she added quickly.

'Well, Garv said he'd cover the mortgage for a month and I've my credit card. No way of paying it off, though, until I get a new job.' For some reason this worry wasn't as potent as it usually was. 'And I've a bit in my current account.'

In fact, my Ladies' Nice Things account was quite healthy. Though I'd been spending too much lately, I'd been doing it from our joint account and it struck me that maybe I'd been stockpiling money in my own account, somehow anticipating the split with Garv. It wasn't a comfortable thought.

'Why are you asking me about money?'

'I was thinking you might like to hire a car while you're here.'

'Can't I get the bus?'

A funny noise made me look up. It was Emily, laughing.

'What did I say?'

'"Can't I get the bus." Next you'll be offering to walk places. You're a tonic!'

'I can't get the bus?'

'Not really, no one gets the bus. The service is beyond shite. Or so I'm told, I've never actually experienced it first-hand. You need a car in this town. There are some great pick-up trucks for rent,' Emily said dreamily.

'Pick-up trucks? Do you mean jeeps?'

'No, I mean pick-up trucks.'

'You mean . . . like hill-billies drive?'

'Well, yeah, but new and shiny and without hogs sitting up front.'

But I didn't want a pick-up truck. I'd been entertaining a pleasant vision of zipping around in a foxy little silver convertible, my hair flying out behind me, lowering my heart-shaped sunglasses and making eye contact with men at traffic lights. (Not that I ever would, of course.)

'Only tourists and out-of-towners drive convertibles,' Emily scorned. 'Angelenos never do. Because of the smog.'

I remembered that Emily had picked me up from the airport in a huge, jeep-style, four-wheel-drive type of yoke. She'd looked as if she was driving a block of flats, and I'd almost needed a rope and crampons to get up to the passenger seat. 'Pick-up trucks are very now,' she advised. 'And if not a pick-up truck, then get a jeep like mine.'

'But I just need something to get me from A to B.' And it was all right for her, living in year-round sunshine, but when would I get another chance to take the roof off my car and not get soaked to the skin?

'You see, your car is how you're judged in this town. Your car and your body. It doesn't matter if you live in a cardboard box, so long as your car is cool and you're in the terminal stages of anorexia.'

'Well, I think convertibles are cool. That's the car I'd like.'

'But —'

'My marriage has broken up,' I said, playing dirty. 'I want a convertible.'

'OK.' Emily knew when she was beat. 'We'll get you a convertible.'

*

Just before we went out, my mother rang. 'That entire seaboard could fall into the Pacific at any moment.'

'Is that right?'

'I'm only saying it for your good.'

'Thank you.'

'Is it sunny there?'

'Very. I have to go now.'

The beach was no distance, I could easily have walked it. If I'd been allowed. I abseiled down out of the car and away Emily drove, perched high and tiny in her mobile block of flats.

The scene ahead of me looked like a postcard. Bathed in citrus light, lines of high, spindly palm trees brushed the jaunty blue sky. Stretching far away in both directions was a wide expanse of powdery white sand, and beyond that was the glinting rush of the ocean.

We've all heard that Californians are gorgeous. That through a combination of good-living, health-consciousness, sunshine, plastic surgery and eating disorders they're skinny, muscled and glowing. As I arranged my towel on the sand I suspiciously watched other people on the beach. There weren't that many – possibly because it was a weekday – but there were enough to confirm my worst fears. I was the fattest, saggiest person on that stretch of sand. Possibly in the entire state of California. God, they were thin. And I was filled with resolve – tinged with despair – that I was going to start exercising again.

Two Scandinavian-looking girls took up a position far too near for my liking. Immediately I wondered if either of them were divorced; I was driving myself mad speculating about the marital status of everyone I met . . .

They whipped off their shorts and tops to reveal tiny bikinis, flat stomachs and golden thighs, shaped and curved with muscle. You never saw two people more comfortable with their bodies; I dearly wanted to shoo them away.

Their arrival meant that I couldn't remove my sarong. Time passed, and when I had managed to convince myself that no one had any interest in me, I slid it off. I held my breath, wondering if the lifeguard would jerk with sudden shock and break into a slo-mo, red-rescue-pack-under-his-arm, pounding-rock-soundtrack run towards me and order, 'I'm sorry, Ma'am, we're going to have to ask you to leave. This is a family beach, you're upsetting folks.'

But no drama erupted and I slathered myself in factor eight and prepared to bake; skin cancer seemed the least of my worries. God, I was white! I should have lashed on some fake tan before I came. Immediately this made me think of Garv – I always snapped on surgical gloves before applying fake tan and he used to say, 'Oooh, matron, a surgical-glove moment!'

Oh, God. I closed my eyes, lulled by the rhythmic rush and suck of the waves, the yellow heat of the sun, the short-lived, skippy breezes.

It was actually quite pleasant until I turned over on to my stomach and found that there was no one to put sun-tan lotion on my back. Garv would have done it. I suddenly felt very lonely and the feeling hit anew, *My life is over*.

As I'd packed, the night before I left Ireland, I'd told Anna and Helen the very same thing. 'My life is over.'

'It's not.' Anna had been visibly distressed.

'Don't patronize her,' Helen had urged.

'You'll meet someone else – you're young,' Anna said doubtfully.

'Ah, she's not really,' Helen interjected. 'Not at thirty-three.'

'And you're good-looking,' Anna struggled on.

'You know, she's not bad,' Helen admitted grudgingly. 'You have nice hair. And your skin isn't bad. For your age.'

'All that clean-living,' Anna said.

'All that clean-living,' Helen echoed solemnly.

I sighed. My living wasn't that clean, it just wasn't as *unclean* as theirs, and my good-for-my-age skin was thanks to slathering on so much expensive night-cream that I used to slide off my pillows, but I let it go.

'And . . .' Helen said thoughtfully. I leant forward on the bed, all the better to be praised. '. . . You have a lovely handbag.'

I sat back, disappointed.

'Funny that,' she mused. 'I'd never have put you down as an expensive-handbag kind of a girl.'

I tried to protest; I *am* an expensive-handbag kind of a girl, I'm almost sure of it. But I wasn't getting into another row with Helen, where I tried to convince her I was irresponsible with money.

Besides, as it happens, it had been Garv who had given me the lovely handbag in question.

'In your granny!' Helen had chuckled. 'You expect me to believe Mr Peel-an-orange-in-his-pocket would shell out over a ton for a *sac à main*. That's French, you know. Anyway, you know the way your life is over? You won't be needing your handbag any more, will you?'

But I wouldn't surrender it, which led her to remark suspiciously, 'Your life can't be *that* over then, can it?'

'Shut up, you're getting my car,' I said.

'But it's only for the month. And I have to share it with *her*.' She jerked her head at Anna.

Then I heard something which catapulted me right back to the present. 'Ice-cream sandwich!'

I sat up on my towel. A young man was passing by, staggering under the weight of ice-cream that he hadn't a hope of selling; not to this crowd of anorexics.

'Popsicles?' he called desolately. 'Blue Gelatos, Cherry Iceys?'

I felt sorry for him. And hungry. 'Go on,' I said. 'Give me an ice-cream sandwich.'

We conducted our business briskly, then he was once more on his profitless way. I wondered if anyone ever shouted abuse or threw stones at him as he plied his high-fat, high-sugar goods along the beach. 'Garn! Clear orf.' The way people do to drug-pushers in other communities.

And then I was alone again. Suddenly I was very glad I was in California, because I could blame the horrible feeling of being out of step with the rest of the human race on my jet lag. It made it not my responsibility, and I could always try fooling myself that I'd feel perfectly normal in a few days.

Watched hungrily by the two Scandinavian-looking girls, I ate my ice-cream. Their expressions were so avid I felt quite uncomfortable. In fact I nearly offered them a bite. I couldn't help feeling that if this was a book, *someone* would have invited me to join in a game of volleyball or at least struck up a conversation with me – the lifeguard or another sunbather. But the only person who spoke to me all day was the ice-cream seller. And I suspected I was the only person who spoke to him.

8

Late afternoon, Emily picked me up from the beach. When we got home there was still no phone call from David Crowe. Her desperation filled the house.

'No news is good news,' I tried.

'Wrong,' Emily said. 'No news is bad news. They keep the bad news from you and cover themselves in glory with any good news.'

'Well, you ring him then.'

A bitter laugh from Emily. 'It's easier to get an on-set pass to a Tom Cruise movie than to talk to an agent who doesn't want to talk to you.'

But she rang him anyway. And he was 'not at his desk right now'.

'I bet he wouldn't be "not at his desk right now" if it was Ron Bass on the line,' she said gloomily.

I took it that Ron Bass was some hot-shot screenwriter.

'I feel a strange but compelling urge to get bollocksed-drunk,' she said. 'Could your jet lag handle going out this evening?'

'What have you in mind?' Would I be forced to go out with a gang of girls and dance to 'I Will Survive', as always seemed to happen to women who'd just split from their men?

'How about dinner somewhere nice?'

'Lovely!' Relief that there would be no Gloria Gaynor made me sound more enthusiastic than I felt.

'That's the spirit. You know what?' she said thoughtfully. 'What you need to do is let your hair down a little.' Even though Emily was very fond of Garv, she'd always thought that I'd missed out on the necessary rites-of-passage high-jinks by getting married so young. 'Go a bit mad for yourself while you're here.'

'I'll see,' I said noncommittally. Jesus, little did I know . . .

'We'll call Lara. Lara likes a drink. And Connie. And Troy. And Justin.'

A quick round of phone calls, and then she just went and got that really pulled-together look. Just bang-bang-bang, like it's easy or something. The dress, the heels, the bag, the hair, all smooth and shiny, shiny, shiny.

Then she opened her wondrous make-up bag and shared with me some of her knowledge. Lotion was smeared on my lips, 'to get that bee-stung look'. My eyelashes were curled with a little machine (I believe it may have been called an eyelash curler). Then she produced a little tube and said, 'This'll get rid of your jet-lag bags.'

'No need,' I countered smugly. 'I have my Radiant-whatchamacallit.'

'Radiant, schmadiant. Wait till you try this.' She dotted some cream under my eyes and – dramatically – I actually felt my skin contract.

'What is it?! Who is it by?' I was all set to run out to a cosmetic counter and hand over the small fortune this magic gear would undoubtedly cost.

'It's Anusol.'

'Huh?'

'Piles ointment. Five dollars a tube, works a dream, all the models use it.'

Do you see what I mean about her always being ahead of the game?

Then a few seconds on my hair with the straightening tongs, and some aloe vera on my ring finger – I'd burnt the tender skin where my wedding ring used to be (which sounded like the title of a particularly maudlin country and western song).

Emily marched to the door, all snappy little sounds. The *tap-tap* of her heels, the *crack* of her handbag clasp, the *click* of her lighter, the *clack-clack* of her nails. I loved it.

We were going to some place on Sunset, she said. The Troy person couldn't come, nor could Connie, who was up to her tonsils in wedding arrangements, but apparently Lara the jarhead and Justin could.

'Are either of them married?' I asked casually.

Emily laughed, 'God, no. Both single.'

'Single single?'

'Is there any other kind?'

'Divorced single.'

With a sympathetic look she said, 'No. They're single single.'

As we drove along, palm trees were silhouetted against the skyline. The sun was setting and the sky was layered with colours: pale blue low down, rising and darkening overhead to a deep luminous blue, in which the first stars twinkled like pinholes in fabric.

We passed the neon lights of gas stations, motels offering waterbeds, billboards in Spanish, used-car lots, signs for Mexican food, chiropractors and houses with really high numbers. There couldn't possibly be 22,000 houses on this road. Could there?

'Maybe,' Emily said. 'Sunset is about twenty miles long.'

Sunset. She means Sunset Boulevard. *I'm driving along Sunset Boulevard*, I thought, feeling like I was in a film.

At some traffic intersection a man stood holding a ragged piece of cardboard, which said in big, crooked letters WIFE WANTED. There was even a phone number. He looked presentable enough, that was the weird thing.

'There we are, Maggie,' Emily indicated him. 'May the best woman win.'

'I'm already married,' I said automatically.

Funny how you forget.

We pulled up in front of a big, white hotel, then some young men were upon us. For a mad moment I thought it might be because of my bee-stung lips and curly eyelashes, but they turned out to be valet parkers.

'So you give them your car key and they park the car and bring it back when you want it!' I'd heard of such a thing, but never before seen it in action. I find parking immensely stressful so I raved with praise for this most civilized of notions.

'But you pay, they're not doing it out of the goodness of their hearts,' Emily said hastily. '*And* you've to give the driver a tip. In we go.'

It was a packed, vibey place. Everyone looked tanned and buffed and gorgeous. However, I wasn't asked to leave. I liked them for that.

As soon as we were seated, Emily said, 'Here's Lara.'

There was a tall, blonde woman swinging herself past tables, and all I could think when I looked at her was: rolling fields of wheat. She had a gilded quality, as if she'd been dipped in golden syrup. There were a lot of beautiful people in that restaurant and she was possibly the best looking of them all.

'Heeeyyy,' she exclaimed at me, when Emily introduced us.

'Hey,' I replied. Normally I'd say 'Hello' or 'Nice to meet you', but I was keen to fit in.

The waiter arrived. Or should I say, the curtain went up. I'd been told that all waiting staff in Los Angeles were resting actors, and this Adonis was so beautiful and so 'on' that he just had to be a thesp.

'Hey ladies,' he dazzled. 'My name is Deyan, I'm your server this evening and I'm going to give until it hurts.'

'Who *is* that?' Lara's face, as she gazed at him, was puzzled. 'Kevin Kline in *In and Out*? Or that guy from *Will and Grace*?'

Not you again, went Deyan's alarmed look. 'It's my interpretation of Jack from *Will and Grace*,' he admitted reluctantly.

'I knew it!' Lara was radiant. 'You know what, Deyan? I'm not really in the mood for Jack tonight. Serve us in the style of . . .' She swept a blue light over me and Emily. 'Who do we want? Choose an actor. Arnie? Ralph Fiennes?'

'I like Nicolas Cage,' I confessed.

'How about it?' Lara questioned Deyan.

'Which movie?' he asked sulkily.

'*Wild at Heart*?' I suggested tentatively. '*City of Angels*?'

He became still and faraway, and I thought he was disgusted at my suggestions. Then his entire body assumed a lanky, boneless quality. 'Rockin' good news,' he drawled. He had Nic's heavy-lidded charm right down!

It was only when I heard myself laugh that I realized it was a long time since I'd found anything funny.

'C'n I git you beautiful ladies a drink?' Deyan husked slowly.

'Vodkatini with Gray Goose, no ice and four olives,' said Lara.

'Apple Martini with Tanqueray and cracked ice,' Emily decreed.

'The same,' I mumbled. 'The apple one.'

'Peanut, you got it!'

I had to admit to being absolutely astounded by this Lara. When I'd first clapped eyes on her swingy, honey-streaked hair and her taut, gold-leaf body, I'd immediately decided that if you looked up 'Airhead' in the dictionary, you'd see a picture of her. But she was intelligent as well as beautiful. I wasn't entirely convinced this was fair.

Across by the bar, Deyan stopped abruptly, dropped as if he was about to kneel on one knee, but stopped about a foot from the floor, swivelled his body back to us, pointed a finger and winked. He mouthed some words, one of which was definitely 'peanut'. I had to hand it to him, he was really working hard.

Then he was back with the drinks. Still in character he began, 'And today's specials are . . .'

Right away my brain went into screensaver mode. I couldn't help it. I wanted to know what the specials were, but something to do with maintaining eye contact for such a long time seemed to interfere with my hearing. It always happened.

'. . . blah blah blah done in a blueberry blah . . .'

'Ooh,' I murmured appreciatively, nodding my head, still locked in that hideous eye-meet.

'. . . blah blah blah served with blah blah and blah.'

'Did anyone listen to that?' Lara asked when he was gone. 'I always get ADD when they start.'

Overjoyed that it wasn't just me, I exclaimed, 'It's like when someone gives me directions. All my energy goes into nodding my head and looking attentive.'

Lara declared. 'You go!' (Big US of A compliment.) 'Me too. I always get the start – "Make a right." Then it's like they scrambled the words and I only get, like, one in twenty –'

'– "Second set of lights,"' I chipped in.

96

'– "Left on Doheny." Where d'ya find her?' She looked at Emily and pointed at me. 'She's great!'

Her effusive friendliness was over the top, but it still burnt off some of the sense of my own defectiveness. Who was this Lara? Apparently, she worked in a production company.

'A movie-production company?'

She gave me a surprised look that said, *Are there any other kinds?* before nodding. 'Sure, a movie one. An independent.'

'That means,' Emily said, 'they make intelligent movies.'

'But not much money,' Lara laughed.

'Busy week?' Emily asked.

'No. Next coupla weeks I'll be pulling together the launch party for *Doves* but right now I'm taking some down time.'

'I've had way too much down time,' Emily sighed.

I listened attentively. 'Down time' – it seemed to mean 'quietish patch'. One of the things I love about coming to the States is getting the new slang before it comes out in Ireland. To my knowledge, I was the first native of the Blackrock hinterland to use the phrase 'no-brainer', acquired on a trip to New York to see Rachel. It's a bit like seeing all the big films six months before they come out at home.

'I'll probably have nothing but down time for the rest of my life.' Emily was becoming maudlin. 'Bastard agent.'

'It's three days!' Lara admonished. 'Give the guy a chance.'

'Five days. He's had it since last Friday.'

'Three working days. It's nothing. And how's the new script going?'

'Badly. Very badly.'

''Cos your confidence is so low. Hey, here's Justin.'

Justin wasn't what you might call a looker. He had glasses, short, tight black curls, and he was sort of plump. Although to be fair, all he was was probably a pound or two over his optimum weight, but because everyone else in LA was so slender he looked tubby by comparison.

'Sorry I'm late, guys.' His voice was quite high-pitched for a man. 'Desiree's real depressed and I didn't want to leave her.'

I thought Desiree must be his girlfriend, but it turned out to be his dog.

Emily told me that Justin was an actor.

'Would I have seen you in anything?' I asked him.

'Maybe.' But he didn't seem to be taking the question too seriously. 'I play expendable fat guys. You know when they beam down to a planet and one of the crew gets zapped by an unfriendly native? That's me. Or a cop who gets killed in a shoot-out.'

'Don't knock it,' Emily said. 'You've got more work than you can cope with.'

''Sright! In Planet Movie fat guys needed to be expended a lot.

'So!' he said to Emily. 'What happened with your blind-date dinner party on Saturday?'

'Oh God,' Emily groaned. 'Well, I get there and Al, the guy they'd lined up for me, looked OK.'

'Always a bad sign,' said Lara drily.

'He tells me he works in the organ-donor business, and I decided I *had* to fall in love with him. This man saves lives, I thought. So I said, "Tell me about your work."'

'Big mistake in this town,' Lara said to me. 'You ask someone to pass the water jug and you get a ten-minute monologue about how great they are.'

Emily nodded. 'He has to go to car wrecks to check out the dead people's organs, so he starts going on about an accident site. The man had been – this is *awful* – decapitated. "His head was thirty yards away," Al says. "They didn't find it until the next day. It was off the highway, in someone's front yard. The dog found it."'

'Ew,' Lara and Justin shuddered.

'He enjoyed telling me just that bit too much,' Emily agreed. 'I had to go to the bathroom. And when I came back in I heard him telling the entire room, "THE DOG FOUND IT IN THE FRONT YARD". Mind you, I got on really well with this other guy, Lou. He took my number. But he hasn't called me.' Suddenly sobered, she observed tightly, 'I can't have a relationship. No one wants my work. I'm the biggest failure I ever met.'

'No, you're not,' I consoled desperately. I swallowed hard and made myself say it. 'I'm about to get divorced. I can't think of a worse failure.'

'At least you've been married,' Emily said gloomily. 'Although right now I'd settle for sex. Thanks to Brett's botch-job penis enlargement I haven't slept with a man for nearly four months. How about you, Maggie?'

'Not quite that long.' I was much too embarrassed to discuss it in front of Lara and Justin. It had been hard enough admitting I was getting divorced.

'Well,' Lara beamed, 'I haven't slept with a man for *eight years.*'

She had to be joking. All was still as I waited for the punchline. I mean, this woman was off the scale. And if she couldn't get a fella, what hope was there for anyone, anywhere?

'Are you serious?'

'Sure.'

I'd heard about women like her. Emily had said Los Angeles

was full of them – stunningly beautiful, intelligent, nothing too neurotic going on, but they'd been hurt by so many men, who could just take their pick of beautiful women in this town, that they'd decided to throw in the towel and totally shut down emotionally.

'But why?'

'I'm gay.'

Gay. Lara was a *lesbian*. I'd never met a real-life lesbian before. Not knowingly, anyway. Plenty of gay men, of course, but this was a new one on me and I had no clue what to say. Congratulations? Get lost, you're too good-looking?

'I'm sorry.' Lara roared with laughter. 'I shouldn't have done that.'

'So you're not gay?' Suddenly I was comfortable again.

'No, I am.'

9

The following morning dawned bright and sunny. I was beginning to spot a pattern here.

'How are you today?' asked Emily, handing me my breakfast smoothie.

How was I? Goofed, knackered, fearful, disoriented . . . 'Jet-lagged,' I settled on.

'Give it a couple of days, then you'll be fine.'

I could only hope so.

After breakfast, Emily took me to hire a car, but to my disappointment it wasn't as foxy as the one in my imagination, because the foxy one transpired to be about ten times as expensive as the non-foxy model.

'Get it anyway,' Emily urged.

'I shouldn't,' I said. 'I'm not earning.'

'Tell me about it.'

Then the pair of us went to the beach and whiled away several hours, dissecting all sorts of inconsequential stuff, like what a total gobshite Donna's Robbie was – we got great mileage out of that one – and how Sinead looked much better since she'd gone blonde the previous year.

'I'd never have thought it would suit her.'

'No, me neither. Not with her colouring.'

'No, not with her colouring.'

'But she looks great.'

'She really does.'

'And if she'd told me what she was planning to do, I'd have tried to talk her out of it.'

'Me too. I would never have thought it would suit her.'

'No, me neither. I have to say I really didn't think it would.'

'But it's fantastic. Really natural looking.'

'*Very* natural looking . . .' And so on. Lovely, no-brainer stuff, where I didn't have to be clever, or even coherent. Extremely comforting.

But when we got back from the beach, our sleepy, lazy mood changed and we were suddenly encapsulated in a ball of anxiety. The first thing Emily did after she'd opened the door was to skid towards the answering machine, hoping for a message from David Crowe.

'Well?' I asked.

'Nada.'

'Oh, poor Emily.'

'It's too late,' she said the following morning, as she made us our smoothies. 'If it was going to happen it would have happened by now.'

'But your script is brilliant.'

'It makes no difference.'

Despite having perfectly valid problems of my own, I couldn't help but be affected by Emily's hopelessness.

'Isn't life very unfair?'

'Too right. I'm so sorry that all this stuff is going on with me,' Emily said. 'I'm sure you could do without it.'

'Ah, you're OK,' I shrugged.

The thing was – though I'd never have admitted it – that it was almost a relief to be around a big drama that wasn't mine.

Now and again Emily made another half-hearted effort to quiz me up and down about Garv, but I was resistant and she hadn't the energy to persist.

'So what would you like to do today?' Emily asked.

'Duh!' I gestured at the window and the dazzling day beyond it. 'Go to the beach, of course.'

'I'll get my bikini,' she offered, gallantly.

I shook my head. 'There's no need. Stay and do some work, you'll feel better.'

Emily had always been a grafter, and though she claimed she wasn't making any progress on her new script, I knew how guilty she felt if she didn't put in the hours. She'd even done some work the previous evening.

Mind you, as well as writing, Emily spent half her life on the phone, hopping from call waiting to call waiting, like a juggler keeping several balls in the air. There was no such thing as a short conversation.

Connie – whom I still hadn't met – seemed to take up a lot of her time, on account of having drama after drama with flowers, caterers, hairdressers, bridesmaid dresses . . . It made me queasy to overhear. I didn't want anyone ever to get married, I wanted the whole world to get divorced – even single people – so that my life wouldn't feel like such a rare and conspicuous fiasco.

Connie's most recent wedding disaster related to her honeymoon. In a strange version of life imitating art, the resort she'd picked for her honeymoon had been invaded by disgruntled local militiamen, who'd kidnapped seven of the guests. Connie's travel agent was refusing to return her deposit, and though Emily hadn't an ounce of legal knowledge, she was urging Connie to sue. 'You've got rights. Who cares if it wasn't in the contract? Oh hang on, there's my call waiting . . .'

'I'll be back later,' I said, flinging a book into my beach bag.

'Are you sure you're OK?' Emily asked.

'Yes.'

Well, I wasn't too bad – I'd been in Los Angeles for three days and not once had I rung Garv. I'd had two really compulsive urges, but luckily they'd both happened when it was the middle of the night in Ireland, so I'd convinced myself not to act on them.

'You're getting a great tan,' Emily said, sitting cross-legged on the couch and switching on her laptop. 'Drive safely.'

On the way to my car I saw the New-Agey next-door neighbours, obviously on their way out to work. An incongruous pair: she was African-American, haughty and graceful, with a swan-like neck and elbow-length extensions, whereas he looked like Bill Bryson – bearded, balding, bespectacled and kind of jolly. I gave them a nod. Smiling, they approached and introduced themselves: Charmaine and Mike. They seemed very pleasant and didn't mention my aura.

As I said goodbye and turned away, I saw one of the neighbours from the other side, returning from buying coffee for himself and his house-mates, if the Starbucks tray he was carrying was any clue.

'Yo,' he yelled at me, as he marched along in knee-length cut-offs and a torn vest. Even if Emily hadn't already told me the lads were all students, I think I could have figured out that this one wasn't exactly an insurance salesman, judging from his shaved head, many facial piercings and elaborate facial hair. In my few short days in Los Angeles I'd decided that next door could well be a halfway house for Goatees Anonymous. There appeared to be dozens of blokes – although Emily said there were only three – and they all seemed to be afflicted. Some just had wispy, bum-fluff efforts; others, obviously the more hardcore cases like this guy, wore cultivated Fu Manchu mini-beards.

Outside their house sat a long, low, orange car. It looked so clapped out I thought it had been abandoned, but Emily told me it belonged to the boys. It had only cost them two hundred dollars on account of none of the doors opening, so entry and exit was by means of the windows. They called it their Dukes of Hazzardmobile.

'Hey,' I replied, climbing into my car.

I drove the shamefully short distance to the beach and parked. The vista ahead of me was as picture-perfect as it always was. The sand, the sun, the waves, the clear, golden light. Pity I was so wretchedly lonely. Worse still – and I was ashamed to admit this – I was unsettled without the routine and structure of a job and, really, I can't tell you how annoying this was, because I felt like I'd spent most of my working life fantasizing about winning the lotto, jacking in the job and having endless free time to loll around in the sun. Now that I had it, I was afraid of it. Of course, over the years, I'd taken holidays, but this strange, uncharted hiatus wasn't a holiday. I wasn't sure what it *was*, but I knew what it wasn't.

I noticed that my left ring finger no longer looked so weird – the raw-dough colour was becoming more normal, the sunburn had gone down and the outline was plumping out to fit with the rest of the finger. It was like writing in the sand being washed away by the waves.

I spread out my towel and sat in the invisible plastic bubble that kept me cut off from the rest of the world – apart from Rudy, the ice-cream man. He hadn't shown up the previous day. His day off? I asked.

No, he said. He'd been at an audition.

'So what'll it be today?' he asked.

'What do you recommend?' I was keen to prolong the contact.

'How about a Klondike bar?'

A Klondike bar it was, and away he went.

I watched him slog along the beach, getting smaller and smaller the further he went. Where did he put the ice-creams at night, I wondered. Was there a big place they all lived? Like a bus depot, but for ice-creams? Or did he have to bring them home with him? And if so, was he worried about members of his family eating them? It wouldn't matter so much if they paid for them, it'd save him trudging along the beach while people threw stones at him. But they probably wouldn't cough up . . . I drifted off to sleep.

As far as I was concerned, there was no such thing as too many zeds. I was still sleeping that same dead-person's sleep as I had been at home – at least I did once the loudest telly in the Western hemisphere was switched off. Being asleep was a blessed release, and waking up was like being delivered into hell. Each morning when reality hit my first thought was one of terror. 'I can't believe this has happened. I can't actually believe I'm here.' But not long after waking, the horror usually dispersed, just leaving a wispy residue of dread.

When I got back around six-thirty, Emily had fallen asleep on the couch, her laptop on her stomach, and there was a flashing light on the answering machine. One message. Not for me.

A man's voice, speaking in that laid-back, Californian, sing-song way, like this call wasn't a matter of life and death. 'Yeah, hey Emily. This is David. Crowe. Your hardworking agent.' He got particularly sing-song at that bit. 'I just got a call from Mort Russell at Hothouse. He's read your script and he's veeeeery excited.' Another little tune. 'Call me.'

'Emily! Wake up!' I tugged her by the arm and tried to pull her up. 'Wake up, you have to listen to this!'

Her face blank and dazed, I played the message again. Then she was off that couch and on that phone so fast . . .

'Who's Hothouse?' I asked. 'Are they good?'

'I think they're part of Tower,' she mumbled, punching numbers. 'Don't have left for the day, oh still be there, *please*. Emily O'Keeffe calling for David Crowe.'

She was put straight through.

'Yeah,' she said and nodded. 'Yes . . . Right.' Another nod. 'OK . . . When? . . . OK. Bye.'

Slowly she put down the phone. Even more slowly she let her body slide down the wall until she was on the floor. Everything in her actions screamed catastrophe. She turned a strained face to me. 'You know what?'

'What?'

'They want me to pitch it to them.'

It took me a moment. 'But that's good!'

'I know. *I know*. I KNOW.'

Then she wept as I've never seen another human being weep. Torrents. Buckets. Convulsions. 'Thank God,' she bawled into her hands. 'ThankGodthankGodthankGodthankGod . . .'

'You artistic types,' I said, indulgently.

'I have to talk to Troy.' She was suddenly urgent.

A quick phone call – at least it was quick by her standards, a mere twenty minutes or so – then it was all hands on deck. Hair and make-up and dresses and heels; we were meeting Troy at Bar Marmont at eight-thirty. Apparently Troy was a director and he would advise Emily on Mort Russell, Hothouse, pitching and self-esteem, among other things.

'Is he married?' I asked, as I asked about everyone.

This sent Emily into fits of laughter. 'Troy? Yeah, Troy is married all right. To his work. But other than that he's single. Single, single. Single, single, single. The most single person you've ever met.'

'What films has he made?' I asked, as we sped along the 405.

'None that you'd have heard of.'

'Is he no good then?'

'He's brilliant. But he works in the independent sector. He's too uncompromising to survive in the studio system – at least at the moment. He's waiting for his reputation to be good enough so he gets total artistic control on a big-budget block-buster.'

'God, would you look at them!' We'd passed a gym with floor-to-ceiling glass windows, so that everyone on the tread-mills was visible to the whole world. Not only would I hate to have passing motorists witness my red, sweaty shame, but it was eight-thirty on a Friday night! Had they no bars to go to?

'Loads of gyms do that window thing,' Emily said. 'There's always the chance that Steven Spielberg might be passing.'

Bar Marmont was dark and gothic and very un-LA. Plaster serpents snaked up the walls and even the mirrors reflected back gloom.

'There he is.' Emily marched over to a man sitting on his own. After they had greeted each other very excitedly, she introduced me to him.

'Hi,' he said shyly.

'Hi.' I was staring at him. I knew I was, and all I could do was wonder, *What makes a man beautiful?*

I knew there were certain conventions. Big jawlines, prominent cheekbones, long, thick eyelashes. Everyone likes a good set of gleaming white choppers, while soulful puppydog eyes do it for some people (although I'm not one of them). And noses? No. Noses are meant to take a back seat. Everyone thinks it's just better if they keep out of the way.

However, sometimes a person breaks all the rules, and they still end up being devastating. Troy's long face was dominated by his nose. His mouth was a straight, underscored line which gave nothing away. But the light bounced from his olive skin and his dark hair was shorn GI short. His eyes were, perhaps, hazel-coloured. A sidelong glance across the room, as he looked across at the bar, and a greenishness blazed.

'You girls like a drink?' he asked softly.

'Sure,' Emily said. 'White wine.'

'Maggie?' And the eyes were on me. More khaki than hazel.

'Something.'

'You want to narrow it down for me some?' A little upward curve of his mouth.

'Aaah. Something frosty. With alcohol.'

'Something frosty with alcohol. You got it.' He smiled. Oh, and there we are. Gleaming white choppers, all present and correct.

I watched him crossing the room. He wasn't very tall, but there was a careless grace to his movements, as if he wasn't terribly interested in himself.

'Y'OK?' Emily asked.

'Er, yes.'

She rummaged in her handbag, smiling a private smile.

Then he was back. 'Frozen margarita, Maggie. The best in town. So what brings you to LA?'

'Just . . .' I hated this question, just hated it. Then I knew what to say! 'Just taking some down time.'

No one looked at me funny. No one burst out laughing. Looked like I'd managed to use the new slang successfully.

Then it was debriefing time. According to Troy, Mort Russell was 'Insane, but not in a bad way . . . Not *always* in a bad way,' he amended.

'And he's really EXCITED about my script,' Emily twinkled.

'I love your work,' Troy crooned at her. 'I troooly love your work. I want to have sex with your work I love it so much.'

'I love *your* work,' Emily said. 'I'm getting all hot just thinking about it . . . That's the way they go on,' she explained to me. 'Mort Russell probably hasn't even read my script.'

'They just drop a love bomb on you,' Troy said. 'Two days later they won't even take your calls.' Not that that was going to happen to Emily, he insisted.

'So what do you know about Hothouse?' Emily asked.

'They've good people and a lot of energy. You know they made *The American Way*?'

'Was that them?' Emily looked alarmed. 'That wasn't so great.'

'Yeah, but only because they kept firing the directors.'

'You know *Glass Flowers*?' Emily went off on a tangent. 'I heard they had *sixteen* writers on it.'

'True. And it shows. Whatja think of *Sand in Your Eyes*?'

'Not as bad as *Obeying Orders*. Like, I managed not to walk out!'

While I sipped my frozen margarita, Emily and Troy batted high-speed banter about movies they'd seen recently. Mostly they dissed them, but now and again they poured praise.

'*Great* cinematography.'

'Really tight script.'

After a while, I got the rules. If I'd heard of the movie, they didn't tend to like it, but if it sounded obscure, preferably foreign, then it got praised.

'So pitch me your movie, Emily,' Troy said.

'OK. I'm thinking *Thelma and Louise* meets *Steel Magnolias* meets *The Thomas Crown Affair* meets *Lock, Stock and Two Smoking Barrels*,' she said in a rush. 'Only joking. I haven't had time to work on it yet.'

'We have until Wednesday,' Troy said. 'But you know? You'll be great. You,' he pointed at her, 'are Good in a Room.'

'Good in a Room?' I asked.

'It's what they say,' Troy said, 'about someone who's got the art of the pitch. Emily tells a great story, she's Good in a Room. Another frosty drink with alcohol?'

'It's my turn.'

Three drinks later, Troy looked at his watch. 'I gotta take off. Early start.'

'Breakfast roller-blading date?' Emily asked.

'Seven a.m. spinning class,' he replied, and they both laughed.

'They all do that as well,' Troy said to me. 'It's kind of a macho thing, having your personal trainer come by before sun-up.'

Out we went to the valet station and handed over our tickets. I must have been a little bit tipsy, because I couldn't stop going on about how great the whole notion of valet parking was. I told everyone – Emily, Troy, the valet man, the couple waiting next to us – and they all seemed slightly amused. I saw nothing amusing about being a crap parker and scraping cars against pillars in multi-storey car parks. Although I didn't do that in every car, just in . . .

'Here's mine.' Troy's eyes were trained on a valet guiding a jeep towards us. He swung an arm around Emily. 'Baby girl, we'll talk.'

Then an arm around me and a touch on my cheek from the steep-trap mouth. 'And you, Maggie, enjoy your down time.'

He slipped the driver a dollar, swung himself up into his jeep and was gone.

It was midnight. As we drove down Sunset we passed one of the gyms with floor-to-ceiling glass windows. There were still people on the treadmill running to nowhere.

10

The next day was a Saturday and the tight wires of my work ethic unwound and gave me a little relief. Today I really *could* go to the beach and sunbathe legitimately without feeling like a skiver just about to be caught.

David Crowe's call had utterly transformed Emily. Her hopeless lethargy had completely disappeared and activity was the name of the game. After breakfast, we climbed up into her car and drove the two blocks to the aircraft-hangar-sized supermarket. From my years in Chicago, I knew how fabulous American supermarkets were, but even so, I was sure they didn't carry the magnificent array of fat-free products they had here. Everywhere, packaging screaming '0 per cent fat' jumped up and accosted me. I'd found it impossible not to be affected by the pervasive body-beautiful ethic, and virtuously bypassed the occasional cluster of full-fat doughnuts or ice-cream, and instead bought blueberries and salad and sushi. And wine, of course. Emily insisted. 'I must take good care of myself at this important time,' she said, flinging a few bottles into our trolley.

As we wheeled our purchases back to the car, I was startled by someone yelling, 'Hey you!' I turned to see a dirty, bearded man, dressed in rags. 'Hey, you girls, are you listening?' he called angrily. 'A body lies under a fire escape. Male, Caucasian, mid-thirties.'

'What's up with him?' I asked nervously.

'He's always here.' Emily wasn't even interested. 'Roaring and shouting about mad stuff. He's bonkers, God love him, but quite harmless.'

We were barely home and unpacking our groceries when Lara burst through the front door and flung herself so hard at Emily that the pair of them scooted halfway across the room. 'You the maaaaaan!' she cried. 'I'm so happy about the pitch!'

Apparently she was in the neighbourhood because she'd been to her yogilates (whatever that was) class. She offloaded flowers and an affirmation card and a Native American something on to Emily to celebrate the good news.

Then she turned, saw me and exclaimed, 'Go girl! You look so *tan*. Hanging out at the beach?'

'Yeah,' I said shyly, flattered by her admiration. It was good, coming from her, a walking ray of light.

Lara stepped closer and said thoughtfully, 'You know what? Your hair is *so* great.'

Already I'd started to pick up on LA intonation. Telling someone that something is '*so* great' is actually a criticism. 'Your script is *so* great,' – but we're not buying it. 'Your friend that I went on the blind date with is *so* great,' – but she bored me to death and I hope I never see her again.

So when Lara told me that my hair was *so* great, I was pleased for a second, then I wasn't. '*So* great,' she repeated. 'But your bangs' (she meant my fringe) 'are too long. Hello,' she laughed softly, parting my fringe with her long nails, moving hair out of my eyes. 'Are you in there? Hey, there she is!'

'Hi.' I was close enough to see her contact lenses.

'You know what?' Consideringly, she weighed the end of my hair, curling it under with her palm. 'We've gotta get you to my hairdresser. Dino, he is like, the *best*. I'll call him now.'

Already she was halfway across the room, fishing in her handbag, and I breathed out. She'd been standing too close but I'd been afraid to move, what with her being a lezzer. If it had been anyone else I could have stepped back, no bother, but I didn't want her to think that I was uncomfortable around her and her lezzerness. Political correctness is a *minefield*. The palm pilot was out, she was tapping on her little cellphone, then talking. No waiting around. They do everything so *fast* here.

'Dino? Kiss, kiss, baby. I want to schedule in my girlfriend with you. She has the *best* face and she needs a great cut. Tuesday?' She looked up at me with her aquamarine eyes. 'Maggie, Tuesday, six-thirty?'

I felt overrun, taken over. I quite liked it. 'Sure.' Why the hell not? 'Tuesday is good.'

'I got reason to celebrate too,' Lara said, clenching a fist in the air. '*Two Dead Men* has finally dropped out of the top ten!'

'Rock on!' Emily exclaimed, and a general air of celebration prevailed.

Two Dead Men was a spoof gangster comedy film. What had it ever done to Lara?

'Tell Maggie the story,' Emily urged.

'You want to hear it?'

'Course!'

'OK! As you know, I work in a production company, and one of my many, *many* duties is to do script reports. Like, read them, say what the chances of making a good movie are. Anyhoo, two years ago I get this script on my desk, it sucked and I totally trashed it. And the name of this piece of crap? *Two Dead Men*. Only one of the biggest comedy movies of the year!' Her high spirits were infectious. 'The day I read in *Variety* that Fox were going into production on it was one of the worst days of my life. I have prayed so HARD for it to bomb. I have SWEATED when I've seen the weekend grosses. And I came this close –' she held up her thumb and first finger, leaving a tiny space between them, '– to losing my job.'

'But you're entitled to your opinion,' I said.

'Nuh-uh.' She shook her head. 'Not in Lala land. One strike and you're out.'

'I saw the original script too,' Emily said. 'And Lara was right, it was crap. I don't think the writer meant it to be a comedy, but because it was so bad everyone assumed he *had* to be joking.'

'But it's all OK now,' Lara beamed.

All of a sudden a low, rumbling vibration began. I felt it before I heard it and it built with alarming intensity. For a minute I thought it was an earthquake and that my mother had been right. How very annoying.

'Gaaaagghh,' Emily groaned. 'They're at it again. Drumming to the Rhythm of Life. Gobshites!'

'Who?'

'Next door. Mike and Charmaine and a load of professional adults who should know better. Banging Native American drums and hoping to find happiness. They do it on purpose to annoy me.'

'You should never have stolen their "Armed Response" sign,' Lara said.

'Don't I know it! Well, I'm left with no choice but to go shopping and buy something to wear to The Pitch. Any takers?'

Shopping! Apart from a sun-product splurgette in the duty-free, I hadn't bought anything for ages – not since my life had gone belly-up. I experienced a little rush, feeling alert and almost normal, which intensified when it transpired that they

116

both wanted to go to Rodeo Drive. Going to Rodeo Drive was what I *should* be doing, what anyone who came to LA would do, instead of sitting like a lost soul on a lonely beach. OK, so maybe it was a little out of my price range, but a girl could always dream. And use her credit card.

As we left the house, the Goatee Boys were also going out.

'Hey, Lara!' The one with the shaved head exploded in admiration. 'You are the bomb, man, toadally the bomb!'

'Thank you, Curtis.'

'No, I'm Ethan. That's Curtis.'

'Hey.' Curtis shyly raised a plumpish hand.

'And I'm Luis.' A pretty, Latino boy, with Bambi eyelashes and a neat little beard, also waved. 'And you *are* the bomb.'

'I was really hoping,' Emily said wistfully, 'that when term ended they'd pack up and leave and we'd get some proper neighbours in. But it looks like we're stuck with them for the summer.'

The Goatee Boys were going out in their orange wreck. Luis placed his hand on the car roof, vaulted daintily through the open car window and arrived neatly in the driving side. Then Ethan placed his meaty hand on the roof on the other side and also swung in, feet first. But things weren't so easy for plump Curtis, who got stuck Winnie-the-Pooh-like in the window space.

After we'd helped shove him in, we got into Lara's car (a shiny silver pick-up truck about a mile long). The sky was blue, the silvery palm trees were swaying in the gentle breeze and I had a bit of a tan – all in all, things weren't so bad.

I'd half imagined Rodeo Drive to be a type of celebrity compound. Almost a theme park that you'd pay an entrance fee into. Instead, like Sloane Street or Fifth Avenue, it was just a road of famous, expensive shops, staffed by those skinny, snotty cows from central casting. I was well out of my league – I'd worn my very best 'city-girl' get-up and was ostentatiously carrying my expensive handbag like an Access All Areas badge of accreditation, but I was fooling no one. After the first two or three places I confided gloomily to Lara, 'I hate the people who work in these shops, they always make me feel like shit.'

'There's a trick to it,' she sympathized. 'You gotta march in like you own the place, look evil and bored and never, *ever* ask the price of anything.'

So in the next sparse, high-ceilinged emporium, I picked up a handbag – because handbags are the new shoes – and tried to look evil and bored, as instructed. But I can't have been too convincing, because the starved, glam-haired assistant dismissed me with a contemptuous eye-sweep. Then her radar picked up Emily, the label babe, and everything changed. 'Hi there! How are *you* today?'

'Good!' Emily said. 'How are YOU?'

Do you know, for a minute, I thought they actually knew each other, until your woman continued, 'I'm Bryony. How may I help you today?'

On the rare occasions when those girls do speak to me, I'm far too intimidated to answer. In fact I usually leave immediately. (And what's with the 'today' thing? When else was she planning on helping? Next Tuesday?)

I replaced the beautiful bag on its plinth. But clearly I hadn't done it right, because Bryony shot over and, with brisk, angry swivels, moved it half an inch back to its correct position. Then she took a little cloth and polished off my handprints. I felt so humiliated that for a minute I thought I might cry.

'Just remember,' Lara murmured into my hair, 'her clothes

are borrowed. She couldn't buy that sweater she's wearing if she worked here for a year.'

Meanwhile, Bryony had descended on Emily, who was flicking through the hangers with a trained eye. Then Emily was being led to the changing-room, where she started trying things on, flinging them off again and firing them back in crumpled balls at the snotty cow.

'You look GREAT,' Bryony insisted over and over, but Lara kept up a constant stream of 'Hmmm. Let's see it in a different colour. What about the longer skirt? Does that come in a cross-over style?'

Bryony was run ragged carrying out her suggestions.

Eventually I tentatively suggested, 'How about a smaller size?'

'Yeah,' Lara praised, when that sent Bryony racing back to the rails. 'Now you're getting the hang of it.'

We made Bryony bring different styles and different sizes – even shoes and handbags – until it seemed that Emily had tried on every item in the shop several times. Painstakingly, she narrowed her selection down to a shirt-dress and jacket, then beckoned us both into the huge changing-room and shut the heavy wooden door. 'I'm skint,' she hissed. 'Is it very wrong to spend a month's rent on a suit?'

I was all for telling her that of course it was and that she could get a perfectly fine get-up in Banana Republic for a tenth of the price – and not just because I didn't want Bryony to get the commission, I'm not that mean, but out of concern for Emily's finances – when Lara said solemnly, 'You've got to spend money to make money. Gotta look the part for the pitch.

'Sorry Maggie,' she said to me. 'I'd love it to be like that bit in *Pretty Woman* –'

'"Big mistake",' I quoted eagerly.

'"Big HUGE mistake." Yeah.'

Then Emily understood. 'Oh God, was Bryony a bitch?'

'Yes,' said Lara. Then to me, 'But Emily's pitch is totally important and she does look great in these clothes . . .'

'Oh-kay.'

'So what's it to be?' Lara asked Emily.

'I'll get the suit, but not the shoes.'

'Your call.'

'Well, maybe the shoes, but not the bag.'

'Whatever.'

'No point spoiling the ship for a ha'p'orth of tar, I suppose.'

'Ex*cuse* me?' Cow-face had returned.

'I'll take the lot.'

Just before we left, Lara picked up 'my' handbag, manhandled it roughly and put it back all askew and covered with handprints. 'Thank you,' she beamed over her shoulder at Bryony.

'Thank *you*,' I said to Lara.

As we wandered along the street, Emily laden with carrier bags, I indicated a man strolling past us. 'Isn't he the image of Pierce Brosnan? He could get a job impersonating him.'

Lara and Emily took a look. 'It *is* Pierce Brosnan,' Lara remarked, and they continued up the street, clearly unimpressed.

'Where next?'

'Chanel?'

But the Chanel shop was closed because some famous person was inside buying the place up. Madonna, according to a small crowd of Japanese tourists clustered outside. Magic Johnson, a rival group insisted. No, no, a third cluster were adamant, it was Michael Douglas.

Perhaps it was for the best that it wasn't open, Emily said. She'd done enough damage.

'It's five o'clock, let's go for a drink,' Lara suggested.

'The Four Seasons?' Emily said. 'It's close by.'

'Sure.'

'Don't!' I exclaimed.

'What?'

'Don't suggest going for a drink at the Four Seasons hotel in Beverly Hills like it's *not a big deal*.'

'Sorry,' Emily said humbly.

'Yeah, sorry,' Lara said.

The Four Seasons had classical art and huge vases, swagged curtains, thick carpets and mucho, mucho gilt. It all seemed very *patternedy*. My mother would have loved it. As we walked into the bar, a man holding court around a table shouted, 'Billy Crystal is the best goddam director in the whole world!'

'Just in case we didn't know you worked in the movie business,' Emily muttered.

We found a squashy couch and ordered Complicated Martinis and they brought us a little dish of Japanese crackers. As the drink took hold we got a bit carried away.

'It's all starting for you,' Lara promised Emily. 'Look at Candy Devereaux. One minute she's waitressing and thinking about getting the bus back to Wisconsin. Then she writes a dream script and now she's charging a hundred thousand dollars a week, doing script surgeon.'

'Prada will send a truck of stuff over and whatever I want will be mine to KEEP,' Emily said gleefully, stretching out on the couch.

Fantasy stuff and yet . . . In other jobs you're supposed to toil

121

away patiently and incrementally better your lot. But I got the feeling that things worked differently in this town: your luck could turn on a sixpence and you could shoot from the gutter to the stratosphere very, very quickly. I was distracted by a girl passing by with a cleavage as deep as the Grand Canyon. Talk about silicon valley – those breasts couldn't *possibly* be real . . .

'Can I have a part in the movie?' Lara asked.

'Sure!'

'When Lara first came to LA, she was an actress,' Emily told me.

'So how come you're not now?'

'I didn't have what it takes.' She tipped her head back and funnelled crackers into her mouth from her fist. 'I wasn't thin enough. Or beautiful enough.'

'But you're *really* beautiful.'

'She's hot for me,' she drawled.

Emily gave her a stern look, which was interrupted by Lara's cellphone ringing. An animated chat ensued, then Lara snapped her phone away. 'It's Kirsty, she's nearby, she's going to join us for a quick drink.'

Emily made a face. 'A quick alcohol-free, dairy-free, sodium-free glass of water served with a slice of organic lemon in a lead-free glass.'

'She's OK,' Lara said.

'Yeah. She's just so virtuous and humour-free. And she thinks she's gorgeous.'

'But she is.'

'That's no reason to go round showing off.' Emily directed this to me. 'We were all talking about who would play us in the story of our lives – yeah, I know, but it's an LA thing – and Lara there, *beautiful* Lara there, says Kathy Bates. I say ET in an afro wig, Justin says John Goodman, and even Troy says Sam the American Eagle from *The Muppet Show*, and who does Kirsty say would play her? Nicole Kidman, that's who. Says people are always mistaking her for Nicole. She wishes. Well, before she gets here, can I show you something?'

She opened her handbag and slowly produced a keyring. I recognized it. It was from the shop where she'd bought the clothes; it even had the logo, picked out in rhinestones.

'I've been a bad girl,' Emily said, but she couldn't hide a grin.

'Oh my God,' Lara groaned. 'You have *got* to stop!'

'You stole it?'

'Liberated it, I prefer to say. Hey, I'm really stressed right now.'

'I know, but could you not just do a relaxation tape or something?' I said.

'You're just jealous,' Emily accused.

'I know,' I admitted humbly.

I'd only shoplifted once in my whole life – a choc-ice from a newsagent's. I hadn't even wanted it, I much preferred Cornettos, but they didn't have any and Adrienne Quigley had dared me to do it. Anyway, wouldn't you know it? – I got caught. The man was very nice about it and said he'd let me off if I promised never to do it again. Which meant I had to spend the rest of my teenage years looking on enviously as everyone else returned from trips into town with their bags crammed with all sorts of stolen booty: earrings, lipsticks, glittery nail polishes, a length of electrical flex and a handful of screws from a hardware shop. It was Emily who'd nicked the screws and the flex, because she just shoplifted for the thrill, whereas Adrienne Quigley shoplifted to order. I was sick with envy at their daring (and the free stuff, apart from the screws and the flex), but I knew for certain that if I tried it again, I was bound to get caught – and bring everyone else down with me too. There's just something about me. Each of my sisters could get away with brazenness because Claire was feisty, Rachel was funny, Anna was away with the fairies and Helen was fearless. But me – all I had was obedience, it was my only survival tool.

The arrival of Kirsty put paid to my sudden introspection, and actually she did look quite like Nicole Kidman, all tendrilly strawberry-blonde hair and alabaster skin. (Also, she was as thin as a rail, but you could have guessed that, I'm sure. *How do they all manage it?* These women are in their thirties, traditionally not the age to be as insubstantial as a sixteen-year-old. It's a mystery to me.) Kirsty was sparkily vivacious and I couldn't understand Emily's antipathy – until the waiter came and she made him list every mineral water they carried.

Then I offered her a Japanese cracker and she all but shuddered.

'They've only four calories each,' Emily said. 'The waiter said.'

Kirsty quirked a know-all eyebrow around the table. 'They've been sitting there for the longest time, with everyone's hands in and out of them. You wanna eat other people's germs? Go right ahead!'

Instantly the mood became subdued, even shamefaced. No one went near them after that, and when the waiter finally took them away, relief loosened us.

A girl with a tiny pink T-shirt stretched to the limit over a HUMUNGOUS pair of boobs strolled through the bar. Out and proud, it was like the breasts were taking *her* for a walk. Everyone knows LA is Plastic Surgery Central, but when you see these human Barbie dolls with your own eyes, it defies belief . . .

Emily grinned meaningfully at Lara, who regretfully shook her head. 'Too phoney. The fake ones don't feel as good.' She looked down at her own golden cleavage. 'And I should know.'

'Too much information!' Kirsty chided. 'We so do NOT want to know.'

There she was wrong, actually. Was Lara saying she'd had a boob job? I was fascinated, but too embarrassed to push it. Was it true that sometimes they burst on planes? That if you shine a light underneath them they turn green? That in a swimming pool they float like armbands and you can't get them beneath the surface for love nor money?

'Tell Kirsty your news,' Lara prompted Emily.

Emily succinctly told the story of the forthcoming pitch, and in all fairness to her, Kirsty seemed delighted.

'Heeeyyy!' she said. ''Bout time. We've been worried about you, stuck in your little house, becoming a total loser.'

'Excuse me?'

'I love your sandals! Where did you buy them?' Lara hastily said to Kirsty.

'You know what? I bought them last summer and, on purpose, I never wore them,' Kirsty said happily. 'Now everyone wants to get a pair and they can't! Anyway, guys, I gotta take off. Troy is coming over tonight to hang out with me.'

Emily looked like she'd got a crack on the skull from a frying pan.

'Like, really?' Lara interjected. 'Are you and Troy . . . ?'

'Like I'm going to tell you!' Kirsty replied, in high good humour.

Lara walked Kirsty to the valet stand and Emily fumed at me, 'Troy is *my* friend. She only met him through Lara. What the hell does Lara see in her? And what does Troy see in her? Stingy bitch, didn't even pay for her drink. And that stuff with the sandals. Hiding them in a drawer for a year – what was *that* all about?'

'Lara's coming back,' I warned.

But instead of that shutting Emily up, she said 'Good!' then laid into Lara, who was very grown-up about it all. Emily didn't own Troy, she said. Troy could hang out with whoever he wanted. Yeah, the thing about the sandals was a bit weird, but Kirsty's job as a gym receptionist didn't pay much . . .

'Let's get another drink,' she suggested.

After another Complicated Martini, Kirsty's traces had been washed away.

'You coming to Dan Gonzalez's party on Monday night?' Emily asked Lara.

'I thought you weren't going to go!'

'Yeah, well, it's different now. I can hold my head up. I'm a player. So, you coming?'

Lara shook her head. 'Nuh-uh. I'm going on a date.'

At this point, Emily got all screechy. 'Tell us!' she ordered. 'You never said! Where did you meet her?'

'At a club.'

To be honest, I was sort of embarrassed. I just didn't know what to say. If it was a girl going out with a man I'd have been all agog for details, but . . .

'She's way cute,' Lara said. 'She used to be a dancer.'

'A dancer, wow! Hot body?' Emily asked.

'Hot.'

Lara went on to describe the girl, the way men usually get described. How good-looking she was, how sweet she'd acted, how she'd really seemed to like Lara . . .

I pushed away my embarrassment and matched Emily screechy noise for screechy noise. I am a woman of the world, I thought.

11

Slowly I shifted the sole of my foot along the fluffy bathmat. The squashy clumps of wool were balm to my aching feet. I shifted the other foot and felt the touch of every fibre against my over-sensitized skin . . . *so soft, so kind* . . . Then back to the first foot again.

How long had I been standing here? Too long. Maybe I should finish drying myself. Someone else might want to use the bathroom.

As I stumbled to my bedroom to get dressed, I knew one thing for sure. *I'm never drinking Complicated Martinis again.* Clearly, Emily was a bad influence. I wasn't what you might call a party animal, but I'd been drunk twice in two days. And I'd never before had a shower while wearing sunglasses – what did that tell me about the company I was keeping?

I wouldn't mind, but I was the only one who was in shreds. I'd woken at eight, feeling like I was coming round from a coma, my habitual terror on waking even more pronounced, and I'd found Lara and Emily sitting in the kitchen, drinking smoothies and chattering, just like normal people. Hardy creatures.

'Y'OK?' Emily had sounded concerned.

'Fine,' I said. 'It's just . . . I can't actually open my eyes. The pain is too bad.'

Emily gave me sunglasses and some painkillers, and suggested

I take a shower. Which hadn't really helped, although the bathmat had, at least while I'd been standing on it.

As I got dressed the sunglasses fell off, but when I bent to retrieve them from the floor, black patches scudded before my eyes so I had to leave them. Then I emerged into the living-room, where the sound of my feet slapping on the wooden floor was too much. I was half-looking for a pillow or blanket on the couch, signs that Lara had slept there, but when I peeped into Emily's room, Lara's clothes were flung on the floor. She must've slept with Emily.

Not *slept* slept. Just slept, slept. Oh, you know what I mean . . .

I got the land of my life to see that while I'd been in the shower Troy had arrived on the premises. I squinched a look at him from my aching eyes. Still strangely beautiful, in a slab-of-granite kind of way.

'Hey, Maggie,' he nodded.

'Howya,' I said, too shattered to be bothered with this 'hey' business. I had to lie down. Carefully I lowered myself on to the couch, flattening my back against the cushions, but even when I'd stopped moving, I still felt as though I was sinking, sinking . . .

Emily and Lara and Troy were discussing the pitch. From far away I could hear their murmuring voices. I found that if I softly moved strands of my hair along my cheek, the pain in my face-bones lessened briefly. Again and again I stroked the feathery strands from my nose to my ear and back again.

'Y'OK, Irish?' Troy was standing over me. 'What's the deal with your hair?'

Too out-of-it to be embarrassed, I told him. Then I told him about the rug in the bathroom.

'What you need is a massage,' he concluded. 'Work those pressure points.'

'From you?'

'No,' he laughed softly. 'From the master. You wait.'

Minutes later the front door opened, bringing a great big bright dazzling morning into the room.

'Close it,' I begged.

It was Justin, beaming and wearing a yellow and red Hawaiian shirt. I actually thought I might vomit.

A clicky skiddy noise on the floorboards alerted me to a second presence. A little white Scotty dog chasing dust motes and generally being cute. Desiree, I supposed.

'Right on time, buddy,' Troy said to Justin. 'Lady here needs help.'

'Oh yeah?' Justin asked in his highish voice. 'What appears to be the problem?' He knelt by the couch and theatrically took my pulse at the wrist.

'Hangover,' I said, flinching at his shirt.

'My fault,' Emily apologized.

Justin laced his fingers together and flexed his hands back and forth, like he meant business.

'OK, where does it hurt?'

'Everywhere.'

'Everywhere. OK, let's fix everywhere.'

I was afraid I might have to take some clothes off, but it turned out it was only my feet he was interested in: reflexology. I'm not proud of my feet. Whenever I'd had reflexology before, shame of my hard skin and my second toe being longer than my big toe had interfered with my enjoyment. But the great thing about feeling like I wanted to die was that the state of my feet didn't seem to matter.

And Troy was right. Truly, Justin was the master.

As he pushed and kneaded with pleasurable firmness, my

pain gradually receded further and further until, to my great surprise, I was restored to myself.

I sat up. The birds were singing, the world was shiny and bright and bearable. The sun was no longer a malign yellow goblin, but once again a dearly loved friend. I could even look at Justin's shirt.

'You,' I said in awe, 'are a miracle worker. You could do that for a living. Is that what you did before you became an actor?'

'Nah, it's just a hobby. I learnt how to do it to try to get a girlfriend.'

'Did it work?'

'No.'

'Not yet, you mean.'

'Nah, I've given up. I'm not just the expendable fat guy at work, I'm the expendable fat guy, period. Now I live just for Desiree. Although,' he added cheerfully, 'I only got her so as I could meet women. I thought I could hang around the dog parks and look for a girlfriend, but that didn't work either.'

'It's IMPOSSIBLE to find love in this town,' Emily interjected. 'Everyone is so into their work. And there's no place to meet anyone.'

'What about bars? Or clubs?' I was sure I'd heard my sisters and friends in Ireland telling millions of stories about going out to a club and waking up the next morning with a strange man in the bed. It seemed to be worthy of comment on the rare occasions that it *didn't* happen and used to make me wistful for the single life.

'Friends of friends is how you usually meet people in LA.' Emily gave Troy a meaningful look. But if she was hoping he'd spill the beans about how he'd got on the night before with Kirsty, she was disappointed.

He loped over to me. 'OK, feeling better now?'

Flat on my back again, I nodded up at him. 'Great. Ready for my ten-mile run.'

'I wouldn't joke about that kind of thing round here,' Emily's disembodied voice said. 'Come on, are we going to work, or what?'

They gathered around the kitchen table like a council of war. Even Desiree was sitting on a chair, paying rapt attention. I later discovered she'd been in a couple of movies.

The doors and windows were all open, bringing the smiley day into the house. At midday Emily rang for brunch from a nearby restaurant and half an hour later enough food to feed an army arrived.

'D'you want any?' she called to me. 'Or would you boke?'

'I suppose I could manage a couple of mouthfuls.' My head pains were gone but I still had the vestiges of hangover nausea.

Troy brought me a plate and when I tried to sit up, he said, 'No need to,' and carefully tried to balance it on my chest. But on account of having breasts and on account of them being, by their nature, wobbly, the plate wouldn't come to rest.

'Maybe you'd better hold it,' he decided, with an embarrassed half-smile. 'Got it?' Then he flashed a direct hit with those greeny eyes and, all at once, he didn't seem a bit embarrassed – and suddenly I was.

When he'd gone, I tried a few cautious mouthfuls and marvelled as they stayed down.

Some time later, Troy reappeared.

'You done?'

I don't know why, but I waited a beat, looking into his face, before saying, 'Yeah.'

Then he lifted the plate from my chest, somehow managing to glance the edge of it off one of my nipples. Instantly both of them contracted and hardened, leaping 3-D-like under my T-shirt towards him.

He looked at them, then looked at me. I knew I should laugh but couldn't. Then I was watching his retreating back, as he returned to the others.

I stayed on the couch, half-flicking through what I thought must be *Daily Variety* but actually turned out to be the *LA Times*. All the news seemed to be about the movie world. Nothing about wars or massacres or natural disasters – only innocuous articles about opening weekends and weekly grosses . . . My eyes closed.

Emily was improvising her pitch, and now and again a remark floated over to me.

'. . . Emily,' went Troy's gentle sing-song, 'you're not convincing me . . .'

'. . . Don't compare it to *Drop Dead Gorgeous* . . .'

At some stage the phone rang, and then Emily was looming over me.

'Are you awake?' she asked. 'Phone call from home.'

Something in the way she said it immediately alerted me and, too quickly, I sat up. It was Garv, right?

Except it wasn't, it was my dad. I'd been about to attempt getting to my feet and walking to another room for privacy, then decided to spare myself the trouble. It was only Dad. But I should have realized something was wrong. Dad hated the phone, he normally behaved as if it gave off noxious gases, so why was he ringing me?

133

He had something to tell me, he said, halting and mortified. 'Though it mightn't be news to you at all.'

'Go on.' My heart was still pounding from the expectation of talking to Garv.

'Tonight we were coming home in the car . . .'

'Tonight?' Oh yes, Ireland was eight hours ahead. 'Go on.'

'. . . and I saw Paul . . . er . . . Garv. He was with a young woman and the pair of them, they looked . . .' Dad stopped. I was holding my breath and I wished I'd taken the phone into the bedroom. Too late now – dread had paralysed me.

'They looked, um, fond of each other,' Dad went on. 'Your mother said it wouldn't achieve anything by telling you, but I thought you'd prefer to know.'

He was right. In a way. The idea of being made a fool of isn't one that appeals to me. And I'd known anyway, hadn't I? But suspecting very strongly wasn't the same as knowing for sure.

'Are you all right?' he asked awkwardly.

I said I was, but actually I had no idea how I felt.

'Did you recognize the girl?' My heart rate increased dramatically.

'No, no, I didn't.'

I blew out a stream of air. So at least it wasn't one of my friends.

'I'm fierce sorry about this, pet,' he said miserably.

You fucker, Garv, I thought. Doing this not just to me, but to my poor dad.

'Don't worry, Dad, it was probably his cousin.'

'Do you think?' he asked eagerly.

'No,' I sighed. 'But it doesn't matter anyway, it really doesn't.'

Punch-drunk I hung up. What the hell did 'fond' mean? What were they doing? Snogging in the street?

I turned to see a frozen tableau of stares. Even Desiree's head was to one side in compassionate enquiry.

'What's happened?' Emily asked.

I was too shocked to dissemble, and the response from all of them was immediate and steeped in kindness. Lara poured me a drink, Emily lit me a cigarette, Justin rubbed the pressure points on my temples, Troy recommended deep breathing and Desiree gave me a consolatory lick.

'You had already split up?' Lara asked.

'Yeah, but . . .'

'I know. Yeah, but . . .' she repeated, with understanding. 'We've all been there.'

In the middle of the fuss, the phone rang again and Emily answered it. Her face was a picture of reluctance. 'It's your mum.'

I took the phone and made for my bedroom.

'Margaret?'

'Hi, Mum.' I closed the door behind me.

'It's Mum.'

'I know.' And I know why you're ringing.

'How are you getting on? Is it still sunny?'

'Yes. And I still haven't fallen into the San Andreas fault.'

'I've something to tell you and I'm going to give it to you straight. No point beating round the bush. If someone's got something to say, they might as well say it . . .'

'Mum . . .'

'It's that Paul you were married to,' she blurted. 'We passed him tonight in town. He was walking along Dame Street and he was with a . . . a . . . girl. They looked quite enamoured with each other.'

So it's *enamoured* now. *Fond* was bad enough. I swallowed

with effort. The bastard, I thought. The bastarding bastard.

'Your father was all for keeping it from you, but you're like me, you've your pride, you'd rather know.'

True perhaps, yet it still made me angry.

'I'm very sorry.' She sounded suddenly teary. 'And I'm sorry I didn't understand when you said you'd left him. If there's anything I can do . . .'

Abruptly I remembered how, a couple of times, I'd had the urge to phone him; I was transported with insane gladness that I hadn't. Could you imagine if she'd been there? If she'd *answered*? I'd have been so humiliated.

'Did you recognize her?'

'No, no I didn't.'

When I emerged, Troy observed, 'Your mom? Good news travels fast.'

Emily squeezed my trembling hands, trying to stop the tremors, while a flurry of comforting platitudes rained down on top of me. I'd get over it. The pain would pass. It was horrible now, but it would get better . . .

The phone rang again. We all looked at each other. What now?

'Helen,' Emily said, giving me the phone. 'Her sister,' she explained to the others.

Once again I found myself in my bedroom. 'Helen?'

She sounded uncharacteristically halting. 'You're probably wondering why I'm ringing and, in a way, so am I. Something has happened and Mum and Dad said that under no circumstances was I to tell you, but I reckon you should know. It's that prick you were married to. I know I've made things up about him before, but I'm telling the truth this time.'

'Go on.'

136

'We saw him in town tonight. He was with a girl and he was all over her like a dose of scabies.'

'In what way?' I *was* curious to know what they'd been up to.

'He had his hand on her waist.'

'Is that all?'

'Well, lower down, actually,' she admitted. 'Sort of on her arse. He was squeezing it and she was giggling.'

I closed my eyes. Too much information. Yet I wanted more.

'What was she like?'

'Disfigured.'

'Really?'

'Well no, but I can arrange it.'

'For God's sake, Helen, it's not her fault.'

'OK, him then. I can get someone to hurt him badly. It could be my birthday present to you. Or I'll swap it for your handbag.'

'No. Please.'

'We could burn his house down.'

'Don't do that. It's half mine.'

'Oh, yeah.'

'Promise me you won't do anything. I can live with it, I swear.'

'I'm very sorry,' she said, sounding it. I was touched. 'You could at least let me organize to have his legs broken,' she added.

Within seconds of me putting the phone down, it rang again. Anna.

'Another sister,' I heard Emily say to the assembled listeners as, for the third time in ten minutes, I closed the bedroom door behind me.

'Hi Anna,' I said briskly, keen to preempt her pity and

awkwardness – I'd had enough of it. 'Thank you for ringing, but I know all about Garv and his new girlfriend.'

'*What?*'

'I know all about Garv and the girl. Mum, Dad and Helen have all rung me separately about it. What took you so long?'

'Garv has a new GIRLFRIEND?' She sounded appalled.

'You didn't know?'

'No.'

'Oh.' I suppose she'd never been the sharpest knife in the drawer. 'So why were you ringing?'

Big long pause, then an audible gulp. 'I crashed your car.'

Another big long pause, then an audible sigh. 'Badly?'

'What does "badly" mean?'

'Did you kill anyone?'

'No. I drove into a wall, no one else was involved. The front is a bit mashed but the back hasn't a scratch on it.'

I took time to digest all this. I should care, but I didn't, it was only a car.

'But, Anna, what were you *doing*?'

'Uh,' she sounded confused, 'driving.'

After a few expensive seconds of cross-continental silence I said, 'Are you hurt?'

'Yes.'

Concern half-heartedly flared in me. 'Is something broken?'

'Yes.'

'What?'

'My heart.'

Right. Shane. But much as I loved Anna, I'd no comfort to give, I was too messed up myself. Time for a platitude. Luckily I had several to hand, as a result of my own circumstances. 'Just hang on in there, it'll get better,' I lied. 'And with the car, I've insurance. Can you sort it out?'

'Yes, yes, I will. Thank you, sorry, I won't do it again. I'm so sorry.'

'It's OK.'

This sort of serious situation called for more of a response than that, but the best I could manage was, 'Anna, you're twenty-*eight*.'

'I know,' she said wretchedly. 'I know.'

12

The news about Garv had devastated me, there was no getting away from it. And the others wouldn't let me ring him.

'Not when you're sore,' Emily said firmly.

A bit wild in myself, I wanted answers. How had this happened? Where had it all gone wrong?

'Had you any idea about this other girl?' Lara asked.

'Yes.'

'But you hoped it would burn out and you two'd get back together?' Troy suggested.

'No.' In all honesty, I hadn't been holding out for a reunion – but there was a big difference between a strong suspicion that something was going on and knowing *for definite*. And knowing for definite meant that I was destroyed, distracted, lost to myself. I began reconstructing my last visit to the house – when I'd been picking up clothes and stuff for Los Angeles. I hadn't noticed any evidence of torrid carry-on. Mind you, I'd told Garv I'd be coming, so he would have had time to clean the Häagen-Dazs stains off the sheets. '*I* left *him*, you know.' My attempt at bravado didn't really convince. Especially when I tagged on, 'Well, it was really a case of constructive dismissal.'

'Let's go out!' Emily suggested, when she saw me looking longingly at the phone again. So we went to a movie. All of us except Desiree, who stayed in the house, wearing a long-

140

suffering, stoical, I'll-watch-it-when-it-comes-out-on-video face.

There seemed to be several hundred cinemas in Santa Monica, a bit like the way pubs are in Ireland. I sat between Justin and Troy, who tried to ply me with foodstuffs. I shook my head when Justin tilted a bucket of popcorn the size of a dustbin towards me and I waved away Troy's bumper pack of twizzlers.

'No?' he whispered in surprise.

'No.'

'Gimme your wrist.'

I extended my arm and carefully he tied a thick, red liquorice lace around it. 'In case of emergency,' and his teeth flashed in the dark of the cinema.

There was never any chance that I'd lose myself and forget my troubles in the film. Especially when it turned out to be a stylish, violent, highly complicated thriller, with bad cops and good villains double-crossing and even triple-crossing each other. I was too dazed to keep up with the myriad changes of allegiance. Unlike Troy, who seemed thoroughly immersed in it: when someone who'd been a baddy turned out to be a goody, he laughed a delighted 'Aha!' and made me jump. On the other side of me, Justin's hand moved from his popcorn bucket to his mouth and back again in a regular rhythm which I found deeply soothing. He only paused from this pattern to whisper, when an innocent – and I must admit, quite plump – 'regular Joe' got caught in crossfire, 'That should've been me!' Or when a goody-turned-baddy's dog's ear got severed by a baddy-turned-goody-turned-baddy, he confided, 'Ew! Boy, am I glad Desiree isn't here to see *this*.'

As we all trooped out at the end, Troy asked, 'Did we enjoy that?'

'I couldn't really follow it,' I admitted.

'Yeah,' he sighed sympathetically. 'Concentration shot to hell?'

'I'm not sure that's the only reason,' I confessed. 'To be honest, I can never really keep up with the twists and turns of that kind of movie.' And I always got Garv to explain it to me at the end, I thought, but didn't say.

It's funny what strikes you, but what seemed terrible and final and wrenching was not that I'd lost my life companion, not that Garv and I would never have a baby, but that I'd have to go through the rest of my life not understanding thrillers. That, and never getting the hang of exchange rates: Garv was like a calculator made human. 'There's three of them to the pound,' he'd explain, giving me a load of foreign currency at the start of a holiday.

'OK, so to find out what things really cost I multiply by three.'

'No, you divide by three,' he'd say patiently.

So as well as not understanding thrillers, all I had to look forward to was an empty future being swizzed by souk traders.

'You've got to talk about it,' Emily insisted, once we were home and everyone had gone. 'I know you don't want to but it'll help, I swear to you.'

You see, now that things were going well for Emily, she had renewed energy to focus on me and my drama.

'You Californians,' I scorned. 'You talk about everything. Like it helps.'

'Better than putting a lid on things and trying to bury them.' Emily knew me too well.

'What good will talking do?' I said helplessly. 'Maybe I should never have married him.'

'Maybe you shouldn't,' she replied evenly.

She'd said it at the time to me. When I'd got engaged, instead of shrieking with excitement and making vulgar jokes about seeing my ring, she'd said soberly, 'I'm afraid you're playing it safe by marrying Garv.'

'I thought you liked him!' I'd said, wounded.

'I love him. Look, I just want you to be sure. Think about it.'

But I didn't think about it because I thought I knew what I wanted. In retrospect, I'd sometimes wondered if maybe she'd been right. Maybe I had settled, maybe I had played it too safe. But it hadn't all been bad . . .

'We had a lovely time together for years.' I could hear my voice shaking.

'So what happened?'

I was silent for too long.

'Go back to the beginning and talk it right through. Go on, it'll help to make sense of it all. Start with the rabbits,' she prompted. 'Come on, you've never told me fully.'

But I didn't want to talk about any of it. Especially not the rabbits. Because you can't really tell the rabbit story without people laughing, and I was in no state to start making fun of the reasons why my marriage had broken down.

It had begun, innocently enough, with a pair of slippers. What happened was, one Christmas someone gave me a pair of slippers which looked like black furry rabbits. I was extremely fond of them. Not only did they keep my feet warm, but they were cute and cuddly without the shame of them actually being cuddly toys. In the event of any confusion, I could point out that they had a function and that I wasn't one of those women who crammed her bedroom window-sill with an army of fluffy dolphins, pastel donkeys and squashy chickens, who looked down with their button eyes on people calling to the house and freaked the life out of them. Oh no. I had a pair of slippers, that's all. They were made of fake astrakhan, and when Garv gave them personalities, he was obviously influenced by the astrakhan because they were both Russian. Valya and Vladimir. I could never tell them apart, but Garv said that Vladimir had a funny ear and Valya's nose was shaped like a cross-section of a bit of Toblerone. (Why he just couldn't have said triangular, I'll never know.) Valya was a bit of a femme fatale and often said stuff like, 'I hef hed menny, menny luffers.' Sometimes she gave me advice on what to wear. Vladimir – who sounded almost identical to Valya – was a Party apparatchik who'd been stripped of his privileges. He was very gloomy, but then so was Valya.

Garv began to conduct the occasional conversation through the medium of the astrakhan slippers. He'd stick his hand inside and wiggle it about and say, 'I em goink to the Vestern-style supermarket. I em queueink for menny, menny days. Vot vill I get for you?'

'Who'm I talking to? Valya or Vladimir?'

'Valya. Vladimir's the one with the funny ear and –'

'– Valya's nose looks like a cross-section of a Toblerone, I know. We need pizzas, toothpaste, cheese . . .'

'Woadka?' Valya suggested hopefully. Valya had a bit of a problem. So, coincidentally, did Vladimir.

'No woadka, but you might as well get a couple of bottles of wine.'

'Bleck-Sea caviar?'

'No.'

'Bleck bread?'

'Actually, we *could* do with a loaf of bread.'

'I em helpink you.' Valya was pleased with herself.

I didn't mind. To be honest, I thought it was cute. Up to a point. But perhaps I should never have indulged him, because after that it was only a short step to the real rabbits.

As briefly as I could, I told Emily about the slippers. Then, ignoring her complaints that the story was only hotting up, I begged to be allowed to go to bed, on the grounds that I'd scratched my arm so much it was bleeding.

13

The phone woke me. I was out of bed and into the living-room before I realized it. In the wake of the previous day's phone calls my nerves were like taut elastic – I was waiting for someone like my first primary-school teacher or the president of Ireland to ring, to tell me about Garv and The Girl.

'Hello,' I said suspiciously.

A sweet, squeaky voice rattled off, 'Mort Russell's office calling for Emily O'Keeffe.'

'One moment please.' I matched the girl's efficient tone.

But Emily was in the bathroom, and when I knocked on the door she wailed, 'Oh no. I'll have to call them back. I'm dehairing my legs and I'm at a vital point.'

When I returned to the phone, some instinct stopped me from sharing this with Mort Russell's office. 'I'm afraid she's away from her desk right now. Can I help?'

'Could Emily call Mort?' the sweet, squeaky girl requested.

I wrote down the number and said, 'Thank you.'

'Thank *you*,' she replied, sunny as you please.

Unlike me. I'd woken at twenty past three, my heart pounding with an irresistible need to ring Garv. I'd tiptoed into the living-room and, in the dark, dialled our home number. I just wanted to TALK to him. About what, I wasn't really sure. But there had been a time when he'd behaved as though he loved me more than anyone had ever loved anyone. I think I needed to know that even if he loved this new woman, it wasn't as much as he'd once loved me.

With a click and a rush of static, the phone began to ring on another continent, and agitatedly I gnawed at the twizzler around my wrist. But there was no one at home: I'd done my sums wrong. Ireland was eight hours ahead, so Garv was at work. My desperation had already begun to cool by the time I was put through to his desk, so when it transpired that he wasn't there and that all I could do was leave a message on his voicemail, it threw me. *Leave a message after the tone.*

I decided not to. I crept back to bed, finished the twizzler and wished I had several hundred more. I'd had some black times in my past, but I wasn't sure I had ever before felt so wretched. Would I ever get over it, would I ever feel normal again?

I seriously doubted it, even though I'd seen other people recover from terrible things. Look at Claire: her husband leaving her the same day, *the same day*, that she'd given birth to their child. And she'd recovered. Other people got married and got divorced and got over it and got married again, and talked about 'My first husband' in calm, easy-going tones, as if not one twinge of pain had ever been felt getting from then – when he was actually someone who mattered – to now, when he was just a walk-on part from your past. People adapted and moved on. But as I curled into a tight ball in the dark, I had a profound fear that I wouldn't. That I'd stay stuck, just becoming older and weirder. I'd stop getting my hair dyed and I'd end up moving back home to look after my aged parents until I was old myself. No one on our road would talk to us, and when children called to the house on Hallowe'en we'd pretend we weren't in. Or else pour buckets of cold water from an upstairs window on to their masked and sheeted finery. Our car would be twenty years old and in perfect condition and the three of us would wear hats when we went out for a drive – when Dad would insist on taking the wheel, even though he'd have shrunk so much that all the other drivers would be able to see of him would be the top of his hat peeping over the dash. People would talk about me: 'She was married once. Used to be quite normal, they say. Hard to believe now, of course.'

The phone rang again, jolting me back to the present. Emily's agent, this time. Well, not actually David Crowe in person, of course, but some lackey who worked for him, setting up a lunch-time appointment.

Eventually, Emily emerged from the bathroom. 'Not a single hair remaining. Now where's his number?'

I handed her the piece of paper, which she kissed. 'How many people would KILL to have Mort Russell's direct line?'

She made the call, got put straight through, laughed and said, 'Thank you, and I totally love your work *too*,' a whole lot.

Then she hung up and declared, 'Guess what?'

'He trooooly, trooooooly loves your script?'

'Yip.' Then she seemed to notice me. 'Oh, sweetheart,' she said, sadly.

'There was another call,' I said. 'David Crowe's office. Will you have lunch with him at the Club House at one o'clock?'

'The Club House?' She clutched me, as though something terrible had happened. 'He said the Club House?'

'It was a "she" actually, but yes. What's the problem?'

'I'll tell you what the problem is,' she called, disappearing and fast reappearing with a book. She flicked through the pages, then read, '"The Club House. Power-brokers' lunch-time haunt where Hollywood's main men break bread and cut deals. Good steaks and salads . . ." Never mind that – but you heard what it said. "*Power-brokers' lunch-time haunt*". And I'm going there!'

With that, she burst into tears, the way she had when she'd first found out Hothouse wanted her to pitch. When the storm of tears passed, she surprised me by asking, 'Would you like to come?'

'But I couldn't. It's a working lunch.'

'So what? Would you like to come?'

Might as well, what else would I be doing? Sitting on the beach on my own, trying not to think about my failed marriage? 'Yeah, OK. But will he let you bring me?'

'Sure! This is the honeymoon period, when they can refuse me nothing. Might as well make the most of it. I was too clueless to capitalize on it the last time. We'll pretend you're my assistant.'

'Won't he think it's weird that I know almost nothing about Hollywood?'

'Well then, don't ask any questions. Just laugh and nod a lot. Please come.'

'OK, go on then.'

A quick phone call later and the deal was done.

The weather had changed. Instead of blue skies, the sun shone through thick cloud cover, glaring at the world with a dirty mustard light. My first five days in LA seemed like a charmed time, by contrast. Not only had the weather been benign, but so had my state of mind. At the time I'd thought I was unhappy, but I was far messier now. And to make matters worse, I could no longer get away with blaming any of my feelings of fear or alienation on jet lag. These were *mine*.

Emily and I drove along Santa Monica Boulevard towards Beverly Hills, and the filthy sky got worse the more we drove inland. Smog, I understood, with a sudden leap of near-excitement. *So* LA. As iconic as palm trees and plastic surgery.

'Is he married?' I asked. 'David Crowe?'

Emily fell silent, then said, 'Please stop doing this to yourself. Lots of people get divorced, you're not so unusual.'

The Club House was noisy and full. Almost entirely with quartets of men who were, incongruously, eating salads and drinking Evian. Emily and I were ushered through the throngs of men to our table. David Crowe hadn't arrived yet.

I suddenly, urgently wanted a glass of wine, but when I asked Emily if that was OK, she regretfully shook her head. 'Sorry, Maggie, but you're supposed to be my assistant. Though, God knows, I could do with several myself. And twenty untipped super-strengths.' Nervously, she clacked her nails on the table until, in a frenzy of frayed nerves, I grabbed her hands. She looked at me in surprise.

'It'll be fine,' I said, pretending that I was holding her hands in reassurance.

'Thanks,' she said, extricating herself and giving the tabletop another good hammering. 'Oh, thank God, here's David.'

Thank God indeed.

She pointed out a clean-cut young man, who looked affable and sure of himself. This meant he was probably a neurotic mess who'd never had a meaningful relationship and who spent five hours a week in therapy. Such, I am told, is the Hollywood way. He gave us a wave and a big, BIG smile. He was no distance from us, yet it took him ten minutes to cross the room, so busy was he stopping at tables, shaking hands, exclaiming with pleasure and generally bonhomieing.

Finally he arrived, held my hand between his two and stared into my eyes. 'So happy to meet you, Maggie.'

He turned to Emily. 'And how's my main girl?!'

All smiles, down he sat, and displayed what a regular at the Club House he was by not even looking at the menu. 'Cobb salad, hold the avocado, dressing on the side,' he efficiently told the waiter. Then he launched into gossipy and entertaining conversation about our fellow lunchers. He was almost like a tour guide.

'As you know, the hierarchy of power in this town shakes down every Monday morning,' he told me.

'Depending on the opening weekend grosses,' Emily said.

'Right! So see that guy over there, in the suspenders. Elmore Shinto. As of this morning, his career is over. Executive producer of *Moonstone*, a ninety-million-dollar project. Word on the street said it sucked. They reshot the ending four times. Opened this weekend and TANKED. Studio's going to take a huge hit on it.'

I was keen to get a look at him, mostly because I was interested in getting a gawk at a man who showed up in public wearing suspenders. As if the Club House was the Rocky Horror Show. Then to my disappointment I remembered that 'suspenders' was American for 'braces'. From the way Elmore was chatting and laughing, he didn't *look* like a man whose career was over.

'That's the way they do things round here,' Emily remarked. 'Always dress it up with a brave face ... Until you're found rocking in a corner, crazed with cocaine psychosis, and you're carted off to the farm,' she added, with a laugh. '*Then* there's no hiding anything.'

'Er, yeah,' David said, a little uncertainly, then launched into

151

movie gossip. '. . . saved the studio from takeover . . . brought in the original producer . . . three-picture deal . . . script picked off the slush pile . . . ten years to get a green light . . .'

The commentary continued through our unbelievably speedy meal: no starter, and *certainly* no dessert. Since I'd arrived in LA, I hadn't ever once been offered anything other than coffee after my meal. I suspected that if I got a longing for a slice of banoffi, they'd have to ring the dessert chef and get him out of bed.

Over the lunch, David and Emily had discussed pitch tactics a little, but as we left the restaurant the real work began: David stopped at several tables and introduced Emily to meaty-handed moguls.

'Emily O'Keeffe. Hugely talented writer. Pitching her new movie, *Plastic Money*, to Hothouse on Wednesday. You wanna piece you gotta get in there fast!'

I hovered in the background, smiling nervously. The response to Emily varied. Some of the men were patently disgruntled at having their cobb salads and Evian water disturbed, but others seemed genuinely interested. But even with the ruder ones, David – and indeed Emily – smilingly stood their ground, as if they were the hottest stars in town. There was something very exciting about the buzz that David was whipping up before our very eyes. When we finally neared the door, David said quietly, 'That last guy, Larry Savage, has already passed on the script, but betcha he calls.'

'They hate the feeling they're missing out.' I tried to sound knowledgeable.

'They also hate their asses getting fired when Hothouse makes the movie into a big hit and their studio finds out they passed on it.'

Then I heard myself exclaim, 'Oh, holy Christ!'

'What?' Emily asked.

'It's Shay Delaney.'

'Where?'

'There.' I indicated the man with the dark-blond hair, at a table with three other men.

'That's not Shay Delaney.'

'Yes it is! Oh no, you're right, it isn't.' The man had just turned to the room and for the first time I saw his profile. 'But it looked really like him,' I said defensively. 'The back of his head was identical to Shay's.'

14

That afternoon there were two further phone calls from the sweet, squeaky girl at Mort Russell's office. First to know if Emily had any special requests for Wednesday's pitch.

'Like what?' I asked curiously.

'Audio-visual equipment. Herbal tea. A special chair.'

'Well, I'm afraid Emily is in a meeting right now.' She'd gone to her gyrotonic – whatever that was – trainer. Everyone in LA seemed to have a constant parade of appointments with accountants, nutritionists, hairdressers, trainers of strange disciplines and, top of the list, therapists. 'I'll have her call you back.'

Then the girl rang again to give very complicated instructions for parking on Wednesday afternoon. Among other things, she needed the reg. number and make of Emily's car.

'She made a right song and dance about it,' I told Emily on her return.

'That's because in movie studios, parking places are like sincerity,' she remarked.

'Huh?'

'Very, very rare. Anyone else call?'

'Just my parents. They say they're worried about me.'

'They're not the only ones.'

'I'm OK,' I sighed. At least my middle-of-the-night panic had abated. 'And I rang Donna and Sinead.' Once I'd known for sure that neither of them were Garv's girl, I'd felt OK about talking to them. Both of them sounded delighted to hear from me finally, and neither knew a thing about Garv's affair. That was a relief – so at least all of Dublin wasn't discussing it.

'What are you going to wear tonight to Dan Gonzalez's party?' Emily asked.

'Dunno.' I was glad we were going out. Constant activity was what I wanted, to keep ahead of myself and my thoughts. But there was something I had to ask. 'Will Shay Delaney be there?'

A pause. 'He might be. If he's in town.' Another pause. 'Would you mind if he was?'

'Ah, no.'

'OK.'

'Have you ever met his wife?'

'No, she doesn't come with him, I don't think. I suppose with the three children she wouldn't be able.'

'Does he . . . you know . . . play around? Or is he faithful to her?'

'I don't know,' Emily said earnestly. 'I don't see him that often or know him that well. Which would you prefer? That he's faithful or unfaithful?'

'Don't know. Neither.'

Emily nodded thoughtfully at this piece of illogical nonsense. 'Look,' she said slowly, 'you've let him live rent-free in your head for a long time.' Then she stopped. 'I'm sorry, forget I opened my mouth. I don't know . . . I suppose I *can't* know what you went through. Sorry,' she repeated.

'It's OK.'

Then she went to get ready and that was the end of that.

*

155

Half an hour later she reappeared in pink and black leopard-skin jeans, dominatrix stilettos and some sort of jerkin top. But it wasn't just the clothes: there were bracelets and hair slides and shiny make-up . . .

'How do you do it?' My brow furrowed as I studied her. 'You're like Wonderwoman, the way you transform yourself.'

'You look great too.'

I'd done my best, but I hadn't brought many glitzy clothes to LA (mostly because I didn't have them), and in my black 'party' dress I felt like a mourner next to Emily's exotic plumage.

'Oh why,' I berated myself, 'do I have brick-shithouse tendencies, else I could borrow your clothes. Curl my eyelashes, would you, with your magic eyelash curler?'

Emily could do better than that: she did my make-up so that I was nearly as shiny as her, then gave me some spare hair slides and bracelets.

And then off we went.

The party, in a Spanish-style mansion in Bel Air, was one of those highly organized glamorous ones. Electronic gates with burly types checking your identity, ten Mexican men to park your car and fairy lights winking and twinkling through the trees. In the house, good-looking, talkative people circulated in the high-ceilinged, airy rooms, and enormous vases overflowed with abundant arrangements of lilies. The light glinted off trays of champagne *and* – rather disappointingly, I thought – trays of mineral water. As it was a Hollywood party I'd come expecting drugs, hookers and general high-jinks, and I wasn't prepared to relinquish that vision. Surely that ebony princess looking for the ladies' room was *really* off to snort a gram of cocaine? That alarmingly young-looking Hispanic girl *had* to be a prostitute.

Emily went to pay a fealty visit to Dan Gonzalez, the host, and I stood sipping champagne and watching, hawk-eyed, for signs of debauchery.

'Hi!' A burlyish, youngish man wearing a wing-tipped collar walked up to me. 'Gary Fresher, executive producer.'

'Maggie Gar – Walsh.' They were certainly friendly here!

'And what do you do, Maggie?'

'I'm just taking some down time right now.'

Then, so quickly that I could hardly take it in, he said curtly, 'Nice meeting you,' turned his back and walked away.

Whaaat?

I should have had a job. He wasn't interested in talking to me because I couldn't help him. The realization shocked and depressed me. Party, my granny. More like a dreadful networking convention. Next, people would be exchanging business cards. Oh, hold on, they already were, and Emily O'Keeffe was one of them. There she was, in the thick of things, glossy, confident, talking the talk, walking the walk . . .

No sign anywhere of Shay Delaney. He mustn't be in town.

'Hi! I'm Leon Franchetti.'

A startlingly handsome man had materialized in front of me, his hand extended.

'Maggie Walsh.'

'And what do *you* do, Maggie?'

'I'm a pet groomer.' I just couldn't run the risk of being snubbed again and that was the first job to come into my head. 'How about you?'

'I'm an actor.'

I admit it, I was quite impressed. Not as much as I once would have been when my feelings were normal, but . . . 'Cool.'

'Yeah, things have been going pretty good.' I was spellbound

157

by his matinée-idol smile. I was about to ask what he'd been in, but he beat me to it. 'I've just finished a pilot for ABC, should be screening in the fall – I've got a totally great character, with lots of room for growth, I could really stretch myself with it –'

'Excell –'

'Before that I was in *Kaleidoscope.*' Another hypnotizing smile.

'Were you?' I'd seen it, but I didn't remember him from it.

'Not a huge role, but it got me noticed. Oh yeah, it got me noticed.' He flashed me another handsome-devil smile. Oddly, this one didn't affect me like the others had. 'I've also played Benjamin in the House of Pies commercial. "*Where do I get my pie?*"' He stuck out his bottom lip, suddenly looked woebegone, then delivered, with a beam, '"*In the House of Pies, stoopid!*"' It appeared to be the catchphrase from a very crap ad. 'It didn't screen in California, but it was totally HUGE in the midwest. Even politicians were saying it. "Where do you see yourself in ten years time?" "In the House of Pies, stoopid!"'

It was around then that I realized how superfluous I was to the conversation. Emily rescued me, but within minutes I was boxed in by another walking résumé, who gave me chapter and verse on his entire acting career. He asked me one question and one question only: did I work in 'the business'?

When he'd finished with me, I stood alone and watched the room. All the glitter had rubbed off and the people moving and smiling and talking looked like sharks in a shark pool. It was true what Emily had said: it would be impossible to find love in this town. They were all too into their work. Within me a space opened up; there was nothing to distract from my thoughts of Garv. Depression began to circle and settle . . .

Then my heart thrilled at the sight of an old friend across the room: Troy, with his long face and implacable mouth. OK, so I'd only known him since Friday, but compared to this awful crowd of humourless egomaniacs he was one of the closest friends I'd ever had. I hurtled through the throng.

'Hey,' he exclaimed, looking as happy to see me as I was to see him. 'Having a good time?'

'No.'

He turned my wrist to him. 'Uh-oh. The emergency happen?'

I nodded. 'I rang him, he wasn't there. Thank you for the liquorice lace.'

'Twizzler,' he corrected. 'It help?'

'It sure did. I could have done with twenty more.'

'Buddhists say that everything is impermanent – that's a comfort. But not as much as refined sugar. So you're not having a good time?'

'No,' I said hotly. 'I've been monologued at by countless thesps. Such egomaniacs!'

'Acting is a savage profession,' Troy explained softly. 'Every day you get told that your voice is wrong, that your look is over. You get so many blows to your ego that the only way to survive is to overdevelop it.'

'I see.' I was momentarily humbled, then I remembered another wound. 'Wait till you hear what happened when I first arrived!' I related the story of the man walking away when he heard I didn't have a job. 'Where I come from,' I scorned, 'people aren't interested in you because of what you do.'

'No, they're interested because of what you look like,' he said drily.

I paused. 'Fair enough,' I conceded. 'And I haven't seen one person snorting cocaine. Call this a Hollywood party. Although do you think she might be a hooker?' I indicated the very young Hispanic girl.

'That's Dan Gonzalez's daughter.'

I could feel the disappointment on my face and Troy laughed a low, gentle laugh. 'You're not going to find drugs and sketchy stuff at this kind of party. They're here to work. But,' he said, 'if you want I'll take you out some night and show you a different side to LA.'

'Thanks,' I said, coolly. Irritated by the flood-tide of heat that roared up my neck and exploded in bright colour in my face.

As Emily and I drove home, I was oddly mesmerized by the freeway traffic. Five lanes of cars streaming forward, everyone proceeding at the same speed, with the same distance between every car.

Sliproads fed newcomers into the main body. They settled into their place with balletic grace, without missing a beat. At the same time, cars were leaving, extricating themselves smoothly and zipping up sliproads until they disappeared from view. Constant motion, constant grace – I found it beautiful.

What was wrong with me? Finding traffic beautiful. Finding big-nosed, slab-of-granitey men beautiful.

I was covered in confusion. It was a long, long time since I'd found someone other than Garv attractive and I couldn't help but worry about my unconventional choice.

15

A mild crisis had arisen. David Crowe wasn't able to make Emily's pitch.

'Something's come up,' Emily said bitterly. 'Some*one*, he means. More important than me.'

But Mort Russell's 'people' still wanted the meeting to go ahead as arranged.

'So David said I'm to bring my assistant with me.'

'What assistant?'

'You!'

'Me?'

'You get nothing for nothing in this town,' Emily mourned. 'You'll be paying for that caesar salad at the Club House for the rest of your days.'

'But Emily, I'll be no help. I know nothing about pitches.'

'You don't need to. You just have to flank me and laugh at the funny bits. Maybe carry a clipboard.'

'But . . . But what'll I wear? I didn't bring any suits, I'll have to buy something.'

'Third Street Boulevard is only five minutes' drive from here – go now!'

Obediently I obliged – like shopping was a hardship – and spent a couple of hours going round the normal shops where the assistants acted pleased to see me, unlike the snotty cows in Rodeo Drive. But, as we all know, the first law of shopping says that when you're urgently looking for something specific, you've no hope of finding it. The few suits they had had the peculiar effect of making me look like a prison warder. Half-heartedly I picked up some stowaways: an embroidered denim skirt and a white vest top.

Then I stumbled upon Bloomingdales. I know it's naff, but I love department stores – so much better than those funky little boutiques where you've to ring a bell to get in. The type where they only have eleven items of stock, which you can survey and dismiss in 2.7 seconds but have to spend fifteen minutes going 'Mmmm, lovely,' in order not to seem rude in front of the assistant, who is never less than ten inches from you, explaining how the silk was handspun in Nepal, cold-dyed in natural plant colours, etc. It's excruciating and I often end up buying something just to extricate myself.

So what I love about department stores is that it's operation free-flow. Apart from an occasional woman jumping out and trying to spray you with perfume, no one bothers you. And there must be a moral in that somewhere, because within seconds I'd pulled out my wallet and welcomed aboard another stowaway: a face gel that promised to make me look radiant. Then followed a brief moment of madness when I almost bought Garv some Clinique for Men stuff – my head turned by the free gift that was on offer – then luckily I remembered I hated him.

But the bottom line is that I wasn't any better off in the suit department. My other purchases made me feel good only for about forty seconds, and by the time I got home I was needled by guilt – I shouldn't be buying stuff while I had no job – and also by fear – Emily was a little volatile at the moment. Tentatively I broke the no-suit news to her, and she responded by snuffling like a warm-up act for full-blown hyperventilation, so I said very quickly, 'Couldn't I borrow something?'

'Who fucking from? Charles Manson? The Easter bunny?' Wildly, she appraised me, then visibly calmed. 'Let's see, you're about the same size as Lara. Except maybe in the chest area.'

'Did she really have a boob job?'

'She was an actress.' Emily sounded as if that explained everything. 'Anyway, could you call her and borrow a suit?'

'Well, I'm seeing her later, anyway. She's taking me to get my hair cut, remember?'

'Is she?' Emily looked a little startled. 'When was that decided?'

I thought back. It had been a morning. Sunny. But that was no help, they were all sunny. But hold on, Lara had been off work . . .

'Saturday, remember?'

'Oh, yeah, of course, sorry.'

At six o'clock, Lara swept me off in her silver pick-up truck to Dino's salon. 'OK sweetheart, let's make you even more pretty than you already are!'

Whizzing up Santa Monica Boulevard, I said – daringly, I thought – to Lara, 'So how did your date go last night?'

'Good,' she said cheerfully. 'It's totally too soon to call it, but she's a funny girl and we had a good time. She said she'd call me. Like, she'd better!'

Lara parked the pick-up truck in a space that would have held three normal cars and ushered me into a white, Grecian-style salon. Lots of urns and ivy and columns.

'Dino!' she called.

Dino was huge, with enormous sideburns and tight, flamboyant clothes. Ropes of muscle rippled beneath his skin. Gay? Not necessarily.

'The beautiful Miss Lara!'

Lara pushed me towards him and said, 'This is Maggie. Hasn't she got the BEST face?'

'Yeeaaah,' Dino drawled with interest, and ran a hand parallel to my cheek, conveying that he found huge potential in me. Hope stirred. I was going to be changed for the better. 'Hey, I gotta tell you my news,' he said to Lara with such anticipatory drama that I thought at the very least he'd won the state lottery. It transpired that he'd bought a tongue-scraper. 'I do not know how I lived without it up until now. My breath is the FRESHEST.' He breathed a big 'Haaah!' into Lara's face to demonstrate.

'Fresh,' she agreed solemnly.

'You gotta get one, it'll change your life,' he predicted.

Now that he mentioned it, I had seen ads for them. But I'd dismissed them as silly nonsense, in the same category as vaginal deodorants. Could I have been wrong?

'Sit here, in my special chair. The light is better,' Dino guided me. Then with frowning concentration he was mussing my hair, lifting the ends to chin level, changing my parting to the middle, pulling my fringe back from my face . . .

By my side, Lara watched the variations in the mirror.

'She's totally got a great jawline,' Dino remarked, with professional-sounding dispassion. 'The best!'

But I haven't. I've got a very mediocre jawline, and I know it.

'Look at those eyes,' Dino ordered.

I looked. They were just my eyes, nothing to write home about. But they were an awesome colour. Leastways, that was what Lara said. From the way the pair of them were love-bombing me, you'd swear I was gorgeous.

'I think we're gonna go pretty short here,' Dino said. 'Your head shape is good enough to take it.'

I opened my mouth to object, then realized that I didn't have to.

It was Garv, you see.

Despite popular opinion, he'd actually been very easy-going. At least, about most things. But there was some stuff that he simply was not open to negotiation on.

1. He would have no truck with electric blankets – dying of cold was preferable. He insisted that if you stayed in an electric-blanket-warmed bed for too long you'd – and I quote – 'pop up like a slice of toast'.

2. He hated me getting my hair cut. Visits to the hairdresser were fraught, because even when I only got a blow-dry, Garv used to examine me on my return and insist that they'd lopped off four inches. And getting a trim was a total nightmare – no matter how often I explained to him about split ends and what Bad Things they were. While his insistence on long hair used to irritate me, I indulged him, because when I could never find time to go to the gym and so lost most of my muscle tone, he didn't once complain.

But as Dino's hands sketched shapes around my face, I suddenly saw that I was free to do whatever I liked with my hair. I could shave my head if I wanted.

'I don't want it too short.'

'Your face can take it.'

'But my hair can't. It goes into awful curls if it's shorter than three inches. I look like a cauliflower.'

There have been many hairstyles over the years: the Shingle; the Bob; the Purdey; the Rachel. Well, I lived in terror of the grim halo of curls they called the Irish Mammy.

'I hear you,' Dino said, clicking open and closed a huge pair of steel scissors, practically pawing the ground.

'You've got to wash it, first,' Lara murmured.

'I *know*.'

As dark clots of wet hair fell to the white tiles, the weight on my head noticeably lightened. It felt strange: it was ten years since I'd had anything other than a trim. Now and then anxiety leapt, as I forgot how much my life had changed. Garv would *kill* me. Then I remembered he wouldn't. He couldn't.

'How'd your date with the dancer go?' Dino asked Lara. 'Gimme the 411 on her.'

As the old me fell away, the pair of them chatted easily. Then I was being blow-dried with my head upside-down, then finally I was being turned to the mirror, face to face with a sleeker, sparklier version of myself. By comparison, the earlier me seemed pathetically crude and lumpish – and very long ago.

Words finally found me. 'I look different. Younger.'

'The right cut is as good as a facelift,' Dino said.

And almost as expensive. It cost a staggering one hundred and twenty dollars! With a twenty-dollar tip! I could have got four haircuts at home for the same amount and had enough change for a bag of Maltesers for the drive home. But if that's how they do it here . . .

As we left, Dino said, 'You know what? You have great

eyebrows, but they could use a shape . . . You know what I'm thinking?' he questioned Lara.

'Anoushka!' they declared together.

'Who?'

'Eyebrow shaper to the stars,' Dino explained.

In a by-now-familiar scenario, Lara already had the palm pilot and the cellphone out. 'Madame Anoushka? My girlfriend is having a brow crisis.' She looked at my eyebrows. 'It *is* an emergency, Madame Anoushka.'

For some reason I couldn't be bothered being offended.

Lara paced anxiously, then, 'Saturday, five-thirty?' She turned to me. 'OK?'

I nodded. Why not?

Next stop, Lara's Venice apartment to pick up clothes for the pitch. I liked Venice. There was something bleak and charming about the clapboard houses with their peeling paint, the secret, hidden little streets which darted away from the road, the dusty trees weighted low over front yards, casting a mysterious, sub-aquaish light.

Lara's apartment took up the entire top floor of a big, wooden house. From her windows you could hear the swish and roar of the ocean.

'My closet is through here.' She marched into her bedroom, me in her wake. Then I took one look at her bed and all I could think of were porn film titles. *Hot Lesbian Love Action. Ladies Who Munch. City Lickers.*

I couldn't help it. This was the first lesbian bedroom I'd ever been in – I defy anyone not to have the same reaction.

Blithely unaware, Lara was pulling clothes from the closet – not a pair of dungarees in sight.

'There's this pant suit. Or how about this skirt and jacket? Lemme show you the shirt that goes with it . . . Try this on,' she kept urging. 'Try that on.' And when I finally got round to doing so, she stepped out of the room while I got changed.

Then, my arms full of business-like clothes, Lara gave me a lift – or ride, if you prefer – home to Santa Monica. Night was falling and the light draining away. As we drove down an avenue lined with palm trees, their silhouettes black against the fading sky, I noticed again how lanky and skinny they were. They say some people get to look like their dogs. Well, Angelenos get to look like their flora.

As I ran in home, I glanced through the window into Mike and Charmaine's front room. To my great surprise there were loads of people there, sitting amongst flickering candles. They all had their eyes closed. In fact, they were so still I wasn't even sure they were breathing. With a strange thrill, I wondered if I'd stumbled on a Jim Jones grape-flavoured-Kool-Aid mass-suicide-pact-type thing.

While I'd been out, Emily had gone into a pre-pitch frenzy and tried on every item of clothing she owned. They were scattered on the bed, the floor, the chairs, flung over her television, and she was on her hands and knees pawing hysterically through them.

'I have nothing to wear tomorrow!' She didn't even look up.

'But what about the lovely things you bought on Saturday?' She shook her head. 'I hate them. They're all wrong.'

Only then did she notice my hair. 'Holy Christ, I'd hardly recognize you! You're BEAUTIFUL.'

'Listen to me. There's something funny going on next door –'

'Police raid?'

'No, the other next door. Loads of them, not moving. They look dead! Should I call 911?'

'They're meditating,' she said. 'They do it every Tuesday night. Listen, Mammy Walsh rang.'

'She's worried about me and I'm to come home?'

'She's worried about you and if it doesn't stop raining soon she's going to wind up in the mental hospital.'

'Nothing about me coming home?'

'Nothing.'

'Good.'

'So did Lara give you a suit for tomorrow?'

'Yes.' I picked a shirt off the floor. 'Come on, I'll help you hang up some of this stuff.'

'All right,' she sighed, grabbing a bundle of hangers. 'Lara has a great apartment, hasn't she?'

'Yeah.' Then I thought of those porn film titles again. 'You know, Lara's the first lesbian I've ever met,' I admitted. 'At least, knowingly.'

'Me too.'

'I wonder . . .' I trailed off.

'What they get up to in bed?'

'No!' Well, yes.

'Dildos, I imagine. Oral sex. Christ, I wouldn't be into it myself,' Emily said with distaste. 'It'd be like licking a mackerel.'

I hung up a few more items, then I said, 'But everyone is a little bit bi, aren't they? That's what scientists say.'

Emily paused in her hanging-up and she gave me a forbidding look. 'No,' she said firmly. 'Don't even go there.'

16

When the real rabbits had finally showed up, at least Garv hadn't pretended they were a present for me. I'd heard stories of other men doing that – buying a kitten or a puppy which they'd really wanted for themselves and presenting it to their girl. Thus adding insult to injury, because the girl not only has to share her home with an unwanted animal, but has to feed and clear up after the little shagger also.

Garv arrived home from work one evening carrying a cardboard box lined with straw, which he placed on the table.

'Maggie, look,' he whispered, clearly about to burst with excitement.

Torn between dread and curiosity, I looked in, to see two pairs of pink eyes looking up at me, two little noses twitching.

'Funny-looking pizzas,' I said. He was supposed to have brought home our dinner.

'Sorry,' he said, full of good nature. 'I forgot. I'll go back out.'

'They're rabbits,' I accused.

'Baby ones,' he grinned. A girl at work had had some going spare, he said. 'We don't have to keep them if you don't want, but I'll do all the taking care of them,' he promised.

'But what about when we –'

'– Go on holiday? Dermot will mind them.'

Dermot was his younger brother. Like most younger brothers, he'd do anything for a couple of bob.

'You've thought it all through.'

Instantly, his glow began to fade. 'I'm sorry, baby. I shouldn't have just landed them on you like that. I'll give them back tomorrow.'

Then I felt *awful*. Garv loved animals. He was affectionate and indulgent and he wasn't just saying he'd return them so that I'd relent. His contrition was genuine.

'Wait,' I said. 'Let's not be hasty.'

And so began the Year of the Rabbit.

The black and white one was a boy and the pure white one was a girl.

'What'll we call them?' Garv asked, holding them both on his lap.

'I don't know.' *Bloody nuisance?* 'Hoppy? What else do rabbits do?'

'Eat carrots? Ride rings around each other?'

Eventually we decided that the girl would be Hoppy and the boy would be Rider.

I would have preferred not to have had two (well, I would also have preferred not to have had one), but Garv said it would be cruel to keep just one, that he'd be lonely. And because I didn't want them breeding like . . . well, *rabbits*, I insisted that they got done. The first of many visits to the vet.

Before we did anything else, though, we had to buy them a hutch.

'Can't we just keep them in the garden?' I asked. But apparently not. They'd burrow under the garden wall and into the next-door neighbours', then off out into the wide, blue yonder. So we bought a hutch, the biggest in the pet shop.

Most days, after work, Garv let them out for a run around the garden, to give them a taste of the wild. Although trying to catch them to put them back in the hutch was like trying to put toothpaste back in the tube. They were *impossible*. I remember standing at the kitchen window watching Garv belting around outside in his sober charcoal suit. Each time he'd almost caught up with one, it would spring away from his outstretched arms and the chase would begin again. All we needed was the Benny Hill theme music and for someone to fling a sack of ball bearings at them. It was hilarious. Sort of.

Don't get me wrong, they were very cute in their way. And when they hopped over to see me when I got home from work, it was sweet. And Garv had a way of carrying them, with their head over his shoulder, the way you'd burp a baby, that used to have me in convulsions. Especially, for some reason, when it was Hoppy: she did a great wide-eyed expression of surprise that was very funny. We ascribed them personalities, the way we had with the slippers. Hoppy was a mischievous flirt, Rider a smooth ladies' man with an arsenal of cheesy chat-up lines.

But on one of their turns around the garden the little bastards ate my lupins, the lupins that I'd planted myself, with my bare hands (nearly), and I'm afraid I slightly took agin them. I also resented having to shop for them – if we hadn't managed to get to the supermarket for ourselves we could just get an Indian delivered. But we couldn't get away with ordering a couple of extra onion bhajis for them. Instead, we were obliged to make regular trips to the Bad Place for their bags of carrots, bunches of parsley and funny pellet yokes.

Then came the day when Garv marched in, waved something at me and declared, 'Present!'

I whipped it from his hand, tore off the paper bag . . . and stared. 'It's a bit of wood,' I said.

'To gnaw on,' he said, like he thought he was making sense.

'To gnaw on,' I repeated.

He understood before I did, and couldn't stop laughing. 'Not for you. For Hoppy!'

More presents followed: a ball, a mirror for the hutch, a baby-blue clutch bag (for me, so I wouldn't feel left out). And one day, I got home from work to find half the garden dug up.

'What's going on? Have you murdered someone?'

But the truth wasn't much more palatable – Garv was making something called a run, because he felt it was cruel to confine the boyos to a hutch.

In a way, it was a relief that Garv had dug up the garden to make the run: at least we'd never have to worry about cutting the grass again. But in another way, it wasn't a relief at all. I thought he was getting too fond of Hoppy and Rider. But when I mentioned it to Donna, she told me to cop on to myself. Who ever heard of anyone being jealous of a pair of rabbits?

Not long after, Hoppy got sick and Garv was clearly worried. He took a morning off work to take her to the vet, who diagnosed an infection due to – of all the weird things – misaligned teeth. It was no big deal: the vet clipped her teeth and prescribed a course of antibiotics. But a few days later, we went out for dinner with Donna and Robbie, and Garv began telling them about Hoppy's bout. About how he'd known something was wrong, because she was normally alert and reactive, but she wouldn't even gnaw on her new bit of wood. Donna and Robbie made sympathetic noises, and Garv went on about Hoppy's high temperature and how Rider had tried to tempt her to eat a bite or two of onion bhaji. (One very busy week, when we hadn't had time to go to the supermarket, we'd discovered that they actually quite liked them.)

As Garv went on, Donna and Robbie's indulgent expressions

faded and hardened, and I had a tight place in my stomach that no amount of wine-swallowing would dissolve.

'How's work?' Donna eventually cut across Garv.

'Work?' He sounded confused. '*My* work? But you never let me talk about my work, it's too boring.' As enlightenment dawned, he began to laugh. 'Oh right, I see. I'll shut up about them, so.'

Donna rang me early the next day and said, 'Maggie, I think you might be right, he *is* a bit too devoted. Stick him on to me there, I'll tell him myself.'

The crunch came not long after, when my sister Claire came to visit and remarked on the amount of rabbit paraphernalia lying around. Garv was putting them into their travelling baskets to bring them to the vet for their jabs.

'Jabs?' Claire exclaimed. 'It's almost as bad as having a child!'

17

*SCENE: Sunny day. White clapboard house,
with small front yard. Front door opens.
Two women emerge. One, tall, carrying an
empty folder and wearing a jacket that
bags slightly in the chest area. The
other, short, skinny, well-dressed,
smoking manically.*

SHORT GIRL. I need to go to the bathroom
again.
TALL GIRL. No, Emily, you don't!

*They cross the lawn, just as the
sprinklers spurt high jets of water from
the ground, catching the short girl and
extinguishing her cigarette. She shrieks.
Like a reaction in a scientific
experiment, her glossy, shiny hair
immediately begins to fuzz and bulk.*

Cue laughter.

Oh, stop!

I couldn't stop thinking in screenplay speech. Emily had
practised on me long and hard into the night, and, between

appointments at the hairdresser's and reiki practitioner, through the morning also.

We were both in shreds.

I was *literally* having a bad-hair day. As usual, I'd woken up feeling like it was the end of the world. And that was even before I went to the bathroom and saw my hair – what remained of it. When I thought of all the hair I'd lost, the eight or nine inches which had dropped to the floor and been peremptorily swept away, I cried. Interestingly enough, I wasn't crying because my haircut was symbolic of the end of my marriage. I'm fairly sure I was crying because in all my excitement at Dino's I'd only gone and signed up for a high-maintenance cut, and now it was too late.

Fecking hairdressers. It always looks great when you leave the salon. (Well, it doesn't, but let's not get into the times when we've been fighting back tears even while we've been shoving them a tip. I'm talking about the rare occasions when we're actually happy with what they've done.) Everything is dandy until the first time we wash it, and then for love nor money we cannot re-create that just-out-of-the-salon look. Despite all the hype, there is one way and one way only to achieve that just-out-of-a-salon look and that's when you're just out of a salon. Even now, all I'd done with my hair was sleep on it funny and already I'd lost control of it. It took water, styling wax and a hairdryer at its highest setting before I could bring it to heel.

Emily had taken the precaution of bringing her own hair to the hairdresser's. She returned briefly and walked around the house saying, '. . . camera pans over a pair of breasts in a T-shirt . . .' Then she went out again.

While she was gone, the sweet, squeaky girl from Mort Russell's office rang for her.

'I'm afraid she's away from her desk right now.' She'd gone to her reiki – now I knew what *that* was – practitioner. 'Can I help?'

This time she wanted to know, for identification purposes, what our DNA make-up was. Well, almost. She needed me to fax over copies of our driving licences, because she needed to see our photos.

'I'm sorry to bother you like this,' she said. 'But we've got to be security conscious.'

I could well believe it. There was every chance that crazed scriptwriters, desperate for an appointment, could try to break in, hold studio chiefs hostage and force them to listen to their pitch.

'See you at three-thirty,' she said.

She'd been so lovely every time we'd spoken that, on impulse, I asked her her name.

'Flea,' she replied.

Instantly I realized my mistake. I'd been far too friendly. Crossed professional boundaries. Stung, I mumbled a goodbye and hung up. Flea, indeed! Oh, make fun of the poor Irish eejit just off the plane. And what's your surname, lovey? Pit? Bite? Bag?

'. . . Camera pans over a pair of breasts,' I heard. Emily was back.

'My chakras were in a terrible state,' she announced. 'Good job I went.'

Then she started muttering to herself in the mirror. 'The universe is benign, they will option my script, the universe is benign, they will option my script . . .' She varied this affirmation with, 'The perfect pitch is twenty-five words or less, the perfect pitch is . . .'

'I thought you didn't believe in chakras,' I said. 'And don't you hate all that New Age stuff?'

Her answer humbled me. 'When you're desperate, you'll try anything.'

In the end, I talked Emily into wearing her new outfit. She brushed her hair for the millionth time, put on the umpteenth layer of lip-gloss, then we squared our shoulders and sallied forth. Just in time for the sprinklers to spring into sudden life and launch their jets directly at Emily. As her hair expanded like bubble bath, she almost had hysterics.

'It's a disaster,' she shrieked. 'I'm going to have to cancel!'

'Quick, back to the hairdryer,' I suggested.

'We don't got time,' she wailed. 'The only thing I can do is to keep combing it. But I've got to drive!'

'We'll take my car.'

'We can't bring your crappy hire-car – what'll they think of us?'

'Actually, we can't bring my crappy hire-car because our parking space is allocated for your reg. number,' I remembered.

'I'll drive, you comb.'

We sped across LA, Emily talking to herself, her face like flint, me combing energetically and doing my best to ignore the startled looks we were getting at stop lights.

The studio, like most of the studios, was in a place called 'The Valley'. From what I could gather, most people would rather live in a cardboard box in Santa Monica than in a five-bathroomed mansion in The Valley. Apparently it was naffer than Liebfraumilch, Andrew Lloyd Webber and mullet hairdos put together, and one of the worst insults you could level at anyone was 'Valley Girl'.

After we'd been driving about forty-five minutes, Emily interrupted her affirmations. 'This is The Valley.'

For all the talk, it didn't look that remarkable, to be honest. People weren't lining the streets guzzling Blue Nun, dancing to *Phantom of the Opera* and teasing their neckcurls, as I'd almost expected.

'Nearly there now,' Emily said, heaving a breath from her diaphragm.

Just then we ran into heavy traffic.

'Come on, come on, come on! Oh, Jesus!' Agitatedly, Emily pounded her steering wheel, then handed me her cellphone. 'Give Flea a buzz and tell her we'll be five minutes late.'

'Flea? You mean that's really her name?'

'Yeah, Flea.' Emily sounded impatient.

'Like the insect?' I couldn't let it go.

'No. F-L-I. It's short for something. Felicity, maybe.'

'Right!' Short for something. Felicity, maybe. *Not* making fun of the poor Irish eejit just off the plane!

Then we were driving through the gates, then the man was checking our name was on the list, then we were parking in the special space that had been allocated for us. It was like an out-of-body experience and, despite my anxiety, a long-forgotten feeling stirred – excitement. For months – though it felt more like for ever – my positive feelings seemed to have been running on half-power; I hadn't been able to spark up any genuine unbridled joy or excitement.

But I couldn't get too carried away, because I knew how important this was to Emily's life. She was nearly out of money and chances, and she'd be going back to rainy Ireland and working as a checkout girl if she didn't pull this one off.

179

Then we were walking through the glass doors – for a moment, I thought Emily was going to faint. Then we were looking at posters on the wall of box-office-breaking movies the studio had produced – which was my cue to think that *I* might faint. Then we were introducing ourselves to the nauseatingly thin, beautiful, unfriendly receptionist hidden behind the enormous flower arrangement on the curved wooden desk. As soon as she heard Emily's name, her implacable expression lit up.

'Hiiiiii. I'm Tiffany. I love your script,' she said warmly.

'You've read it?' I was impressed. Even the receptionist had read it.

A startled, caught-in-the-headlights look skipped across Tiffany's gorgeous face, and when she spoke she sounded as though she'd been inhaling helium. 'Sure,' she squeaked nervously. 'Sure. I'll tell Mr Russell you're here.'

As Tiffany clicked down the marble-floored hall, Emily said, between angry lips, 'She hasn't read it.'

'But she –'

'*No one* has read it. Except the person whose job it is to reduce 190 pages of screenplay to three lines.'

'Shush, she's coming back.'

'Mr Russell will see you now,' Tiffany said.

Emily and I rose slowly and followed her back down the hall, passing more framed posters of famous movies as we went. My ears pounded and there was a loose-hinged wobbliness about my knees. I couldn't even begin to imagine how Emily must feel. So much depended on this.

Tiffany opened a door into a tastefully understated room, where three men and a dinky blonde girl – Fli? – were grouped around a table. They stood up and one of them, all teeth and

tan, extended his hand and announced himself to be Mort
Russell. He was a lot younger than I had expected, but he had
that fear-generating charisma that very powerful people have.

'Emily O'Keeffe,' he proclaimed, making it sound like an
accolade.

'Guilty as charged.' Emily stepped forward with a confident
smile, and I relaxed just a tiny bit. She seemed to have a handle
on things.

After Mort had loved-up Emily a little, he introduced her to
the other people there. The girl was indeed Fli and the two
other men were vice-presidents of some ilk. Which wasn't
necessarily as impressive as it sounds. In the States, you could
be a tea lady and be called Vice-President of Beverage Providing.
(Indeed, I'd once been a vice-president myself.)

Then Emily shoved me and my empty folder at them and
they professed themselves to be 'So, *so* happy' to meet me. You'd
swear it was one of the nicest things that had ever happened to
them.

'Nice to meet you,' I replied. I was under strict instructions
to say nothing else.

Coffee was offered and accepted – no Hobnobs, or bikkies of
any kind, unfortunately, but other than that the mood around
the table was friendly and informal, and the four of them
couldn't have been nicer. Loudly, enthusiastically, they all professed how much they loved *Plastic Money*.

'It's, ah . . .' Mort sketched a shape in the air. 'Gimme a word,'
he ordered one of his boys.

'Edgy.'

'Yeah, edgy.'

'But commercial,' the other provided.

'Oh yeah, gotta be commercial.'

'And funny,' the first one supplied.

'Funny is good. We *like* funny. So pitch it to me,' he suddenly ordered Emily.

'Sure.' She smiled around the table, shook back her hair and started. 'I'm thinking *Thelma and Louise* meets *Snatch* meets . . .'

To my horror, you could actually *hear* how dry her mouth was. Every word was accompanied by a type of clicking noise as she unpeeled her tongue from her hard palate.

Fli slid a glass of water towards her.

'Water,' Emily explained, with a goofy grin, before taking a quick gulp from it. Then, to my giddy relief, the velcroey sounds stopped and suddenly she was like a hare let out of a trap.

All the practice had been worth it. She did her 'twenty-five words or less' summary. Then she did a longer description of everything that happens, and even though I'd heard it all before, she was so good that for a moment or two I almost forgot where I was and nearly enjoyed myself.

She finished by saying, 'It's going to make a great movie!'

'All right!'

They all clapped and I wondered if I should join in or whether it would be seen as applauding myself, but they'd finished before I could decide.

Then Mort spoke, and I could hardly believe the words that came out of his mouth. 'I see this as a big, BIG movie.'

A thrill flamed through my entire body and I shot the fastest look at Emily. Her smile was restrained.

Above his head, Mort made a screen shape with his hands and we all obediently looked up at it. 'Big budget, big stars. Seventy million dollars, minimum. I see Julia Roberts and Cameron Diaz. Am I right?'

The others all nodded enthusiastically, so I did too.

'Who're we gonna get to direct our movie?' Mort asked the lads.

They named a couple of Oscar winners. Then came talk of fast-tracking it, green-lighting it, opening on three thousand screens across the country. It was the most exhilarating thing that had ever happened to me. Then we were shaking hands and Mort was promising that he was looking forward to working with me.

As Emily and I walked back down the hall, I literally couldn't feel my feet.

Another flurry of goodbyes in reception, then we were walking away. Aware of their eyes on our backs, neither of us said anything. I was shaking with unexpressed elation. Still in silence, we got into the car, where Emily lit a cigarette and sucked at it, like it was a thick milkshake coming through a narrow straw.

'Well?' I eventually said, and waited for the pair of us to SCREECH and hug with excitement.

'Well,' she said, consideringly.

'But that was fantastic! You heard the man! Julia Roberts! Cameron Diaz! Three thousand screens!'

'Don't forget, Maggie, that I've been here before.'

I thought she was being very negative and told her. 'So now what happens?'

'Now we wait.'

'Now we wait,' I repeated, feeling cheated and resentful.

'Mind you,' she conceded, 'we could get drunk while we're doing it.'

18

An impromptu party was what was called for, Emily decided. She spent the drive home with her phone clamped between her shoulder and ear, inviting people over. 'I don't know if we're celebrating,' she kept saying. 'But we're definitely partying.'

Lara was under instructions to come round at six, to accompany Emily to the Liquor Locker to buy up the place. Every time I saw Emily spending money, I got a pang of anxiety, but this time for once felt no worry. The good times they were a-coming.

We were home by five-thirty. As I hung up Lara's suit, I asked Emily if tonight's do would be a dress and heels affair.

'Christ, no. Shorts and bare feet.'

Shorts and bare feet it was. While she waited for Lara, Emily tapped and fidgeted distractedly. Then her face fixed on a thought.

'Look,' she said defensively. 'There's something I want to do. Don't laugh, but will you run in to Mike and tell him to come with his smudge stick?'

'I won't laugh,' I assured her earnestly, 'because I haven't a clue what you're talking about.'

'Mike, next door – beardy New Ager?'

'Oh, Bill Bryson? Go on.'

'He's always offering to banish the negative energy in here. It's called smudging. I just feel that maybe I'd have a better chance of getting good news if the house was full of positive vibes.'

I didn't laugh. Instead I felt the full force of her terror. She must be out of her mind with worry to contemplate doing something she had such contempt for.

'Will you go?'

I was happy to. Constant activity was keeping me one step ahead of myself. Sooner or later, I knew the bubble would burst and I'd be flung down hard against the ground. But not just yet. So out I went and rang next-door's bell, but no one came. I rang again, and still the door remained unanswered. Then I gave the large wind-chime which hung in the porch a smack, setting off a mad tinny jingling, but that got no response either. At this stage any sensible person would have given up, but the thing was I knew he was there. I knew he was there because I could *see* him. There was a big pane of glass in the front door, through which he was clearly visible, sitting on a floor cushion, making 'O' shapes with his thumbs and middle fingers. I'd just decided to leave and promise Emily I'd get him for her another time when I saw him get to his feet and amble to the door.

'Hi,' he smiled. 'I was finishing a meditation. Come in.'

To my surprise there was no flurry of 'Sorry to keep you waiting's. Maybe spiritual people don't apologize.

I stepped into the dim room, to be hit by a sweet smell. Rose oil? Or lavender? How would I know? In the background I could hear the plinking of more wind-chimes. From somewhere else came the rush of running water, which in any other house I'd assume was from a burst pipe – but, somehow, not here.

Dreamcatchers dangled from the windows, embroidered throws decorated the chairs, and wooden carvings – mostly of men with bulging eyes and disproportionately large penises –

hung on the walls. Every object looked like it meant something, and from the odd placing of the furniture I was prepared to bet that the place had been Feng Shuied to within an inch of its life.

'Hi, Bill,' I said.

'Mike,' he corrected, with a gentle smile.

Cripes! 'Oh, sorry, Mike. Emily sent me.'

'She'd like to be smudged?' It sounded like he'd been expecting this. 'I'll get my stick.'

The effect of the house – the smells, the sounds, even the men with the big mickeys – was immensely consoling, and as we left I said as much.

'It's a safe place,' Mike agreed, slamming the front door behind him with such force that it sent the porch wind-chime swinging away with a wild jangle. Just as quickly it was pendu-luming its way back – and heading directly for my face. Before I knew what was happening, it had delivered a smart belt to my right eye: pain shot through my socket, red exploded behind my eyelids and all I could hear was a riot of discordant notes – like a broken piano.

'Whoops. Shouldn'ta slammed the door,' Mike laughed softly. 'Y'OK?'

'Great!' I exclaimed, wondering if I'd been blinded, acting the way you have to act when you get injured in front of someone you don't know very well. Even if your head falls off you have to say things like, 'Just a scratch! Besides, I never use it much anyway!'

As it happened, I *was* fine. My eye watered a bit, then stopped. But I felt very close to tears and maybe Mike was aware of it, because he held my arm as we walked the short distance between the two houses.

Emily let us in and, clearly torn between embarrassment and vulnerability, she explained her situation.

'Sure,' Mike said cheerfully. 'Is now a good time?'

'How long will it take?'

He sucked his teeth and shook his head regretfully, just like a swizz-merchant builder would. All that was missing was a cigarette tucked behind his ear.

'Let me guess, you haven't got the parts,' I heard Emily mutter.

'Sure I have!' He waggled his stick and Emily had the good grace to pinken. 'But the energy in here is so bad one session won't clear it. But, hey! Twenty minutes now and we're ahead of the game, right?'

Intrigued, we watched him carry out his juju. Smudging appeared to involve lighting tapers, waving the stick into corners of rooms, muttering incantations and doing a type of hopping Red-Indian-on-the-Warpath dance.

'You know, you don't need me, you could do this yourself,' Mike panted at Emily, his belly rising and falling with each hop.

'Ah, I'd never get the dancing right.'

'But the dancing is optional!'

After Mike finished, he assured Emily with great kindness, 'This'll give you a fighting chance, but if they don't buy your movie, it's not the end of the world.'

'It IS the end of the world.' Emily was very firm on this.

Mike laughed gently, much the same way he had after I'd been savaged by his wind-chime. 'Be careful what you wish for – you might get it,' he said, then left, promising to drop in later with Charmaine.

Not long after, Lara arrived and Emily went out with her to buy the drink.

'Can't I come?' I asked, discovering how very reluctant I was to be left on my own.

'But you don't have a connoisseur's interest in alcohol, the way Lara and I do,' Emily said. 'And we need someone here to let people in.'

'Woman sits alone in room,' I said, resentfully. 'Unhappy. Clearly abandoned by friends.'

Lara laughed but Emily replied, 'Camera tracks her as she gets up, opens a couple of bags of peanuts and fires them into bowls in order to be helpful.'

I was sure that no one would arrive while they were out, but they'd only been gone five minutes when Troy walked in.

'Hey, Irish!'

'Young man, casually dressed,' I said.

Troy stood by the door, his poker face confused.

'Stands by door, looking confused,' I said.

'Crosses room,' Troy replied, quick as a flash. 'Notices girl has had her hair done. "Cute," he says.'

I laughed, delighted at how fast he'd got it.

His straight-line mouth quirked in acknowledgement. 'Coming right back atcha!' He threw himself into a chair, and flung his leg over the arm with loose-limbed ease. 'So how'd it go today?'

I sat on the day bed, my legs stretched out in front of me, and related everything that had happened in Mort Russell's office. All the time, Troy watched me, nodding intently when I mentioned anything good.

'Were they all lying when they said they'd read her script?' I asked.

'No. If they've seen a twelve-line résumé, they honestly think they've read it. For real.'

'So what do you think?' I finished with, keen to hear something other than Emily's negativity.

'Could be good.' But he sounded more thoughtful than hopeful. 'Could be good.'

He lapsed into faraway silence, and into the quiet I asked, 'Where do you live?'

'Hollywood.' He pronounced it 'Hoh-hollywoooood,' and spread his fingers to demonstrate sarcastically the name in lights. 'Only the name is glamorous. Sketchy neighbourhood, which means rents are low.'

'And is that far from here? I've no idea where anywhere is in relation to anywhere else in LA.'

'I'll show you.' He unfolded himself from his chair and came to balance on the bottom of the day bed.

'OK, this is the ocean.' He pointed to a cushion. 'This is Third Street Promenade, and you live here.' He jabbed at a spot on the day bed. 'Make a left on to Lincoln and drive for, oh, 'bout a mile.' He dragged his finger in a line along the fabric. 'Excuse me,' he said, as his finger bumped up on to my bare shin. 'Until you get to the freeway entrance. Take the 10, going east.' His finger did an abrupt left turn and was no longer crossing my shin, but was whizzing up to my knee. I was a little surprised, but he didn't seem to think it was a big deal, so I took my cue from him.

He paused, with his finger on my knee. 'Then when you get to downtown, you change on to the 101, going north.' Now his finger was speeding up the bare skin of my thigh. 'To Cahuenga Pass, which is about here.' He paused, his finger resting unnervingly near the top of my thigh. 'Actually, no, more like here.' He moved his finger marginally higher. 'Then,' he took a breath, his expression determinedly innocent, 'you make a right.' His

189

finger curved on to the soft, hidden skin of my inner thigh. We both looked down at his hand, then quickly looked up at each other again. 'Just for a coupla blocks.' His matter-of-fact tone was confusing. He was giving me directions, right? But his hand was between my legs.

'And I live right here.' He demonstrated his whereabouts by gently circling the tip of his finger on my tender white flesh. 'Just here,' he repeated, continuing to stroke the inside of my thigh.

'Thank you.' I was sure he could feel the heat coming at him from down there.

'You know what?' His smile was suddenly wicked. 'I live pretty near to the Hollywood Bowl, but if I showed you where it was, I bet you'd slap my face.'

It took a moment to understand what he was talking about.

'Prob'ly,' I managed, while a small, sweet spasm jumped from my Hollywood Bowl.

One final touch from his feather-light fingertip, a regretful look at my denim crotch, then he was getting to his feet. 'Do you want a beer?' he asked as he headed to the kitchen.

Tons of people came. There wasn't even time for the obligatory standing around in the empty house, looking at the acres of drink, feeling fearful and friendless, the way people usually do when they have a party.

One of the first to arrive was Nadia, Lara's new girlfriend. She was a lollipop girl, her head big with dark, swingy hair, her limbs shrunken sticks. I wasn't surprised by her sexy glamour – after all, meeting Lara had dissolved my subconscious precon- ception that all lesbians look like Elton John – but I was surprised by the instant dislike I took to her. Two seconds after

190

being introduced, she snapped gum in my face and confided loudly, 'Right this afternoon, I got me a Playboy wax. There is totally not one pube left on me!'

'Lovely!' I said, mildly mortified. 'Will you have a peanut?'

She shook her enormous head, barely drawing breath before launching into an account of how she'd had to get on her hands and knees and stick her butt high in the air so that the beautician could properly get at her. Then she'd had to lie on her back and put her ankles behind her head. They'd tell you *anything*, these Angelenos. Compulsive Disclosure Disorder, that's what they had.

Then came Justin and Desiree, who brought two jockish men and three dogs with them. They'd all become friends when they'd gone to the dog park, trying to meet girls. Next at the door was Emily's friend Connie, a short, strident, bandy-legged Korean-American: sexy the way very sure-of-themselves people are sexy. She was accompanied by her sister Debbie, her friends Philip and Tremain, and her fiancé Lewis, who barely spoke – I suppose she was such a great talker that his ability had simply atrophied. This was the first time I'd actually met Connie, and I hadn't wanted to; something to do with her imminent wedding. Emily had been my bridesmaid and she was going to be Connie's too, and I felt on the wrong side of the being-married divide. Connie had a happy future ahead of her, while my happy future was far behind me.

Tendrilly Kirsty showed up and unsettled me by making a beeline for Troy. Mike and Charmaine showed up too, as well as a load more people whom I didn't know from a plate of chips. Even David Crowe dropped in briefly, charmed his way past everyone, then left again.

'He didn't stay long,' I remarked.

'Are you kidding me?' Emily grabbed Troy away from Kirsty and ordered him, 'Tell her the joke. The agent joke.'

Deadpan, Troy began. 'Man gets a visit from the cops. "We've bad news, sir," they say. "Someone broke into your house and killed your wife and child." The man is distraught and says, "Who could do such a terrible thing?" And the cop goes, "I'm sorry to have to tell you, sir, that it was your agent." And the man says, "My agent? My agent came by my house?! Oh boy!"'

'See?' Emily said.

'I see.'

The house was full and the party had spilled out into the backyard. Somehow, in the warm, twinkly-blue night, I ended up in conversation with Troy and Kirsty. Kirsty had just been to a two-hour power yoga class and was extolling the benefits of exercise, when I said vaguely that I really should go to a gym while I was in LA. To my astonishment, Kirsty said, 'That's a neat idea.' She looked me up and down and concluded, 'You could drop, say, five, six pounds.' She swept a critical gaze from my feet to my upper arms. 'And you could use some toning. It's worth doing,' she said with utmost seriousness. 'I mean, look at me. I work out and I –' she did a little wiggle of her little hips, 'am in purr-itty good shape.'

OK, so most of it was for Troy's benefit and it was probably all true. Of course I'd be delighted if I woke up one morning and found I'd miraculously lost half a stone during the night – who wouldn't? But nevertheless, I was speechless. I'd never before come across a woman who claimed, by her own admission, to be in good shape – I thought it was simply Not Allowed. That you say it about everyone else, whether it's true or not, while berating yourself for being a hippo/heifer/Jabba the Hutt, even if you've been on the grapefruit diet for the past month.

All right, maybe it's dishonest, but it somehow seems less offensive.

In that moment, I hated Kirsty so much I wanted to hit her, and for the first time in ages I got a stab of pain up into my back tooth. Even though I'd only spoken to her to prevent her having a one-on-one with Troy, I had to get away. Muttering some excuse, I promptly got buttonholed by Charmaine.

She was nice, if a little intense. Yes, she stood just a teensy, weensy bit too close to me, and whenever I moved back a little, she moved forward a little more, until my head was almost fully immersed in a lilac bush, with only my nose peeping out, but no one's perfect. She wasn't exactly a laugh a minute, but I got the feeling she was broadly sympathetic to me, so I ended up telling her about me and Garv.

'Do you still love him?' she asked kindly.

'I don't know,' I said despairingly. 'How would I know?'

'How did you know when you were sure?'

'Dunno. It just sneaks up on you, doesn't it?'

'No one event?'

'No.' But then I remembered something. 'The snail!' I exclaimed.

'Huh?'

I explained. Garv, being a man, had been the one in charge of all insect removal: spiders in the bath, moths around lights, wasps on window-sills were all his department. I never used to lift a finger, just used to yell, 'Gaaarv, there's a wasp!' and he'd come with his rolled-up newspaper and do battle. But he had a thing about snails, a bad thing; he was so grossed out about them, he was almost phobic. And when we'd been going out about six months, a snail crawled up his car's windscreen, then settled in for what looked like a long stay. (On the driver's side, too, at eye-level just to make it worse for Garv.) A high-speed burn along the dual carriageway didn't budge it, so in the end I put on some rubber gloves, lifted it off and threw it at a passing Nissan Micra, packed with nuns. I wasn't wild about snails either, but I did it because I loved Garv, and ever since then I'd been head of snail extermination.

'So right now, would you remove a snail from his windscreen?'

'Probably not.'

'There's your answer.'

'Right.' That made me improbably sad.

Then – emboldened by drink – I made some reference to Charmaine reading auras.

'Yes,' she said.

'Do you?'

'Yes,' she repeated.

'So what's mine like?'

'Are you really sure you want to know?'

Well, after that I *really* wanted to know.

'It's a little toxic,' she said.

All of a sudden I was upset, despite the fact that I didn't actually believe that I – or anyone else, for that matter – even *had* an aura.

'Toxic – that's bad, isn't it?'

'Good and bad are just labels.'

That old cop-out.

'You should learn not to be so judgement-based,' she instructed, in a manner which sounded very judgemental.

I disentangled my head from the lilac bush and went back inside, to discover that the Goatee Boys had got wind of the knees-up. They had commandeered the stereo – replacing

Madonna with some Death Metal racket – and had formed an impromptu mosh-pit in a corner of the front room. Luis, the small, dark, pretty one, showed a great aptitude for moshing. While the others just ran straight at each other and violently bounced stomachs, Luis invested his moves with delicate steps and socket-defying hip-swervage.

To my surprise, beardy Mike was in the thick of it, having what looked like the time of his life. I suppose he had the belly for it. Every time he gave someone a good mosh, he sent them flying halfway across the room. A particularly enthusiastic bump scooted little Luis several feet and he only stopped when he crashed into a chair.

Once they'd picked him up and established that he wasn't badly hurt, they tried body surfing, passing one of them over the heads of the others, but it all fell apart when they tried to hoist Mike up and found they couldn't.

They dispersed, to reveal the shaven-headed one, Ethan, in a corner, gloomily bent over the coffee table. Because he had the most hardcore goatee – a pointy, satanic beard and a long, Zapata-style moustache that extended to his chin – I'd always thought of him as the leader of the other lads. Closer inspection revealed that he was playing with a penknife. He had his hand splayed, palm down, on the table and he was flinging the penknife at the table, aiming between his fingers. Sometimes he missed his hand but, as evidenced by the cuts between his fingers, sometimes he didn't.

'Stop it!' I exclaimed.

'It's my hand, man.'

'But it's Emily's table!'

'I'm bummed out, man.' Mournfully, he looked up at me. 'This is what I do when I'm bummed out.'

'But –' I said helplessly, worried about the table. Then I had a solution. 'If you want to self-harm, could you not try burning yourself with cigarettes?'

'Smoking, ew! Totally gross.' He sounded mortally offended.

It transpired that he was hurting because he'd tried to get off with Nadia and she'd spurned him. But as soon as I told him she was gay, he brightened. 'Yeah? For real? With Lara? Oh, wow, man. What do they do?'

Something I'd been wondering myself, actually.

'I don't know,' I said sternly. 'And leave the table alone!'

Back out to the garden to check on Troy and Kirsty. They were still talking to each other. Before I could decide how I felt, Lara and Nadia, arm in arm, skipped over to me.

'Having a good time?' Lara beamed.

'Yes . . .' I trailed off, as Nadia snaked her hand under Lara's arm and began caressing her breast.

'Hey!' Lara laughed. 'Cut that out.'

Nadia withdrew her hand but only to lick her finger and recommence stroking. Lara's erect nipple appeared through the damp cotton and I felt acutely uncomfortable. If a man did that at a party everyone would loudly condemn him as a lech and a gobshite, but because Nadia was a lesbian I had to behave as if I was totally down with it.

All night, I was aware of Kirsty talking to Troy. Even when I couldn't see them, I could sense their closeness and it didn't make me happy. So the high point of my evening was that they didn't leave together. She effed off around midnight and I was hard put not to stand in the middle of the road, roaring after her car, 'You can't be in *that* good a shape, now can you?'

Troy stayed quite a bit longer and when he finally left I

half-expected a special goodbye. But he kissed Emily and said, 'Baby girl, we'll talk,' then he kissed me in exactly the same friendly way and said, 'Night, Irish.'

Bit by bit, the crowds drained away until it was nearly just Emily and me left. While we were arranging all the bottles to be recycled, sweeping the splinters off the coffee table, wrapping broken glasses in newspaper, I blurted – the drink talking, 'I've a confession to make. I have a . . . crush.' Yes, that was the right word. 'Troy. I find him attractive.'

'Take a number and get in line.'

'Oh. It's like that?'

She pointed her finger, winked and said in an Elvis-type voice, 'Don't fall in love with me baby, 'cos I'll only break your heart.'

'Don't tell me he said that!'

'Not as such.' She seemed amused. 'It's just the way he acts. You'd swear everyone's mad about him . . . Although,' said with less certainty, 'maybe they are.'

'But he has a big nose,' I protested.

'Don't seem to bother the ladies none.'

'What ladies?'

'With Troy there are always ladies.'

'Are you talking about Kirsty?'

'Sure.'

'But do you know for a fact that there's something going on with them?'

'*Intuitively*, I know for a fact.'

Then I got it. 'Has anything ever happened with *you* and Troy?'

'Me and Troy?' She began to laugh. It started as a quite normal chuckle, then progressed to where she was leaning on the kitchen counter. 'Sorry,' she said, her face contorted with hysterics. 'It's just . . . the idea of me. Me and Troy!'

She was off again. I picked up a bin liner and started flinging cans into it.

Later, in bed, I thought about Troy. I'd been surprised, indeed almost put out, when he'd touched my leg. But now I thought about it differently. I savoured the memory, replaying it again and again. The heat of his hand running up my bare skin, the leap of desire at the moment his finger had reached the top of my thigh and turned inwards. Again. His finger reaching the top of my thigh and turning inwards, his finger reaching the top of my thigh and turning inwards . . .

A dreamy weakness began to steal through me. I'll take my chances, I thought. I've played it safe for too long. I *will* fall in love with him and he's *welcome* to break my heart.

In that halfway state between waking and sleeping, my defences slipped for a moment and in rushed thoughts of Garv and Truffle Woman and their public displays of affection.

Immediately I thought of Troy.

'Ha!' I said to myself, with sleepy defiance.

19

It must have been all that talk of falling in love, because that night I had The Dream. I'd had it on and off since I'd been eighteen: maybe once a year, perhaps not even that often, and it was nearly always the same. I'd spot Shay Delaney in a crowded street and I'd start running and pushing, trying to catch up with him. Above the January-sales throng I'd see the back of his head, moving further and faster away from me, and I'd try to go quicker, but more and more people would get in the way, tangling themselves in my legs, tripping me up, blocking my path, until he was gone.

I used to wake up swollen with longing, dreamy with re-membered love, irritable and snappy with Garv. For the entire day following the dream, these feelings would wrap themselves around me like a hangover, and it was only once they'd worn off that I worried about them. I hardly thought about Shay from one end of the year to the next, but did these dreams mean that I still loved him? That I didn't love Garv?

Consolation came via an unexpected route: a science pro-gramme I watched one bored Sunday evening, maybe eight or nine years ago. It was about the earth's relationship with the sun. The commentary said that even in the depths of winter, when our side of the earth is facing away from the sun, its draw is so powerful that we're still pulled to it. Once in a while the cold side of the earth gets its way, which is why we sometimes get days of bizarre warmth and sunniness in the middle of February.

Maybe I'd misheard it, because when I thought about it properly it didn't really make much sense, but it still operated as a consolation: a weight lifted from me and I understood that of course I loved Garv, but that there were times when I'd still be drawn back to Shay. It didn't mean anything.

But this night the dream was different, because when it started it was Shay I was running after, but at some stage he became Garv. I ran as hard after Garv as I ever had done after Shay. It was so important to catch up with him, I was tender, *sore* with love for him – that giddy, lifting wonder of when we'd first fallen in love. I *remembered*, I felt it with such clarity. But he slipped through the crowds and my legs wouldn't go fast enough, then he was gone. And I awoke with tears on my lashes, carrying years' worth of loss.

In the sunny kitchen, Emily was already up and hyper with it. 'I've been awake since six,' she announced. 'Waiting for that phone to ring!'

Oh, right, news of her pitch. The dream was still with me, so I was finding it hard to be present in the here and now. I was like a badly tuned radio which was picking up two frequencies. One in the foreground, another more ghostly one fading in and out in the background.

'But it's only nine now,' seemed to be the right thing to say. 'They're hardly likely to be at work.'

'Lazy, LAZY bastards! Anyway, Mort has David's home number – he could have called him last night or early this morning, if he was very keen. Every second that passes without news is another nail in the coffin.'

'You're being overdramatic. Is there any coffee?'

Two mugs of muscular coffee managed to shake away some of the wraiths that were wrapped around my mood, and life came into clearer focus.

'This place doesn't look bad, considering we had thirty people here last night, drinking their heads off. You'd hardly know.'

'Yeah,' said Emily. 'Apart from the souvenir on our couch.'

Oh cripes! A cigarette burn? Or had someone puked? Had anyone been that drunk? Could have been a bulimic, mind you.

'Worse,' Emily said. 'It's Ethan. I don't know how we missed him last night. I've already tried waking him up and he growled at me like a dog. Little prick.'

Sure enough, Ethan was curled up on the couch, clutching his penknife between his paw-like hands, five o'clock shadow bristling on his skull. In slumber his goateed, bemetalled face was sweet.

'That boy needs to get home to shave his head. Give him a kick,' Emily urged.

'Couldn't we just shake him?'

'More fun to kick him.'

'OK.' I tried a tentative jab on his shin, but he shifted and muttered something about nailing my motherfucking head to the table.

I looked enquiringly at Emily. 'Best leave him for a while,' we agreed over-enthusiastically. 'A young man needs his sleep. More coffee.' We headed back to the kitchen.

On top of the fridge was an open bottle of white wine that we'd missed in last night's clear-up. I noticed that a cork was still wound around the corkscrew. That could be used to seal the bottle for later.

'Pass me the sesame,' I said to Emily.

A long stare from Emily, and a bottle of sesame oil arrived in front of me. I looked at it, realized what I'd done, and saw that she was already subjecting me to an are-you-quite-sane examination.

'What d'you want sesame oil for? To stir-fry your raisin bran?'

'Ah no, I meant can you pass me the corkscrew.'

'That's not what you said. You said "sesame". Unless I'm going mad, and I'm really not in the mood for that.'

I contemplated lying – it'd be easy enough to convince her she was halfway around the bend – but saw how unkind that would be. 'It's just a word. That Garv and I used to say,' I explained, awkwardly. 'When we opened a bottle of wine, we'd say "Open Sesame". So the corkscrew got called "sesame". I'm sorry, I forgot.'

'Is that why you keep putting my toothpaste on my toothbrush for me every night? It's something you and Garv did?'

'Wh-at?' I stuttered.

'Every night since you've got here,' she said patiently, 'after you've gone to bed, I've gone to the bathroom and my toothbrush is waiting, with toothpaste on it. If you're not doing it, then who is?'

I had to admit it. 'It is me. I hadn't realized I was doing it. I can't believe it.'

'And it's something you and Garv did?'

'Yeah. Whichever one of us went to bed first would get the toothbrush ready for the other person.'

'That's the sweetest thing I ever heard,' Emily glowed, then quickly quenched it when she saw my face.

The grief I'd felt when I'd woken up was back. I was carrying the full weight of a lost language and all the rituals that would mean nothing to anyone else, but were part of whatever had bound Garv and me together. And there were loads of them: when he made my dinner and put it on the table, I had to rush into the room and declare, 'I came as soon as I heard!' And if I forgot, he'd withhold the nosh and prompt me, 'Say it. Go on – I came as soon as I heard!'

Trying to explain why that was funny or comforting would be like trying to describe colour to a blind person. Not that I'd ever have to, because now it was all gone. An entire way of life.

Clearly, I was pumping out waves of regret, because Emily urged, 'It's OK to say it.'

'Say what?'

'That you miss him. Even *I* miss him.'

'OK,' I sighed. 'I miss him.'

But I missed more than him. I missed me. I missed the way it used to be, when I didn't have to pretend to be anything other than me. Now there were all these people around, and I was tired of having to act. Even with Emily I wasn't as fully me as I once was with Garv. And it showed up in the smallest of things, like the telly being on too loud. With Garv I'd just roar at him and he'd turn it down, but with Emily I had to keep my mouth shut and burn holes in the lining of my stomach instead.

'I had a dream,' I announced. I sounded like Martin Luther King.

'Tell me,' Emily said, then thought to add, 'Marty.'

'Well, you know the plot already.'

'Is this the Shay Delaney dream?'

'Yes, and it started with me running after Shay, but he turned into Garv.' I described the frantic running, the desperate need to catch up with him, the terror as he slipped further and further away, the bereft grief when I understood that he was gone. 'So, go on,' I ended. 'Make me feel better.'

Emily's very good at that sort of thing.

'We process things in our dreams that we're not able to in our waking hours,' she said. 'You were married for nine years, of course you feel shite. The end of any relationship is a wrench. I mean, even after I've been going with someone for three months, I feel suicidal when it's over. Unless I ditch them. Then I'm over the moon.'

I was beginning to feel a good deal more normal, then Emily ruined it all by asking, 'Is there any chance, though, that maybe you and Garv could try again?'

The room seemed to darken.

'I know he's had an affair,' Emily said.

'Having,' I corrected. 'He's *having* an affair.'

'It could be over, for all you know.'

'I don't care. The damage is done. I'd never be able to trust him again.'

'But it could be worked out – other people have done it.'

'I don't want to. Since February . . . I can't describe it, Emily. It was like . . . like being locked in a car boot with him.'

'Jesus!' she said, startled at my imagery. I was quite startled myself, to be honest. I'm not normally good at that sort of thing.

'A car boot that was shrinking,' I added, just to outdo myself.

Emily gasped, her hands to her throat. 'I can't breathe!'

'That's exactly how I felt,' I said thoughtfully. 'Anyway, I'm just having a bad day . . . Another one,' I added.

'Let it go, man,' a dopey voice interrupted. It was Ethan, leaning against the door frame, clearly enthralled. 'If it don't come back, it was never yours. If it comes back, it's yours to keep.'

204

'Out!' Emily ordered, her arm straight, her finger pointing. 'We've enough armchair philosophers around here.'

As he loped to the door, Emily checked the time again. 'David has *got* to be at his desk by now!'

And he was – but he couldn't really tell her anything. As was his way, he made positive noises. 'They really loved you!' But she wanted hard news. A yes or no. Are they in or are they out? And he couldn't tell her.

'He's scared,' she surmised, hanging up the phone.

'Why would he be scared?' I forced joviality.

''Cos this town runs on fear. If Hothouse pass, it'll reflect badly on him and his lousy judgement in backing a loser. Makes him a loser by association.'

Food for thought. I'd always thought of agents as kind of impartial catalysts. Middlemen who brought people together but who remained unaffected by the process. I'd been wrong.

'And Mort Russell is probably scared that if he buys it, the head of the studio mightn't like it,' she continued gloomily. 'And scared that if he *doesn't* buy it, someone else might and make a hit of it. Meanwhile, I'm fucking terrified that *no one* will buy it. How do you feel, Maggie?'

I checked my anxiety levels. Same as they always were. 'Scared stiff.'

'Welcome to Hollywood.'

A ring on the doorbell had us making enquiring faces at each other. Emily nearly broke her neck skidding across the floor, spurred on by visions of Mort Russell standing on her doorstep holding a your-worries-are-over cheque.

But it wasn't Mort Russell, it was Luis, one of the Goatee Boys. Up until now, they'd only existed for me as a blur of interchangeable facial hair, but at last night's party they'd come into separate focus. There were indeed only three of them. Ethan: big, meaty and shaven-headed. Curtis: blondy, balding, plumpish, with the least impressive goatee of the lot. It was wispy and flyaway, as though he'd been crawling under a bed and had got a load of fluff stuck to his chin. I found something slightly odd about him, but that might just have been because Ethan had told me that in high school Curtis had been voted pupil 'Most likely to go postal in a public place with an automatic weapon.'

And, standing in front of me, Luis. Neat, pretty – and polite! He'd come to thank us for the party and to invite us over for dinner some time. He claimed to be an excellent cook – a result, apparently, of his Columbian heritage. 'Call by whenever,' he invited.

'Sure.' Emily brusquely closed the door.

'Don't you want to?' I asked.

She rolled her eyes at me. 'Oh, come on!'

Muttering something about being thirty-three and not fifteen, she grabbed the phone and spent several unbroken hours on it, hopping from call waiting to call waiting, discussing the pitch, having the same conversation again and again, speculating and, in effect, saying nothing.

I could have gone to the beach or reverse-shopping – I'd decided to return the embroidered denim skirt, because when I tried it on at home it made my knees look funny – but instead I listlessly watched a telly evangelist, weighed down by the return of my earlier, regret-filled mood. I thought about Garv. He'd had a lot of good points. But then again, plenty of bad points. They ping-ponged around so much in my head that in the end I grabbed one of Emily's yellow pads and wrote them all down.

List of Good things about Garv

1. Understanding exchange rates and the plots of thrillers.
2. Having a lovely, tiny bottom. (It was really gorgeous, especially in combats.)
3. Thinking I am the most beautiful woman on the planet. (Though he probably doesn't any more.)
4. Seeing the good in everyone. (Except for my family.)
5. Doing his own ironing.
6. Bringing me to jazz concerts and such like, to further my cultural education.

List of Bad things about Garv

1. Bringing me to jazz concerts and such like, to further my cultural education.
2. Loving football and being proud of me because he thinks I understand the offside rule. (I don't.)
3. The electric blanket business, obviously.
4. And the way he was about my hair.
5. Not talking to me about Things. (I know all men refuse to talk about Things and shrug, 'Ah sure, we're grand,' when a nine-year marriage is falling apart, but it still distressed me.)
6. Sleeping with other women.

But my childish list of facts made no impact on my gloom. I still felt spooked – heavy with sorrow and a hope-flattening sense that I was a failure. That I was a mess and my life was a mess. And my future was a mess. And my past was *definitely* a mess.

Realizing that the day was shaping up to be a write-off, I

took a towel out to the backyard for a spot of sunbathing, and within seconds I was mercifully asleep.

I awoke choking on a jet of water – the sprinklers had started – and came back inside to find Emily still on the phone. She was getting directions from someone. 'Oh, I know it. The block where all the plastic surgeons are? Right.' She hung up. 'Coming out for dinner tonight?'

'Who'll be there?' I tried to sound casual.

'Lara, Nadia, Justin, Desiree, you and me.'

No Troy?

'Troy's got to work,' she said kindly, sensing my unasked question. 'He's meeting some producer guy. And you know what he's like about his work.'

I didn't, but anyway. I was disappointed – and still no word from Mort Russell. Although, while I'd been asleep, Helen had phoned. I was touched by her concern. Until I discovered there wasn't any. All she'd done was try to discuss sexy surfers with Emily. 'And she wouldn't believe me when I said I didn't know any!'

As we drove through the dazzling evening to Beverly Hills, we came upon a little commotion outside a mini-mall. Two boys were being arrested. They had their hands on the roof of the black and white and one officer was frisking them, while another swung handcuffs, ready for use. I'd never before seen someone being arrested. It gave me a little living-on-the-edge thrill, of which I was immediately ashamed.

The restaurant was mostly outdoors, the tables beneath a pretty green and white striped awning, separated from the street by a white trellis. Nadia and Lara were already waiting at our street-side table. As Emily and I wove through the tables to get to them, I felt there was something slightly odd about the place, but I couldn't put my finger on it until Justin arrived, Desiree trotting by his side.

'Thanks a lot, guys.' Thin-lipped and high-pitched, Justin chided Lara and Nadia. 'You invite me to a dyke restaurant. I could get lynched.'

And then I realized what was so strange: the clientele were all women. Justin was literally the only man. Suddenly the open staring, the two winks and the one wide smile I'd received all made sense. And I was beset with anxiety; had I been wrong to wink back? Giddily, Nadia 'fessed up that coming here had been her idea. 'I love this place. Isn't it the greatest?'

'The greatest,' Justin muttered, mortified. 'Let's eat.' As he perused the menu, every now and again he flashed an 'I'm just an expendable fat guy, you have nothing to fear from me' look about the place, but he couldn't relax.

We ordered, everyone except me asking for things that either weren't on the menu or for the menu description to be customized. It seemed to be the LA way to be as awkward as possible in restaurants. Then, just as I was about to tuck into my dinner, my fork froze in my hand as I saw something that didn't fit with the rest of the world. A woman, her entire head and face swaddled in bandages, was being led along the sidewalk by a young, great-haired babe. As they got closer, we could hear the girl murmuring tenderly, 'OK, Mom, there's a step coming up. Two more steps, then down again. OK, here's the car.'

They stopped at a four-wheel drive parked only a few yards from our table. In silence, we watched the woman stand blind and passive, waiting for the car door to be opened.

'What happened to her?' I muttered queasily. 'She looks like a burns victim.'

209

Instantly I was fixed with indulgent smiles all round. Even Desiree's liquid eyes looked kindly and amused.

'Plastic surgery,' Lara said, *sotto voce*. 'Looks like she got her whole head lifted.'

'Really?'

'Sure.'

But why not? LA was a shrine to beauty and every paper I opened urged me to GET those saddlebags sucked conveniently away, HAVE every hair on my body burnt off with a laser, DEFINE those blurry cheekbones with no-fuss collagen injections. (And who CARES if after six months the collagen slips down to your chin and you look like the ELEPHANT man and you have to have LIPOSUCTION on your COLLAGEN?)

'Take it easy, Mom.' Gently the woman was being guided into the passenger seat, but she didn't lower her head enough and managed to bump her face on the door surround. A little squawk escaped the mouth slit and a spontaneous flinch rippled through the entire restaurant. Everyone had stopped eating.

Then the woman was in. As her daughter scooted round to the driver's side, she sat in her four-wheel drive, looking like *Return of the Mummy*. I had to be careful about slagging off plastic surgery, what with Lara's fake jugs, but what *must* that face be like under those bandages? A raw steak? I couldn't help wincing, 'It looks barbaric.'

'Hey!' Lara playfully shook my arm. 'Don't faint on us. She's happy. She'll spend a couple of days in bed, then she'll have a launch party for her new face.'

'What about her daughter?' I don't really know what I meant by that. I just thought it must be terrible for her to see her mother in such a state.

'Don't worry about her!' Emily comforted. 'She'll be OK

soon. At Beverly Hills High they get nose jobs for their sixteenth birthday present!'

'I got a nose job,' Nadia announced proudly. 'Not just for me, but so my kid will be born with, like, a totally great nose.'

A paralysed silence descended. Desiree actually got down off her seat and trotted away. Lara smiled at me but she looked a little sick.

'What? WHAT?' Nadia had picked up on the atmosphere and was looking from one of us to the next. 'What'd I say?'

Then, 'Oh, I get it. It's because I'm gay. You think gay women can't have children. Well, get over yourselves.'

'Sperm donors!' Emily declared and conversation erupted, a bit too enthusiastically.

20

There was something I'd forgotten to put on my list of bad things about Garv. Now, what was it? Putting empty orange-juice cartons back in the fridge? Pronouncing 'certainly' as 'certintly'?

No, it wasn't either of those, it was:

7. Wanting to have children when I was afraid of it.

Claire had been bang on the money when she'd remarked that the rabbits were almost as much trouble as children. Of *course* Garv's fondness for Hoppy and Rider was something to do with wanting children. Even an amateur psychologist who'd failed all his amateur psychologist's exams could have figured that one out. And I sort of knew it myself, even if I did my very best *not* to know.

Before Garv and I got married, we'd discussed the subject and decided that, while we both wanted children, we also wanted a few years on our own first. That suited me fine, because at twenty-four I felt too young to be a mother. (Even though I knew other twenty-four-year-olds had lots of kids; the only explanation I could come up with was that I was immature.)

The thing was – and I'd have been the first to admit it – I was terrified by the thought of having a baby. And I wasn't the only one. Most of my friends were of the same mind, and we spent many happy hours perplexed by the notion of natural childbirth. Occasionally a horror story was produced about some girl – a distant cousin, someone one of us worked with, no one too like *us*, if you know what I mean – who'd recently had a baby without pain relief. Or stories of nice, normal women who'd had epidurals lined up for months, but who got to the hospital too late and had to have an eight and a half pound baby without so much as a junior aspirin to take the edge off the agony. Such conversations usually came to an abrupt conclusion by someone begging, 'Stop! I'm going to black out!'

But the ink was barely dry on my marriage certificate before both Garv's and my parents mounted a round-the-clock Pregnancy Watch. Soft cheeses were whipped away from in front of me. If I so much as belched (not that I ever dared to in front of his mum and dad), it generated a Mexican wave of pleased, knowing eyebrow raises. When I ate a dodgy mussel and spent two wretched days lying on the bathroom floor, they were practically knitting bootees. Their expectations made me feel panicky – and resentful. Just because I'd never stepped out of line before didn't mean that, just to please them, I was going to start dropping sprogs like I was shelling peas.

'They can't help it,' Garv said. 'It's just because we're the first one in each family to get spliced. Humour them.'

'Will it all be OK?' I asked anxiously, bothered by visions of my in-laws holding me down and forcibly impregnating me with a turkey baster.

'It'll all be OK,' he reassured.

'Everything?'

'Everything.'

'*Everything* everything?' (You know the way you can get, sometimes.)

'Everything everything.'

And I believed him. Broodiness, I was sure, was one of those things that belonged Sometime in My Future. A change that automatically occurred with the passage of time; like all of a sudden wanting to sit down in pubs, when standing up, being goodnaturedly pushed and shoved, had been fine – indeed *enjoyable* – for years. I'd watched it happen to other people – I saw no reason why it wouldn't happen to me.

We hadn't been married long when we moved to Chicago, and suddenly I was studying at night and we were both working very long hours, trying to get a toehold on our respective career ladders. Having children would have been out of the question; we'd barely have had the time or energy to conceive the poor creature, never mind take care of it.

Then, astonishing news came from London: Claire was pregnant. On the one hand, it was a blessing because my mother would have her longed-for grandchild and the pressure would be off me. But on the other hand, I felt peculiarly usurped. It was Claire's job to reduce my parents to hand-wringing despair; it was my job to please them. All of a sudden, she's puking day and night and cutting my most-well-behaved-daughter's legs out from under me.

And Claire had been one of the greatest party animals of our time, so what had prompted the decision to have a baby? I asked her, hoping she'd confide that James, her husband, had said it was a good tax break. (That's the kind of man James was. It was a godsend when he had the affair and left her.) But the hardest fact she could come up with was that it 'felt right'. This I liked the sound of: if it 'felt right' for a wild woman like Claire, the time would definitely come when it would 'feel right' for me.

A few days before Claire's due date, I happened to be in London for one day's work. It was months since I'd seen her, what with me living in Chicago, and when she collected me from the tube station I barely recognized her. She was enormous, easily the most pregnant person I'd ever seen – and she was proud, excited and mad keen to involve me in the whole process. The minute we got back to the flat, she ordered gleefully, 'Look at me, I'm HUGE!' Then she whipped up her sweatshirt and gave me a full frontal.

I was delighted for her happiness, but as I looked at her gigantic, blue-veined belly, I felt a little squeamish at the thought that there was a human being in there. But what made me even more squeamish was that it had to get out, through an orifice which it was clearly far, far too big for.

I found myself wondering just what *had* Mother Nature been thinking of? The process of gestation and giving birth was definitely one of her poorer ideas – the biological equivalent of being painted into a corner.

However, one of the plus sides of being around a heavily pregnant woman was that her flat was full of food. Cravings food – an old biscuit tin was an Aladdin's cave of different chocolate bars, and there was a freezer crammed with ice-cream.

We parked ourselves before the biscuit tin and ate our fill (this took some time), then we were ready to lie on her bed and watch telly. But before we did so, Claire pulled off her sweatshirt. And why not? It was her home. And why should she have a problem undressing in front of me? I mean, I'm her *sister*. But as I stretched my neck to see over her bump to the screen (put it this way, if it had been a subtitled programme we'd been watching, I wouldn't have had a clue what was going on), I tried to blank out the colossal belly which rose, like Ayers Rock, from her body. I began to wish we lived in Victorian times. Modesty, there's a lot to be said for it.

'I shouldn't have eaten that second-last Bounty. The baba's got the hiccups,' she said tenderly. And indeed, before my aghast eyes, her bump convulsed with rhythmic twitches. 'Do you want to feel?' she said. If she had asked me if I'd like to stick my hand in a blender I'd have been as enthusiastic – *more*, probably – but I couldn't think of any way to refuse without giving offence.

I produced my hand and let it be guided, and when she placed it on her stomach a shudder shot up my arm to my scalp. I couldn't help it. I'd have preferred to take the giblets out of a turkey.

She passed my palm over something bumpy. 'Feel that? That's her head,' Claire said, and it was all I could do to suppress a whimper.

Then, as if I wasn't finding things hard enough, Claire remarked idly, 'She could come at any minute.'

Sweat popped on to my forehead. *Not tonight, God*, I prayed. *Please God, don't let her come tonight.*

Claire had always sworn that if she was ever 'unlucky enough' (her words) to have to give birth, she'd start mainlining heroin the minute her waters broke. But when I tentatively enquired how many lines of defence she'd prepared for her fight against labour pains – Pethidine? Epidurals? Heroin? – she shook her head and said, 'Nada.' My horror must have been stamped on my face, because she roared laughing and explained, 'Having this baba is the most exciting thing that's ever happened to me! I want to be fully present for it.'

Clearly she'd gone over to the Dark Side – which I found strangely consoling. If someone like Claire could be contemplating a natural birth, then there was great hope for a scaredy cat like me.

All the same, the following morning I was awake and dressed a full hour before I needed to leave, and not even the charms of the biscuit tin could persuade me to linger. Claire wandered around the flat yawning and muttering to herself, 'I'm ready to pop.' Eventually, she lumbered to the car to drive me to the Tube, and when I saw the underground station, relief made me light-headed. Long before the car had come to a halt, I had the passenger door open and my foot on the road, sparks flying from my heel.

As I leapt out, I blurted, 'Thanks for all the chocolate and good luck with the excruciating agony of childbirth.'

I hadn't meant to say that. I tried again. 'Er, good luck with the labour.'

She had the baby two days later, and no matter how hard I tried, she wouldn't admit that it had hurt that much. It was around then that I realized there was some sort of conspiracy afoot. Whenever I tried pumping any woman who'd had a baby for specifics on agony, pain relief etc., they wouldn't play ball. Instead they just said dreamily, 'Ah yeah, I suppose it stung a bit, but afterwards you've got a baby. I mean, a BABY. You've created a new life, it's miraculous!'

I expected that the passage of time would take care of my fear, that I'd grow out of it. So what I did was I told myself I'd have a child when I was thirty. Partly, I suspect, because I thought thirty was so far away it would never come.

21

'As the crisis in Santa Monica moves into its second day . . .' I woke with my usual horrible jolt to the sound of Emily talking to herself, '. . . conditions inside the house are bad. Morale is low among the hostages . . .'

So I could take it that Mort Russell hadn't arrived in the middle of the night, with a contract under his oxter.

But shortly after I got up, someone rang. Someone who caused Emily to giggle a lot and wind her finger in her hair while talking to him. It was Lou, the guy she'd met at the dinner party where the organ-collecting bloke had been her date.

'I'm going on a date with him tonight,' she said, when she finally hung up. 'He's taken nearly two weeks to call, he's given me no notice, but I don't care. I'm going to go out with him, have sex with him, then never hear from him again. That,' she said with satisfaction, 'will take my mind off Mort Russell not calling!'

I was staring out the window.

'What are you looking at?' she asked.

'Curtis. He's after getting stuck again.' I stared a while longer. 'They're calling us to help.'

'Oh, for God's sake!'

After we'd helped dislodge Curtis – this time he'd been trying to get out of the car, not in – we returned home. I'd half-planned to spend the morning taking a turn around the Santa Monica mall – my knees still looked funny in the denim skirt – until I saw Emily producing an armload of cleaning products from under the sink and pulling on rubber gloves. Housework! What with staying with her rent-free and all that, I felt obliged to help. Or at least to offer and hope she said no. But to my disappointment she said, 'If you wouldn't mind, the floor could do with a wash.'

Ah well, it'd be good exercise for me. As I filled a bucket with floor cleaner and water, Emily sighed, 'Thanks. Conchita is coming on Monday. I like to have things nice for her.'

'Who's Conchita?'

'My cleaning lady. Comes every fortnight. Goes mad if the place isn't clean.'

There was no need to challenge this piece of seeming illogicality. I don't know anyone who doesn't clean up before their cleaning person comes. I started mopping my way across the wooden floor and was working up a good satisfying sweat when the front door opened and in came Troy.

'Right across my nice clean floor,' I scolded.

'Whoops! Sorry.' He laughed softly but there was an urgency about him. 'Guess what?!'

'What?' Emily had appeared.

'Cameron Myers!'

Cameron Myers was a box-office heart-throb. Young and pretty.

'What about him?'

'You know I met with Ricky the producer last night? Well, I'm in his house, and Cameron Myers pays him a visit! Turns out Ricky's an old buddy of Cameron's. But this is the best bit. I tell Cameron my name and he says, "Didn't you direct

Free-Falling?"' A quick aside to me – 'That was my first movie, Irish. Then he says that it rocked!'

Emily went hysterical and I did my best to match her, but Troy silenced us. 'It gets better. Today's his birthday and he's taken the penthouse in the Freeman to hang with his homies tonight. And this is where it gets *real* good – he told me to drop by! And bring a date!'

Anticipation began to stack up inside me. I felt my shoulders tense and my whole body move forward . . .

'So how about it, Emily? You might get to meet some people. Sorry, Irish,' he lifted his arms helplessly, 'I only get to bring one person.'

The sensation of defeat was acute, but in an unexpected reversal of fortune Emily was shaking her head. 'I can't come. Got me a date.'

'A date?' Troy stared at her, then revealed his perfect teeth in an amazed laugh. 'Who *is* this guy, that you're turning down Cameron Myers' birthday party for?'

'No one special, but I'm burnt out from all this movie stuff.'

Troy gave her an enquiring look and Emily turned her mouth down apologetically. 'Maybe I'm just not tough enough for this town.'

A few seconds of silence, then Troy concluded, 'Or maybe you just need a day off.'

'Thanks,' she said, with weary relief. 'Why don't you bring Maggie tonight?'

'Would you come with me?' He sounded surprised, even humble – which in turn surprised, then touched me.

'Yes.'

'You mean you'd come out with me alone?'

If you'll do that thing on my leg again. Except, of course, I didn't say it.

'Emily hasn't warned you about me?' Now he was joking. And flirting. 'I am baaaaaad news.'

'I'll risk it,' I said, wishing I didn't sound so prim.

'Great.'

'What's Cameron Myers like?' I asked.

'Mmmm,' Troy said thoughtfully. His eyes roamed across the ceiling while he contemplated. 'Let's see. What's Cameron like?' The searching silence endured a good time longer, then finally Troy decided. 'Short! I'll pick you up at eight.'

As soon as the door had closed behind him, all my hope and fear was distilled to one sentence. 'I've got to get my hair blow-dried.'

But I didn't know Dino's address. Besides, I couldn't afford him.

'Go down to the corner to Reza,' Emily said. 'She's as mad as a brick, but she'll do in an emergency.'

I hurried to the end of the street, where a small hairdresser's was sandwiched between the Starbucks and the surveillance-equipment shop. The salon was empty save for a magnificent, exotic-looking woman of indeterminate age. Brick-mad Reza? Very dyed black hair bouffed to her shoulderblades and many gold chains nestled in her wrinkled but full décolletage. She glared, as if mortally insulted, when I asked if she had a free appointment, then surprised me by saying, 'Now!'

'No?' Had I misheard?

'No! Now!'

'Um . . . great.'

'I am Reza,' she declared.

'Maggie.'

I explained that I wanted my hair to be smooth, full and shiny. Reza bunched her blackberry lips and said, in an interesting accent, 'You have this bad hair. Fat . . . ?' With expanding hand gestures she sought the right word.

'Thick?' I offered.

'Coarse!' she concluded triumphantly. 'Very bad. The worst kind. Is very hard work to get this bad hair shiny. But I am strong!'

Excellent.

The wash she gave me was so thorough I'm surprised that she didn't draw blood with her nails. 'Strong hands,' she grinned grimly, then proceeded to give me whiplash as she vigorously towel-dried.

As she revved up the dryer – for some reason making me think of a logger about to cut down a tree with a chainsaw – she asked from which godforsaken place did I hail, to end up with such dreadful hair.

'Ireland.'

'Iowa?'

'No, Ireland. A country in Europe.'

'Europe,' she said dismissively. She might as well have said, 'Pah!'

'And where are you from?'

'Persia, but we are not bullsheet Persian. We are Bahai. We don't mess with the bullsheet politics, we love everyone. NO!' She turned to yell at a girl who had appeared at the door. 'No appointment today! We are FULL UP!'

Crushed, the girl disappeared, and without missing a beat, Reza turned back to me. 'We give all peoples their respect. Rich, poor, black, white. Hold your stupid head! You have this BAD hair!'

More than once in the next half-hour my ear lay flat against my shoulder, as she tugged and pulled the coarseness from my hair. Finally, my neck feeling as though it had been pummelled by a baseball bat, Reza switched off the dryer and turned me to the mirror. 'You see.' She couldn't hide her pride. 'Is good. I am strong!'

And my hair *was* nice. Except for my fringe. However she'd managed it, it was almost circular, as if it had been wrapped around a sausage roll. But I saw no point in mentioning it, she would have just laid the blame at the feet of my bad, fat hair.

Then came the delicate matter of payment and she was surprisingly expensive. Perhaps it was extra for hair as terrible as mine.

'OK,' I sighed, proffering my Visa card – which she energetically spurned. 'Bullsheet credit cards,' she muttered. 'Only cash.'

Then came more muttering about 'Bullsheet IRS,' and I passed her some notes and left.

I made my way home pressing my fringe against my forehead, and had the bad luck to be spotted by Ethan, who opened a window and yelled, 'Hey, Maggie! Your bangs look kinda weird.'

Within seconds all three of the boys were on the street, examining me.

'You look like Joan Crawford,' Curtis concluded.

'And your goatee looks like candy floss, only I'm too polite to say it,' I replied. Before I even had time to be appalled at my crassness, they all ROARED laughing, and already Luis had a plan to help me.

'You gotta flatten the hair and keep it flat. Come inside.'

One of the features of this strange post-Garv time was that I seemed to have no power to resist doing things I didn't want to do. I found myself accompanying them into their dim, smelly

223

house and letting Luis ease a pair of tights on to my head, the waistband snug around my fringe. The only saving grace was that they were new tights, straight out of the packet. Ethan told me they kept such stuff on the premises in case any of them got lucky with a girl.

'Keep them on until you have to go out tonight,' Luis advised.

I thanked the three of them – I mean, what else could I do? – and carried on home, the legs of the tights dangling down my back. When I let myself in, Emily looked up from her laptop and remarked, 'Jesus, Reza has lost it altogether.'

And still no word from Mort Russell. Emily abandoned her writing and, humming calmly to herself, pottered around the house, polishing the mirrors, doing her nails. Now and then she rounded on the phone and shrieked, 'Ring, you fucker! Ring, RING, RING!!!!!' Then it was back to the humming.

Meanwhile, I was fretting about what to wear to the party and wondering if I should race down to Santa Monica to try and find something, but I was all too aware of the first law of shopping and knew I hadn't a hope.

'How about that new embroidered denim skirt?' Emily suggested.

'I can't, it makes my knees look funny.'

'No, it doesn't.'

'Yes, it does.'

'Try it on and show me.'

'Come into my room.'

Twenty-nine seconds later, a perplexed Emily was forced to admit, 'Christ, it does. I don't know how. Normally your knees look fine.'

She began rooting through the suitcase on the floor, looking at my clothes and commenting, 'That's a lovely skirt . . . I've that T-shirt in pink.' Then she paused and groaned, 'God, these are gorgeous.' I looked. She'd found my turquoise sandals and was pulling them out from under a pile of socks. 'Gorgeous. And they're new. Look, the price-sticker is still on them. How come you've never worn them?'

'Just waiting for the right occasion.'

'Which I believe might be this evening.'

'Ah, no,' I swallowed. 'Not tonight.' At her sharp look, I explained, 'They're high and uncomfortable. I want to be relaxed this evening.'

I wasn't sure she really believed me, but she let it go.

In a mutation of the laws of physics, the day was interminable, but it also went far too fast. Each individual second endured for quite some time, yet all of a sudden it was five-thirty – too late to get news. Emily spoke to David, who said that Hothouse were obviously taking the script seriously, that the time-lag indicated that Mort was discussing it with his bosses. But Emily wasn't reassured.

'He didn't get enough of a buzz going,' she said sadly. 'I've seen what happens when the hype works. The agent rings the executive in the morning and fires him up so much that he's shelled out two million dollars by lunch-time. Often without having even seen the script.'

'I don't believe you.'

'Honest to God. I can give you four separate instances where a studio paid shedloads without having read a single word. The agent offered them a one-hour window to make a pre-emptive bid. They all came through – too terrified of someone else getting the chance.'

'But what if it's a bad script?'

'It often is, but by the time the studio discover they've paid two million dollars for a dog, it's too late. The writer's sunning himself in the Caribbean and is already on his next project.'

'That's insane.'

'It's an insane kind of town. Anyway, might as well try and enjoy my weekend,' she said sensibly. Then she put her face in her hands and screeched, 'I can't fucking BEAR this.' She emerged with a shaky smile. 'Just taking a moment. Right, where's my make-up bag? C'm'ere till I do your face.'

'But you've to get ready for your date.'

'Ah, it's as easy to do two people as it is to do one. And it's not every night you go to a movie star's birthday party in the penthouse of LA's most fabulous hotel.'

When she put it like that . . . 'Look, are you *sure* you don't want to go?'

'Quite. There's a good chance I'll get laid tonight. A bird in the hand and all that. Are you sure *you* want to go? You don't seem very thrilled.'

She was right. Going to Cameron Myers' birthday party was dream-come-true stuff and I wasn't as fizzy as I should be. As I once would have been. I felt ashamed of myself. The only time I'd come close to feeling any real excitement lately had been at Emily's pitch – and I was starting to wonder if I'd been mistaken about it.

'I just don't seem to be great at enjoying myself at the moment. Everything, even the brilliant stuff, is a bit flat.'

'You're depressed. This whole thing has really taken its toll on you. Naturally enough.'

'The part I'm most looking forward to is going out with Troy,' I admitted.

'It's great you're his date,' she agreed. 'He might have asked Kirsty otherwise.'

'That bitch!' I exclaimed. 'I never told you what she said to me at the party . . .'

I related the story, while Emily did her usual stunt with the make-up and hair slides and stuff. I ended up wearing the same black dress I'd worn to Dan Gonzalez's bash – I'd nothing else – but Emily did something to me with a chiffon neck-scarf and said my look was 'very Halston'. Then came the moment of truth: we finally removed the tights from my head – and my fringe was as flat as Holland. I owed those boys.

At half-seven, as Emily clacked out the door, a fragrant, glittery vision, she paused and turned back to me. 'Just in case you were thinking . . . about Troy. A word of advice. Human Teflon.'

'That's two words.'

'Wonderful to have around, but . . . he's non-stick. Enjoy yourself, but don't expect anything. Promise?'

I promised, then promptly forgot about it. I had to take my enjoyment where I could find it.

22

The Freeman was new, the most glamorous hotel in a town crammed with glamorous hotels. We could hardly get into the noisy lobby, so jammers was it with people meeting for drinks, waiting for dinner and tripping over sculptures. Everyone was astonishingly good-looking – and most of them were staff. It took a long time to get anyone's attention – like Troy muttered, they hadn't been hired for their ability – but eventually we were directed to a special elevator, which was policed by two bouncers who frisked us for cameras and tape-recorders.

The elevator shot us straight to the top floor, playing havoc with my already swoopy stomach. And when the lift doors opened, straight into the penthouse, I nearly got snowblindness. It was all white. White walls, white carpet, white tables and huge, white-leather sofas. I got a fright to see a disembodied blonde head floating in mid-air above one of the couches – then I realized it was just a girl whose white-leather catsuit had merged in with the white leather of the couch.

Troy and I stepped reticently from the lift and exchanged a nervous smile. 'Where's Cameron?' he murmured.

I looked around: there were only about a dozen people there, but never had I seen such a condensed distillation of gorgeousness. It was like walking into an episode of *Beverly Hills 90210* – girls displaying lots of bare, tanned, toned flesh and boys with square teeth and noticeably well-cut hair, all laughing and holding Martini glasses. *What on earth am I doing here?*

This impression intensified when my sweep across the room landed on Cameron Myers. And I have to say that, despite my excitement-facility not operating at full capacity, I did go a bit dizzy and starstruck, as though a plane had flown just two inches over my head. He was on his knees in front of a plain white hole in the wall, a very modern fireplace.

'Hey!' He scrambled to his feet when he saw Troy – and I must admit he did look much shorter and dinkier than he does on screen. 'You came!'

'Happy birthday, man. Thanks for inviting us. This is Maggie.'

'Hello.'

I was almost on a level with Cameron Myers' perfect symmetrical face, with the white-blond hair, the blue, blue eyes, and the tight, evenly tanned skin. He was nearly as familiar to me as one of my family, and yet . . .

Wait till I tell them back home. They'll never believe me.

I realized I was staring, so I shoved four orange orchids at him. 'These are for you.'

He seemed genuinely touched. 'You brought me flowers!'

'But it's your birthday.' I gestured at the room. 'I'm sorry they're not white.'

He laughed a sweet laugh and I had the urge to pick him up under my arm, start sprinting and not stop until I had him safely locked in a cage. He was so cute, like a puppy.

'There's frosty drinks in the kitchen. Help yourselves.'

'I'll get them,' Troy said, and headed off across the room, leaving me alone with Cameron Myers.

'Hey, do you know how to do this?' He gestured helplessly at the instant-fire packets at his feet.

'Er . . . yes, it's easy.'

'I love a real fire. It's kinda homey. Will you help me?'

What could I say? It was July. It was Los Angeles. It was eighty degrees out there. But he was Cameron Myers and he wanted a fire.

'OK.'

Once the fire was crackling brightly and Cameron had rung down for marshmallows, Troy handed me a Martini, murmured, 'How about this place,' and took me on a walkabout. It was huge. The 'reception room' (as they say) must have been sixty foot long, and there were three enormous bedrooms, so full of dazzling white cotton it hurt to look at them. There was a kitchen, an office, countless bathrooms – even, would you believe, a screening room. All around were dotted soft, white, cashmere throws, white, suede cushions, white porcelain vases. Maybe it was good Emily hadn't come. She might have been tempted to start nicking stuff.

'Who are all the other people here?' I whispered. 'Any of them famous?'

'Don't think so. Wannabes, Maws –'

'Maws?'

'Model-actress-whatevers. Another word is "mattresses" – models-actors-waitresses. Now, get a load of *this*!' He opened a door on to a roof garden. 'Wow.'

We stepped out into the sultry night – far hotter than in the air-conditioned rooms – the air dense and musky with the smell of flowers. There was a hot-tub, steaming into the night. But most impressive was the astonishing view.

'No smog tonight,' Troy observed, as we leaned over the balcony, staring, awestruck. Far below us were pristine Spanish-style homes, neatly parked cars, the springy tops of palm trees and the jewel-bright turquoise of underlit swimming pools. The pools were like stars – at first I only noticed one, then another, then suddenly, popping up out of nowhere, there were too many to count. They dotted away randomly into the distance, until they became too small to see. Beyond the nearby streets, the megalopolis of Los Angeles was laid out like a grid of Christmas lights, a city of the future which stretched for miles until it blurred into a horizon of electric colour.

The odd thing was that I couldn't see a single human being. But they were out there – countless hopefuls caught on the grid, like so many flies in an endless spiderweb. Infinitesimally, I felt the collective weight of all the dreams on that net of light: the beautiful girls waiting tables, while waiting for their one big break; the would-be actors, writers and directors who'd poured into this reclaimed desert from the four corners of the globe; hundreds of thousands of individuals hoping that they'd be one of the pitifully few who made it. Such longing, such dogged determination: I imagined I could nearly see it, rising into the night sky like steam.

'Awesome?' Troy quirked his straight mouth.

'Scary.'

'Yeah. Want to sit down?'

There was a wide choice of wicker chairs and top-of-the-range sunbeds (with about twenty different inclines), but '*This* is the one for us.' Troy seemed amused by a squashy, swinging sofa suspended by ropes from an overhead beam.

After a twinge of fear that the ropes wouldn't hold our weight (*my* weight, really. Could you imagine the shame if I clambered aboard, only to yank the hooks out of the beam and send the whole thing crashing to the floor?), I got totally into it. We took an end each, and curled on the cushions, our feet almost touching.

Look at me, I thought, amazed by myself – swinging in the warm night, high above the city, sipping a Martini with a sexy, sexy man.

Yes, now about the 'sexy, sexy man'. They say that you don't know how sad you've been until you feel happy once more. Similarly, you don't realize how much you haven't fancied anyone until it happens again. Troy's easy grace, his greenish eyes, his very nearness, generated something in me – what I could only describe as readiness.

'I could get to like this,' he said softly. From his tone and the accompanying sidelong glance, he wasn't just talking about the view/frosty-drinks/swinging-sofa set-up. I might have lived a fairly sheltered life, but I'm not a complete ditz.

'Me too.' I kept my inflections neutral.

'You're sure? You really do feel OK? You know, after those phone calls about your husband?'

'Fine.' Well, I felt fine at that precise moment.

He nodded. 'Cool.'

'Tell me about your meeting last night.' Emily had implied that his work was important to Troy, so I wanted to know.

He told me a little about the three projects he was trying to get off the ground, the various setbacks, how hard it was to get finance, and I encouraged and commiserated where appropriate, but it was like we were speaking in code.

If only he'd touch me. The skin on my leg almost tingled with the need for his hand . . .

'Is there a Maggie here?' Someone had stuck their head around the door. 'Cameron needs ya. His fire has gone out.'

The mood broken, Troy made a regretful face and said, 'Better go in.'

Back inside, more people had arrived, but there were still

only about thirty of them. Cameron beckoned me across the chilly tundra and yelled raucously, 'Come on baby, light my fire!'

'Lord,' I murmured, 'what have we missed?' It looked like the high-jinks factor had gone up several gears while we'd been outside. But as soon as I'd fixed the fire and Troy and I had commandeered one of the white-leather sofas, I discovered how mistaken I was. Cameron's boisterousness was about as rowdy as things got: as parties go, this one was very well-behaved. And as movie stars' parties go, it was a bitter disappointment.

'No one's had their face slapped, there's been no jiggery-pokery in the hot-tub, not one television has been thrown in the swimming pool,' I said sadly. And apart from a couple of slender joints doing the rounds, there wasn't even any obvious drug-taking.

'Irish, you're obsessed!'

I shrugged. 'Just trying to make up for lost time.'

Around the fireplace, weaving in and out in a tight knot, all of the 90210 crew seemed to know each other. And while they were perfectly cordial to Troy and me, they weren't overly friendly. For once I didn't care, because Troy was the only person I wanted to talk to. He resumed telling me about his work while I widened my eyes and licked my lips and looked up from under my lashes – and then realized I was sipping from an empty glass. Had possibly been at it for quite some time.

Troy indicated it. 'Another?'

'I'll get them.'

I crossed the vast expanse of whiteness to the kitchen, but as I got there, the door was shut in my face. Behind the door a girl gasped, 'Do you want *everyone* to see? And where did you get it?'

I paused, my hand frozen on the door knob, as a male voice tempted, 'Want some?'

'I can't! You shouldn't!'

'A little isn't going to hurt.'

'Jeez, listen to yourself!'

I was afraid to go in. What manner of illegal mood-alterer were they indulging in? Cocaine? Angel dust? *Heroin?* But my curiosity got too much, so I opened the door – and found the pair of them bent guiltily over a tub of Ben & Jerry's Chunky Monkey. They looked up, a picture of shock, and the girl actually said, 'This isn't how it looks.'

Full of glee, I skittered back to Troy and, with my mouth intimately close to his ear, confided what had happened. 'Not exactly rock and roll, is it?' I couldn't stop grinning.

'No,' he laughed. 'This isn't such a great party, is it? Come on, suck down that drink, I'll take you home.'

The words were out of my mouth before I'd even known I was going to say them. 'Whose home?'

Instantly, I dropped my eyes, afraid to look at him. I was shaking with hope, with my own audacity, with dread . . .

'Maaaggie,' he whispered, and cautiously I peeped up again.

His expression was quizzical. He was wondering if he'd mis-understood, then saw that he hadn't. He laughed – a funny, regretful laugh. 'Oh, boy.' He sounded almost weary. With a heart banging with nerves, I watched him stand up and sling an arm towards me.

'Let's go.'

23

In his jeep I faced away and stared out of my window, because I couldn't bear looking at him and not touching him. In silence, he drove too fast. But when we got caught at a red light, I made the mistake of turning and glancing at him, and then his mouth was on mine. I hadn't known what kind of kiss to expect, because his mouth was hard but he was gentle – but when it happened I was actually shocked by the quality. It wasn't just my being out of practice that made me think he was an expert kisser. He was teasing, tantalizing and more than a little dirty.

We kissed through three changes of the lights. At the time, I didn't know that was what was happening, but afterwards I made sense of the noises I'd been faintly aware of – the mad beeping must have been when the lights changed to green and we didn't move. The sound of acceleration was us being overtaken, then a fresh burst of mad beeping must have been when the next lot pulled up behind us on the red and the lights went to green again.

Somehow we were driving again, even faster, then we were parked on a trash-strewn street, he was opening a graffitied metal front door and we were going up some concrete stairs. His apartment was tiny and untidy, full of books and piles of manuscripts. Then we were lying on his bed, facing each other.

'Are you sure you want to do this?' he murmured, stroking

along my hairline with his thumb, sending little shivers through me.

All my life I've been cautious and held off on things until I'm sure they're right. But this could not happen fast enough.

'I'm sure.'

'You've just broken up with your husband . . .'

I had no interest in playing games, holding on, hoping to drive him mad. I wanted this and I wanted it now.

'It's been six weeks. And it's been over for much longer than that.' I was breathless. Not just with longing, but with fear that he was going to turn me down.

'Because I am bad news,' he said gently.

'So you've already told me. D'you want me to sign a dis-claimer clause?'

He laughed, and I took his hand and placed it on my shin. 'Show me again how to get to your apartment from Santa Monica.'

'I can do better than that.'

He pulled off his T-shirt and his chest was shiny-smooth and hairless. Then went the rest of his clothes, to reveal a body that was narrow-hipped and sinewy, and blessed with that perfect, olive skin. If I tell you that he was the most beautiful man I'd ever seen, I'm probably exaggerating, but you get the picture.

Then he was helping me out of my dress and telling me how much he wanted me.

Claire had told me about the first time she'd had sex after she'd split up with James, how nervous she'd been with the new person. And after I'd left Garv, I'd found it impossible to imagine ever sleeping with another man – literally impossible. But this was a lot easier than I'd ever expected.

236

'You're beautiful,' he whispered, gently unknotting my 'Halston' scarf from around my neck, then just as gently tying it around my wrist – then tying the other end to his bedpost. Oh my God! 'Stay there,' he ordered, disappearing and – oh, Jesus! – returning with slender ropes. 'This OK?' he asked, tying my other wrist to the other side of the bed.

'Don't know. I've never done it before.'

''Bout time you did,' he laughed, then he was holding my foot in his hand and attaching a rope to my ankle. Soon all four limbs were tied and I was spread-eagled on the bed.

And now I was afraid. What if he was a serial killer? What if he was going to torture and kill me?

Then he was inching his way up my leg with his tongue, taking his own sweet time, lingering on my kneecap, and by the time he'd got to my thigh, I'd decided that if he was a serial killer, I didn't care. Up, up, he moved, still not high enough, up a little more, then back a bit – I nearly choked – then finally he'd arrived where I wanted him to be.

I'd forgotten how fabulous sex could be. Put it this way, it had been a long time since Garv and I had had sex on the kitchen table. (The fact that we were still waiting for it to be delivered didn't help, of course.) This was pure, selfish pleasure, all for me. The circles began to build, pleasure stacking and intensifying, reaching for the almost unbearable sweetness until it got to the top. I quivered on it, helpless, until the burst dispersed and I returned to myself, striving for breath.

'You're very good at this,' I half-laughed.

He grinned and drawled, 'I practise a lot.'

Then he was kneeling between my legs with an impressive, angry-looking hard-on and swinging the tip against me, then removing it, then it was in half an inch, then out again, then in a bit more, then out again, and all I wanted him to do was thrust right up into me and fill the need. But in the midst of it all was the worry about contraception – the last thing I needed was to get pregnant by Troy.

Then he was pulling a foil square from a drawer, rolling a condom on in one fast, unbroken motion, then he was plunging into me, and it was wild. Though my arms and legs were tied, I flipped with desire beneath him. Then he was whimpering, 'Oh Jesus, oh Jesus.' His eyes shut, his head arched back. At the moment of climax his body spasmed into paralysis and nothing moved except his spurts pumping inside me.

Limbs suddenly floppy and weak, he collapsed on to me, our chests heaving. Then he pulled himself up on to his elbows and looked at me with amusement. 'Jeez,' he said, softly. 'You love this, doancha?'

He untied me, and the second time we took it slower – a lot slower. Side by side, barely moving, locked at the groin, we ground further into each other with the smallest of actions and I stared into his eyes and forgot who I was.

The sun was already starting to come up when we got to sleep, then suddenly I was awake and the yellow light of full-on morning was filling the room. Panicked, I turned my head on the pillow and there he was. Awake and watching me. He rolled closer, fixed me with sleepy green eyes and said, 'Our first morning together.'

His lazy drawl made everything sound like a joke so I laughed, then moved my hands under the sheet until I found what I wanted – velvety skin over iron – and slithered down the bed to it. 'Your turn.'

Afterwards he insisted on returning the favour, then said

with a regretful sigh, 'I'd love to do this all day, but I got work to do. C'mon, I'll drive you home.'

Coming out of his apartment, we stumbled across a cluster of tourists, laden with maps and Leicas, wandering around the manky streets looking bewildered. Wasn't Hollywood supposed to be glamorous? As we climbed into Troy's jeep they studied us over-hopefully, desperate for us to be famous, and we pulled away with them still staring hard.

On the drive to Santa Monica, neither of us spoke. I had my eyes closed as I basked in a great sense of well-being. Then Troy's voice was saying, 'Wake up, Irish, we're home.'

I opened my eyes. We were outside Emily's and all the Drummers to the Rhythm of Life were streaming out of Mike and Charmaine's and into waiting Mercs and Lexuses.

I roused myself. 'Thanks for the lift, and the party and, you know . . . everything.'

'My pleasure.' He slid a hand under my hair to the nape of my neck, and touched a brief kiss to my mouth.

'Call me,' I yelped, hopping down out of the jeep.

'Sure,' he grinned. 'I'll write you every day.'

24

The sunlit house was unexpectedly silent; Emily wasn't home yet. She'd obviously got lucky also. For once, I didn't mind being on my own, I didn't mind *at all*. I was aglow – with my sore wrists and ankles and my stiff inner thighs, I'd never felt more alive. After a shower, where I looked in awe at the bite mark on my stomach, I drove to the beach to catch some rays. I liked this picture of myself. A convertible-driving independent woman, happy with my own company.

I'd only been stretched out for a few minutes when along came Rudy, laden down with ice-creams.

'Where'd ya go? Been worried about ya,' he said.

'Busy week,' I said. 'Any tri-colour Klondikes?'

As I arranged myself and my ice-cream beneath the dazzling sun, a vision of a fresh start wound around me seductively. This place had everything: great weather; fantastic location; lovely people. I could put my disastrous life in Ireland behind me, begin again and, this time, get it right. After my time in Chicago, surely someone would employ me and sort out a green card for me – there must be thousands of jobs in the studios for people with legal experience.

Then I let the door open on a secret, exciting hope: maybe Troy would be part of my new life. I revelled in a happy idyll of me and him, laughing happily together. Strolling through a fruit and veg market – in films, people who've just got off with each other spend a lot of time wandering amongst fresh produce, and it's always OK to stroke aubergines suggestively without a stallholder shouting, 'Oi, no 'andling the goods!' Or for the man to pluck a juicy, red strawberry from a stand and feed it to the woman without getting arrested for theft.

I entertained myself thus for most of the afternoon, and it only came to an end when I had to go home because I was dying to go to the loo.

Back at the house, I raced to the bathroom and was surprised at the stinging sensation. Then I remembered what had caused it and suddenly it became pleasant. Oh yeah, of course . . .

Still no sign of Emily, but there was a message on the machine from her. She'd spent the day with Lou, they were going out again tonight, I wasn't to expect her home. 'Call me on the cellphone if you've any problems.' As if it had just occurred to her, she added, 'But maybe you're not back either. I'll try you at Troy's.'

That was the only message. At least it was the only message for *me*. There were about ten thousand for Emily. Justin and Connie, someone called Lamorna, another person going by the name of Dirk.

It was then that the implications of Emily's message began to filter through: I'd be spending the evening alone. That was OK, I could ring Claire – then I remembered I couldn't because of the time difference. Fine, I could ring Rachel in New York, and afterwards I could compound my happy, independent-woman status by going to the movies on my own. Doubtfully I thought, yeeess, I could do that. Then I let myself think the thought that had been begging to be formed – unless Troy rang. There might be a possibility of repeating the fantastic sex of the previous night and this morning . . . Suddenly, I was in a state of raging arousal.

There was a noise at the door and I looked up in wild hope. Could I have conjured up Troy? With a pistol in his pocket?

Not quite. It was Lara. 'Ready?' she beamed. 'For Madame Anoushka?'

I froze. 'Oh Lord, I'd completely forgotten!' Madame Anoushka, who would save me from my terrible eyebrows. I had an appointment with her for five-thirty. 'Give me ten minutes,' I begged, and bolted to the shower to wash off the day's sand.

Three minutes later I was dragging a towel over myself, and while I foraged for clothes Lara came in to talk to me. As I located a bra, I had a panicky moment of wondering how I'd put it on without her seeing my chest, then was too rushed to bother. Let her see it. Nothing she hadn't seen before! Hadn't I always been annoyed by homophobic men who acted as if every gay man they met was going to come on to them? And wasn't I behaving in exactly the same way?

Anyway, I didn't for one second think she was going to make a move on me. I suppose I just wondered how I measured up, if she thought my jugs were nice.

I was dressed in under nine minutes – 'I'm impressed!' Lara said – then into the silver pick-up truck, once more heading for Beverly Hills. Sure, I was hardly ever out of the place! As we drove, she asked about Cameron Myers' birthday party and I told her about the apartment, the view and Cameron's fire, but she didn't ask if anything had happened with Troy, and I didn't quite know how to bring it up.

Madame Anoushka was an icy white Russian who was shocked by the poorly plucked state of my eyebrows. 'Bed,' she pronounced. 'Werry bed.'

So bed that she had to sit down for a moment and heave a deep, heartfelt sigh. Then she rose to her feet and the challenge. 'Ve fill do fot ve ken,' she said, painting some molten wax on my eye socket. Her accent was reminding me of someone, generating a maelstrom of hard-to-place nostalgia. Then I remembered: Valya and Vladimir. Garv and his shopping lists. It was as though a door to a draughty place had opened inside me. Then, mercifully, Anoushka ripped off a strip of wax and the agony wiped out the memories.

The process was preposterously unpleasant. As Anoushka plucked, it was like being assailed with a thousand little darts, my eyes dribbled water and I hovered uncomfortably on the edge of a sneeze. All the while, she gave orders in her Valya accent.

'Tveezers,' she barked, like a surgeon in *ER*. 'More wex.'

I pushed down an impulse to ask if she'd had menny, menny luffers. Anyway, I'd say she would have had, she was a fine-looking woman.

After what felt like ages, the plucking frenzy started on my other eye and it was, if anything, worse than the first. I prayed for it to be over.

Eventually everything went still – like the calm after all the popcorn has popped – so I opened my eyes and began to struggle to my feet. Only to be stopped by Anoushka insisting, 'No!'

Obediently I lay back and shut my eyes again. But nothing happened, and I cautiously squinched open one eye to find Anoushka studying me with great concentration.

'The hardest part is knowing when you're finished,' Lara said admiringly. 'All the great artists say that.'

Over the next ten minutes, a single hair was plucked from

my right eye and none from my left, then Anoushka saw fit to declare, 'Finish!'

Sitting up, I looked into the mirror: my nose was red and my eyes were rheumy, as though I'd been crying for a week. I reminded myself of someone. Who? Oh, *myself*. Last February. But my eyebrows were lovely, no doubt about it.

'Better than a facelift,' Anoushka said. Now where had I heard that before? And once again, it was almost as expensive.

When we got back into Lara's pick-up truck, a change occurred. All of a sudden, she was uncomfortable, and the feeling filled the small space. 'There's something I've got to say to you,' she said, then picked up my hand. Alert, I stared into her blue eyes. Oh God, here it comes. Lezzer snog! Senses instantly heightened, I noticed that she smelt of strawberries, that her legs were so long her car seat was as far back as it could go . . . She pulled my hand to her face. Was she going to kiss it? And then me?

'I feel bad saying this,' she sighed, 'but you have the worst nails. You have *got* to get to a nail bar.'

It took me a perplexed moment to realize she'd returned my hand to me. No lezzer snog. Just another instalment in Lara's mission to groom me to LA standards.

'Have you, like, *ever* had a manicure?'

'Of course I have.' I'd had one when I'd got married, hadn't I? And other times too, I'd say.

'But not in a while, right? OK, there's a place in Santa Monica, on the corner of Arizona and Third. Nail Heaven, Taiwanese girls, they're the best! Tell them I sent you.' I waited for her to grab her palm pilot and book me in, but she didn't.

'You're not . . .' I tried to sound normal, 'getting me an appointment?'

244

'You don't need one, not for nails. This is a civilized country! Hey, you don't hate me, do you?'

'No.'

'Phew! So what'll we do now? Go for a drink, or get some dinner, or . . .'

Before we could decide, her cellphone rang. 'Yes –' Her eyes slid to me, 'I've got her.'

It was Troy! Tracking me down! Mad for sex with me!

But it wasn't. It was Justin. Emily had called him and he was under instructions to take care of me that evening.

'Can I come too?' Lara asked.

'No Nadia tonight?'

'No.' Suddenly subdued, she switched on the ignition, and we drove over to Justin's house – a red-roofed mini-hacienda, with lots of Spanish archways and wrought-iron window shutters. He wore a blue and green Hawaiian shirt that I hadn't seen before. He must have hundreds.

'Hi, how are you?' I asked.

'Pretty sore,' he answered, his voice even higher than usual.

'Why, sweetie?' Lara asked with concern.

'Some other guy keeps getting the parts I'm up for. Look at him!' He hit a copy of *Daily Variety* with the back of his hand, then showed us a little photo of the other guy. It was uncanny – he was so similar to Justin, they could have been brothers, but this guy was just that little bit plumper and cuter and his face was even more open and uncomplicated than Justin's.

'All I can do is be fat and expendable,' Justin said, slumped in depression. 'If I can't do that, I've no job. I'm a total loser.'

Lara and I pitched in, reminding him he could give great foot massages and was an excellent cook (according to Lara), until eventually he perked up. 'Aw, I'm sorry, guys. So what'll we do? We could catch a movie?'

'Suits me.' Going to a film was always a great opportunity to eat loads of confectionery under cover of darkness.

'How about *Flying Pigs*?' Lara said.

'Nah, I hated his last one,' Justin said.

'Which? *Introspection*?'

'No, *Washday Blues*.'

'Did he do that?'

I tuned out as the pedigrees of the many, many films currently showing in greater Los Angeles were discussed – this is the one complaint I'd have about hanging around with people who work in the film industry, they know too much – and tuned back in only when they'd finally nominated a candidate. Something called *Seven Feet Under*.

'A black comedy,' Justin explained. 'Directed by the guy who made –'

'Grand, whatever.' I was more interested in the bag of M&M's I'd be eating while I watched it.

On our way out of the house, I noticed the name on Justin's mailbox: Thyme.

'Justin Thyme? That's a great name. Is it –?'

'No.' He beat me to it. 'Not my real surname. I made it up to try and stand out from the thousands of other expendable fat guys out there.'

By Sunday morning, I was itching for Emily to come home.

And for Troy to ring me.

When was he likely to? What were the rules? Perhaps it was way too soon – it had been less than a day. Then I checked my watch – OK, just over a day. Nothing, no length of time. I could ring him, of course. That's what people did, normal people that I had to start behaving like. But I didn't have his number.

Aimlessly, I opened a couple of cupboards, found nothing of interest, then sat staring at the floor, wishing Emily would come home from her sexathon with Lou. Sundayitis – the same wherever you are.

When the phone rang, the adrenalin rush felt like a heart attack. Nerves a-jangle, I picked up on the second ring. But it wasn't Troy, it was my mother.

'Are you all right?' she asked.

I nodded assent, too disappointed to speak.

'Is it nice there?'

Quickly, I got it together. 'Lovely, *lovely*!' I so didn't want any pressure to go home. 'Nice people, gorgeous weather –'

'Is it sunny?' she cut in.

'Sunny? Splitting the stones!'

'I'd love a bit of sun,' she said wistfully.

I got a strange little inkling and began backtracking. 'Mind you, it can be smoggy too. Very overcast. And there's always the chance of an earthquake.'

'It hasn't stopped raining here since the day you left. I'd prefer an earthquake.'

'Ahaha,' I laughed nervously, changed the subject, then said goodbye and resumed staring at the floor.

Emily got home around two o'clock. Lou had love-bombed her all weekend: taken her out for fabulous meals, practised his shiatsu on her, then last night they'd driven up to Mulholland Drive to watch the lights of the city and he'd said that this was something they'd tell their grandchildren.

'Classic commitmentphobic,' she said gaily.

'What are they?'

'They do instant intimacy – just add water and stir. Then you never hear from them again.'

'You almost sound happy about it.'

'It's nice to know there are some things you can depend on . . . Unless he actually *meant* all that stuff about telling our grandchildren,' she added scornfully. 'That'd be even worse!'

No need to tell her that Mort Russell hadn't called: she'd checked her messages several times.

'So how are you?' she asked.

How was I? Troy still hadn't rung, which had whipped up a ball of anxiety in my stomach. But hadn't I always been one for deferred gratification? When he finally came through, the wait would have been worth it.

'You look . . . different.'

Oh my God, was it that obvious?

She studied me thoughtfully. 'Your eyebrows!'

'Oh, ah, right. Lara took me to Madame Anoushka.'

'Tell me about Cameron Myers' birthday party.'

'Weeelll,' I said, unable to keep my delight from spreading right across my face. 'It was great.'

'How? Tell me everything.' Then her expression altered. 'Oh, shit.' She looked surprisingly shocked. 'You slept with Troy.'

'What's wrong with that?'

'Nothing,' she insisted. 'Nothing . . . OK,' she admitted, 'it's just a bit weird for me. Like, for nine years you've been Garv's wife, you've been here – how long? – less than two weeks and you're sleeping with other men. And you were never a goer – not really – and, you know, it's a bit hard to get used to, that's all.'

'I've got used to it.'

'Great.' She made a very obvious attempt at being fine, and with a big smile asked, 'Was it fun?'

'Fun isn't the word.'

'Fair play to you.' For a second, it looked like she was about to say something else, then she stopped.

25

About three years ago, two things that I never thought would happen, happened. My thirtieth birthday arrived and, after five years in Chicago, Garv was offered a promotion in the Dublin office and we decided to move back to Ireland. Garv settled into his new managerial position, I got a six-month contract at McDonnell Swindel and suddenly it was baba time!

But, to my distress, I still didn't feel 'ready'. It was great being back in Ireland, but I missed Chicago. In addition, adjusting to my new job was stressy; I hated the insecurity of a short-term contract, but that's all that anyone offered me. *And* we had nowhere to live: we'd expected our return to the Emerald Isle to be the traditional one of an Irish person who goes to Ameri-kay: they make good, then come back and dispense largesse like it's going out of fashion. So it came as a big shock to discover that while we'd been away, Ireland had had the temerity to go and get an economy for itself.

Dublin was boomtown and the price of property had gone through the roof. We arrived back at the very zenith, when shoeboxes were changing hands for several million quid and if someone stood still long enough, someone else would apply for planning permission to build sixteen apartments on them. The upshot of all this was that instead of snapping up a city-centre mansion with the proceeds of our Chicago apartment, it took us five months before we managed to buy a house in the suburb of Dean's Grange, several miles from the city.

Before us, it had been owned by an old lady – the kitchen and bathroom were museum pieces and small, gloomy rooms were the order of the day. So we fashioned plans to modernize: new kitchen, new bathroom, knocking through walls, adding skylights and all that. Lord Lucan Construction duly arrived, knocked down most of the house, then promptly disappeared. And every day that the pile of cement in the front 'garden' stood unattended was another day that I didn't have to commence babymaking.

But all the time the net was tightening. Just before we'd left Chicago, nearly every couple we knew were having children, and we'd barely touched down in Ireland when I noticed they were at the same lark there. Only a week after our return, Garv's sister Shelley had a baby boy, Ronan. Garv and I went to visit her in hospital, a bunch of grapes under our oxter, where we found that Shelley's partner Peter had conjoined with a bottle of Power's to celebrate the birth of his first child. 'GARV!' he shouted, when he saw us coming down the corridor. 'Garv, Garv! C'mere till you see the fruit of my loins!' He thrust his pelvis at us with such vigour that he almost fell over, then, bouncing between the shiny green walls, he got Garv in a headlock, dragged him to the infant's cot and berated him, 'De murkil 'f new life. 'Sa MURKIL!' I was mortified for him, especially when he was asked to leave as he was upsetting the other fathers. But Garv seemed quite moved by it all.

I hadn't been able to avoid noticing that Garv was keen on sprogs. He liked them and they liked him back. They were particularly fond of messing up his hair and pulling off his glasses and poking him in the eye. When they cried, he held them and spoke sweetly and they stopped crying and looked at him with a kind of wonder and everyone said (except my family), 'He'll make a great dad.'

Sure enough, Garv started making noises about us reproducing, and I cursed my bad luck. In other relationships, it seemed to be the women who wanted to have children while the men would do anything to get out of it. In fact, according to popular folklore (and women's magazines), these child-shy men riddled the landscape like landmines. Every time Garv brought up the subject, I always managed a legitimate reason why now wasn't the right time. But it dawned on him that my reluctance wasn't simply temporary, one weekend when we were babysitting Ronan. (Well, I say weekend, but it was only Saturday night, all that Peter and Shelley dared leave him for. And they rang about eighty times in that twenty-four-hour period.)

It was the first time that we'd minded Ronan for more than a couple of hours, and we weren't at all bad at feeding, burping, changing and cajoling him. It was good fun because, you see, I had nothing against babies *per se*. Just the idea of having them myself. When Ronan cried a couple of times in the night, Garv got up without complaint. Then in the morning he brought him into bed with us and sat him on his lap facing us. Already Ronan was chortling, and when Garv held on to his chubby wrists and blew raspberries at him, Ronan nearly shrieked his head off. Garv was laughing almost as much, and with his bare chest and off-duty hair, he looked like the hunky man in that Man and Baby portrait. I got such a pang of confused yearning, it almost hurt physically.

A great day was had by some and when Peter and Shelley came to collect Ronan, they asked, 'Was he good for you?'

'Good?' Garv said. 'He was brilliant! We don't want to give him back.'

'You'll have to get working on a little cousin for him, so,' Shelley said.

Quick as a flash, I indicated the raw walls and said, 'How could we bring a baby into this building site?' They laughed and I laughed and Garv laughed – but his laugh wasn't as loud as ours. Even then, I knew that it had been one excuse too many and not long afterwards the rabbits showed up.

Time passed and I still didn't feel 'ready'. Some of my fears had lessened, specifically the one about the pain of childbirth; I knew enough women who'd had children to know that it was definitely survivable. But whenever I heard stories about people having their first baby at thirty-nine, it brightened my day. Then there was something in the paper about a woman of sixty having a baby using some artificial process and that, too, was good news. But, a lot sooner than I expected, my thirty-first birthday arrived and tipped me into panic: I'd said I'd have a baby when I was thirty and I was now a year older than that. When would my full-blown maternal instinct arrive? I was running out of time. If it didn't get a move on, it would show up just in time for my menopause.

Like I say, Garv is no fool. And finally, he sat me down gently – but firmly, mind. He can be firm when he wants to be – and made me talk about it. *Really* talk about it, instead of fobbing him off as I had been doing for the previous twelve months.

'I'm just not ready,' I admitted. 'And it's not really the pain any more, I'm a bit better about that.'

'Good woman, we'll get you the finest epidural that money can buy. So what is it, then?'

'Well, my job.'

Once I said it out loud, I realized what a problem this was. For over five years, both in Chicago and Ireland, I'd been working very, very hard, pushing against the current, and I was still waiting for my job to plateau, to get to a position where I felt 'safe'. Where I was established enough to be able to take maternity leave, sure that I'd be re-employed, and free from the worry of my colleagues undermining me in my absence and poaching my work. But I was on my third temporary contract.

'You'll get maternity leave and . . .'

'But how easy will it be to get back in? And what will it do to my promotion prospects? If I take four months off, how will I ever get to be Frances?'

'So you can sleep under one of the desks and wash in the staff toilets like a bag lady? Anyway, they can't discriminate against you, it's against the law.'

Easy for him to say. He hadn't heard a partner at my firm (a man, of course) complain about someone on maternity leave, 'If I took four months off to sail around the Med, and expected to be paid for it, they'd laugh in my face!'

This was what I was up against. Compared to his, mine wasn't much of a career, but it was important to me. Even though it drained and stressed me, to a certain extent I defined myself by it.

'OK. Anything else?'

'Yes. What if it turns out to be like one of my sisters? Like Rachel and the drugs, say? Or Anna and the insanity. Or Claire and the rebelliousness. I'd never be able to control them, they'd have my heart scalded.' I stopped. 'Listen to me, I'm already sounding like my mother. Anyway, I'm too irresponsible to have a child.'

That made him laugh. 'You're not irresponsible!'

'I am! You and me,' I urged, 'we have a lovely time. We can go away for weekends at the drop of a hat. Think of Hunter and Cindy!' Friends of ours in Chicago, who'd had a baby and, overnight, had their life up-ended. Once upon a time the four of us had gone on trips together, but post-baba they'd seemed perpetually ensnared by their screaming child, while Garv and I had swanned off to the lakes for the weekend, feeling guilty and relieved. 'We couldn't leave a baby with Dermot, the way we can with Hoppy and Rider. And parenthood never stops,' I pointed out. 'Not until the babies are grown up. And maybe not even then.'

'OK, a baby will cause you agony, have your heart scalded, finish your career and destroy your social life for the next twenty years. Other than that, have you any objections?'

'Yes.'

'Tell me.'

'It sounds stupid.'

'Tell me anyway.'

I made myself voice it. 'What if . . . like . . . anything happened to it? What if it got bullied at school? Or if it died? What if it got meningitis? Or was knocked down? We'd love it so much, how could we bear it? Sorry for being so mad,' I added quickly. I'd never met anyone else who felt like this. Friends who'd got pregnant had admitted to mild regrets, but they'd all been along the lines of 'Well, that's our last romantic weekend away for the next three years,' or 'I'm reading as much as I can now, because you can't concentrate on a book for the first two years. Your brain just goes.' No one had expressed the kind of morbid misgivings that I had. The closest anyone had got was when they said, 'I don't care if it's a boy or a girl, so long as it's healthy.'

But Garv said, 'I do understand how you feel.' And I knew he did. 'But if we thought that way all the time, we'd never love anyone.'

For a moment, I was afraid he might suggest that I had therapy. But of course he didn't – he was an Irish man.

Unlike most of my friends, I'd never had therapy. Emily said it was because I was too afraid of what I'd find out. I agreed – I said I was afraid of finding out that I'd paid forty pounds a week every week for two years to entertain a stranger with the story of my life.

'Can you see anything positive at all about getting pregnant?' Garv asked.

I thought long and hard. 'Yes.'

'Yes?' The hope in his voice shamed me.

'Chocolate.'

'Chocolate?'

'Food generally. I could eat as much as I liked and never feel guilty.'

'Well,' he said, with a heavy sigh. 'It's a start, I suppose.'

Another year passed, I turned thirty-two and I still didn't feel 'ready'. More than I had, admittedly, but not quite enough. Until one day, feeling like I was giving up after years on the run, I just crumbled. I knew I had to. The silent struggle was exhausting and I suspected that things with Garv and me had gone a bit weird since Hoppy and Rider had arrived. I loved Garv and I didn't want things getting any worse.

When I turned myself in, Garv almost burst with happiness. 'What changed your mind?!'

'I don't want you becoming one of those women who steal babies from outside a supermarket,' I said.

'You won't regret this, I promise,' he enthused.

And while I suspected that I probably would, my resentment was defused by the knowledge that he didn't understand how great my qualms were. That he genuinely thought that once he'd knocked me up, all my trepidation would be washed clean away in a great tide of oestrogen.

'So will I buy a thing that tells me my temperature and all that?' I asked.

Garv looked startled. 'No! Can't we just . . . ?'

So we just . . .

The first time we had sex without contraception, I felt as if I'd jumped out of a plane without a parachute, and even though we'd been told it could take between six months and a year, I was still watchful of my body.

But despite the risks we'd taken, my period arrived, and not even the squeezing cramps could dampen my relief. I relaxed a little – I'd bought myself another month. Maybe I'd be one of the women who could take up to a year.

Not a hope. I conceived in the second month; and I knew about it within minutes. I didn't immediately start demanding peanut butter and wasabi sandwiches, but something in me didn't feel settled, and when I abruptly took agin Tesco Metro BLTs, I *knew*.

Mind you, I'd been fairly sure the previous month too, when I *hadn't* been. But within days it was clear that this was no neurotic imagining. I really was up the pole. How was I so sure? It might have had something to do with the fact that until after eight in the evening I couldn't even keep down water. Or if anyone passed within three feet of my boobs I wanted to kill them. Or that I was chalk white. Except for when I was mint green. It was all wrong. When Shelley had been five weeks pregnant, she'd gone on a walking holiday in the Pyrenees (Why, indeed? Your guess is as good as mine), covered ten gruelling miles a day and never once felt lightheaded. Claire hadn't even known she was pregnant for the first month and was out partying day and night, without recourse to a single bucket.

But I was the sickest person I'd ever met, which was especially hard for me because I didn't usually get sick often. Even my brain was affected – I couldn't *think* straight. Just to make it official, we did a pregnancy test and when the second blue line rose to the surface, Garv cried, in a manly, I've-an-eyelash-caught-in-my-eye sort of way. I cried too, but for different reasons.

Sick though I was, I just about managed to keep working – though God only knows how much use I was to them, and the only thing that kept me going was the vision of my bed at the end of the day. By the time I reached home, almost whimpering with relief, I'd make straight for the bedroom. If Garv had got home before me, he'd have already flung back the covers and all I had to do was crawl in between the cool, forgiving sheets. Then Garv would lie beside me and I'd grasp his hand and tell him how much I hated him.

'I know,' he crooned, 'I don't blame you, but I promise that in a few short weeks you'll feel better.'

'Yes,' I whispered, gratefully. 'Thank you, yes. And then I'll kill you.'

Sooner or later, I struggled to sit up and Garv knew the drill. 'Puke bowl?' he'd ask solicitously, as we prepared for yet another round of dry retches.

'Watching the game, having a Bud,' Garv murmured, as I

Whassup'd into the pretty fuchsia basin he'd bought specially for the occasion.

It was after the first month that something began to ripple through me, a sensation so unfamiliar that I couldn't categorize it.

'Indigestion?' Garv suggested. 'Wind?'

'No . . .' I said, in a daze. 'I think it might be . . . excitement.'

Garv cried again.

Call it hormones, call it Mother Nature, call it whatever you want, but to my great surprise I suddenly really wanted the baby. Then, at seven weeks, when we went for the first scan, my love just exploded. The grainy, grey picture showed something tiny, a little blob that was slightly darker than the other blob-biness around it, and it was our baby. Another human being, new and unique. We'd made it and I was carrying it.

'It's a miracle,' I whispered to Garv as we studied it.

'De murkil 'f new life,' he agreed solemnly.

In wild, celebratory mode, we took the rest of the day off work and went for lunch at a restaurant that I sometimes went to with clients and consequently had never been able to enjoy before. I even managed half a chicken breast without barfing. Then we wandered around town and he persuaded me to let him buy me a JP Tod's handbag (the one that Helen now covets). It was so expensive I'd never have been able to buy it for myself, not even out of my Ladies' Nice Things account. 'Last time we'll have the money for this kind of thing,' he declared skittishly. Then I bought him a CD of some saxopho-nist whom I knew nothing about but whom he loved. 'Last time you'll get the chance to listen to music,' I declared, also skittishly. It was one of the nicest days of my entire life.

That was when we decided to give Hoppy and Rider to

Dermot. He'd become very fond of them, and though we were sad to lose them, we'd decided they'd have to go anyway when the baby arrived. We'd heard enough horror stories about jealous animals attacking babas, and even though Hoppy and Rider had never shown signs of narkiness, we felt we couldn't take any chances. So, tearfully, we waved them off to Dermot's, promising to visit them regularly.

Around then, other things changed too. I'd never been mad about my body. I mean, I didn't hate it enough to starve or cut it, but it had never been something to celebrate. But with my pregnancy came a profound shift; I felt ripe and gorgeous and powerful and – I know this sounds funny – *useful*. Up until then, I'd regarded my womb in the same way as the keyring on my Texier handbag: it was neither decorative nor useful, but it came with the rest of the package, so I was stuck with it.

Another by-product of my pregnancy was that I felt blessedly normal; for so long, my lack of maternal instincts had had me thinking I was almost a freak. For the first time in a long time, I felt in step with the rest of the world.

You're supposed to wait until after the twelfth week to tell people, and I'm normally very good at keeping secrets, but not in this instance. So on week eight we broke the news to our families, who expressed delight – most of them, anyway. 'I reckoned you for a Jaffa,' Helen coldly told Garv.

'What's a Jaffa?'

'An orange which doesn't have any seeds.'

He still looked confused, so she elaborated. 'I thought you were firing blanks.' Then she added, 'When I could bear to think about it at all.'

Next I rang Emily, one of the few people who'd known the full extent of my reluctance to get pregnant – and only because she'd been of the same mind. She was one of those people who, if you asked if they liked children, would reply, 'Love them! But I couldn't manage a whole one.'

I broke the news that I was eight weeks pregnant and when she asked me, 'Are you happy?' I heard myself reply, 'I've never been so happy in all my life. I was a fool to have waited so long.'

There was silence, then a sniff. 'Are you crying?' I asked suspiciously.

'I'm so happy for you,' she wobbled. 'This is wonderful news.'

It was on a routine visit to the bathroom one Saturday afternoon when I saw it. This wasn't the spotting they'd talked about. This was crimson and *everywhere*.

'Garv,' I called, surprised at how normal I sounded. 'Garv! I think we'd better go to the hospital.'

Out by the car, I decided I wanted to drive myself. I was quite insistent, something to do with control, probably. And Garv, who rarely loses his temper, stood in the street and yelled, 'I'LL FUCKING DRIVE.'

I remember every part of the journey to the hospital in almost hyper-reality. Everything was acutely sharp and clear. We had to go through town, which was so thronged with Saturday-afternoon shoppers we could hardly get the car through the streets. The sheer number of people made me feel entirely alone in the world.

At the hospital, we parked in an ambulance bay and to this day I could still tell you what the woman on admissions looked like. She promised that I'd be seen as soon as possible, then Garv and I sat and waited on orange plastic chairs that had been nailed to the floor. We didn't speak.

When a nurse came for me, Garv promised, 'It'll be OK.'

But it wasn't.

It was a nine-week foetus, but I felt as if someone had died. It was too early to tell the sex and that made me feel worse.

A shared loss is harder, I think. I could handle my own pain, but I couldn't handle Garv's. And there was something I had to say to him before the guilt devoured me whole. 'It's my fault, it's because I didn't want it. He or she knew where it wasn't wanted.'

'But you did want it.'

'Not in the beginning.'

And he had nothing to say to me. He knew it was true.

26

On Sunday evening, Lara came over.

'Not out with Nadia?' Emily asked.

'Nah, she got her butthole bleached and can't sit down.'

'Excuse me?' I spluttered. 'Her butthole? Bleached?'

'It's the latest thing in plastic surgery,' Lara explained. 'Lots of girls do it. To make it look pretty.'

'Like getting your teeth whitened,' Emily chipped in. 'Except it's your butthole instead.'

'You're making this up!'

'We're not!'

'But who'd see . . . when . . . ?' I stopped. I was better off not knowing.

'I got me a present.' Lara thrust a box at us.

'Lovely,' Emily enthused. 'What is it?'

'It's my new state-of-the-art caller display. So sophisticated it can almost tell me what my caller is thinking. Listen to the functions!'

As she listed out all the things it could do, she reminded me of Garv – boys and their toys – and I wondered whether there was a link between loving gadgets and wanting to have sex with girls.

We took ourselves and a bottle of wine out to the sunloungers in the fragrant back garden, where Lara tried to quiz Emily on her thirty-six-hour date with Lou. But Emily tetchily dismissed him: 'I had a good time but he's not going to call.' She was far more interested in analysing her work situation.

'The new script just isn't coming together, so if Mort Russell passes on *Plastic Money*, that's it. Game over.' She blew into her hands and her face was pale. 'I've got no other choice, I really am going to have to go back to Ireland.'

Lara shook her head. 'I've been thinking about this. There must be other work you can do.'

'Yeah, I hear they're hiring at Starbucks.'

'No, other *writing* work. Script polish.'

'What's that?' I asked Emily.

'I take a poxy script that's about to go into production, make it coherent, add jokes and make the main characters three-dimensional and likeable. For that I get a pittance and someone else gets the credit.' Emily sighed. 'Obviously I'd love it, but there are so many writers in this town and we're all chasing the same pieces of work. David says he's tried for me.'

'Agent, schmagent. The time has come to get out there and hustle yourself,' Lara encouraged.

'I do!'

'You need to do more than look pretty and give out your cards at parties. You've got to *bother* people. That's if you really don't want to go home to Ireland.'

'I really don't.'

'OK. I'll see if I can swing something and so will Troy. And what about that Irish guy? You know the one from Dark Star Productions. Shay something? Shay Mahoney?'

'Shay Delaney.' Beside me I could feel Emily's sudden awkwardness.

'Yeah, him. Wonder if he's got any shit Irish films that could use a polish.'

264

'I'm sure he's got plenty of shit Irish films that could use a polish,' Emily said. 'But no money to pay for it.'

'You never know,' Lara mused. 'Call him. Convince him.'

Emily made noncommittal noises and I was relieved. I didn't want her to ring him.

'Oh, enough doom and gloom already!' Emily declared. 'We need cheering up. Lara, will you tell us your "I'm OK, you're OK" story?' She snuggled into her lounger, like a child preparing for their bedtime story. 'Off you go,' she encouraged, with the air of someone who'd heard this many, many times. '"I'd been nineteen for seven years and it was starting to show . . ."'

Lara took a deep breath, and began. 'OK, I'd been nineteen for seven years and it was starting to show. I'd been the prettiest girl at my high school, and seven years earlier I'd come to LA hoping to be the next Julia Roberts.'

Emily was happily mouthing the words along with her.

'But LA was full of chicks who'd been the prettiest girls at high school and I was nothing special.'

I began to object that Lara was *very* special, but she stopped me.

'Tell it to the hand. Look around you, this town is full of babes. They are everywhere and a thousand new ones arrive every week, can you *imagine*? But at the time I didn't know this. So I start looking for work, hit a brick wall and end up having to do pay theatre.'

'What's that?'

'Productions you pay for a part in.'

'*You* pay *them*?'

'Yeah, but there's always the chance that some hotshot director will spot you and you get to put something on your résumé. Anyhoo, after that, I got a few walk-on parts where *they* paid *me* and I thought I was on my way. In between acting jobs, I waited tables and got my boobs and lips done.'

'Biggened,' Emily explained. 'And some casting director told her to drop ten pounds –'

'Was her name Kirsty?' I asked sarcastically.

At that point, the story of Lara's life stalled while Emily had a little rant about Kirsty telling me I needed to drop ten pounds. (I had exaggerated to make her seem worse.) Lara soothed and smoothed, then Emily resumed. 'Right! Some casting director told her to drop ten pounds, though she was already x-ray skinny – so she upped her exercise to four hours daily. Then she began starving herself and only ate twelve grapes and five rice-cakes a day.'

I didn't believe her. No one could survive on that.

'It's true,' Lara confirmed. 'I was constantly hungry.'

'Even though you were on pills,' Emily reminded her.

'That's right. I knew every doctor who gave fake pre-scriptions. I took so much speed – that's what diet pills are – my mouth was always dry, my heart was racing . . .'

'. . . I was permanently homicidal,' Emily chimed in with the last bit.

'I was so poor and so unhappy. Six days out of seven I managed to stick to my diet. But – and it was like Russian roulette, I never knew which chamber was loaded – on one of the days I broke my diet. And how! Three pints of ice-cream, a pound of chocolate, four bags of cookies . . . then I made myself puke it all up.'

'Bulimia,' Emily intoned gravely at me. 'For all the good it did her.'

'You got it. Instead of graduating to speaking parts, even the walk-on parts stopped happening. They said my look was over. Big, blonde Aryan types were out and wide-eyed waifs who looked like they'd been abused as children were in.'

She paused and Emily prompted her, '"I'd been to twenty-three auditions in a row without a single call-back."'

'I'd been to twenty-three auditions in a row without a single call-back and I hadn't had a paying acting job in over two years. I'm stony broke and all the time I'm getting older, my ass is slipping, my face is getting lines, and every week a thousand *real* nineteen-year-olds are getting off the bus and hawking their fresh teenage bodies round town. I can't, just can't go back to waiting tables, so I slept with a director – a *man* – who promised me a part. It never happened. Then I got so desperate I slept with a *writer.*'

'Why's it worse to sleep with a writer than a director?'

Emily and Lara both chuckled. 'Because writers in Hollywood have no power,' Emily explained. 'They're the amoebas of the Hollywood food chain, even further down the scale than the caterers on a movie set.'

'Then,' Lara bit her lip, 'just when I think it can't get any worse, my girlfriend threw me out. She'd found out about me sleeping with the director. I had no job, no money, no girl, no self-respect – no rice-cakes, even. The long, dark cocktail hour of the soul.' She laughed, but saw fit to add, 'It was horrible – I can't tell you. The dream was over, I knew I was beat and it just about broke my heart. I saw myself going back home to Portland on the bus and I felt like the biggest failure in the history of the world. So there you go – my sordid life as an actress!'

'At least you never did a porn film,' I comforted.

'Oh, I did.' She sounded surprised. 'I even put it on my résumé. For a while.'

'But the moral of the story,' Emily prompted. 'Let's not get sidetracked.'

'The moral of the story is I thought I would never be happy again,' Lara said. 'I was twenty-six years of age and all washed up. I'd had plastic surgery, I'd given years of my life, I'd used up every bit of my hope and I had nothing to show for it. I hated myself and I wished I was dead.'

'She tried slitting her wrists,' Emily said.

'But I couldn't even do that right. Did you know you're supposed to do it longways instead of crossways?'

'Yes.'

'Smarter than me. But here's a thing – my life did get better. I made the decision to let go of my dreams, because they were killing me, and I stopped asking the impossible from myself. I changed my attitude and decided to focus on what I had rather than what I didn't have. And most of all, I decided I wasn't going to be bitter.'

'So you went back to school,' Emily said.

'So I went back to school and two days – *two days* – after I got those little letters after my name, I got hired by a production company. So I still got to work in the movies, right? I hadn't wanted to work behind the scenes, I'd wanted to be in front of a camera, but I sucked it up and got with the programme. And yeah, there are times when I see a girl's face on the silver screen and I wish it was me,' she said. 'But most times I'm down with it. I love my job – except for when I nearly got canned for missing *Two Dead Men*. I love the movies I work with and I got over the girl. So there you go.'

'I love that story,' Emily sighed. 'Makes me think that whatever happens, I'll be OK. And so will you, Maggie.'

We lapsed into a silent glow of hope and, for the first time, heard a conversation floating over the hedge from next door. The Goatee Boys were also taking the evening air in their backyard.

One of them said, '. . . crusty and kinda green . . .'

This gave rise to groans and 'Oh man!'s.

'Like peeing razor blades,' the first voice said, and more groans ensued.

'Venereal disease,' Emily whispered, her face alight with disgust. 'Ssshhh, listen. One of them has VD.'

Sure enough, we listened and there was more talk of peeing fire and a visit to the quack.

'Which one of them is it?' Lara asked. 'Ethan? Curtis?'

'Betcha it's Ethan.'

'It doesn't sound like him.'

'And Curtis is too weird, who'd sleep with him?'

'You'd be surprised.'

We earwigged a bit more. Whoever it was, their winkie was like a war zone and the doctor had only added to the grief because he'd put a type of furled umbrella down into the afflicted willy – then opened it! Behind the fence, cries of horror rose up into the night and I myself felt the first signs of queasiness.

'It's not Luis,' I insisted. 'He's too sweet.'

'So who is it, then?'

'I've got to know.' Emily pulled her lounger across, stood on it and poked her head over the fence. 'Which one of you is it? *Luis?* I'm surprised.'

Still standing on the lounger, she turned back to us. 'It's Luis, and they want to know if we want to come over. They're doing tequila shots. Dude, that's most excellent!'

Despite her sarcasm, she seemed happy enough to go round. So did Lara, and I had no problem at all with it: nearly everything I did in Los Angeles was strange and new, this was no different. But as we passed through their darkened house, I got the fright of my life when I saw a seven-foot-tall figure looming blackly out of a corner. It transpired to be a cardboard Darth Vader – Curtis's most prized possession. 'I got a C-3PO too, and a Chewbacca suit,' he boasted. 'And three of the original posters.'

God, he was peculiar. To humour him I said brightly, 'So you're a Trekkie.'

'*Star Wars.*' He sounded appalled. 'Not *Star Trek.*' Under his breath I heard him mutter with contempt, '*Girls.*'

Indeed.

They'd dragged their flowery old sofa out into the back, where Luis was installed, with a slight air of the invalid about him. His hands seemed to hover and flutter protectively over his groin. Or maybe it was just to fend off prying eyes: Emily, Lara and I all stared long and hard at the diseased area.

'You girls look like you got x-ray vision,' he said nervously.

'You'd better believe it.' Lara gave a menacing wink.

Ethan doled out shot glasses of tequila, then stopped in front of me. 'You look different,' he said thoughtfully.

'No pantyhose on her head.' This from Luis.

'No-o, not just that.' He paused to give Curtis a sharp poke and hissed like a mammy, 'Get off the sofa and let the ladies sit down,' then resumed his scrutiny of me. 'You haven't . . . had your moustache shaved off?'

'She's had her eyebrows done,' Lara contributed.

'Ahhh, gotta be that!'

And so began a pleasant, mellow night which only ended when an argument broke out over who should have the worm at the bottom of the bottle. ('Stop!' I berated Lara and Emily, who were both flushed from the tussle. 'It's Ethan's bottle. He should be allowed to have it.')

Then we all went home and slept soundly.

27

I awoke to find a woman, approximately four foot high, banging a swiffer around my room. Conchita, I could only imagine.

'Sorry I wake you,' she beamed.

'I was awake anyway,' I lied back, grabbing some clothes.

In the kitchen, Emily was hurriedly putting on her sandals. 'Didn't I forget to get Conchita's bun, so I've to run up to Starbucks. She refuses to touch the bathroom unless we give her a sugar hit.'

'I'll go,' I offered, still on my keeping-busy kick.

'Are you sure? Well, thanks. But listen, she won't eat anything with bananas or blueberries,' she yelled after me.

Outside, yet another beautiful day was presenting itself for inspection. Considering it was a Monday morning, the world was suffused with triumphant yellow light, and everything looked picture perfect – the pretty little houses, the even-skin-toned lawns, the velvet petals of the blazing pink flowers.

In Starbucks I got us a chocolate muffin each, even though all Emily would do with hers was to crumble it into bits, then announce she was stuffed. Then I set off for home again, passing Reza's salon as I went. She was within, grimly tugging the hair off someone. I waved at her and she glared at me. Just as it should be! God was in his heaven and all was well with the world.

But the second I walked back into the house, I knew something bad had happened. Emily was shaking on the edge of the couch and Conchita was ministering to her.

'They passed,' Emily declared.

For a confused moment, I thought she was talking about exams or a driving test. Where I come from, 'passed' is a *good* word – the opposite of 'failed'.

'Who passed what?'

'Mort Russell. Hothouse passed on my script. David just rang.'

Shock rooted me to the spot. They couldn't have passed. What about Julia and Cameron? What about the three thousand screens? It took a moment for my hope to dwindle away, to understand that none of it would be happening. The lying bastards!

Emily was hyperventilating with squeaky gasps and she was shuddering as if she was crying, but her eyes were dry. 'What am I going to do? I'm fucked, I'm so totally fucked. I've no money, not a red cent. Oh my God, oh my God!'

From her apron pocket, Conchita produced a little bottle and said, 'Xanax. To calm her down.' I made sweeping, go-for-it, no-time-like-the-present motions with both my hands.

'Can I've two?' Emily asked.

'Ob course.'

But when Conchita shook some pills into the palm of her hand, there was a little ruck and before I knew what had happened Emily had roughly grabbed not two, but four xanax and crammed them into her mouth.

'Sorry,' she mumbled – but only once they were good and swallowed.

Conchita and I exchanged a look. Who were we to deny her?

Another wave of disbelief hit. 'But they were so enthusiastic,' I voiced. 'It sounded like a done deal.'

'That's the way they all carry on.'

'Did they say why they passed?'

'They *said* it's not what they're looking for right now,' Emily gasped. 'But I don't know what the truth is. Probably they just hated it.'

'Sssssh,' Conchita urged, pulling Emily to her bosom and stroking her hair.

'But –' I started up again, a thousand indignant questions forming, but Conchita nitched them with a firm shake of the head.

The three of us sat in silence while the hopeless day ticked by. I was at a complete loss. Everything had been geared around this coming through, and though I'd had my worries, I'd never really considered that it wouldn't. What was Emily going to do now? Come home to Ireland with me? But I didn't want to go home. Especially not now. Now that Troy – It was then that I realized he still hadn't called me. Unless he'd called while I'd been out getting the muffins, and it so wasn't the right time to ask . . .

'Maybe you go to bed?' Conchita suggested and Emily nodded obediently.

'Four xanax, she sleep until Websday,' Conchita told me.

I was on the verge of asking for a couple of pills for myself when the phone rang. My immediate thought was of Troy, but when I answered, a woman's voice said, 'Hold for David Crowe calling for Emily O'Keeffe.'

'She's busy right now.' Having a nervous breakdown. 'I'm her assistant. Can I help?'

But the woman was gone and after a few clicks the next voice I heard was David. 'Hey, Emily!' he chuckled.

'It's Maggie. Emily's a little upset.'

'Sure. But I got good news. Larry Savage over at Empire took a look. He wants to meet with her.'

'Well, that's great! When?'

'Right now.'

'Oh, that's a shame,' I said regretfully. 'She can't go right now. She's just taken four xanax.'

A pause. Not a cordial one.

'Now you listen to me,' he said, all traces of affability gone. 'She needs to get it together *now* and get over to Empire. We can't push this meeting back. She's got to get in today before Larry finds out that Hothouse passed, xanax or no fucking xanax. Coffee, cocaine, I don't care how, but she'd better get it together. And if she can't do it, *you* do it. I've put my ass on the line here.'

All the moisture had retreated from my mouth. It was as dry as carpet. What had happened to David Crowe, charm monster? I was frightened of him, genuinely frightened. He sounded so dangerous, so vengeful.

And I had got the gist of what was happening. Some machiavellian machinations meant David had managed to con Larry Savage into thinking that Mort Russell was still interested. There was a tiny window of opportunity before Larry discovered that Mort had passed. If Larry found out, then David was in the shit. And Emily's last chance was gone. So the pitch had to be today.

I glanced into Emily's bedroom. She was lying down, her eyes closed, Conchita stroking her forehead. There was no point asking her what we should do. And *I* hadn't a notion. I thought of Lara – she could help, even though she was up to her eyes organizing the launch for some movie called *Doves*. Or how about Troy?

'Could you give us a couple of hours?' I glanced at my watch, it was ten-twenty. 'Say until midday?' That should be enough time for either Troy or Lara to get here, and then they could take over, they'd know what to do.

'No. I can't give you five fucking minutes,' he snapped. 'The clock is ticking and news gets round this town way fast. It's this morning, or never. By lunch-time it'll be all over.'

Desperately, I tried to focus, to think intelligently. *Oh, Jesus Christ!* 'Oh, OK . . . what can you tell me about Larry Savage?'

'Larry, Larry, Larry . . . what's to say?' There was a clicking sound like David was banging his pen off his teeth. 'Weeell, he's rumoured to have sex with animals. But, hey, it's only a rumour!'

I pushed down my frustration and asked, 'Any career information?'

'A coupla years back he made *Fred*. Remember it? Old English Sheepdog who saves the circus from closure?'

I remembered it.

'Seen it?'

'No. I was more than five years of age at the time.'

'Cute,' David said unpleasantly. 'Well, lie. Tell him you loved it.'

'OK. Now, can you tell me how to get to Empire?'

Irritably, David gave sketchy directions, and just in case there was any chance that I might calm down, he ended the conversation by saying, 'This is Emily's last chance. Make sure she doesn't fuck it up.'

'Right.' With a pounding heart, I hung up the phone and hurried in to Emily. Who, floating away on a pink xanax cloud, was having none of it. 'Al go ch'morr',' she said sleepily.

'Tomorrow's too late.' Hysteria skimmed my voice as I explained the situation.

Luckily, Conchita displayed an astute grasp of the workings of Hollywood. 'The man find out the other man have passed, he not berry happy!' She hoiked a startled Emily from the bed.

'Emily, you'll have to make yourself sick,' I said urgently.

'Huh?'

'Stick your fingers down your throat and make yourself throw up. To get rid of the tablets.'

Dazed though she was, she looked disgusted.

'I'm sorry. But desperate circumstances call for desperate measures.'

Conchita and I marched her to the bathroom, where despite issuing some impressively inhuman gawking noises from her gullet, she couldn't recall the xanax.

'I'j nevr make ablimic,' she said, slumping against the bowl, her forehead beaded in sweat from her efforts.

'One more time,' I encouraged. 'Just try once more.'

'K.'

But though she strained until her face was bright red and running with tears, there was still no joy. What was I to do with her?

Conchita was on top of things, though. 'Emily, you get in the shower! And you –' she pointed at me, 'make coffee. Strong!'

After her shower, we dressed Emily and tried to get a comb through her hair.

'You look good,' Conchita encouraged.

Emily shook her head and said sadly, 'Everything is wrong.'

'Like what?'

'My 'spensive suit's in jrycleaner's, I haven't been reiki'd, my hair's a Jackson Five special.'

'Nebber mind,' Conchita said, forcing a cup of treacly coffee on her. 'You got a pitch, lady!'

When we were ready to leave, Conchita whipped out a little plastic bottle of holy water and flung generous handfuls of it at us. As a drop splattered on to Emily's face, she turned to me in confusion.

'Maggie, is this actually happening? Or mi jreaming it?'

'It's happening,' I said grimly, marching her to my car and wondering how the hell you got to The Valley.

The drive was horrible. My heart was banging against my ribs and my breath didn't want to be drawn – there is nothing more terrifying than the LA freeways when you don't know where you're going. Lanes and lanes of aggressive cars on all sides of you. My right arm was begging to be scratched. To make matters worse, I was trying to make Emily practise her pitch.

'Camera pans over a breast of pairs . . .'

'Good,' I tried to encourage. 'Good.' I saw a sliproad approaching and peered around, looking for signs. 'Is this where we turn off?' And how did I cut across three lanes of traffic to do so?

By the time I'd discovered it wasn't our turn, Emily had meandered off into silence. I managed to take my eyes off the road just long enough to see her chin nodding on her chest and a delicate trail of dribble heading south to her second-best suit. Christ! That was all we needed. Her falling asleep mid-pitch.

I shook her and begged, 'Drink some Jolt, try and stay awake. Please!'

'Oh my God, Maggie,' she mumbled. 'This is a nightmare.'

I felt for her, because she genuinely understood how serious the situation was, but simply couldn't control herself.

'I can't do it,' she said.

'You can.'

'I can't.' There was a pause and I knew what was coming next. 'Will you do it?'

'What? The pitch?'

'Yes.'

What could I say? With dreadful resignation I said, 'You'd better remind me how it goes.'

So then I was trying to remember the pitch as well as concentrate on directions. My palms were so wet they were sliding all over the steering wheel and I still couldn't seem to get enough air.

Some time, today will be over, I told myself. Some time in the future this horrible day will have ended. Then I changed it to, Some day I'll be dead and at peace and none of this will matter.

More by luck than judgement, we finally arrived at Empire Studios. You couldn't miss it. On top of each of the two gateposts they had twelve-foot-high Freds.

I rolled down the window and gave our names to the man with the clipboard, who confirmed we were on the list. 'Welcome to Empire Studios.'

'Nice dogs,' I nodded at the Freds.

'Oh yeah?' The man laughed. 'Thing is, guy who made them had a grudge against the studio. When it rains, it looks like the dogs are peeing.' Then he cheerfully waved us through.

Empire Studios looked very different to Hothouse. Hothouse had been high-rise glass and steel, but this studio looked like it had been built in the thirties: rows of unassuming-looking, white, two-storey buildings. It reminded me of a holiday camp.

Not that it meant that Empire was any less successful or powerful than Hothouse, it just meant it had been around for longer. And the reception area was covered with posters from mega-successful movies, just like it had been at Hothouse. The only difference was that this time it didn't thrill me. It all felt like a nasty sham and though my knees were wobbling the way they had done there, this time it was from fear, not excitement.

'Take a seat,' the text-book-beautiful receptionist said.

'Are you OK?' I whispered to Emily, as we sat down.

'Yeah, I just feel like I'm dreaming.'

'Try and stay awake,' I encouraged desperately.

'I'll try.'

A few minutes later, we were met by Larry Savage's assistant, a pleasant-looking woman called Michelle.

'I loved your script,' she told us warmly. 'I truly loved it.'

It was all I could do to stop myself from curling my lip at her.

'This way, please,' she said, walking us through the heat to Larry Savage's chalet.

I'd seen Larry Savage – briefly – once before at the Club House, and he looked just like I remembered: an identikit Hollywood executive. He had the tan, good teeth, well-cut lightweight suit and – no doubt – a convincing line in bullshit. I'd become very cynical very quickly.

He was on the phone as we were ushered in. 'I don't freakin' care,' he was shouting. 'We test-screen the ass off it. If no one salutes, then it's straight to video.' An angry pause, then he yelled, 'No, you kiss MINE!' Then he clattered the phone back into its cradle and turned to Emily and me. 'Actors,' he said, with a rueful smile.

'Yeah,' I rolled my eyes sycophantically, then effected introductions.

'All righty. I read your script,' he began.

I almost put my arm up to shield us from the avalanche of fake compliments. Funny, edgy, great dialogue – hadn't we been here before?

'I hated it!' Larry Savage declared.

Now I hadn't been expecting *that*. Then I wondered if it was going to be one of those 'I hated it so much I want to pay you three million dollars for it' riffs?

Unfortunately, it wasn't.

'I hated it,' Larry repeated. 'Me, I like animals!'

'So we've heard,' Emily slurred beside me.

I gave her arm a sharp little pinch.

'Fred, Babe, Beethoven, now *that* was a movie...' Larry sighed wistfully. 'But the studio is looking for smart.' He bitch-slapped the script in front of him. 'This is real smart.' He managed to sound glum about it. 'It's sassy, snappy, pacy. But I got an idea, hear me out here!'

We nodded. Not that it made any difference, he fully intended to have his say. 'These girls in your movie go on the run. How about their pet dog goes with them, stows himself away in the trunk of the car, they discover him when it's too late to bring him back, but they're real happy. Then he tips them off when the rangers are coming. Y'know, he wakes 'em by pulling the bed clothes off with his teeth.' Suddenly Larry started speaking in falsetto. '"What's up, Chip? Had a bad dream, boy? Go back to sleep, boy. Oh, you won't? You think the rangers are coming. Wake up, Jessie, wake up!!!"' He returned to his normal voice. 'The pet doggie saves the day. Got a problem with that?' he barked (appropriately enough) at Emily.

Mutely, she shook her head.

'Terrific.' Suddenly he was all smiles. 'I look forward to working with you. Your people will be hearing from my people.'

Then, an arm around each of our shoulders, he was walking us back out into the too-bright sunshine.

As Emily lurched to the car, she mumbled, 'Did I dream that bit?'

'The bit about the dog saving them from the rangers?'

'No, the bit where he said my people would be hearing from his people.'

'He said it all right.'

'But nobody *ever* says that in real life.'

'This isn't real life.'

It was only when we were clambering into the car that we noticed that neither of us had had to pitch to him.

'After all our practice,' I laughed. 'But it's probably for the best.'

'So how d'you think it all went?' Emily asked, dazedly. 'Any chance he might buy it and save my life?'

I considered it – there had been no talk of fast-tracking, green-lighting, three thousand screens or major stars. But Mort Russell had done all that and it had amounted to nothing, so who knew? And did Emily really want to rewrite her witty, sexy script as *Chip, the Wonder Dog*? But before I got to say any of that, Emily had fallen asleep on me. She slept for the entire hellish journey home, so she never knew that I took a wrong turning on the 405 and ended up halfway to Tijuana, passing turn-offs to all sorts of dodgy neighbourhoods before I managed to turn around.

Once back in Santa Monica, there was still no rousing her, so I had to call in on the Goatee Boys and get Ethan to help carry her from the car. Which was almost more trouble than it was worth, because he made me take her arms and insisted that he'd carry her legs, and I knew, just *knew* it was so he could look up her skirt. Then, when we'd flung her on the bed, he suggested hopefully, 'We better undress her. Like, in case she can't breathe and stuff.'

'No! Thank you, Ethan! Goodbye!'

I wanted to get rid of him fast, because as we'd stumbled into the house I'd noticed there was a message on the machine. It had to be from Troy. And sure enough, when I hit 'play' a man's voice said warmly, 'Hey, baby . . .' I exhaled with relief. But another second in, my reprieve curdled into bitter disappointment. This wasn't Troy. It was Lou, Emily's commitmentphobe. But what the hell was he doing ringing her? According to her prediction, she was never going to hear from him again. And here he was, calling her 'dollface' and suggesting that they catch a movie tomorrow night.

Abruptly all hope departed, like air from a burst beachball. For the past two days I'd been pumping myself with faith, warding off doubt – and suddenly I had no defence. Why hadn't Troy called me? It was Monday afternoon, almost evening – I'd last seen him on Saturday morning and he'd said he'd call me. Well, I'd asked him to call me and he hadn't said no. But I hadn't heard a word. Why?

At that, my worst suspicions began to multiply like bacteria in a Petri dish. Had I a horrible body? Was I boring? Had I not been good in bed? After all, I'd been out of practice for so long that I could have been atrocious and not known. But he'd *seemed* to enjoy himself. Then again, Mort Russell had *seemed* to love Emily's script and hadn't. Was this city just one big hall of mirrors, where nothing was what it seemed?

Immobilized by despair, all I could see ahead of me was an empty, burnt-out future. Then I remembered the vile day I'd had: anyone would feel discouraged after it. I tried hard to generate a tiny amount of positivity. Troy was probably just busy. Emily had said he was fanatical about his work. And the night we'd spent together, he'd really seemed to like me. We'd had fun. He *would* ring me.

Just about convinced, I turned my attention to the telly, and spent several catatonic hours in front of it, too tired even to eat. At around eleven, I heard noises from Emily's room. She must have finally woken up. When I went in, she was sitting up in bed like a princess.

'You know what, Maggie?' And her smile was anxious. 'I had the strangest dream.'

28

The night's sleep wrought an astonishing change in me and I came to full of benign thoughts. Troy was going to ring me today, I just *knew.*

For once, my mood matched the weather. Most mornings since I'd come to Los Angeles I'd woken up with foreboding, shocked on a daily basis at finding my life so altered. But today my expectations were as sunny as the elements.

Emily was in the kitchen cradling a huge, crackly cellophaned bouquet. 'Look,' she said. 'Lou sent them. What's he up to?' She was genuinely perplexed. 'This must be some new mutation of the commitmentphobe syndrome. They knew we were getting resistant to the One Fantastic Night thing, they *knew* we expected never to hear from them again, so they've had to raise their game. He wants us to go out again tonight. Well,' she laughed, 'he must think I'm a bigger fool than I look!'

'You don't think for a second that he could be sincere?'

A firm shake of the head. 'I do not. Because if he did mean all that stuff about telling our grandchildren, that would be the worst. To have grandchildren, you first have to have children and you know my views on – Oh, Maggie, I'm sorry!'

'It's OK.'

'I just wasn't thinking –'

Just then the phone rang and I jumped to answer it, knowing, with the same certainty that one and one equals two, that it would be Troy.

It turned out to be David. Well, I'd never had great psychic powers, that gift had gone to Anna.

David was once again sweetness and light. Not a mention of yesterday's rage – and certainly no apology. 'Hey, Larry loved you two!'

'That's funny,' I said stiffly. 'We barely opened our mouths. Has he found out about Mort Russell passing?'

'Don't know, but who cares now? You girls hooked him.'

'Did he tell you he wants to make it as an animal movie?'

'Details, details,' he dismissed airily. 'I gotta great feeling about this. Stand by for good news.'

When the phone rang again, I let Emily get it. Then I was sorry, because this time it really *was* Troy!

My heart gave one big, almost painful thump and my anticipation built and built as Emily went on for ages, filling Troy in on the dramatic events of the previous day. 'It's *déjà vu*,' she exclaimed at him. 'I'm *still* waiting for the phone to ring. Same shit, different studio!'

I pottered around in her vicinity, waiting for Troy to finish being polite to her and get to the real business of the call. But on and on they went, and I stopped pottering, I was wearing myself out. So I plonked myself in a nearby chair until *finally* she got round to making winding-up noises. I half got up, my arm stretching for the phone, which is when Emily did something unfathomable. She hung up. It seemed to happen in slow motion, her finger hovering over the red disconnect button, then moving in for the kill. Completely at a loss, I goggled at her and at the phone, which should still be connected but for some incomprehensible reason wasn't.

'What?' Emily looked confused.

'Didn't he ask . . . didn't he want to talk to me?'

'No.' Then, still staring at me, 'Oh shit.'

'Oh shit' was right. Troy's message to me could not have been clearer.

'Maggie, I didn't . . .' Emily squirmed and her manifest anguish belittled me. She pitied me and even though she'd commiserated on the end of my marriage, for a reason that I couldn't articulate, this stung a lot more.

'Maggie, I didn't realize you were expecting . . . something from him.'

'I wasn't.' My voice was barely there.

She was wrestling with some dilemma. With mortifying gentleness, she said, 'There's something you're probably better off knowing. When I called him on Saturday, Kirsty answered the phone.'

'You don't know for sure that something's going on with them.' My defiance was pathetic. 'And even if there is, he might decide he preferred me.'

'You're right.'

That did it. 'I think I want to lie down for a while.'

'No, Maggie, please . . .'

But I closed my bedroom door and redrew the curtains that I'd flung open with such anticipation less than an hour before, and climbed, fully clothed, between the sheets. This is what it's like, I understood. This is what it's like to be single and out there. I mean, I hadn't really thought that Troy and I would end up together and that I'd stay in Los Angeles and live happily ever after. Not for more than five seconds, anyway. But I hadn't expected it to be a for-one-night-only extravaganza either.

So much for living dangerously; it wasn't half as nice as

people made out. Unless the fault was in me. Maybe it was an acquired taste, like olives. I should probably just keep at it until I'd learnt to enjoy it.

Some time later, Emily tiptoed in. 'I'm really sorry,' she whispered. 'How do you feel?'

'I don't know.'

'Humiliated?'

'Yip.'

'Rejected?'

'Yip.'

'Betrayed?'

'Yip.'

'Not good enough?'

'Yip.'

'Lonely?'

'Yip.'

'Ashamed that you lay down and gave it up so easily?'

I closed my eyes. Lord, did she have to be so graphic.

'*Not* ashamed that you lay down and gave it up so easily?' She sounded puzzled.

'Yes, ashamed.'

'That's what I thought. Didn't think you'd changed that much. Have I forgotten anything?'

How about missing my husband? I thought, but didn't say. Both losses had merged into one and I was grounded by their combined weight. For a while, when I'd been with Troy, I'd danced on stardust. Now the glitter had fallen from the sky and all was drab and grey again. While I'd been caught up in Troy, I'd flirted with another life, with being someone else.

Now I was back to being me and I longed to scuttle back to the safe haven of marriage, where this humiliation would disappear. But I couldn't even ring Garv – until I'd found out for definite about Truffle Woman, I'd felt that option was always available to me if missing him got too bad. Now that door was closed. Anyway, wanting to go back to Garv because another man had humiliated me was hardly a healthy reason.

'Have you any idea . . . ?' I asked Emily. 'Why . . . Troy . . . might do this to me?'

'That's just the way he is,' she explained earnestly. 'He likes the ladies but he's too into his work, not interested in a relation-ship.'

She didn't say that she'd told me so. She's nice that way. Anyway, he'd as good as warned me himself when he'd said, 'I am baaaad news.' But he'd been laughing when he'd said it and, like an eejit, I thought the laugh meant that he was joking.

'He should have left you alone,' she said. 'You're too vulner-able.'

'Too stupid, you mean,' I muttered, hating myself for being so naïve, inexperienced, out of practice. I'd fallen for the oldest trick in the book – a man had been nice to me and I'd thought it meant something.

'Don't be hard on yourself – this is normal, you're on the rebound! You're on your own for the first time in years, you're more than a bit lost, who could blame you for going looking?'

All of a sudden, I was furious with Troy. Him and his concern and his twizzlers and compliments about my hair and calling me 'Irish'. To think I'd once thought he was ugly, with his long features and his hair-grip mouth. Someone with a nose that size had no right to go round breaking hearts!

And small wonder the sex had been so fluid and unclumsy: he was an expert, the guy had a black belt in riding. Christ, he even had special bondage ropes! What did that tell me about his dedication?

Then I cringed as I remembered the most embarrassing bit of all – to think I'd asked him to . . . to *call* me. All those years listening to my single friends and had I learnt *nothing*? You never let on you want to be called. If *he* says he'll ring *you*, you've to murmur, 'Whatever,' like you so couldn't give a damn. What you don't do is throw your hat in the air and burst into 'Happy Days Are Here Again'. Isn't it funny how we all know the rules, but we never think they apply to us?

I was going about this break-up lark all wrong. The usual procedure is you feel awful, then a little bit better, then another little bit. And then a big bit. But the more time had gone on since Garv and I had split, the worse I felt. How much further did I have to proceed into this heart of darkness before I came out the other side?

How was Garv getting on with the single life? Was he faring better than me? Or was he as miserable too? Probably not: he was a man, they always seem to find this sort of thing easier. And who exactly was his girlfriend? How serious was it? Those tormenting thoughts which had been dormant for a while were now back in force.

'I'm giving up on men,' I said bitterly. 'Do you know what I'm going to become?'

'Oh no,' Emily moaned softly. 'Don't say it, because someone round here might take you up on it. Anyway, you have it all wrong. Lesbians are just as bad as men, as far as I can see. They say they'll call then they don't. They sleep with you, then ditch you –'

'I wasn't going to say lesbian,' I interrupted. 'Although it's a thought.'

'Noooo,' she covered her eyes.

'What I was about to say was I'm going to become one of those fabulous single women who go on about choices a lot.' Bitterly, I pretended to be airy and launched into, '"It's just *great* being single because I can *choose* which side of the bed to sleep on. I can *choose* who I want to spend time with, and who I don't. I don't have to waste time on my partner's *boring* family or workmates. No negotiations, no compromises." It'll be fantastic. I'll have tons of friends, a huge mother-ship hand bag from Coach, linen drawstring pants and beautifully cut but practical hair.' Somehow I'd mutated into Sharon Stone.

'Or maybe I won't,' I finished with a sigh. Maybe I'd just end up moving back in with my parents so we could become our street's version of the Addams Family. I would grow a moustache. Eventually I would bow to the inevitable at the hairdresser's and ask for an Irish Mammy.

I wanted to go home. I was so hurt and embarrassed by the way Troy had rejected me that I wanted to put as many miles as possible between me and him. For a while, the dazzling Californian sunshine had bleached out the sharp contours of my pain, but my eyes had adjusted until my anguish was just as severe here as it had been in Ireland. Like a painkiller that becomes less and less effective the more it's used, Los Angeles had stopped working for me. I'd always suspected this would happen, but I didn't expect it to be so soon. I'd only been here two weeks and my initial plan had been to stay for about a month. Ah, well . . .

I was acutely aware of how much I didn't belong here. Mind you, where did I belong? 'Home' didn't really exist any longer. But there was so much music to be faced in Ireland that sooner or later I was going to have to bite the bullet and return – and in the wake of my humiliation at the hands of Troy, I wanted to leave for the airport immediately. I looked for my suitcase; I still hadn't fully unpacked, mostly because I had no closet-space – it wouldn't take me ten minutes to gather up my stuff and ship out of here. The image of me getting on a plane was as comforting as a padded plaster on a blister.

But what about Emily? How selfish would it be to leave her at this nerve-wracking time? Reluctantly, I concluded that I should wait until we heard from Larry Savage. Either he'd buy her script and she'd be fine, or he'd pass and her adventures in Lala land would also come to an end. Whichever happened, we'd know very soon.

That decision made, I rang my parents to tell them I was homeward bound: the mere act made me feel like I was already on my way.

Dad answered, with his customary terror. 'Which one of you is that? Oh, Margaret.' I waited for him to be overcome with the noxious gas given off by the phone, but to my surprise he stayed talking. 'Have you been to Disneyland yet?'

I hadn't.

'You should go, it's marvellous! And they've other ones too. Some Six Flags place. They say it has the world's highest rollercoaster.'

'Think of your neck,' I said firmly. 'Anyway, how do you know about the Six Flags place?'

'Read about it on the Net.'

'*What* net?'

'The Internet Net.'

'What are you doing on the Internet Net?' I couldn't hide my surprise. Surprise which bordered on indignation.

'Helen set it up.'

'He's never off it,' Mum's voice cut in, on the extension. 'Cruising on the Net, looking at pornography.'

'I do not look at pornography!'

'There's no need to shout. And I know all about what goes on on that Net.'

'I'm not shouting, I only sound loud because you're just upstairs from me. And there's other things go on on the Net besides pornography.'

'Like what?'

'Holidays.'

A pause, then a suspicious, 'Flights?'

'Yes, flights.'

'To sunny places?'

I had a clear and unpleasant insight into where all this was heading, and decided to nip it in the bud. 'I'm coming home soon. In the next few days.'

'*Are you?*' High-pitched and irritated and perfectly in unison.

Just as I'd suspected. Well, hopefully that had knocked that on the head.

But later I spoke to Emily about it. 'I've a bad feeling Mum and Dad might be planning a visit here.'

'Don't be silly,' Emily said.

'No, I'm serious.'

'So'm I. They couldn't come here because they haven't had it booked since last November. They're not exactly spontaneous, are they? I mean, their idea of being mad-cap and spur-of-the-moment would be to plan a weekend break for next spring.'

Thus comforted, I put my fears from my mind.

*

But I hadn't reckoned on Helen and her surfermania and it all came to a dreadful head three short hours later.

'. . . booked the flights on the Internet Net,' Mum was saying. 'No need to bother with travel agents, you just type in your details and they give you all these choices. This Net is a great invention!'

'But I want to go home.'

'Well you can't,' she said pleasantly. 'We'll need you to show us the sights. Sure, what difference can a few more days make, anyway?'

For God's sake. I had to bite my knuckle to stifle a scream of frustration.

'Where will you stay?' Then I added very quickly, 'There's no room here.'

'We wouldn't dream of imposing,' Mum said graciously. 'I spoke to Mrs Emily and she gave me the name of the hotel that she stayed in when she came over. Only down the road from Emily's and very friendly, she says, and the breakfast is nice and you get little yokes . . .'

'What little yokes?' I asked wearily.

'Shower caps, sewing kits, the lend of an umbrella. Not that I'd be needing an umbrella,' she sounded suddenly fearful, 'because I'm coming to get away from the rain. If it starts raining in Los Angeles, I'm just booking myself into the mental hospital and let that be an end to it.'

'Well, you know what they say?'

A mistrustful pause. 'That you shouldn't put butter on a burn?'

'They say, it never rains in California.'

'Good,' she said firmly.

'It pours!'

But even that wasn't enough to deter her.

'They arrive on Tuesday,' I reported to an appalled Emily.

'Oh, good Christ.'

29

I clung grimly to sleep as though to the side of a cliff. Reluctantly I rose towards consciousness until I was covered only by a thin veil of sleep, but still I refused to surface. It was the sound of the ringing phone that finally made me give in and face the day.

God, was I sorry that I had. My first thought was of Troy and his horrible, humiliating rejection of me. The second was that, with my family coming to visit, I was trapped in Los Angeles.

Unless ... unless they'd messed up their Internet reservations. The more I thought about it, the more I saw that the chances of them either a) getting seats on a flight that actually existed or b) booking themselves on a flight to Los Angeles instead of say, Phnom Penh or Tierra Del Fuego were very slim indeed.

I began to cheer up, and when Emily tapped quietly on my door I was able to smile at her. Until she handed me the phone and whispered, 'Mammy Walsh.'

Within seconds, my worst fears were confirmed. It was a perfectly straightforward American Airways flight from Dublin to LAX – and they were definitely booked on it. 'I rang this morning and got confirmation,' Mum said cheerily. She even had a flight number. In fact, she'd even reserved their seats and a vegetarian meal for Anna! Which was the first I'd heard of Anna coming.

'How long will you be staying?'

'Helen's got to be back to do Marie Fitzsimon's wedding – seven bridesmaids, three flower girls, the bride, the mother of the bride and the mother of the groom – so we won't get the full two weeks –'

'*Two* weeks!' I'd have to stay here and face Troy for another two weeks! For the love of Christ!

'– so twelve days is how long we're coming for. Now have a word with your father, he wants to know should he bring his shorts.'

As soon as I was off the phone, things got worse; Emily wanted to have a little 'chat' with me. 'As you know,' she began awkwardly, 'I still haven't heard from Larry Savage and I'm not holding out much hope. Lara made a suggestion the other evening –'

I already knew what was coming.

'– about me looking for other work doing script polishes.'

I couldn't bear it any longer. 'Ring him,' I said.

'She suggested several people, one of them being . . . Oh! Do you mean it? Shay Delaney – you wouldn't mind if I rang him?'

'Why would I mind?' Like, what grounds did I have?

'Maggie, please be honest with me. Just say the word and I won't go near him.'

'Go for it.'

Anxiously she asked, 'Are you sure?'

'Completely.'

'Thanks, thank you. I'm just so desperate for work and I know it was a long time ago, you and him, but first cut is the deepest, as they say. So I was afraid you might be cross with me, and –'

'It's fine,' I interrupted, a little too brusquely. 'Just fine.'

Quickly, she said, 'I won't ring him. I'm sorry I even asked you, it was wrong of me.'

'Ring him, I don't MIND!' The yell hung in the air, shocking us both, then I took a breath and forced a more reasonable tone. 'I don't mind, I promise. Just don't make me keep saying it.'

Bu–'

'Nnnneh!'

'Are you sure?'

'Yes.'

'OK.'

I was hoping that she'd take days to get round to it, but she rang him immediately – so I went to my room, where I could listen avidly without being observed. She didn't get to talk to him, but when she said, 'So he *is* in town right now?' I watched my fingers begin to tremble, although nothing like as badly as the day I'd met him and I hadn't been able to undo the zip on Dad's anorak afterwards. Emily spelt out her name for whoever she was talking to, 'O'Keeffe. O-K-E-E-F-F-E, yeah, O'Keeffe. It's Irish. No, *Irish*. So if you could have him call me, that would be great. Bye.'

Then she came looking for me. 'Maggie? He wasn't there.'

'Wasn't he?' I said neutrally, like I hadn't been standing behind the door, holding my breath in order to overhear and slowly turning purple.

'No. No, he wasn't. So what would you like to do today?' she asked solicitously. 'We could go to the beach or for a drive – or how about we go out for lunch?'

'You've work to do.'

'I can skip it.'

I couldn't help laughing. 'I'm O-K!'

'Bu–'

'Nnnneh!'

She was clearly reluctant to let it go, but at least she didn't start disagreeing with me again.

'Do some work,' I urged.

'All right.' She switched on her laptop and disappeared into her writing. I switched on the telly, hoping for a similar type of escape, and so began another day without someone buying Emily's script: I had a sudden surreal flash that I was in some sort of Beckettian play, and that the rest of my life was going to be spent stuck in this house with Emily, waiting for good news that never came.

After thirty minutes of unproductive channel-hopping, my nerves couldn't take any more so I decided we needed food, and set off for the supermarket.

The raggedy shouting man was there, like he always was, this time roaring about police shoot-outs and heroes taking a bullet. I must have been giving off kick-me-when-I'm-down signals, because as soon as I got out of the car he lit up, sprinted straight across the parking lot at me and yelled 'Zoom!' right into my face.

My heart pounded with shock. Though Emily had said he meant no harm, he seemed out-of-control crazy. Skirting around him and his manic eyes and his bad smell, I hurried across the tarmac, trying to avoid the indignity of full-blown running. I was close to tears by the time I reached the air-conditioned haven of the supermarket.

Then there was the worry of how to get back to the car without being accosted by him, so when I had finished shopping, half-ashamed of my wussiness, I asked one of the bag-packing boys to escort me. Just as well I did, because as soon as we appeared through the sliding doors, the raggedy man yelled angrily at me, 'You're supposed to be ALONE!'

'He's kinda harmless really,' the boy tried to reassure me, as we put our heads down and rattled the trolley at high speed across the parking lot.

'Mmmm.' But I was no longer that concerned for my physical safety. It was what the nutter had said: 'You're supposed to be alone.' It sounded almost prophetic and I was indescribably depressed by it.

'We've a visitor,' Emily said as I staggered into the house with the shopping bags. I assumed it was Ethan. Since the night he'd slept on the couch, he was a regular guest, under some illusion that he was welcome. He kept showing up to hang out and watch television.

But it wasn't Ethan, it was Mike, armed with his smudge stick and lepping about good-oh.

'Hey, Maggie,' he grinned. 'Just clearing a little more of the toxic energy in here.'

'Good man,' Emily urged. 'Get rid of it all, so I'll get good news from the studio.'

'That's not how it works.' Mike gasped a little from his exertions. 'What it means is the right thing will happen.'

'And the right thing is that they'll buy it for a million dollars.'

'I keep telling you, be careful what you wish for,' Mike grinned.

When he was taking a breather from the dancing, he turned his attention to me. 'And how about you, Maggie?'

'I'm OK,' I said unenthusiastically.

'Yeah?'

'Mmmm.'

He beamed at me, a full-on, beardy beam and said, 'When you're in a dark place, you know what you gotta do?'

I shrugged. 'What?'

'Hold your face up to the light.'

I hadn't a clue what he meant, I don't really get that woolly, mystical talk, but for the second time that day I was a little tearful.

'Be kind to yourself,' he said.

'How?'

'Nurture yourself. Take time out to smell the flowers or listen to the ocean.'

'Um –'

'You'll know what's right for you. Maybe do a little meditation and listen to your own stillness?'

'Ah, OK.'

'Hey, if you girls aren't doing anything tonight, why don't you come by ours? We're having one of our fable-telling evenings.'

Both Emily and I froze as we frantically sought some sort of excuse.

'Er, what goes on at this fable-telling evening?' I asked. It was the best I could do.

'Some beautiful people come by and we tell stories from our different cultures.'

'When you say beautiful people,' Emily said, 'you're not talking about Gucci-sunglasses-streaked-hair-and-speedboat beautiful people?'

Mike laughed. 'I mean beautiful on the inside.'

'I was afraid of that. Anyway, asking me to come to a fable-telling evening would be like inviting a dentist over for dinner, then getting him to do a couple of root canals between courses. I'm telling stories all day long, it's my job.'

Mike shrugged equably. 'I hear you.'

I shoved my feet into my mules. 'OK, I'm off.'

'Where?'

'I'm holding my face up to the light and I'm going shopping. I don't know how I didn't think of it before now.'

'Excellent!' Emily said. 'Good for you.'

I took myself down to Santa Monica, where I spent an unexpectedly happy afternoon wandering along Third Street Promenade in the sunshine, popping in and out of Aladdin's Caves of fabulousness.

So much was happening that I was once again glad to be in LA: a man with a clipboard gave me two tickets for a test-screening of a new movie; I saw someone who might have been Sean Penn buying a packet of Lifesavers; a man painted from head to toe in silver, juggling silver balls, was being filmed by a small crew. All the time the sun shone and the funny-knees-denim-skirt shop gave me a sympathetic hearing. 'Why are you returning this garment?' the girl asked, her pen poised over the form (oh yes, you've to fill out a form when you return things).

'It makes my knees look funny.'

'Makes . . . knees . . . look . . . funny,' she said as she wrote.

Then she went to her manager to see if making knees look funny was worthy of an actual refund or just a credit note. It was close, she told me, it had gone to the wire, but in the end the manager felt that as the garment couldn't actually be regarded as defective, I was only due a credit note.

For the rest of the afternoon, I didn't even do my usual stunt of buying too much of the wrong things. Money changed hands only once – when I bought two little T-shirts with stuff written on them. Emily's said 'I want, I want, I want' and mine said 'Boys are Mean'.

Feeling miles better, I arrived home, where Emily professed herself to be in love with her new T-shirt. 'I'll wear it tonight. Will you come out for a drink later?'

'And play gooseberry with you and Lou?'

'Lou?' she said scornfully. 'He can get lost with his flowers and his phone calls – does he take me for a total idiot?'

'So who's going out tonight?'

'Me. Troy.'

I managed a short, bitter, 'Hah!'

'Oh please, please don't be like that. Troy sleeps with everyone and he stays friends with them.'

'I'm obviously very old-fashioned, then,' I said stiffly.

'Please come out with us.' She was a knot of anxiety.

'Who's inviting me? You? Or him? And be honest!'

'Both of us.'

'Did he say anything about me?'

'Um . . .'

'Don't lie!'

'No, I suppose he didn't.'

Hurt though I was, I could see some good in this; if he was planning to avoid me for the rest of my visit, it would cut down on opportunities for me to feel humiliated.

'You go out,' I urged. 'Enjoy yourself, you've been working all day. And before you ask again, I'm FINE.'

Off she went, and though I had numerous invitations – the fable-telling evening on one side of me or watching a digitally remastered *Rosemary's Baby* on the other – I parked myself in front of the telly, defiantly wearing my 'Boys are Mean' T-shirt. To pass the time, I planned scathing put-downs for Troy, unable to decide between maintaining a dignified silence or shrilly berating him for his alley-cat morals. It was extremely enjoyable.

At some stage the news came on, with a piece about the Irish peace process, and I got the fright of my life: for a moment I thought the colour on the telly was broken. Everything was grey, and the Irish politicians were so pallid, as if their skin had never seen sunlight. And as for their teeth . . .

Oh dear. I'd crossed the invisible line: now I thought glowing skin and expensive dentistry were normal. With a sigh, I resumed my imaginary conversations with Troy.

Some time later, a car screeched to a jarring halt outside, a door was slammed, then came the clatter of heels on the path. I listened to them, wondering where they were going, and located them just as they burst into the room, bearing a mussed and distraught Lara.

'Where's Emily?'

'Out with Troy. What's wrong?'

'Oh my God!'

'A glass of wine?' I suggested.

She nodded and followed me into the kitchen.

'What's wrong?' I asked again. Had she been mugged? Or in a car crash?

'It's Nadia. She called me tonight, and on my new caller display panel her number came up as "Mr and Mrs Hindel". Can you believe it – Mr and Mrs Hindel! She's married. The bitch is married!'

I poured the wine faster and said, 'It could be a mistake. She might have been married once but they could be separated now.'

'Oh no, she admitted it all.' Lara caught sight of herself in the mirror and groaned. 'God, I look like twelve miles of rough road.' In fairness, I'd seen her looking better: her lovely tan was mushroom-coloured. 'She was totally up front about it – she was just a sexual tourist having an adventure.'

After a painful gap, Lara squeezed out, 'She was just using me.' And she began to cry in a contained, dignified way that brought a lump to my own throat. 'I really liked her,' she wept, the way women usually weep about men. 'It hurts just as bad when it's a girl.'

'I know, I know.' Well, I knew now, didn't I?

'I thought she was someone special.'

'You'll meet someone else.' I stroked her hair.

'I won't!'

'Shush, you will. Of course you will. You're beautiful.'

'I feel so bad.'

'You do now, but you'll get over it. She wasn't the one for you.'

'Yeah, you're right.' With a watery smile, she said, 'I'll give myself a week to obsess about her, then I'll get over her.'

'That's the spirit,' I encouraged.

'Thanks.'

Foreheads almost touching, we shared a rueful, can't-live-with-them-can't-shoot-them look and, all of a sudden, she was taking my face in her hands and kissing me softly on the lips. I was startled, but even so I noticed that it wasn't unpleasant.

That was the moment, of course, that Emily chose to come home. I saw her shock before I saw her face; white and appalled, it loomed through the night-time window at me. In more of a hurry than usual, she burst into the house and looked, in confusion, from Lara to me.

'What's going on?' she asked.

'You're not going to *believe* this.' Lara began her tale of woe.

Both Emily and I listened intently to Lara, but we weren't meeting each other's eye much. Not at all, in fact. We didn't even exchange words until eventually I said, 'I'd better go to sleep. I need my full fourteen hours.'

Then Emily called after me, 'Troy says hey.'

'Does he? 'Night.'

I went to bed and shut my eyes and for once I wasn't thinking about Garv. I wasn't even thinking about Troy. I was thinking about Lara.

30

The next morning, in the time between chopping the bananas for my first-thing smoothie and putting them in the blender, we were informed of Emily's salvation – Larry Savage had bought her screenplay!

Naturally enough, she nearly screeched the house down with relief. And nothing, not even the proviso that she had to rewrite the script to include Chip the dog, could dent her joy.

'I'll change my entire cast to orang-utans if he wants!' Emily declared. 'So long as he gives me the money.'

'How much will you get?' I asked, feeling pretty uplifted myself.

'Writers' Guild minimum, the stingy bastard,' she said airily. 'It's nearly an insult!'

But an insult that ran to almost six figures. With the promise of half a million dollars if they actually made the movie.

The thing was, though – *would* they make it? I knew from my own small experience that this was impossible to gauge; no matter how enthusiastic a producer was, they still had to convince the studio executives and the Green-Light Guy that it was a movie worth making. And that was easier said than done. But still, we wouldn't worry about that today . . .

Emily surgically attached herself to the phone and began a ringathon: that night we were having another party, a *proper* party, and this time we really had something to celebrate.

Meanwhile, the good news was criss-crossing amongst her friends, and those that hadn't already spoken to her were ringing in, so call waiting was doing overtime. 'Hold on a minute, the other line is going,' I kept hearing.

And one of those call waitings was Shay Delaney. I knew immediately: the air molecules around Emily seemed to re-arrange themselves into a guilt-filled configuration. What a terrible pity he hadn't rung the previous night and left a mes-sage, because I could have wiped it and Emily would never have known. And what an even worse pity that I'd never have the guts to do something like that.

When the telephone frenzy had played itself out, Emily approached me as I sought out a clean T-shirt in my suitcase.

'I invited Shay Delaney to come tonight,' she said apologetic-ally. 'In the heat of the moment, it just slipped out. Do you mind?'

'Bit late if I do,' I said briskly, continuing to rummage in my suitcase.

'I could uninvite him.'

As if.

'I'll do it right now.'

'No, it's OK.' Tonight was Emily's long-awaited celebration, I had no right to spoil it. And Shay Delaney was ancient history.

Emily decided the party should be catered. I was doubtful – my only experience of caterers was of acquiring dozens of sample menus, taking six weeks to deliberate over them, then finally deciding it would be cheaper to pay my mother to make ham sandwiches and apple tarts. But in Los Angeles, you just pick up the phone and say, 'I want Vietnamese finger food, miniature pastries and pink champagne for forty.' And four hours later, three buffed out-of-work actors are efficiently transforming your house into a white-clothed, crystal-glinting venue, bursting at the seams with Vietnamese finger food, miniature pastries and pink champagne. As smooth and speedy as Formula One engineers changing a tyre, they were, and the moment the last champagne glass was placed in the triangular configuration and the last sprig of coriander placed on the pile of glass noodle spring rolls, they were on their way again.

'Off to save someone else's party?' Emily asked.

'You got it.'

'Well, thank you Super Caterers, how can we ever repay you?'

'Just doin' our job, ma'am.'

'And the invoice is in the mail.'

'And we know where you live.'

'We'll be back for the glasses and stuff in the morning. Enjoy!'

Once they'd gone, Emily decided we'd try the pink champagne. 'Just to make sure it isn't poisonous.'

We clinked glasses and Emily said, 'I couldn't have done it without you. To my lovely assistant, Maggie.'

'To a brilliant script!' I said gallantly.

'To Larry Savage!'

'To Chip the dog!'

'To a cast of orang-utans!'

In the dreamy, happy silence that followed, I heard myself ask, 'Does he know I'm staying with you?'

'Who?'

'Shay Delaney.'

'No. Well, I never mentioned it.'

Just like that, my bubble burst and I was at the mercy of all the stupid feelings you get when someone was once your sole preserve but now you're out in the cold, excluded and irrelevant.

And speaking of excluded and irrelevant, 'Is Troy coming tonight?'

'Yeah.' Emily looked uncomfortable. 'I know you don't want to see him, but he's been my friend for a long time and he's helped me so much with the script. I couldn't not invite him.'

I saw her point, but this put paid to my hope that Troy would have the decency to steer clear of me for the rest of my stay and thereby spare me any further mortification. It stung that I wasn't even worthy of being avoided!

'Well, if Troy's coming,' I said, whipping off my 'Boys are Mean' T-shirt, 'I'd better find something else to wear.'

'Why?'

'In the words of the song: He's so vain, I bet he'll think this T-shirt's about him.'

Shortly after seven, people started arriving. Justin and Desiree were the first to show up. Next, bearing a bottle of champagne, came Lou the commitmentphobe, who was swarthy, sexy and extremely pleasant. When I whispered to Emily how nice he seemed, she replied, 'Oh, these guys are clever, I'm not saying they're not.'

Then I saw Troy's jeep parking across the road, and to my shame I immediately began wishing for the best: that he might take me to one side and whisper an apology about how he'd been too busy to ring me – even though I knew for a fact *it wouldn't happen.*

And how right I was! As he alighted from his car, I got a pain in my stomach when I saw that he was accessorized by Kirsty. Then they were crossing the road and coming through the door. Before I had time to wonder how he'd behave, he was walking straight over to me. My heart constricted with hope . . . then he was planting a brotherly kiss on my cheek and saying, real goofy and friendly like, with none of the innuendo I'd come to expect, 'So Irish, you were the one driving the getaway car!'

'What?' I asked shrewishly. Funny that, I'd *meant* to sound calm and cool.

'You saved the day on Monday, right? Driving Emily across town to Empire. Even offered to do the pitch, yeah? If it hadn't been for you, well, who knows . . . Oh, thanks,' he took a drink from Justin. 'Hey guys, how about we raise our glasses to Irish?'

Justin and Lou obediently raised their glasses with Troy and chorused, 'To Irish!'

Interestingly enough, mind, Kirsty's glass of low-fat water didn't budge and her lips remained zipped.

'Hey, we haven't met – I'm Troy, Emily's friend.' Troy thrust his hand at Lou by way of introduction.

'Lou,' Lou replied evenly. 'Emily's boyfriend.'

'Oh,' Troy said. 'Yeah, right.' He was looking at Lou and Lou was looking at him – what I recognized as an Alpha-male moment. If they'd been lions they'd have been circling each other, sizing up their respective strengths.

'So where is she?' Troy looked around for Emily.

'Here!' she called, emerging from her bedroom.

Both Lou and Troy stepped forward, but Troy got there first and spread his arms in homage. 'The success story! Need a director?'

'Eat my shorts,' Emily laughed.

'So what's the catch?' Troy asked.

'Why should there be a catch?'

'C'mon Emily, you know these guys, there's always a catch. How bad is it?'

'Chip the dog gets a part.'

'You happy to do that?'

'If the man is happy to give me the money.'

'Whatever happened to art?' Troy teased. 'Whatever happened to principles?'

'Amazing how easy it is to compromise when you're broke and scared,' she grinned.

'Yeah, I know,' Troy smiled. 'Congratulations, baby girl, I'm way happy for you.'

At this point, Kirsty decided that there was too much grinning and camaraderie going on with Emily and Troy, so she stepped between them and started whining to Troy about her mineral water having the wrong size bubbles, or something.

They arrived in their dozens: Lara, David Crowe, Mike and Charmaine, Connie and her entourage, Justin's two friends from the dog park, a gang of scriptwriters from Emily's Learning Annex class, another bunch from gyrotonics. It was so much like a rerun of last week's premature shindig that when I found the Goatee Boys moshing in the front room, I groaned, 'Groundhog day.'

Everyone brought presents: the studio had sent half a garden of flowers earlier; David Crowe had arrived with an arrangement only marginally smaller. It was a happy night, a night of celebration. Most of the people present were connected in some way with the world of movies, so Emily selling a script gave everyone a lift – a victory for one was a victory for all.

But I didn't feel happy or celebratory, not even close: I was burning up from Troy's treatment of me. Bad enough to use me for a one-night stand, but I wasn't even important enough for him to hide his carry-on with Kirsty from. At least he respected *her* enough to lie to her. And I was complicit in my own humiliation – by keeping my mouth shut, I was going along with it and making it easy for Troy.

It was all wrong, but I could see no way to make it right. What would be achieved by telling Kirsty I'd slept with Troy, then bitch-slapping her like we were on the *Jerry Springer Show*? Apart from the fact that I'd enjoy it?

So not only did I hate Troy – and Kirsty – but I hated myself. And, though I didn't like facing it, I was angry with Emily for inviting Shay Delaney. Small wonder that I felt I hated the whole world. My sole consolation was that I didn't hate Kirsty just because Troy was dancing attendance on her; luckily I'd already hated her.

I wandered around ungraciously shoving trays of food at people who seemed indignant at the implication that they occasionally ate. If it hadn't been for Justin I'd have had no takers at all.

'Gotta take care of this,' he said, wobbling his belly and popping a jumbo prawn into his mouth. 'I got my job to think of. Now, what about you, Princess?'

'Sure, another three or four more can't hurt,' I said, reaching for a prawn.

But he was talking to Desiree, tempting her with a spring roll, which she disdainfully turned her nose up at.

'See that?' he asked anxiously. 'She usta love Pacific Rim.'

'Maybe she's sick. Why don't you bring her to the vet?'

'She's not sick. It's worse than that.'

'What do you mean?'

'I'm scared she has anorexia.'

'Anorexia? But . . . but she's a *dog*.'

'Dogs can get anorexia,' he said sadly. 'There was a thing in the *LA Times* about it.'

'Please tell me that you're joking.'

'Maggie,' he said sadly, 'I wish I was.'

I picked up my tray and set off on another thankless circuit and wondered: What kind of place was this where even the dogs got eating disorders?

'See you at the pastries in five,' Justin called after me.

Justin and I kept bumping into each other in the garden at the tray of pastries. They'd lured me back so often I was actually beginning to get embarrassed and, sure enough, a short time later, Justin and I both showed up beside them.

'We've got to stop meeting like this,' I said, and in the hope that if I couldn't see them, I wouldn't be as tempted to eat them, I turned my back – and came face to face with Troy and Kirsty. *Shite.*

'Having fun?' Troy asked.

'Um, yeah.' I turned around, located a thumb-sized chocolate eclair and threw it at my mouth. I just couldn't help myself.

'Great news for Emily, huh?'

'Yeah, um . . .'

Then, like I was possessed by a sugar demon, I was picking up a dime-sized doughnut. (When you ask for 'miniature' in LA, that's exactly what you get.) Kirsty watched it carefully, following its journey from the tray to my mouth, then asked with fake sympathy, 'That's, like, number *at least* seven. Are you pre-menstrual?'

The taste of rough sugar vanished from my mouth, to be replaced with the taste of hatred.

'You know what you gotta do?' she carolled. 'You gotta try zinc. Zap those sugar cravings! But forget glucose, forget candy! I got something even better!' A statement like that was bound to attract a lot of attention in Los Angeles. Several heads turned

313

to her and when she was satisfied that her audience were hanging on her every word, she continued. 'Better'n all of them is – a frozen grape! Just buy grapes at the market, put them in the ice compartment, and any time those old sugar cravings come calling, scare 'em away by eating a frozen grape. Totally sweet and zero, read my lips, *zero* calories.'

All I could say was, 'Grapes have more than zero calories.' A poor attempt, but better than nothing.

'She's right,' Justin said, making mischievous eye contact with me. 'Grapes are very high in fructose. You're looking at fifteen to twenty calories a grape.'

'More,' I lied. I hadn't a clue. 'Depending on the size of the grape. If it's a big one and has a particularly high sugar content, you could be looking at as many as –' I paused for effect, '– FIFTY calories.'

'Seems to me you should stick with pastries,' Justin concluded, reaching for a tiny custard pie. 'Better for you!'

With that, Justin and I exchanged a high five with our eyes, then peeled away, leaving Kirsty with her reputation as a food guru in tatters.

Just when I thought I was in the clear, Shay Delaney arrived.

All evening I'd been as tense as an exam hall, wondering if he'd show, but the more time had passed the less likely it had been that he'd appear. Naturally enough, the minute I decided he wasn't coming was when I spotted a tall, dark-blond head across the garden. It couldn't be . . .

It was.

Every one of my muscles tensed as I waited for him to notice me. And waited. And waited . . .

He seemed to know almost everyone. Heads were thrown

back and laughter floated at me as he worked the garden and chewed the fat with David Crowe, Connie, and Emily's friend Dirk. Well, they say the movie world is very small.

Finally, unable to bear the suspense, I placed myself in his path.

Just like the last time, he looked gratifyingly shocked. 'Maggie Garvan!'

'Walsh,' I corrected, defiantly – the last time we'd met I'd have died if he'd found out about the breakdown of my marriage, and now I was determined that he should know about it.

'Walsh?'

'Yeah, Walsh.'

'Oh. So, what are you doing here?'

'Taking some down time.'

'Staying with Emily?'

'Yes.'

And then – just like the last time – 'Well, *great* to see you,' and he stuck out his hand for me to shake, then off he went, leaving me in a huge pool of anti-climax. I wanted to call after him, *Don't you want to know what happened? Why I'm Walsh now instead of Garvan?*

My mood darkened further. It was no fun being at a party where I'd been rejected by two of the men present. Why didn't they just fly Garv in to complete the set? Even though I'd had a laugh at Kirsty's expense, she was the one with Troy by her side. And there was Shay Delaney, hail-fellow-well-met-ing his way around the party, but he wasn't coming within a mile of me.

Well, I thought with a sigh, maybe he feels guilty. And maybe he should.

Without warning, Curtis bumped into me, jogging my drink and squeezing his weight down on to my toes. As sticky champagne slopped over my hands, rage leapt in me and at that moment I'd have had the strength to throttle him with my bare hands.

Maybe Kirsty was right, maybe I *was* pre-menstrual.

Tetchily, I sucked the champagne off my fingers and, all of a sudden, I got that tingly, hair-lifting feeling you get when someone is staring at you. I looked up and around the garden and my gaze landed on Lara. She was watching me. When she saw I'd noticed her, her face changed and she playfully rolled her eyes after Curtis, then flashed me her radiant smile, which seemed more radiant than usual. I smiled back, feeling a little head-spinny, a little off-balance, and a funny anticipation began to flicker in the pit of my stomach.

Most people left around midnight. Most people except for those I really wanted to see the back of: Troy, Kirsty and Shay arranged themselves in the kitchen around Emily, talking excitedly and roaring laughing. While, glowering with resentment, I trudged back and forth from the garden, carrying glasses, bottles and leftover food. Lara and Ethan flitted around me, loading the dishwasher in Lara's case and finishing any half-drunk glasses in Ethan's. Both, in their way, were helping.

'Excuse me,' I said, pushing past Troy to get to the bin and accidentally-on-purpose sticking a fork into the back of his leg.

'Ow!'

'Sorry,' I said, trying my very best not to sound it.

As I crumpled a paper plate into the bin, plans were being made for the following night: Troy, Shay and Emily felt that they could help each other out in their respective careers, and they were going out for dinner to discuss it.

'You'll come too, won't you, Maggie?' Emily invited.

'You might find it kinda boring, Irish,' Troy said, a little too quickly for my liking.

'Probably.' I straightened up from the bin, looked at him hard and tried to invest my tone with unpleasant meaning.

But before it got any nastier, Lara interjected cheerily, 'Hey, Maggie, come out with me tomorrow night. Those guys are going to be talking work, but you and me – we can have fun!' She winked flirtatiously at me and confusion dulled my reactions. I wasn't imagining this. Was I?

No, I wasn't, because next thing she was sliding her arm around my waist. 'Don't worry, guys, I'll take care of Maggie. Real good care. Right, Maggie?' She tickled my waist with her fingers and I twisted around to look into her aquamarine eyes. As so often with her, I felt railroaded – and I liked it.

'Right, Lara,' I said, with a huge, happy smile, then brazenly moved to kiss her. It was quite chaste – i.e. no tongues – but had a sweet, lingering quality, so that when we opened our eyes and turned back to the others, we were slap bang in the middle of what could only be described as an 'atmosphere': Troy, Kirsty, Emily and Shay were pictures of disbelief and confusion.

'Oh man,' Ethan groaned, rearranging his crotch.

As soon as they'd all gone home, Emily pounced. 'What's going on with you and Lara?'

'I don't know. Nothing.' But honesty compelled me to add, 'Yet.'

'Yet? Maggie! You mean you're planning . . . ?'

I nodded. 'Yeah, maybe. Probably.'

'But you're straight!'

After a stretch of silence, I made myself say it. 'I'm not sure I am, you know.'

'What the HELL are you talking about?'

'Well . . .' It was difficult for me to voice this. Very difficult. 'You know –' I swallowed hard. 'You know if you're watching a porn film?'

Emily's face was a picture. Though we'd discussed almost everything else that had ever happened to us, pornography was a neglected area.

'Please don't look at me like that!' I implored. 'It's not like it sounds. I don't have any, but if I'm away in a hotel with Garv and they have it on the in-house movies, then sometimes . . .'

'Mmm.'

'I've never admitted this before, but I wasn't interested in the men in the films.' I looked at her, hoping for some sort of encouragement, but she was expressionless. 'They were just plastic-looking, over-developed bodies. To be honest, I actually found them quite repulsive.'

'That's because they *are* repulsive, with their mullet hair-dos and their bushy moustaches.'

'How did you know that's what they looked like?'

'They're all like that.'

'Are they really? Right. Well, apart from Garv I've never told anyone this ever before, but . . .' I stopped, not sure if I could continue. Then I almost choked as I blurted out, 'Emily, it was the girls that I wanted to look at. I fancy them.'

'You don't fancy them,' Emily said in despair. 'You just want to *be* them! Everyone feels like that. It's normal.'

I shook my head. 'I don't think so. I might be a lesbian. At the very least I'm bi.'

Emily's exasperation drained away and she assumed an expression of concern. 'Maggie, I'm worried about you. I mean it. Think for a moment about all you've lost in the last while.

It's no wonder you're looking for love, or affection or whatever. Especially after the way Troy rejected you.'

'Troy didn't reject me.'

'Sorry, wrong choice of words. When he didn't . . . When he decided not to . . .'

'He didn't reject me, because you can only be rejected if you *let* yourself be rejected.' I'd heard something similar to that recently and I'd liked it. Trouble was, I didn't think I had it quite right. Troy had definitely rejected me.

'Right, but what I'm saying, Maggie, is that after all you've been through it's no wonder you don't know what you want. Last week it was Troy –'

'Now there was a mistake.'

'– and now you think you want Lara. But you don't.'

'That's where you're wrong.'

'I'm not! You're all confused.'

'I'm not confused. Listen to me, Emily – Lara smiled at me tonight and something good happened in me and for the first time in ages I felt . . .' I sought the right word. '. . . OK. It felt right. I'm sorry you're finding this so hard, but I can see why. You've always known me as heterosexual and you've got slightly homophobic tendencies . . .'

'Now just a minute!'

'But you do! You said you'd hate to lick someone's mackerel.'

'Lara is one of my best friends, I love her to death. Just because I don't want to do what she does in bed doesn't mean I disapprove. I mean, I'm not that keen on anal sex either, but I don't care if anyone else does it.'

Emily put her face in her hands. 'This is all my fault. I told you to let your hair down.'

'And I'm glad you did. I've played it safe for far too long.'

319

'Put it back up,' she implored. 'Before you do yourself any more damage, put it back up.'

'No.'

'Today is Thursday,' Emily whispered to herself. 'They're coming on Tuesday.' She bit her knuckle and whimpered, 'She'll kill me. Mammy Walsh will kill me.'

31

Larry Savage proceeded to extract his pound of flesh – with immediate effect. No sooner had her celebratory hangover kicked in than Emily was summoned to his chalet to 'bounce around' some script changes.

'This morning's not so great,' I heard her say, then she put her hand over the speaker and mouthed desperately at me, 'Alka Seltzer, please!' Then, after a little pause, she said, 'Yes, sir, I understand sir. Eleven o'clock. I'll be there.'

Hanging up, she rushed to me. 'Maggie, how good is your shorthand?'

I handed her a fizzing glass. 'Non-existent.'

'Oh. How good are you at writing fast?'

'Not bad.'

'Get dressed. We're going to The Valley. We've got us some face time with Mr Savage.'

But first it was my unpleasant duty to call to the Goatee Boys' darkened house and rouse one of them to wait in for the catering guys to collect their stuff. I was afraid of seeing any of them naked, but especially Curtis.

Luckily, the only one who showed any sign of life was a half-dressed Ethan, who pulled on a singlet and announced that he was considering a career change.

'But don't you first need a career,' I suggested gently, 'before you can consider changing it?'

Entirely unfazed, he told me his great idea: he was going to start up a new religion.

'Come on,' I beckoned him to the door. 'Hurry.'

'My mom says she doesn't care, so long as I pick something and stick to it. She says I've got to stop changing courses and I think starting a new religion is a pretty cool career move.'

I wasn't so sure. Don't you end up being crucified, that sort of thing? But far be it from me to rain on his parade.

'And what kind of things would you believe in?' I asked, opening our front door and ushering him in. 'Or haven't you got that far?'

'Sure I have!' Then Ethan outlined the cornerstone of his new faith, which was that the disciples have to have lots of sex with Ethan.

'Oh, Christ,' Emily muttered, putting on her lipstick in the mirror.

'"Oh, Ethan" is what you'll be saying soon,' Ethan cheerfully corrected her.

'I don't think so,' she said stonily. 'The catering guys will be here inside an hour, then you can go home. And just to let you know, I have my underwear drawer arranged in a special way. I'll know if someone's been through it. Capisce?'

'Capisce. Hey, Maggie, are you really going to go out with Lara tonight?'

'Yes.'

'Woooh! Lesbianism rocks!'

Emily sighed, but said nothing.

Out at Empire, we were given a warm welcome by Michelle, Larry's assistant.

'Congratulations,' she said, hugging first Emily, then me. 'It's a great script, we're all really excited about it.'

The door to Larry's office was closed, but he could be heard, clear as a bell, shouting at someone, 'Sue me! So freaking sue me!'

'Larry's just on to his mom,' Michelle smiled. 'He won't be long.'

Sure enough, one final valedictory bellow, then the office door was wrenched open and Larry emerged, full of beans.

'Have we got a deal or have we got a deal!' he beamed at Emily. 'Congratulations, kiddo.'

'Thank you for buying it,' Emily beamed back. 'And thank you for the flowers.'

Larry waved away her thanks. 'Don't mention it. Studio always does it. Standard procedure.

'OK.' With an arm around each of us, Larry guided Emily and me out into the sunshine. 'This morning we're meeting with two studio executives. We gotta get these guys on side if we want this movie to be made. Got it?'

We nodded energetically. Oh, we got it all right.

At the boardroom chalet, the two executives – a stick-thin blonde called Maxine and a clean-cut, square-jawed man called Chandler – both gushed at Emily about how much they loved *Plastic Money* and how it was going to make a great movie. For a trillionth of a second I was excited, then I copped on to myself.

As we gathered around the table, Larry produced a copy of the script, and when some of the pages fell open there were thick, red lines scored through paragraph after paragraph and in some cases dragged across entire pages. I can't describe the feeling. I hadn't written the script, so I wasn't attached in the same way that Emily was, but I still felt sick. For some reason, it made me think of visiting someone in prison and seeing them bearing obvious signs of beatings.

Michelle distributed photocopies of *Plastic Money* to the rest of us and Larry called the meeting to order. 'OK. Let's try and knock this into shape! First off, that whole plastic surgery stuff has to go. Too weird, too edgy.'

'But that's the whole point,' Emily explained calmly. 'It's an exploration of society's fixation with the body beautiful, it makes important points about our value system –'

'Well, I don't like it. Get rid of it. All of it!'

Shock had my jaw swinging like a sign in the wind. I'd heard about studios buying scripts then proceeding to eviscerate them. But I'd always thought such accounts were wildly exaggerated to generate sympathy or laughs: clearly they weren't.

Emily swallowed hard, then she asked, 'So what's their motivation for holding up the bank, then?'

Larry leaned across the table and sing-songed at her, 'Well, I don't know. I'm not the writer!'

Emily went white.

'How about a blind girl needs an operation to restore her sight,' Chandler suggested.

Larry clicked his fingers. 'I *like* it!'

'Or a bunch of underprivileged kids have a ball park,' Maxine said, 'but a big corporation wants to turn it into duplexes, so they need the money to buy it?'

'Yeah,' Larry said thoughtfully. 'Could work.'

'If there's no plastic surgery, the name will have to be changed,' Emily said, slightly shrilly. '*Plastic Money* makes no sense now.'

'Yeah, you're right. We'll change the name to *Chip*.'

Emily looked even more upset and I was dismayed; I'd hoped

that he'd intended Chip only to have a bit-part, not the starring role.

'If the name is *Chip*, you don't think people might think it's a movie about *a* chip?' Maxine wondered.

'Would they?'

'Maybe – after *Chocolat*.'

'So we call it *Chip the Dog*,' Larry said.

'That's great!' Chandler said. 'That's so great. But what about those animal-rights guys? They see a movie called *Chip the Dog*, they're going to tell us that people might see it as an order. Like, you *gotta* chip the dog!'

'Unless we change the dog's name,' said Michelle.

'I like Chip.'

'Yeah, I like it too.'

'How about Chuck?'

'*Chuck the Dog*? Bad as *Chip the Dog*.'

'How about calling him Charlie?'

'So now it's a drug movie!'

As the discussion raged, Emily maintained a flinty silence. I was forbidden to speak, but even if I'd been allowed I wouldn't have wanted to, muzzled by a potent mixture of depression and boredom.

Larry announced that we were 'working through' lunch, so at twelve-thirty enough food to feed a multitude was delivered to the chalet and laid out prettily – and very quickly – on a table in the corner.

I was starving, but everyone else put tiny amounts of food on to their plates: one strand of noodle; half a baby tomato; four pasta shells; one rocket leaf. So we were taking a little and often approach – OK, I could do that too . . .

We all sat back down with our food and Larry continued to

demand suggestions from us, so it took me a while to notice that I was the only one who'd cleared my plate and that there were no signs of anyone paying a return visit to the buffet. I forced myself to be patient, perhaps they were just slow eaters ... but then the plates were being absently pushed aside as ideas were scribbled in the margins of our scripts. Lunch was over. Over before it had begun, and I was still so hungry.

I wondered if I could just get up and help myself. But we were all sitting down and fully immersed in work. Could I just get up and walk over and put more food on my plate, then put that food in my mouth? What would they think of me?

Wistfully, I looked at the table. Its legs were almost buckling from the weight of uneaten food on it. An entire quiche – *untouched*. A deep-pan pizza, its perfectly circularity unbroken. It was the pizza that did it. All at once, I was pushing back my chair and straightening my knees.

Larry Savage looked at me in surprise. 'Where ya going?'

My resolve departed abruptly. 'Nowhere,' I said, sitting right back down again and studying my script.

My regret was immense. If only I'd known I only got one chance, I'd have made the most of it.

Suddenly that sounded very profound.

We worked through until two-thirty, then Larry wrapped things up. 'Time out, guys. My acupuncturist just got here.'

Her head bowed, Emily straightened the papers in front of her. 'I'll get writing.'

'You do that. We need these rewrites fast.'

'By when?'

'Say, Friday.'

'*Next* Friday? Or the Friday six weeks from now?'

'Haha. Next Friday.'

'No, Friday's not so good for me.'

'Thursday, then. Or Wednesday?'

'Oh. Oh, OK then, Friday's fine.'

Exhausted, we got into the car. Emily was grey.

'Are you OK?' I whispered.

Her face was wretched. 'Why did he buy it if all he wants to do is butcher it?'

'I don't know.'

'What was it that eejit next door said?'

'Follow me and I will get jiggy with thee?'

'No, the other eejit from the other next door. Mike. "Be careful what you wish for," he said. Well, he was right – I wished for someone to buy my script and now I wish they hadn't.'

'It might be a great film. You never know.'

'No, it's going to be a piece of shit,' she said, and tears began to spill down her face. 'My lovely script that I worked so hard on until it was perfect, perfect, perfect. I was so proud of it and now it'll never see the light of day. No one will ever see it. Seven months I slaved on it, to make it wonderful, and now he wants it totally rewritten in a week. It can't be done! And he's taken out all my one-liners, all the funny stuff is gone, and any of the touching moments now involve a fucking DOG!'

I rummaged for a tissue while she howled like a child. 'I'll be ashamed, Maggie, I'll be so ashamed to have my name on a cheesy, schmaltzy, moralizing movie about a dog.' She tried to catch her breath. 'About a dog called *Chip*.'

'Could you pull out?' I suggested. 'Just tell him to stick his money and you'll find someone else to make your movie, thanks very much!'

'No. Because no one else does want to buy it. I know all that and I need the money to live on. But there's no doubt that everything comes with a price tag.'

'Just refuse to make the changes,' I urged. 'Tell him this is the movie he bought and this is the movie he should make!'

'Then he'll fire me and I'll get paid almost nothing, but they'll still own my script. They'll just get some other writer in to make the changes.'

'They can't do that!' But I knew they could; in my time I'd worked on enough contracts to know how much power the big studios retained. I'd just never seen it in action before.

'They don't just buy your script, they buy your soul. Troy is right to try and get all his work produced independently.' Emily's sobbing began to quieten down and she smiled regretfully. 'You make a deal with the devil, no point complaining if you get a pitchfork in the arse.' Then tears began to spill again. 'But that script was like my baby. I loved it, I wanted the best for it, and it kills me to see it torn apart like that, my poor baby.' Aghast, she stopped. 'Oh, Maggie, I've done it again. I'm so sorry.'

32

When you have a miscarriage, you get given a huge amount of information, but you actually discover very little. People bombarded me with well-meant advice, which varied too much for comfort: some said we should try again immediately; others insisted it was vital that we grieve the loss before moving on.

But nobody could tell me the one thing I wanted to know, and that was: Why had it happened? The best that Doctor Collins, my gynaecologist, could come up with was that fifteen to twenty per cent of pregnancies routinely end in miscarriage.

'But why?' I persisted.

'It's nature's way,' he said. 'Something must have been wrong with the foetus, so that it wouldn't have been able to survive on its own.'

I'm sure that was meant to be comforting, but instead it enraged me. In my mind's eye, my child, wherever it was, was perfect.

'But it won't happen again?' Garv asked.

'It could. It probably won't, but I'd be lying to you if I said it couldn't.'

'But it's already happened to us.' Meaning we'd had our quota of bad luck.

'Just because it's happened once is no guarantee that it can't happen again.'

'Thanks a bunch,' I said bitterly.

'Another thing,' he said warily.

'What?' I snapped.

'Yeah, what?' Garv echoed.

'Mood swings.'

'What about them?'

'Expect them.'

I went over the past nine weeks with a fine-toothed comb, searching for the thing I'd done wrong. Had I lifted heavy objects? Accidently gone on a loop-the-loop rollercoaster? Booked myself into a German measles hospital? Or was it just down to the fact – now unimaginable to me – that I simply hadn't wanted it and he or she had known?

They provided a nurse-counsellor-type person, who told me that there was no way that the baby would have known that it hadn't been entirely welcome. 'They're thick-skinned little creatures,' she said. 'But it's natural to blame yourself. Guilt is one of the emotions everyone feels when this happens.'

'And what else?'

'Ooh, anger, grief, loss, frustration, fear, relief –'

'Relief?' I glared at her.

'Not for everyone. And did I mention irrational rage?'

Because we'd told so few people that I was pregnant, there weren't many who knew I'd miscarried. So almost no one made allowances for us as we tried to fill the hole in our lives.

And it was a hole. We'd already thought up names – Patrick if it was a boy, Aoife if it was a girl.

The due date had been April 29th and already we'd started looking at baby clothes and planning the decoration for the bedroom. Then overnight we no longer had any need of teddy-bear wallpaper or revolving lamps that throw patterns of stars on the walls, and that was hard to get used to.

Even more painful was that I'd been excited about getting to know my child. I'd been looking forward to a lifetime with this new person, who was part of me and part of Garv – and abruptly it had all been whipped away.

You know how it is when your boyfriend ditches you – out of nowhere the world is full of loving couples, holding hands, kissing, clinking champagne glasses, feeding each other oysters. In the same way, as soon as I'd lost my baby, out of the woodwork suddenly emerged busloads of heavily pregnant women, ripe and gorgeous, carrying their swollen bellies with pride. And worse still, there were babies everywhere I turned: in the supermarket, on the street, by the sea, at the optician's. Perfect little creatures with their dolphin-smiley mouths and lustrous skin bursting with freshness, flapping their pudgy arms, clapping their sticky hands, kicking their socks off and making high-pitched, swooping, singing noises, like bald mini-Bjorks.

Sometimes it was too painful to look at them, but at other times it was too painful not to, and Garv and I used to eyeball them with hungry gazes, thinking *We nearly had one of them.* Then Garv usually whispered, 'We'd better stop, we're being weird, the mother will call the peelers on us.'

My instinct was to get pregnant again immediately, so that we could almost pretend that the first loss had never happened, and Garv said he wanted to do whatever made me happy. So I went straight out and bought a temperature thing, because I wanted to leave nothing to chance. My life was pared down to just one all-consuming need, and terrible fear tormented me. What if this time it took a year? What if – unthinkably – it

331

never happened? But we were lucky: I'd miscarried at the start of October, and I was pregnant again by the middle of November. It's hard to describe the giddy mix of relief and happiness I felt when the blue line appeared on the stick; we'd been given a second chance. Breathless, we squeezed each other and we both cried, as much for the loss of the other child as the joy of the new one.

But almost straight away the joy was overtaken by anxiety. Blind terror, actually. What if I lost this one too?

'Lightning doesn't strike twice,' Garv said, even though it does, and it wasn't lightning anyway.

I became so very, very careful; I stopped going to pubs, because I was afraid of inhaling cigarette smoke; I drove at about fourteen miles an hour (quite fast for Dublin, actually), so there'd be no danger of any sudden braking; I refused to give cream cheese house-room, and I never permitted myself the luxury of a belch – quite understandable when you consider that I even worried about *breathing* too hard, in case it dislodged the baby.

Horrible dreams dogged me: one night I dreamt that the baby had died and was still inside me, another night I dreamt I gave birth to a chicken. And this time round, there was no skiving off work and buying handbags from JP Tod's; we'd been so badly punished the last time for being happy that we were scared of doing anything that smacked of celebration. Mind you, I wasn't at all as sick the second time – apart from when I found something very funny (almost never), and my laughter segued seamlessly into dry-retching. (I was a model dinner-party guest.)

We cautiously took the reduced nausea as a good sign. Though there was no medical basis for it, I said to Garv that the terrible sickness the first time round had probably been a sign that something was wrong. Then he repeated it back to me and thus we tried to reassure each other and ourselves.

But every twinge in me could indicate the onset of disaster. One night I got a really bad pain in my armpit and I was absolutely *convinced* that this was it. Garv tried to restore calm by pointing out that my armpit was miles from my womb, but I countered defiantly, 'Yeah, but when people have heart attacks they get a pain in their arm,' and then I could see I'd put the fear in him too.

But we survived that night, and in the seventh week we went for our first scan, where anxiety stripped the event of the joy we'd had with the first baby. I kept asking if everything looked OK and the nurse said over and over that it did.

But how could she tell? If I was completely honest, the picture they gave us looked more like a poor black-and-white photocopy of 'Starry, Starry Night' than a baby.

As we approached the ninth week, the tension built and built. During the ninth week itself, time slowed down to the ticking of each individual second. We breathed as though the air was rationed. Then – unbelievably – it had passed without incident and we'd moved into the clear blue waters of the tenth week. The cloud lifted and suddenly we were gulping breaths like the air was chocolate-flavoured – you could actually *see* the change in us. I remember smiling at Garv and watching him smile back at me and being shocked at how unfamiliar it was.

Week ten passed. Week eleven arrived and we went for our second scan, where we were a lot giddier and lighter than at the previous one. Then something happened which upped the ante more than I could ever have imagined – as I was lying on the table, the nurse indicated that we should be quiet, she flicked a switch, and the sound of our baby's heartbeat filled the room. A lightish pitter-patter, so fast it was absolutely belting along. It is impossible for me to convey the depth of my wonder and joy. I was transported with it. As you might expect, we both cried buckets, then we had a little laugh, then shed a few more tears. Our awe just knocked us sideways. And the relief was glorious: it had a heartbeat. Things must be fine.

And just as soon as we were over week twelve, we'd really be in the clear. 'Two days to go,' I said that night, as we squeezed hands before we went to sleep.

The pain woke me. There hadn't been pain the last time, so I wasn't immediately alerted. Then when I understood what was happening I went into a dreamscape: *I can't believe this is happening to us.*

When bad things happen, I'm always taken by surprise. I know some people react to disaster by stomping around shouting, 'I knew it, I just fucking KNEW this would happen!' But I'm not one of them. Bad things are supposed to happen to mythical 'other people', and it comes as a shock when I discover that I am one of the 'other people'.

As we hurried out to the car, I looked up to the night sky, silently begging God not to let this happen. But I noticed something that seemed like an omen. 'There are no stars tonight,' I said. 'It's a sign.'

'No, baby, it's not.' Garv slid his arms around me. 'The stars are always there, even in the daytime. Sometimes we just can't see them.'

The sense of déjà vu as we drove to the hospital turned reality into a nightmare. Then we were sitting on the orange chairs again, then someone was telling me that everything would be OK, and once again it wasn't.

It was still too early to tell the sex, not that I cared. All that mattered was that this was the second time I'd lost a child: a ready-made family, gone before it had arrived.

This time it was far, far worse. Once I could live with, but not twice – because the one thing we'd had the last time, that we didn't have now, was hope. I hated myself and my defective body that was failing us so terribly.

People provided stories that were supposed to be comforting. My mother knew a woman who'd had five miscarriages before carrying to term and now she had four fine children, two boys and two girls. Garv's mother could go one better: 'I know a woman who had *eight* miscarriages and then she had twins. A lovely pair of boys. Mind you,' she added doubtfully, 'one of them ended up in prison. Embezzlement. Something to do with a pension fund and a villa in Spain . . .'

Everyone tried to instil optimism back into Garv and me, but I didn't buy it. Hope was utterly absent and I was in the grip of a burgeoning belief that this was all my fault. I'm not given to fanciful nonsense, talk of hexes and jinxes and the like (that'd be Anna you're thinking of), but I couldn't chase away the conviction that I'd brought all of this on myself.

33

I opened the front door. Emily was on the day bed bent over her laptop, working hard.

'Hi,' I said cautiously.

'Hi,' she replied, equally cautiously. 'Good night?'

'Yes. You?'

'Yes.'

'How were Troy and Shay?'

'Fine. Helpful. They both say hey.'

I nodded at the computer. 'So, ah, how's *Chip the Dog* going?'

'Nightmare. I'm getting cramps in my stomach from writing this stuff. Did you get off with her?'

A pause. 'Yes. Sorry.'

'Not at all, whatever floats your boat. So what was it like?'

'It was . . . different.'

'Like licking a mackerel?'

'It was only the first date,' I said. 'What kind of girl do you think I am?'

'Jesus Christ,' she said faintly. 'And what did you do?' Then she hit her forehead. 'Doh! Not like that!'

'We went to a movie. Look, I'm going to have a shower and get some rest.'

'Sure, you must be exhausted. I mean, I'm not saying . . . Oh Christ,' she clicked, 'see you later.'

I went into my bedroom, closed the door, then sat at Emily's desk and wearily flicked through some of her unsold scripts, looking to be distracted.

I wasn't exhausted; I was terrified. I was way, *way*, WAY out of my depth here. This business with Lara – what had I been *thinking* of?

I wasn't a lesbian. I suspected I wasn't even bisexual.

The whole night had been a disaster, starting with Lara turning up looking radiant; her hair was swingy and shiny and she wore a clingy jersey dress. Nothing wrong there – until I suddenly understood that she'd *made a special effort*. She'd made a special effort *for me*. Momentarily I was flattered and seconds later I was freaked out.

We went to Santa Monica to a movie where neither of us understood the plot, and when we got outside into the sweltering night it transpired that each of us hoped that the other would be able to explain it. That didn't bode at all well, and I had a powerful compulsion to ask Lara what she knew about exchange rates, except I was afraid of discovering that she was as clueless as me.

'What now?' I asked. 'Will we go for a drink?' There were hundreds of very attractive-looking bars and restaurants all around us. But Lara firmly shook her head and said, with a message-laden smile, 'Nuh-uh. My place.'

It was as though a full cage of butterflies had been released into my stomach. *Nerves*, I told myself. *Not terror. Nerves.* On account of my shyness and inexperience, of course. But Lara would be masterful enough to take control and make it easy for me.

So back to her place we went, where she opened a bottle of wine, put some soft jazzy-type music on the stereo and lit scented candles. It was the scented candles that brought home to me the full extent of my mistake. It was so *romantic*. She definitely meant business. A lead ball displaced the butterflies and there was no longer any ambivalence about how I felt. I wanted to go home, I wanted to run away as fast as I could – but instead I had to curl up on the sofa, sip Chardonnay and exchange mischievous glances in the flickering light.

Valiantly, I tried. I managed to dredge up a sickly smile each time Lara warmed her eyes at me, but as she moved closer along the sofa, my panic built.

Desperately, I tried to keep talking but I was so uptight I sounded like I was interviewing her for a job. 'How many screens will *Doves* be opening in? Is it fun organizing the launch party for it? Oh, a nightmare, is it? Oh dear.'

I longed to leave, but couldn't see how I could possibly extricate myself; the words that might release me wanted to be uttered yet remained locked in my throat. What was stopping me was that I'd gone into this with my eyes open. As soon as it had been offered, I could have told Lara to get lost, but instead I'd given every appearance of fancying her – because at the time I had. Now, though, was a different story, but I felt I'd no right to tell her I'd changed my mind.

A glass and a half of Chardonnay in and Lara suddenly leant right over to me, almost on top of me. *Here we go.* Automatically, I shrank away from her and the relief was intense when I realized she was just refilling my glass. With a shaky hand I picked it up and gratefully gulped back most of it.

'Hey, don't get too drunk on me,' Lara chided sweetly.

'Er, no.' And my anxiety started anew.

I actually prayed, offering to do a deal with God: if he'd get me out of this, I'd never do anything risky again. But God must have been on the other line, because next thing Lara had moved closer and was stroking my hair away from my face. Then she'd kissed me, which hadn't been too bad, and put her hands under my top and caressed my breasts, which hadn't been too bad either. At that juncture I felt it was my turn to do something, so I kind of pulled at her shoulder strap to show willing. But I wasn't expecting her to shrug her dress off her shoulders, down to her waist, then whip off her bra and weigh her breasts in her hands. As soon as she touched herself, her nipples sprang at me and it would have been sexy in other circumstances, but I was paralysed by the inappropriateness of it all. 'Don't be chicken,' she said, so I took a deep breath and gingerly started caressing her breasts, partly to return the favour and partly because I was curious about what implants felt like – but as I'd never felt anyone else's breasts except my own, I'd nothing really to compare them to.

A bit more caressing and clothing removal ensued; Lara was beautiful, there was no doubt about it, and she was soft and downy and sweetly fragrant. And yet, when we were pressed crotch to crotch, it felt all wrong – we were both too flat. I realized how much I liked men's bodies.

Whatever bravado or curiosity or neediness had propelled my initial response to Lara had all drained away and I was keenly aware that I'd bitten off more than I could chew. Not that I was chewing anything – God, no! No power on earth could have persuaded me to do any mackerel licking.

They say that only a woman can truly know what another woman wants and Lara certainly did her best. But I couldn't divorce my body from my mind and just let go and give myself to any pleasure that might come from the experience. I felt like an out-and-out fraud and, worse still, I felt silly.

Luckily, Lara had seemed to really enjoy herself and waved

away any of my inhibitions with an airy, 'Hey, it's your first time.'

'Thanks,' I said humbly.

'Soon,' she said, 'we'll have you strapping on a twelve-inch dildo!'

Jesus Christ!

I'd barely slept all night. Then she'd dropped me home this morning on the way to her yogilates class. The Drummers to the Rhythm of Life were just arriving – one or two of them said hello, clearly getting used to seeing me arrive home on a Saturday morning, still in last night's clothes.

'I'll call you tomorrow,' Lara said, driving off. 'We'll go out. Tell Emily I said hey.'

And now here I was, flicking through Emily's old scripts and unable to concentrate on anything. So what was I to do? I couldn't break it off with Lara – not only did she really seem to like me, but I'd have to 'fess up to just being a sexual tourist. And after Nadia had let her down so badly! I simply couldn't do it.

Anyway, I'd no idea how to go about breaking it off with someone, it was so long since I'd done it. What do people say? 'It's not working out'? 'I need some space'? 'Can we still be friends?'

But if I didn't break it off with her . . . ?

I could see my future unrolling itself in front of me. I'd have to stay in Los Angeles for ever and be a lesbian. I couldn't see any way out of it. I'd have to do all sorts of lezzery things that seem enticing in the occasional fantasy, but not that alluring in real life. And I'd be worn out from the regime of personal grooming that Lara would expect from me: my hair and eyebrows would need twice-weekly maintenance, and she'd brought up the question of my raggedy nails again. She'd make me go for the Brazilian wax and God knows what else.

How had I ended up in this mess? Having sex with a *girl*? This wasn't me, this wasn't the way I behaved – someone must have led me astray. But much as I'd love to, I could blame no one but myself. I forced myself to face one of the reasons I'd flirted – yes, flirted – so shamelessly with her: I'd been *showing off* in front of Troy and Shay. I'd been hoping to shock them or hurt them or something, because they had both, albeit in very different ways, hurt me.

What had I become? Before Lara there had been Troy, and even though the sex itself was fantastic, the entire experience left me feeling bad about myself.

At least one thing was pretty clear, I thought wryly: any suspicions I'd ever harboured that I was a bad-girl peg jammed uncomfortably into a good-girl hole had been allayed. I'd often told myself that it was a shame I'd got married at twenty-four, that I'd done myself a disservice by forgoing anonymous sex with mysterious strangers. Deep in my heart I'd felt that if I was presented with the opportunity to showcase my dormant wild-girl side, I'd be able to misbehave with the best of them.

But I'd been wrong. I wasn't cut out for one-night stands. Unlike women like Emily or Donna, casual sex didn't excite me; it depressed me. God, how disappointing that I was what I'd always behaved like: a dyed-in-the-wool serial monogamist. Well, who knew? Emily was right to be worried about me: I was out of control.

In despair, I sat at the desk for an indeterminate amount of time. Then I began to think of Emily, who was desperately trying to cram seven months' work into a week. I got up and went out to her. She was still at her laptop, typing furiously.

'Emily, can I do anything to help?'

She paused, her shoulders hunched and her purple-ringed eyes giving her the look of a raccoon.

'I could make you something to eat. Or I could rub your neck. But not in a lezzery kind of way,' I added, lest there be any confusion.

Slowly, she lowered her shoulders. 'You know what, there is something you could do. I need to get out for a few hours this evening. I don't care what we do so long as we do something. You decide.'

'OK.' I thought about it. And I knew exactly what I wanted to do. 'I'd like to go out with a gang of girls and get drunk and dance around our handbags to "I Will Survive".'

'Fabulous,' Emily breathed. 'Who would you like to come? Lara, obviously –'

'No, she's busy! Um, how about Connie?'

'Connie? I didn't think you liked her.'

'Ah,' I shrugged.

'Is it all the wedding arrangements?'

'It doesn't matter as much now.'

'*And* you've stopped asking me if everyone is married. Maggie, I finally think you're on the mend. Now if you'd only stop getting off with people . . .'

'I will, I promise. There'll be no more.'

Connie was on for it and so was her sister Debbie. We got very glammed up in short skirts, heels and shiny make-up and went to the Bilderberg Room – so naff it had suddenly become very cool – where the men were aggressively forward and fashionably attired in Starsky and Hutch retro. We were barely in the door when one said to me, 'Here I am! What were your other two wishes?' I jostled away from him, and moments later I was running my hands through my hair when I encountered another hand in it. Belonging to a brat called Dexter, who then asked me to go home with him.

But all four of us were there to dance, not to meet men, and we deflected assholes like Wonderwoman deflects bullets – which only made us even more popular. Complicated Martinis kept being bought for us, which we drank but didn't say thank you for. And although our handbags were small enough to swing from our shoulders without injuring bystanders, for the sake of tradition we placed them on the floor beneath the glitterball – Emily's Dior saddlebag, Connie's mother-of-pearl Fendi, Debbie's LV clutch and my JP Tod's special – and danced around them.

When Connie decided she wanted to fix her lips, all four of us steamed haughtily across the floor, ignoring offers of drinks and/or fabulous sex, and went to the ladies' room, which was a landscape of brown-cork tiling – even on the walls. The woven wicker chairs were like a 'Readers' Wives' special and the smoked-glass mirrors were very 'Last Days of Disco'. Highly stylish, of course, but not so great if you were trying to see if you'd got lipstick on your teeth.

There was only one other woman in there, squinting at the smoky glass and trying to reapply her mascara. On the washstand, beside her handbag, lay something slightly odd – a pair of handles like the ones usually found attached to expensive carrier bags, the type of handles that are made of hard plastic and clip together along their length. They weren't odd in themselves, what was odd was that there was no bag attached. But I

343

only noticed all this on the edge of my consciousness, until the woman threw her mascara back in her handbag, tucked it under her arm, then – I thought I was seeing things – picked up the handles and swung them as if there was an invisible carrier attached. The Emperor's New Bag.

In silence, we all turned to watch her leave, and as soon as the door had shut behind her, Emily, Connie and Debbie erupted into excited talk.

'It was, wasn't it?'

'Got to be!'

'Who? What?' I asked, realizing that the woman wasn't, as I'd thought, a poor lost soul and mad as a bike.

'Doctor Hawk's handles!' From their shining eyes it was clear I was meant to know what they were talking about. Slowly I shook my head and Emily explained.

'You know how we all carry baggage from our past?'

I had to admit I did – in fact, I was beginning to realize just how much stuff I was carrying.

'So Doctor Lydia Hawk is a shrink who's got this, like, pioneering approach. She translates emotional baggage into physical baggage. For the first month you see her you've to carry a proper suitcase.'

'And it can't be one of the ones with wheels,' Debbie elaborated. '*And* it's got to be full of stuff – Doctor Hawk packs it so it's way heavy and you've really got to carry it. Ev-err-y-where. To the drugstore, to work, out on dates . . .'

'And as you get better, the bags get smaller. Until you're shrunk enough to get given Doctor Hawk's handles. You've got to carry them for a whole year as a reminder.'

'And they cost a thousand dollars.'

'Ten thousand,' Connie corrected.

'That's insane!' I said. 'They're only plastic handles. You could just tear them off any carrier bag that you get for free.'

They all disagreed, three heads of big hair swishing emphatically from side to side. 'Nuh-uh. Got to be the special Doctor Hawk ones, else they don't work.'

'There are only twenty pairs in the whole world,' Connie marvelled. 'They are totally the coolest things.'

Sometimes I thought I was getting the hang of how they do things in Fantasy Land. Other times, like right then, I felt as clueless as the day I'd arrived.

But never mind – back out for more dancing! The music was unreconstructed seventies disco – 'Mighty Real' and 'Disco Inferno' and other wonderful stuff that I remembered from my childhood – and the high spot was when Emily had a word with the DJ and next thing 'I Will Survive' was bouncing off the mirrored walls. One of the braver blokes tried to break into our circle just when the song got to the 'Go on now, Go!' bit, so we shouted it at him until he withdrew again, then we danced like there was no tomorrow.

34

I found myself certainly wishing there hadn't been one the following day, when Emily announced, 'Lara's on her way over.'

'To see you?' I asked hopefully.

She gave me a funny look. 'No, to see you.' She spelt the words out like I was a moron. 'Her. Girl. Friend.'

Oh Lord.

The day had begun very nicely, starting with Lou taking us both out for breakfast. Lou had arrived last night when Emily – loosened by several free Complicated Martinis – rang him at two a.m. and invited him over. He'd arrived within twenty minutes and claimed that he'd spent the evening watching a ball game on TV and praying she'd ring.

'Sheesh,' Emily had exhaled, making a meal of being disgusted by his insincerity.

Then in the morning he'd taken us to Swingers, a cool, crowded diner where the ambience was vibey and flirty, even at ten o'clock in the morning – long, hot looks being exchanged over blueberry pancakes, and that was just the waiters – where he was fun, entertaining and as nice to me as he was to Emily without in any way coming across as sleazy. He insisted on paying for us both, and on the drive home stopped at a drugstore and bought cigarettes and sweets for Emily, gave her three good suggestions for *Chip the Dog* and told her to call him if she needed anything. 'And I mean *anything*,' he stressed, with unmistakeable meaning.

As he drove away, I had to say to Emily, 'I think he's really nice.'

'Only because you've been out of the game for too long,' she said, booting up her laptop and arranging herself at the kitchen table with an ashtray, coffee cup and packet of Mintos. 'But he's actually evil.'

'Evil! That's a terrible thing to say.'

'And it's not terrible to cold-bloodedly set out to make a woman fall for you, then do a disappearing act?'

'But are you *sure* that's what he's doing?'

''Course I am.' She scrolled down her screen and muttered, 'Now where did I get to? Oh here we go. Chip the dog has just bitten the property developer.' She flung her face into her hands and whimpered, 'I can't believe I'm writing this stuff. I hate myself!'

'Think of the money,' I replied, just like she'd told me to. 'Think of all those lovely things, like being able to eat, and pay rent, and put gas in your car.'

'Thank you, thank you.' She began to type and everything was grand until Lara rang to say she was coming over.

Half an hour later, Lara burst into the room, as golden and gorgeous as always, except instead of filling me with admiration it now terrified me. She stopped at Emily and looked over her shoulder at the screen. 'Hi, sweetheart, how's it going?'

'I've gone beyond shame, Lara. I'm a Hollywood whore.'

'Hey, who isn't? Emily, would you mind if I spent a little time with Maggie in private?'

Emily winced but managed, 'Work away.'

347

'I know this is a little weird,' Lara said softly.

Emily just shrugged and, feeling wretched, I took Lara into my bedroom, closed the door and braced myself for passionate snogging.

'So whatcha do last night?' she asked, moving around the bed and sitting at Emily's desk chair.

'Went to the Bilderberg Room with Connie and Debbie.'

'Sounds great!'

'Er, yes, it was. Good music.'

'Like what?'

I listed some of the songs and all the time I was wondering, *When is the snogging going to start?*

'I went for dinner at Shakers,' Lara said. 'Up in Clearwater Canyon. Great food. You should go.'

'OK.' The waiting had got too much to bear, so I stood up – I had to because she was quite a way from me – forced her to her feet and pulled her to me. But before I could plant my lips on hers, she'd placed the palm of her hand on my chest and straightened her arm.

'No.'

'No?'

'I'm really sorry, Maggie, but I don't think we should do this.'

''Cos of Emily being outside?'

'No. I don't think we should do it, period.'

I mouthed her words, repeating them back to myself until it sank in. 'You want to break up with me?'

'Um, yeah, you got it.'

'But *why*?' What was wrong with me? Why did I keep getting rejected?

She fixed me with her blue laser beams and said candidly, 'I was sore after Nadia and I was curious about you. It seemed like a good idea at the time, you know . . . ? I'm way sorry.'

'So didn't you fancy me at all?'

'Sure!'

'Since when?'

'Since . . . ah, since the night I found out about Nadia and you were real nice to me.'

'Not since I first came to Los Angeles, then?' I didn't know why this was so important, but it was.

'Not straight off, no. See, you're a little confused right now, 'cos of your marriage and Troy, and I'm real sorry but I think I took advantage of you.'

'Um . . .'

'Like, you're great, you're really great.'

'But not great enough.'

'It's not that, it's like . . . I don't know how to say this . . .'

'I'm not your type?'

'Don't be pissed at me,' she said sadly.

Very hurt, I swallowed. 'So what is your type? Girls like Nadia, I suppose.'

'Yeah, I suppose.'

'And why? She had a great body?'

Uncomfortably, Lara assented.

Now, I wasn't expecting that. I thought men made choices based purely on physical attraction, but I expected girls to be less shallow. Doesn't a good personality count for anything any more? I wondered bitterly.

'You've got a great body too,' Lara said, so nicely it took some of my mortification away. 'But because she usta be a dancer, you know . . . And, like, she really took care of herself.'

'It was my nails, wasn't it?'

'It didn't help,' she admitted.

349

'And . . .' I made myself say it, 'was my . . . you know . . . bum . . . um, bit . . . the wrong colour?'

She shrugged. 'I didn't really see it. But Maggie, it's not about that. I'm pretty sure your natural inclination is not to be with girls . . .'

There, she'd said it.

'. . . and I swear to you that if I didn't break up with you, you'd break up with me real soon.'

I paused, wondering if I should play the pity card or go for pride. Pride won. 'Actually, I wanted to do it today, but I didn't know how.'

'*What?*' she said sharply. 'And here I am feeling totally like the worst person ever!'

'Yes.' All at once the silliness of the situation struck home and I began to laugh. 'Tell me, Lara, tell me honestly, was I terrible?'

She stared at me and a smile creased her face as she filled up with mirth. 'No, but I've gotta say I've had better.'

'Me too.'

And suddenly we exploded into convulsions, huge belly laughs of relief and liberation and the full-on insanity of it all.

When we eventually quieted down I said, 'But we'll still be friends, right?' And that was enough to start us all over again.

'Keep Wednesday night free,' she said, before she left. 'For the première of *Doves*.'

When the door had shut behind her, I cornered Emily. 'I've good news for you. It's all off with me and Lara.'

She stopped her frantic typing. 'What happened?'

'She broke it off with me. Says I'm not her type.'

'So what's the story? You hate her now like you hate Troy and every time she comes over here you'll stick a fork in her leg?'

Aghast, my heart pounded. 'No, we're friends.'

'That's a relief.'

'Emily, I'm sorry.'

'For what?'

'Sleeping with all your friends. I won't do it again.'

'You can sleep with who you like. It's the bad atmosphere when it doesn't work out that I don't like.'

'I won't be sleeping with anyone else. I was off the rails and out of control, but I'm OK now. I'm sorry. It's back to being clean-living Maggie – I'm just not cut out for anything else. I might even join an enclosed order.'

Emily shook her head. 'Some sort of middle ground might be nice.' Then she added, 'But thank Christ you knocked that lezzer lark on the head before the arrival of Mammy Walsh. Else we'd have all been in the soup.'

I heartily agreed.

35

After the second miscarriage, I cried for four solid days. I know people often say things like 'I cried for a week,' when they mean they cried on and off for a few days, but I really did cry non-stop for four days. I even cried in my sleep. I was hazily aware of people coming and going, tiptoeing around my bed and whispering to Garv, 'How is she now?'

By the time I stopped crying, my eyes were so swollen I looked like I'd been beaten up and the surface of my face was white and crusty like those dried-out salt lakes that you see in the desert.

In the past, when I'd heard about women having miscarriages, I couldn't imagine their sadness, because I suppose I wondered how you could miss something you'd never had. I could identify with other losses – if one of my friends got dumped by their boyfriend, I felt lonely, rejected and humiliated for them. Or if someone belonging to a friend died, I could go some way to understanding the shock, the grief and the very weirdness of death, even though my grandparents were the only people I'd loved who'd died.

But I hadn't been able to imagine the grief of losing a baby. Not until it had happened to me. Not until it had happened to me twice.

And the funny thing is that in ways, it's similar to the other losses. I felt as lonely, rejected and humiliated as if I'd been dumped – lonely for the person I'd never get to know, rejected because they didn't want to stay in my body and humiliated by my very defectiveness. And I also felt shock, grief and weirdness, like someone had died. But there was an extra dimension to my sadness, something that went to the very essence of my humanness. I had wanted a child, and the longing was as visceral and inexplicable as hunger.

Throughout it all, it was as though a pane of glass separated me from the rest of the human race, so isolated was I. I felt almost no one could understand the exact nature of my pain. Those who'd miscarried would – although I didn't know anyone – and those who were unsuccessfully 'trying' for a baby, and maybe some people who'd already had children would. But the vast majority wouldn't get it. I intuited that, because for a long time I'd thought the way they did.

The one person who truly shared my loss was the one person I could barely look in the eye – Garv. Having to go through it all with him made it worse and I couldn't figure out why. Until I realized that I couldn't stop thinking about something that had happened when I was about twenty: a child from the neighbourhood had run out from between two parked cars and been knocked down and killed by a motorist who hadn't had a hope of stopping in time. The parents of the dead boy were devastated, of course, but there was also a lot of sympathy for the man who'd been driving. I overheard several people say, 'My heart goes out to the driver – the poor man, what he must be going through.'

Well, I was the same as the driver. I was responsible for Garv's grief – it was my fault, and it was horrible living with it.

But Garv coped a lot better than I did. In the fortnight after the miscarriage he kept the household running, monitoring my visitors, replacing my *Mother and Baby* magazines with *Vanity Fair*, and ensuring I ate. I flailed around, failing to reclaim normality, and refused to talk about what had happened. I couldn't even use the word 'miscarriage' – when anyone started on about it, I interrupted and called it a 'setback'. And when they said, 'OK, setback,' and continued trying to probe me, I'd say, 'I don't want to talk about it.' I was so resistant that even the most dedicated of friends kind of gave up.

Then someone came up with the idea that Garv and I should go on holiday. All of a sudden, everyone was in agreement that a holiday was a great idea, and it felt like everywhere we turned there was another spooky face intoning, 'It'll dooo yooou the world of gooood.' Or 'A few days lying by a pooool reading a crappy booook and you won't knoooow yoooourself.' It was like a horror film. 'You yourself were conceived on holiday, Margaret,' Mum said, accompanying this information with a wink and a disconcerting leer. 'Don't tell us, for God's sake, don't tell us,' Helen begged.

In the end, Garv and I felt we'd no choice. I had no energy to resist everyone's urgings and the idea of staving off real life for another week was too tempting to resist.

So off we went to a resort in St Lucia, spurred on by visions of silvery palm trees, powder-white sand, hot yellow sun and goldfish-bowl-sized cocktails. Only to discover that three days before we'd arrived, they'd had a hurricane – even though it wasn't the hurricane season – and their beach had fallen into the sea, along with most of their palm trees. Not only that, but my bag, crammed with gorgeous, newly purchased beachwear, never turned up on the airport carousel. Salt was rubbed vigorously into the wounds by the JCBs which commenced work rebuilding the beach every morning at seven a.m. outside our window. And the icing on the cake was the fact that it pelted rain, and no, it wasn't the rainy season either.

But the cherry right on the very top of the icing on the cake was the attitude the hotel staff took to my missing bag. No matter how hard I tried to convince them that I wanted my stuff urgently, it didn't seem to cut any mustard. Every morning and every evening Garv and I made enquiries as to its where-abouts, but nobody could ever give us any hard information.

'They're so laid back here,' I complained.

'Laid back?' Garv said grimly. 'They make the Irish look as hard-working and efficient as the Japanese.'

On the fifth day, it all came to a head when we showed up, once again, at the front desk. Even though we'd gone through the whole missing-bag thing with Floyd every morning for the previous four days, Garv had to explain it all afresh to him.

Unconvincingly, Floyd pressed a couple of keys on his key-board and looked at his screen. I twisted my head trying to get a look at it, because I harboured a suspicion that the computer wasn't even switched on.

'Be comin' tomorrow,' he drawled.

'But you said that yesterday,' my jaw was clenched, 'and the day before.' I thought of Garv having to wash my T-shirt and shorts in the handbasin again tonight and me having to put them on damp in the morning and be laughed at by the other well-dressed girls there. Then I thought of my bag, filled with jewel-coloured bikinis, flower-splashed sundresses and, worst of all, my new unworn sandals, and I became a little hysterical. Even now, when I think of those sandals my gut twists with pain. Not because I'm a shoe junkie – my first love has always been handbags, really – but because Garv went to so much trouble to get them for me. I'd seen them in a shop in town the

355

week before we'd come away. I'd even tried them on and was all set to buy them when into the shop came a woman with a baby. It was tiny, clearly a newborn, its delicate eyelids fluttering with sleep, its marshmallow hands curled into fists.

I had to leave. I'm not exaggerating, I *had* to leave, or I would have lost it and started crying again – and once I started I found it very hard to stop.

At home, I collapsed on Garv. 'It wasn't just the baby,' I said. 'I know it's stupid, but it was the sandals too. They were perfect, they would have gone with everything. And I left them . . .' I hovered on the brink of a great crying torrent.

'I'll get them for you,' Garv offered, and a muscle leapt rhythmically in his jaw. 'Where were they?'

'No, it's OK.' Anyway, I couldn't remember which shop – all I knew was it was in Grafton Street. Next thing I know, Garv is placing a pad in front of me. 'Draw them,' he says. 'Put down colour, size, everything you know about them.'

I tried to talk him out of it, but he was insistent. Which only made me feel worse. It was a sign of how bad things were, of how close we were to toppling over the edge, if he had to employ such extreme measures to try to make me happy.

Like a private eye, he pounded the pavements in the centre of Dublin, armed only with my diagram. He went into shoe shop after shoe shop with the folded bit of paper, asking people, 'Have you seen these shoes?'

He tried Zerep, who didn't have them, but thought that Fitzpatrick's might. Fitzpatrick's hadn't seen them either and tried to send him to Clarks. But Garv said I wouldn't have been in Clarks, that their shoes were too comfortable, so they suggested he try Jezzie. Who tried to fob him off with a pair that were too low and didn't have a ridged sole. Off his own bat

Garv tried Korkys, and though the staff couldn't help, a customer – a shoe aficionado – overheard and insisted that the sandals were in Carl Scarpa. And sure enough, paydirt was hit in Carl Scarpa.

'I just hope they fit,' Garv said, opening the bag when he got home.

'They'll fit.' I was quite prepared to chop my toes off, if necessary. I was so appalled at the trouble he'd gone to, especially in view of my unworthiness, that I wouldn't have been able to admit to anything being wrong.

He held them up. 'Are they the right ones?'

I nodded.

'Your ruby slippers,' he said, handing them over. And though they weren't ruby – more of a turquoise, really – or slippers, I put them on, clicked my heels together three times and said, 'There's no place like home.'

Tightly we held on to each other and for a while there I thought we might make it. Isn't it strange that sometimes the memory of an act of kindness can cause more pain than the cruel stuff?

Meanwhile, Floyd just didn't give a damn whether the bag containing my sandals and everything else ever turned up.

'Where is it?' I begged. 'It's been lost for nearly a week now.'

Floyd fixed me with a dazzling melon-wide grin. 'Relax, mon.'

And maybe in other circumstances I would have. Perhaps if I'd had a proper night's sleep in the previous month, if my nerves hadn't been stretched see-through, if I hadn't hung so much hope on this holiday. Instead I heard myself shout, 'No, I won't fucking relax.'

Garv put his hands on my shoulders and firmly marched me

to a pretty white bench. 'Sit here,' he ordered. Resentfully I sat while Garv leant over the desk at Floyd. 'Now listen to me,' he threatened. 'That's my wife. She hasn't been well. She's come here to feel better. There's no beach, the weather is shite, the least you could do is find her bag.'

But despite his macho intervention, the bag didn't turn up till the final day and our mood didn't turn up at all.

At the airport coming home, the pall of depression that hung over the pair of us could almost have been photographed. We'd thought the holiday would heal us, but it had only highlighted the divisions. Not only was I not pregnant but we were further apart than we'd ever been.

As I thought about all the terrible things that had happened with the weather and the bag and the food poisoning (oh yes, two gippy tummies, one overworked bathroom, let's not go there), I wondered if Garv and I were jinxed. Then an unexpected terror got me as I understood that the disasters had actually been the best thing about the holiday – because they meant Garv and I had had things to talk about. The only times we'd been animated or in agreement had been when we were venting about what a kip it was or when we were planning the various tortures we'd inflict on the JCB drivers or Floyd or the chef who had given us the dodgy swordfish.

For the first time ever, as far as I could remember, Garv and I were running out of things to say to each other.

36

The exity bit of LAX, where the recent arrivals emerge, was choked with people waiting. As well as the Dublin plane, a flight had recently landed from Manila, and another from Bogota, and it looked like thousands of relatives had turned out to greet the passengers. I'd already spent almost forty minutes standing with a stretched neck, being jostled and shunted by the vacuum-packed throng. Every time the glass doors slid back to reveal yet another family group, a happy wail went up from some-where, and a fresh heave had me stumbling all over my neigh-bours as people sought to burrow through to their visitors.

The more time that passed without my lot appearing, the more lighthearted I became – they must have missed the plane. Great, I could go home to Ireland. What a pity I hadn't thought to bring my stuff with me, I could just have left there and then. But at the exact moment I'd decided they definitely weren't coming, my senses pricked up and my hopes slid away. I still couldn't see them, but I knew they were about to show – not thanks to any sixth sense, but because I could *hear* them, their voices raised in disagreement.

And then they appeared. Mum with a mysteriously orange face – the mystery was explained later when I saw the palms of her hands, also a browny-orange colour. She'd been at the fake tan again. No matter how many times we told her she just couldn't handle it, she wouldn't listen.

I caught a quick glimpse of Dad, almost invisible behind an overladen trolley. He was wearing khaki shorts. Fetchingly accessorized with varicose veins, argyle socks and black lace-ups. Behind him came Anna, and I got a surprise – actually, a shock – when I saw her. She'd had her hair cut – *styled*. She looked great. And then came Helen, her long, dark hair glossy, her green eyes sparkling, her mouth curved in a contemptuous smile as she surveyed the waiting multitude. Even from a distance, I could see what she was mouthing: 'Where the fuck is she?' With a sigh, I positioned my elbows outwards, like I was about to do the Birdie Song, and prepared to push.

The reason for the delay? One of Anna's bags hadn't turned up, and only after they'd filled out the forms was it spotted taking a twirl for itself on the Bogota carousel. Also the trolley wasn't helping. Capricious and unpredictable, it had caused skinned ankles and bruised calves all round. Put it this way – if it was a dog, you'd have muzzled it.

But I was happy to see them, happier than I'd expected, and I had a moment of feeling protected – Mum and Dad were here, they'd mind me. But something about Dad's thin, white and blue legs was telling me it wasn't fair to expect to be taken care of. Instead, because I'd been in LA for three weeks already, I'd be responsible for their welfare – even though I hardly felt able to take care of myself, never mind the four of them.

With much barking of knuckles I got their huge amounts of luggage into Emily's block of flats and, under a blue, blue sky, we headed for the freeway to Santa Monica while they discussed my new look.

'Your hair hasn't been that short ever.'

'It must have been short when she was born,' Helen said.

'No, it wasn't.'

'How would you know? You weren't there. I have to say, Maggie,' Helen mused, 'you look great. Your hair really suits you that length and you've a gorgeous tan.'

I waited for the catch. However, the trap wasn't for me, but for Mum.

'A gorgeous tan,' Helen repeated. 'Nearly as gorgeous as Mum's. Hasn't she a great colour?' she asked unkindly.

'Yeah, lovely.'

'I've been sitting out in the garden at home,' Mum said.

'Between showers,' Helen twisted the knife.

'The Irish sun can be very strong,' Mum persisted.

'Must be, if you can get that sort of colour when it's pissing down.'

The sniping continued until – a mere six blocks from Emily's – we got to the Ocean View hotel. To my surprise, it was accurately named: you *could* actually view the ocean from it. All that separated it from the vast, twinkling expanse of the Pacific was a road, a line of palm trees and a cycle path.

'Look,' Anna said, all excited, as two six-foot, toffee-tanned, pony-tailed blondes rollerbladed past. 'Welcome to California.'

Inside, the hotel was nice and bright and had a swimming pool and the advertised umbrellas, but Mum seemed edgy and distracted, moving around her room, opening drawers, touching things. She only relaxed when she discovered that they hadn't hoovered under the bed. She's a bad housekeeper herself and she hates feeling out-cleaned.

'It's quite nice here,' she finally conceded.

Helen was less impressed. 'We came this close,' she held up her thumb and forefinger, 'to staying in the Chateau Marmont.'

'She told me it was a convent,' Mum said indignantly. 'If it wasn't for Nuala Freeman, who told me the kind of place it really was –'

'Glamorous,' Helen interrupted. 'Full of the stars of screen and stage. It would have been great.'

One of the reasons they – at least Mum and Dad – had come to LA was out of concern for me, and they hadn't even unpacked before I was called to provide an account of my emotional health. Somehow, Mum had backed me into a corner, thrust a concerned (and orange) face at me and asked softly, 'How've you been these past few weeks, since . . . you know?' Up close, her neck was streaky, but her eyes were kind and I wondered where I should start – 'I found out for sure that my husband has someone else, then I had mild bondage with a big-nosed man who didn't call me, then I ran into Shay first-cut-is-the-deepest Delaney again, who did his best to ignore me even though we'll always be linked, at least in my head, then I had sex with a woman with breast implants and she rejected me too. I've been to very dark places and behaved so out of character that I've scared myself, and I'm still no wiser about what's going to become of me and my life and my future and my past.' So which bit should I tell her first? I mused. The lesbian sex? Being tied to Troy's bedpost?

'I'm fine, Mum,' I said weakly.

Her loving expression remained on me and I noticed she'd missed a patch just below her ear. For some reason this squeezed me with hopeless tenderness.

'Are you sure?'

'Yeah.'

'Thank God,' she sighed. 'I was afraid you might go . . . a bit mad for yourself.'

'What news from home?' I was keen to change the subject.

'Well, you heard about us being broken into, did you?'

'No! What happened?'

Moving her orange face even closer to mine, Mum told the story. Apparently, one morning as Dad was going downstairs to make Mum's cup of tea, he met an unfamiliar youth climbing the stairs. 'Morning,' Dad said, because an unfamiliar youth climbing the stairs was, in itself, nothing unusual. With five daughters, the chances of this sort of encounter of a morning were high. But then Dad noticed that the youth had two of his golf trophies under his arm. And that the microwave was by the front door. And so was the telly. 'What are you doing with my golf trophies?' Dad had asked uncertainly.

'Ah fuck!' the youth had said moodily, bouncing the trophies on to the ground, bolting down the stairs and out into the wide, blue yonder. It was then that Dad saw the key still in the front door – left there when Helen had come home the previous night. The youth was no swain of one of his daughter's, but an opportunistic, early-morning burglar.

'It was the mercy of God that your father got up,' Mum said. 'Or else the bed would have been stolen out from under us. And another night Anna came home scuttered, put some beans on the ring, then fell asleep.'

'I was still there when that happened.'

'Oh, were you? We could all have been burnt in our beds. Mind you,' she said ruminatively, 'I suppose we could count ourselves lucky to still have beds to be burnt in, the way things were going . . . Now tell me,' abruptly Mum changed the subject and dropped her voice to a hiss. 'Is my face a bit much?'

'No, Mum, you're gorgeous.'

'Only it's fake, you see. I was putting it on and nothing was happening and I put some more on, a good handful, and when

I looked in the mirror this morning this is what I was greeted with.'

'But you know the colour doesn't come up immediately, Mum, we keep telling you, you have to wait.'

'I know, but I'm always afraid that I haven't put on enough. Anyway, I think it's marvellous to have a bit of a colour, but Helen has been at me, making fun.' She paused, swallowed, then made herself continue. 'She's been calling me Outspan Head. Kept telling the air hostesses, "Outspan Head can't work her earphones, Outspan Head wants another blanket." She even told the man at immigration that that was my real name, not the name on my passport, and it wasn't funny, they can't take a joke, those men.'

'Maybe Helen's jealous.'

'Jealous!' Suddenly it all made sense to Mum. 'Sure of course she is! That's what's up with her. But you're OK yourself? And you're coming home soon?'

Then Dad made the same sort of enquiries about my general well-being, though of course, being a man and worse still being an Irish man, he did it more obliquely and without eye contact. 'You're looking . . . healthy.'

'I'm fine, Dad.'

'You've been . . . eating properly and all that?'

'Yes, Dad, I'm fine and you're not to worry about what you told me about seeing Garv.'

'It *was* his cousin?'

'Ah no, it wasn't. But don't worry, it's still OK. Right, I'll go on home. I'm sure you're all knackered, I'll see you to-morrow.'

From the clamour of disagreement that ensued, this was clearly the wrong thing to say.

'But it's gone midnight in Ireland,' I protested. 'What about your jet lag?'

'The best way to deal with jet lag is to try and stay awake, then go to sleep at the normal time,' Mum said knowledgeably. I looked at her in wonder. Since when had she become such an expert traveller? 'That's what Nuala Freeman said.'

'Oh well, if Nuala Freeman said it, it must be true,' Helen said bitterly. And I had to agree with her; Nuala Freeman sounded like a right pain in the bum.

'And we have to have our dinner,' Mum said. 'How can we go to bed before we have our dinner?' They are creatures of routine, my parents.

'Is it too late to go to Disneyland today?' Dad asked.

'It's half-four, you old fool,' Helen said.

'But it stays open till midnight,' Mum supplied. 'Nuala Freeman said.'

Before Helen could round up a lynch mob for Nuala Freeman, I quickly told Dad that it was a two-hour drive to Disneyland and that we'd be better off going another day. I suggested that they unpack and spend some time by the pool, then we'd go out for an early dinner.

'What about you?' I asked Helen and Anna. Surely they'd want to go out, get pissed and look for surf gods? But they decided to come – they had to eat and Dad was paying.

'And what about Emily?' Mum asked. 'I told Mrs Emily I'd look in on her and make sure she's eating properly and looking after herself.'

'Emily's very busy,' I said, but Mum had got that look.

'All right,' I caved in. 'But I'd better bring her car home in case she needs it. I'll tell her to expect us all later.'

'Then you'll be right back?'

'Yes.'

I whizzed home, warned a knackered-looking Emily that they'd be calling in to her for a quick drink before dinner, then returned to the Ocean View, where we whiled away a not-unpleasant couple of hours, unpacking and bickering.

At six o'clock, we walked the six blocks from the hotel to Emily's. Even though this was Santa Monica, where people were occasionally spotted getting from A to B without vehicular assistance, the sight of five people walking on their hind legs caused almost as much of a stir as it must have done when the prehistoric tree-dwellers first came down to terra firma and decided to give it a go. Cars kept slowing down to stare at us, like we had two heads each. 'What's up with them?' Mum tisked, as yet another car beeped us. 'Helen, what have you been doing?'

'Nothing!' She didn't sound innocent, so I relaxed. It's when she sounds innocent that you really have to worry.

When we got to Emily's street, Helen noticed the surveillance-equipment shop at the end of it and made us all go in, where she quizzed the man up and down about what the stuff was for.

'Mostly domestic use,' he said. 'We got hidden cameras and tiny microphones if you suspect that your husband is having an affair and want to tape his . . . like . . . activities.'

The jokey way the man said it meant he thought it was out of the question that a husband of Helen's would ever have an affair and need to be taped, but a pall suddenly settled on our little group and everyone avoided meeting my eyes.

'And I supply quite a few private detectives.'

'Private detectives!' Helen's already glowing face lit up even further. 'I wouldn't mind being a private detective.'

'Right, we'll be off so!' Dad said, fear in his voice. I don't think he could take another career change from Helen just yet.

Back on the street, as we passed Mike and Charmaine's, Mike stood up and had a good, decidedly unspiritual gawk at us through his window. Then, as Helen and Anna filed up Emily's short path, the dirty, torn sheet that passed for a curtain in the Goatee Boys' front window twitched. Convulsively.

Emily, God love her, was still labouring away at *Chip the Dog*, and she was exhausted.

'Hello Mrs Walsh. Gosh, you've a great colour.'

Mum hesitated, then preened. 'I take the sun well.'

We all filed into the front room, where Justin and Desiree were sitting; they'd come by to help Emily with some of the doggier parts of her screenplay.

'How's Desiree's anorexia?' I asked, sucking in my face to indicate great thinness.

'Way better,' Justin said happily, then added, 'since she started on Prozac.'

Right. For a minute there I thought normality had come to pay a visit. Clearly I was wrong.

Wine was uncorked and introductions were effected.

'What do you do?' Dad asked Justin. Dad could only relax with people once he knew what job they did. He was at his happiest in the company of local-government officials.

'I'm an actor, but –'

'That's right!' Mum said appraisingly. 'I've seen you.'

'You have?' Clearly this had never happened to Justin before.

'I have. In *Space Hogs*, wasn't it? They sent you down to that planet and the scaly plant thing ate you.'

'Er, yes. Yes!' Justin's dinner-plate face lit up. 'That was me.'

'You gave an excellent performance, but to be honest I thought it was idiotic beaming you and the other space corporal down like that. Wouldn't anyone with an ounce of sense know that you wouldn't last five minutes with that scaly plant thing?'

'Yes! Totally right! But the way it works is . . .'

As Justin explained the whole expendable-fat-guy thing to Mum, I was surprised to see Mike and Charmaine had arrived. They *claimed* they were coming to see how Emily was getting on with her desmudged house, but if I didn't know better I'd think they'd just come in out of nosiness.

Dad was very pleased that Mike worked in health insurance – which I hadn't known. I'd always thought he'd have some airy-fairy, touchy-feely form of employment. Then Emily brought Mike over to meet Mum.

'This,' Emily said dramatically, 'is Mammy Walsh. And this –' She turned to Mike, but Mum interrupted and with her most charming smile said to him, 'Oh, I know who you are.'

'You do?'

'You've so many famous friends,' Mum complimented Emily, then turned back to Mike. 'You write those travel books, don't you? And didn't you have your own TV series for a while? What's that your name is?'

'Mike Harte,' Mike said politely.

'No, no, it isn't. It begins with a "W". Oh, it's on the tip of my tongue – what is it?'

'Mike Harte,' Mike repeated, just as politely.

'No! I have it – it's Bryson, Bill Bryson, isn't it?'

'No, Mammy Walsh, it's not.'

'Are you . . . are you sure?'

'Sure I'm sure.'

An uncertain silence followed, and Mum became a strange purplish colour. I could only assume she was blushing beneath the tan. 'Sorry, you look very like him.'

'Hey, that's OK,' Mike said, extremely nicely.

'I have news!' Emily attempted a very clumsy diversion. 'Lara phoned!' Automatically I winced, certain that the mere mention of Lara's name would bestow Mum with psychic knowledge that I'd slept with her. '*Doves*, the movie Lara's been working on, is having its first screening tomorrow night and you're all invited!'

Naturally enough, this caused considerable excitement and semi-papered over the Bill Bryson faux pas.

'Will there be famous people there?' Helen wanted to know.

'Maybe, but do you know who *will* be there?' Emily screeched, still on her hostess-with-the-mostest kick. 'Shay Delaney! You remember Shay Delaney, Mammy Walsh, don't you?'

'Indeed I do.' Mum was quickly recovering her aplomb. 'And a lovely boy he was, too. I'll be delighted to see him again.'

I swallowed it away, pushed it down. I wasn't going to feel it, whatever it was that wanted to be felt. I'd enough to cope with.

In no time, Mum was back on top, and even though it was Emily's house, she was the one who was filling people's glasses, checking they were OK, acting in every sense the Irish matriarch. The Mickriarch. But when she tried to refill Charmaine's wine glass, Charmaine protested, 'I've already had one.'

'Have another,' Mum pressed her, the way Irish mammies do. 'A bird never flew on one wing.'

Charmaine tilted her head to one side and repeated slowly, 'A bird never flew on one wing. But that's beautiful. Such wisdom.'

Was she being sarcastic? I wondered. But there wasn't one bit of badness in her.

'Excuse me,' she said. 'I gotta tell Mike that.'

'That one's all sweetness and light,' Mum said mistrustfully, watching Charmaine's slender back and swinging braids.

'She's a very spiritual person,' I said.

'Oh, she's a Catholic?' Mum perked up.

'No, she said she was a *spiritual* person,' corrected Helen, who'd been following the entire exchange.

After that, Mum had clearly become of great interest to Mike and Charmaine, because they kept watching her. When Anna began to droop with jet lag and Mum chivvied her, 'Snap out of it, you're like a tree over a blessed well, there,' Mike elbowed Charmaine and, with a look of wonder, they mouthed at each other, 'A tree over a blessed well!'

A short, intense conversation ensued, then Charmaine gave Mike a little push and said, 'You ask her.'

'No, you ask her,' Mike said back.

Their heads were together again and they had another little mutter, then Mike was touching Mum on the shoulder. 'We gotta go, tonight's our meditation night.' He sounded disappointed. 'But it was a great pleasure to meet you, Mammy Walsh, and we were wondering if, while you're here in LA, you'd like to join us for one of our fable-telling evenings.'

Of course, she was thrilled. Just *delighted*. But she had to pretend that she wasn't – that's the way it's done in her world. 'I'll be very busy while I'm here, I'm going to a film premeer tomorrow night and my husband wants me to accompany him on Thursday.' She was doing a good job of sounding important and gracious until she added, 'To Disneyland.'

'We can work around your schedule.'

'How about Thursday night, when you get back from Disneyland?' Charmaine suggested.

'I can't promise,' Mum said solemnly, 'but I'll do my best.'

'We'll look forward to it.'

37

'So what does today hold?' Emily was in her pyjamas, drinking Jolt and smoking the first of that day's sixty cigarettes.

'Chauffeuring them round Beverly Hills with the "map" of the stars' houses, then on to the Chinese Theatre to see the stars' handprints set in concrete.'

Emily cringed at the naffness. 'For the first time, the idea of *Chip the Dog* doesn't seem so bad. It just goes to show, there's always some poor bastard worse off than yourself.' She gave a feeble smile, but she was so exhausted the skin beneath her eyes looked bruised.

'I wish I could help you,' I said fervently.

She shook her head. 'It reminds me of cramming for exams – no one can really do it except me. And I can't complain, I'm getting well paid for it.' But she looked so woebegone, my heart went out to her. 'It's the shame that I can't take. I'm cringing with every word of the schmaltzy crap I'm having to write. That's what's really depressing me. And the conference calls don't help.' She gave the phone a vicious glare – Larry Savage kept ringing, looking for progress reports and making her have conference calls with him and Chandler while they forcibly suggested cuts and additions. 'If they'd just let me get on with it, it mightn't be so bad. But every time I finally manage to sew up a scene, they make me change it, so I feel like I'm getting nowhere.'

'Do you think you'll be able to come tonight?'

'Ah, yeah. I'll need a break.' She suddenly remembered something. 'Look, sorry about telling you about Shay Delaney like that. I sort of panicked with the Bill Bryson thing and couldn't stop talking.'

'It's OK, no biggie,' I said quickly, keen not to dwell on it. 'Who else'll be there?'

'Do you mean Troy?'

I winced. 'S'pose.'

'He'll be there. How do you feel about him now?'

'Oh, you know,' I said airily, 'mortified, embarrassed.'

'Do you still want to sleep with him?'

'Are you insane? Last man on earth and all that.'

'That's great. You're not so messed up that you've become a rejection addict.'

'And what's that, oh pop-psychology one?'

'You know – the more he pushes you away, the more you want him.'

'God, that'd be worse, no doubt about it. As it is, I just feel really stupid.'

'You're not the first woman to have been taken in by a man and you won't be the last, so go easy on yourself. All that's wrong with you is that you're out of practice,' she added with a smile. 'Soon you'll have been duped by tons of men, and Troy will fade into nothing!'

'Speaking of being duped, how's Lou?'

'Clever, I'll give him that. Playing at being Mister Perfect. But I'm several steps ahead of him.' Coolly she blew out a plume of smoke.

Down at the Ocean View, they'd all been awake since four a.m. and were looking for kicks. Spirits were high as we set off beneath a cloudless blue sky for Beverly Hills and purchased a 'map' of the stars' houses. Everyone knew the maps were, at best, inaccurate and out of date, but who was I to ruin anyone's excitement?

First stop was Julia Roberts' house, where we spent a good twenty minutes parked on a well-kempt deserted road, trying to see through solid metal gates.

'She'll have to come out some time,' was Dad's reasoning. 'To buy a paper or get a pint of milk or something.'

'You haven't a clue,' Helen scorned. 'She has people to do that. She probably even has people to read the paper and drink the milk *for* her.'

We resumed our silent vigil.

'This is really boring,' Helen said. 'Although it's good practice for when I set up my private-detective agency. A lot of that will be surveillance work.'

'You're not becoming a private detective,' Mum said tightly. 'You've got Marie Fitzsimon's wedding on Monday week and you'll send her down the aisle looking like a princess, or you'll have me to deal with.'

'Don't you need qualifications to be a private detective?' Anna said.

Helen thought about it. 'Yep. First, I need to develop a drink dependency. Shouldn't be any problem considering the gene pool I come from. Secondly, I need a wacky family.' Helen swept an approving eye over the assembled group, over Mum's patchy face, Dad's argyle socks and Anna's I-get-dressed-in-the-dark chic. 'Once again, ladies and gentlemen, we appear to be in luck!'

'Someone's coming out. Someone's coming out!'

'Calm down, Dad.'

But it was just a Mexican gardener with a leaf-blower.

Dad rolled down the window and shouted at him, 'Is Julia around?'

'Hooleeya?'

'Julia Roberts.'

'Thees ees not Mees Roberts' khouse.'

'Oh,' Dad said in consternation. 'Well, do you know which one is?'

'Yes, but eef I told you, I would have to keel you.'

'Fine help you are,' Dad muttered, rolling the window back up. 'Come on, who's next?'

After visits to the 'houses' of Tom Cruise, Sandra Bullock, Tim Allen and Madonna had yielded nothing but views of electronic gates and Armed Response signs, we gave up on it and went to the Chinese Theatre, which was overrun with tourists seeking their favourite actors' handprints, then putting their own hands in and having their photo taken. Dad paid homage to John Wayne's hands, Mum couldn't get over the tininess of Doris Day's shoes and Anna seemed very touched by Lassie's paw print. Helen, however, wasn't so impressed.

'This is boring,' she said loudly and tagged a passing official. 'Excuse me, sir, where can I find Brad Pitt's arse?'

'Brad Pitt's arse?'

'Yes, I heard it was here.'

'Didja? OK. Hey, Ricky, where can this lady find Brad Pitt's arse?'

'What's an arse?'

'An ass,' Helen translated helpfully. 'A butt, if you prefer.'

'Do we have Brad Pitt's butt? Hey, LaWanda, where's Brad Pitt's butt?'

But LaWanda wasn't as stupid as the rest of them. 'We don't got it,' she snapped.

'Did someone steal it?' Helen asked sympathetically.

LaWanda eyed Helen angrily. 'You weird.'

'Because I want to see a concrete copy of Brad Pitt's arse? It'd be weird *not* to want to see it.'

'Brad Pitt ain't gonna come on down here, drop his pants and sit his ass in wet con-*crete*. He a star!' By now LaWanda was giving the hand and doing that side-to-side, head-popping thing they do on Jerry Springer. I knew what usually followed. Before Helen got the crap beaten out of her, I moved her on.

Later, I dropped them back to the Ocean View, with instructions to get ready for the film screening, then to come round to Emily's.

'And we're to get dressed up?' Dad asked, hoping the answer would be no.

'It's a film premeer,' Mum scolded. 'Of course we are.'

'Are we?' he asked me again.

'You might as well.'

Though *Doves* was only an independent film – which meant no household-name stars and no one in Ireland being impressed because they'd never hear of it – all the same, it was worth looking our best.

And then, I don't know what got into me, but I decided I'd take a trip to Arizona and Third and get my nails done.

I found Nail Heaven easily. Not only was it on the corner of Arizona and Third, just like Lara had said, but it had a pink-neon hand in the window and a blue-neon sign that said 'nails, nails, nails' (only the 'n' wasn't lighting properly so what the sign actually said was 'ails, ails, ails', but what harm?). Down a couple of steps and in I went.

It was run by Taiwanese girls, Lara had said. The best. Behind a desk sat a beautiful, doll-like receptionist, whose name badge said 'Lianne'. As I explained myself to her and apologized for not having an appointment, I was distracted by her nails – they were about two inches long and each one was individually painted with the stars and stripes. All at once, a wealth of nail-related possibilities opened up – maybe I'd get mine done the same!

'You don't need appointment,' Lianne said – just as Lara had promised – then she grasped my hand and bent over it to examine it. 'Ooohhh,' she breathed, sounding quite shocked – and suddenly I saw what she was seeing; the uneven, crooked nails, the scraggy cuticles, the general air of neglect. I'd never thought it had mattered before. How wrong I was!

Just in case I wasn't already feeling ashamed, Lianne began to laugh – childish, sweet hee-hee-hees – before lifting her glossy head and excitedly summoning her colleagues to have a look. In seconds I was surrounded by slender, white-coated girls, high-pitched garrulous chatter and lots more laughter as they examined my hand, as if it wasn't attached to me, but was a strange object found abandoned in the street.

'On vacation?' one asked.

'Yes. From Ireland.'

'Ah,' she nodded, like it all made sense now. 'Iowa.'

Quick-fire questions in Taiwanese began to hop between the girls and the word 'Mona' kept appearing. Finally, when some conclusion had been reached, Lianne said, 'Mona will do you.'

'Which one of you is Mona?' I asked, looking from blossom-like face to blossom-like face, and for some reason this question was enough to start the laughter all over again. I could sort of understand why when Mona emerged from some back room, a heavy-set lady quite a bit older than the other beauticians.

'She very goo',' one of the young girls whispered respectfully to me.

'She rike a charrenge,' whispered another.

Mona examined my fingernails. 'The feet too?' She leant over for a look at my toes poking through my sandals and all but winced.

'I'm not sure I have the time.'

'We do them same time as hands. One girl hands, other girl feet,' she said scornfully.

'OK then.'

She summoned one of the younger girls, and in no time they had my hands and feet soaking in soapy water.

'You need the hot wax. It's goo' for your skin,' Mona said.

'Fine.' If the job's worth doing, it's worth doing properly, right?

Just then a tall, well-kempt woman stalked in, wearing a beautifully cut trouser suit and an air of panic. She had a quick word with Lianne, who shouted a few urgent-sounding imprecations around the salon and within moments people were rising from their work stations and gravitating to the front of house. There was an atmosphere of importance, of professionals falling into well-rehearsed roles, and for some reason it reminded me of the time, years ago, when I'd had to go to Accident and Emergency with a badly sprained ankle. I'd been in agony, my foot had swollen up to the size of a football and I was whimpering in pain, when out of nowhere gurneys were rattling past me, bearing bodies that were losing blood hand over fist. Paramedics were running beside them, holding drips and shouting stuff like, 'He's still breathing.' Apparently there had been a terrible car crash on the Stillorgan dual carriageway and my sprained ankle, painful though it was, was suddenly (and rightfully) bottom of the priority list.

From the minute the well-dressed woman had rushed into Nail Heaven, there was the same attitude that this was a *real* emergency. While she told the terrible story of her 'prize nail' and how she'd got it caught while changing a toner cartridge, Mona rose to her feet, followed by her assistant, and a path opened up for them.

'Oh, Mona, thank God!' The woman thrust the injured nail at her. 'Can it be saved?'

When Mona had taken stock and eventually concluded, 'It's bad. I'll do what I can,' I almost expected them all to start scrubbing up and donning green gowns and masks.

While the worthier woman was being fast-tracked to full nail health, I sat abandoned, my hands and feet in basins of soapy water. Some kind-hearted soul placed a magazine on my thighs, but, on account of my hands soaking, I couldn't turn the pages. Then I moved my foot a fraction and the magazine slid off my knee and down into the basin of water that my feet were in.

'Sorry,' I muttered, as the same kind-hearted soul retrieved it and shook out its swollen, pulpy pages. I wondered if she'd bring me another.

She didn't. I looked at the two other women there who were having their hands and feet done. Neither of them had let their magazines fall into the soapy water. What was it about me that I sometimes felt I'd been born without life's rule book?

Eventually, after she'd saved the prize nail, Mona returned to me bringing her helper and they set to work, filing, buffing, pushing back cuticles, rubbing at callouses, and then it was time for the hot-wax treatment. A basin of molten wax was placed on the floor in front of me and I was told to put my foot in. But the second I came in contact with the wax, I hopped my foot right back out and yelped, 'It's much too hot!'

'But it's goo' for your skin,' Mona cried, clamping a vice-like hand around my knee and trying to force my foot back down into the basin.

'But missus . . . Mona, it's too hot.' We struggled for a few seconds, me pushing my knee up, her pushing it down, then Mona cheated by standing up and giving herself extra leverage. Right away my foot was plunged back into the scalding wax.

'It hurts,' I begged.

'It's goo' for your skin,' Mona repeated, her hand steady on my quivering knee.

All the other girls were in convulsions, shrieking with laughter behind beautiful hands.

After a short but agonizing wait, I was allowed to lift my foot out. But as soon as a layer of wax had cooled and whitened around my foot, she plunged me back in again. The laughter started anew. In, out, in, out went my foot. The pattern was repeated four or five times, each time as painful as the first.

Some years ago, there was a programme on the telly called *Shogun*. In it a man is dunked repeatedly in boiling water until he dies. For some reason I thought of that. And funnily enough, I thought of it again when we did the second foot.

Then they wrapped my be-waxed feet in plastic bags tied at the ankles with pink ribbons, and if I hadn't seen this done before I'd have been looking around for the hidden cameras.

Ten minutes later, when they peeled off the white wax, to my surprise my feet weren't in need of urgent skin-grafts but were soft and petal-like. Then they painted all twenty of my nails in a pretty ice-cream pink – they'd laughed indulgently but shaken their heads when I'd asked for the stars and stripes – and sent me on my way. Already I was a convert, promising myself that I'd definitely have it done once a week from now on. The way you do.

Back at home, Emily was hiding her worn-out pallor beneath a mask of make-up. I don't know how she does it, but when she'd finished she looked fantastic – radiant and shiny and not at all like a sleep-deprived, stressed wreck who'd been working flat-out and living on cigarettes and Lucky Charms.

My family were due to arrive at Emily's at seven, and when they hadn't arrived by twenty-five past, I was a ball of anxiety.

'They've got lost!'

'How could they get lost? It's six blocks, it's a straight line!'

'You know what they're like. They've probably ended up in South Central and are already in a street gang. Gold chains and uzis and bandannas.'

'Could you imagine your Dad in a bandanna?' Emily got sidetracked.

'Could you imagine Mum in one?' For some reason, we were suddenly snorting with uncontrollable laughter. 'An orange one.'

'She'd look like a space-hopper.' And we were off again, shaking with mirth. It was lovely.

'Oh God,' Emily sighed happily, scooping an expert finger under her eye and removing a little pool of mascara, 'that's fabulous. Hold on,' she cocked an ear. 'I hear them.'

The four of them burst into the house, bringing their collective bad humours with them.

'It's her fault we're late,' Mum glared at Helen.

'We're here now, that's the main thing,' Dad tried.

'And you all look lovely,' complimented Emily.

Indeed they did. We were a glitzy, perfumed lot (except for Dad), and it came as no surprise when, almost immediately, the Goatee Boys appeared at the door.

'We're just going out,' Emily said shortly, trying to bar them entrance.

'Hey, I'm Ethan.' Ethan bobbed up and down, trying to see around Emily and make eye contact with Helen and Anna.

'Oh, let them in for a second,' I said.

'Go on, then.' Emily stood by narkily as the three of them filed in and stood shyly in front of the girls. I did the introductions and for a few minutes left them to sniff around each other like dogs, then we really did have to go.

'What do those lads do?' Dad asked, as he hoisted himself up into Emily's jeep.

'Catch VD,' Emily muttered.

'They're students,' I said.

'Yeah,' Anna said, 'but Ethan, the one with the shaved head, he's going to be the new Messiah.'

Mum's lips tightened. 'Oh, he is, is he?'

38

The première of *Doves* was taking place off Doheny, in a wonderful old-fashioned movie theatre with red velvet seats and art deco mirrored walls, a throwback to a more glamorous age. I was glad we'd made an effort with our appearance, because everyone else looked fairly ritzy. There were even a few photographers hanging around. 'More likely to be from *Variety* than *People*,' Emily said, but all the same.

Emily went off to network – 'Just a quickie before the movie,' and I shepherded my charges to our allotted seats. I was just settling myself in comfortably when, a couple of rows ahead, I noticed Troy and Kirsty and instantly shrivelled. Seeing him – and worse still, seeing him with Kirsty – reminded me of my stupidity, of how naïve I'd been. But then I remembered what Emily had said: I wasn't the first woman who'd let herself be made a fool of and I wouldn't be the last, and all of a sudden I felt a bit lighter, freer. Perhaps I'd always nurse a desire to stick a fork in his leg, but that wasn't the worst way to feel about someone.

Troy turned around to check the place out and I lowered my eyes, but too late. He nodded coolly at me, I nodded even more coolly at him – I like to think my head didn't move at all, just some of my strands of hair – then his look slid over me and arrived at Helen, where it lingered speculatively. Brazenly, Helen winked at him and he grinned back. Kirsty, alerted by some sixth sense, also twisted around and when she saw who Troy was looking at, her whiny voice started up in some attempt to distract him. At least I wasn't like her, I thought – at least I no longer wanted him.

Then Emily took her seat, the lights went down and the movie began.

'What kind of film is it?' Dad whispered hopefully. 'A horse opera?'

'Is Harrison Ford in it?' Mum asked into my other ear.

Harrison Ford has cross-generational appeal in my family; Mum is as keen on him as the rest of us. In fact, even my niece Kate stops crying when Claire plays her the bit in *Working Girl* when he takes his shirt off – arguably his finest hour.

Well, I can tell you that *Doves* didn't star Harrison Ford and it wasn't a horse opera. I'm not quite sure what it was. It could have been a love story, except the hero kept murdering his girlfriends. It could have been a comedy, except it wasn't funny. It could have been a porn movie, except it was mostly filmed in black and white so that we'd know the sex wasn't gratuitous but was essential to the plot. (It really is intensely uncomfortable watching graphic sex scenes while sandwiched between your parents.)

It was the kind of film which makes me feel incredibly thick, which reminds me that I didn't go to university, that I haven't read any Simone de Beauvoir, that I thought Kieslowski's *Three Colours: Red* was complete tosh (and I'd only gone because *When a Man Loves a Woman* had been booked out). I spent most of it a) wishing the sex scenes would end and b) trying to think of things to say to Lara afterwards about it, other than 'pile of shite'. It took me the full 120 minutes of running time to decide that 'Interesting' was a good neutral phrase. After two dreadful hours – and seemingly midway through a scene – the credits began to roll, the lights went up and the clapping and whoops began. Mum turned, smiled brightly at me and declared, 'Marvellous!' Then muttered in an undertone, 'The oddest thing I ever saw. I thought *The English Patient* was bad, but it was nothing on this yoke.'

As everyone stood up to applaud the director, Dad remained sitting, staring straight ahead.

'It's not actually completed, is it? This isn't the actual thing people will pay money for into the cinema?' He was almost pleading. 'Maybe they've shown us the out-takes, the funnies that turn up on *It'll Be Alright on the Night*?'

'Where's the drink?' Helen demanded.

'I've to go to the loo, I'll investigate.' As I excuse-me-excuse-me'd through the audience out into the lobby, I overheard someone describing the movie as 'very European'.

'Brave,' someone else said. 'Challenging,' yet another person said. I filed the phrases away, they'd come in very handy the next time I wanted a euphemism for 'pile of shite'.

'Maggie, Maggie!' Lara, luminous in a copper-coloured, floor-length, beaded sheath and big Barbarella hair, was beckoning me over. 'Thank you for coming. What did you think?'

'Yeah, great. Interesting, really interesting. Very European.'

'You think? You hated it!' She laughed with delight.

'No, I . . . oh OK, it wasn't really me. I'm more of a chick-flick kind of girl.'

'That's OK.' Then she noticed. 'Hey, *great* nails. You went to Nail Heaven? Who did you?'

'Mona.'

'Mona? Wow.'

'Why "wow"?'

'One of the greats but she's kinda in semi-retirement. Only does the special cases. I better go talk to some journalists, but I'll catch you later.'

She shimmied away and I felt happy – at least things were OK with Lara. I still wanted to keep her away from my parents, but there was no residue of awkwardness from our brief dalliance.

After I came out of the ladies', I found the glittering room where the hooley was being held, full of glinting trays of champagne and tables bearing finger food. I took a glass of champagne and made my way through the tanned, glam throng to Emily, who was standing in a little knot with Anna, Kirsty, Troy and – surprise, surprise – Helen.

'Weren't those old velvet seats like totally grungy?' Kirsty said.

'I loved them, it's a great theatre,' Emily said and we all made noises of agreement.

'Eeuw!' Kirsty exclaimed, in elaborate disgust. 'You're gross! Don't you think of all the butts that have been in them before you . . .'

I tuned out, and not just because I hated her; there was something weird going on with the food. The quantities were disappearing fast – each time I turned away from it, then looked again, it had diminished even further – but try as I might, I couldn't see anyone actually putting any of it in their mouths. *No one* was visibly eating – except for my Dad, who was leaning against one of the tables, going for it – but he wasn't eating it all. And turning around very fast gave me no clues, just got me a couple of funny looks. It was as if people were eating using something like the Vulcan mind-meld.

'So howja like the movie, Short Stuff?' Troy asked Helen, looking at her from under meaningfully lowered eyelids.

Christ, he already had a nickname for her! I almost felt sorry for Kirsty.

But was I jealous? I wondered anxiously. I so didn't want to be, I'd been doing well on the emotions front and didn't want a setback. So I had a good rummage through my feelings, and all I could find was a mild interest in what might happen. Perhaps I should have been protective of Helen, but I was sure she could take care of herself. I reckoned Troy was the one who'd want to watch out.

My pride in how well I was coping took a bit of a knock, though, when I saw who my mother had engaged in intense conversation – none other than Shay Delaney. That hadn't taken her long. He was leaning his dark-blond head down to her level and his tawny eyes were fastened so attentively on to hers that I had a strange urge to laugh.

As though he knew I was watching him, he suddenly looked up and gave me a stare that went straight to my stomach. Mum craned her neck to see who he was looking at and, when she saw me, beckoned me over – and of course I went. Out of obedience? Politeness? Curiosity? Who knows. But I found myself standing beside him where, big and kind of shaggy and smiling and charming, he was being *very* Shay Delaney.

'Look who I found!' Mum was skittish and over-excited. 'We were just reminiscing on old times. It only seems like yesterday that I had Shay Delaney sitting in my kitchen, eating . . . what were they again, Shay?'

'Bakewell tarts!' the pair of them said simultaneously.

'You were the only one who ate any. None of my lot would touch them.'

'I don't know why,' Shay's eyes twinkled. 'They were delicious.'

But he would have said that even if he'd gone home and promptly died of food-poisoning. He'd always been this way: full of compliments, and he went out of his way to make everyone feel good about themselves. Except for me. My look lingered on the golden stubble on his jawline and I swallowed a sigh.

'And you're married, I hear,' Mum probed.

'I am, six years ago, to a girl called Donna Higgins.'

'The Higgins family from Rockwell Park?'

'No, the Higgins from York Road.'

'Malachy Higgins or Bernard Higgins?'

'Neither, although she does have an Uncle Bernard . . .'

A brief detour to establish exactly which branch of the Higgins family Shay's wife hailed from, then Mum was off again. 'Margaret's marriage is after breaking up, but sure these things happen. You're no one these days if you don't get married more than once. We have to move with the times, isn't that right? What's the point in having divorce if we don't use it? Use it or lose it, as they say.'

With each passing sentence, my surprise stacked up until it became fully fledged shock. My mother is the woman who cried when divorce came to Ireland and said it was the end of civilization as we knew it. And how tactful it was of her to bring it up in front of Shay, considering his background.

'And your wife?' she asked Shay. 'Is she with you right now or back . . . Oh, back in Ireland. I see. And you're out here for work a lot? It must be tough when you don't see that much of each other. Well, who knows, you could be one of the fashionable types who have more than one marriage, if you're not careful!'

I thought I was too old to be embarrassed by my mother. Well, there's a turn-up for the books.

'It seems no length of time since you were teenagers,' Mum said wistfully. 'Where do the years go?'

Silently, Shay and I looked at each other and suddenly I was right back there, remembering one particular afternoon. Him lowering me into a patch of sunlight on his bedroom carpet. The heat, the light, the rare touch of his naked skin against mine. I'd been almost unable to bear the pleasure.

He remembered too, or something very similar, because the atmosphere thickened almost visibly.

I'd tried to keep my teenage romances secret from my parents. Naturally, they'd suspected when I first went out with Garv when I was seventeen. But at the time I never confirmed it – or that we'd split up. Nor did they ever know for sure that I went out with Shay, either. Not that I ever went *out* with Shay – all we did was have sex. What I remember of that time was the constant waiting and yearning for his mother to go out so I could slip into his house and out of my clothes. I was in a state of constant arousal and even when his mother and younger sisters were home, all we did was have sex, although a little more surreptitiously – we pretended to watch television while I had one hand in his jeans, one eye on the door handle and my pants under a cushion. Sometimes his nervy, beleaguered mother cracked under the constant badgering and let us go to his room to 'listen to music', where we had sex with most of our clothes still on: my skirt pulled up, his jeans pulled down, dreading the footfall on the stairs that had us leaping to our feet and hastily covering up our flushed skin. Even when we went to parties, it was just an excuse for him to lock me in a bedroom and screw my brains out on the pile of coats.

'I'll leave you two to catch up,' Mum said with a warm smile, and promptly turned on her heel, pushing through the crowds. I hadn't ever thought I'd see the day when my mother was pimping for me.

'When did she get so liberal about divorce?' Shay asked.

'In the last ten minutes.'

I hated the pause that followed. I couldn't think of anything to say. I was stripped of all conversational skills, which was a shame because there was so much I wanted to talk to him about.

'Right,' he said, and I knew what was coming next.

'Time up, is it?'

'What?'

'You've talked to me on my own for more than five seconds, so it's time you stuck out your hand and said, "Well, great to see you again." Isn't it?'

He didn't like that. He seemed startled – because he'd been caught out not being perfect? I was rather startled myself; I'm not normally so forthright. But we'd once been so close that maybe I still felt I had the right to say anything I wanted to him.

'It's not like that.' He stumbled over the words. 'It's . . . I mean . . .' He looked anxious, as if he was pleading to be understood.

But before we got any further, Dad spotted Shay and came running joyously. 'Shay Delaney, as I live and breathe! It's great to see someone from home!'

I swallowed another sigh. Dad had been away from Ireland less than two days. What is it with Irish people? Rachel, my sister, says we can't even go on a daytrip to Holyhead without singing maudlin songs about how we were forced to leave the

Emerald Isle and how much we wish we were back there. Do we share some sort of inherited memory, so that whenever we leave the country it triggers recollections of being deported to Van Diemen's Land for stealing a sheep?

'We're all heading back to the hotel now on account of the jet lag, but I'm taking everyone out for their dinner on Friday night,' Dad told Shay, 'and I'll take it as a personal insult if you won't join us.'

39

On Thursday evening, Mum, Dad, Helen and Anna arrived unexpectedly at Emily's. They'd gone to Disneyland for the day and I hadn't thought they'd be home till midnight. Right away, I knew it wasn't just a casual call because Mum had on her best cardigan and her 'going-out' lipstick, i.e. a ring of lipstick that was wider than her lips. She looked like a respectable clown.

'Come in, come in,' I said. 'How was Disneyland?'

Mum silently stood aside to reveal Dad. Wearing a neckbrace.

'Oh.'

'That's how Disneyland was,' Mum said. 'He stood up on that log thing again. He wouldn't listen. He never listens. He has to know it all.'

'It was worth it,' Dad said, having to turn his entire body to glare at her.

'Dad, when you came here with the other accountants, did you wear your suits?'

'Suits?' He sounded shocked. 'We were ambassadors for our country. Of course we did.'

'Did you have a good time at Disneyland?' I asked Helen.

'Yeah, because we didn't go. We went to Malibu looking for surf gods.'

'You've no car,' Emily said to Anna. 'How did you and Helen get to Malibu? Surely to God you didn't . . . get the *bus*?'

But Anna shook her head. 'No. Ethan and the other lads from next door drove us in their Dukes of Hazzardmobile.'

'But you only met them last night.'

'*Tempus fugit*,' Anna said knowingly. 'No time like the present.'

The whole room fell silent and stared, because Anna was the girl whose motto had always been, 'Don't do today what you can put off till tomorrow. Or preferably some time next year.'

'Anna fancies Ethan,' Helen said.

'No, I don't.'

'Yes, you do.'

'No, I don't.'

'Yes, you do.'

'Do you really?' Emily asked, agog.

'No!'

'She does,' Helen insisted. 'We'll just have to torture her to get her to admit it. Emily, have you anything we can give her an electric shock with?'

'Look in the kitchen. While you're at it, bring out some wine and glasses as well, would you?'

'Could you not just tell us, pet?' Mum asked. 'Electric shocks can really sting.'

'I don't fancy him!'

From the kitchen came the sound of rattling and rummaging in drawers. 'Emily, all I can find is an electric carving knife,' Helen called. 'We could cut off bits of her.'

'If you torture me, I'm going home,' Anna said.

'Leave it so. Just bring the wine.'

'And what did you do today?' Mum asked me.

I'd had a funny kind of a day, assailed by all manner of nostalgia, cast back in time to when I was seventeen and first involved with Shay. So much had come back to me, remembered with bitter-sweet pain . . .

Mum's voice cut across my thoughts, returning me with a jolt to present-day Los Angeles.

'Am I talking to the wall?' she said sharply. 'What did you do today?'

'Oh, sorry. I washed clothes. Went to the supermarket.' Got shouted at again by the raggedy man, something about a car chase with 'Lala' getting a bullet in the thigh. This time I didn't take it personally. Bought loads of lovely food, then wondered why it is, no matter whether it's in a supermarket in Ireland or one six thousand miles away in Los Angeles, that I always end up standing behind the Person Who Gets a Big Surprise When They Realise They Have to Pay. Their stuff is all packed in bags, which are sitting in their trolley to be pushed to the car, then when they get told the amount they act amazed, and only then do they begin patting their pockets or opening their handbag, looking for their wallet. Eventually paying either with a credit card whose swipe doesn't work or counting out the exact amount in small change.

Then I went next door to the drugstore, bought a tongue-scraper and waited hopefully for my life to change.

'And when I got home I helped Emily.' Well, I'd made her a blueberry smoothie, given her another word for 'growled', and answered the phone to Larry Savage and told him that Emily was at her colonic irrigation person when she was just lying on the couch smoking and crying.

'Last night was marvellous,' Mum said. 'Apart from the film. Shay Delaney hasn't changed a bit, it did me the power of good to see him. And he's going to come out with us all for dinner tomorrow night, Dad says.'

'He won't come,' I said. 'He was only being polite.'

'He will come,' Mum insisted. 'He said he would.'

Dad had practically held a knife to his throat, of course he'd said he'd come.

'I think he's a bit creepy,' Helen said. 'He was looking at you, Maggie.'

'He was looking at all of us,' Mum said smartly.

'No, I mean he was *looking* at her. *Looking*. With his *eyes*.'

'What else would he be looking at her with?' Mum snapped. 'His feet?'

Before I could separate and label the clump of feelings this engendered, Anna said something surprising. 'He wants everyone to like him.'

'What's wrong with that?' Mum asked. 'Anyway, everyone does like him.'

'I don't,' Helen said.

'You're just contrary.'

'Go home, old woman, I'm tired and you're annoying me.'

'I'm going, but only because I want to. C'mon, you!' Mum summoned Dad as though he was an obedient dog. 'Let's get this over with.'

'Where are you off to?'

'In next door to their fable-telling evening.'

When we'd all finished laughing, I said, 'Why are you going if you don't want to?'

'Sure, what could I say?' Mum said indignantly. 'That Mike put me right on the spot the other night.'

'Just don't go,' Helen suggested. 'Let him fuck off.'

'No.' Suddenly Mum was all hauteur. 'If I say I'll do something, I'll do it. I'm not the kind of woman who goes back on her word. We'll go for an hour to be polite, then we'll say we've another engagement.'

'Say you're going to the Viper Room,' Helen suggested. 'It's oldies' night.'

'The Viper Room,' Mum repeated. 'Right you are. And if we're not out in an hour and a half, come and get us.'

As soon as they'd gone, Helen said, all business-like, 'Now, the bloke with the big schnozz? Troy? I find him strangely attractive.'

'Take a number and get in line,' Emily said, just like she'd once said to me. 'Don't fall in love with me baby 'cos I'll only break your heart.'

'Fall in love,' Helen scoffed, highly amused. 'That's a good one. So who's slept with him?' She looked eagerly at Emily. 'Surely you have?'

'Ask Maggie.'

'OK. Who's slept with him?' I shrugged and Helen gave me a gimlet look. '*You?*'

'Yes, me.'

'But . . . you're a lickarse, a good girl.'

'Is that right?'

She gave me a mistrustful look, then pressed on, 'But you and this Troy, you're not an item?'

'No.'

'Well, do you mind if I have a go of him?'

'Nothing to do with me.'

'You might want to run it by his girlfriend.' Emily sounded unexpectedly sharp.

'Who? That ringlety one?' Helen laughed softly. 'I don't anticipate any problems with her. Now tell me all about Lara. The lads were saying she's a lesbo. I wonder what it's like to

395

have sex with a girl,' she said dreamily – only because she wanted to cause a bit of a furore. 'I wonder what they get up to in bed.'

'Ask Maggie,' Emily said.

'HAHAHAHA!' went Helen. Then stopped as if she'd just driven into a granite wall. The colour vanished from her face. 'I don't believe you.'

I shrugged again. 'Up to you.' I was enjoying this.

'When?'

'Last week.'

'I don't believe you. I'm going to ask Lara.'

'Ask away,' I said equably.

Helen spent the next hour staring at me as though she'd never seen me before, then shaking her head and murmuring faintly, 'Jesus Christ. Jesus *Christ* . . .' She only stopped when Emily looked at her watch and exclaimed, 'What about your Mum and Dad? It's been nearly an hour and a half. Should we go and rescue them?'

'Right, come on.'

We filed out, stood on the street and looked through the window into Mike and Charmaine's front room. Mum was sitting majestically on a chair, while all the others were clustered at her feet. She was talking and smiling. Dad was propped on the couch, his head in his neckbrace, unnaturally still. He was smiling too.

I knocked on the glass of the front door and a slender, beardy type tiptoed over and held a finger to his lips. 'It's the story of Famous Seamus. How he won the love of the doctor's daughter.'

Emily, Helen, Anna and I exchanged baffled looks, followed him in and took our place on the floor. Straight away, I was worried. Mum's accent was more Irish than I'd ever heard it before and the 'Musha' and 'Wisha' hit rate per sentence was alarmingly high.

'. . . Wisha, me prime boy Seamus could do it all. Reversing tractors, making reeks, and as for the dancing! Musha, he was the tidiest dancer you ever saw, he could dance on a plate . . .'

I was mortified, she was making such a show of herself. But a glance at the assembled faces gave me pause for thought: they were spellbound. Every person there was angled towards her as though she was a magnet and they were iron filings. You could have heard a pin drop.

'He could jive, he could line dance, he could do an eight-hand reel. But he had brains too, musha, brains to burn! Great, he was, at the book-learning . . .'

'"*Book learning*"?' Emily whispered. 'What is she *like*?'

'Sshhh,' a poster girl for tie-dyeing hissed fiercely at her.

'. . . he'd the heart of every woman in Ireland broke. Every mother in the townland had her eye on him.' A professionally timed beat. 'And not just for their daughters!'

Much laughter ensued and I took advantage of the disturbance to make wind-it-up gestures at her. She saw and acknowledged. Mind you, she looked disappointed.

'Ladies and gentlemen,' she cut across the laughter, 'ladies and gentlemen. As you can see, my daughters have arrived and want to take me away to the Viper Room.'

Instantly, several heads snapped around and glowered.

'So reluctantly I have to take my leave of ye.'

'"*Ye*"?' Helen questioned. '"*Ye*"?'

'Couldn'tja wait five minutes?' a large pony-tailed man turned to us and asked aggressively. 'We wanna hear the end of the story.'

'Yeah,' someone else called. '*Let* Johnny Depp wait.'

How was it we were getting the blame? 'Fine,' I said. 'Makes no odds to us.'

'Wisha,' Mum acted coy. 'I'd no idea ye were enjoying it so much. Sure, if ye insist . . .'

'WE INSIST!' the room erupted, then one of her front-row acolytes touched her gently and said, 'Carry on, Mammy Walsh.'

Mammy Walsh carried on for quite some time, and by the time they finally let her go, she was floating on air and so was Dad. Unfortunately, things got a little ugly out on the street when she discovered that she wasn't really going to the Viper Room, that it had only been a ruse – agreed upon by herself, we had to remind her – to get her out.

'I want to go to the Viper Room.' She sounded like a spoilt child.

'You can't, you're too old!' Helen said.

'You said it was oldies' night.'

'It was a joke. And we're knackered, our jet lag has caught up with us, we're going home to bed.'

Mum turned an Et Tu, Brute? look on Emily and me. 'I've a screenplay to write,' Emily said nervously. 'I need my zeds.'

'And I'm helping her. 'Night all, see you tomorrow.'

Emily and I hurried into the house and closed the door behind us, but from the street we could still hear her plaintively insisting, 'But I'm on my holidays. You lot are no fun.'

40

The holiday that was supposed to do Garv and me the world of good did the exact opposite. We returned frayed and shrouded in a dreadful suspicion that everything we did together would go wrong, that we were travelling on a non-stop, one-way ticket to disasterville, and that the more we struggled to extricate ourselves, the more trapped we'd become.

The atmosphere remained strained on our return and once or twice I caught Garv looking my way, with blame in his eyes. But about ten days after we got back, we had an appointment with Dr Collins, my gynaecologist, where we tried once again to find a reason why I'd miscarried twice. It was in that room that the final prop was removed for Garv and me. I can pinpoint, almost to the second, the exact moment that my marriage keeled over and died.

However, often when fatal things are happening, you don't know at the time that they're fatal. You get an inkling that they're Not Good, that they Haven't Helped, but only the passage of time will reveal just how bad they are.

I blame routines. Routines mask disaster. You think if you're getting up in the morning, putting on clean clothes, going to work, eating from time to time and watching *East-Enders* that everything's under control. And we were doing all that, but dragging the weight of our moribund relationship with us.

After the first miscarriage, we'd both been eager to try again immediately. We'd had a lot of hope that a new pregnancy would erase our sadness. This time was different. I think I was afraid of getting pregnant again, in case I miscarried once more. But nevertheless, I consulted my temperature thing daily, and Garv and I dutifully had sex if the signs were auspicious. Until one day something that had never before happened, happened. We were in bed and Garv was about to enter me, when I noticed that he was having trouble. His erection had gone a bit bendy and flippy.

'What's wrong?' I asked.

'It's just a bit . . .' he said, trying again to hit the target.

But he hadn't a hope, and before my eyes it got softer, softer, softer, shrinking in seconds from a hard baton to a shy marshmallow.

'Sorry,' he said, rolling away from me and staring at nothing. 'It must be the drink.'

'You only had two pints. It's me, you don't fancy me any more.'

'It's not you, of course I fancy you.'

He rolled back to me and we lay wrapped around each other, rigid in our separate miseries.

The next time we tried, it happened again and Garv was wretched. I knew, from *Cosmopolitan* and sessions with my girlfriends, that this was the worst thing that could happen to a man, that he felt his very manhood was failing him. But I didn't have what it took to provide comfort. I was wound too tightly around myself; sore that he'd rejected me and angry at his uselessness – how could we ever have a baby with this carry on?

We had one more disastrous attempt, before reaching a silent, mutual decision not to chance it again. From then on, we barely touched each other.

One Sunday night, we were watching a video – I think it was *Men in Black* – one about the world being about to end unless someone does something heroic very quickly. It was near the end of the film, time was running out, urgent music was playing, it was all very tense . . . And suddenly Garv says, 'Who cares?'

'Sorry?'

'Who cares? Let the world end. We'd all be better off.'

It was so unlike him that I took a good look to see if he was joking. But, of course, he wasn't. I watched this person slumped on the sofa, his hair flopping over his dark, mutinous face and I wondered who he was.

The following morning, I'd got up, had my shower, had my coffee and got dressed, and he was still in bed.

'Get up, you'll be late,' I said.

'I'm not getting up. I'm staying in bed.'

He'd never done that before.

'Why?'

He didn't reply and again I asked, 'Why?'

'For tax reasons,' he mumbled, turning his face to the wall.

For a short time I stood looking at the inert mound of him under the duvet, then I left the room and went to work. He wouldn't talk to me and I was barely even frustrated. Upsets no longer sent me plummeting with despair, they simply settled calmly on top of the others. Probably because there was no place left for me to plummet to – I was as low as it got.

Apart from the occasional day skipping work – but never together – our routines kept us running like rats in a wheel. We thought we were moving forward, but all that was happening was that we were marking time, getting nowhere. It was around then that I started drinking my contact lenses.

Click, click, click, the days passed. We paid our mortgage, we marvelled at how expensive our phone bill was, we discussed Donna's love life – all familiar stuff, the lifeblood of normality. We went to work, had the occasional night out with friends where the pretence was maintained, then went to bed without touching, and got a few hours' sleep before waking at four a.m. to worry. And yes, I did wonder when things were going to get better. I was still convinced that this horrible patch was temporary. Until the night, shortly before it all went pear-shaped, when I was afflicted with sudden x-ray vision. I could see straight through the padding of the daily routine, the private language and the shared past, right into the heart of me and Garv, into all that had happened. Everything was stripped away and I had a horrible, too-clear thought: *We're in big trouble here.*

Somehow, three months had passed since the holiday in St Lucia.

The day we were supposed to be going out with Liam and Elaine dawned no differently from any of the others. No one could have predicted that today was the day that the whole rickety structure would come crashing down. Then, inexorably, the series of events kicked off – the flat-screen telly falling on Liam's toe, the phone call where I said I'd pick up some food, the box of truffles in the chilled compartment – ending with the awful tableau of Garv lifting the chocolates out of the shopping bag and exclaiming, 'Hey, look! Those sweets again. Are they following us?'

Then I was looking at him, at the box, then back at him. Baffled.

'You *know*,' he insisted happily. 'The same ones we had when –'

And then it all went see-through and I *knew*. He was talking about someone else, another woman.

I felt that I was falling, that I would go on falling for ever. Abruptly, I made myself stop. The gig was up, the end had come and I just couldn't do it. I couldn't bear to watch the downward spiral of my marriage begin to catch other people and spin them into the vortex too.

41

On Friday, Dad went to the chiropractor and Mum, Helen and Anna went to Rodeo Drive. Mum had insisted on going, even though we'd told her it was very expensive. No doubt she'd enjoy it, or at the very least she'd enjoy tut-tutting about the outrageously high prices when she returned.

I couldn't go with them because, as Emily put it, I had to help her hammer the final few nails into the coffin of her rewritten script. Larry Savage wanted it by lunch-time and it was all hands on deck. We worked through the morning, reading aloud, looking for inconsistencies and checking for continuity. Then at midday – High Noon, Emily kept calling it – we printed it out, the courier came, and Emily kissed the bundle of pages goodbye, 'Good luck, you poor bastard.'

Straight away, an exhausted Emily went to bed. With Lou. I found myself at an unexpectedly loose end. It was too hot to sunbathe, there was nothing on telly and I was afraid to go shopping in case I bought stuff.

My thoughts turned to that night's dinner. I was pretty sure Shay wouldn't show; you'd want to have seen his face when Dad had strong-armed him with his invitation. Not keen – he'd just said yes so he wouldn't give offence, and it would come as no surprise to get a message saying he'd been unavoidably detained at a meeting or something.

But what if he did come? Then what?

In no time at all, I'd decided to get my hair blow-dried. My only real option was Reza; she was strange and narky, but she was only two minutes down the road and, apart from the way she'd gammied up my fringe the last time, she'd done a fine job. I'd just wear tights on my head for a couple of hours when I got home and I'd be grand.

I rang for an appointment, and when I showed up at the salon it was no surprise that Reza wasn't friendly – but she wasn't as brusque as she'd been the other time, either. In fact, she seemed a little subdued. A few times while she was lathering my hair she exhaled wearily on to my scalp, then as she started tugging the head off me with the blow-drying brush, she gave a big, heavy, despair-sodden sigh.

Seconds later came another huge sigh, gathered up from her toes and released like a hurricane all over me. Then another. Eventually I had to ask, 'Are you OK?'

'No,' she said.

'Er, what's wrong?'

Another sigh was on the way. I could feel it, being collected, climbing its way through her body, expanding her chest, then being exhaled. It took so long I thought she wasn't going to answer me. Then she found words. 'My kusband is cheeedink me.'

God, was I sorry I'd ever risen to the bait. 'Cheedink you? Out of money?' I asked hopefully.

'No!'

Oh dear, I didn't think so, and I simply couldn't bear to discuss unfaithful husbands.

'He has found another love.'

To my horror, a tear zoomed down her cheek, then another and another.

'I'm very sorry to hear that.'

'But still he sleeps in my house and eats my food and rings this *whore* on my phone bill!'

'That's really terrible.'

'Yes, my sorrow is great. But I am strong!'

'Good for you.'

Then she seemed to notice my hair for the first time in ages. 'Your bangs are too long,' she said mournfully.

'Ah, no they're fine!'

But it was too late. She was reaching for the scissors, then she was cutting and all the while tears filled her eyes, blinding her vision. *Blinding her vision.*

It only took two or three seconds for the terrible damage to be done. One second I had normal hair, the next my fringe was a pure diagonal, as if I was a New Romantic. At its shortest point it was less than an inch long. Appalled, I gazed into the mirror. Reza might as well have gone the whole hog and given me a Mohican. And what could I say? I could hardly berate her, a woman in her condition. (Not that I would anyway. Don't we all know that it's harder to be honest with hairdressers than it is to get a camel through the eye of a storm, or whatever it is.)

Feeling sick, I paid up. Then, my hand over my forehead, I hurried towards home. But as I passed the Goatee Boys' house, Ethan opened a window and yelled, 'Hey Maggie, your bangs look kinda weird.'

In no time, in a reprise of my last visit to Reza, the three lads were on the street examining me.

'I think it's cool,' Luis said.

'I don't. I'm too old for novelty hair-dos. Have you any suggestions for fixing it?'

Luis studied me thoughtfully. 'Yeah.'

'Great. Tell me.'

'Let it grow.'

At least the whooping noises from Emily's room had stopped. They must have gone to sleep. The sky had clouded over and it was fearfully hot, so I turned the air-con up full, watched telly and willed my hair to grow. This was like a sign: I'd never impress Shay Delaney. It just wasn't going to happen.

Around five, Emily emerged in her robe and wandered about yawning and smoking, then saw me and stumbled in fright. 'What happened to your HAIR?'

'Reza.'

'Why did you go back after the last time?'

'Because I'm a fucking eejit,' I said disconsolately. 'Is there anything you can do?'

She tried to pick up the shortest bit of the fringe. 'Hmmm,' she said speculatively. 'Let's see. I'll get some stuff.'

Minutes later, she emerged from the bathroom with a ton of gear for taming unruly hair – gels, wax and spray – and rummaged through them. 'I think we'll need warp factor ten. Class A. The hard stuff.' She showed me a tin of wax. 'They use this on horses, you know.'

While she was coaxing the lard-like horse wax through my butchered fringe, the phone rang and she said urgently, 'Don't answer. Let the machine get it. It'll be Larry the Savage, getting me to rewrite more of that fucking script and I'll lose my reason.'

We listened, but it was a hang-up. 'Another one,' frowned Emily. 'There's been a fair few over the last day or so. Don't tell me I've got a stalker, on top of all my other troubles. There now, how's that?'

I looked in the mirror. She'd done a very good job of sweeping the fringe over to one side and making it look almost normal.

'Great. Thanks.'

'You'll need a lot of wax and hairspray to keep it in place, but it should work. And don't go back to that woman *again*.'

'No, I won't. Sorry. Thanks.'

The dinner that evening was in some outdoor place in Topanga Canyon, and the cast of characters were me, Emily, Helen, Anna, Mum and Dad – proudly sporting his brand new clicked-back-into-place neck. ('I thought it was a gun shot but instead it was my own neck!')

We had all squashed into Emily's jeep and the restaurant, when we got there, was beautiful. Lanterns were strung through the trees, a rushing sound indicated a stream nearby, and it was mercifully cooler than it had been on lower ground.

No sign of Shay. We were herded into the bar to wait for him and I nervously went to the bathroom to check my fringe, but I shouldn't have gone because when I came out Emily and Dad were squaring up to each other and the atmosphere was tense.

'Mr Walsh,' Emily said, 'I really don't want us to fall out over this.'

My heart sank. What was happening?

'I have my pride,' Dad said.

'Let me make this very plain,' said Emily. 'I will buy the first round. I live here, you are the guests, it's appropriate that I buy the first round.'

Sulkily Dad said, 'And what about the second?'

'One of you can get it.'

'Which one?'

'I don't know. You can fight it out amongst yourselves.'

But as it happened, the first round was bought by Shay, who strolled in, blond and hunky, suavely flicked some sort of gold card at the bartender, then smilingly said hello to us all in turn.

'Hi, Maggie, you look beautiful. And so do you, Emily. And there's Claire. Oh, sorry, Mrs Walsh, I thought for a minute you were Claire.' Then he moved on to Helen, who was more beautiful than the lot of us put together, but she bared her teeth in a silent snarl and all his words disappeared. He never got to Anna. Instead Dad locked him into a conversation, proudly boasting about how loud his neck fixing had been. ('I thought a gun had gone off, so I did.')

After our drinks, we were led to a table beneath the stars and surrounded by rustling, fragrant trees. Our waiter was the usual full-on experience.

'Where you guys FROM?' he shrieked.

'Ireland.'

'Iowa? NEAT.'

'No – oh never mind.'

Then we had the performance about that day's specials. Vegan this, lactose-friendly that and zero per cent the other. The waiter addressed most of it to Shay, who made murmury, approving noises until the guy went away and then said, 'God, it'd wear you out. Why does it always have to be so complicated? But that's LA, I suppose.'

'Do you like it here?' Mum asked him.

'Yes,' he said thoughtfully. 'So long as you realize that this town is all about movies, nothing else matters. Like, remember when the American hostages were released from Iraq?'

Everyone nodded, though I'm sure they didn't.

'I was in the Grill Room that day for lunch with two agents

and one of them said, "Did you hear they released the hostages?" And the other guy says, "Released it? I didn't even know they'd started shooting it." It's that kind of place. Hey, Mr Walsh,' Shay urged, 'tell the snooker story.'

'Will I?' Dad asked shyly, acting like he had a crush on Shay.

'Ah, do,' we all urged, so Dad told the story of the only day in my entire life that he persuaded me to do something wrong – to take a day off school sick because he'd got tickets to the snooker final and no one to go with – and how it ended up being on the evening news. Really, it did; as the champion potted the winning shot, right behind him, clear as day, clapping like an eejity seal, is me. I am more in focus than the champ and the clip got shown on the six o'clock news, again during sports round-up, then a longer piece on the nine o'clock news, and even though I didn't see it myself, I'm told it was on the late news too. It got run on the following day's lunch-time news, then at the weekend when they were doing a review of the week. Even at the end of the year, when they were showing the year's sporting highlights, once again I could be seen. In fact, only about a year ago, when the player announced his retirement, they ran the clip again and there I was, the fifteen-year-old me, with my terrible fifteen-year-old hair, grinning and clapping happily. Everyone in the whole country saw me at least twice, and included in their number were my teachers. Some were sarcastic – 'Feeling better now, Maggie?' – but more of them were confused. 'I'm surprised at you,' several said. 'You're normally so good.'

Dad told the story so well that we were all crying with laughter.

'I'm terrible at being bad,' I agreed, wiping my face. 'Every time I do something dangerous I get caught.'

I couldn't help it. I looked at Shay and he was looking at me and our smiles kind of faded. I looked away, and the next thing there was a right kerfuffle as a cordon of people surrounding another person moved as one well-oiled machine between the tables.

'Celebrity alert,' Emily said.

The whole restaurant was trying to look without seeming as if that's what they were doing, then a word began to ripple, almost as if it was being carried on the wind. Faint and whispery at first, '. . . hurll . . . hurll . . . hurley . . . lishurley . . . lishurley . . . Liz Hurley.'

'It's Liz Hurley,' Emily hissed, and that was our cue to dislocate our necks looking. It was hard to see through the wall of minders, then one of them moved slightly, the light from a lantern caught her face and it was! It was Liz Hurley.

'Does anyone dare me to go over there and ask for her autograph?' Helen asked.

'Does anyone dare me to go over there and tell her to wear more clothes?' Mum asked skittishly.

Shay shook his head admiringly. 'I'm not daring you, Mrs Walsh, because I know you'll do it. You're a wild woman.'

'The nerve of you. I'm a respectable married Catholic.'

'You're a wild woman.'

As Shay and Mum twinkled at each other, I watched with bittersweet amusement. Mum and Dad were mad about Shay. What would my life have been like if I'd married him instead of Garv? A lot easier with my family, that was for sure. Mind you, Helen didn't seem to like him any more than she'd liked Garv.

'OK GUYS.' The waiter was back, doing his interpretation of the dessert list. 'Fat-free ice-cream, anyone?'

'Ice-cream?' Shay asked me softly.

Mutely I shook my head.

'Some other time,' he said. It sounded like a promise.

It was a nice night, apart from the row over the bill. Shay tried to pay it and Dad nearly had a fit, then Emily threw her oar in, insisting that the evening was on her. Eventually, some kind of compromise was reached and we made our way to the car valets.

They brought Shay's car around first, and next thing Mum piped up, 'We were very cramped in Emily's jeep coming up. Would you be able to drive one of us home?'

'Sure.' Shay offered her his arm. 'Shall we?'

But there was no fear of that.

'I'd better go with himself,' Mum nodded at Dad. 'Why don't you bring Margaret.'

'No, I –' I started.

'Ah, do.'

I was acutely embarrassed. Even more so when Helen said loudly, 'I was reading a thing in the paper about some country where mothers sell their daughters. Where was it again? It began with "I".'

'India?' Anna said.

'Yes! Or was it Ireland?'

I was perspiring from every pore. I wished the ground would open up and devour me whole, then Shay smiled at me, a smile packed with sympathy, understanding, even amusement. He knew exactly what was going on and he didn't seem to mind.

'OK,' I said. 'I'll go.'

As we drove away, I said, 'I'm sorry about Mum.'

'No problem.'

But he said nothing else, so eventually I asked, 'How long more are you in LA for?'

'Until Tuesday.'

'Long time. You must miss your wife.'

'Ah,' he shrugged easily, 'you get used to it.'

I didn't know what next to say, and we maintained silence – not entirely comfortable – until, in an astonishingly short space of time, he was pulling up outside Emily's, the engine still running.

'Thanks for the lift.' I reached for the door handle.

'You're welcome.'

I already had the door open when, out of the blue, Shay asked, 'Do you hate me?'

I was so shocked I gave a funny bark of laughter. 'Um, no.' I tried to recover myself. 'I don't hate you.' I couldn't have told you what I did feel, but it wasn't hate.

But if we were asking leading questions, I had one that I'd wanted the answer to for years.

'Do you ever think about him?'

Shay paused for such a long time, I thought he wasn't going to answer. 'Sometimes.'

'He'd be fourteen now.'

'Yeah.'

'Nearly the same age as when we first met.'

'Yeah. Look, Maggie,' he flashed me a quick smile. 'I've got to go. Early start in the morning.'

'Even on a Saturday? Tough schedule.'

He was handing me a business card. 'I'm staying at the Mondrian. Out of office hours,' he scribbled quickly on the card, 'you can get me at this number. 'Night.'

''Night.'

413

Then I was out of the car and standing in the humid, flower-scented night, listening to the screech of his tyres as he drove away.

42

I rang him in the morning, as soon as was civilized. I'd been awake since six, my arm itching like crazy, but made myself wait until five past nine before calling. Shay answered, sounding asleep.

'It's Maggie.'

Silence.

'Garv . . . Walsh,' I explained.

'Oh, hi,' he laughed. 'Sorry, I haven't had any coffee yet, brain not engaged. So, ah, last night was good fun.'

'Yeah, it was. Listen. Shay –' I said, at the same time as he said, 'Look Maggie –'

We managed a laugh and he said, 'You go first.'

'OK.' My blood was pounding in my ears and I plunged into what had to be said. 'I was wondering . . . can I see you? Just for an hour or so.'

'Today's not so good. Or tonight.'

'Tomorrow? Tomorrow night?'

'OK, tomorrow night. Call here around seven.'

'See you then. Thanks. And what were you going to say to me?'

'Oh, nothing, doesn't matter.'

My agitation calmed. I'd see him tomorrow night.

When Emily got up, we went to the supermarket for more supplies (mostly wine). As usual the raggedy man was in the parking lot, and when we abseiled down he yelled, 'Interior

415

shot. Night. Jill takes a box from under her bed and opens it. Camera lingers on the gun inside . . .'

'Oh my God, Maggie,' Emily clutched my shoulder. 'Listen to him.'

'What?'

'Can't you hear it?'

'What?'

'He's doing a pitch. He's pitching a movie.' She was walking over to him and I was hurrying behind.

'Emily O'Keeffe,' she stuck her hand out.

'Raymond Jansson.' He extended his filthy hand with its long black fingernails and gave her a good firm shake. From a yard away I could smell him.

'Is that your movie you're pitching?'

'Yeah. *Starry, Starry Night.*' His eyes were bright in his smeared face.

'Has someone picked it up?'

'Yeah, Paramount, but the producer got fired, then Universal did but they closed that division down, then Working Title came on board but they couldn't get the financing.' Suddenly he didn't seem at all mad, until he said, 'But I've got some meetings set up and I think I'm gonna get another deal real soon.'

'Good luck with it,' Emily said, linking me and moving away.

'Jesus,' she muttered, tears filling her eyes and overflowing down her cheeks. 'This is an awful town. Is that what's going to become of me? Going loopy from disappointment and pitching to the fresh air. That poor man, that poor, poor man.' She wept all the way through fruit and veg, breakfast cereals, baked goods and dried pasta and didn't stop until we reached savoury snacks.

Back home, we were unpacking the groceries (mostly wine) when the phone rang.

Automatically I went to answer it and what happened next was like the bit in a film where a child is about to get run over by a car, and the hero flings himself, in tortuous slow motion, into the road and an echoey 'Nooooooo!' is heard. Emily threw herself bodily across the room and screamed, 'Noooo, don't answer it! I'm waiting for the other shoe to drop. It'll be Larry the Savage and I need the weekend off.'

But it was another hang-up. 'Definitely a stalker. I'm a fully fledged LA woman now.' Emily sounded cheered.

'We're wilting in this heat,' Mum gasped, flinging herself on to Emily's couch and waving her hand in front of her face.

Anna, Helen and Dad trooped in behind her, their faces pink from the five-minute walk from the hotel.

'It's very oppressive,' Emily agreed. 'I think we might be due a thunderstorm.'

'Rain?' Mum sounded alarmed. 'Oh God, no.'

'Sometimes in Los Angeles you can have a thunderstorm without any rain,' Helen said.

'Is that a fact?' Mum asked.

'No.'

Shopping at the Beverly Centre was on that afternoon's agenda.

'Let's get going.' Emily jingled her car keys.

'I've been practising my signature.' Helen flexed her hands. 'For all the credit-card slips I'll be signing.'

'Go fecking easy,' Dad barked. 'You're up to your neck in debt as it is.'

'I don't know why you're coming shopping,' Mum said to him. 'You'll have an awful time.'

'I won't.'

417

'Oh, but you will,' Helen promised. 'D'you know what I'm thinking?' she asked dreamily. 'I'm thinking underwear. Lots of revealing, lacy underwear. Half-cup bras and thongs and ...'

'He doesn't know what a thong is,' Mum said. 'To be honest,' she admitted, 'neither do I.'

'Let me *explain*,' Helen said, and launched into an eager exposition. '... no VPL and though everyone says that they're like bum floss –'

'Oh, those ones,' Mum said sourly. 'I've washed plenty of them. When did they stop being g-strings?'

As it happened, the Beverly Centre lift disgorged us not at an underwear shop but at the next best thing – a swimwear shop. In we all tramped, Helen leading, Dad bringing up the reluctant rear.

It was a class act: not just swimming togs, but coordinating wraps, sarongs, overshirts, hats, bags, sandals, sunglasses ... Not cheap, mind. The bikinis cost more than the week in the sun they'd be bought for, the changing-rooms were bigger than my bedroom and the shop assistants were those determined, terrier-like helpful ones that you couldn't fob off by murmuring, 'Just looking.' The type that riposte, 'For what? An all-in-one? We have some great Lisa Bruce pieces that would be perfect on your figure.' And before you know it, they're frogmarching you to the changing-room, sixteen wooden hangers belonging to sixteen different pairs of togs clanking in their arms. These women were the type who'd squeeze in the door of the changing-room to get a gawk at you. The sort who'd double-bluff you by saying that one didn't suit you – so you thought they were honest – just to tell you that the next one (the more costly one, of course) was wonderfully flattering. And if they saw you were in any way unconvinced, they'd call five or six of their fragrant, Twiglet-thin colleagues to press the message home.

I knew this to my cost. There was a boutique in Dublin with the same air, where I'd ended up buying an expensive chiffon skirt – that I'd never once worn – just to get out of the place. And I wouldn't mind, but I'd only gone in because it had started to rain and I'd no umbrella/hood/hat/nice hair that looked better after it had been drenched in rainwater. I'd have been better off going to the small chemist's next door and buying thrush ointment (or something else that involved a time-wasting question-and-answer session).

However, despite all of this, I felt an adrenalin rush as soon as we entered the swimshop; everything was so beautiful. Helen, Anna, Emily, Mum and I instantly split up and spread out, alighting on our favourite colours like bees on flowers. Dad hovered by the door, staring at his feet.

Within seconds, I was well on my way to talking myself into a swimsuit-wraparound skirt-visor ensemble, when my attention was caught by an exchange at the cabana-hut-style changing-room. From the number of discarded bikinis and fluttering assistants in evidence, a choosy customer was within.

'Marla,' a laden assistant called over the straw door, 'is the DKNY totally great on you?'

'Totally great,' Marla's disembodied voice said. 'But my breasts are still too high.'

Too high? All of us out-of-towners ceased our browsing and turned, as one, to exchange what-on-earth? looks. What did she mean, 'too high'? Too big?

We regrouped in the centre of the room – even Dad – and Helen went to the cabana hut for a gawk. 'Too high,' she confirmed on her return. 'So lifted, her nipples are almost on her shoulders. A halter-neck is her only hope.'

'Ah here,' Dad murmured, squinting up from his feet, 'I think I'll just go to the pub and have a pint and read the paper.'

'There aren't any pubs round here,' Emily said. 'Just some strip joints.'

'Don't let any of the girls sit with you,' Anna advised. 'You'll be charged for it.'

'No,' Mum said firmly. 'Find a coffee shop, that's good enough for you.'

'It's Saturday night tonight. I'd love a bit of glamour, girls,' Mum sighed. 'Where's a good place to go?'

'There's the Bilderberg Room,' Emily said doubtfully, but I shook my head. I knew where to bring Mum. I'd known it was her sort of place the first (and only) time I'd gone there: the Four Seasons, Beverly Hills.

Dad refused to go. 'Feck this for a haircut, I'm sick of getting dickied up. I want to watch sport and eat peanuts.'

'Fine. Stay at home then, we don't care.'

I needed the horse-hair wax to fix my hair for the Four Seasons, so I picked my way through Emily's bomb-site bedroom.

'It's on the dressing table,' she said.

But the dressing table was crammed with stuff and when I lifted the wax, I dislodged a heap of photos, which slithered to the floor. 'Sorry.' As I gathered them up, I saw that they'd been taken at a party eighteen months before, when Emily had been home. Instantly intrigued – I love looking at photos – I shuffled through pictures of Emily and her friends in various states of disarray. One of her winking, another of me and her blowing

420

kisses at the camera – 'The state of us,' I held it out to her. 'And we thought we were gorgeous' – Emily with Donna, Emily with Sinead. One of me, waving a bottle of Smirnoff Ice, my pink, shiny face and red, Satan eyes happy and carefree; me again, slightly more demure; then a picture of Emily with the cutest man. He had lovely cheekbones and shiny, dark hair flopping over his forehead and he was laughing mischievously into the camera.

'Christ, who's he?' I asked in admiration. 'He's yum!'

'Hahaha,' Emily deadpanned.

Before she'd even finished, I'd recognized the man – of course I'd recognized him – and I started to shake with reaction. Emily was staring carefully at me. 'Did you really not know who he was? Or were you joking?'

'Joking,' I said. 'Of course I knew who he was.'

It was Garv.

I was almost afraid to turn to the next photo, because I suspected I knew who it was of – and it was: Garv and me, head-to-head, together and happy. And for a second I could remember what that felt like.

'Come on, then,' I said, my heart rate returning to normal. 'Fix my hair.'

Mum loved the Four Seasons, fingering the swagged curtains and saying with respect, 'I'd say they didn't come cheap.' Next to be admired was the couch. 'Isn't it a bee-yoo-tiful shade?' Then she asked in awe, 'Would you say those statues are antiques?'

'Pretty old,' Helen said. 'Not as old as you, obviously, but good and old.'

When the waiter came, Emily, Helen, Anna and I ordered

Complicated Martinis and urged Mum to have one too. 'Should I?' Her eyes were alight at her daring. 'All right, so. Lord above!' Her attention had been hooked by a pair of high, enormous breasts, which had walked past attached to a child's body. 'She's very well developed.'

Maybe it was because it was Saturday night, but the breast-implant girls were out in force.

'It's as good as a cabaret,' Mum said, after a particularly ginormous pair passed us. 'Just as well your father didn't come. He'd probably banjax his neck again.'

'Look at her,' Emily said in an undertone, indicating a woman wearing HUGE big sunglasses.

What was it? Someone famous?

'Nah, that Jackie O look is so over. No, she's had her eyes done. Any time you see someone wearing those glasses in-doors, they've just had their eyes lifted. Will we get another drink?'

We'd just embarked on our second round of Complicated Martinis when, across the room, I saw someone I recognized. 'Oh. My. God.'

'What? Who?' Emily asked.

'Look,' I nudged her. On a nearby couch, no more than twelve feet away from us, sat Mort Russell. He was on his own, ostentatiously reading a script, just so everyone would know he was in the Business. Gobshite. He hadn't noticed us.

'Who's he?' Mum, Anna and Helen clamoured.

Maybe we shouldn't have said anything but, like I said, we were garrulous to the tune of one and a half Complicated Martinis, so Emily and I spilled it all: the story of the pitch; the wild enthusiasm from Mort and his acolytes; the talk of Cameron Diaz and Julia Roberts; the possibility of opening on three thousand screens across America . . . and how it all came to nothing.

'But why?'

'Dunno. He might have meant it at the time.'

'Could have been he was just being cruel. Leading you on, like,' Helen posited, her eyes narrowed thoughtfully.

'That's no way to behave,' Mum scolded. 'And letting your poor mother buy that navy spangledy dress under false pretences. And it was a shocking price. Even though it was at –'

'– forty per cent off,' we all finished for her.

An attempt to explain that Mort Russell had had nothing to do with Mrs O'Keeffe's navy spangledy dress, that that was the fault of an entirely different and unrelated executive, was fruitless. All Mum cared about was that Mrs O'Keeffe had been swizzed into buying an expensive dress to wear to a film and that, as yet, no film had materialized.

'She's had to wear it to the Christmas party *and* the Lions' fundraising barbecue to try to get the wear out of it. And her manning the sausages.' Tight-lipped, Mum shook her head at the injustice, the downright *indignity* of it all. 'Getting it splashed with some honey marinade stuff. I've a good mind to go over there and tell that pup what's what.'

'Haven't we all?'

The five of us were looking at Mort Russell so hard I was surprised that he hadn't intuited it. Perhaps he was used to it. Maybe he thought our stares were admiring ones.

'Do you know what? I will go over to him!'

We tried to talk her out of it. 'No, Mum, don't. It'll only make things worse for Emily.'

'How could it make things worse for Emily?' she asked with irrefutable logic. 'Didn't he waste her time, lead her up the garden path with false promises, then turn her down? And hasn't she a contract with someone else now?'

She had a point.

'Listen to me,' Emily said quietly. 'Just don't humble him in front of anyone else.'

My head snapped back to Emily. She was giving the OK!

'They can live with humiliation so long as none of the people they want to impress know about it,' she explained to Mum. 'Try and find out why he passed on my script. And Mrs Walsh, if you can make him cry, I'll make it worth your while.'

'You're on!'

And without further ado, she was up and off! Appalled and thrilled, we watched her go.

'It's the Martinis,' Anna muttered. 'It was too much for her delicate, two-spritzers-a-month constitution.'

My mother isn't a small woman, and I almost felt sorry for Mort Russell as this Irish battle-axe descended upon him, bristling with righteousness.

'Mr Russell?' we saw her mouth.

Mort assented, his face withholding friendliness. Then Mum must have explained who she was, because Mort twisted his head to have a look at us, and when he registered Emily his tan retreated by a couple of shades. Emily wiggled her fingers at him in a travesty of sociability and then the berating began: a wagging finger, a voice high with indignation.

'Oh God,' I whispered faintly.

We followed the action closely and our anxiety was tempered with glee. Mort's face was sullen and hostile. I'm sure they never have to deal with the consequences of their wild promises, these Hollywood types.

We could hear most of what Mum was saying. 'There's a

name for people like you,' she scolded – then abruptly faltered. 'Except it's usually for girls . . . But never mind!' Back on track, the dressing-down resumed. 'A tease, that's what you are. You should be ashamed of yourself, getting the poor girl's hopes up like that.' Then she told him about Mrs O'Keeffe's navy spangledy dress, with no mention that it had been at forty per cent off.

Mort Russell mumbled something and Mum said, 'So you should be,' then she was back.

'What did he say?' we clamoured. 'Why did he make all those promises and not follow up?'

'That's just his way, he said. But he said he was very sorry and he won't do it again.'

'Did he cry?'

'His eyes were wet.'

I didn't really believe her, but so what?

'I think this merits another round of Complicated Martinis,' Emily said gaily.

43

I was already awake when the doorbell rang at eight-thirty on Sunday morning. I went to answer it but Emily was ahead of me, pulling up her pyjama bottoms and complaining about the earliness of the hour.

'Why are we both awake?'

'Worry?' I suggested.

'Guilty conscience?'

I didn't answer.

Mum and Dad were at the door. 'We're going to Mass,' they chorused cheerfully. 'We wondered if you'd like to come.'

I waited for Emily to hastily assemble an excuse, but instead she hitched her pyjamas even higher – so that she looked like a fifty-four-year-old psycho man who lives with his mother and wears his waistband up around his chest – and said, 'Mass? Why not? Maggie, how about it?'

And then *I* thought, why not?

I hadn't been to Mass for so long I couldn't remember the last time – perhaps when Claire had got married? I was a foul-weather Christian, and only prayed when I was afraid or when I desperately wanted something. Same with Emily. Seemed like we were both afraid – or desperately wanted something. So we pulled on some clothes, stepped out into the butter-yellow day and walked the four short blocks to the church.

Mass, LA style wasn't how I remembered it from home. The young, handsome priest was standing outside making people shake hands with him on the way in, and the pleasantly cool church was packed with good-looking – and here's the weird bit – *young* parishioners. As we squeezed into a polished pew, someone was intoning, 'Testing, testing,' into the altar microphone, then a manic woman shrieked, 'Gooood Mor-naane! Welcome to our celebration.'

A bell jingled and a girl with swishy hair and Miu Miu shoes walked slowly up the aisle, holding a huge Bible above her head like someone about to do an exorcism. Following her dramatic lead came the priest and a coterie of the handsomest altar boys I'd ever seen. They climbed the marble steps and suddenly it was SHOWTIME!

Were there any visitors to Santa Monica, the padre asked, or anyone who'd been *away*? The *away* was said meaningfully, so I took it not to mean 'away' in the geographical sense. Someone stood up, then everyone started to clap, so several more stood up. 'Out-of-work actors,' Emily murmured. 'Their only chance of applause.'

Mum, who'd stretched up like a cobra, checking out the standers, turned to me – to cuff me for talking, so I thought – but she whispered, 'That last fella was in *Twenty-One Jump Street*. Got taken out by the mob.'

Another few people stood up and got clapped. Beside me, I felt Mum get twitchy. 'No,' I begged. 'No.'

'We're visitors,' she hissed. 'Why shouldn't we?'

'No,' I repeated.

But, dragging Dad and me with her, she was rising to her feet and smiling around graciously. 'We're from Ireland,' she told the congregation, meaning: *We're REAL Catholics.*

427

Everyone put their hands together for the über-Catholics from Ireland and then I was allowed to sit down again, my face burning.

Next we had to turn to the person on our right and greet them. Dad turned to Mum, Mum turned to me, I turned to Emily, and Emily, who was at the end of the row, refused to look across the aisle.

Then it started. My clearest memory of Mass in Ireland was of a miserable priest droning at a quarter-full church, 'Blah blah blah, sinners, blah blah blah, soul black with sin, blah blah blah, burn in hell . . .' But this was more like *Mass: the Musical*. Lots of singing and melodramatic acting-out of the readings – I suppose you never knew when a hot-shot producer might be in the audience – sorry, I mean congregation.

I wasn't exactly comfortable with so much unbridled zeal, and Emily and I nudged each other and sniggered a fair bit, as if we were nine years old. The upbeat and celebratory mood reached its cringy zenith in the Lord's Prayer, where the people in each row held hands and sang. Emily smiled smugly, letting her end-of-aisle hand swing emptily. But her smirk turned sickly as the man across the way stretched out his hand and clasped hers, pulling her out of her seat and me with her. In the row in front of me, a slender young man with a disproportionately large bottom sang the whole thing into his girlfriend's avid eyes. It was creepy.

At a certain sentence ('And lead us not into temptation,' if I remember correctly), we had to raise our joined hands above our heads. I couldn't help thinking that if you'd had a camera on a pulley above the crowds it would've been a really good shot, like a Busby Berkeley musical. Maybe.

No sooner was the mortification of the Lord's Prayer over

than the padre uttered words that struck new dread into my heart. 'Let us offer each other the sign of peace.' All of a sudden, I remembered that this was the main reason I'd stopped going to Mass. It's an awful thing to do to people, make them be affectionate, especially on a Sunday morning. In Ireland we do the bare minimum – touch paws, mutter 'Peace be with you,' and defiantly refuse to make eye contact. But I suspected we wouldn't get away with that here, and sure enough, we ended up practically having sex with the people around us. People were stepping out of their pews, confidently crossing the aisle and giving bear hugs all round. It was horrific. I got smothered into the shoulder of the boy with the big arse who'd sung to his girlfriend.

But then the priest invited us to bow our heads and pray for our 'special intentions', and the we're-only-here-for-the-laugh air abruptly lifted from Emily and me. Emily buried her face in her hands; no prizes for guessing what she was praying for. And me? I knew what I wanted, but I was afraid to pray for it.

The comfort I'd hoped to get from going to Mass evaded me, and for the rest of the day a nervy excitement hummed within me. When the Goatee Boys invited everyone over for an evening barbecue, I had to take Emily aside. 'This barbecue tonight,' I said, flooded with anxiety in case it scuppered my plans, 'I can't go, I'm sorry.'

'Why, what are you doing?' Emily was alert – and alarmed.

'I'm going to see Shay.'

'On your own?'

I assented.

'But Maggie, he's married! What are you at?'

'I just want to talk to him. I want...' I picked a word I'd heard on Oprah, '... closure.'

In exasperation she said, 'We all have ex-boyfriends – it's called life. We can't go tracking them down and getting closure off every one of them. We just live with it. If you'd had more boyfriends in your time you'd know all this.'

'He's not just an ex-boyfriend,' I said. 'And you know it.'

She nodded. I had her there. 'But I still don't think you should see him,' she said. 'It's not going to help.'

'We'll see about that,' I said, then went to my bedroom to try on everything I owned several times.

The Mondrian is another of those hotels where you'd get snow-blindness; any colour so long as it's white. The lobby was overrun with chiselled, bronzed men in Armani suits, and they were just the staff. Kitchen porters, probably. I jostled my way through them to the desk clerk and asked him to call Shay's room.

'Your name, please?'

'Maggie ... um ... Walsh.'

'I have a message for you.' He handed me an envelope.

I tore it open. It was a slip of paper, with a typewritten message. 'Had to go out. Sorry. Shay.'

He wasn't there. The fucker. My tense anticipation flipped into hollowed-out let-down and I was so disappointed I wanted to kick something. I'd dressed so carefully, I'd spent so long taming my hair, I'd been so buzzy and hopeful. All for nothing.

Well, what did you expect? I asked myself bitterly. What did you expect after the last time?

I am bad at being bad. Terrible, actually. The one time I tried shoplifting, I got caught. The one time I sneaked in Shay

Delaney when I was babysitting for Damien, I got caught. The day I bunked off school to go to the snooker with Dad, I got caught. The time I threw the snail at the Nissan Micra packed with nuns, they pulled over, got out and told me off. So you'd think that that would have taught me that I couldn't get away with stepping out of line. But it didn't, and the one time I had unprotected sex with Shay Delaney, I got pregnant.

Perhaps it wasn't the only time it was unprotected – the way we had sex was often so fraught and hurried that slips and spills might have happened anyway. But there was one definite occasion when we didn't have a condom and we couldn't help ourselves. Shay had promised that he'd pull out in time, but he didn't and somehow I ended up assuring him that we'd be OK, as if my love for him was so powerful I could tame my body into obedience.

When the time for my period arrived without anything happening, I told myself that it was study stress that was keeping it away – I was due to sit my Leaving Cert in less than three months. Then I tried the trick of telling myself that my period wouldn't come until I stopped worrying about it not coming. But I couldn't stop fretting – every twenty minutes I ran to the bathroom to check if it had arrived yet, and I analysed everything I wanted to eat to see if it could be classed as a 'craving'. But that I might be pregnant was literally almost unimaginable.

I couldn't bear the not knowing, I had to find out that I wasn't pregnant, so when I was three weeks late I went into town and – anonymously, I hoped – bought a pregnancy kit, and while Shay's mum was out, we did the test in the Delaneys' bathroom.

We grasped sweaty hands and watched the stick, willing it to stay white, but when the end of it went pink I lapsed into deep shock. The kind of shock that people end up going to hospital and getting sedation for. I couldn't speak, I could barely breathe, and when I looked at Shay, he was almost as bad. We were terrified children, the pair of us. Sweat broke out on my forehead and gaps began to break up my vision.

'I'll do whatever you want,' Shay said dully, and I knew he was just acting a part. He was petrified as he watched the bright star of his future implode. A father at eighteen? 'I'll stand by you,' he said, like he was reading from a crappy script.

'I don't think I can have it,' I heard myself say.

'What do you mean?' He tried to hide his relief, but already it had transformed him.

'I mean . . . I don't think I can have it.'

The only thing I could think of was that it didn't happen to girls like me. I know unplanned pregnancies happen to lots of women; even then I knew it. And I'm certain most people are distraught and wish it hadn't happened. But I felt – and maybe everyone feels this – that it was somehow *worse for me*.

I suspected that if someone wild and breezy like Claire had got pregnant at seventeen, it would be as if everyone had almost expected it from her, and would just sigh a little and shake their heads, 'Oh, Claire . . .'

But I was the well-behaved one, my parent's comfort, the one daughter they could look at and not have to say, 'Where did I go wrong?' The idea of having to break this news to my mother was unimaginable. But then I thought of having to tell Dad and I shrivelled entirely. It would kill him, I felt.

I was gripped by intense panic. Being pregnant felt like one of the most frightening things that could ever happen to anyone.

Within the boundaries of my middle-class world, it was as bad as it got. I thrashed around like an animal in a trap, torn asunder and trapped ever deeper by the ugly realization that no matter what choice I made, it would have terrible implications that I'd have to live with for the rest of my life. There was no way out – every one of my options was terrible. How could I have a child and give it away to someone else? It would break my heart wondering how it was getting on, if it was happy, if the new people were looking after it and if my rejection had scarred it. But I was also terrified of having a baby and keeping it. How would I take care of it? I was only a schoolgirl and felt young and incapable, barely mature enough to take care of myself, never mind a helpless scrap of life. Like Shay, I too felt my life would be over. And everyone would judge me: the neighbours, my classmates, my extended family. They'd talk about me and scorn my stupidity, and they'd say I'd got what I deserved.

Fifteen years later, I can see that it wouldn't have been that much of a disaster. It was all survivable – I could have had the baby, taken care of him, eventually sorted out a career for myself. And of course, while my parents wouldn't have hung out the flags, they would have got over it. More than that, they would have loved him, their first grandchild. In fact, as the years passed I saw people live with far worse stuff than being presented with an illegitimate child by their best-behaved daughter. Keiron Boylan, a boy from our road a few years younger than me, got killed in a motorbike accident when he was eighteen. I went to his funeral and his parents were beyond recognition. His father was, quite literally, wild with grief.

But back then, I was seventeen and knew none of that. I was inexperienced at life, at standing up to people, at going against expectations. I had no capacity to be rational and I was in the grip of extreme fear, which woke me on the hour every hour through the night and turned my days into lucid nightmares.

I dreamt about babies. In one dream I was trying to carry a baby, but it was made of something like lead so it was far too heavy to carry, but I still struggled. In another, I'd had my baby but it had an adult's head and kept talking to me, challenging me, exhausting me with the strength of its personality. I was constantly nauseous, but I'll never be sure if it was because of the pregnancy or the accompanying terror.

Shay kept parroting that he'd stand by me, no matter what I decided, but I knew what he wanted me to do. The thing was he'd never say it straight out, and though I wasn't able to put words on it, I hated feeling that I alone was responsible for the dreadful decision. I'd have preferred him to yell at me that I'd better go to England and get myself sorted out pronto, instead of him acting all caring and 'mature'. Even though he looked like a man and was the head of the Delaney household, it began to dawn on me that perhaps he *wasn't* as mature as he seemed; that it was merely role play. And despite us being inseparable, I felt oddly abandoned by him.

Three days after I'd done the test, I broke the news to Emily and Sinead, who were appalled. 'I knew something was up with you,' Emily said, her face white. 'But I thought it was exam worry.'

They kept shaking their heads and breathing, 'Jesus!' and 'I can't believe it!', until I had to tell them to shut up and advise me on what to do. Neither of them tried to convince me to have the baby, they both thought that not having it was the best – or least bad – option. Their eyes were so full of pity and relief that it wasn't them, that once again I yearned for all this to be a terrible dream, for me to wake up, shaky with relief that I'd imagined it all.

They decided my best option was to go to Claire, who was in her final year at university and very vocal about women's rights and what bastards the priests were. In fact, she used to go on so much about the right to abortion that Mum often sighed, 'That one'll get up the pole and have an abortion just to prove a point.'

So I told Claire about my condition and she was staggered. In other circumstances it might have been funny, but at the time nobody was finding anything amusing. Claire actually cried and, peculiarly, I ended up comforting her. 'It's very sad,' she wept unconsolably. 'You're so young.'

Through her welfare officer, Claire was able to get information for me and Shay, and with unexpected ease the arrangements were made. A load lifted off me – I wouldn't have to have the baby and face the consequences – and then a whole host of new, horrific worries bobbed to the surface. I'd been brought up as a Catholic, but somehow I'd managed to avoid a lot of the accompanying fear and guilt. I'd always thought God must be a decent kind of bloke and I'd only suffered mild agonies of guilt about having sex with Shay because I figured He wouldn't have given us an appetite if He didn't want us to use it. It had been a long time since I'd believed in Hell, but all of a sudden I started to wonder, and reactions that I didn't recognize as mine began to play out.

'Am I doing something terrible?' I asked Claire, dreading the answer. 'Am I . . . a murderer?'

'No,' she reassured me. 'It's not a baby yet. It's only a bunch of cells.'

I clung uneasily to that thought as Shay and I got the money together. It wasn't hard for me because I was a saver, and it wasn't hard for him because he was a charmer. And on a Friday evening in April – my parents under the impression that I was on a study weekend with Emily – Shay and I left for London.

Plane fares were out of our price range, so we went by ferry. It was a long journey – four hours on the boat, then six on the bus – and I sat bolt upright for most of the way, convinced I'd never sleep again. Somewhere outside Birmingham I nodded off on Shay's shoulder and I remember waking up as the bus was driving past red-bricked mansion blocks in a London suburb. It was spring and the trees were startlingly green and the tulips were out. Even to this day, I shy away from London. Whenever I have to go there, I relive those feelings, my first glimpse of the place. Those red-bricked mansion blocks are ubiquitous and I always wonder, *Were these the ones I saw?*

I rose back into consciousness, like swimming to the surface, and I heard myself crying. A noise that I'd never before made was tearing itself from my gut. Stunned and still part-anaesthetized, I lay and listened to myself. I'd stop soon.

And pain. Was there pain? I checked, and yes, there was, a low-down, pulling cramp. When I'd finished letting these yelps come out of me, I'd do something about the pain. Or maybe someone would come. In this hospital that wasn't a hospital, surely a nurse who wasn't a nurse would hear me and come.

But no one came. And almost dreamily, as if someone else was making those sounds, I lay and listened. I must have fallen back to sleep, and the next time I woke I was silent. Bizarrely, I felt almost OK.

*

On Saturday evening, when Shay collected me and brought me to the B&B where we were spending the night, he was immensely tender. I was relieved, yet I cried – only when it was all over and safe could I afford to let myself get sentimental about the baby. For some reason I'd decided that the baby had been a boy, and as I wondered out loud if he would have looked like me or him, Shay was clearly uncomfortable.

We left for Ireland on Sunday morning, arriving back that evening. Unbelievably, less than two days since I'd left, I was back in my bedroom, where everything looked deceptively – almost bafflingly – normal. My little desk was piled high with textbooks requiring my urgent attention. This was my future, it had never gone away, all I had to do now was re-embrace it. Immediately, in fact that very night, I knuckled down and threw myself into my work, it was only six weeks to my exams. But over the following days, weird stuff began to happen. I could hear babies crying everywhere – when I was in the shower, when the bus was moving – but when the water stopped running or the bus came to a halt, the faint wailing stopped too.

I tried to tell Shay, but he didn't want to know. 'Forget it,' he urged. 'You feel guilty but don't let it beat you. Think about the exams instead. Just a few weeks to go.'

So I swallowed my need to talk about it, to convince myself I'd done the right thing, and instead forced myself to list how many hours of study I'd managed. When the urge to talk about our baby got very bad, I'd ask Shay something about *Hamlet* or the early poetry of Yeats and he'd earnestly explain, mostly regurgitating study guides.

I got through the suspended animation of exam time and then it was all over. I'd left school, I was an adult, my life was about to begin. While we waited for our results, Shay and I were almost never apart. We watched a lot of telly together – even on the warm, sunny days when the celebratory sunshine made the corduroy couch and brown carpet look ridiculous, we stayed inside and watched the box.

We never had sex again.

Mid-summer, we got the results of our Leaving Cert – Shay did brilliantly and I did badly. Not disastrously, but I'd worked so hard that everyone's hopes for me had been high. My parents were confused and immediately set about reducing my failure into something unimportant. How were they to know that I'd spent the last six weeks before the exams sitting in my room straining to hear imaginary babies crying behind the ring of a burglar alarm?

The aftermath lingered for a very long time. Almost from the moment I was no longer pregnant, guilt and regret arrived and I began to think that having the baby wouldn't have been so bad. (Although I was just about together enough to understand that if I was still pregnant, I'd be yearning not to be.)

Contradictions pulled me this way and that. I felt I'd had the right to have an abortion – but I was still bothered by horrible uneasiness. No matter how cleanly I lived the rest of my life, till the day I died this would always be with me. I couldn't exactly find the right description: 'sin' was the wrong word, because that was about breaking someone else's laws. But a part of me would always be broken and I would always be a person who'd had an abortion.

I felt so trapped by this irreversibility that I thought about killing myself. Only for a few seconds, but for that short time I sincerely wanted to. It was like being shackled to something shameful and painful for ever. Not like having points on your licence or a criminal record that lapses after five years or ten. It could never be fixed. It would never be fixable.

And yet . . . I was relieved that I didn't have a child to bring up. What I really wished was that I'd never had to make the decision to begin with. And of course it was my fault, I should have kept my legs closed in the first place, but life isn't like that – even then I knew it – and it's easy to be wise after the fact.

Occasionally, anti-abortionists paraded through the streets of Dublin, campaigning to make abortion in Ireland more illegal than it already was, carrying rosary beads and waving placards with pictures of unborn foetuses. I had to look away. But when I listened to them condemning abortion so vehemently, I wanted to ask if any of them had ever been in my situation. I would've bet money that they hadn't. And that if they had, their commitment to high-minded principle might have wavered.

What bothered me most were the men – men protesting against abortion! Men! What did they know, what *could* they ever know, of the terror I'd felt. They couldn't get pregnant. But I never voiced any of it at home, because I didn't want to draw attention to the issue. And – at least when I was there – Claire never said anything either.

At the end of September, Shay went to London to do his degree in Media Studies. That had always been his plan, because Irish universities didn't offer such imaginative courses.

'This changes nothing,' he promised me, as we said goodbye at the ferry port. 'I'll write lots and see you at Christmas.'

But he never wrote. I'd had a premonition this might happen – I'd already started having dreams about trying to catch him even before he'd left – but when it did, I refused to believe it. I watched the post every day and after seven wretched weeks I took my pride in my hands, visited his mother and gave her a letter to give to him. 'Maybe I've been sending them to the wrong address,' I said. But she checked and the address I had was the right one.

'Have you heard from him?' I asked, and flinched when she said, in surprise, that of course she had, that he was getting on great.

I regrouped my hopes and instead hung everything on him coming home at Christmas. From the twentieth of December onwards I was a ball of adrenalin, waiting for the phone or the doorbell to ring. But when they didn't I began walking past his house, up the hill, down the hill, shaking with cold and nerves, desperate for a sighting of him. When I saw Fee, one of his sisters, emerge, I nabbed her and in a high, wobbly pretence of unconcern said, 'What day is Shay coming?'

Looking confused, she broke the news. He wasn't coming, he'd got a holiday job. 'I thought you'd know,' she said.

'Oh, I thought there was still a chance he might get here for a couple of days.' My humiliation had me stuttering.

Easter, I thought, he'll come home at Easter. But he didn't. Or for the summer. I waited for him long after most people would have given up hope.

In the meantime I'd got a job, where I'd made a new friend, Donna. Like my other friends, Sinead and Emily, she went out a lot, on the hunt for men and good times. I used to tag along and, with them urging me on, if some decentish bloke asked me out I'd say yes; nothing much came of any of them. There was someone called Colm who gave me an engraved lighter for my birthday, even though I didn't smoke. Then, for about six weeks, I saw a DSS worker who kept coming across his dole claimants working in the pubs he took me to; he ditched me when I wouldn't sleep with him. After him was a cuteish one called Anton, even though he wasn't foreign. I towered a good three inches over him and he kept wanting us to go for walks. I actually went to bed with him – probably, I later suspected, because I found it so embarrassing to be upright with him.

But no matter how I tried, I just couldn't get worked up about any of them.

The current of life was trying to drag me forward, but I resisted. I preferred the past, not yet convinced that that's what it was – the past. And I would never have believed when I'd said goodbye to Shay at the ferry port that it would be fifteen years before I saw him again.

44

I drove from the Mondrian back to Emily's. Roars of laughter and a smell of burning were coming from the Goatee Boys' back garden. Ignoring it all, I let myself into the mercifully empty house, and made straight for the couch. I didn't even turn on the lights, I just lay in the dark, feeling flattened, soulless, lost to myself.

As time passed after Shay's departure for London, occasional news reached me of him: he was spending the summer working in Cape Cod; he'd graduated; he'd got a job in Seattle. At some stage I understood that it was over, that he wasn't coming back to me. I tried my best with the other men I met, but I couldn't move forward. Then one night when I was twenty-one I bumped into Garv in a pub in town. It had been more than three years since I'd seen him. Like Shay, he'd gone away to college – Edinburgh for him. Now he was back, working in Dublin, and as we swapped autobiographical details, I felt so guilty about the way I'd treated him that I could barely look his way. Mid-small-talk I blurted out a shamefaced apology and, to my relief, he began to laugh. 'It's all right, Maggie, take it easy. It was a lifetime ago.' And he looked so cute that for the first time in a long, long time, I got a *feeling*.

It was a great surprise to find myself going out with him again, the boyfriend I'd had when I was seventeen, my first-ever boyfriend. I was wildly entertained by the novelty of it, as indeed was everyone else. But then it stopped being funny the day I lifted a snail off his windscreen and threw it at a passing car of nuns – because I realized I'd fallen in love with him.

I loved him so much – he was such a good man. Though he didn't have Shay's quicksilver charm, he enchanted me nevertheless. And I thought he was gorgeous. Again he didn't have Shay's full-on hunkiness, but he had subtler good looks that had worked their way under my skin, so that whenever I looked at him I got a rush. His eyes, his silky hair, his height, his big hands, the way he smelt of ironed cotton – I was mad about him. Above all, we were mates – I could tell him anything. He even got chapter and verse on myself and Shay and was nothing other than entirely sympathetic. Not even a flicker of judgement came from him.

'I'm not a murderer who's going to burn in hell, am I?' I asked anxiously.

'Of course you're not, but no one's saying it was an easy decision.'

And I felt so, so relieved to have met a man as benevolent as Garv was.

But some people went a bit weird when we got engaged. Emily, in particular. 'I'm afraid you're playing it safe by marrying him,' she said.

'I thought you liked him!' I said, wounded.

'I love him. But you got so badly burned by Delaney, and Garv is so cracked about you . . . Look, I just want you to be sure. Just think about it.'

I promised I would, but I didn't because I knew what I wanted.

So we got married, moved to Chicago, moved back to Dublin, got the rabbits, started trying for a baby, had one miscarriage, had a second miscarriage, then watched my past come back to haunt us.

For a long time, I was the only person I knew who'd had an abortion. Then, when she was twenty-five, Donna had one and Sinead's sister had one when she was thirty-one. Both times I was called on to relate how it was for me and I told them honestly what I thought: it was their body and they had the right to choose. They shouldn't give any credence to those pro-life bullies. But – at least if they were anything like me – they shouldn't expect to emerge unscathed from the experience, but should brace themselves for fall-out. Every emotion from guilt to curiosity, shock to regret, self-hatred to wretched relief.

Though I was glad no longer to be the only one, both those terminations churned up memories, so I almost felt as if I'd gone through it all again. But it passed and, mostly, I lived with being someone who'd had an abortion. As the years went by, I thought about it less. Except for every anniversary, when I felt awful, sometimes without even realizing why, at least not immediately. Then I'd remember the date and understand, and wonder what the baby would be like now, aged three, six, eight, eleven . . .

But I thought it had been absorbed safely into my past – until that last visit to Dr Collins, the day of reckoning, when I had to vent the worry that had been gnawing away at me.

'Could I keep miscarrying because . . . because . . . I've damaged myself?'

'In what way, damaged yourself?'

'By an operation?'

444

'What kind of operation? A termination?'

I flinched at his bluntness. 'Yes,' I mumbled.

'Unlikely. Very unlikely. We can check but it's highly unlikely.'

But I didn't believe him and I knew Garv didn't either, and though we never discussed it, that was the very moment our marriage keeled over and died.

Some time later – I don't know how long – the phone rang in the darkness of Emily's front room; I had no intention of getting it. I let it ring, waiting for the machine to pick up, but someone had switched it off so, cursing, I dragged myself over to the phone.

The second I answered, I remembered Emily's ban and said a silent prayer that it wouldn't be Larry the Savage. But it was Shay.

'Oh, hi.' He sounded surprised. 'I thought I'd get the machine.'

'Well, you got me instead.'

'I'm real sorry about tonight.' He sounded so contrite that my bitterness began to melt. 'It was a work thing, it came up suddenly.'

'You could have rung me.'

'Too late,' he said easily. 'You would have already left.'

'You're going back on Tuesday?'

'Yeah, so we're out of time.'

'But there's tomorrow. Or tomorrow night?'

'Bu –'

'Just for an hour or so.'

He was silent and I was holding my breath. 'OK,' he finally said. 'Tomorrow night, then. Same arrangement.'

I put down the phone feeling marginally better and decided

to pop next door and see how the barbecue was going. To my great pleasure, I was given a hero's welcome, as though it was years since they'd seen me, instead of a few short hours. Then it dawned on me that they were all scuttered; red-faced and rowdy, exhibiting the kind of aggressive drunkenness engendered by drinking tequila on an empty stomach. The smouldering grill was abandoned and a dozen shrunken, blackened things that might once have been burgers lay upon it. When Dad sidled up and asked if I'd any chocolate in my handbag, it transpired that no one had been fed.

Troy and Helen were curled up on the flowery couch, looking very cosy; there was no sign of Kirsty. Either Troy hadn't brought her, or she'd refused to enter the house on the grounds that it was a health hazard. Anna, Lara, Luis, Curtis and Emily were ensnared in a hard-to-follow discussion on the merits of brunch over TV. I would have liked to join in but I was so patently on a different wavelength to everyone else, i.e. not psychotic drunk, that it was pointless.

'You get freshly squeezed orange juice with brunch,' Lara said hotly. 'When has your TV ever done that for you?'

'But you can watch *The Simpsons* on TV. Gimme that over French toast any day,' Curtis retorted.

I wandered away, over to Mum and Ethan, but they were toe-to-toe in a barney.

'Who died for our sins?' Mum asked shrilly.

'But –'

'Who died for our sins?'

'Hey –'

'Tell me, come on, tell me. Who died for our sins? Just give me the name.' It was like being in an interrogation cell. 'His name, please!'

Ethan hung his head and mumbled, 'Jesus.'

'Who? Louder, I can't hear you.'

'Jesus,' Ethan said angrily.

'That's right, Jesus.' Mum almost smacked her lips with satisfaction. 'Did you die for anyone's sins? Well, did you?'

'No, but –'

'So you can hardly go around being the new Messiah, can you?'

After a pause, Ethan admitted, 'No, I suppose not.'

'You suppose right. Carry on with your computer studies, like a good lad, and less of the blasphemy, if you don't mind.' Then she turned the force of her personality on to me and slurred, 'Where's Shay?'

'Working.'

'Ah, feck,' she said moodily, lurching away.

I went and sat with the others, and then we noticed that Troy and Helen had disappeared.

'Where are they?' Emily clutched me.

'I don't know. Gone, it looks like.'

'Gone,' she wailed, clapping a hand over her mouth. 'Gone! He's going to fall in love with her.' Her face crumpled with sudden, drunken tears and she was snorting and coughing from crying. When she hadn't stopped a full five minutes later I said, 'C'mon, I'll take you home,' and led her, bent almost double from hopeless sobbing, back to her own house.

'I'm just very tired,' she kept saying. 'I've been working very hard and I'm very tired.'

I put her to bed, but before I put her light out she said, 'Wait Maggie, I want to talk to you.'

'What?' I asked defensively. She was going to tell me off again about Shay Delaney and I so wasn't in the mood.

447

'I'm going to ask Lou to marry me and have my babies.'
'Oh. Oh. Why?'
'Because I don't want to see him ever again.'

45

Conchita was due to come on Monday morning, so as soon as I awoke, I began a hurried clean-up. But then she rang to say she was sick and not coming and instantly I abandoned the housework. Only to recommence it about an hour later out of boredom – Emily was still sounders and there had been no visits or calls from any of my family. So when someone knocked on the door at ten past twelve, I nearly wrenched it off its hinges, so delighted was I to have company. It was Anna.

'Come in, come in,' I said. 'Tell us, did Helen come home?'

'Yeah, about half an hour ago.'

'Oh my God, she must have slept with Troy.'

'She did. Do you mind?'

'No, not a bit.' Although Emily clearly did; what was going on there? 'Sit down,' I urged Anna. 'What did she say about it?'

'He tied her up, it was great. Um, listen, I've got to talk to you about something.'

'Oh.' I'd got a bad feeling.

'You've to promise not to kill me.'

'I promise.' I didn't mean it, I only said it, so she'd tell me whatever she had to tell me.

'I've got a job.'

'And?'

'In Dublin.'

'Good for you.'

'In Garv's firm.'

Ah.

'Well, Dublin's a small town, coincidences happen.'

'It wasn't a coincidence,' she said in a little voice. 'He got me the job.'

'*What?* When?'

'After I crashed your car – sorry, sorry, sorry! – I couldn't find anything about insurance in your room, so I rang Garv and he told me to come over to get the stuff from him.' She looked at me almost questioningly. 'He was asking me how I was getting on without Shane and I told him how poxy it was and how I felt left behind by everyone and he was really, really kind.'

'Was he?' I was tight-lipped. So Garv managed to stop riding Truffle Woman for long enough to be nice to Anna?

'Really kind. He said that if I'd like to get a proper job he'd try and help me – he wasn't being, like, manipulative or anything, I promise. You know him, he's not like that. He was just being decent. So I got my hair cut and he set up an interview.'

'Big of him,' I muttered. I was suddenly very bitter.

'Yes, it was,' she said gently. 'That's exactly what it was. So they've offered me a job in their post room.'

That Garv was being so nice to one of my family while at the same time doing the dirty on me filled me with hot fury. I had to wait for the bad feelings to pass before I could speak.

'Congratulations.'

'Thank you,' she said with dignity. 'And I'm sorry.'

'Ah, it's OK,' I said, as the poisonous rage began to drain from me. 'And if you're really that sorry, you can do something for me.'

'What's that?'

450

'Tell me if you fancy Ethan.'

She thought about it. 'Kind of. But I'm not going after it. He's too young and flaky. There'd be no future in it.'

'It never stopped you before.'

'I know. Well . . . I'm different now.'

'Jesus Christ.'

'People can change,' she said, with most un-Anna-like defiance.

'Did I hear right?' Emily emerged from her bedroom, mascara crumbling from her lashes and her hair like a fur ball. 'She fancies Ethan? Oh God, it's all too much.' Banging around the room, making coffee, she muttered something that sounded like, 'They come over HERE.' Bang! 'They take our JOBS.' Bang! 'They steal our MEN.' Bang! Then a violent coughing fit overtook her and she inhaled deeply on her cigarette. 'I'm not long for this world. Thank God.'

Before I could explore her bad humour – which I was pretty sure had something to do with Troy – Mum and Helen arrived. I was dying to ask Helen all about Troy, but couldn't with Mum there. Instead I had to make sympathetic noises as everyone compared hangover symptoms.

The atmosphere was tense. Emily was smoking heavily and saying very little, just flicking Helen narrow-eyed looks from time to time. 'OK,' she uncurled herself with a sigh from the sofa, 'I'm going to call Lou.'

'Are you really going to tell him you want to marry him and have his children?'

'Yes,' she said shortly. 'If that doesn't scare him away, I don't know what will.'

She went into her bedroom and closed the door a little too loudly for comfort.

451

'What's up with her?' Helen snapped. 'Narky bitch.

'Oh Jesus!' She suddenly remembered something. 'You'll never fecking guess who rang last night for you.'

'Who?'

'Slimebucket. Creephead. Gobshite of the year.' At my puzzled face she shrieked, 'Garv! Do I have to spell it out for you?'

'Garv rang? Here?' I knew I sounded stupid, but I couldn't help it.

'Yeah. I told him you were out with ridey Shay Delaney. Even though I don't think he's ridey, of course, but there's no need for Garv to know that. He sounded good and pissed off,' she said with relish. 'It was three o'clock in the morning in Ireland when he rang. He's obviously having trouble sleeping. Good enough for him!'

'What were you doing answering the phone? Didn't Emily say we weren't to?'

'Red rag to a bull, I'm afraid,' she said regretfully.

Emily came back out of her bedroom.

'Well?'

'He said yes,' she said faintly. 'Oh my God, now what am I going to do?'

'In my day,' Mum said, 'if you broke off an engagement you were sued for breach of promise.'

'Thanks a bunch.'

Various unspoken hostilities filled up the room and when Mum decided to go to the bathroom, they spilled over into an actual row. All of a sudden, Helen and Emily were leaning into each other, trading clipped barbs – concerning Troy.

'If you like him that much, why don't you do something about it?' Helen scorned. 'Like, if you don't stake your claim on him, you can't blame anyone else if they do.'

452

'It's too late,' Emily muttered. 'Now that he's met you.'

'Don't be so stupid, I'm leaving in a week.'

'I bet you'll decide to stay for him.'

Helen barked with laughter. 'Are you joking me? I'm going back to Ireland to set up my detective agency. Why would I bother staying here?'

'Because of Troy.'

'He's not that special.'

'Emily,' I had to cut in, 'what do you care about Troy? You're just friends with him. Aren't you?'

She shrugged sullenly and I had my answer: she was in love with him. I'd suspected the previous night and now I knew for sure.

I withered with shame; I'd been so wrapped up in my own problems I hadn't seen what was under my nose. I'd been so dense. Worse, I'd been so selfish.

'Well, why didn't you say before now?' I pleaded. 'Then we mightn't all have slept with him.'

'I haven't,' Anna said.

'I'd get in there fast,' Helen said.

Mum had come back from the bathroom but the argument was too advanced to knock it on the head. She picked up on it immediately. 'What did I miss?'

We all lapsed into tight-lipped silence.

'Margaret?' she demanded. 'What's going on?'

'Ah, um . . .'

'It's about Troy,' Helen supplied. 'Emily's mad about him.'

'And he's mad about her,' Mum said. 'So what's the problem?'

'No, you stupid old woman,' Helen said. 'He's mad about *me*.'

'Troy?' Mum confirmed. 'The one with the nose? That one? Yes, he's mad about Emily.'

'No, he's not,' Helen repeated. 'Just because the crowd of nutters next door think you're some sort of wise-woman-guru type doesn't mean you actually are.'

'Helen, you were just a diversion to the chap. And I suppose he thought it was no harm to make Emily jealous.'

'But –'

'Am I right, Emily?' Mum asked. 'He's got his eye on you?'

'Well, once he had,' she conceded, then coyly went further. 'He said he was in love with me.'

'When?'

'About a year ago.'

'And were you mad about him then?'

'Yes, probably.'

'So what,' Mum demanded in exasperation, 'in the name of GOD was stopping you?'

'He was too into his work,' Emily mumbled. 'I'd always be second. I thought it wouldn't work, then we wouldn't even be friends.'

'And now?'

A head-bowed reluctant mumble. 'I've changed my mind.'

'But in the meanwhile he started "getting off" – is that the phrase? – with all of your friends?'

'Yeah, except Lara.'

'Why not Lara?'

'I'll tell you some other time.'

'And you were jealous of these other girls?'

''Course.'

I closed my eyes at the memory of Emily realizing I'd slept with Troy, of her in convulsions when I asked if anything had ever happened between them. God, it must have been horrible for her.

'But I didn't totally mind, because I knew he liked me more than any of them and that his work was still his main love. But . . . but . . . I was worried about Helen.'

'Don't be,' Helen said. Not exactly pleasantly. 'You can have him.'

'He mightn't want me any more.'

'Only one way to find out,' Mum said.

'You mean ring him and ask him?'

'I do not!' Mum was appalled. 'I never rang anyone and told them I fancied them and I had my pick of the men. No, flirt with him, wear perfume, maybe cook him his favourite meal . . .'

'Ring him and ask him,' Helen, Anna and I chorused.

'OK,' Emily said thoughtfully, lighting another cigarette. 'I will.' She took the phone and the ashtray into her bedroom and closed the door, and ten minutes later she came out again. She was dressed, made-up and happier looking. 'I'm going out to meet him,' she said.

'Act coy,' Mum advised.

'Be straight,' I urged.

'Be straight yourself, Maggie,' Helen said slyly.

Mum darted me a suspicious look.

'Now what'll we do?' Mum asked, when Emily's block of flats had screeched away. 'Tell a joke, someone.'

We were all a little too fragile to want to do much else. Helen told a joke, Anna told one too but got the ending wrong, and I was garnering laughs by making my fringe stand out at right angles from my head when there was a knock on the door.

'The Goatee Boys, I suppose,' I said. 'Coming to apologize for not feeding you all last night.'

I opened the door, and there, standing outside, was someone I recognized but who didn't belong here. Garv.

Words deserted me.

'Hi,' he said.

'What the hell are you doing here?'

'You said if you weren't home in a month to come and get you. It's a month.'

It was actually only four weeks, not a full calendar month, and I knew that the real reason he was here was because he'd heard I'd been out with Shay Delaney. The bloody cheek of him, after his carry-on with Truffle Woman.

He looked the way people do when they've been trapped on a desert island for a while. His hair was longer than I'd ever seen it and was sticking up in tufts, three-day beard growth shaded his chin and jaw and, in the harsh glare of the sun, his eyes were lit blue – at least the bits that weren't bloodshot were. Even his jeans and T-shirt looked like he'd slept in them, and if he'd just got in on a flight from Ireland, I suppose he probably had.

'Who is it?' Helen asked.

'It's the adulterer,' I heard Mum say.

'Before they stone me,' Garv said, 'could we talk?'

'Come on,' I said wearily. 'We'll go for a walk on the beach.'

46

I was looking forward to this encounter with Garv about as much as a repeat of the time when I was sixteen and having hundreds of glass slivers removed from the tattered flesh of my knee. Nevertheless, we managed to maintain cordial chat while walking the six blocks to the beach.

'You cut your hair,' he said. 'It's nice.'

'Ah, you hate it really, admit it.'

'No, I like it. It's very . . . groovy. Especially the fringe.'

'Oh, please, don't mention the fringe. Have you somewhere to stay?'

'Yeah, it's near here. I rang Mrs Emily and she recommended the place she'd stayed in –'

I stopped him. 'The Ocean View. My family are staying there too.'

'Ohh-kaay. So I'd better have my breakfast in my room if I don't want to be pelted with rotten eggs in the dining room.'

'It might be for the best. So tell me, why didn't you just ring instead of coming all this way?'

'I did ring, loads of times, but the machine was always on and I felt weird about leaving a message . . .'

'Oh, so you're Emily's stalker.'

'Am I? God, my secret double life, I never knew. Anyway, I thought that some stuff is better said face-to-face.'

Up till then I'd assumed that Garv's appearance was in

response to Helen telling him I was out with Shay Delaney. But all of a sudden I was wondering what Garv had to say that merited a face-to-face visit? Could there be any further bad stuff to discover? Yes, actually, there could be: his new girl could be pregnant. The thought was such a shock that, as I stepped on to the beach, I stumbled.

'Are you still going out with that girl?' I asked.

To his credit, he didn't give me any wide-eyed 'What girl?' crap. He just waited a while, obviously weighing up what to say, then exhaled.

'No, I'm not.'

Relief was the first thing to hit, but immediately after, a wave of jealousy slapped me. So it was real. Really real. I forgot all about the two flings I'd had in the past month and I felt hollow and betrayed. A gathering sense of unreality surrounded me.

'Who was she?'

'Someone from work.'

'What was her name?'

'Karen.'

'Karen what?'

'Parsons.'

Driven by a self-destructive prurience, I wanted to know everything about her. What did she look like? Was she younger than me? Where had they done it? How many times? What kind of underwear had she? 'Was it serious?'

'No, not a bit. It lasted no length.' His every word hit me like a dart.

'Did you sleep with her?' I desperately wanted him to say no, that it had only been hand-holding and flirting. But, after a tense pause where I held my breath, he said, 'Yes, twice. I'm sorry, I'm sorry. I so wish I hadn't but I was off the wall.'

'Why's that, then?' I asked stiffly, jealous bile sickening my stomach.

'I was very depressed. They were my babies, too. But no one was interested in what I felt. I know it was harder for you, but it was killing me too. Then you and me stopped talking and the loneliness was unbearable, and then,' his voice dropped so low I could hardly hear him, 'when I couldn't get it up with you, I felt such a failure.'

'You'd no bother with her, I suppose. Your fancy woman. And look at what you've turned me into,' I cried. 'Someone who says things like "fancy woman".'

'I'm sorry,' he whispered.

'When did it start?'

'Not until you'd gone. Left for LA.'

I had a good snort at that. 'Something was going on long before then.'

'No, we were just . . . friends. I swear to God.'

'"Just friends." I can imagine. Flirting and sharing fucking truffles. You don't have to sleep with someone to be unfaithful, you know! You can be unfaithful with your emotions.'

He bowed his head.

'Was it the first time you did this to me?'

'Of course!' He sounded shocked.

'Your only fancy woman?'

'My only fancy woman.'

'But one too many.'

'I know, I know. I wish I hadn't. I'd give my left arm to go back in time and change things,' he muttered feverishly.

'You blamed me, didn't you? For the miscarriages?'

'How? It was hardly your fault.'

'It was. Maybe I'd . . . damaged myself . . . when I'd had the

459

abortion. That day in Doctor Collins's office, I knew you blamed me. But that was OK, because I blamed me too.'

'I didn't blame you. You were the one who was angry with me.'

'I was not.'

'You felt I'd forced you into trying for a baby. And if we'd never tried, we'd never have had all that misery with the miscarriages.'

I clamped my lips together, unwilling to admit anything, but the feelings were too big.

'OK, I was angry.' Still was. Furious, actually, I'd just discovered. Our life together had been fine until he'd opened that can of worms. 'But I wasn't the one who had an affair,' I said, consumed with bitterness.

'No, you just came to Los Angeles because of Shay Delaney.'

'What –? I did fucking not,' I stuttered indignantly.

'Yes, you did. You could have gone to London to Claire or New York to Rachel or you could have stayed in Dublin, but you came here.'

'Because of Emily.'

'*Not* because of Emily. Or not just because of Emily. There was that thing in the paper about Dark Star Productions and the work they were doing in Hollywood. You could have guessed he'd be here. I've been honest with you, why won't you be honest with me?'

We marched on in angry silence. The bloody audacity of him trying to shift the blame for *his* affair on to *me*. Somewhere in the recesses of my brain, a thought began to swim upwards, reaching to break the surface. Before it did, I turned on Garv. 'Why do you still hate Shay Delaney so much?'

He stopped, sat on a rock, put his head in his cupped hands, breathed deeply a couple of times, then looked up. 'Surely it's obvious?'

'Tell me.'

'Right, this is why. You are the most precious person in the world to me and Shay Delaney treated you like muck. When you told me about the abortion and all, I wanted to kill him. Then we got married, and it was fine when we were in Chicago, but then we moved home . . . every time Delaney's name got mentioned you went white.'

Really? I hadn't realized his effect on me was that evident.

'Yes, really.' Garv confirmed my unspoken query. 'And any time we drove past his mother's house, you turned and looked.'

Really? I had no knowledge of that either. Well, now that he mentioned it, maybe I did sometimes. Not every time, just sometimes.

'I used to go the long way round just so we wouldn't pass his old house. I felt like we were never going to be free of the fucker. Please try and imagine it the other way round – if every time some old girlfriend of mine was mentioned, one I'd ditched you for, I went funny. You wouldn't like it, would you?'

'Stop trying to blame me.'

'Then there's a thing in the paper about Dark Star Productions, then four days later you leave me, and the next time I hear from you, you're on your way to Los Angeles.'

'I didn't leave you because of reading anything about Dark Star Productions,' I said furiously. 'I left you because you were having a fucking AFFAIR. And you didn't even try to stop me –'

'Well, I'm doing it now,' he said grimly.

'All you did was say you'd pay the mortgage, then you helped me PACK, for God's sake.'

'I did try to stop you. I'd been trying to talk to you for days, but you ignored me or came home too drunk for there to be any point. The day you left I was all out of fight and I'd figured that you were going to leave me anyway.'

'How d'you reach that conclusion?'

'I suppose things had been desperate for so long. And you wouldn't talk to me.'

'*You* wouldn't talk to *me*! It was your fault.'

'I was hoping we could try and get beyond all that. Could we not just say that neither of us were perfect . . .'

'Speak for yourself. I didn't do anything wrong.' I was shaking with anger. 'So let me sum up what you've told me – you had an affair, but it was OK because it was all my fault.'

Then Garv did something he didn't do often – he lost his temper. He seemed to swell with it. His muscles were taut and his eyes were livid blue as he brought his face close to mine.

'That's not what I said.' He bit the words out. 'You KNOW what I said. But you don't want to hear it, do you?'

I looked at my watch and said coldly, 'I have to go.'

'Why?'

A pause. 'I have to meet someone.'

'Who? Shay Delaney?'

'Yeah.'

Garv went the colour of chalk and my anger got wiped away, to be replaced with the deadness I remembered from the first weeks of separation.

'Garv, why did you come here?'

'To try to persuade you to come home in the hope that we might rebuild us.' He smiled a little twist of a smile. 'Looks like I've had a wasted journey.'

'You were unfaithful to me. How could I ever forgive you? Or trust you again?'

'Oh, God.' He rubbed his hand over his eyes. I thought for a moment he was going to cry.

'Tell me one thing,' I said. 'Was she beautiful, this Karen?'

'Maggie, it wasn't like that, it wasn't about that . . .' He was in agony.

'Just a simple yes or no,' I cut in. 'Was she beautiful?'

'She was attractive, I suppose,' he admitted miserably.

'Oh yeah?' I grinned and he watched me warily. 'Well, I bet she wasn't as attractive as the girl I got off with.'

It took a moment. I could almost see the words being processed, then understanding dawn and when it did, he laughed out loud. 'Really?'

Garv was the only person – other than Emily – who knew how the girls in the porn films had affected me.

'Good for you,' he said. Then a little more sadly, 'Good for you.'

In a gesture that belonged to another life, he touched my head and hooked my hair behind my ears, first one, then the other. Then he noticed my red, flaking arm. 'Christ, your poor arm,' he said unhappily. Surprisingly, it seemed natural to hug one another and as I turned my face into his shoulder, he smelt of something that I couldn't identify. A huge sadness was mushrooming inside me, filling me up so I couldn't breathe.

'We really messed things up,' I choked into his T-shirt.

'No,' he said. 'No. We were just unlucky.'

47

This time Shay was waiting for me, smiling a slow, lazy smile as he watched me walk across the lobby. When I saw him, a thought flickered just beneath the surface, but I pushed it away and smiled back at him.

'Let's have a drink at the bar,' he said.

But the bar at the Mondrian was no ordinary hotel bar, devoid of character and atmosphere. It was the Sky Bar, hang-out of celebrities and beautiful people. Open to the warm, night sky and set around a luminous, turquoise swimming pool, a sexy decadent atmosphere was created by the scattering of huge silk cushions and low-slung day beds. The only lighting was from flame torches, which cast a mysterious glow and made everyone dewily beautiful.

FBI types in shades and walkie-talkies manned the reception desk – Fort Knox probably has less security – and only when Shay had produced his room key were the pearly gates opened.

We wandered amongst the silver, six-foot-high pot-plants looking for a seat, but all that was left was an enormous, white, satin mattress. Gingerly we placed ourselves upon it and one of the most beautiful girls I've ever seen took our drinks order.

Then Shay and I were alone, sitting on a mattress, looking at each other.

'I was afraid you were going to cancel me again tonight,' I blurted, out of need to say something.

'Look, I told you, last night was work, I couldn't help it,' he said, so defensively that for the first time I wondered if he was lying. And he'd tried to get out of meeting me tonight. And when he'd rung last night he'd been hoping to get the answering machine . . .

'I make you uncomfortable,' I said sadly.

'Not a bit of it.' Accompanied by a gorgeous smile.

'Ah, I do,' I teased. 'All that shaking hands with me, then running away.'

He half-laughed, 'Maybe I feel guilty.'

'For what?'

'For, you know, when we were teenagers. But it's all in the past and you don't hate me, right?'

'I don't hate you.'

He smiled with relief.

'But when you went away and never wrote to me,' I surprised myself by saying, 'I nearly lost my reason.'

He looked like I'd slapped him. 'I'm sorry, I thought it would be better that way. Less painful, to just let it all fade away.'

'Well, it wasn't, not for me. I spent years waiting for you.'

'I'm sorry, Maggie. I was only eighteen, young and stupid. I hadn't a clue. If there's anything I can do to make it up to you . . .' He stretched out, lay on his elbow, and placed his hand over mine. We sat in silence.

'Shay, tell me, are you happily married? Do you love your wife?'

'Yes and yes.'

'Are you faithful to her?'

'Yes.' Then a beat later, 'Mostly.'

465

'Mostly? What does that mean?'

'I am in Ireland,' he said awkwardly. 'But, like . . . when I'm working here . . .'

'I seeee . . .' I said speculatively, letting it hang in the air.

'Maggie, I want to tell you something.'

There was something about his tone that had me on the alert.

His tawny eyes were on mine. 'Maggie, I want you to know . . .'

That he'd always loved me? That every day since he'd said goodbye to me at the ferry port, he'd yearned for me?

'Maggie, I'll never leave my wife.'

'Um . . .'

'My own dad left us and I saw what it did to the family.'

'Ah . . .'

'But you and I . . . I come to LA a lot – if you're still here, maybe we could . . .'

I understood what was happening: I was being offered a part-share in Shay Delaney. A consolation prize: *We apologize that your life was damaged by the abrupt withdrawal of Shay Delaney, but please accept this voucher to be redeemed by Shay Delaney at your convenience.*

Unexpectedly, I started to laugh. 'You're one of the good guys, aren't you, Shay?'

'I try. It matters.'

'Your wife is so lucky, having a husband who'll always stay with her.'

He nodded.

'Even though he rides rings around himself on his business trips.'

His face darkened and he half-sat up. 'Hey, there's no need to be like that. I'm just trying to . . .'

466

'What? Please everyone?' That started me laughing again.

'Trying to be fair.'

'Fair. Like you're a prize.'

He stared at me. He looked surprised, and I realized how very glad I was that I wasn't his wife, waiting at home six thousand miles away, taking care of three children and wondering anxiously what her handsome, charming husband was up to. And I knew something else – I wouldn't take a snail off his windscreen.

'You try to be everything to everyone; you can't say no. Don't you get tired?'

He wasn't happy. Not one bit.

'I thought this was what you wanted,' he sounded confused. 'You know, all that ringing me, insisting on seeing me. You knew I was married . . .'

Oh Christ, when he put it like that. He was right: I'd almost stalked him over the past couple of days.

'Why did you come here?' he asked. 'What did you want from me?'

Good question. Very good question. Being around him was like staring at the sun for too long: it temporarily blinded me. I'd gravitated to him, like a moth to a light, but with only the vaguest idea of what I'd hoped to get.

'I wanted to know why you never wrote to me.' But I already knew that, it was hardly rocket science: he'd outgrown me and didn't have the guts to tell me. No biggie, it happens all the time, especially at that age.

'And that's all?'

'Yes.'

'Sure,' he said, slightly scornfully. 'You wanted a lot more than that from me.'

I hadn't. I hadn't known what I'd wanted, but now I was certain of what I didn't want. I didn't want a relationship with him, part-time or otherwise.

'Honest to God, I just wanted closure.'

'Well, you've got it,' he snapped.

'I have, haven't I?' I grinned.

'You're in great form all of a sudden.'

'I am.' I felt light and free. Shay Delaney was just a guy from another life, the repository of hopes that were years past their use-by date.

Suddenly I found myself thinking about those people who break into the pyramids looking for treasure, but when they get there the tomb is empty because someone had got there long before them.

'Did you ever see *Raiders of the Lost Ark*?' I murmured.

He looked at me as if I'd cracked up completely. 'Of course I did.'

And the thought that had been striving to make itself known broke the surface, ready to be claimed – Garv had been right when he'd said that Shay was one of my reasons for coming to LA. It hadn't been a conscious decision, it had definitely been decided lower down in the sneakier part of my brain. But my first night in Los Angeles, when Emily had told me that Shay spent a lot of time there, I already half-knew – and even then I'd wondered if that was why I'd been so keen to respond to the invitation to stay with Emily.

You don't have to sleep with someone, you can be unfaithful with your emotions – and I was the one who'd said it.

Poor Garv. And what about the dreams I'd occasionally had about Shay? Garv didn't know about them – unless he did. He seemed to be several steps ahead of me.

Poor Garv, I thought again. What must it have been like, knowing that his wife still held a pocket of love for someone else? How lonely he must have been through the miscarriages, mutely carrying his grief and partaking in all the fuss around me. How humiliated he must have been when he became impotent. How frustrated when I wouldn't talk to him – because he was right, I had stopped talking to him.

Then I thought about him and Truffle Woman and a lick of anger touched me; I'd been adamant that I'd never forgive him. But what mattered more – my self-righteousness, or the truth? And I had to admit that I hadn't been perfect either.

That's the thing with relationships, I understood. It doesn't mean we don't hurt one another; how can we help it sometimes, we're only human? But if you love someone, you get hurt and you manage to forgive. And be forgiven. Garv had come to forgive me and I'd given him the bum's rush.

I rolled on to my back and stared up at the purplish night sky. Then I realized what Garv had smelt of when I'd hugged him goodbye earlier. He'd smelt of home.

'No stars tonight,' I said.

But the stars are always there, even in the daytime. Sometimes we just can't see them.

I sprang up. 'I've got to go.'

48

I drove fast, but all the stoplights were against me and it took nearly an hour to get to the Ocean View. I did one of my worst pieces of parking ever on the sidewalk outside and hurried into the tile-floored lobby. And who should I meet? Only Mum, Dad, Helen and Anna. I later discovered they'd been to the cinema.

'I thought you were out with Shay Delaney,' Mum said in surprise.

'I was.'

'Then what are you doing here?'

'Looking for Garv.'

'What for?' Her face was suddenly mutinous.

I didn't answer and she said hotly, 'If he can be unfaithful once, he'll do it again.'

The desk clerk followed this exchange with great interest. 'Hi,' I said. 'Can you ring Paul Garvan's room for me, please?'

'He checked out.'

My heart thumped hard. 'When?'

'About an hour ago.'

'Where was he going?'

'Home to Iowa.'

'Right, thanks, I'll get him at the airport.'

But when I turned around, Mum was blocking me. She drew herself up to her full height. 'You are not to go after him!'

'Don't, pet, for me,' Dad beseeched.

'Margaret, you're not to go!'

I stared at the two of them, stared long and confused, then said, 'My name is Maggie and just watch me.'

As I raced back to the car, there was the clatter of feet running after me. It was Anna. 'I'll come with you,' she said breathlessly. She jumped in beside me, slammed the car door shut and pulled on her seatbelt. 'Hit it!'

The journey seemed to take for ever, the traffic was very heavy for that time of night and, despite the spells Anna muttered, the stoplights were still against me.

'What airline do you think he flew?' I asked Anna, hoping for some sixth-sense action.

'American Airlines?'

'Maybe, unless he came through London, like I did.'

'Maggie, what about the other girl?'

'Gone.'

'But will you be able to forgive him for it?'

'Yeah, I think so. I hope so. The thing is, I wasn't without fault either.'

'And that makes it easier?'

'Yes, I love him, we'll work it out.' Then I added, 'Mind you, if he ever does it again, he is so dead.'

'Good for you. I always thought you and him were perfect for each other.'

'Did you?'

'Didn't you?'

'I have to say,' I admitted, 'there were times I had my doubts. I sometimes wondered if I was a wild girl who'd settled for a safe marriage.'

Anna sniggered and I gave an inquiring look. 'Sorry,' she said. 'It's just you . . . wild. Sorry.'

After a few seconds I said, 'It's OK. Because while I've been here I've tried being a bit wild and I just couldn't take to it.'

'Did you really get off with Lara or were you just winding Helen up?'

'I really did.'

'God Almighty.'

'But the point I'm making is I wasn't playing it safe when I married Garv. This is the way I really am!'

'Plain yoghurt at room temperature?'

'Um . . .'

'Plain yoghurt at room temperature and *proud of it*?'

I thought about it. 'How about plain yoghurt with raspberry puree at the bottom? I'd settle for that.'

'More interesting than you initially seem?'

'Exactly.'

'Has hidden depths.'

'Yes! I might even get a T-shirt saying it.'

'Two. One for Garv as well.'

'If we find him,' I said, my stomach tightening with fear. 'And if he doesn't tell me to fuck off.'

We finally reached LAX, and after some more truly atrocious parking, we ran into Departures. But when I asked the American Airlines check-in girl if she could tell me if Garv was on the flight, she said, 'I can't give out that information.'

'I'm his wife,' I begged.

'I don't care if you're the Dalai Lama.'

'It's urgent.'

'So is my need to use the bathroom, but there's nothing I can do about that either.'

'Come on,' Anna pulled me. 'We'll see if we can get him at the gate.'

LAX is huge and always crowded, no matter what time of the day or night it is. Panting, Anna and I ran through the throng, bouncing off people like pinballs. For a few frustrating minutes we got entangled in a flock of Hare Krishnas, and had to slow down to their pace, as they hopped and chanted. One of them even tried to give me a tambourine, before we managed to break free and begin sprinting again.

'What's he wearing?' Anna gasped.

'Jeans and a T-shirt. At least, that's what he was wearing earlier – he might have changed.'

'Is that him?' Anna said and my heart nearly jumped out of my mouth. But the man she was pointing at was an African-American.

'Sorry,' she said. 'I just saw jeans and T-shirt and jumped to conclusions.'

We raced in and out of all the shops and bars in Departures, and Garv was nowhere to be seen. The only place left to check was his actual gate, but without boarding cards we couldn't get past the barrier and the woman official was so not interested in our story.

'Security. You could be terrorists.'

'Do we look like terrorists?' I pleaded, hoping she'd see reason.

She snapped her gum a few times and drawled, 'Yeah, you do.'

I stared at her, trying to psych her into giving in. She stared back, bland and unaffected, and with each empty second my hope dwindled away. But I wouldn't give up.

'Let's check the shops and bars one more time.' But there was no sign of him. Sweating, my heart pounding, my blood fizzing with awful hope, I skidded back and forth like a headless chicken, Anna doing her best to keep up, and I only stopped when I ran myself into exhaustion. Still I didn't want to leave. 'Let's just hang around a bit and see if he comes.'

'OK,' Anna said, stretching and scanning like a meerkat on guard.

But when time passed and passed, I filled up with despair.

'Come on,' I eventually said. 'We're not going to find him. We might as well go.'

I drove home feeling like a waxwork model of myself. The streets and houses of Los Angeles disappeared and I was driving through a wasteland.

'You can call him,' Anna encouraged. 'The minute he gets back to Ireland.'

'Yeah,' I mumbled, but a lump of cold terror was lodged in my stomach. I knew I'd left it too late. He'd come, I'd chosen Shay, he'd gone. I'd had my chance and blown it. The realization was like that moment on a plane when your ears pop and everything is clear again.

'It was silly thinking I'd catch him at the airport,' I said wretchedly. 'That sort of thing only happens in movies.'

'Starring Meg Ryan,' Anna nodded gloomily.

'He would have vaulted over the barrier.'

'And everyone would have clapped and cheered.'

We both sighed and, in silence, continued the drive to nowhere.

For a long time I'd thought of my marriage as a horrible, dark place where I didn't want to go. I hadn't been able to remember anything good about it – but all of a sudden I could think of loads. Like, when we used to get ready to go out for the evening, Garv would appear before me in his Calvins and an ancient pair of cowboy boots and say, 'I'm ready!' And I'd frown and say, 'You can't go out like that. It's cold, you need a jacket.' Then I'd dot my foundation all over my face but not rub it in and he'd say, 'Exquisite, my dear, you're like a flower. But might I suggest a soupçon of lipstick.' So I'd put a streak of red on my chin or forehead and he'd declare, 'Perfecto!' Then hand me the cotton wool to rub it off.

And Friday nights used to be lovely – we'd get a video and a takeaway (no change there) and lie on the couch and unwind after the week. And before the second miscarriage, Friday night had always been sex night too – that's not to say we didn't sometimes do it at other times, Sunday mornings could be nice – but Friday night was always a given. And even though, like I said, it was a long time since we'd had sex on the kitchen table, I'd had no complaints. It had been wonderful being with someone who knew my body almost as well as I did.

Then I remembered the way we used to do each other's toothpaste. And how, whenever we went to the local Tex-Mex place, we used to share a basket of chicken wings as our starter, a basket of chicken wings for our main course and a basket of chicken wings for dessert. And the time . . .

Memories, each one happier than the next, tumbled into my head and presented themselves for inspection and I had to put my fist into my mouth to stop myself bawling with loss. I'd often heard it said, but never thought it would apply to me – you never know what you have until it's gone.

When we arrived back in Santa Monica, I'd no real idea of how I'd got us there.

'Do you want to be dropped at the Ocean View?' I asked Anna.

'No, I'll come to Emily's with you.'

I shoved my key into the lock and half-fell into Emily's front room – where so many people were sitting quietly that my first thought was, 'Who's dead?' In a second I'd taken in Emily, Troy, Mike, Charmaine, Luis, Curtis, Ethan . . .

'You got a guest, man,' Ethan said coldly, indicating the person beside him. Who happened to be Garv.

'I thought you'd gone back to Iowa.' Surprise made me sound stupid.

'Couldn't get on the plane. I only had a stand-by ticket. How was your date?'

'Short. Ludicrous. I went to the airport to try and catch you.'

My face was burning with emotion and everyone was staring, boring holes into me with their eyes. And was it my imagination or were they all clustered protectively around Garv – and sending me hostile vibes?

Emily stood up. 'How about we give them some space?' And after a brief, reluctant pause, everyone trotted meekly behind her towards the front door. As Curtis passed, he pointed to Garv and said angrily, 'This guy's a way better man than the jazzy dude with the toney wheels who gave you a ride home Friday night!'

'How do you know about that?' Emily asked.

'He's got a telescope,' Luis said.

'Ugh,' Emily groaned.

'This love thing, it's not like a haircut,' Luis leaned into me, as he left. 'You fuck it up, it's not going to grow back, right?'

'Er, right.'

'If it don't come back, it was never yours,' was Ethan's contribution. 'If it comes back, it's yours to keep.'

'Be careful what you wish for,' Mike nodded meaningfully. He was right there – I'd wished for Shay.

'Think of the snail,' Charmaine said.

'Huh?!' several of them exclaimed.

'The *snail*?' I heard Emily query. 'What's that all about?'

Then everyone had left and Garv and I were alone.

'What's going on?' he asked wearily.

'You were right. I'm sorry.'

'Right about what?'

'Shay Delaney. I was still sort of hung up on him – but I didn't know about it, I swear. Not really.'

Garv rubbed his eyes – he looked exhausted. 'This is one time I'd have been happy to be wrong.'

'I'm sorry. I'm so, so sorry.'

'I'm sorry too.'

The way he said it started alarm bells ringing; it was the wrong sort of 'sorry'. It sounded final and defeated. 'What for?' I asked, too quickly.

'Everything. For Karen. The awful months when we didn't properly talk. For keeping my mouth shut about Delaney and hoping it would go away.'

'It has gone way.' My breath was short. 'I swear.'

'Why did you come to the airport?'

'Because . . .' How did I say it? How to encapsulate the shift where everything came into focus and Garv was centre? 'I'd thought it was over with us, I really thought it was gone for ever. Then after seeing you today it all flared up again and every feeling was still there and I knew I'd always take the snail off your windscreen. And not off anyone else's.'

I finished on a gasp and, as Garv said nothing, my nerves stretched to the limit. I felt like a prisoner waiting to hear the verdict of the jury.

'Let me put it another way,' I tried. 'I love you.'

'Do you?'

'Yes, honestly. I mean, of *course* – would I have gone to the airport and tried to be Meg Ryan otherwise?'

And he surprised me by saying, 'The flight wasn't really full – I just said it to try to hold on to the last shred of my self-respect. I got to the airport and thought it was stupid to come all this way and give up so soon.' He shrugged. 'I came back to give it one more go with you.'

'Oh. Oh. Well. Great! Why?'

He looked away to one side as he thought about it, then laughed softly and faced me. 'Because you're my favourite.'

'Well, you're *my* favourite.'

'Make up your own compliments.'

'Sorry. OK. I love you.'

'I love you.'

'Now you're at it.'

'That's because I've very little imagination.'

'That makes two of us. We've a lot in common.'

'Yeah.'

'What would you have done,' I asked cautiously, 'if I hadn't come home? If I had . . . you know . . . stayed with Shay?'

'Dunno. Gone mad. Started eating lightbulbs.'

'Well I didn't, so the lightbulbs are safe.'

'Yeah.'

'Yeah,' I swallowed. And all of a sudden, the way he was looking at me made me nervous and shy. 'So . . . um . . . what happens now?'

'Well, we're in Hollywood,' he said, taking a step closer to me, 'So . . . ah . . . we could drive a car off a cliff?'

'Or run down a hill in slow motion?' I shifted nearer until I was close enough to get his delicious Garv smell.

'Or I could take you in my arms and kiss you until the room starts spinning around.'

'I like the sound of the kissing,' I said, barely above a whisper.

'Me too.'

So we did.

Epilogue

A week later, Larry Savage got the sack from Empire – just came in one morning and without explanation was told to clear his desk, then was escorted off the lot. Par for the course if you're a movie executive, they say. Emily's script is languishing on a shelf at Empire and the story of Chip the wonder dog looks likely never to be told. Which would have been a blessing, Emily said, except it also meant she only got paid half of her fee. So great was her fear of turning into the man shouting outside the supermarket that she resolved to get out of the scriptwriting game altogether. But Troy put an end to that by getting financing for an independent production of her newest script. Apparently, it's brilliant, really dark – Emily says it's thanks to the fact that she was so depressed and scared while writing it. Some producer from another small studio is interested in reviving *Hostage!* And one way and another, the wolf is being kept from the door, even if Mrs Emily still hasn't had a chance to wear her navy, spangledy dress to a première. However, she might get a chance to wear it in the near future. Not to a film première, but to a wedding – Emily and Troy's. I will admit to having had my doubts over Troy's fidelity, but since Emily hooked up with him, he's been a model of good behaviour.

Lou half-heartedly stalked Emily for a couple of weeks, then gave up, but when Kirsty heard about Troy and Emily, she turned to food. Apparently she put on fifteen pounds in as many days. I'd laugh, except it would be mean.

Lara continues to be a great big golden ball of fun. She hasn't yet found the right girl, but is having a fantastic time looking. Justin is still living a shut-down life with Desiree, but things picked up recently for him when the other expendable fat guy contracted glandular fever and lost a ton of weight.

Reza kicked her husband out and told him to go and live with 'his whore'. He was back within the week, prostrating himself with contrition.

The poor mad scriptwriter is still hanging around the supermarket shouting set directions at the people buying their groceries.

Luis's little problem cleared up on the second lot of antibiotics. Himself, Ethan and Curtis finished college, shaved off their goatees, grew their hair (those who were in the habit of shaving their heads) and got respectable. The Dukes of Hazzardmobile was sent to the wrecker's yard.

Charmaine and Mike are still Charmaine and Mike. Before I left, Charmaine told me my aura wasn't as toxic as it had been. Occasionally the fable-telling group ring Mum and ask her to come back. She sent them a copy of *The Tales of Finn McCool* and hopes that they'll now leave her in peace.

Connie got married and didn't get kidnapped on honeymoon.

Helen, to everyone's astonishment, really did set up a private-detective agency when she returned to Ireland. She specializes in 'domestics' – i.e., she traps cheating spouses – and she's kept busy. Anna got on so well in her new job that they promoted her from the bowels of the post room to the bright lights of the front desk. She no longer mentions Shane and apparently she gets the occasional e-mail from Ethan. Sometimes, to upset Mum, she says he's going to come and visit as soon as he gets time off.

Dad's neck is better now. So are my relations with him. It took a while, and even longer with my mother.

Dark Star Productions went to the wall, but Shay already has a high-flying new job in another film company. As Claire said – almost admiringly – when she heard, 'There he goes again. Falling into a pit of shite and coming out smelling of Paloma Picasso.'

I was watching telly the other day and it was previewing a glossy new drama series from America, when I saw someone who looked familiar. It took me a moment; he was a lot more shiny and packaged than the last time I'd seen him. 'It's Rudy!' I yelped. 'It's the ice-cream seller from the beach in Santa Monica. I used to buy Klondike bars off him.' No one believed me, of course.

Is that everyone? Oh, me. I'm in bed, unable to move, on account of being eight months pregnant and huge. I haven't seen my toes for weeks and once I lie on my back, I can't turn over or get up without Garv sliding a stick in under me and leaning on it. I've promised Helen that I'll tell her how agonizing the birth is and that I won't fob her off with any talk of miracles.

Garv and I are very together. It hasn't always been easy; we've had the occasional shout at each other as we've ironed everything out, but, at this stage, we're sure our bond is strong enough to survive the blips. Even though we were separated and angry with one another, we were still linked.

As he says himself, the stars are always there, even in the daylight. Sometimes we just can't see them.